TALES OF DOHRYA

The Southern War

by

Mark A. Smith

2016
Auctoritas Publishing LLC
Springfield, Missouri
Auctoritaspublishing.net

ISBN-10: 0-9858017-7-8
ISBN-13: 978-0-9858017-7-9

This is a work of fiction. Any resemblance between characters herein and any person living or dead is a coincidence.

First Edition, Paperback

DEDICATION

For Lane

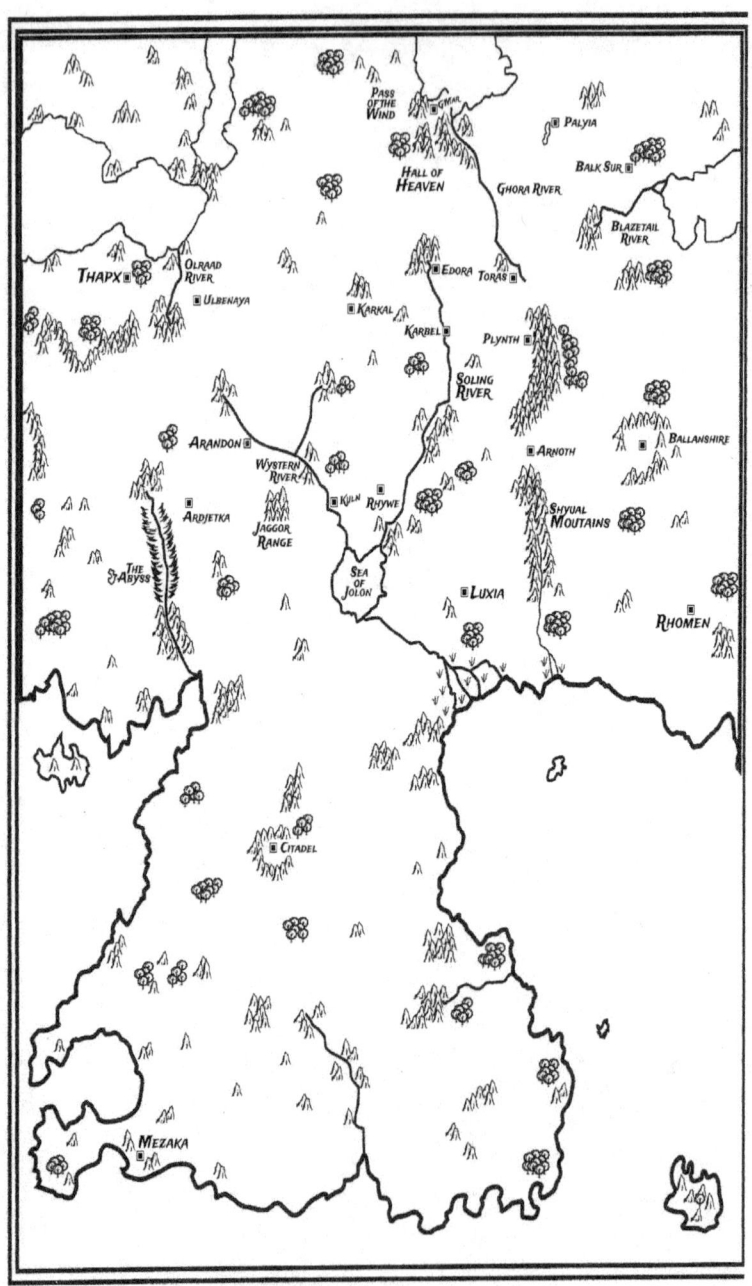

The Beginning
An Unlikely Savior

G'mar

The group moved through the tunnel at a hurried pace, eyes constantly flicking between what might lie ahead or behind them. The sound of their boots echoed dully in the wide stone lined passage. Being quiet was not an option, speed was essential. Smoke from torches carried by those in the front and back of the group rose to disappear in the darkness that masked the ceiling after the torchlight moved away. It mixed with the dust that trickled down to further foul the air.

The flickering shadows that the torches threw across the walls and floor were a grotesque mockery of the images. Apart from the torches, light in the tunnels was sparse; many of the torches and lamps that were normally lit to illuminate the passageway were out or missing entirely. At first as they moved into the passages, from above the sounds of fighting could be heard. But it faded as they moved deeper into the tunnels that ran underneath the bastion.

Taranh, the senior majic user and leader of his people, clutched the burden of scrolls and sacred books he carried tighter to his chest as he moved quickly through the warren of tunnels, guards pressed close around front and back. The thought that he had failed was never far from his mind. *How did we come to this* a small voice in his head asked. He glanced to the left and then had to turn his head to look a little behind him to see what he was looking for: Anagir, one of his junior majical apprentices. The pair who were in the middle of the group were already moving at nearly a run as they were being hustled through the semi darkness toward their destination, a storage room near the center of the underground tunnel web that ran beneath the massive fortress.

A blast from somewhere above shook the ground causing more dirt to filter down from around the blocks that formed the tunnel ceiling. The ground rocked for just a moment making footing treacherous and then it was steady again. Dust from the explosion caused several of the party to cough as they tried to breath in some cleaner air and their lungs found only dirt. The group never stopped, only slowed; their mission was too desperate to allow for delays or the luxury of breaks. Hurry, there is no time.

Two more turns brought them to yet another tunnel and the group started down the passage when the leading guards suddenly stopped. Taranh pushed forward to see what the problem was. Fearing the worst, flickering torch light revealed the grim news. One arm protruded from the mass of loose soil and stone blocks from the collapsed ceiling that filled the entire avenue before them. The smell of fresh soil was thick in their noses.

There was no time for sentiment for whoever it was that had been buried. The commander of the guards immediately ordered the formation to turn around and then turn left at the end of now shortened passage.

Anagir blanched at the sight of the arm. The fingers of the hand were stretched outwards as if reaching for help. No help had been coming and no help was necessary now. *What if that had been me?* the young majic user thought. His feet seemed to fail as the order to turn around came. He didn't move when the others did, it took a less-than-friendly shove from one of the guards to get him moving again. The young majic user was so engrossed the sight of the buried corpse he completely overlooked that one of the guards had dared touch him. Anagir stumbled forward, his eyes never leaving the sight of the outstretched hand until the light faded returning the area to darkness.

As he stumbled along the thought *that could have been me* went through his mind over and over. The last two days had been a blur of fighting, running messages and errands, no sleep and seemingly ever-present death. The easterners had pressed their latest assault forward despite horrific losses.

It had worked. They had managed to breach a section of the wall and were pouring into the massive fortress. The defenders were fighting desperately but the effects of a long siege had reduced their numbers and sapped their strength. Anagir had witnessed incredible acts of courage on both sides. Some of them were selfless acts of sacrifice that he knew he could never be capable of.

The group moved forward through a different passage trying to find a way to reach their destination. Taranh, too, felt the despair of the others; it was nearly a physical presence there in the tunnel with them. He knew without a doubt that they would all do their duty but their hearts were heavy with a sense of failure and fear. Time seemed to drag out like a long scream, it grated at the mind. None of them knew how much longer it would take to get where they were going and how much time it was before the invaders reached the tunnels and when that time came fortune would turn against them, if it hadn't already. They continued on without pause moving further into the darkness that lay beyond.

It took longer than expected to arrive at their destination due to fatigue and disorientation but they finally reached their goal. Once at the door to the storeroom Taranh looked at the senior soldier on the guard detail. He caught his leader's eye and with a great sense of dignity bowed his head and lifted both hands palms up in an Image of Order movement that Taranh approved of with the full measure of his spirit. The sight of one of his people displaying that level of dedication despite the certain doom that awaited them lifted his heart, he felt a small spark of new hope about what they were going to try to do. The discipline level among his people had always been high and now he reaped part of that reward. It helped to restore a measure of his spirit.

Anagir, taking one of the torches, was already inside the room having been given the books, so did not see what took place in the hallway. Without speaking a word the one in charge of the guards assured his leader that while they lived no one would enter the room. Taranh then bowed his own head and placed a closed fist to his chest over his heart to honor the commitment to duty the younger one was displaying. He held the pose for longer than was usual for one of his position acknowledging someone of a lower station. He then turned to enter the room as well to rejoin Anagir. The detail leader came smartly to attention then turned to ensure that the meager force he had with him was positioned as well as they could be in the area of the storeroom.

Once inside Taranh secured the door as best he could. Anagir was near a stack of crates waiting for someone to tell him what to do, the precious scrolls and books casually tossed on one of the crates that held assorted supplies. The elder majic user was disheartened once again, the lift he had felt from the dedication of the guard leader was suddenly dashed by the lack of conviction that Anagir, the most junior apprentice he had brought with him to G'mar, was showing. It was as if the younger one was bored by what was going on.

Taranh had Anagir with him now only by chance; the young one was the only majic user that Taranh had been able to find when it had become apparent that something drastic must be done to secure the sacred material. The Council members were already dead or taken by the invaders. The more senior apprentices were all involved in the fighting or dead. So, the task would fall to this one. The greatest risk in all their history and it would all rest on a novice mystic who in the name of AllFather was as useful as a bucket without a bottom.

Taranh cursed the easterners again for their interference, that his people would have to rest their hopes on the likes of this one was almost too much to bear but circumstances dictated that exact situation. So be it.

***

Gritting his teeth in resolve Taranh called to Anagir -- who missed it completely, so absorbed in what was happening to *him*. He barely acknowledged the second time that his master spoke. Taranh stepped over to him and grabbed him by the shoulder which caused him to snap his head around and look up into the face of his master. It was not a pleasant sight, eyes flashing with anger and a snarl that curled up one side of the mouth as the older one tried to give voice to the fury he felt.

Only part of it was Anagir's fault. The battle and the failure to carry out the ceremony that they had come here to do was the rest. But Anagir and his attitude were here, now, on display in front of him while above and around them more of their people were fighting and dying every moment. All for the belief in what they had come to do. And that this one would be so weak…

Anagir saw the anger and shrank down but couldn't escape this time, the powerful hand on his shoulder gripped tighter and tighter as more of the anger took control. The squeeze was painful and growing more so by the moment. It felt as if his bones were being crushed in a vise, the pressure was mounting until he could no longer contain the sound of his pain.

"Master, enough!" He wailed as he fought to twist out of the strength of the grip.

The sudden movement and sound of pain in the voice was enough to cause Taranh to stop closing his fingers. The anger faded some from his eyes and he quickly took in two deep breaths in an attempt to regain some control. He chided himself but given the circumstances he did not regret it. The older figure numbly pointed to the books then stepped toward the rear wall of the store room grabbing the torch from the holder where Anagir had placed it. He then grabbed two other torches from a pile laying atop one of the other crates. The room was one that they had used to store a variety of equipment and food stuffs. Once these were lit and thrust into holders on either wall the room brightened up considerably. Anagir scrambled to gather the mystic tomes and waxed parchment scrolls together as quickly as possible to avoid another brush with the master's anger. His shoulder ached from where the hand of Taranh had squeezed.

The tall majic user reached the back wall and moved over closer to the right side of the wall. He turned his gaze to the side wall looking for a specific stone. Counting in his head he stopped when he reached the fourth one over and fifth down from the top. A steady push on the selected stone caused it to slide into the wall; the sound from the hidden machinery that operated the wall could be faintly heard coming from somewhere deep within.

The rear wall began to move, sliding to their left as they watched. A gap appeared at the right edge where the two walls met and grew slowly in size. It took nearly to the count of ten for the wall section to open to its limit; as the wall moved down the metal track on which it rode it another chamber was revealed in the smoky torch light. It was about ten paces wide and half as many deep.

The discovery of the hidden room had been a complete accident, when the supplies and equipment were being moved into the storage area a crate had slipped from its resting place and had fallen against the proper stone triggering the mechanism. A careful search of the other rooms beneath the fortress had found two other rooms such as this as well. Taranh was sure that there were others but they had remained hidden. The news of the discovery of the rooms had been strictly limited; the senior majic user had quickly thanked his ancestors that the one who found the first one had the sense to keep it to himself before bringing it to the attention of one of the Council members. That information was cautiously shared only with Taranh. Both the finder and the Councilor were now dead, killed the previous day during one of the assaults.

Taranh stepped into the now exposed space. The torch drove away the darkness. The pale flickering light reflected dully from the metal of three doors set into the stone of the back wall. Heavy iron strapping surrounded each of the three, with rivets as large as a palm width driven into the rock that formed the room. Doors that appeared as sturdy as the rivets surrounding them were closed but appeared unsecured.

Anagir stole in holding the books and scrolls. He had watched the wall slide away into its resting place with wonder. He had previously explored the fortress as much as he could during their time there and had encountered many interesting things, but this was by far one of most arresting. The time he had used for exploration stolen from when he was supposed to be sleeping or studying his mystic arts.

This was a truly a wonder of engineering; Anagir had seen few broken examples of the mysterious equipment left by the builders of the large bastion. In two locations above them in the buildings near the courtyard there were huge stone panels engraved with long lines of text, written in a tongue that none of them could speak or read. He had spent no small amount of time standing before the panels intrigued at the sight.

Stepping over to the wall Taranh fit the torch into a holder then moved to the iron door farthest to the right of the three. He quickly lifted the guard bar and opened the portal. He took a step back and to the side to allow the door to open all the way. A metal lined chambers about four feet in depth and three feet in the other dimensions shown empty in the guttering light of the torches. This vault and the others were once used to safeguard treasures beyond the dreams of men. Now all they held was a thin layer of dust.

Anagir stood waiting, the books and scrolls clutched tightly to his chest. He felt lost, out of touch with what was going on, he wasn't sure why his master was here or what he was doing. A part of him wanted to ask, to try and figure out what was happening but fear kept him from saying anything. The young novice majic user simply stood there, a living bookcase. Waving the younger one forward Taranh turned to take the load of written material from him. Anagir walked forward barely lifting his feet as he covered the space between him and the now impatient leader.

Taranh placed the written material in the vault with the exception of one thin scroll which he handed back to Anagir. Resting one hand on the tomes, the gathered work of a dozen lifetimes, Taranh knew that this would be the last time he would touch them. His destiny was written, the plan set in his mind for two days now, and he knew what must happen for the material to be kept safe. The bitter taste of defeat and despair rose in his mouth and for a moment he waded in the pool of self-pity that suddenly rose up from his soul. He was the leader of his people, the senior majic user, it had been up to *him* and now it had turned to ashes despite all their efforts. One faint hope remained, it was all he had left and so it must succeed, it *must*.

Enough - with a strong, decisive movement he withdrew his hand from the books then swung the door to the vault closed and secured the lock bar. He took one step back, drew in a deep breath and began to focus, sharply, without hesitation. The spell series he was about to undertake was the most complex he had ever attempted. Taranh began to slowly open himself up to the nearly limitless supply of mystic energy that saturated the region. It had to be done slowly or else the mystic power would wash them away destroying all they were trying to make safe.

He tried to keep his mind clear, sharp and focused on what was being worked. For the most part he was successful. The wounds of earlier, including a large burn on one cheek courtesy of a fireball that passed too close, taunted him with their pain and discomfort. Sweat running down his face stung the burn but he ignored that. He began the spell series; it would take some time since he was mixing several different spells and then binding them into one, he hoped. Much rested on his years of experience and training. Drawing in more power, careful to ensure that it was enough, just enough, for the sequence he was working through.

***

Anagir had remained silent since Taranh had released his shoulder.

He stood watching as his teacher locked the books away and now was beginning to cast a spell. The young student of the mystic arts was at a loss as he tried to figure out what was happening.

He had been looking for a place to hide, someplace where the enemy wasn't when Taranh found him. The leader of their people assumed he had been on an errand or some type of official duty, why else would he have been so far from the fighting? Taranh didn't ask and Anagir wasn't about to volunteer the information about what he had been doing. He had been told to follow and so he did. Taranh was accompanied by fifteen or so guards which Anagir was glad to see. If there was fighting then it would be them and not him that would bear the risk of injury or death.

The nimble fingers of Taranh worked the intricate majical patterns back and forth as he pulled more and more power from the natural sources around him. Faintly at first but growing in strength, Anagir could see the fingers weave trails through the air. The glowing traces of majic faded quickly but were lasting longer as it wove deeper into the sequence of power that Taranh worked. The temperature in the room began to rise, slowly but steadily as more mystic energy was drawn into the small space.

There was power here, power for every majic user in the world it seemed but right now one majic user was enough. The novice took a half step to his left to better see what his teacher was attempting. He could sense the power being drawn in, the substance of the spell, the taste of it changing as Taranh fought to bend the mystic forces to his will and those of the spell series he was working to invoke.

It was warm in the room now, the combination of the extra torches and the energy bleeding off the spell series did it. Taranh with about one third of the way through the series. He could sense that he did not have sufficient energy in him to finish. He knew the risk of that, an incomplete spell series, especially one of this magnitude, could be disastrous. The forces he had so far channeled would be released in one moment which could leave nothing save a crater where they now stood. He turned his head slightly to call Anagir to him. For once the younger one needed no prompting, he moved over right away.

"Infuse yourself," Taranh said. It was a fairly simple task, one learned early on in the mystic arts so that the user could get used to the feel of the mystic energy and become familiar with its nature. Anagir placed one hand on the dominant shoulder and the other palm open over the heart of his master. Bowing his head in concentration while opening himself up more and more to the energy around them directing it through him into the older one.

Despite maintaining his focus on the series Taranh could feel the power flowing into him, strength rose and continued to climb. He did note with no small measure of disappointment the level of power though. It should have been higher, much higher. Anagir had been shirking his lessons again. The only way to increase skill was daily, sometimes hourly practice and it was all too apparent that the student now with him had not been doing that. In spite of that the power should be enough to allow him to complete what he had started. Now well over half the series had been accomplished, time seemed to speed up as more and more power flowed into the web of spells that surrounded the holy tomes resting inside the vault.

As Anagir continued to feed his master power, he saw the effects. The metal around the vault containing the books sparkled somewhat, there were flashes of color within the metal itself. Slender ribbons of pale yellow that changed over to blue-white raced along the surface of the metal and then without effort disappeared into the heavy iron. As more and more of the ribbons flowed into the binding strips a pale glow rose from it. With his training Anagir could see, literally *see*, the network of protection webs that were now wrapped around the vault on all sides. The protection spells were overlapping, some were intended to prevent an intruder from tearing away the wall itself, and other words were there to keep majic from being used against it. The webs grew tighter and tighter as Taranh continued the conjuring.

Through their connection Anagir could feel a measure of the fatigue that Taranh felt and brushes of the forces he was grappling with. It was like standing on the edge of cliff and looking at the scene far below, you could get a measure of it but the true nature of what you were looking at was beyond your touch.

The ancient race that had constructed the immense fortress had not chosen this location randomly, it sat at a nexus of five mystic force lines, three airborne and the other two soil bound. Having that much power available was almost beyond imagining. Anagir had seen numerous places in his travels where two of the energy lines crossed, rarely – very rarely three -- but five!

The glow from within the metal now faded and within moments was gone as if it had never been. Taranh, now finished with the protection spells allowed the student to continue infusing him with power. He was tired, his arms were as stone so little strength were left in his limbs. His head drooped until his chin was nearly resting on his chest his breathing coming in deep draughts.

The power coming in from Anagir and what he was drawing in on his own were restoring but it would take some time, time that he could not allow himself if the rest of what he had planned was to come to fruition. Lifting his head he told Anagir to stop what he was doing and come around to his other side. When the youth's hands were lifted off him it was as if a tap was closed and no more liquid came forth.

Anagir slowly slid around his master until he was standing nearly against the wall by the vault. He unconsciously avoiding touching it. Taranh noticed this but it couldn't be helped for the next part was the true challenge.

"Turn around. Place your hand on the vault door." Anagir was surprised to hear the strength present in the voice of his master. He slowly turned and with a degree of hesitation raised one hand slowly while the fingers opened and closed several times with nervous abandon. Touch the door? What madness was this, he knew that there were protection spells in place. *Kill me, he's trying to kill me to keep me quiet,* Anagir realized with a panic. His eyes darted around looking for a way out, any way, but the strong grip of Taranh locked his arm in place and then slowly raised it to rest the anxious hand on the door.

Anagir waited for the moment of agonizing death -- but it didn't come! The door and the spells ignored him as if he was not there.

Taranh spoke once again, "Remember these words, for only these words will undo what I have set in place. Do you understand?" The senior majic user waited for a response but got nothing.

"Anagir, do you understand? You must listen and remember or else we are lost. Only what I am saying now, Our Hope in Sorrow, will unlock the guard spell." He then made the student repeat it as he concentrated on connecting the phrase to the spell that would serve as guardian for the books.

As Anagir repeated the words he felt an odd tingling sensation in his hand, it was like an itch but worse, it was if his whole hand was burning. But it was not heat, more like water flowing over his hand. The sensation grew stronger and stronger, light again began to shine from within the metal. With a start Anagir realized that he could no longer see his hand, a wrap of glowing energy had covered it and was slowly enveloping his arm a little at a time as he watched. He tried to turn, lift his hand, jerk his arm away but nothing worked. He was stuck there as if he was now part of the door.

The energy wasn't painful but he was scared of what it was doing to him. Tiny tendrils of mystic origin pierced his skin in hundreds of places where the glowing mass shrouded his skin. He could half sense something in his mind. Shadows of images, of something flittered around behind his eyes and he tried to make sense of what he was seeing, feeling, and what was being done to him. His arm wouldn't come loose. Out, he wanted out, but nothing he was doing allowed that to happen.

Gone. It was suddenly gone, the light, the energy that wrapped his hand and arm, the images in his head. It was just the two majic users and the crackle of the torches burning. Anagir jerked his hand off the metal and absently rubbed it with the other hand but nothing was wrong with it.

Taranh slowly turned the student around gently; Anagir was facing his teacher. The senior looked down on his charge and gently asked him if he was well. Anagir nodded without thought, his mind trying to grasp what had just happened to him.

"What is the phrase you must remember?" Without effort the phrase leapt forward in his mind and he spoke it aloud, "Our Hope in Sorrow".

Taranh made sure that was looking in the younger ones eyes, "Good, good, now hear me. What has been done here is more important than anything in our history. It is the hope of our people. You, only you, can unlock the door without fear. Do you understand?"

Anagir didn't really, but he said "I understand." For his part the senior one didn't think his student really did but there was no time to wonder about it. He sensed that they had been occupied for some time and it was likely that the underground had been penetrated by now and that they would have to leave soon, very soon. He turned and crossed the room to unlock the door.

He pulled the portal open. Cautiously, he looked outside and saw that the guards were present and alert. The one in charge of the others hurried over as soon as he heard the door move. He bowed once more to his leader and Taranh motioned him inside. The man took a quick look around before going through the door, which was closed behind him. The warrior moved to the center of room and waited. Taranh looked at the two others with him now and felt the weight of the moment and his decision to bring it about.

Taranh, speaking for the first time since re-entering the room asked the warrior his name; he answered at once, "Lykan Tee of the Family Brahaan." The elder majic user nodded once and with a measure of dignity told the younger one that he did indeed know of the family and their proud history. Lykan bowed deeply to his leader in gratitude for the honor paid to his line.

"Lykan Tee of the Family Brahaan, I am about to give you the most difficult order I have ever issued. It will be hard to do but harder still for you to bear, but for our people to survive and one day return to our place I must do this thing." He nervously wet his lips and paused as if to hold the inevitable off for a moment, just one moment, longer.

Squaring his shoulders and taking a deep breath Taranh looked the warrior in the eye and told him, "You are to guard this one. This majic user is the hope of us all," pointing to Anagir who was silent but keenly watching the events that would shape the future of their people.

He then continued, "In order to do this you must avoid fighting, no matter what the situation if it means that any harm may come to him." To never avoid a fight was their highest law and for Taranh to order the warrior to break this was without precedent in their history.

To his credit Lykan merely flinched slightly as he heard the order and the implications that it carried. Anagir was shocked; he couldn't imagine that it would come to this. The young apprentice was just beginning to understand how serious the situation was and the role he was to play in it. Reality had come crashing down on him and nearly did him in.

Taranh told the pair to quickly check the boxes for any food items. Lykan immediately turned and pulled the nearest box open with one powerful yank. The box contained nothing edible so he moved on to the next one. He was opening his third crate before Anagir moved forward to help. Their combined effort allowed them to quickly locate several crates of preserved foodstuffs and even a pair of barrels containing water that appeared to be at least drinkable if not completely wholesome.

The elder one knew that the spell series now protecting the books would be strong; he had tied the spells into the mystic lines that converged here at the fortress. Since the energy of the lines was neutral it was possible for any majic user to draw on them. The power that was available was beyond belief. It was why Taranh had risked virtually everything to move such a large number of them here to perform the rite. Now it was lost.

The power of the lines would seep into the spells at a faint trickle and over time the spells would be self-sustaining requiring only a fraction of what they drew in now. The majic users of the enemy would find it nearly impossible to use the power to locate the cache now hidden within amid all the energy that the fortress teemed with. In addition the use of so much majic by both sides would further muddy the water in a manner of speaking, adding additional confusion to any efforts. No, if they wanted to find what they had just secured they would have to do it the hard way, searching by hand throughout the massive fortress. A task that he hoped was beyond even their cursed determination.

***

Taranh ordered them to move these supplies into the smaller chamber; again the soldier complied without hesitation while the novice majic user lagged behind. Within a very short time a decent size pile of supplies occupied about a third of the smaller chamber and Taranh pointed out the proper stone on the inside of the hidden room that would open the wall from that side.

Lykan noted this and then grabbed several more torches to add to the pile of material. His leader bid him to stay there, which he did. His steady demeanor was a blessing to the senior majic user that he would never know of. The plan he had devised was fraught with flaws not the least of which was now standing next to him.

He turned to Anagir and told him with all the firmness and authority he could place in his voice, "Listen well to this soldier, he will protect you but you must not allow yourself to be killed or we are all lost. Do what you must to survive. This is the most important thing you will ever do in life. Use the scroll wisely and keep it hidden, even from our own people."

Turning his gaze to the soldier, "In two days' time leave this room and surrender yourselves to the enemy. Do nothing that will alert them to who you are and what you guard." Lykan bowed deeply placing one hand across his massive chest to accept the charge that his leader had decreed.

Pushing the young majic user toward the smaller chamber Taranh could sense the hesitation that his student felt. In a gentler voice than he had used in some time the teacher tried one last time to get Anagir to understand. "The two of you will hide here while the enemy tears the place apart looking for what we have taken here. In two days you will surrender and disappear among the masses of our people blending in which will allow you to survive. Do you understand?"

Lykan answered at once, "My Lord, it is not for me to understand but to obey and this I will do." The words warmed the heart and raised the tattered spirit of his leader.

Anagir was finally coming to understand that Taranh meant to leave him, to go away. That was why he had gotten the soldier to come in; he was leaving him behind to die. He tried one last time, "Master, stay here and hide with us, you are too important to be lost." The plea was much like that of a child, earnest and innocent but the senior majic user understood the reasoning behind the plea. He felt the disgust rise in him as he cursed the fate and especially the hated easterners again for bringing this to bear. That this one should be the one was almost too much for him to choke down. The anger washed over him for a moment then he regained control swallowing twice and took in several deep breathes to clear his mind.

Taranh understood as did Lykan -- who had figured that the books he had seen the pair with earlier were the reason for coming here -- that the elder could not be found anywhere near here. If he was then the enemy would figure out where they had hidden the books and all would truly be lost then. Taranh knew he had overstayed his time and pushed Anagir toward the room. Feet dragging the younger one stumbled toward the rear of the room then stopped. Lykan moved forward to take him by the arm and if needed drag him in.

Nearly at the door leading out Taranh turned one last time and told Anagir, "When the time comes you will personally remove any discredit that falls to Lykan regarding his conduct, do you understand?" The question hung in the air with a great sense of expectancy.

Anagir drew himself up and with a voice that surprised even him with its conviction told Taranh, "I will do this on my word and my life" The senior one was more than a little caught off guard by the promise and waved them to their places. Lykan waited for a moment and then gently taking Anagir by the arm led him into the smaller room. He never hesitated; as soon as the majic user was inside he walked over and pushed the stone covered release to return the wall to its place. The sound of the hidden machinery could again be faintly heard as the wall began to emerge from its resting place. Lykan watched his leader as the wall continued across its path. Anagir couldn't make himself look. Just before the wall closed Taranh suddenly yelled to the pair to keep the door unlocked to not arouse suspicion. Lykan quickly waved in acknowledgment and then was gone as the wall returned to its proper place.

Leaving the room and making sure it was not locked Taranh closed the door behind him and tried to quell the growing sense of hopelessness he was feeling. He called for the guards to rally to him. The sounds of booted feet striking the stone floor could be heard as the well trained soldiers hurried over in response to the summons. Taranh's grin was savage in the harsh light of the torches as he gathered the guards to him. Once all of them were with him he looked around the circle of the loyal ones there, some were wounded and all of them tired.

Their leader spoke, "I go Deathwalking," a tradition among them that called for no quarter and no return. "Who goes with me?" The question was delivered with a note of promise and challenge, death to their enemies and entrance to the halls of the ancestors was all that was left for them.

Several of the guards pulled daggers and slashed their cheeks to answer the question. This was to allow the spirit a way out of the body when death came. With a measure of determination, the leader of his people pointed down the long tunnel and the group started on their way. He knew he had to get as far from this place as possible and the prospect of venting his frustration on the enemy was suddenly upon him. They would pay dearly before he went down of that he was certain.

…Nearly Two Thousand Years Later…

Chapter One
Travel Mercies

West of Karkal

The caravan was slowing again, it was the fourth such delay since they had risen for the day and taken the road west some four hours earlier. Radhan Triadl, a merchant and trader from the city of Edora turned in his saddle to try and determine what the slow down had been caused by this time. Every delay kept them from reaching their destination on time and that cut into his already thin profit margin.

He looked upward at the mid-morning sun and pulled a linen hand cloth from his pocket to wipe his bare brow. The day was warm but not overly so; the forty or so extra pounds he carried that spilled over his belt made him easy prey to the sun's warming rays. His riding cloak had already been removed and lashed to his bag.

Unable to locate the problem he turned to get the attention of one of the caravan guards who pointedly ignored him and kept riding. Berating himself for hiring this particular group of sell swords the portly merchant turned his horse to the side and rode toward the man who now had no choice but to acknowledge the fat fool who thought he knew everything.

Radhan had taken this route back and forth a great number of times over the years but it was only in the last year or so that it had been a problem. Two caravans belonging to some of his competitors had been sacked with a great loss of life and goods. To keep his creditors, of which he had many -- too many if you asked him -- happy he had to agree to provide guards for the lengthy trip.

Prior to leaving he had spoken to several firms in Karkal that provided these services. One such firm, operated by a former Legion officer used exclusively former Legionnaires had quoted Radhan a price. The merchant had offered up a counter proposal. The soldier, he still thought of himself that way, merely looked at the merchant and told him that was the price, period.

Radhan couldn't believe what his ears were telling him, it was nearly a third of the value of the entire wagon train, that it wasn't negotiable was ridiculous, *everything* was negotiable. When he realized that the man was serious he got up and walked out without a word.

The one time officer watched the merchant leave his office. He hoped that the fool wouldn't come to a bad end. He'd shaken his head once and then returned to the paperwork that needed his attention.

Now, Radhan was informed of a problem with one of the wagons belonging to a small family near the rear of the column. It had long been an unwritten rule that those wishing to join a caravan were free to do so. Radhan, in an attempt to offset the cost of the guards, had charged a fee for joining the wagon train. Several families and two other merchants recanted their desire to join when informed of the fee. Radhan had explained it was a small fee and since that caravan was well guarded what could it hurt? The explanation was weak at best but several others paid it and now one of them was slowing down the whole group.

Radhan urged his horse, already suffering from the weighty burden it carried, to go faster so he could get to the guard quicker. He wanted the man to go and see what the problem was and get it fixed so they could continue on their way. It was a long enough journey to Ulbennaya, a large Dwarf settlement on the northeast frontier of the Dwarf kingdom, as it was.

Ulbennaya hosted a large regional market that carried a wide variety of goods, clothes, food and numerous examples of the fine metalwork that the Dwarf craftsmen were renowned for. Trade was brisk and prosperous if the goods were of quality. The Dwarves guarded their own territory fiercely but not being great lovers of the horse due to their smaller stature did little to patrol beyond their own borders.

Delays, like this wagon problem, only added to the expense.

***

Two sets of eyes carefully watched the caravan as it made its way along the track heading west. The eyes belonged to members of one of the nomad tribes that rode through the vast grasslands, sometimes they stayed in the eastern reaches. Others times, like now, they favored the more southern marches of the plains.

The nomads were hunters. Their game was plunder and their prey was the hapless travelers who were unaware that they were being stalked.

One of the two watchers spoke quietly to the other who nodded and slid down of the slight rise on which they perched to watch the wagon train. He rushed over to his horse being careful to keep himself and the horse out of sight. He galloped away south and then angled to the west to report the sighting. Another caravan, unsought, but still a rich prize.

There were guards but they were lazy and so posed no threat. The fools didn't even have any outriders. It was a mistake that would cost them if the leader decided to attack this group which he likely would.

Within the hour the raiders had silently and with increasing numbers surrounded the caravan at a distance and rode pace with them while staying out of sight. They waited until the wagon train was passing through some scattered groups of trees to converge. They could approach quickly using the trees as cover. As the caravan moved out of the trees and into a large clearing the nomads struck. Death came swiftly to some but eluded others for far too long.

The region was not well populated or extensively traveled by those other than merchants so it took some time before the slaughter was discovered. Another trade caravan traveling the same route as yesterday's caravan, with some of those who had forsaken the offered trip with Radhan for a fee discovered the fate of the fallen.

Smoke, more than would come from casual cooking could be seen rising in air to the west and so a half dozen of the better armed members of the group rode forward to see what they could find out. Others rushed getting the wagons into some semblance of a defensive arrangement. Weapons were made ready as women gathered up children. This caravan leader had hired the guards employed by the former army officer, so the situation was much different than the outcome of the caravan of Radhan.

The half dozen former Legion soldiers who knew their business well rode carefully forward toward the smoke watchful for any signs of any ambush or other trouble. The wind moved the leaves and branches of the trees and when it blew from the west a smell of ash and char came with it. The ex-soldiers knew the smell well but said nothing.

They found the source of the smoke a few moments later as they broke out of the cover of the trees. Up ahead what remained of several wagons were burning but not with great vigor, the majority of the wood already consumed by the fire and drifted away in smoke.

The six spread out slightly and rode forward a little faster; eyes constantly on the move checking the area. The horses didn't like the smell of the smoke and some got a little balky as they approached the site. Nervous hands patted the broad necks trying to soothe the nerves.

Debris of all types littered the area, some clothes, broken crates, pieces of some of the wagons, tack from the horses that were missing, and bodies. The bodies of many of those who had composed the caravan party were strewn throughout the area. The men rode slowly through the scene taking in the sights. Arrows were stuck here and there, some in the bodies of those they had killed.

The leader of the six men stopped his horse when he came across Radhan. The merchant had tried to defend his goods to the end and it had cost him. He had been singled out for an exquisite and horrific death. A frame work of stout boards had been lashed together in an X shape to one of the wagons and he had been tied to these. Once secured a small fire had been built between his feet. The heat would have slowly eaten his flesh away, a very painful and slow way to die. His corpse was charred up to near mid chest level, the pain he felt clearly visible on the death mask of the body.

The smell coming from the body was overwhelming, a sickly sweet odor that was unmistakable. One of the men turned away and noisily deposited the contents of his stomach onto the grass. He had seen action many times in the service of his realm but this went beyond that.

At the same time the others had found more of the handiwork of the raiders. At least a dozen men with their throats cut along with several older teen age boys, these would have proved the most troublesome for the nomads and so they were killed. It also kept them from being able to tell anyone where the raiders went when they left. The men included the old and one infirm who was minus an arm. He would have been of no use sold as a slave; he couldn't do the work of a whole bodied man and as such had no value.

It was the last body that did it; one of the men noticed a flash of color in the grass. He rode over and when it was apparent what it was he choked off a cry that brought several of the others over. He sat on the horse looking at the figure, tears filling his eyes burning from the salt of the eye water. Three of the others hurried over and the sight stopped them as one.

The quartet sat looking sadly at what had very recently been a pretty red headed girl of about fourteen summers. Her nude body was on its back with the legs splayed open, the remains of her clothes a few feet away in the grass. The swine had chosen her to sate their sexual appetites, at least temporarily. Her throat had been sliced apparently when the nomads were ready to leave, she may have fought them or they simply chose not to bring her along having already gang raped her lowering her value at the auction block.

One of the four slowly dismounted and never taking his eyes from the girl pulled a cloak from his saddle pack. He opened it and with a gentleness that was all too late for her covered the still form.

The girl was about the same age as his niece, the daughter of his favorite sister whom he suddenly wanted to see and hug. The thought of this happening to her was too terrible to deal with right now. What was covered up on the ground near him was too painful and he felt helpless. The senior of the six rode up just before the girl was covered. He saw the results of the nomads work and hung his head briefly in a short prayer to the spirits for the girl and the others.

He had seen enough. He had been stationed in the north for several years and knew the signs of many of the nomads. Judging by the arrow fletching he reckoned these to be plainsmen like the Running Horse or Chowon tribe, both of them nasty little groups that favored this kind of work. It was time to get back and report. There was nothing that they could do here so they needed to get back.

The man who had covered the girl took one last look, mouthed a silent goodbye and then remounted his horse. The six then turned and broke out at a gallop heading back to the east. Somebody needed to be told about this and as soon as possible. There was big trouble in the area and they were too few to deal with it. Time to turn this caravan around and he didn't give a good damn if the merchant didn't like it. They were going back to Karkal and that was that, he prayed they made it.

He prayed hard.

Chapter Two
His Majesty's Strikers

The Palace, Karbel

"Bad news, always bad news. Why cannot the day start with good news once in a while?"

The speaker of these words stood near one of two windows of the room looking intently at the room's only other occupant, who by now was well used to the tirades. It was part and parcel of being both advisor and friend to the king.

The other man replied with a smile splitting his face, "Something like the Assembly building collapsing on them?" The tone was light and utterly without seriousness.

Thadar Skye, ruler of Karbel, scowled as he heard the question. "That is not what I meant and you know it!" Despite his anger a small smile began to creep into Thadar's features as the mental image of that even happening filled his mind's eye. Both men knew that wouldn't necessarily be a bad thing, especially if a few dozen of the more disagreeable Assembly members happened to be in the building when it collapsed.

The Assembly, originally put together to help Thadar when he first came to power nearly twelve years earlier, had once been a useful and necessary entity. Now it was a power hungry group of noblemen whose main concern was their own wellbeing.

The king, with his anger slackened by the sharp wit of his friend, was still somewhat angry but more focused on the matter at hand. "Tell me the tale, I am sure I know it but tell me anyway." He asked of his companion, his voice was tired, the strain of running such a large realm was taxing even during good times. And these were far from good times.

The other man Gunnar Norstaad began, "It was well west of Karkal on the road to Ulbennaya. Raiders surrounded a trade caravan then looted it, took most of the travelers as slaves, killed the rest - this happened three days ago or so."

At hearing that the king's head came around to fix his gaze squarely on his advisor, "Three days? What happened, why so long for the news?" Thadar's anger was back in full bloom and this time Gunnar wisely allowed it to flourish. No humor would stifle it this time. The large kingdom possessed an excellent heliograph system, well in excess of a thousand towers and their companion messenger stations dotted the landscape allowing for rapid transmission of news.

Gunnar had no answer for the questions so said nothing. He felt much the same as his friend as he considered the toll, over a hundred dead or missing, goods and coine worth thousands taken. For those unlucky enough to be taken prisoner, there would be slavery, abuse and rape.

The king turned to look out one of the windows and absently began to rub a long scar on his left forearm as he gave the matter additional thought. Gunnar noted this and recognized it for what it was. Whenever Thadar was faced with sending some of his troops in harm's way he agonized about for a short time before giving the order. The scar was a constant reminder of the price that must be paid at times to ensure freedom. The Northman knew the story better than some even though he had not been present at the time the king had received it.

It had been not long after Thadar had come to power twelve years earlier following the death of his father in a battle on the western frontier. During this time there were no special security measures in place to protect the young king. Security was the function of regular army troops. Thadar and a group of his friends had been returning to his quarters in the palace from a party in the city.

A group of assassins had been waiting for him, having slipped past the palace guards earlier and hidden themselves near the royal quarters. They had not anticipated his being accompanied by a half dozen or so of his friends but they attacked anyway. A wild melee ensued. Two of his friends died and all of them were wounded defending him while managing to slay several of the would-be killers with the help of late arriving guards.

The scar was from a deep cut, courtesy of a knife slash he deflected with his arm before it could slit his throat. Thadar was not even aware of the fact that he often traced the line of the scar which was over a hand span in length and very disfiguring. It did not affect the ability to use his arm, which was tan and muscular beneath the short sleeve mail shirt he often wore.

The king was silent for several moments before speaking to his friend again, "Send for Balkon and Steele".

The king's companion said nothing but was curious about this. He understood the need for one but both? This could prove interesting he told himself, life in the service of royalty. He was not a stranger to life working in the house of a king but that was another life he reminded himself and pushed the issue away, again.

Gunnar remained silent as he dropped the sheets of parchment on the rich surface of the table, rose from his chair and walked to the door. It was but a few steps from his former position. Once there he pulled steadily on the portal, the door was well built of heavy timber backed with several iron straps and so was somewhat heavy. It resisted the strong arm at first but as more muscle was applied it gave way, silently since the hinges were well maintained.

Once open enough for him to stick his head out he asked one of the guards outside to summon the men the king requested. The guard, one of Thadar's elite bodyguards, known as Strikers, smartly came to attention, saluted and headed down the hall way to send word of the king's order. Gunnar nodded to the remaining three troopers who repositioned themselves to cover for the missing man.

The one closest to the door, an Elf, nodded once in response and returned his full attention to the corridor in front of him. Closing the door Gunnar walked back over to the table and then returned his attention to the other matters on the daily list.

Trade talks with the Dwarves were going well while the report on the emissary mission to the Federation of Clans was less than encouraging.

The Federation was a large but loose association of tribal clans situated to the northwest of Karbel and they occasionally raided into the kingdom. Thadar had sent an emissary to speak with several of the clans regarding trade talks; he was in favor of trade rather than another long bloody war. There had been several of those in the hundred or so years since the founding of Karbel.

One such war had cost him his father when he was twelve. The battle had been a solid victory for Karbel, killing thousands of the gathered Clansmen at the cost of nearly a quarter of a Legion, over two thousand men and their king.

Darnel Skye had fallen while leading a charge of horse against a flank of the clan army that caved in the wing of their force and led to the rout of the clansmen -- who had not bothered Karbel for a number of years after. That time appeared to be coming to an end, small raids and occasional skirmishes had been reported several times during the previous months with no rhyme or reason why.

The death of Darnel had placed Thadar on the throne at an early age but he had managed to stay in power and rule his realm through war and peace, drought and bounty. Sometimes, when he was alone Thadar grew angry at father for dying when he did and forcing him to take over as ruler when he did. The king had known his whole life that he would one day be in a position that he would have to rule the large realm but to do it at the age of twelve had been asking much. Now, twelve years later the trouble that had taken his father was returning.

The two men resumed their discussion regarding matters until a knock on the door interrupted them. "Come", Gunnar said, and at that the door was swung inward.

One of the guards from the hallway stepped in, came to rigid attention and waited by the door as two officers entered. The first was slightly over medium height dressed in a well cut uniform of gray and red that managed to mostly hide the fact he was well past the middling weight for a man his age, the uniform marking him as a member of the army of Karbel. A rich cloak covered his shoulders with the left side tossed back to reveal his medals which were displayed prominently above the breast pocket one row wide. His hair was short and immaculate, not a lock out of place while a finely combed beard framed his mouth. The highly polished boots he wore reflected the light streaming in from the window. He stopped short of the table and looked casually bored.

The second man was a little taller than the first and was dressed in the black and silver uniform of the king's bodyguard troops. His hair was long and gathered at the back with a black scarf shot through with streaks of silver.

The Striker was as lean as his counterpart was plump. The high boots worn over the trousers of black were scuffed and mud stained. Steele had reported to his ruler directly from the training field where he had been overseeing one of his units conducting drill when the summons came. A shirt of fine chain mail, black in color, the armor was dipped in oil and then baked to give it the darkened hue could be seen underneath the tunic, the sleeves of the armor extended down the arms to nearly the elbow. A set of back-and-breast plates completed his armor. Heavy leather bands circled both of the wrists, a common fighter's tactic to protect the important joints from incidental blows or slashes.

Once both men were inside the guard exited the room pulling the heavy door closed behind him after bowing once more to his king.

Legion Marshal Serus Balkon was first to salute the king, ever one to try and curry favor he was a far better politician than he was a soldier. Everyone in the room save him knew that. Laen Steele was but a heartbeat behind his Legion counterpart in rendering honors to his liege but his was much crisper and done with a degree of sincerity that Balkon couldn't match in two lifetimes of service.

Thadar came to attention, heels touching at an angle, left arm straight down with the fingers curled into the palm, thumb along the seam of his finely tailored trousers. His right arm brought across his chest with the closed fist resting over the left side near where his heart was. The king disliked the formal trappings of power and ceremony and so avoided them whenever possible but this was one of those times when it was appropriate. Anything less would have been insulting.

Formalities completed, Thadar waved them to seats around the table. Balkon stopped long enough to remove his cloak and drape it carefully over the back of the chair he then occupied, wondering if this would take long. Steele sat opposite him while Gunnar took the chair to Thadar's left, the king taking the seat at the head of the table. There was one empty seat between Gunnar and Balkon who shared the same side.

The ruler of Karbel didn't waste any time, "I imagine that you both have heard about the latest nomad attack on the caravan?" There was a noticeable note of fatigue present in the timbre of his voice. Balkon nodded as did Steele, was this all the king wanted? For this he was called away from his morning briefing? That it was mid-morning and he had only just arrived at his office while all of the others present had been hard at work for hours never occurred to him. He was a man who enjoyed his station in life and took full advantage of it whenever he saw fit which was often to the detriment of his duties.

Seeing an opportunity the Legion Marshal spoke up first. "My Lord, we have hunted these vermin repeatedly and have yet to bring them to battle sufficient to inflict the losses we desire on them. They are elusive and more of an annoyance than a threat, do we really need to concern ourselves with them?"

Gunnar, who had been a member of Thadar's inner circle for going on three years, had thought he had heard it all but this was something new. He turned away from looking at Balkon to hide the astonishment that he felt sure covered his face.

The king of Karbel blinked hard once at the words of the man who commanded his Legions. That a soldier could so easily dismiss the suffering that even this moment someone was undergoing as casually as that was nearly beyond him. Steele said nothing and didn't change his expression.

The king wasted no time in framing his reply, "Yes General, we do need to concern ourselves with them, they are killing our citizens; which is something that the army is supposed to prevent, would you not agree?" The last words were dripping with sarcasm that Balkon did not fail to notice.

Even when he was angry Thadar did not use contractions, it was something that his father had instilled in him. Speak clearly the first time and he would not have to repeat himself. Balkon had misread the king's mood and smoothly changed his previous track to more in line with what he felt the king wanted to hear, the quicker to be free of this meeting and then on to his luncheon at Valerio's in the city. He thought quickly of their fine menu and extensive wine selection. The Legion General who was no stranger to the finer things in life was so involved in thinking about lunch it took him a moment to realize that the others were waiting for him to answer the question.

Coughing to cover his gaffe the portly General excused himself and then started, "My Liege, we could mount a punitive expedition, using troops from the northwest garrisons and the Eighth in Karkal. We simply flood the area with cavalry, find them and dispose of these pests once and for good." Pleased with the solution he had come up with so quickly, Balkon leaned back, confident of the plan and the praise it would bring him personally for coming up with it. He had no intention of leading the units that would be involved -- that was the job for men junior to him. Besides, campaigning was often hot, dusty work and he had better things to do with his time.

Thadar couldn't believe what he was hearing. It was a half assed plan at best and even that was being very generous. The king was careful not to blurt out how stupid he thought the plan was, before he could say anything Gunnar, in his role as advisor, spoke up. "How is it that you would force battle on those you canna' find?"

The tension in the room went up measurably. Balkon was caught off guard by the question and more so by the source of the question. He wondered why the king surrounded himself with these people of such obviously low station of birth. The senior army leader responded to the verbal jab.

"We will find these raiders, have no fear of that." He tugged down on his spotless tunic to further straighten it as he settled deeper into the chair he occupied.

What Balkon didn't know was that Gunnar came from a long line of military leaders; his uncle, Thindor, was Warlord, senior military advisor, to the ruler of Vankard, a human kingdom well to the northwest of Karbel. A post that Gunnar had been groomed to take over in due time but he had left Vankard much to the dismay of his family.

The king was silent during the exchange and seeking a way to keep things moving along turned to the man who commanded his bodyguards. "Colonel Steele, what is your opinion on this matter? You have not said a word since coming in." The remaining eyes in the room moved to take in the man that the king entrusted with his life and that of his family.

Steele was as opposite from the man he sat across from as he could be. The two men who controlled the military forces of the kingdom were simply cut from cloth totally unlike one another. The Striker leader was first and foremost a fighter, it was his way. He told himself to be careful, while he had no respect for Balkon as a soldier or for that manner, a man; he did respect the Legionnaires that he commanded. Getting into a personal issue with the general would be a distraction. He mentally shrugged and told himself, go ahead.

"Sire, it be foolish and a waste of time to send a large cavalry force after the nomads." After hearing the statement Balkon was angry and growing more so by the moment, he wondered again what Steele was doing at the meeting.

He did not feel the same respect for the Strikers that Steele had for the Legions. He thought them little more than thugs in fancy uniforms. He made sure that Steele could see the anger he felt. Part of his dislike for the king's bodyguards went back twelve years to when the young king had nearly been killed during an attack on him in the palace.

At the time Balkon had been the commanding officer of the Tenth Legion, one of the two units which had been charged with protection of the city including the palace. The guards on duty that night had been his men. After the attack and the subsequent uproar that followed it Balkon had been hard pressed to distance himself from the blame being tossed about regarding the near success of the assassination attempt. He had gone to incredible lengths to remove himself from the glaring eye of public scrutiny following the attack.

Many of those directly involved found themselves transferred to distant postings or discharged outright to keep as much of the stain of what happened away from him. Several promising careers were cut short to save Balkon's precious reputation.

The man who commanded all of the Legions of the realm had worked hard over the years to gain control of the position he now held and felt strongly that this situation, bringing in the thrice damned Strikers, was a slap in his face. It was a job for the army or no one.

Thadar wasn't surprised by the bluntness of Steele's statement; in fact he had been counting on it. Balkon was not his choice for the position of Marshal of the Legions, he was a political appointee foisted off on the king by the Assembly.

"Why a waste of time Colonel?" Gunnar stayed silent but leaned forward slightly in his chair to hear the answer.

"My Liege Lord, be likely that the raiders have spies out following the patrols. Recall the patrols which should fool the spies, send a unit of

Strikers from Edora to the area to find the nomads and deal with 'em. Then the Legion patrols may be assigned as the garrison commander sees fit." That, thought the king is one of the longest speech I have ever heard him speak at one time in all the years I have known him, strange times we live in.

Balkon couldn't believe what he was hearing; he leapt to his feet knocking the cloak off the back of the chair, "Recall? Recall? You want to recall the only troops protecting the area? Are you mad?" His face was red and his breathing rapid as he stood looking at Steele who returned the gaze but said nothing.

The Northman advisor to the king took up the question, "It would seem that they aren't protecting much, eh General?" The caustic remark scored heavily against the vain officer. He whirled to face his attacker self-control nearly at an end. He now felt that this had escalated into a personal attack against him and his position.

The king was satisfied with what he had heard. He told his senior army commander, "Sit down General." Balkon held his place for the longest delay that protocol would allow before resuming his seat.

Gunnar liked the plan for its craftiness and boldness as well; he communicated this to his friend with a look and a barely perceptible nod. Thadar looked over to the senior general who had his gaze fixed straight ahead. So be it, his army had their chance. Now it was up to the Strikers.

The Northman spoke first, "How soon could they get going Colonel?" The response was immediate; they could leave first thing in the morning, early.

The king wasted no more time with this, "Send the orders."

Chapter Three
Hunters

The Northern Plains

A large group of soldiers were gathered beneath one of the group of trees that dotted the vast grass plains that dominated this part of the continental mass. Their horses were tied and still, enjoying the shade they waited in not far away; the soldiers wanted them close at hand.

This was not the typical group of soldiers someone might encounter if they rode through the various states and realms that dotted the face of Dohrya. They numbered nearly three hundred which wasn't unique or even interesting but these numbers included members of several different races, Humans, Elves and even an Ogurth, one of the Mountain Trolls of the deep south all riding beneath the banner of the king of Karbel which helped to set them apart from others who followed the way of the warrior.

The group was slightly spread out with most seated among the trees eating a hasty meal of cheese, fruit and some dried meat washed down with water from nearby canteens. This was not the time for a hot meal; that would come later; right now a quick bite would have to suffice. The horses had already been fed and watered; the soldiers knew the value of keeping their horses well cared for.

Their leader sat apart from the main body nearly finished with the morning food. He was tall, thin for his height with long dark hair gathered at the back with a cloth tie. The man sat with his back to a tall oak watching the distant western horizon and more importantly the heavy black clouds that were slowly rolling closer, a sure sign of more rain to come. More rain was not something the scattered inhabitants of the region wanted or needed. The streams, waterholes and other water bearing features of the area were already full, many of them overflowing. The grass of the plains was lush and long due to the extended moisture. Now it seemed certain yet more water was coming. A knobby piece of bark was trying to irritate him by being between his shoulder blades but ignored it as best he could.

The lanky officer, now finished with his repast took a long drink, never taking his eyes from the discolored sky to the west. He figured they had at best five hours until it was raining again and that only a guess, it could start raining in the next hour or two. The rain had been a nearly constant companion, at least since they had arrived in the area nearly nine days earlier seeking the nomads that had been raiding farms, caravans and small settlements. It had been nineteen days since they had departed Edora, nineteen days was a long time to look at grass especially when grass was all you could find. The spirit accursed nomads had vanished without so much as trace of a trail.

Having finished the long pull on the canteen he replaced the cork stopper and situated the canteen at his belt while he was standing. "Parun," he called out.

The soldier in question was nearby, having stood when he saw his commander do so. A figure of medium height and indeterminate age that even a casual glance would reveal that he was of mixed parentage, human and Elven. The fine features of the face and slightly pointed ears and above average size for an Elf were giveaways but it was the long dark hair, something unusual for Elf whipping about in the breeze that was the biggest clue.

"Sir?" The lean soldier waited for his officer to let him know what he wanted done, although Parun had a pretty good idea. He had served with Shorin Tallon for nearly two years now and had a better than average idea of how the man thought. Shorin spoke again, "Get 'em up, replace the outriders and let's go. Break's over."

Parun felt the corner of his mouth curl up in small grin as he nodded once and saluted. He had been right again. He turned and in a measured voice relayed the orders to the group where it was echoed by the section leaders. Very little prompting was necessary, they were elite troops and it made life much easier on Shorin that they didn't want or need their hands held to get things done. To a man they all wanted to find the raiders, finish them then return to Edora where they were stationed.

For his part Shorin wanted to finish this task up because he knew that he had orders waiting for him, orders to transfer him and a few others to the south east frontier, the quietest of the borders that Karbel shared with those surrounding it. It would be nice to get to a quiet area for a while. This posting had been adventure filled to say the least and so he was looking forward to it.

The raiders the Strikers hunted were likely one of the numerous nomadic tribes that roamed this part of the world. The raiders had been getting bolder with their attacks, striking at larger targets as the opportunity presented itself. Some villages were spared while others suffered. Those that could afford to had built walls and other defenses as they could. This was not something that every collection of people living together could do and it proved the undoing of some. Legion patrols in the area were thin since it was quite a distance from any regular border outpost and the land did not technically belong to Karbel. It was open range for any who wished to brave it.

Shorin, having stowed his canteen and the remainder of his meal began to stretch as he usually did before riding. He had found through long experience that it helped ease the discomfort that spending long hours in the saddle produced. He shrugged his shoulders to get the chainmail shirt he wore to ride better across his shoulders. The weight, while familiar was still pressing. Wearing the heavy armor was a necessary part of his life, the strong muscles of his shoulders and back bore the weight but the damned thing chafed in places and that was irritating as all that.

Once finished with his short workout he let his eyes drift over the scene as he walked over to his horse and absently loosened the reins from the branch where they were tied, then rubbed the horse gently on the neck.

Nearly all his troops were mounted and the small two wheel supply wagons that accompanied them were ready as well, their three horse team allowed them ample speed to keep up with the fast moving troopers.

One of these was used by Luth the Troll, in place of a single horse. Luth was the shortened version of his name, Q'Kaln'Luth which in the language of his people, the Ogurth meant Bearer of Duty. No single horse could carry the massive soldier, originally from the deep south he was now a soldier of the north.

The senior Striker swung himself up into the saddle with ease and long practice; he had been a soldier for nearly eight years despite the fact that he was only twenty three. Originally from a small farm well east of Edora, Shorin had been found wounded among the bodies of his family and several nomads who had attacked his family's farm when he was fifteen. The attackers had burned the once thriving farm nearly to the ground, livestock killed or taken. The Legionnaires took the teen with them when they left to get him proper medical treatment for his wounds. He enlisted in the Legions the week after his wounds had healed enough to allow him proper movement of a sort. No one thought to ask him his age, he was big for his years and he certainly didn't volunteer the information.

Shorin quickly proved to be an excellent soldier and within two years had been promoted to a junior officer in no small part due to his ability to read and perform his mathematical sums. It wasn't long after that when a recruiter for the Strikers found him and now he was here. Shorin still owned the land where the farm once stood. It had not been occupied since the day he had left, he had only returned once since then.

It was time to get going, looking back toward his men he quickly raised one hand over his head, circled it once and then thrust it forward to signal the formation to move out. He lightly dug his heels into the horse's flank to get it going. The well trained mount responded immediately and the whole procession started forward. They rode slightly north of west for nearly two hours before it started raining again. Hooded cloaks of durable cotton, dyed green and brown that had been waxed to repel water kept close at hand were put to use again. The rain fell at a steady pace, never too heavy but constant enough to keep them miserable. The horses had no such cover and so suffered from the climate. Visibility was down to about two hundred paces or so and that was often generous. At times the rain fell in heavy sheets that were hard enough to sting any exposed skin it found.

The troop rode for another hour or so in the rain when one of the point riders suddenly appeared out of the gloom ahead. He headed directly toward Shorin once he saw the formation. Grateful for the interruption the Under-Captain signaled the column to halt and sent word for his senior sergeant. The Striker rode up to his commander, stopped his mount and saluted. Shorin returned the salute and waited for the man to speak which didn't take long.

"Sir, horse and wagon tracks, heavily borne just ahead, be going to the southwest."

Southwest? Shades, why would they be going that way he wondered. The nomads usually faded into the vast grasslands to the north and from there melt into Federation territory. He was about to ask the question when he saw Parun riding up, he had been checking on the wagons.

The Striker officer studied his sergeant again as he had many times since the two had been together. The lean frame of the half Elf was wrapped in the grass colored water resistant cloak that the bodyguards all favored. A sword and a brace of dagger were strapped to his waist over the coat to allow for easier access should the need arise, an Elven long bow of dark ash was in a case lashed to the side of the mount as well. There is a story in that but Shorin didn't know what it was and Parun wasn't telling. In the two years since being together the young human had found out several things about his senior sergeant.

Parun was half elven as a result of the rape of his mother by a human nomad following a raid on her farming village; he passionately hated his father and all like him. The rest of his mother's family had been killed during the attack as had many in the village. Parun had told his commander the story a few months after being assigned together. Shorin had felt it necessary to speak to his senior enlisted man after watching the utter disregard for his own safety Parun displayed during a fight to capture a fortified smugglers outpost. Parun never endangered any of the Strikers but fought with a will Shorin had never seen before or since.

After the fight the veteran Striker explained to his leader that every nomad he killed kept what happened to his mother from occurring to someone else and since several of those present at the outpost had been nomads of the Running Horse clan, the same clan that had attacked his mother's village he was merely saving someone the trouble of killing them later. Shorin recalled the blunt wisdom of the statement. He also knew that Parun was very dedicated to his mother and sent part of his pay to her on a regular basis, visiting when he could. She lived in the same small village west of the capital where she had lived since first coming to Karbel.

Shorin told him about the sighting as Parun rode up. The veteran Striker merely grunted at the news and then looked at the scout. "How many be they?" The answer was immediate, "Rounds three hunnerd, maybe three fifty but no more'en that for sure." The estimate was delivered with a note of confidence born of years of tracking experience.

Both the other men heard the statement, looked at one another then the scout again. That couldn't be right, the average war party for nomads were usually about a hundred or so, sometimes one fifty and even that was unusually large but three hundred? He, no they, couldn't believe what they were hearing. The point man saw the looks and told them, "We all took count apiece -- all agreed, no more than three fifty." He nodded as he spoke, water flying off his hood to join the rain that already filled the air.

Parun didn't like the odds at all. They had nearly three hundred troopers with them but had not counted on finding such a large party. He wasn't afraid just cautious.

"Well, sitting here does us no good, just wetter. Parun, take five men and find 'em. First though, double the flank guards. I don't want any surprises, kill any nomads they find." He looked hard at his leading sergeant as he spoke; the tone of his voice was decisive.

Parun never hesitated; he merely wheeled his mount around to carry out his orders. Shorin nodded at the scout who turned and rode off with Parun to return to his mission.

This left the young Striker officer alone for a moment with his thoughts. He wasn't afraid of battle, he cared little if he lived or died so long as the job got done. Fighting was all he knew how to do and he did it well. He despised the waiting before combat; the time ate at him and grated his nerves like a rasp shaping wood. He lowered his head until his chin nearly rested on his chest, he absently noticed the rain hitting the back of the cowl as he sat there, just him alone in that moment.

Parun then rode up with the five men he had selected and as they passed their commander the senior sergeant sounded the motto of the Strikers, "King and Karbel" which was echoed by the quintet he led. Shorin's head came up sharply at hearing the words that the elite bodyguards held higher than their own lives.

This is what they served for; this was what life was about, service in the name of a good king and death to those who declared themselves his enemy by either words or actions. The six men rode forward and were shortly swallowed by the misty darkness. Shorin watched until he couldn't see them anymore.

***

The next senior sergeant, a veteran named Hain Peerce moved up from his normal position in the column to take Parun's place at the head of the formation since the senior enlisted man was absent. Shorin turned and told Hain to order the column into a column-on-line formation. The acting command sergeant signaled the order and then waved the troop forward.

As the column started forward the riders immediately behind the first four in line began to spread out and the others behind them moved up until the nearly three hundred mounted troops were arranged in a series of blocks twenty five riders wide and three deep riding abreast. The formation was three blocks of riders wide with the supply wagons safely tucked into the heart of the neatly formed pattern. The allowed them to cover more ground and provide a better defensive arrangement should they be attacked.

They continued their ride forward following the directions given them by the scout. Time faded to nothing as they rode. Weapons were readied but kept covered to protect them from the weather.

As the main body of Strikers had ridden forward they passed the bodies of several nomads that the scouts had killed earlier. Shorin barely gave them a look, they were dead and that was enough. Food for the wolves and carrion birds was all the nomads were good for anyways, dead or alive. Be a shame if the wolf got sick from eating it…a small chuckle at the thought.

Parun and others located the main nomad camp, and sent one of the scouts back to inform the Strikers. They gathered together at the base of one of hills. That camp was in the valley just the other side of the hill. Waiting for his commander, Parun double checked the area once more. The rain had fallen off to nearly nothing again but that could change easily.

He thought he heard something, his head came up and he lowered the cowl of his cloak to better hear. His heightened sense of hearing, courtesy of his mother's heritage, served him well here. Yes, there it was again -- horses and they were close. Trotting, not riding hard out. Shorin

41

knew his business, in weather like this sound wouldn't carry far. You could trot to cover ground quickly but not ride full out.

Shorin saw his senior sergeant up ahead and signaled for the unit to return to a walk. If the Elf was already dismounted then they were close and he didn't want to risk discovery by riding in hard, fast and worst of all, noisy. He chafed a bit at having to wait that much longer for the word. The situation would be revealed soon enough. Don't rush it, take what is given and use it. An old axiom serving him well here as he bid his nerves to calm down. The familiar rush of battle loomed.

Covering the remaining distance between them, Shorin pulled in on the reins to stop his mount and quickly slid out of the saddle to speak with Parun. One of the scouts rapidly stepped over to take the reins to Shorin's horse. He nodded his thanks and returned his full attention to the half Elf.

The veteran sergeant filled his commander in on what details he knew and then what he suspected to be true. The young Under-Captain, a rank similar to Senior Lieutenant in the Legions couldn't help but smile a bit, Parun always did that. Told him what he knew the facts were and then followed it with his hunches.

It helped the decision making process tremendously to be able to make choices based on facts rather than supposition. The hunches weren't unimportant because sometimes they worked out better than the facts did but the older Elf always gave the facts first. He was a soldier and so things were done in an orderly fashion. He kept his gear the same way, everything clean, working and placed in the same location every time.

Parun waved up at the hill they were next to. It was about a hundred or so feet high, the sides and top covered in grass that was slippery from the rain, the two discovered as they began to climb up. Cavalry boots were not the best footwear for hill climbing it would seem. More than once one of them was forced to grab hold of the other for support or leverage as they made their way up. It took them a little time to get to the top; there was little fear of immediate discovery since the nomads were being lax with their security. Parun had told Shorin before they started climbing. The unit leader was curious about the statement but said nothing. If they wanted to get sloppy now that was fine with him, any advantage he could get he would happily take.

As they approached the top of the hill they slowed and crouched down to avoid being seen. They needn't have worried. The two lay at the feet of the "sentry" who was shuffling back and forth with his head down and arm wrapped around his chest just as a bored, wet guard would. He traveled a short path back and forth, the slow pace took him about fifteen strides in each direction, at times he was lost to view in the mist that blew over the hilltop.

The clouds were low, low enough that from time to time they covered the top of the hill which was how he had been able to get close enough to kill the nomad assigned to stand watch up there. The Striker pointedly ignored the two men who were looking over the valley from a few feet away. The man he had killed was lying at the base of the hill where the Strikers had gathered, no longer needing the cloak that now hid the distinctive black and silver uniform of the Strikers from view from the valley beyond.

Shorin could see the valley landscape during the breaks in the cloud cover as it passed over the hilltop. Several small hills formed the southern boundary with no gaps between them while a small entrance fed into the valley from the east; the three nomads there had been killed and replaced by his men as well.

On the northern side of the valley several small hills shouldered a large group of trees that filled in most of a large gap between the two larger hills forming that side of the natural feature. Parun nudged him as the cloud cover lifted somewhat higher allowing a better look at what lie below, Shorin peered over and then at what the half-Elf was carefully pointing at.

At the far end of the valley beyond where the nomads were gathered a bridge could just be seen, it appeared large enough to be able to handle modest size transports. The Striker leader was puzzled by that, what was it doing here of all places? There were no settlements of any kind for some distance yet there was this man-made construction. Strange was the right word and the only one he could think of for a bridge being here in the middle of nowhere.

It was another fact dumped into the mix in his head; he had been trying to sort out the nomad plan for some days now and had yet to figure it out. The raiders had not been following the usual pattern and it had caused Shorin several sleepless nights while tracking them.

A long train of approximately thirty or so large wagons were lined up along the rutted track that ran more or less through the middle of small valley. Shorin returned his attention to the nomads. The main group was located near the first wagon under a collection of awnings stretched out to provide at least some shelter from the rain which took that moment to return, a steady drizzle coming down again.

The awnings had not been strung with great care and so didn't cover as much as they should but at least it was more than the captives had. He took another count as best he could based on what he see of breathing bodies and mounts with saddles. He did the tally twice to make sure of the count. Cursed sakes, it seems that his scouts were right, about three hundred and fifty or so of the nomads. What the spirits forsaken offspring was that many of them doing together he wondered not without some passion.

Shorin continued to look the scene over trying to catch every detail. Here and there some of the raiders walked about but for the most part they kept to the sparse shelter of the tents or awnings as the rain strengthened. There were three groups of captives gathered together in tight masses near the middle of the wagons. They appeared to be shackled together which would only make sense. It was the easiest way to move a large group like this. Shorin guessed that the captives numbered at least one hundred, maybe a little more; he could see men, women and a few children, mainly those in their teens. That made sense, old enough to be workers for the boys, for the girls... he left the thought unfinished.

The wagons were piled high with spoils, most of it unseen, covered by haphazardly tossed cargo blankets that kept at least some of the rain off. Shorin and his senior sergeant lay on the wet grass of the hilltop for several more minutes studying the scene. The activity level seemed right for the weather and those involved, the nomads were not the most industrious people that breathed the air of Dohrya.

All at once Shorin had a thought, the reason everything the nomads had done things different, it all made sense now. He shook his head in anger and cursed himself for a slow witted fool. Parun caught the look and asked, *what?* The young officer nearly had it figured out and waved his sergeant down impatiently as he fitted the last pieces in place.

The bridge, the bridge was the piece of the puzzle that he had been lacking in order to understand it. He recalled the map of the area, long committed to memory. They had traveled basically west for nearly two ten days since leaving Edora. This course had brought them close to the north-east border of the territory claimed by the Federation of Clans.

A bridge being in a place where it had no business being could only mean that this location was used at least semi regularly as a meeting place. It seemed likely that the nomads were in league with at least some of the Clans to furnish them with slaves and to trade their captured spoils for items they wanted. The Clansmen used slaves for labor to harvest crops and the like. If the nomads were here then those coming to meet them… Shorin quickly turned and explained his suspicions to Parun who listened intently. He nodded in agreement and told his superior, *we have to hurry before they change the guards.*

All right, thought Shorin, here's what we are going to do. The two quickly discussed their plan. Shorin tapped Parun on the elbow and the two slid back away from the crest of the hill. Shorin quietly reminded the "sentry" to keep up the good work. The Striker smiled and chuckled with a low sound as he continued his rounds. They didn't know when the sentries on the various hills were due to be relieved so attacking soon as possible was essential otherwise the element of surprise would be lost and given the nomads numbers that could prove disastrous and fatal to the captives.

Getting down the hill proved to be no problem at all. The two soldiers slid on the wet grass tucking one leg underneath them. Stopping once at the bottom was another matter entirely. Several of the Strikers alert to their plight grabbed them once they had slid off the hill. The wet grass was an excellent lubricant. Standing with all the dignity he had remaining and ignoring the grins and laughter of his men Shorin pulled his tunic down and straightened his belt. He turned to Parun who was already standing without mussing any part of his clothing or equipment.

Shorin waved all of the nearby section leaders over and then began to give out orders. It was high time to pay a call on their neighbors in the valley beyond. Once the orders were issued some of the equipment was redistributed and what wasn't needed was stacked and covered with wax coated cotton covers that doubled as tent sections when needed. Only what was needed was to be taken, the task ahead called for quickness. The Strikers worked rapidly to carry out the plan.

Parun led his group north along the creek bank and when necessary through the creek itself. His group had moved around the hills that formed the lower edge of the valley along the southern line and were now west and south of the main enemy camp. The water, about ankle deep in most places was cold and chilled their legs quickly but there was no time for thoughts of comfort. Time was essential so they moved ahead with as much speed as they could.

The only delay came when it was necessary to move one of the men to the bank and hide him among some large bushes. The Striker had slipped on some mossy rocks and fallen hard, breaking at least two ribs on a sharp rock, the chainmail shirt he wore helping to spread the force of the impact, but it still hurt.

The proud trooper winced some as he was helped up and out of the water. He nodded as the others made him as comfortable as possible and rushed to rejoin the others. The man wasn't concerned about himself. The Strikers never left their own, they would be back after they took care of the nomads. He was simply angry at missing out on such an important mission due to something as stupid as falling on a rock. He pulled himself a little farther up into the concealment of the greenery to ensure his presence wouldn't be detected. The effort was not without cost, sharp pains shot through his mid-section forcing the air in his lungs out in a burst that left him winded and in a great deal of pain. He crawled up a little farther but slower this time.

The remainder of Parun's group continued north as quietly as possible. The rushing water of the stream did much to cover up what errant noise they created as they moved into position.

Shorin progressed with his group around to the north. The plan called for them to come through the gap by the trees once they heard the signal from Parun's group. Scouts had already cleared the hilltop to their left of what nomad sentries had been present so they could move into position unobserved by less than friendly eyes.

The remaining group of Strikers were to take their horses to the top of the hill that Shorin and Parun had just left and wait for the signal before advancing down the opposite side of the rise and on into the raider camp from behind. The gap at the east end of the small valley was narrow and would slow down the last group from being able to deploy quickly enough to carry out their part of the plan.

Three groups approached the nomad camp from different directions. The rain continued, more drizzle adding to the discomfort of the day. The group heading up the creek carefully moved along the bank staying in the water as much as possible. The lead Strikers neared the poorly built bridge, a pair of large logs laid over the running water with some roughhewn boards of oak for planking hastily notched into place and further secured with rope bindings.

Parun slid his body up the bank to peer through some long reeds growing along the water's edge. One hand pulled the slender green stalks aside enough to allow him to see more clearly. High grass occupied the ground between the creek and the nomads. A long water resistant case was propped up against the bank next to him holding his bow and a large quiver of the long, gull feathered arrows he favored.

A small party of six nomads were gathered around a meager fire that struggled to keep alight, gnawing at the damp fuel given it. A small pot was laying in the sparse coals possibly for cooking purposes. The half dozen men were draped in cloaks and blankets trying to keep warm and dry, their attention focused on that task and they paid no attention to anything outside their immediate concerns. Two of the cloaks were likely from spoils taken from some hapless village or farm, the hue, cleanliness and condition of them made it unlikely that they had in possession of the current owners long.

The six were assigned to watch over the crossing that served as entrance to the western side of the encampment. All of them were cold, wet and tired; none of them were concerned with anyone other than their contacts showing up. It had been a long raiding trip and they were all eager to return to their own territory. Dry huts, warm food, full pockets and willing women were a powerful draw despite the victories that they had enjoyed.

***

More of the Strikers were in position now; Shorin's group was nearly where he wanted them while the third group, under the command of Hain had managed to walk nearly half their mounts up the slippery slope. They were running out of time and Hain knew it. He quietly urged his men to hurry up. Several of those who already had their mounts up near the top of the hill passed their reins over to someone else and went to help their fellow troopers.

Hain had to quiet several groups who were struggling to get the wary mounts up the hill. Noise now would be disaster and kill the plan before it even got started and worse likely the captives as well. The nomads wouldn't hesitate to kill the prisoners if something went wrong.

Parun withdrew his hand from the reeds and then looked to either side of him to check on the progress of his men. Another group was moving under the bridge to get into position. He silently pointed to six of the king's men and made a cut throat motion across his neck. Each of the Strikers nodded and with practiced movements drew their daggers and slid carefully out of the creek into the high grass to close the distance between them and the soon to be dead nomads.

Shorin's group was now in place and he was checking their alignment while he waited anxiously for the signal from the bridge group. He had originally intended to lead that group but Parun talked him out of it. The half Elven trooper had argued that if the plan needed to be modified at some point, it would have to be Shorin's doing.

He couldn't allow himself to be tied down with the bridge group, it was too isolated from the rest of the valley and he told his commander that the goal was the freedom of the captives. Killing nomads was the not the main concern although that was a nice way to spend a day. Smiling at the line that his sergeant delivered with a straight face brought a bit of levity to a serious moment.

Grudgingly the young Striker officer recognized the truths among what he was being told and changed his mind, he didn't like it but that didn't matter. His job was to lead.

***

In the main nomad camp their leader, a large, leathery skinned brute named Shaddara was preparing to eat when suddenly a long horn call was heard. The clear notes cut through the air without effort, the notes like wind whipping away smoke. The nomad was surprised and then grew quickly angry, what fool did that? He would have the man's sac for a trophy, it was not time for the contacts to arrive and that was the wrong call anyway.

He felt it unlikely someone would hear but the time to collect their money was near and he was always anxious when money was involved, especially money coming to him.

A call came again as he was walking out of his tent, the notes this time were different from the first call. What idiot is doing that he wondered, a large joint of roasted lamb forgotten in one large hand as he tried to find out what was going on. Numerous other tribesmen were milling about as well wondering what the commotion was.

One of the sub-chieftains came running over to where his clan father was standing. The man had seen something that disturbed him greatly and seeing his leader knew he had to tell him. The nomad leader looked to where his follower was pointing. At the far end of the valley in front of the bridge standing shoulder to shoulder stood six hands of men, soldiers. Dressed alike as they were they could only be soldiers.

On the ground in front of them what could only be the bodies of six of his tribesmen. His anger level jumped at seeing this. One of the soldiers, a few paces in front of the others had a horn and lifted it again to his mouth. The notes of the call cut the air, the tune was unmistakable. It was the Song of the Dead, the same tune used throughout the various lands. The message was simple, no quarter, no surrender, a challenge to all of them. Kill me if you can.

Shaddara couldn't believe it, the sacs that this one had to come to his camp, kill his men and then *taunt* him? Death was too kind a fate for all of them.

The brawny nomad flung the joint of meat in his hand away; it landed fifteen paces away and was pounced on by one of the mongrel dogs that the tribe kept around. It tore into the rich prize with gusto; this was far better fare than the mutt usually ate.

Shouting for his men to mount, Shaddara rushed back into his tent to grab his favorite weapon, a long sword. The blade alone was nearly four feet in length. He tossed away the scabbard and ran back outside to climb aboard his horse which had been brought over to him by one of his retainers. He hurriedly mounted and waving the immense sword overhead screaming at his men to charge the enemy.

***

Parun watched carefully as the nomads rushed toward them, a churning mass of riders strung out along the wretched example of a road. So far the plan was working -- the nomads were not spreading out across the width of the valley which likely would allow them to break the Striker line. So far they were riding in a long column about six riders wide or so in places. When they reached a point that he had noted earlier he turned his head and shouted, "Now!"

As soon as they heard that the remaining sixty or so Strikers leapt up from their places of concealment along the creek bed to join the others.

Shaddara saw this and became even angrier, how many of these accursed soldiers were there? He then noticed what the first group had been doing. They were readying long bows; the nomads hated long bows. They felt that the oversized arrows launchers were a cowardly way to fight. It was best to look someone in the face as you killed them. Up close was how real men fought.

The veteran Striker knew that timing for this would be critical, he raised his hand and as he did the Striker archers drew back on their arrows. He held his hand up for heartbeat and then dropped it. At the first instant of movement down the archers released. The thirty or so long, metal tipped shafts were all aimed at the leading riders of the approaching nomads; the trailing riders not yet clear of the camp.

When the projectiles struck chaos ensued among the riders. Because they were riding so tightly together over a dozen men and horses were struck by the deadly metal tipped missiles some of them several times.

When they were struck the riders fell which caused a ripple effect. One rider went down, then the two right behind him and the five behind them and so on until the original twelve that had been struck had tripped or someway interfered with three times that many.

A second flight of arrows, this time nearly fifty, was in the air just moments after the first. These arrows were aimed to strike all over the nomad group and many found flesh. The weighty shafts sometimes passed through their victim before finding something more substantial to stop them, such as the horse -- dropping both.

Shouts and screams resounded.

The second flight created more havoc than the first. The nomad charge was nearly broken due to the work of the archers. Those riding in the front of the group suddenly found themselves without support at their immediate back as the confusion of the fallen took hold.

The downed riders, most of them dead but some still clinging to life, had shattered what cohesion the charge had contained. The nomads were barely a hundred paces from the Striker line milling about trying to redress their line. More of those who had been behind the ones struck down made their way forward now around or through where the fallen were.

Parun watched the scene carefully. He and Shorin had discussed this part of the plan carefully. It was crucial that he and his group had to draw the majority of the nomads out of their camp and hold them at the end of the valley. To do that they would have to sting them and then draw them in, once engaged they had to hold them long enough for the other two groups to attack. It was risky, there were at least nine score riders arrayed against them while the blocking group numbered about ninety.

Parun had been very specific with some those he had chosen to take with him. One more surprise awaited the plainsmen but it wasn't time for that one just yet. A cruel smile curled up as he thought about seeing how that played out when the time came.

If they just used bows to try and shoot the nomads down the raiders would withdraw to their camp and likely harm the captives. No, it had to be this way, hurt them, gall them and then holding them by the nose, kick them square in the ass.

Shaddara was beside himself with anger and wonder. The fury at what was being done to them tearing at him, the guard commander would have much to answer for after this. He would kill the man right now but not with enemies before him would he stop to take the blood of a tribesman. That matter would wait until these ones were dealt with.

The nomads were still milling a hundred paces or so from the Strikers. The men in black and silver were waiting; no more arrows flew at the mass of riders. The elite soldiers were waiting for their enemy to do something, not the best plan but the best one they had.

The nomad leader could see that his men were disorganized but that they still outnumbered the soldiers and so he screamed at his tribesmen to ride them down. Only a part of the mass of riders heard and understood the command, they tried to move forward as a group but the press was still a shambles, in places groups of ten to fifteen did break out and charge.

***

Parun had moved back into the line with his men and saw the nomads charge. He quickly lifted the horn once again and had time to sound a single note which was enough. Sixty of the Strikers quickly bent down and grabbed the pikes they had laid in ready. A bristling wall of sharpened steel rose from the grass as the soldiers stood.

The charging riders had no time to change directions, speed, or momentum, and distance worked against them. The soldiers braced themselves for the force, grounding the butt end of the long spears against the ground and stood with one foot on it, points aimed at chest level of the rapidly approaching horses.

The rest of the nomads had gotten the idea after seeing their fellows ride toward the Strikers and had done the same. Those in front struck the line of waiting infantry and were slaughtered. The steel points of the pikes, a clever design of pieces that could be broken down for easier storage, stabbed deep into flesh, human and equine.

The air was torn with the screams of man and beast, as the Striker weapons bit. In two places the nomads pushed through only to be shot down by the waiting archers. One nomad was the unwilling recipient of four of the long arrows; he spilled out of the saddle and landed in the grass with a boneless bounce and then lay still. The remainder of the raiders smashed into the line immediately following that and the line broke under the weight of the charge.

The fight then broke down into a hundred individual melee's as each side tried to kill the other and survival was the only rule.

The veteran Striker sergeant judged the strength of the fighting and weighed that the time was right for his little surprise. He turned back toward the creek bed and shouted at the top of his lungs, "A'nok Sha!"

As soon as Parun had yelled out the words he had carefully learned during his time with Luth, the massive Troll burst from his place of concealment along the creek bed and rushed forward with a savage yell.

Parun had been very specific to include him in his group. He felt that the advantage that he could offer was too great to pass up and since the other two groups were to fight mounted, it would be better if he was with him. By using the Ogurth speech there would be no mistakes given the noise of the fight, it was only one of the tongues that the long time soldier could speak at least some of.

In one large hand the towering figure, wrapped in heavy scale armor, carried a mace while in the other, a great two headed axe. The axe had been a gift to the fearless Troll from Thadar himself in recognition of his service to the throne. As he emerged from where he had been waiting several of the nomads caught sight of the angry leviathan now rushing toward them screaming unknown oaths. Trolls were virtually unknown among those of the far north so the sight of the armored giant bearing down on them caused several of the nomads to turn and run. Two of these were struck down as they turned away in fear.

Luth waded into a knot of fighting where the numbers were on the side of the raiders. One swipe with his right hand hewed the head from a nomad while the mace crushed the skull of another. The number advantage the nomads enjoyed a moment earlier disappeared like smoke in a stiff breeze.

The Striker trumpeter sounded martial airs to encourage his brethren while the fighting grew in earnest. The horn calls also served to try to dampen the noise from the other groups of Strikers as they moved into position, keeping the full attention of the bridge group. No quarter was given by either side. A Striker was hit by two arrows that winged in from the side of the melee, as he turned to fall he was hacked by a curved sword nearly taking off his arm. The man died noisily in the mud as the battle raged on.

The half Elf bodyguard was a whirlwind of energy and death, sprinting from place to place lending his sword arm where it was needed, but always watching the progress of the fight. His eyes scanned over the scene and he caught sight of one of the nomads who was still astride his horse wielding the largest blade Parun had ever seen.

The nomad had just killed one of black and silver clad troopers. Parun shouted in anger. He rushed toward the man as he yelled at the trumpeter to send the signal. The horn was lifted again and the man blew a three note call twice and then again.

***

The sound carried far. The senior Strikers had discussed the use of horns for signals prior to the attack. It was a legitimate concern that the sound would be heard for great distances but it couldn't be helped. If someone else was around they would hear it and that could spell trouble but it couldn't be helped. There was simply no other practical way for the groups to signal one another. It was horns or risk the communication breaking down. Since the plan was complicated enough Shorin opted to run the risk.

Shorin and the group under the command of Hain both heard the signal. The unit leader waved at his men to move forward just as he had explained to them earlier. They began riding forward toward the enemy first at a trot then the line some thirty men wide and three deep picked up more speed. Hain ordered his men to mount and took another look over the crest of the hill they waited on to watch the activity below before hurrying over to where his own mount waited. Almost time he thought...

Parun was running toward the mounted nomad, who noticed the soldier approaching. He spurred his horse forward and the two rushed toward each other. Shaddara raised the blade intending to sweep it down and cleave the soldier in two where he stood.

Parun kept running and just before the blade swung down he slid to his knees. With a powerful cut, he severed the right front leg of the nomad's horse which caused it to spill. The long blade passed through the air just over the head of the Elf, Parun felt his hair move from the force of the swipe. Shaddara was thrown over the horse's neck as the mount stumbled badly now minus a leg, landing heavily on his back sword flying from his hand. The horse rolled over and shrieked with a full measure of pain as it began to die.

Parun quickly looked around to check the scene, fighting was still taking place all around but he could sense the tide was turning in favor of his Strikers. The experience of the veteran soldiers was having an effect in the battle. The nomads too were experienced fighters but it was often against those with far less knowledge than they had and who were usually poorly armed if at all.

To be forced to stand and fight against heavily armed, well trained soldiers in armor was something altogether different. The weight of arms was having its way and it wasn't in favor of the nomads. Parun saw a sword find an exposed nomad throat and open it with a spray of crimson. The Striker sergeant quickly returned his full attention to the man laying several paces away.

Shaddara shook his head to try and clear the cobwebs that fogged his thoughts. He saw his sword on the ground several feet away and scrambled on his hands and knees across the distance to grab it. Rolling over and using the momentum to get to his feet he looked over to where the man he had tried to kill waited.

The ringing of steel, sword on sword filled the air along with shouts and curses. Due to the extensive rains of late there was no dust to worry about.

Parun recognized the nomad for what he was, an experienced fighter and one with greater physical strength than his own; he knew he needed to keep his wits with him and to try and shake the nerve of the other if he could. He taunted the big man in his own tongue, the Striker was fluent in five languages and knew more than a smattering of a handful of others, "Come keeper of goats, kill me if you can!"

The bruised tribesman couldn't believe his ears. Those who spent their lives tending animals were among the lowest of creatures in the eyes of the nomads who favored freedom and as little physical work as possible. To toil while raising crops or the like was considered unmanly among many of those who rode the plains -- so the remark did have some effect.

Goat keeper, eh? Something else to make the little one pay for thought Shaddara as if there wasn't enough already. The two foes began to slowly circle each looking for an opening. The tall nomad struck first trying a bull rush that nearly succeeded in bringing the Striker down. He was able to twist away at the last instant taking the force of the powerful swing full on his blade, the shock of the blow ran up his arms, sharp and painful.

***

Shorin's group began their turn which would bring them through the gap in the trees north of the nomad encampment. The far right side of the line began to gallop now, the extra speed necessary to ensure that they could keep up in the turn having farther to go and the formation would stay aligned, this was crucial. If they encountered resistance, Shorin was sure that they would, the men of Karbel had to be in proper place or what strength the formation had would be lost.

Hain watched as he could through the clouds that were now passing over quicker, the wind having picked up. He found that he was eager for the signal from Shorin, he had been a soldier for nearly fourteen years, a Striker for almost six of that and like his commander it was the only thing he had found that he was good at. In life some men were favored by the plow, others the quill pen, for Hain a good sword was his tool.

***

Near the bridge the fight between Parun and Shaddara was taking on epic proportions, each had wounded the other at least twice with neither conceding anything. This was to the death with each one sure it would the other paying the ultimate price.

Some of the nomads were trying to head back toward their camp being pressed by the men in the black and silver. Some of those from Karbel had stopped long enough to try and provide rudimentary medical aid to their own; the nomad wounded lay where they had fallen. Thought one Striker as he tended to a nasty sword slash, *Gods curse their wounded*; he would. Led by Luth more and more of the bridge group were moving down the valley toward the nomad camp having handled their own scraps and now lent their swords to others.

The lean half Elf noticed that when the big nomad slashed horizontally his guard was open for just a moment, maybe it would be enough. His arms ached from the fight, the powerful blows of the bigger man having an effect. He fought off another slash and with a twist of the wrist brought his blade back around scoring a cut on the upper arm of his foe.

Baiting the nomad wouldn't be easy the man was an experienced sword fighter, Parun was sure of that. The burning he felt from the two slashes he had received so far was proof enough of that. Time to try something different and not altogether smart, he appeared to stumble as he moved forward and the heavy blade sailed through the air looking for his neck. The veteran Striker fell to one knee pivoting on the other foot as he did so and rammed the sharpened point of his saber backwards with all the force he could muster.

Shaddara saw the bastard Elf trip and knew he had him; he swung for the neck and was astounded when the smaller man adroitly twisted underneath the cut. The burly nomad suddenly felt pain in his stomach, the sensation like fire and it felt like his insides, all of them, were ablaze as if he had swallowed a pan of hot coals.

He looked down and was shocked to see the saber of the soldier wedged deeply in his middle section. When he saw the blade the pain doubled and kept increasing, it robbed him of strength, his breathing became labored and the big sword dropped clumsily from his hand.

He staggered back and fell heavily landing on one side and coming to rest on his back. Blood filled his mouth and ran out one corner as death took him. Parun watched as life left the big nomad. He rose heavily favoring his right leg which sported a long slash courtesy of the now deceased raider. Parun moved over to collect his sword which was protruding from the midriff of the nomad.

***

The Striker officer and his group had made the turn and were aimed at the gap when he signaled the trumpeter riding two men over. The man lifted his instrument to his lips and sounded the call for charge, a forgone order but it was not intended for the Strikers.

In the main camp of the nomads a number of ears perked up when the call was heard, most of those previously there were engaged at the bridge but a good three score remained having been gathering horses and arms to ride to the bridge when the horn call came from the north.

The senior leader present ordered his men to horse and pointed in the direction he wanted them to go. He had correctly determined where the threat to them was coming from riding out of the camp to meet it.

The Striker charge was now at full speed and they fit, just barely, in the gap between the groups of trees. Emerging they saw the numerous nomads heading their way. Each of the Strikers carried a pike similar to those the men at the bridge had used earlier. The design allowed for additional sections to be added or deleted as the user needed. The ends carefully carved out to allow the sections to fit one inside the other meaning it was easy to transport them via wagons or horseback. Simply put the number of sections you wanted together and it was done.

Passing through the trees the men kept the pikes upright, resting the weight atop their right boot but now with the enemy in sight the deadly spears were swung down to serve as lances. Eighty three long shafts of death were aimed at the approaching throng of riders who were not in any kind of formation at all, just a mass of riders heading the same direction. Shorin shouted at the trumpeter and another call went out, this one for Hain.

The last group heard the signal which ordered them to move. Hain had already moved back to where his horse was and along with his men was anxiously waiting for the word. It was here at last and when it came he stood in the stirrups and with a wave of his sword ordered his men forward and down the hill. It might have been better to use the small opening into the valley but Shorin was concerned that trying to get a body of mounted men through it would take too long and leave those at the head of the formation exposed if the nomads counterattacked in force. So he had his men use the hill, it would give them the added advantage of momentum.

The northern group with Shorin hit the nomad charge like a honed scythe trimming ripe wheat. Organized and aligned, the heavy mass of soldiers rode down their enemies, felling nearly half of them in the first pass.

The young officer aimed his lance with care and it passed the buckler shield wielded by the man finding its way to his chest. The force lifted the victim clear of the saddle, the point of the pike lodged deeply in the ribs and stayed there after ripping one lung open.

The man fell heavily tearing the pike from Shorin's hand who through experience had learned not to try and maintain his grip. The Striker quickly drew his sword and wheeled the horse about to check his flank, it was clear. He spotted a lone nomad and headed toward him shouting orders as he went. The trumpeter sounded the notes for Rally Here. Those nomads still mounted were being pressed by the king's guards.

***

When the second nomad group rushed out of the camp it left just a handful of their own behind, mainly the guards for the prisoners. One of these, a bit of a slow witted brute -- which meant he often got the guard duty -- had turned to silence one of the prisoners. This one, a woman recently captured, had had enough -- the noise of the fighting, the capture, the horns and the treatment she had endured pushed her over the edge. She began screaming hysterically, wretched screams of pain and fear shook her when she saw the last group of Strikers pouring down the hill. She thought they were more nomads.

Several of the others who were chained saw them as well but said nothing knowing that this likely salvation recognizing them as soldiers. They tried to calm the woman but she was beyond reason, the events of late that had destroyed her life had taken hold.

The nomad, armed with a spear and a sword swung the butt end of the spear toward her head connecting hard enough to knock her unconscious. She slumped over and was grabbed as best as possible by the nearest prisoner who was limited by the chains that linked them together in groups of ten, shackled at the neck.

The guard, proud of how he handled the woman turned when he heard something behind him, his eyes grew wide at the sight of the third

Striker charge. He yelled for some of the others who were nearby who turned and noticed the approaching cavalry. They rushed over forgetting about the prisoners -- which turned out to be a serious mistake. Believing the captives too cowed to be a threat, the dozen or so nomads suddenly found themselves under attack, as groups of ten pulled their chains to the limit to give them as much room as they could.

Hain was watching intently for any signs of resistance. He had carefully chosen not to use horns with his charge to try and keep the surprise element. It worked to a point. He could see a group of the raiders rushing toward them when they were suddenly attacked from the back, since his group was nearly on top of the nomads when it happened the result was unavoidable. Riders plowed into the melee of nomad and captive adding to the confusion tenfold.

***

At the bridge, the fight was essentially over. Parun, having retrieved his sword from the body of the former nomad leader was issuing orders to various Strikers, help the wounded, find Shorin, kill the wounded nomads, there was no time for prisoners or gentle care. This was the frontier and this was what the nomads would have done to them if the situation was reversed.

He ordered three of men to grab some horses and to head across the bridge and scout as far as they could. He told another six to stay by with their bows to cover the bridge in case trouble showed up ensuring one of them carried a horn to sound a warning if necessary.

The rest of the men he sent toward the main camp to help there. He was going there himself in a few moments but first he had to make sure that what they had done to the nomads wouldn't happen to them.

It was Shorin's concern that these nomads were here to meet with one or more of the Federation clans to sell off the goods and captives. It was the only reason for there to be a bridge here in the middle of nowhere and for the nomads to have traveled this far west. If a large group of clansmen was coming it would mean trouble, serious trouble.

The Strikers were not likely to be able to fight another major engagement so soon. The scouts had already crossed the poorly built bridge and were well on their way. If someone was coming they would get word back.

Time to go and check on rest of the fighting. He had heard the sound of the horn calls from Shorin's group, and knew that Hain and his men would have come over the hill he had been on earlier.

A number of the Strikers from the third group were forced to dismount to sort out who was who amid the piles of squirming humanity, while others rode headlong into the main gathering of tents and shelters striking down anyone showing their faces and bearing a weapon. Strong arms pulled at the mass of struggling bodies until they reached those without iron collars about their necks. These were unceremoniously grabbed and flung away from the soon-to-be released captives.

Other Strikers had taken up positions bows in hand to cover the approaches to the wagons. A few shafts were sent out as stragglers from Shorin's attack tried to get away, unaware of the soldiers now holding their camp.

The Strikers fighting in the north had managed to kill or subdue the majority of the three score riders who had come out to face them, killing most of them. Several of them had dropped their swords and raised their hands in a gesture of surrender. They were dragged from their horses and carefully searched; it was possible to hide any number of weapons on your person if you knew where to do it.

***

Seeing that his men had the situation in hand Shorin stopped his horse. He realized that once again he had survived the trial of arms. He lowered his head and rubbed his forehead for a moment to work out the tension present. Then he lifted his eyes to survey the scene around him again. The sword in his hand seemed to be three times as heavy, the adrenaline of fighting now fading drawing him down.

A number of nomad bodies dotted the grass, horses wandered aimlessly here and there. Prisoners, a few anyway, were being taken care of, and the wounded Strikers were being attended. He could see the bodies of several of his men who would not be rising to serve again.

It was the loss of men that ate at the soul of the soldier. He knew that it was part of a soldier's life to risk death but every time that one of his men paid the price, he felt it. He was tired, the years of fighting and killing was beginning to wear on him.

He knew that orders sending him to the south east frontier were waiting for him when he returned to Edora and he was very much looking forward to it. The south east, an area known as Eastmarch was reportedly a peaceful, beautiful area where there was little trouble. He hoped so; he could use a break from this. Blowing out his frustration he returned his attention to the matters at hand, wounded, scouting, prisoners and list went on.

***

Hain noticed that all the remaining nomads who had them had pulled their daggers. The seven men leapt toward his Strikers who shot them down without regard. The hum of bowstrings filled the air for a moment replaced by the sound of arrows finding their way into flesh; Hain had heard the sound many times in his life, an arrow biting deeply into flesh was unmistakable. As were the results, this time was no different. The seven fell to the ground and lie still, each having been hit, some of them twice and one of them showed the accuracy of three different archers.

As the last one fell Hain thought to himself, *that is what I would have done too.* He then turned to find his commander and report in. Behind him the wind stretched out the banner of the nomads, a running horse depicted in black against a field of green.

Chapter Four
A Time for Instruction

The Citadel

The fortress sat atop a large mesa that rose from the floor of one of the vast fertile valleys that made up much of the deep south of the main continent that spanned the planet. In size and scope the fortress had been a massive construction project, covering nearly a square mile on the inner bailey alone. The outer walls, built of huge blocks of dark stone quarried in the western mountains soared to over fifty feet in height and were nearly eighty feet thick at the base.

High towers, their gleaming stones reflecting the light of the morning, lined the walls at regular intervals surrounded the entire fortification. Construction had taken nearly eighty years and thousands of lives. The ground around the fortress had been cleared and leveled to the edge of the mesa save for the roads leading out. A garrison force of thousands maintained and defended the enormous house of war.

For over a mile in all directions the land around the base of the mesa was open as well. Wide roads ran out from the mesa like the spokes of a wheel, all of them precise and clean. Beyond the cleared area villages and military camps surrounded the bastion on all sides. Carefully constructed roads climbed the steep sides of the mesa, each switching back on themselves so that each ascending level overlooked the just traveled path. At each of the curves a series of gates stood silent sentinel ready to be swung shut at a moment's notice to isolate the fortress above from attack.

The fortress was known as the Citadel. It had, for over a thousand years, been the seat of power for the Varshon. It did not rival the architecture of Imalla, the former home of the Varshon in the far north prior to their defeat at G'mar so many years before.

The fortress had never fallen to an enemy force; no invading army had ever made it that far. Many did not even know it existed, some said it existed only in legend, and to some less than that. The deep south had long been a place of mystery and danger among those of the other races. This fact had been used by the Varshon to their benefit, adding to those legends whenever possible to keep their existence secret for as long as possible. That the Varshon felt that much of the population of the known world were stupid, superstitious peasants only helped.

In one of the rooms high on the north face of the inner bailey that faced their distant enemies, the wind blew the dark curtains away for a moment and then lay still. As the curtains fell slowly back into place, the corner of a table caught one of them leaving one side of them partially open. A larger measure of light spilled into the pool of darkness that filled the room, softening the darkness to a milder tone. The lone occupant of the immense room sat behind a desk situated well back from the windows.

Distractions thought the large figure, *always distractions*

The ancient writing table where he was working was covered with maps and pages of notes, his and others. A single oil lamp on one end of the desk barely broke the darkness.

Bookcases stretched into the ebony void lining two of the walls stretching floor to ceiling. Each shelf contained works that the world's scholars would sell their maiden daughters virtue for if they had known they still existed. The works had been carefully gathered, purchased when possible, stolen when necessary. Rich furniture of dark wood tastefully graced the room. The other wall was covered with maps, tapestries and paintings. A rich thick carpet of the finest hand woven Tabir'l fiber from distant Ardjetka covered the floor.

Soon, Anagir mused, very soon now after all these long years, the time fast approaching. How strange that something you have waited on, planned for, worked toward for nearly two millenini can suddenly seem to sneak up on you. He thought quickly of how little time meant of someone of his age. *Fool,* he told himself, *there is no one of your age.*

You are the last. Yes, I am the last but I am still young enough for this! A sudden flash of anger that he quickly squelched and tossed aside. Curse the Elves! *I remember and so shall they and all those who oppose me!* He promised himself and moved on to other thoughts.

"Two thousand years." The words filled the room as he spoke them slowly, his voice filled with menace. The light spilling in the window and banked curtain was steadily lifting the darkness from the corners of the room as the morning deepened. Anagir looked up once more from his work and slowly surveyed the room.

This room, his private retreat for longer than he cared to think about, somewhere he could escape some of the duties and cares of leading his people, if but briefly. The work of dozens of generations was gathered here. The furniture as rich and well cared for today as when it was made many years earlier and presented to him after one of his awakenings from the Spirit Sleep. Murals depicting the glory of better times hung from the walls. *Yes*, he thought as he looked over his favorite, *times shall be glorious again.*

The memories of the bitter defeat and exile so very long ago ate at him. The old mistakes will not be repeated. Never again shall we underestimate the humans. Mistakes are the price of the folly of youth. Many generations of raiding and border clashes have removed much of our youth and all of our folly. Dozens of generations have been spent in preparations for what lie ahead. It *will* be different this time! With that thought he could be content to wait.

Curse the Elves! He took in and held a deep breath to help shed the anger which he knew was a distraction and foolish, especially at his age. A wry smile unseen by another living creature crossed his face. Enough of this! He knew it was nearly time for the regular session he spent with the younger majic users so Anagir rose from his desk and left his place of contemplation to attend to that and other matters.

Crossing the room he said the word *door* aloud and the heavy portals swung open immediately of their own accord, a simple spell long infused into the materials that formed the doors. Anagir nodded to the guards and passed through the doorway. The two doors closed silently behind him.

One pair of the Troll guards followed him, their size nearly filling the wide corridor while the remaining pair stayed in place to watch over his quarters. Anagir had a pair of the ever vigilant Trolls with him at all times, it was a holdover from earlier times when his life had been threatened by other Varshon fearful of his growing power and despite the gap of centuries from then to now the tradition continued. The trio moved through the fortress headed for the courtyard and the group of students who awaited him.

The class provided a welcome respite from the endless reports and studying he was forced to occupy his time with. He wondered idly as he walked, if the leaders of the other nation states and kingdoms were as cursed with paperwork as he. Probably. It seemed to be part and parcel of the job of ruling. He cursed that part of his job too.

***

"Master?" the question from one of the older students.

"Yes, Pailan?" This part of the class was Anagir's favorite. After the students had spent two cycles of the sand clock learning new spells and practicing their existing ones under the watchful eye of the elder majic user he always allowed a question and answer session. It was another tool he used to ensure the loyalty and hence the control of the majic users, long the key to his power.

"Would you tell us something of our history? Something not spoken of in our studies?"

The faces around him were eager with ambition and the desire for bigger things. Anagir liked that, it gave him strength to see the youngest generation of the Varshon respectful of their past and anxious for what lie ahead. He could use the strength.

In spite of the spirit sleep that he had used over the centuries to survive through the long wait he was still well beyond the medium age for those of his race. The aches and stiffness of age came a little more often these days. It had been nearly two dozen years since he last awoken from the mystic sleep that prolonged his life and gave him energy. There had been too much to do to return to it.

He had worked hard over the centuries to guarantee that the generation that would go north be given additional discipline training to harden them for the task ahead. In addition, as they had been coming of age numerous tales of the Varshon history had been ever present for them to hear and wonder at. It served to keep them eager to serve and seize a piece of history for themselves. Anagir had long ago mastered the art of controlling the masses, this was but another tool for him to use.

"Hmmm, what tale indeed?" The elder majic user thought for a moment, settled on a topic and drew the moment out to prolong the anticipation. He leaned forward in his seat and the others did so also without thought.

Anagir said, "I will tell you of a brave warrior and the truest Varshon I have ever met. Will that do?" He looked from face to face judging what he saw there pleased with the results in spite of knowing ahead of time what the results would be.

A chorus of *yes, yes* was his answer. He leaned back to begin his story. "This all begins with battle, a great and terrible time for us." The Varshon leader knew that they had been told the story of the fight for G'mar and the Long Walk during their studies but he wanted to give it to them from the perspective of one who was there.

Anagir had gone to great lengths over the centuries to ensure that he alone passed from the old hands to the time of renewal which approached; all the better to hide his secrets while adding to his own legend. He had many secrets to hide and a healthy ego to feed.

"This is the story of Lykan Tee of the Family Brahaan. He was a warrior who served all the Varshon proudly." The statement was delivered with just the right amount of dignity to convey the spirit of the message he intended to get across.

"This warrior was personally selected by Taranh, our leader and greatest of all majic users to fulfill a special task," at the mention of the long dead leader the students all bowed their head once in proper deference as they had been taught. Anagir continued, "…a task that came with great hardship and risk. He completed this with skill and brought great honor on his house. Do any of you know what this was?"

The teacher waited while the group tried to find an answer. When none of them could answer Anagir found he was slightly disappointed. Had he been neglecting the education programs? He made a mental note to discuss this with the head training master. The sea of young faces were waiting for him to speak, none of them dared to say anything until he did. The sense within him that this was the way it should be was strong.

After pausing for a moment longer he began his story. He began with the reason for the Varshon moving into the immense fortress at G'mar. The rebirth ceremony was the centerpiece of their myth and hope. If the ceremony was completed it would increase the Varshon ability to work the majical arts to levels currently unknown in the world. Their majic users would be supreme, no power or army could stand against them. The Varshon would rule the world with all the others would be dead or enslaved.

Before the ceremony could be completed an army of Elves and humans attacked the fortress and killed the majic users including Taranh. Anagir explained that he alone had been entrusted with the knowledge on how to recover the hidden material that lay waiting for the Varshon to return. Near the end of the battle Lykan Tee had been ordered by Taranh to guard Anagir and ensure that no harm befell him no matter the circumstances.

Anagir asked if they knew what other order had been given to the warrior. None of them knew the answer; this caused Anagir to strengthen his resolve to speak with the head training master regarding some of the history lessons.

The Varshon leader looked at each of the students and told them. Taranh had ordered Lykan not to fight to carry out his mission. The students were shocked, the first Varshon Principle, the one most holy to them was fight, always fight, never retreat. Some of the students were trying to speak but speech failed them.

Finally Pailan, *it would be Pailan*, thought Anagir, spoke up. "Master, why did our most revered leader do this, how could he order a warrior to disobey the Law?" His tone plainly spelled out what he thought of the order despite his best efforts to keep the look of disbelief and loathing from his face.

"Being wise as he was, Taranh knew that fighting alone was not the key to delivering the hope of our people, the salvation of the Varshon and their might from the hands of the enemy. It would be another power that would deliver us victory, the power of majic, our power." The tone of the statement, strong and confident seized the students just as Anagir intended.

"After our arrival here in the south we had to start over. We had virtually no food, no tools or the means to make them." The young students were silent as they thought on the work that had been necessary to deal with those circumstances.

Several of them were deep in thought while they mulled the

situation. Anagir noted this and was pleased; he had them thinking --
always one of the goals of a teacher. That it stroked his own ego was of
no small consequence either. Anagir had not schemed all these centuries
to achieve his position for nothing.

"After a while Lykan felt it best to return to the north and try and
reach Imalla." Several eyes lit up at the mention of the rightful capital of
the Varshon which lay deep in the far north. What was once the greatest
city and home of all the Varshon, a city that only Anagir of all the
Varshon living in the south had ever seen personally. To the rest it was a
near mythical place, a place revered to them.

Over the centuries Anagir often wondered what had happened to the
city of his birth. Once they finished at G'mar he intended to find out,
returning home after so long would prove interesting. No party sent north
to reach the city had ever returned in all the years that the Varshon had
been in the south.

The Varshon leader told them of how long they lingered in the south
while many died of hunger and sickness as the years passed. Anagir told
of how Lykan convinced several dozen of the others to go with him and
attempt to reach the capital. Each of them knew that the journey would
be long and dangerous but agreed none the less.

That Anagir had long been planting the seeds for Lykan to leave and
go north he spoke nothing of. Only Lykan knew of Anagir's fear, the
deep, nearly numbing fear that nearly unmade him during The Long
Walk as the Varshon called it. That truth was his deepest secret and
greatest weakness; he was a fraud, a junior majic user who had been
given the responsibility simply because he was the only one that could be
found at the time. The fear of someone discovering this was nearly a
physical thing that gnawed at him even here, now, after nearly two
thousand years.

Lykan had been the only reason he had made it to the south,
ensuring that Anagir was warm, had food and drink, often giving up his
own portion to make up for the meager ration that the Elves provided
them as a way of keeping them weak and thereby docile. He protected
his charge from both the Elves and other Varshon who preyed on those
they could cower, seeking their food or what scraps of clothing they had.
He had never failed in his mission.

Anagir remembered the taunts that Lykan endured at the hands of others, "wizard's pet" chief among these. That Lykan would not fight was another source of contention. He was called coward and Elf lover for his apparent lack of courage.

Once they were in the south and the Elves released them to their devices Anagir took revenge on some of those who had dishonored the proud warrior. It was often little things, conjuring a double handful of ticks to fill a bedroll, turning someone's drink into a foul smelling mass as they drank it causing them to spit up usually all over themselves. These torments were designed to cause the victim as much public embarrassment as possible. He was careful not to do this too openly so that it would seem that Lykan needed someone else to stand for him. In fact the warrior often was completely unaware of the turns taken against those who had spoken or acted against him.

Eventually word began to get around not to cross words with the proud soldier from the Family Brahaan. It wasn't worth it. Once a more permanent settlement was established further south of the Elven outposts designed to spy on them Anagir revealed himself fully and declared himself leader. When the first challenge to his assumed power came he turned to Lykan who had been released from his order of avoiding a fight from Taranh by Anagir. The young warrior killed no less than eleven challengers who sought to take over the role of Varshon leader. By the sixth duel it was Lykan who was the favorite. If any of them still had issues with the past they kept to themselves lest they run afoul of the *wizard's champion* as he was now known.

Anagir knew all along that Lykan would venture back to G'mar along the way to Imalla. He was counting on it. He had carefully laid down the scenario that would end the life of the one Varshon that could undo what he had become, leader of his people. The power, prestige and privileges that came with being the leader were a great deal better than what the average Varshon was able to partake of so he was loath to give that up.

He had confided in Lykan how to open up the vault that contained the records that lay within. At least that was what Lykan believed. Anagir knew that when Lykan touched the vault door, that the warrior would make it to the fortress; it was his way, that the guardian spell would kill him. With Lykan dead the secret of his fear and the only other witness to what happened that day would be gone. Taranh had told him once that two could keep a secret if one was dead; he intended to be that one despite his debt to the warrior.

Anagir told the students that after gathering what supplies and equipment he could that Lykan and the others headed north. They slipped around the Elven patrols with little difficulty then using a route that took them far to the west of the Homelands they made their way through the wilderness. The group encountered wild creatures, nomads and battled the elements until at last after a journey of nearly a year they reached the fortress.

Once there the group, now reduced to less than half their number, were forced to fight a battle with a group of nomads that had moved in and set up temporary housekeeping scavenging what they could. Among the Varshon only Lykan and two others survived after the few remaining nomads fled.

After the fight Lykan tried to open the vault and was killed by the guardian spell that protected the books. The remaining two Varshon vowed to finish the quest. One agreed to return all the way to the south and bring word to the others of what had happened. The remaining Varshon was to head north and try and reach Imalla.

Many months after leaving G'mar to return south, the Varshon, a warrior named Otakin, made it through the Elven lines to deliver his tale. He was weak and sick, wracked with fever from his wounds and travel. He staggered into the communal dining hall one evening and the tale poured out. Those gathered spread the word to others and within two days the tale had spread to every one of the survivors. This ended a great deal of speculation regarding leaving the south; many vowed that they would never leave again.

Just as Anagir planned, if they returned to the north and Imalla then his new power would vanish in the face of the council members who hadn't traveled with them to G'mar.

***

The students sat rapt in the tale as Anagir kept them on edge until he finished. Of the Varshon who went north no word of him ever reached the south, no one knew to this day if he made it back to Imalla or what fate befell him. Anagir suspected but didn't know for sure. Either way it wouldn't matter. Lykan was long dead and his secret was safer.

The shadows of afternoon had deepened considerably by the time that Anagir released the students to their other duties. Their allotted time was long over but who would object to it? He was pleased with himself and that he could still weave a tale that captured the listener.

After the students paid their respects and departed he rose from his seat and with his ever present escort headed back toward his room. There was still much to do.

Chapter Five
Visions

Vankard

The man suddenly sat bolt upright in bed as he wrestled with the images of what was shown to him.

The dreams had returned again, it was the seventh night of seven his sleep had been visited. A thin film of sweat covered his brow and his breathing was heavy from the exertion during his sleep. The rumpled covers and scattered pillows bore mute testimony to the strength of his struggles.

The weak light from the still burning fireplace across the room gave everything in his limited view a reddish tint, shadows stayed deep in the corners of the bed chamber hidden from sight.

Vode Anners, High Priest of Vankard, slowly swung his feet out of bed as he lowered his head to rest it in his hands. He worked to control his breathing, fast due to the exertion during his sleep.

The priest, senior member of the order that served the kingdom, began to quietly chant one the mantra's used by those of his order to promote calm. The effect was nearly immediate; the deep breathing of moments earlier slowed and became more regular, his heart rate evened out and he felt better and more alert. The tired man blinked several times to help clear his mind even further and remove the gritty feel of the dried moisture from his sight organs.

After completing the short repetitive chant he called for his chamber man, the door to his private bedchamber swung open nearly immediately. Vode was not terribly surprised to see Levas Hoosen, his senior acolyte come in the room in place of his regular night staff member, one of the junior priests who rotated the duty. The elder student carried a lit oil lamp which brightened the room considerably softening the red tint of the fireplace. The younger man crossed the room quickly and arriving at the side of his mentor placed the lamp on the side table, studying the face of the High Priest.

Something, someone, or some power was giving Vode these signs and so being here tonight, as he was last night, doing what he felt was his duty. Levas was the senior acolyte and so care of the High Priest was his given duty. That he himself was tired was of no concern, his purpose was to serve and if being tired was what was required, then so be it. This was merely another test for him to pass -- as were many of the daily tasks that the priests were expected to handle.

Many of their order possessed the skills to invoke powerful spells and with that power came great responsibility. The Gods in which the northmen believed were hardy warriors and beings of great strength so it was natural to assume that they wished for their believers to be of the same vein that they themselves were.

With one glance Levas could tell that the dreams had once again visited his master, the flushed complexion and sweaty brow were certain signs. The senior student knew about the dreams and the effect it was having on his master. Vode had been unusually withdrawn for several days now as he wrestled with the portents he was seeing nightly. The acolyte had been told that several times over the course of the previous nights the High Priest had been calling out in his sleep; Levas could see the fatigue from lack of rest wearing at his mentor. His face was drawn and there a slightly noticeable slump to the shoulders that had carried many a burden over the years.

The acolyte who had been in service to the Order for nearly twelve years began to cluck over Vode as was his way; the High Priest had long ago given up trying to change the younger man of his almost motherly ways. He rose from the bed and quickly dressed; no point in trying to return to sleep this night, not sure he wanted to even if he could.

Vode had it in his mind that these sights he had seen, the people, were all trying to tell him something. He had to figure it out and he was now sure what the next step in that process must be. Once properly dressed in the robes of his position, he and Levas walked out of the bed chamber and through the suite of rooms belonging to the High Priest. The younger man opened all the doors for the High Priest as was proper for one of his station.

When the pair reached the main door Levas opened that one as well, stepping to the side to allow his mentor to pass through. The two junior priests who were on duty outside in the hall should the High Priest require anything during the night bowed deeply in respect to Vode as he exited into the hallway. He returned the bows with the proper amount of decorum, deep enough to be seen but not as deep as theirs. After all, he was High Priest.

Levas closed the door and took up his place behind Vode and one pace to the left. The pair of priest apprentices fell in stride one pace behind the senior acolyte as the leader of their order strode down the hall, his pace never hurried or too sedate. It was the steady gait that long years of authority had brought on. It wouldn't be seemly for the High Priest of Vankard to be seen scurrying through the hallways like some buffoon. Scurrying wasn't on his mind; running through them was another story. He wanted to get to his destination as soon as he could but decorum must be observed. So a small test of his patience as he walked.

***

As the foursome made their way through the quiet hallways Vode was thinking more about the visions. The images he had witnessed this night were different than those of the other nights, more powerful, real enough that he felt if he had extended one hand they would have felt solid to the touch. Each night he had seen many of the same sights, the previous six nights the scenes had been flashes, quick images of places, usually a massive fortress repeated over and over but from different angles and it seemed different times.

Sometimes the scenes were heavily populated with what seemed to be humans, tall and fair; the area around them was rich with life and bright with colors as they moved through carrying on with their various lives, shopping, trading, crafting incredible metalwork and more.

Other times the scene he was given was the same location but empty of life, the surrounding area showing heavy signs of decay, overgrown foliage, fallen stonework and the like. It was as if the visions were trying to impart some lesson, what the lesson might be he didn't know, he suspected much but had yet to give voice to it.

The fortress in the visions was not located in Vankard, of that he was sure. Extensive travel throughout the realm over the years had exposed much of the country to him. Even their history failed to speak of such a place and none of it was similar to what he had seen in the dreams. It must lie in the lands beyond their mountains; that realization caused a small wave of doubt, or even fear to ride through him.

The ways of the world outside the kingdom of the northmen were now little known. The people of Vankard kept to themselves and let the troubles of the world beyond the mountains bother others.

It had been that way for decades, ever since a fever, some said brought by a traveler from beyond the mountains, swept through the kingdom killing thousands. The plague lasted for nearly a year and spared no town or village it seemed. After burying their dead many felt that what happened beyond the border was not their concern and began to distance themselves from the rest of the world. Some reactions were extreme, in some places luckless travelers were killed simply because they were foreigners, in most cases reason in some form prevailed and the visitors to Vankard were shown to the borders and told to leave, never to return.

It was a memory that Vode wasn't proud of, the actions of some of his countrymen, even now after six generations couldn't be forgiven. Understood to a point, fear has a terrible power, but not forgiven.

Could it be time to go beyond the frontier? The question rose in his mind and left him uneasy, more so than he was comfortable admitting. A small measure of him was concerned that was in fact what must happen. But for now he commanded it to not be so. How effective his control over that desire was yet to be seen.

Tonight though, it had been different with the dream, the images sharp but slow, penetrating and lasting much longer, almost as if they were meant to leave a more permanent memory. For what purpose he didn't know but needed to find out, if for nothing more than to get a good night's sleep.

The senior priest suspected a great deal but lacked the information he felt he needed to form the whole picture. The nature of his deep faith kept Vode believing that the images must have some significance, that the reason for the return of the dreams was real.

**

The High Priest had decided after rising from his disturbed slumber to try and locate a clue in the store of written materials that the northmen maintained there in the castle, he was walking in that direction with his followers close at hand. The four priests continued to make their way through the castle that served as the home and seat of power to Odell Baragull, the current ruler of Vankard.

Two days earlier the senior priest had given thought to going to the library and seeking out some answers. He felt that was being foolish but now; after what he had seen and for want of other words, felt tonight he had decided that he no longer had a choice. He then ruefully asked himself if he had ever really had a choice regarding this. For this Vode had no answer and so gave himself none.

Two of the guards on patrol stopped and bowed with respect to the High Priest who returned the gesture with a minimal one of his own. He was too deeply involved in thought to worry about matters of courtesy. Once the quartet of holy men had passed, the guards returned to their rounds protecting the keep and its occupants.

The priests made their way through the castle heading down to the lower levels where the great repository of knowledge lay waiting. They had left the more comfortable and better decorated areas of the castle seen by visitors and guests. The priests were now at the level where the dungeons were and moving lower still, their destination was the Great Library. It housed a huge collection of written works painfully gathered over the centuries since Vankard was founded.

The stone steps that formed the stairs were wide and angled slowly to their right as the men descended. A few torches were kept lit to provide a measure of illumination but there were large areas that stayed shrouded in the heavy cloak of darkness.

The four men kept going down following the curve of the stairs until it ended at a broad landing. The walls of the landing were handsomely carved with intricate figures and symbols that told of long ago battles, kings now turned to dust and their triumphs. Two hallways led off from the landing, Vode motioned to the one ahead of them and the group continued. Conversation was at a minimum as they walked. Vode was still grappling with the mental images and their possible meaning.

They walked the thirty steps distance which brought them before a matched set of massive oaken doors banded with broad straps of iron that glinted dully in the flickering light of the torches. The door towered above the priests, each of the portals easily twelve feet in height. A small alcove had been carefully notched in the living rock to the left of the doors and it contained more torches.

Levas withdrew a stout key from within his robes and received a nod from Vode which granted him permission to open the entrance. To even the most casual observer it was plain to see that the craftsmanship was such that no gap was visible where the doors met.

Walking forward Levas moved over to a spot on the left wall that appeared to be solid rock. It was in fact a majical protective spell used to hide the key slots. With a murmur Levas issued the spell to remove the deceptive spell. A group of five slots now appeared in the wall. Levas moved so his body blocked the view of the junior priests, they were not yet of sufficient standing in the Order to see what he was about to do. Vode of course knew the sequence to unlock the doors. He too had once been senior acolyte charged with the keys that his aide now carried. Selecting the first of the three slots that must be unlocked in order Levas inserted the key and gave it a hearty turn.

For the briefest moment nothing occurred then a heavy rumbling could be heard from within the wall. The key then slowly changed its color from a dull black to something resembling burnished silver. He withdrew the now lighter colored key then inserted it into the next slot necessary.

Again a hearty turn the rumbling grew a bit louder but continued without pause. The key then changed color again, this time a gleaming golden in appearance. Waiting the appropriate interval, Levas pulled the key out and placed it in the last of the necessary slots. Repeating the turn he watched in awe as he did every time he infrequently had to unlock the library as the final transformation of the key took place.

The key slowly but steadily lost the golden luster of moments earlier and become shining crystal. Levas could see through the key to his fingers underneath. He smiled at the sight.

The rumbling within the wall stopped and several metallic *pops* and *snaps* could be heard as the locking rods were disengaged. Once all the machinery sounds ceased Levas withdrew the key which was still crystalline in appearance. He carefully returned the key to within the folds of his robe while stepping away from the locking panel. A murmur from the acolyte and the spell to recloak the wall was restored.

At the same time he did that, the sound of hidden gears could then be heard and the massive doors began to open up. Vode and the others moved back to avoid being caught between the steadily opening doors and the walls. First one door then the other reached the limit of their hinges.

The doors were designed to be opened outward in case of attack; it was harder to pull with force than to push inward. Several heavy latches and crossbars could be seen on the inside of the doors themselves which could be secured from inside if needed. Two men could easily secure all the locks from the inside making the doors virtually impossible to force inward since the doors were backed by a low hanging ceiling right at the entrance. A stone archway butted right up against the upper part of the doors.

The High Priest watched as the great doors opened and then stepped forward to enter the library. The others followed close behind, lights held aloft to illuminate the way.

Once inside Vode paused to marvel once again at the display he had witnessed many times during his service to the Order. The light from the torches sparkled and danced in the crystals contained within the rock that formed the cavern where the repository resided. The flickering of the flame teased and taunted the colors into boldness and then quickly back to shyness as the light left them to find others. The room shimmered and danced in the flickering lights. Supple multi-colored flashes shimmered about the room as the torchlight flickered.

The effect was dramatic, a hundred hues and shades all fighting for attention at once. The High Priest stood just inside the door and simply watched as the students moved to light the lamps carefully placed about. As each new lamp was ignited the pattern of swirling colors was changed.

The chamber that the housed the library was a large one and so the mix of sparkling color and darkness from areas not yet illumed was stark, only adding to the beauty. More light slowly reached into the fog of darkness pushing it further back. In the far corners the deeper dark remained, restrained for now by the light from the lamps.

Finally after several minutes all of the lamps were lit and Vode was forced to tear himself away from the sight to return to his reason for coming in the first place. He moved deeper into the center of the large room which was tastefully decorated with rich wood furniture and high rows of shelving holding the written history of a score of countries, kingdoms and more, most of them now long gone and all but forgotten save the words preserved here.

Vankard was not always as it was now, isolated and nearly forgotten in minds of men. Once it had been a great trading nation. Her ships rode the waters of world bearing goods to markets great and small. The shipwrights of Vankard had been well known by sailors the world over. With trade came knowledge, books and stories, theories and dreams much of which ended up in the library.

As time went by this changed as the world underwent growth and decline. Nations rose and fell, the oppressed rose up and cast off their chains ending empires while other nations decayed and were lost.

***

Levas sent one of the two other priests back up into the castle proper to fetch food and drink for all of them. Vode was wrapped up in the search for information but like any good Northman he still needed to eat whether he knew it or not. Since it was unlikely that the High Priest would stop to think of it, Levas would take care of it. The second year priest bowed to the senior acolyte and went on his way to carry out his task. Vode had the other student with him to assist in finding the works that he required. The pair walked back and forth among the many book-filled wooden racks seeking out the information called for. Levas joined them to assist.

Selecting a comfortable seat at one of the desks near the middle of the library, Vode began to pour through the various books and maps brought to him. Time slipped by without notice as more tomes were searched. Levas was careful to keep the locations of various works memorized so that his master would need not search long for them if required.

***

The night passed without a definitive answer being found but Vode kept a growing list of clues and notes nearby adding to them as needed. Several more of the junior priests came down to the library immediately following morning meal to be of use if necessary. Levas dismissed the two priests who had been part of the original search thanking them for their efforts. The two bowed to the senior aide who returned the salute. Levas was tired but so long as his master was up he would remain. Being tired was simply another test of will.

None of this was noted by Vode who now felt he was getting closer to finding some answers that would suit him. A forgotten plate of half eaten food was whisked away by one of the priests and the stout mug refilled with fresh tea. Vode absently mumbled his thanks while reading.

The information he was seeking seemed just beyond his grasp. A map, drawn up many decades before lay near his elbow. Books were scattered around his feet. He felt he was close but didn't have that one definitive piece of information, that specific something that would make him certain of what he was seeking.

Vode sat for a time, silent and still as he gave thought to the issue. The maps had confirmed what he already was certain of. The fortress in his visions was not located in Vankard and never had been. He had been sure of that before looking but that meant nothing. He was often telling the students not to take information for granted, seek it out and be certain even if they felt they were sure. This was no different; the maps of the countries surrounding Vankard had been consulted as well. A few hints were present but nothing solid he could point to with certainty.

The High Priest sat quietly deep in though for nearly an hour when a sudden thought struck him. When it did his head lifted and a quizzical expression rode his face. Levas knew that expression, it meant an idea or solution had presented itself.

Vode called for the others as he rose from his seat then headed through the chamber toward the far wall and the single door it held. The men hastened after their leader. The door was simple in appearance; nothing marked it as special which was part of the security for what lie beyond.

The door was unlocked using a different key on the ring that Levas carried. The lock was a little stiff from disuse. A pull on the heavy iron ring did nothing, no movement in the door at all. Levas pulled harder but the result was the same, the door failed to yield. Vode waved the junior priests forward and they hurried to the task. The senior acolyte moved aside to give the others room to work. The High Priest and his charge shared a look, what wonders lay beyond the portal?

Vode knew that a challenge had to be overcome prior to gaining access to the room he intended to enter. Levas knew nothing of this since the senior acolyte would only open the door upon orders from the High Priest. Only he and the king had the authority to order the room accessed.

The trio of priests had gotten themselves arranged and were working at pulling the portal open. The door was stubborn at first, it refused to comply with their exertion but then, ever so slowly a dry grating sound was heard as the hinges began to wind. A sliver of black could be seen between the door and the wall, then it grew wider and wider as the door finally began to move as it should.

The dry hinges creaked one last time then were silent as the three men completed their task pulling the door full open. Each was breathing a little heavier from their efforts but not outrageously so. They moved out of the way as Levas stepped forward with a lamp to enter the room.

"Hold!" The High Priest spoke with authority. He knew the area immediately inside the door was clear of traps but wished no one to enter, just in case.

One of the first and most important lessons he had been given by the former High Priest was how to navigate the traps in the anteroom he was about to enter. Only the senior member of the Order knew the path to walk to prevent being killed in order to gain entrance to the door on the far side of the room. Vode had to memorize the sequence of steps that had to be taken in very specific order and then repeat them back without flaw to the outgoing High Priest to ensure that the knowledge wasn't lost. When his time to relinquish the post he held Vode would in turn teach his successor the sequence.

Levas instantly did as he was told; the only departure was a slight turn of the head in order to better see his mentor. Vode quickly stepped forward reaching out for the lamp in the younger man's hand. Taking hold of the lantern the High Priest stepped partially into the darkened room, holding the light before him.

As the yellow glow of the lantern pushed back the darkness, a nondescript room of average size was revealed. No crystals shone in the rock that comprised the walls or ceiling. The floor was a dull gray. The only feature present was a single door on the opposite wall located at an angle from the entry.

Vode was a bit nervous. The long memorized path he must walk played through his mind. This would be the first time he would have to make use of that information. Telling the others not to enter the room, he stepped off five deliberate paces angled away from the door. Stopping, he turned so that he was directly facing the wall ahead. He couldn't quite see the marker he was searching for.

"Bring more light!"

The junior priests were quick to obey. Retrieving two more lanterns, they brought them to the doorway. Ensuring they were turned up to their brightest setting, both of the metal lanterns were set on the floor just inside the open entry. This raised the illumination level in the chamber to a level Vode was comfortable with.

He could now see the stony outcropping straight across the room -- his next waypoint. Moving forward at a slow but steady gait, the High Priest counted off the proper number of steps…ten, eleven, twelve, thirteen. Once at thirteen, he again stopped.

This next part of the journey was most difficult. A misstep here and it could be lethal. Sweat beads were very present on Vode's forehead as he swallowed once to help gather his resolve.

Without looking back toward the door Vode told the others, "No matter what happens to me do not enter this room. It isn't safe. If I fail then no others are to be risked. Do you understand?"

Levas was loath to give his agreement but he did. The two student priests gave their word also.

At the doorway Levas had told the others to step back. This kept them from being able to see what the sequence of entry was. He himself turned away as well but refused to leave the doorway. His master was in there and while forbidden to enter he could at least be present to offer what support he could.

Less than ready but knowing that he had to proceed Vode stepped off, making sure that it was his right foot that he used first. A series of zig zag steps was the next challenge. First the right foot then the left then another until the required seven paces had been taken.

Now sweating more profusely than he had in some time, Vode turned toward a small alcove visible in the furthest corner of the room from the entrance. Gripping the lantern a little tighter he started off again.

Moments went by as the High Priest slowly but steadily made his way toward the alcove. Nothing was said as step after step was marked off. Finally he was there and once there he blew out a half breathe in relief.

Now that he was there the next part required him to find – ah, there it was. Cleverly disguised as part of the rock wall, a simple lever could be seen. Vode reached out and turned it; once it was at the full travel level a simple *click* was heard. This click signaled that the first set of traps and deadfalls were rendered safe.

Two more legs to travel before he arrived at the door he was seeking. Glancing back toward the entrance Vode saw that Levas was deep in prayer. A light smile as Vode hoped that his senior student was praying for a safe journey for him. That was exactly what Levas was doing.

The next part of the journey was shorter than the last and not so fraught with danger. Vode moved so that he was now facing the rear wall directly and stepped off moving toward it. Nine steps brought him to the next to last resting point before reaching the doorway he wanted so badly to reach.

Nearly there, he told himself, *nearly there*. Patience is the key, relax and all will be achieved.

The next part was a bit awkward and Vode always thought that it was done that way on purpose just to teach those trying to enter the room some humility by making them take the ungainly walk needed. To reach the door the visitor had to side step while facing the wall. It had never been explained why it necessary to face the wall while walking the step. Seventeen steps from the spot he was standing to the doorway, seventeen, no more and no less.

Now facing the wall he began the last of the trials.

Levas, now finished with his prayers, watched as his mentor traversed the final distance to the waiting portal. Seeing the High Priest moving in such an undignified manner made the younger man smile -- which he quickly wiped from his face. Then, he turned away. If asked he could tell Vode, no, he hadn't watched. At least mostly no, anyway.

Arriving in front of the door Vode felt some of the tension in his shoulders relax. He was nearly finished, a small tremble at the thought of what lay beyond the door.

From time to time he had wondered at the mysteries that this room might contain and now he was close to finding out for himself. *Enough!* He shook his head to clear the foolish thoughts and feelings; focus was what he needed now. He wasn't inside yet. There were still several steps that must be accomplished in order to gain entry.

He turned his head toward the door and made eye contact with Levas, who nodded once and stepped out of the doorway to give the High Priest the privacy he desired. Now alone he reached up along the upper left edge of the door frame and began to feel for a button. Slowly his fingers traveled the edge of the frame until he found it. Pressing it down a hard *snap* was heard from within the wall.

Switching the lamp from one hand to the other, Vode began to search the lower right edge of the door frame for another button. This one proved to a little harder to find. It was in a small recess in the frame itself. He pushed it and when he did a small panel popped open in the wall about a hand span to the right of the door handle.

Standing, Vode reached over to the open panel and manipulated the lever he found there. This disabled the remaining traps and deadfalls in the room. Resting his head on the door for a moment, the High Priest worked to collect himself. That had been more taxing on him than he had imagined it would be. Several deep breathes helped to restore some of his composure.

Now to open the room up and go inside. Turning toward the door he called out, "Levas!"

The senior student appeared even before Vode finished saying his name. He looked into the room with a questioning gaze. Vode nodded. The two worked closely enough that often verbal communication wasn't necessary. Levas called to the junior priests with him and all of them entered the now safe room.

The High Priest stepped to the side while motioning to the door. The others understood and moved to open the long secured door. Vode never considered that door might not be stuck like the other one was. The two junior priests set themselves and pulled mightily which launched them -- the door swung open with no effort. The duo landed heavily a few feet away. Levas turned to look at his master with a look that spoke volumes, laughter dancing in his eyes.

Vode raised a gimlet eye toward his charge, "Not a word Levas, not a word." Levas quickly affected a pose that said 'Who me?' and the two shared a laugh. The two priests had recovered and were now standing again.

Vode, his spirits now much higher, took a deep breath and stepped to the doorway, his eyes taking in the contents. The inside of this room had not been seen by a living soul in well over three decade's time.

It was a square room about twelve broad paces on each side. A desk and chair were centered on one wall while the on the wall opposite it was a massive spear resting on two stone holders thrusting out from the wall surface, the spear was easily eight or nine foot long. The shaft was as thick as his arm; the heavy metal end was half as long as his arm.

Vode was shocked, he had never seen a weapon such as that, it would take a very strong man, no, that couldn't be. No man could wield such a thing. Not even from horseback, it must be some type of humorous prop.

But it was the back wall of the room that held the greatest mystery. As Vode was looking at the spear he noticed a glow, it was diffused, almost so he didn't see it amid the light from the lamp but the color was different.

The glow was a light blue, like the sky is during early afternoon. Softly the light rose from a large glass topped case that was along the back wall of the room. He blinked several times to make sure of what he was seeing. Yes, there was light coming from the case.

Vode knew that the castle sat at the junction of two majical force lines, one airborne while the other was earthbound. It was likely that the light was the result of a spell, a spell kept fueled by one or both of the force lines. He had heard of spells that had been kept functioning for terribly long periods by tying them into a force line. Vode wondered if this might be the case. He mused at the wonder of such a spell. His own majical abilities were nothing to be taken lightly but the thought of casting a spell with that manner of power tied to it was no small undertaking.

Walking toward the case the light seemed to grow brighter. He almost missed it but the closer he came it did indeed get increasingly lighter in the room. To test the theory he stopped and stepped backwards for two paces. When he did the light faded noticeably.

Amazing! He had never heard of such a thing and he had been a serious student of the majical arts for more than four decades. Already the room was delivering on the wonders he imagined it might hold. A smile rode his face as he continued on his way to the case.

The case was slightly above waist high, the sides were thick colored glass but the top was clear and free of dust. It allowed him to see that the case contained two books. He rested one hand on the glass lid to consider what the books might reveal.

With a start he jerked his hand away from the case. The power he felt there was strong, so strong it almost physically hurt him. He hadn't considered that the case or its contents would carry a charge but something there certainly did. His fingers were still tingling from the brush with the energy.

Levas looked to his mentor who was absently rubbing his fingers together. Vode pointed with his chin at the case. Levas moved the distance between where he had been standing and extended one hand out. The acolyte was careful to keep himself open to majical energy so there was a greatly diminished but still palpable feeling of power present. A smile creased his face as his savored the sensation.

The tingling of moments earlier had finally left Vode's fingers. Lightly caressing the case he too could feel the power that it emitted.

Levas removed his hand, stepping back to allow his master room, and took the lantern from him. Vode now with both hands on the top saw that it had hinges so he tried to lift the top. The heavy glass resisted for a moment then opened with a minute *pop* and swung up easily.

Vode raised the lid and rested it against the rock of the wall. He gingerly released it to see if would stay in place and it did. The two books the case held were now within reach, each seemed to beckon to him. His extensive knowledge of the written languages of Vankard served him well as he was able to read the cover of both books. The titles were written in a much older form of the language currently in use in the kingdom.

Tracking back and forth from one book to the other to make sure he was reading the titles correctly, *The Book of Iron* was on the right. Its companion volume was titled *The Book of Hope*. It was the book on the right that Vode reached for first.

Just as he was about to touch the leather covering he stopped. He had rushed once before and it gave him pause. A quick lick of the lips before he touched the book. As he did nothing happened. Relief flooded him as he lifted the book from within the case.

Asking the others to leave him for a bit, Vode settled into the chair. Placing the book before him on the desk, curiosity gnawed at him. What would the book tell him, what answers would it provide? He didn't know but was anxious to find out.

Levas and the others filed out of the room to honor Vode's request for solitude. The acolyte decided to use the time to have the others replace the numerous volumes and maps in the main room that Vode had used earlier. If the High Priest needed them again it was a small matter, Levas knew precisely where each of the books went. He and the others set to their task.

***

Opening up the book, Vode was surprised at the fine condition of the volume. The leather of the cover was still supple and smooth, the pages showed no sign of aging. A short introduction took up about one third of the first page.

Vode had to remind himself to go slowly, this form of the language hadn't been used in some time and so he could misinterpret what was written. Going slowly he began to dive into what was written.

His eyes going wider and wider, he realized that the book had been written nearly eighteen hundred years earlier by one of the founders of Vankard! Amazing! The opening page told of Revas Colh, one of the greatest soldiers in the history of the northmen and how he and a group of others had created a new country. The book was a story of how that came to be and had been written by Colh himself.

As a student of history to say that Vode was intrigued wasn't a fair statement. He was captivated beyond anything he had ever read in his life and this was only the first page.

Finished with the short introduction the High Priest flipped to the next sheet. The story began with an overview of what was happening in the world at that time, at least in the north. A great and terrible war was going on between the Elves and a race called the Varshon. The conflict had been raging for nearly eighty years with battles being fought in numerous places, some in the east near the Elven Homelands, a few in the south but the bloodiest clashes taking place in the north.

The reminder to go slowly was forgotten as Vode poured through the pages. Tales of battles filled much of the first part of the book. Revas spoke of how these Varshon had been raiding human settlements across the wide expanse of the grassy plains that stretched from nearly one end of the continent to the other. The number of humans killed, wounded and captured was unknown but Revas wasn't shy about expressing his anger at the atrocities. Colh spoke of how the proud Dark Elves had been nearly exterminated by the enemy.

Dark Elves? Vode realized that all of his life the fragments of stories that spoke of the Dark Elves had not been myths, strange indeed.

Revas had included some detailed drawings of what the Varshon looked like. Vode wasn't terribly surprised to recognize the creatures as some of what he had seen in his visions the previous nights. The priest turned in his chair to rest his eyes on the spear and put the two thoughts together -- the spear had once been wielded by a Varshon.

The next section of the book spoke of great siege and battle that took place at a great fortress known as G'mar. Yes! With only a moment's pause Vode was certain that this was the fortress that he had seen repeatedly in the dreams. Eyes flashed over the hand written pages as he continued his reading.

The Elves were trying to force entry into the castle to, what? Vode stopped and reread that passage again, for the first time since beginning, questioning his understanding of the language. Could that be possible?

> ...to stop the Varshon from completing the
> Cycle of Invocation which would couple their
> majic a tenfold.

Vode was staggered, had he not been sitting he might have fallen over. An increase in majic to that extent could be unstoppable. Fear began to creep into the mind of the High Priest. He knew that Elves were users of white majic, their spells were intended for healing and life enhancement. If these Varshon were enemies of the Elves it would seem likely that their majic would be of a darker, more evil nature.

Vode sat in silence as he contemplated what he had read so far. It shook him to the core of being, the wonder of uncovering mysteries that he had so eagerly embraced previously now seemed to mock him.

Reluctantly he returned to the story. The siege wasn't going well for the Elves. They had yet to be able to create an opening of any size in the defenses that they could force their way into the castle itself. A few sections of wall had been taken but then lost. Time was running out for the Elves as the approach of the ceremony was nearing.

Revas and many other leaders of human tribes and clans across the north had been organizing themselves to unite, at least long enough to attack the Varshon. A massive army of humans was marching north toward the home city of the Varshon when word came to them of the battle at G'mar.

Revas and several of the other leaders rode to see for themselves what the scouts had reported. At first they encountered only indifference and disdain from the haughty Elves who made it clear that they felt they needed no assistance from the small band of humans.

Those of the Elder Race had long felt that the humans were not suitable allies in the war against the Varshon because of their short lives and barbaric methods of warfare. It wasn't until the senior Elven commanders were convinced to send a single trusted scout back with the humans to show them the size of the army they commanded. No amount of talking could convince the Elves that the human force was actually as large as they claimed it was.

Revas and others rode back with the scout using the western pass through the high mountains that isolated G'mar. The Elves focus had been on the southern pass leading to G'mar so their own scouts had not been ranging far since the siege had begun.

Once back at the human encampment the amount of surprise that the Elven scout felt could not be contained. He was openly shocked at the size of the army that the humans had been able to bring together. It outnumbered the Elven army nearly three to one!

He rode back with little regard for the welfare of his mount. The news had to be passed along. An army of this size could make all the difference. The humans waited for word from the Elves. If they did not wish their help with the siege then the humans would continue north to try and locate the Varshon capital and destroy it.

Revas confided in the bold strokes of his written word that later on he realized that the plan to march all the way north was terribly flawed and would likely have failed. The location of the Varshon capital wasn't known and they had no maps to even to be able to properly march north without a major risk of ambush.

Returning to his own people the Elven scout hurriedly explained to his disbelieving officers the scope of the army now camped a few hours to their west. It had taken sending a second scouting party, this one included two senior officers to see for themselves.

After this group had returned their only comment was that the initial scouts report wasn't accurate, the human army was *bigger* than he had stated. Revas and the others were formally invited back to the Elven command tent to discuss the terms of an alliance.

Discussions were a bit testy as both sides wanted certain concessions from the other but the impending deadline of the approaching ceremony forced compromises. The humans agreed to join forces with the Elves with the understanding that they would not take orders from their new friends but would listen to suggestions. The Elves were a bit skeptical of the martial prowess of the humans but the addition of their army could only bolster the attack.

Vode continued to read, the passage of time while he did so was of no concern. Once he started reading he didn't stop. Further and further into the book he pushed on as the story of the siege continued.

Pages of the narrative focused on the battle involving the humans. Vode thought it both interesting and curious that little was spoken of during these passages regarding the Elves. It was instead all about what the humans were doing. How they struggled to learn the intricacies of siege warfare, a skill unknown to them until this time. They proved to be quick studies in this.

The tale continued as days passed with more and more gains being made until the fourth day after the commitment of the human army. A breach in the defenses on the western wall was accomplished that allowed a strong force of humans to flood into the castle itself. The attackers were able to seize a long section of wall and several towers.

More of the former victims of the Varshon rushed into the gap expanding their hold. The Elves allowed the humans to take on the goblins and humans that served as proxy troops for the Varshon. Then when the time was right the Elves swept through the human ranks to strike at the Varshon themselves who had been forced to commit nearly all their number to try and seal the breach.

Now the tone of the words changed as the author spoke directly about their allies in detail. Revas explained how the Elven soldiers were led by the finest surviving fighters of their kind. The tall and brooding Nyreth Wayn who commanded one flank of the onrushing Elves, the other flank was led by Lorthan Dys.

But it was in the center that Elves had their greatest champion, the one Elf that even the Varshon feared in the dark of night, Tyran Kass. He had battled and killed over two hundred of the hated Varshon. It was the name Tyran Kass that Varshon children were told was the enemy in the darkness.

When the Elves swept forward to pit themselves against the Dark Ones their demeanor was more like the humans than they would have cared to admit. *No quarter* was the order of the day; the fighting was intense as more of the castle was overrun. Fighting raged from the heights of the tall towers down into the extensive tunnels that ran like a rodent warren beneath G'mar.

The fighting continued through the day and into the night. The Elves were able to find the Varshon majic users and killed them stopping the ceremony literally hours before it could begin. It was another full day and half before the majority of the Varshon and their minion troops were either killed or captured. The leaders of the alliance met to discuss what to do with their captives.

The humans tried unsuccessfully to get the Elves to kill the remaining Varshon. Those of the Elder Race were shocked; killing unarmed prisoners wasn't their way. The war had decimated Elven numbers to the point it would take many generations for them to recover as well. This was in part due to the fact that since they lived so long they tended to procreate slowly.

The few remaining goblins were released to return north since they were merely subjugated vassals. The humans that had served the Varshon were from the far north and given over to the jurisdiction of Revas and the others. They were enslaved and along with the Varshon made to collect the dead and glean the battle site. A vast store of treasure and other valuables formerly belonging to the Varshon was divvied up with much of the wealth going to the humans.

A solution regarding the remaining Varshon prisoners was reached. They would be sent into the deep south and exiled. Since the home of the Varshon was in the north this seemed acceptable to the Elves. The humans tried one more time to get the Elves to reconsider their position and to kill their enemies but to no avail.

The battle site was cleaned of equipment, weapons and bodies the dead were disposed of in the appropriate manner to each race. The Elves were carefully prepared and were transported back to the Homelands for burial. The human dead were buried in mass graves dug by the prisoners. The dead Varshon and their followers were burned in huge funeral pyres, the smoke filled the upper reaches of the deep dell that the fortress sat in.

Once the dead were dealt with the Varshon were assembled and under the very watchful eye of the Elves were marched south. Some of the humans that lived in that part of the world accompanied their recent allies to assist them at least as far their own homes.

The journey, which became known in Elven lore as The Long Walk took nearly two years to reach a point in the mostly unknown south that the Elves felt comfortable releasing their prisoners. During the long journey a number of Varshon had attempted to escape or attack their captors. A few did manage to elude recapture and a number of Elves were killed or wounded but the combination of little food, sickness and watchful guards kept trouble limited to sporadic outbursts.

***

Vode continued to read as the tale passed from first-hand knowledge of a participant to what he had been told. The High Priest skipped ahead a bit, skimming each page until he found something he had been earnestly hoping for, a map, specifically a detailed map of G'mar and the surrounding area.

He knew that he had been correct, this was in fact the place he had been shown in his dreams for the previous seven nights. There could be no doubt. His finger traced the details of the walls, the mountains and then the passes that lead to the openness of the plains. He was now certain that he knew the location of the fortress. G'mar was located in a circular valley of some size surrounded by mountains on three sides with a large body of water to the north. It was some days riding distance to the east of Vankard but at least now he knew where it was! One mystery solved.

Stopping his reading for now, he leaned back in the chair and was struck by the stiffness of his muscles. He had been sitting without moving, hunched over the book for hours on end. His body was tight with tension and he struggled to move a little without incurring pain.

Unknown to him one of the junior priests had been stationed near the open doorway some time earlier by Levas. Vode turned and twisted his frame to release some of the stiffness, which caused the priest to go and seek out Levas just as he had been told to. Do not disturb the High Priest but when he was done reading to inform Levas immediately.

Vode was trying to stand to better relax his tired body when Levas appeared at the doorway and entered. The acolyte was carrying a large goblet in one hand and a plate of... whatever it was it smelled good. The Northman had not eaten or drank anything for nearly a half day.

Levas set the food and drink down on the desk and helped his mentor to stand up. Vode felt better as soon as he stood. The blood flow to the legs was tingling for a moment but it passed rapidly. Trying to offer his thanks proved a futile gesture, his throat was too dry to speak. A deep sip of the ice wine from the goblet eased the parched membranes allowing him to croak out his thanks. Levas merely nodded in response. He felt he was merely doing his duty in serving the High Priest. Vode drank deeply of refreshing liquid then sat the nearly empty goblet down on the desk.

Moving around a bit to further loosen up Vode was deep in thought trying to assimilate the information he had uncovered. The details of the siege played through his mind. Pacing the room he hardly noticed the stiffness loosen as he moved. Levas said nothing as he watched his mentor.

The pacing continued for several minutes before Vode slowed then stopped walking. Levas quietly urged his master to eat something. Vode nodded his thanks and did in fact sit and begin to eat. Approximately half way through the meal he stopped and pushed the plate away. The food was tasty but he was too distracted to really enjoy it.

There were still a number of questions for which he had no answers. In fact the number of questions that Vode didn't have answers for had increased rather than decreased. One book had given him some answers the other book might give him more. Standing again, he hurried over to the case and with care replaced *The Book of Iron* in the case and withdrew *The Book of Hope*. Levas removed the half empty plate from the desk and told Vode that he would return shortly. The senior majic user nodded his gratitude.

The book was resting on the desk with one of his hands absently caressing the leather as he looked at it. Vode knew that he needed to find the answers; the hunt for whatever reason behind the visions was too powerful to ignore. Almost reluctantly Vode opened the cover of the book; he squared up his shoulders and rolled his neck to better focus.

Similar to the first book the first page held only a short amount of text. What was written was intriguing, when he read it through the first time he almost didn't catch it. When he was on the fifth sentence Vode stopped, something wasn't right. Some of the words were written differently from those next to them. He looked the words over again and thought he saw something. Turning the book slightly it was easier to see which words were not like their brethren. Vode focused his attention on the scattered dissimilar words and he saw a pattern, a rhythm to them. A spell, it was a spell!

Being careful to only read and not speak the words he worked through the wording for the spell, he felt it was likely a type of guardian spell. This prevented all of the contents from being read by someone not skilled in the majical arts.

Vode read and then reread the spell sequence until he was certain that he had the timing and inflection correct. Slowly and with no small amount of trepidation he began to utter the incantation. This was a longer spell command than he was used to and so didn't get the entire sequence done properly.

What the High Priest didn't know was that the spell he was trying to work wasn't a guardian incantation but rather a containment spell, one designed to keep someone or something restrained.

At first Vode saw or heard nothing different but a slow swirl of twinkling orange light was visible on the page. The swirl gained speed and intensity. Vode leapt from his chair knocking it asunder as the swirl grew in size; it was now expanding upwards from the book. The High Priest backed up; about that time Levas appeared at the door with a pitcher of ice wine in his hand.

The younger man was startled to see the now funnel shape vortex of majical energy coming from the desk area. He stopped in mid-stride at the sight. The vortex was continuing to expand, within the twisting eddies of majical power Vode thought he could see ribbons of different colors. Levas would later tell Vode he could feel his hair and clothing moving as if being tugged by something.

Suddenly the vortex disappeared in a bright but silent flash of brilliant blue-white light. Both men had to blink hard to shield their eyes from the momentary illumination. When they could see again they could see the book vibrating on the desk. It was bouncing lightly up and down, the vibration caused the goblet to fall over and roll to the edge of the desk. It wound up on the floor ignored by the two priests.

The book stopped moving and with a low but growing tearing sound a light appeared from within the pages. The light was bright but not hard to look at; it seems to well up from within the book much as water comes up from a deep spring. The light twisted and shifted as it grew in size and depth. Vode had never seen the like in all his life. He stood rooted to the floor as if he was part of the stone. He couldn't move, only watch.

A long tendril of the light pulled itself free of the book and as if it was an arm pushed against the desk. As it did more of the light emerged from the book, a second arm like strand became visible. The two wisps of light pulled at the desk then one of them flung itself against the wall where it seemed to latch on. More and more of the bulbous, twisting mass was emerging from the book.

Levas was transfixed, what was this, what was…

The mass stopped moving, in an instant all the twisting and levering ceased entirely. The light form was nearly the size of a good sized man. The men shared a look then looked back toward the desk. There was no movement for several long heartbeats then all at once the light appeared to gather itself and with one effort pulled free of the book which was hovering a hand span or so over the top of the desk. It fell with a solid thump and lay still as if it hadn't moved in a hundred years.

The light form was still moving and shifting. The tendrils released the wall and desk. When that happened the light mass was more of a single form. It was suspended several feet off the floor and began to slide toward the door.

Vode realized that his student wasn't going to move. A long used and often practiced spell quickly came to mind and without conscious thought he formed the spell. It took less than a few blinks and with a thrust of one hand hurled the spell at Levas. The spell which compressed the air into a nearly solid form pushed the acolyte out of the way clearing the doorway.

Levas saw the form approaching, he tried to move, to flee, but he couldn't move, nothing happened when he commanded his limbs to run. Suddenly a rush of air swept him aside and he landed on the floor a few steps backwards no worse for wear. The pitcher of wine lay spilled on the floor a few paces away. Levas watched as the light continued to move.

The form was now at the doorway and increasing the speed it covered ground. Vode found his mobility and rushed after the light. Free of its long imprisonment in the book the entity was seeking a way out. It needed to feed and to return to what it considered home.

Moving out of the room it entered the library where the student priests were working. All of them surprised at the apparition they saw coming out of the back of the great room. Each of them sought to avoid contact, which was fine with the entity. It barely noticed the scurrying figures as it continued on its way. It exited the library heading into the hallway toward the stairs.

Floating up the wide staircase the entity increased its speed, sensing freedom above. Vode and the others were not able to keep up as the light form moved faster and faster. A pair of guards near the top of the stairs noticed the light coming and stopped trying to determine what it was.

They inadvertently blocked the top of the passage but the light form brushed them aside without thought. Both of the Thunderguards were hurled back, one striking the wall with sufficient force to break his arm and several ribs. The others flew down the hallway, landing on a rug which acted as a runner beneath him. The hapless guard slid nearly twenty feet before coming to a stop, battered and bruised.

The entity was eager, almost frantic to escape the confines of the castle. It sensed the open air was near, so near! Resuming its hurried pace it flashed down the corridor until it came to the large dining hall. Two of the night servants were present cleaning when the door flew open with a blast and a mass of shimmering blue-white light shot into the room.

Much of the ceiling of the dining hall was thick glass. The entity didn't care, the air and freedom it craved was there, right there! A loud shriek, so loud it roused everyone in the upper reaches of the large castle. The light circled the room once then like a flaming arrow rose toward the ceiling blasting through two of the large windows.

Broken glass and metal rained down on the now thoroughly mussed dining hall. The two servants dove beneath the large well-constructed table to avoid the falling debris which crashed down marring the wood surface.

After leaving the building the entity roared once again, this time even louder. The volume of it shook windows and shelf contents for miles around. Circling the castle in two ever increasing loops to help gain its bearing the entity then flashed away to the east with such speed some thought it was lightning.

Vode and the others reached the top of the stairs. Levas and the junior priests went to help the wounded guards at the direction of the High Priest. Both were in a bad way needing medical care. The senior Priest of Vankard could only stare down the long hallway and try to figure out what to do next.

Chapter Six
Intentions

The Citadel

As was often the case, Anagir was the first to arrive for the regularly scheduled planning session held by many of the senior members of the Varshon hierarchy. It was necessary for the command group to meet more frequently now since the deadline they had set was bearing down on them. It seemed that a thousand details had risen up and every one of them had to be attended to or it threatened to grow big enough to slow the invasion, at least that's how some of the clerks responsible for the paperwork treated the issues.

The senior Varshon majic user mused to himself that everyone has their own sense of self-importance, even clerks. As each of those attending the meeting arrived they moved through into the room they usually used, this one was high up in one of the main towers of the fortress and so provided a good deal of security along with something even more desirable: privacy.

Once inside the room each paid their respects to Anagir as befitted his position as Elder Majic User, Leader of the Varshon and senior Council member. It was a lofty title that despite his immense ego Anagir was loath to hear over and over. There was a time he enjoyed hearing it, almost demanded hearing it, now, it was noise of no consequence so long as the respect he felt was due him was paid. There were other matters that required his attention.

He paid little mind to the others as they settled in; his focus was on the large pile of reports stacked before him. Anagir was glancing through them filing away the information that he felt was essential, the number of Ogurth available, the estimated rate of travel per day for the army, anticipated losses among the cavalry force and much more.

He read quickly but without pause, long versed in the ability to comprehend and digest large amounts of information. This was merely one more instance of that.

None of the attendees were late, that simply wasn't done. The last two arrived a little before the session was to begin. Each entered the room, paid their respects to Anagir and found their seats.

The elder Varshon majic user looked around the room. The group was seated around a large five sided table of rich wood. Five chairs, each for an important member of the Varshon or their follower. Anagir in one, each of the next three held a Varshon that commanded one of the three tribes of humans that served as soldiers, Arakai, Alush and H'roth.

The fifth chair was for Pon, a human. He had been chosen to be the leader of the southern army. It would be his voice that the three tribes would follow – once, of course, the Varshon told him what they wished done.

Behind each of the three Varshon were the senior members of each tribe. The only other one in the room was standing behind Anagir and no one would mistake him for a human. Leader of the Ogurth, fierce mountain Trolls that had long served the Varshon, Q-tra-All was bodyguard to the elder majic user.

When each of those necessary was present. Anagir nodded his permission for the meeting to begin.

Standing and bowing to his leader, Pon returned his attention to the matter at hand. With practiced ease Pon drew one of his daggers for use as a pointer. He was comfortable, this was his element, command and authority, he never forgot who was in charge but it was *he* who commanded the vast Southern army, it would be his voice that led them to victory over the hated folk of the north.

He began, "As you know the plan is divided into several phases, I'll quickly review since there have been a few small changes since the last meeting.

"As before, the main body of the army will cross the Wystern River using the bridging barges which are nearly complete. Once they're in position we'll cross and move into D'Lohm. Their army is well equipped and trained but small. We feel they'll be no problem. At about the same time a sizable force of Alush will seize the river crossing at Kuln which will keep the southern bank of the river clear of enemy forces protecting our far left flank and the crossing sites."

Pon looked over at the Varshon who commanded the Alush and received a solid nod in return. The senior Alush behind their patron also nodded in understanding. It was an important task and they were eager to do it.

The southern commander then continued, "This will also ensure that the Black Guard will not be able to leave to reinforce the one group, which if properly organized and arrayed could present us real problems - - the army of Karbel."

For many years Pon had studied every report he could get on the army of Karbel. Whether it come from southern spies, merchant tales, made no difference to him, he was like the desert sands when it came to information, he drank it all in.

The general knew that the army of Karbel was a sizable force, well trained with competent leadership. If given sufficient time to mobilize it could be a major thorn in their side. He knew the composition of how each Legion was organized, what their usual supply allotment was, even how many uniforms each soldier typically carried with him. Those details might not seem important to someone else but to Pon it helped him to better grasp the inner workings of the Legions he would have to face in battle.

Anagir asked his general what the percentage of those in the Legions had combat experience. Pon closed his eyes for just a moment to concentrate on bringing up the proper information in order to answer the question.

Ahhh, there it was – "Our best estimates, based on personal reports and stolen documents is no less than one third, which while a significant percentage, it will depend on which particular Legion we face off against. Some of them have a much higher percentage of combat veterans than others. The Fifth, Ninth and Eleventh are the three with the most experience overall, sir. Of these only the Eleventh is of immediate concern because it is garrisoned on the southeast border of Karbel but widely dispersed." Anagir nodded slightly to acknowledge the answer then told Pon to continue.

Returning his attention to the map the point of the dagger returned to D'Lohm and was dragged north. "Once we are in Karbel we will stay in the eastern ranges to avoid the large cities. They are of no use to us and would be a significant drain on our resources if we tried to take them on the way. We don't need them for the trip north to the fortress so we will ignore them.

"I anticipate that we will face at least five Legions total during the march through the eastern part of the kingdom."

One of the other Varshon present asked what this estimate was based on. Pon quickly but thoroughly explained the placement of the Legions in that area of the human kingdom. This seemed to satisfy the Varshon who nodded in acceptance of the answer.

Fully in his element the senior general continued, "In addition to the Legions we may and I stress, may, deal with a few units of the Elven army."

As soon as the name of their eternal enemy was mentioned the younger Varshon hissed and became animated. Anagir allowed them a moment of emotion then turned and looked at each of the three which silenced them immediately. Pon had said nothing during this display; humans do not correct or admonish the masters no matter how senior he might be. It wasn't done. Anagir returned his attention to the map and waved his permission to Pon to continue.

Without missing a beat, "We feel that this is unlikely due to the distance to the west we will be of the Shyval Gap. That is not an area where the Elves regularly patrol and even if we do encounter some, the numbers would be completely in our favor."

Referring to the opening in the massive mountain range that separated the Elven Homelands from their neighbors to the west, Pon had even used the Elven name for them -- which oddly raised no correction from any of the masters.

The wide opening in the long chain of mountains was several days ride to the east of the anticipated direction of march. The understanding that Anagir had given Pon was simple, once the ceremony had been completed and the Varshon majic users infused with their new powers then the Elves and others would be dealt with, harshly and without delay.

"Once we pass through Karbel we will move through this area of open plains, occupied only by a few scattered groups of nomads. There are no cities or towns of notable size. We will then arrive at G'mar. Then we will secure the fortress and begin immediate upgrades to the defenses there. The two passes leading to the fortress, the main one to the south and the much smaller one to the west will be heavily guarded."

He turned at that point to direct his comments at Anagir. "Sir, you and the others in the advance group will then be free to conduct the ceremony unhindered by any outside forces." Pon waited to see if there were any additional questions he needed to answer.

Anagir nodded slowly, he knew the plan, knew it well. *He* had created the plan. That it had been polished by numerous others was of no consequence, it was *his* plan.

"Thank you General." With that Pon sat down.

"It was a thorough briefing of the overall plan." Only two thousand years to do this, Anagir thought on the failures of the past. Three hundred years earlier he had given in to temptation and allowed a large force of Varshon to go north to try and wrest control of the distant fortress. They never got close; a run in with the Elves ended that expedition.

He still chided himself for allowing his emotions to gain the better of him. Varshon losses had been heavy but manageable. It was then that Anagir decided that it would human troops that would bear the brunt of the fighting when the time came.

Discussions went around the room as each of the Varshon explained to their leader what had been accomplished since their last meeting five days earlier. Anagir listened intently to each of his three senior minions. One of them mentioned that several of the troop exercises focusing on command structure had gone well and there had been a marked improvement in unit skills and reaction. That comment triggered something in Anagir's thought process, if there was a way to interrupt the enemy command…

The meeting lasted for another hour or so while reports were made. When the last of the Varshon had finished speaking Anagir looked around the room, taking in each and every face present to gauge their feelings, their level of dedication. He was not displeased at what he saw. "My friends, I thank you for this productive meeting and all the information you have provided. Return to your duties." With that all of the others stood and bowed to their leader. He waved his hand in acknowledgment of their salutes before turning his attention to other matters.

As the meeting broke up Anagir motioned for Q-tra-All who had remained silent during the entire meeting. The massive Troll moved to where his leader was. Despite his size the creature could move quite adroitly which had served him well during numerous skirmishes over the years.

Leaning closer the Troll listened as Anagir explained his idea regarding the use of some of the specially trained troops they had and that now would be a good time to use them and against who. Q-tra-All nodded silently as he too saw the idea for what it was and when Anagir was finished stated that he would personally take care of the details. With a wave of dismissal Anagir sent him on his way.

The elder majic user stayed in the room as the others filed out. Two of the Ogurth were posted outside the room guarding the hallway to ensure his safety and privacy. The last one out of the room pulled the door closed behind him leaving Anagir alone with his thoughts.

Rising from his seat, Anagir pulled the large map that Pon had used earlier over toward him so that he might see it better. One long, scaled finger traced the route that the army would take. It traveled across the Wystern, through D'Lohm up into Karbel across the broad eastern plains, through the nomad lands of the north until the tip of the finger rested on the small square denoting G'mar. He knew the route, saw it in his dreams. G'mar, it was all about G'mar...

Anagir was lost in memory as he absently tapped his finger repeatedly on that point. Images from the ancient battle rose up in his mind, the smell of the smoke, sounds of the clashes as sword rang against sword. All of it was playing out in his mind as it had so many times over the long centuries since they had been forced to leave the north. It would be different this time Anagir was certain of that. He returned his attention to the paperwork before him. There was still much to do.

Chapter Seven
G'mar

Homecoming

The massive fortress was still as night fell, no breeze disturbed the dust. Nothing moved through the enormous halls and galleries that gave the construction its size, even the rodents and other vermin kept their distance from this place. Shadows deepened across the inner courtyard as the sun slid behind the mountains that shouldered G'mar to the west. The bastion sat in a wide bowl ringed by high peaks on three sides while the fourth was an arm of the Wind Sea, a treacherous body of water known for its year round fierce storms once braved by only the hardiest or most foolish of sailors. Only two passes split the mountains giving access to the area, a small one leading in from the west and the other coming up from the south. If one been able to see it from above, it looked for all the world like a funnel lain on its side.

The pass was wide and open at its southern end but rapidly narrowed until it was but barely two hundred walking paces wide by the time it reached the northern apex opening onto the plain southwest of the bastion. The stone walls that formed either side of the pass were smooth and nearly vertical, barren of any foliage.

This pass was once known as the Halls of Heaven for when the region was cloudy, which was often; the low clouds seemed to be supported by the high, thin mountain peaks which took on the appearance of the lofty columns seen in many palaces throughout the land. Someone within the pass may feel as if they were traveling through a long, high hallway. Thus the name.

As night moved on and midnight approached, a flash of brilliant blue-white light suddenly flared high over the western mountains flying at an amazing speed heading straight for the fortress. Clearing the tops of the stone barricade and gaining sight of its destination the entity slowed considerably then shrieked in exultation, a noise that carried for many leagues but heard by few. Those that did hear it clutched tight their cloaks and blankets as if to ward off the effects that the sound rendered. No one wanted to live too close to the House of Quiet Shadows as some had named it.

The former unwilling guardian of the *Book of Hope*, recently freed from its parchment prison in Vankard, was eager to return to its masters and those of its own kind. The entity soared closer to the bastion and suddenly stopped. It could sense no energy of life within the castle; nowhere from inside the great fortress did light show to drive back the night.

It was confused; the masters were ones to always have the fortress lit up at night. It recalled the soaring lamps of polished gold that ringed the high walls, the gilded artwork, each was a masterpiece of the finest artisans work; the lamps could illuminate the area for leagues around if need be. But none were on. All was dark and still within the boundaries that the walls defined.

Where were the Alkushan? G'mar was their capital and the seat of a vast empire that stretched for over a thousand leagues in all directions. What was this? Sensing nothing at this distance the entity, a majical creature of modest power trapped into the pages of a book that would much later become known as the *Book of Hope*, the imprisonment spanning thousands of years. The form of light moved closer and closer to what was once its true home.

Still sensing nothing the figure of blue-white light continued to reduce the distance between it and its objective. Nothing, nothing at all, no lights, no sounds, no noise of any kind save that from a light breeze now beginning to come ashore off the water.

None of its own kind had come out to exchange the words of greeting and challenge. This disturbed it most of all: where were the guardians that shielded the masters from attack? Nearly at the walls now the light form rose in altitude to gain a better view of the area. Still nothing moved within the ramparts.

Passing over the walls it could see the state of disrepair that now marked the once mighty stronghold. Debris and damage was plainly visible in nearly all the areas that could be observed from the high vantage point.

The entity had incredible vision, especially at night. All of its kind did, one of the reasons they were favored by the masters as guardians. Fallen stonework, foliage growing in the courtyard, the general effect of weathering on the area gave it a tired and shabby appearance.

Finally, now hovering over the inner courtyard it at last began to feel the power of the mystic lines that converged here. The confusion of earlier, not finding the fortress occupied had dimmed its senses to its surroundings. The mystic power was one of the reasons that the fortress was situated where it was; there was no place on the planet where the mystic energy more focused than here.

The imprisonment of so many centuries had numbed its innate ability to sense the power so badly that it was akin to a blind man wandering in a fog bank. So intent on trying to determine what was wrong at the fortress the being didn't pay attention to where it was and drifted into the nexus of the five mystic lines. The results were immediate and horrific.

The nearly inexhaustible power of the lines, three of them airborne and others soil bound struck the entity like a thousand bolts of lightning from the hand of the Fire God himself. The sky flashed over and over in a glittering array of colors in all spectrums that lit the entire region to that of nearly mid-day. Had anyone been present they would have been blinded by the display.

The being was helpless, trapped in the raw surge of pure mystic power that poured into it without control or mercy. Being away from a source of power for so long it could not control the rate that the energy flooded in and the pain tore at it at levels that would have killed armies en mass.

The force tossed it like a leaf at the mercy of a windstorm. The being was racked with hammer blows of power over and over until it could barely recognize them for what they were. The light spun and reflected in a hundred directions in all colors. Numbly it fought to keep it presence but the energy was too much as it poured into and through the creature like a jar held under a waterfall to fill it. Ragged screams of agony ripped the silence of the night as the power raced in unchecked and unexpected.

The power was pure and raw racing through it like the sharpest razor's edge multiplied a thousand fold all at the same time in every part of it. The spectacle of light above the fortress was so bright it lit the face of the mountains that ringed the area despite the distance. Sharp, clear flashes of color twisted in the sky visible for many miles. This continued for some time as it fought for some measure of dominance over the situation.

Slowly as the ability to regain some control of the power returned the entity was able to stop being twisted and tossed through the air. It spun itself out of the nexus and hovered weakly off to the side of the convergence while continuing to draw power like a starving man at a great feast. The massive power it had been exposed to did little to replenish it, that process must be controlled and focused in order for the energy to be of use. The force that it had been subjected to was akin to a weak man tossed in a raging river. It allowed him no control over his travel but just enough to keep his head above the water at times; it was much the same for the entity.

Now free of the enormous energy river the creature opened itself up a little at a time to the power that was present. Slowly as more power was taken in, man-like limbs and torso took shape from what had appeared to be a mostly featureless pulsing ball of light. This was not the beings natural form but it was the form that the masters preferred based on their desire to interact with those who at least in form resembled themselves.

The light show of moments earlier now faded and darkness mostly returned, the mountains were again hidden in the curtain of night. The battle with the mystic power had been painful and it would still be some time before entity would be able to regain full use of its own abilities. Abilities that the lack of access to a source of power had denied it for so very long, trapped as it had been.

The glowing figure hovered above the bastion as it continued to absorb some of virtually limitless energy of the lines. The being reveled in the feeling that the renewed power provided it. Energy coursed through it and taking a moment to indulge itself spun off three quick mystic strikes long denied it by the confinement in the book which had dampened the effects of majic severely.

Three bright red balls of light, each the size of a farmer's prize pumpkin, headed for the trees south of the fort. When they hit the trees were blown apart into kindling, some pieces tossed a hundred feet or more into the air. The entity watched in delight as the feeling of regeneration that restored power endowed continued to grow within it. Pieces of what had moments earlier been centuries old oaks continued to rain slowly to the ground as several small fires burned among the stumps and shattered trunks. A wide swath of forest growth had been devastated by the energy.

***

Finally, after a lengthy time, the appetite for power temporarily sated, the creature known among its own kind as Tra'Hak'pulon, drifted down toward the courtyard and into the fortress itself.

It kept a small portal open to continue to draw in the mystic energy that permeated the entire fortress area. This would allow it to continue to feed itself and start to restore its own natural reserves, precious life-giving resources that had kept it alive for so long in its paper prison -- but had nearly run out. The journey here was nearly the last gasp of energy left to it. So powerful was the instinct to return, it had barely fed itself on the flight here despite there being several opportunities.

It was now time to discover the answers to the mysteries before it, what had happened and where were the masters? While still feeding it had continued to reach out for another of its own kind but none of them had appeared.

Tra'Hak'pulon remained aloft a few feet above the ground as it traveled across the broad courtyard. Trees and shrubs grew in scattered groups that varied in size and age. Ancient debris dotted the landscape of the once pristine castle. The creature of majic was deeply confused. Still no lights or sounds came from within, anywhere, and a deepening sense of absence began to settle on the being.

As it moved it began to sense something else, a change of some kind in the majic that saturated the area. It could feel the differences but having been away from here for so long it wasn't able to recognize the changes for what they were. Strong echoes of the deaths that had occurred here were also present, like a steady but light breeze. It was heavier in some areas but present throughout the fortress.

The figure drifted through a large doorways that accessed one of the long hallways running along the edge of the courtyard and headed for the main portion of the castle. The passageway was a shamble of debris, heaped piles of windblown dirt and tumbleweeds in their final resting places. Confusion filled it as the light emitted from its aura cast bizarre shadows through the portico while it moved forward.

Reaching the end of the hall and passing inside, it turned to follow the sweep of a broad stairs that rose and curved to the right. Once, these stairs were showpieces of art, sweeping and gleaming as they rose from the floor to connect gracefully with the upper galleries. Now they were filthy and damaged; two areas were missing steps entirely. This didn't affect the traveler since it was floating several hand spans above the floor deriving its motion from mystic energy.

Once at the top of the staircase it paused to choose a direction of travel. After a brief moment it chose the gallery to its right side and started down the hall to further explore the area. Light emitted from its form shone through the long halls.

The journey took it through various sections, some whole but most damaged and empty in some way, either by the passage of time or what Tra'Hak'pulon had now surmised to be a great battle. Is this what had happened to the masters? What power existed in the world that could have challenged the Alkushan, the mightiest of all races, and triumphed? The creature didn't know but clearly something had laid waste to the fortress and its occupants.

Moving further along the corridor the entity began to extend itself out in an effort to open up to anything familiar. This nearly proved its undoing. Slender ribbons of senses, likened to touch, smell and sight all in one probed in every direction, stretching further and further out as the being became more and more anxious to discover answers.

The invisible tendrils of mystic energy touched something up ahead that the entity didn't recognize. The incredible mystic power that the two sides had used during the Dark War battle fought here had been twisted and perverted in places. In some areas the majic was amplified, a spell unleashed in this area would be orders of power higher than the user was capable of.

In other areas the majic had spun the air itself into a solid mass that lay on the ground, while in other areas the stone that made up the fortress ran like water as it had melted. Great rivulets of the once massive stones looked like a graceful waterfall sculpture in the places that this had happened.

The most dangerous areas to those who used majic were the null areas. These were spaces that no majic would work at all. Any spell or majical energy attempted in one of these areas was snuffed out like a cheap candle, majic would not – *could not* exist within these nulls.

It was one such area that the entity had touched and began to head into. The tendrils it had extended were in contact in several places with something Tra'Hak'pulon didn't recognize. It was the edges of a null area, a large one but the being continued to move forward to investigate. The results were nearly lethal.

As the entity began to enter the null area, the parts of it in contact with the null began to spark and hiss as they were extinguished by the mystic void. These points of contact were horrifically painful. It sought to extricate itself from the unseen force now sapping its very life force away, even as additional points came in contact with the ragged edge of the null.

Tra'Hak'pulon had never encountered anything like this and reacted out of instinct. It attempted to loose a power strike at the force but the null simply swallowed the powerful bolt of energy since it was magically based. Fear was unknown to those of its kind but the sensation coursing through the being was close enough for a comparison.

The struggle continued on for several moments before it was at last able to free up one limb. It turned itself as much as possible and extended the limb like projection toward the wall on the far side of the room and sent a sliver of pure power lancing deep into the stone, like tossing someone a rope. A hole appeared in the stone with a small puff of smoke that quickly dissipated as the sliver hit.

Keeping contact with the wall via the mystic line, the entity used this anchor point as a means of support, pulling itself free of the void that was draining away its life energy. Slowly at first, the being was able to disengage parts of itself from the null. As contact with the siphon was lessened the process moved quicker until the entity was at last free.

The moment that the last part of it was clear from the draining force, Tra'Hak'pulon hurled itself across the room to distance itself from whatever was killing it. The effort slammed it into the wall with enough force to crack several of the stones that made up the wall itself. It slid to the floor. As it lay there a small rain of dust and small rock pieces rained down from the damaged area of the wall.

The being was still in a great deal of pain from the null but it was slowly subsiding. It released its hold on the wall that had saved its life and tried to gather up the energy to rise again. It was battered, weak but alive.

The entity was now more confused than ever, twice in the short time of its return it had nearly been destroyed in a place that once was home.

It carefully opened itself up to allow a greater measure of power to flow in to replace all the energy lost to the void. Using its now expanded senses the creature of majic looked across the room and was able to determine roughly where the edges of the force were lying in wait. It continued to draw in energy while it studied the room.

After some time it was able to rise and resume its journey, injured still but wiser. The entity scouted the null and while it was sure that it extended beyond this room at least it could do something about this part of it.

One arm raised and several strikes were loosed into the ceiling just short of the edge of the null -- which immediately began to collapse. Tons of rock, dirt and debris rained down and buried the edge of the null. That would protect anything else that entered the area. A huge wave of pressure driven air exploded out of the doorway, heavily laden with dust and small gravel pieces. The noise of the collapse rang through the fortress but none but the entity heard it.

Satisfied that at least here the null posed no further danger, it floated out of the room and once again extended the tendrils as before but not nearly as far. Passing through several arches spaced equally along the corridor wall it came at last to a large, open gallery where several passageways and stairs converged.

The area was heavily damaged, two of the stairs were completely destroyed and one of the passages blocked by falling debris. The walls still bore the telling scars of strikes by mystic blasts. Numerous blackened areas, some high up on the walls, told a silent story that the creature found worrisome. A tremendous amount of power had been loosed in this area.

Coming across a picture board, a large story carved into the stone it stopped completely and gazed at the long lines of text and detailed carvings depicting some of the masters and even two of his own kind! What an honor to have been displayed with the masters. The pair must have served very well indeed to have earned such a place.

Tra'Hak'pulon began to read the tale inscribed into the stone. It was an incredible tale and the being was shocked as it read. It told of how the masters became divided and a great war was fought between two of the three families who formed the Alkushan Empire. Disbelief flooded the creature as it read further. *Is that what had happened here?* Never mind, not important for the moment just read!

It moved closer and passed a limb back and forth twice over the board just as the small line of text that ran along one side instructed. Moving back several feet the entity watched as the board slowly changed in appearance. From within the stone light began to shine, slowly at first then the glow got brighter and began to fill in each letter and symbol on the board as water would a glass vessel.

As each word was illuminated it stayed lit and the next word was illuminated from within one letter or symbol at a time. The process started out slowly but gained speed rapidly until words were being filled in faster than the eye could follow. Once all the words were done the tall carved figure of one of the masters began to glow in the same manner as the letters had. The hall where it stood was now bathed in the glow of light from the wall. The light was warm and soft.

Slowly at first but with improving speed a rich voice could be heard coming from seemingly everywhere and nowhere all at the same time. The voice; spoken in a tongue that the being had not heard in many generations, reached out and grabbed it in a way that demanded attention. It was the voice of one of the masters. The voice told the story of what happened at the fortress and to the Alkushan. It was a much more detailed story than the text had provided.

The voice stated that one of the three families that formed the Alkushan Empire had gone west over the seas seeking their own way after a long and brutal civil war. There had been no reconciliation and no peace but this solution seemed to work. The fighting ended and the remaining families tried to rebuild what was left of the empire but the damage was too severe and their numbers, too depleted by the long struggle were not equal to the many tasks at hand. The smaller of the two remaining families decided to leave and try and make their own way in the world but nothing was known of their fate.

The last family hung on for nearly a full generation after the departure of the second group. At last with enemies encroaching on their borders, and some within the family saying that it was time to seek out the other group, it was decided that they too would leave G'mar. No clue was provided as to the location of the remaining family group.

***

Tra'Hak'pulon knew that the group that went west must be found and told of what had happened here. This was the rightful capital of the Alkushan and it belonged to them. Not knowing the location of either of the remaining two families and no clues given by the text the being of majic had no options but to seek out those to the west.

But first it would be necessary to draw in more of the mystic energy. The entity did not eat as other inhabitants of the world would understand it. It was a creature of pure majic and only mystic energy could sustain it.

Returning to the courtyard it selected one of the soil bound energy lines and stepped on it. Careful this time to limit the flow of power into itself, there was no great shock of power. Slowly, very slowly, energy was allowed in and it began to flow. The pace was measured and painless. The process took some time and by the time the being felt it had sufficient power, the sky to the east shown the first hints of rose signaling the approach of dawn.

Pulling itself free of the mystic line the former guardian took flight once again and headed west toward the distant sea, passing first over the mountains that guarded the bastion. Next it streaked over the plains. Several early rising farmers saw the streak of blue white light in the sky and cursed the Gods for evil omens. Little did they realize how right they were.

Tra'Hak'pulon continued to pass over the land not only heading west but seeking any aerial mystic lines that were angled in his direction of travel. Better to replenish as the travel continued. Twice lines were found going in basically the same direction as the journey so it was easy to skim along through the energy while still heading west. Far below the coastal line met the sea and the land that had trapped it for so long quickly passed away behind.

Scattered islands could be barely seen as small dots of green against the vast carpet of blue far below. Capable of moving at great speeds, the being took time to enjoy the sensation of being free, soaring among the clouds and delighting in the flight. It looped and circled as it continued the trek to chase the setting sun. The journey to the west took nearly two full days and nights in spite of the tremendous speed it was capable of. The western sea was very broad; a journey by conventional means such as a deep draft sailing vessel would take as many as five months.

On the third morning a coastline came into view, so the being swooped to a lower altitude to better see what lie below. It did not know where the masters would be now but reasoned that it would be along the coast as the Alkushan had always been sea farers. It was part of their existence in much the same way majic was part of its own. There was no one without the other.

Tra'Hak'pulon swung north to search out the masters. Miles of coastline fell behind as the travel continued through the day. Here and there hints of civilizations could be seen, deserted towns, roads empty of travelers and occasionally small sailing ships that plied the coastal waters. Each of these was investigated and when proved to be of no use, ignored.

The search to the north continued until at last the being reached the edge of the frozen ice pack that extended from horizon to horizon. By now the sun was far to the west and so the entity turned about and headed south, convinced that was now the proper destination.

Not needing sleep the entity selected a nearby mystic line that stretched roughly north-to-south and flew into it heading away from the ice to continue its search. It flew on through the night retracing its path. Just as during the day nothing substantial revealed itself.

As dawn pushed its way west the entity found itself near the point where it had started the search the previous day and so without hesitation it continued south. Tra'Hak'pulon was certain that today it would find something.

The coastline was a jumble of sheer cliffs, rolling hills and gentle beaches. Here and there rivers made their way to the sea to deposit the effects of inland rain and mountain snow. A number of small coastal villages passed below and behind. More signs of civilization could now be seen on a regular basis, roads, towns and well-tended fields were all observed with interest. The creature felt that at last it was getting closer to what it sought. The being continued south until at last a major city appeared on the coast line wrapped around a deep sheltered bay. The being slowed down considerably and flew lower.

The city was full of people and surrounded by a high sturdy wall of stone. A moat ran from one end of the wall to the other. Towers appeared at regular intervals along the barrier that separated the city from the lush jungle that came within two hundred paces of the moat, itself nearly thirty paces wide.

The city was sprawling, noisy and colorful. Several cargo ships were tied up and unloading their contents onto the piers while five vessels that were obviously warships from their structure were positioned to guard the harbor entrance. Much of the building design and coloration seemed familiar. A large, ornate building stood in the southern part of the city and that was where the creature of majic headed. A number of high towers rose gracefully from the building proper and a man could be seen standing on one of the balconies, it altered its path to head there.

***

Da'Haan Tralisk, the current Lagoash, the title reserved for the supreme leader of the Alkushan, stood silently at a high balcony overlooking the deep bay that sheltered Noramth Wielk from the sea. The name for the city in the old tongue meant "the Vengeful Place". His gaze was steady as he absently took in the view that spanned from the far mountains to the sea while he pondered the future of his people.

The Alkushan were masters of all he surveyed and much beyond. Only recently had they defeated yet another enemy along their vast borders which added hordes of slaves, precious stones and gold to their already bulging coffers. The ceremony welcoming home the victorious army had been completed a fortnight earlier. The D'resh, the elite shock troops of the Alkushan, had served their masters well and so were being rewarded in the traditional way.

Lagoash Tralisk absently reflected that the small percentage of slaves being used in this way would be of little consequence compared to what it would bring in the long run -- continued D'resh loyalty, something Da'Haan had little if any worries about. The elite soldiers of the Alkushan had been subjugated many generations before and loyalty to the rulers had been ingrained from the moment they left the birth farms to begin their martial training.

Having settled that now non-issue in his mind, he returned to his earlier thoughts. What challenges would arise to test the Alkushan next? The range of their power already extended from the capital on the south east coast of the continent in all directions for hundreds of miles. Tens of thousands slaves served them and kept the empire running. There had been little fighting these last years. No one was now left alive or free to threaten them. These last ones were from far to west and this had been their last field army. He took great pride in knowing that none had withstood the Alkushan.

His people were progressive, artistic and intelligent. They possessed a gift for warfare but preferred to pursue the arts and to improve themselves; they had come a long way, a long way indeed from the ragged band that had stumbled ashore after leaving G'mar. Now they had the D'resh to serve as soldiers and that allowed them to continue to grow.

The Family of Alkushan that had left G'mar well over two thousand years earlier had been meager in number and resources. The protracted civil war within the Old Empire had been crippling to both sides in terms of casualties. When the survivors had gathered together and determined that the best course of action was to seek other lands for their own they traveled across the great sea and eventually found this place.

Many generations were spent trying to establish and maintain a foothold in the new land. Thousands were lost to disease and battle as their new neighbors tried to push them back into the sea forever. Da'Haan sometimes wondered what had become of the other two families that remained behind. His own forbearers had been Lagoash just as he was now, the line unbroken from the time of arrival.

A streak of light could be seen high over the city and the movement caught his eye. The streak was moving steadily toward him and if his eyes were not failing him it was slowing. What manner of event was this? Curiosity overcame him and he stood still watching as the light came closer. Finally it occurred to him that it was heading right for him and he began to back up keeping his gaze fixed on whatever it was that approached as fear began to creep in touching him with its icy tendrils.

The light form continued to slow down until at last it stopped and hovered a few feet from the edge of the railing. The Alkushan leader had regained some of his senses and all at once the light form changed into a human like shape. No facial features were visible and then a memory of something jumped up. He knew what this was, what this could only be.

Da'Haan could hardly believe was he was seeing. An Entity, a mystic creature that his ancestors had employed as guardians and shock troops, here now, right in front of him. No one had seen one in several dozen generations or more.

The being watched as recognition overcame the man on the balcony. It then floated over the railing and onto the smooth polished surface of the stone. Tra'Hak'pulon knelt as protocol demanded when addressing one of the masters, it waited for the proper commands to be spoken. When the allotted time for the command to come came and went the being stood and waited to see what would happen next.

Licking his lips to rewet them the Lagoash at last spoke, "Greetings noble one, and welcome to Noramth Wielk, home of the Alkushan. I am Lagoash Da'Haan Tralisk."

He bowed his head slightly which was a breach of protocol regarding the entity but he didn't know that. Tra'Hak'pulon was surprised when the man before him, an Alkushan, showed him deference. This was not the Way of Rights; it caused a curious sensation within it. A feeling of doubt; how could this be one of the Masters if he didn't know the Form?

The relationship between the Alkushan and the entities had always been one of great complexity. There were a number of specific protocols that were to be followed depending upon the situation. Lagoash Tralisk found that in his life there was little than he did not either understand or have some control over, this however was completely different, the situation was nearly beyond his ability to grasp.

There was a prescribed method for handling an entity when one first came in contact with one in order to maintain a level of control and servitude. Da'Haan did not know this since many of the old records were lost long ago when an invader succeeded in gaining access to part of the city during a siege. Fires set by the invaders destroyed two of the precious libraries and much was lost including everything regarding the handling of the entities.

Tra'Hak'pulon gave no indication of the breach of established protocol but was curious none the less. It had never before been in the presence of an Alkushan and not had the customs of greeting and loyalty displayed. What was occurring? It did not know but it had come to give a report and so it would.

Da'Haan was nearly beside himself with excitement and curiosity. What had brought the entity here and where did it come from? Where had it been all this time? The surviving written histories spoke of the power that the beings possessed and used at the request of the Alkushan. When he was younger he had read the stories and marveled at them. Now, here, right here in front of him was one of the creatures spoken of by his ancestors.

The creature spoke for the first time, - *Greet you Lagoash. I bear word, word of import. G'mar alone, none there.* - Da'Haan was struck by the curious speech not knowing that the creatures had been taught only simple language skills since their power was in the control of the majic. After a moment, he was able to decipher what he was being told.

"Alone? Do you mean that no one is at G'mar? It is empty?" A hundred questions and more began to surface in Da'Haan's mind and he sought to get them organized to better understand what was happening.

The being of majic listened to the questions and again stated, - *G'mar alone, none there.* -

The Alkushan leader was shocked, what had happened to the other two Families that had remained behind? The thoughts of his Family, a loose term used to identify all those who followed one of the three leaders, the Lagoash, driven from the home so long ago. It burned at him with a deep desire to return to their ancestral home and throw down those Alkushan who they had believed remained there. His ancestors had planned on returning and reclaiming what they felt was theirs but it had not happened. Now it suddenly seemed possible, especially if the fortress, a place of myth and wonder in their history, was indeed abandoned and was ripe for the taking.

He waved a hand toward the opening that led inside the tower and waited for the creature to lead the way. The entity again gave no indication at the breach of form. It rose slightly off the polished floor and floated inside with Da'Haan trailing.

Passing through the gracefully sculpted archway it was in a large room that was well furnished and richly decorated with fine art and other valued objects. A fountain sprayed a fine rain of water, scented with delicate oils into the air, keeping the room cooler and free of odors.

The questions were still bubbling up in the mind of the Alkushan leader as he watched the creature before him. He knew that his guards, all handpicked Alkushan who were carefully hidden in various locations throughout the tower, kept this room under constant surveillance and so word would be sent to his advisors of what was taking place.

Being inside, this room was his personal sanctuary; allowed Da'Haan a measure of comfort that while outside had escaped him. This translated into a fuller control on his thought process and emotions. His mind, long used to cunning, began to turn over the information given it so far.

If the capital was truly abandoned then it was good tidings indeed. He would waste no thoughts of pity for the other two Families; if they had fallen away then it meant that his Family, Tralisk, was the rightful rulers of the empire and that would mean a greater measure of power for him.

He would be AL'Tar Lagoash, Alkushan for Great Family Fatherone, supreme leader of the Alkushan, a title denied him by tradition. Only the Lagoash who rule over G'mar could be wear the mantle of AL'Tar Lagoash.

It was all that Da'Haan could do not to tremble at the prospect. He was strengthened by the knowledge of the past glories and what the opportunity brought to him may represent to his people and more importantly, to him personally. The thought of being the leader that returned his people to their rightful place in the world, the thoughts of G'mar taunted him, teased him. Gave him a nearly insatiable desire. Yes, he would be that leader.

The door from the hallway was discreetly opened but the being had long been aware of the presence of the others hidden about. The secret watching places were well masked from those not familiar with them but to one of its kind it was a matter of no effort to discover them.

Several figures came forward slowly to not disturb their leader and his "guest". Among these figures were members of the advisory council and the Guard Commander. The latter led the group into the creature's presence. Once there they all stopped at a gesture from Da'Haan and bowed slightly to the creature. The entity did not bow as protocol dictated since the men had not followed the established routine; neither would it.

The Lagoash waved at his visitor and told the others that the entity brought news of great joy. He turned to the being and with a wave of one hand bid the being speak of the news again. It stated simply, - *G'mar alone, none there*. - Tra'Hak'pulon in its own stilted manner then asked what had become of the others of its own kind.

Da'Haan told it that no entity had been seen in a very long time. He didn't tell the entity that his kind had been used by both sides in the civil war and their numbers had been decimated as a result.

The creature asked again if they knew where any of its own kind were. Lagoash Tralisk did not know where any others were. His tone was impatient. The being picked up on that right away. It was now sure that this was not a true Alkushan. A master such as it remembered would never act this way. So if this was not an Alkushan then it was owed no further allegiance. It had given the message and would now leave to seek out any of its kind.

It rose higher off the floor and started drifting toward the balcony archway to leave when Da'Haan became aware of what it was doing. He yelled *stop* and was ignored. The Guard Commander moved to step between the creature and its exit. The entity merely flicked a portion of what would be a hand on a human and the Alkushan was hurled aside. He struck one of the decorative columns which snapped his spine like a dry twig. The sound of bones breaking from the impact had its effect on the others who all remained still.

Once clear of the archway Tra'Hak'pulon again rose into the sky and flew off to the west seeking its own kind. The feelings it held for its now former masters were of no consequence. For the first time in nearly three thousand years it was truly free and vowed to remain so. The departure from the tower was witnessed by thousands who saw a great flash overhead and wondered what it meant.

Da'Haan and the others watched the being leave in a flash of blue white light that streaked toward the far horizon. Two of the hidden guards had entered to check on their commander but there was nothing that could be done. He was dead. One of the council members told the guards to remove the body and summon additional men to secure this area. The guards nodded and grabbed their former leader by the feet and under the arms to carry him out.

Several of the others were already in deep conversation with Tralisk regarding what they had heard and what had happened prior to their arrival. For his part Da'Haan used the opportunity to expound on the arrival of the entity. He told them that the being was a messenger sent to bring them word of their need to return. The empire was in chaos and only they could return it to its former glory. He went on to further tell them that this was their chosen time and that it was time to return to their home.

This confused several of the councilmen and they asked what he meant -- Noramth Wielk was home. Da'Haan was angered by their lack of vision and sense of history.

"Home of the Alkushan is but one place, and that place is G'mar. We are going to G'mar." His tone was heavy with decisiveness and authority.

The level of conversation rose immediately as the others grasped what was being told to them.

He allowed them to ramble on for a short time and then with a shout, "Enough! No more of this prattling. We are returning home, all of us. Send out word that I require a Convention, on the morning two days hence."

This was when an elected group of representative came together to hear what the Lagoash wished to pass on to them and to hear other business. They then went out among the people who elected them and passed this word on.

Da'Haan dismissed them and returned to entrance to the balcony where his eyes went at once to the western horizon where the entity had gone. He would order that it was his wish that a great fleet be built and provisioned. Once this was done he would lead his people across the sea. The Alkushan would go east and reclaim what was theirs. He would see to that. He turned back toward the room and called for a scribe, he had a great many things to get done.

Chapter Eight
The King of Fools

Karbel

The pair walked down the wide avenue taking in the sights as they went. The number of people shopping or simply moving through the area was more than was usual for mid-morning but not so many so that walking was a problem. The bustling crowd was noisy and colorful but did little to slow the two as they walked. The husband and wife were talking among themselves as they moved along the street.

A number of silent figures, each heavily armed mirrored the movement of the pair, always keeping them in sight but only two of their number was within arm's reach of the couple. The man and woman stopped several times along the row of businesses to inspect various goods being offered for sale. At each location they were treated with deference and twice were told to take what they wanted free of charge.

The man politely but firmly refused both times choosing not to take advantage of either shop keeper's generosity. The two did make several small purchases as they moved through the area, the items passed over to a waiting aide who quickly secured the items in a cloth bag he was wearing slung over one shoulder. The silent figures continued to shadow the pair as they traveled. They slipped among the crowd not blending in with those present but making no effort to hide amid the bustle.

The other shoppers avoided any type of contact with them, the nature of who and what they were was foreign to some while fearful to others. No one interfered with them or what they were doing. Sharp eyes watched the crowd and the windows above the street for any sign of trouble.

After making their purchases the couple continued their walk down the avenue. Each noticing the strong smell that filled the area, too much sewage, too many unwashed bodies living in close proximity, these were overlaid with the smells of cooking food and animal dung that spotted the cobblestone paved street.

A trench with a grating cover over it that ran more or less down the middle of street channeled what run off that came from the street into it and then dumped it into various sewer pipes that ran underneath the streets.

These pipes in turn led to a series of collection pools just beyond the city wall where the foul cargo was deposited. Once there, prisoners were used to spread the mass out into drying ponds. After drying the blocks were cut and then mixed with animal dung for fertilizer then sold, the smell was powerful and the duty distasteful but it served its purpose while adding to the treasury.

As the two approached an intersection the woman noticed something down one of the connecting streets and laid her arm on that of the man to garner his attention. He turned and she pointed at what she had seen.

The pair turned off the avenue on which they had been and headed toward a sizable crowd that had gathered midway down the street before them. As they approached it was possible to see what had drawn the crowd was a small troupe of street performers.

The silent figures moved with the duo as they changed directions and several of their numbers went ahead to open a path. A number of citizens turned to see the pair as word spread of who it was that had joined them. Several of the crowd were upset that the arrival had interrupted the show since the performers were also now aware of who was watching and had slowed their acts.

The king and queen of Karbel moved through the crowd and when Thadar realized that the show had been stopped on his behalf he waved at the troupe members to please continue. He apologized to several of the crowd for the delay. One man who had been nearby when the king offered his apologies was taken by the fact that the ruler would do that. He nodded in approval as he returned his full attention to the show which was restarting.

The show included a fire breather who had already finished her act and a trio of acrobats who were currently demonstrating their ability to stand on each other's shoulders, placing the uppermost one high above the crowd.

He used the opportunity to wave to a small child who was watching from a second story window overlooking the street. The little girl was completely taken with the man who was making funny faces at her, her giggles could be heard down on the street. The man tossed the young fan a small sweet treat and then launched himself into a back flip to return himself to the street surface.

Spinning while in the air he landed lightly, then bowed to the enthusiastic applause from the crowd. The lithe acrobat turned once more and getting the eye of the little girl, waved once more at her. The man on whom he had been standing did a similar movement to place himself on the ground once more. He in turned bowed to the crowd who applauded the skill. The three men then moved over by the wagon the troupe used as transport and when needed, sleeping quarters, it was a bright, almost garish blend of colors but for the troupe it was their cartage, storage and home.

The last part of the performance was an act by a juggler who was introduced by the fire breather with great pomp and vocal fanfare. As the man stepped up onto the rear of a wagon that was their makeshift stage, Thadar couldn't help but laugh aloud at the clothing worn by the small framed man. Bright red shoes with toes that curled up and adorned with dozens of tiny bells were topped by pants dull gold in color.

It was the shirt or what Thadar supposed was supposed to pass for a shirt that drew his vocal mirth. It was a patchwork of patterns and colors that should have never been joined together. A broad square of white with green swirls bordered a sunny yellow stripe blend while a pink triangle covered area mated up with a pale green patch and so the patchwork continued forming the remainder of the garment.

The combinations were outrageous and it served its purpose catching the eye and was alone enough to draw people in at times to watch, and hopefully tip. Everyone had to eat and if a wild shirt was what you used to get your meal ticket then so be it. Besides the children loved it.

Shay Skye was pleased to hear her husband laugh, it had been a sound absent from her ears for some time. He worked hard to rule and it left little enough time for laughter.

The juggler used a wide variety of materials in his act but the two items that drew the most attention were the last two he used. A number of different kinds of fruit, all bright in colors were being tossed into the air and carefully returned to the clear element as the nimble fingers of the juggler did their work.

The swirl of colors provided by the fruit was a sharp contrast to the drab surroundings. The houses and shops were mostly unpainted and faded due to the sun and weather. The man had the count of objects -- he was working up to seven now and the fire breather was waiting near his side to toss in another when he nodded. The crowd was caught by the spectacle as the nod came. The acrobats were urging the crowd on in a series of silly cheers as the juggler performed.

An eighth piece was added and the circle he was using to keep the fruit going got bigger as he tossed them higher and higher to the delight of those gathered to watch. Applause from the street grew as more and more of the crowd clapped in appreciation for the skill being displayed before them. He tossed the fruit into a small basket near his feet one by one.

Next, as the last of his routines began came a lit torch that one of the acrobats handed him. He accepted the burning item and with a flourish flung it straight up in the air. While it was traveling upwards he was given two more torches, also already lit. These were lightly hurled upward as well but not nearly as high as the first. The crowd's attention was focused mainly on the high flung torch just as the juggler wanted.

As the first one began its descent virtually every eye was riveted on the falling comet-like apparition. Just before it hit the ground it was grabbed and spun, while the other two torches had been sent skyward. The crowd loved it and showed their appreciation in a chorus of "aahs" and "oohs".

He then proceeded to move the firebrands in spectacular display all around his body, over the shoulder, through the legs, balanced on his elbows and much more. The crowd barely took time to breathe being so captured in the performance.

At the last he tossed the three torches skyward once more and as each returned to his hand he deftly dropped them in a small waiting bucket of water to extinguish them. The torches hissed and fizzled when they plunged into the liquid.

The crowd was silent for a moment and then erupted in loud chorus of applause and cheers for the show. Some threw a scattering of coins into a basket placed near the makeshift stage for just a purpose; this was how the troupe members earned their meager living, conducting street shows as they traveled to the various cities, towns and villages. It was never a great deal of money but they usually could afford to eat and that was something. Sometimes they performed in exchange for a meal or two and place out of the weather. Realizing that the show was over, at least for now much of the crowd began to move off.

After the show Thadar waited until the crowd had thinned somewhat before approaching the juggler who was clearly the leader of the troupe, the others deferred to him and he seemed comfortable being in front of the crowd.

A number of the audience decided to wait and see how long it would be before the show started again -- it was a welcome break from the normal, each day filled with toil and little reward. A spot of color and humor was a respite from the harsh reality of the day that the average citizen of the capital endured.

The juggler was bowing to two women who had come to thank him and the others for their show. Shay smiled at the courtly manner that the performer used. The two women giggled as he wished them well and they hurried off to complete their tasks, now delayed by their visit to the show. The two women, neither of which was ugly by any means kept glancing back as they walked and giggling until they had rounded a corner.

As the king approached, the man did not fail to notice the silent forms of the Strikers that shadowed the broad figure who soon stood before him. The soldiers stood a respectful distance away but formed a circle around their charge that was evident for anyone with even one eye to see.

The man who ruled Karbel bid the man hello and introduced himself simply as Thadar, avoiding use of title or last name. The troupe leader knew who the man was -- the silent forms of the Strikers were a large clue. Plus he had heard some of the crowd talking about him, but played along with the low key approach that Thadar was taking. The juggler found himself raising his opinion of the king, but withheld the right to pass judgment later.

The elder male Skye asked the performer his name and was surprised by the answer and how it was delivered.

With a lively flourish and bow the juggler launched into his character as he stated his name. "I am, oh great King of men, Lord of Karbel, known by many names. I am the Duke of Mirth, Prince of Jugglers, Sovereign of Laughter and Regent of Fun. I wear many crowns, support many titles and claim the allegiance of all those who laugh. But king oh my king, I give you leave to call me Turmko, just Turmko."

He stepped back one pace then bowed with a steady grace and dignity that some who attended court would have been hard pressed to imitate. His fellow troupe members who had all heard parts of the grandiose discourse many times before took the time to clap loudly and whistle to support their leader which further added to the moment.

Thadar found himself somewhat embarrassed by the show but since he could do little to stop it even if he wanted to, which he found he did not, simply smiled. For her part the queen found herself greatly amused, *no one,* not even Spree joked with her husband like this and she was enjoying it immensely. The man responsible for ruling the kingdom had not been prepared for the answer he received but did the best he could.

Thadar asked if the troupe was available for hire and with a nod was told that they were. The juggler was sure what was coming next was a summons to the palace which he knew would be hard if not impossible to disregard and was surprised by the next words that the king spoke. The tall man turned and with one hand extended out motioned to the aide that had accompanied them, the aide stepped forward with a heavy coine purse in his grip.

With a flip the king tossed the well filled bag to the juggler who caught it with no effort. He was surprised by the weight of it. Thadar then asked if that was enough to hire the troupe.

Turmko couldn't nod fast enough, he was a shrewd judge regarding the weight of money and he knew that what he held in his hand was a plentiful amount, an amount equal to what the troupe might make in, oh, a hundred and fifty or so performances if the crowd paid well, very well. Turmko had never held the kind of specie he did at that moment before in his life. In fact, it might be as much as he had made in his *entire* life.

Thadar then outlined what he wished, the troupe was to tour the city for as long as the money lasted and when there was enough for one last performance to come to palace and perform there as well.

Turmko for his part was impressed with the man who ruled, placing the people before himself which he felt was unusual, not that he had a great deal of personal experience in dealing with kings but still it seemed out of normal.

The veteran street entertainer, once a promising university student from a well to do family in Rhywe, tossed the heavy purse to the fire breather who barely managed to catch it in surprise. The sharp sound of the coines was an unexpected but welcome sound.

As the royal pair moved off the juggler gave some thought to how the wind of dame fortune could blow in strange directions. He pondered this as a double file of men in robes of red trimmed in white made their way along the street. He wasn't familiar with them but they offered no threat so he ignored them to make his way over to where the others were waiting. They had seen their leader speaking with someone of authority and so were curious about what was going on. A wide grin split the juggler's face, good news for all of them.

***

The priests were members of the minor cult of Dor, who some believed stood at the entrance to the afterlife and passed judgment on those seeking entrance. They continued down the avenue in their distinctive red and white robes. Several nearby residents called good natured taunts after them but the cult members ignored them.

One man respectfully bowed as they strode by. The leader of the eight priests made sure he returned the gesture.

The shopkeeper, who was a follower out of the fear of what came after death more than anything, watched the silent procession as it moved. He felt that hedging his bets in this life was important.

The men were tall, well built, and put forth an aura of power out of proportion to their number. The followers of Dor were never numerous but commanded attention wherever they passed, in part it was due to their martial prowess.

The priests trained extensively with a wide variety of weapons for several hours each day. This reflected their own belief that before they could pass judgment on someone else's entrance into the afterlife that they must first be worthy. Since the world was one of brutality and violence the entrance test to the afterlife must surely be one of combat.

The group continued on its way without further comment or interruption. The avenue they followed would lead them through an older, less maintained district to make its way toward the north end of the city near where their main temple was located.

Chapter Nine
Spear Point

The South

The group of mounted men, guards, officers and the general, passed through the first of the massive gates heading to the west. It was the only opening in the incredibly immense walls, each being nearly eighty feet thick at the base, tapering to their final width of just over fifty feet as they rose three score feet in height was to the east. Traveling in that direction would lengthen their trip unnecessarily and so was disregarded. The riders, who numbered an even thirty, rode in rigid alignment around the man at the center of the formation.

The echoes of the iron shod hooves filled the long stone tunnel which was angled sharply near the middle to hinder an attacker. The passage dim but not totally dark, torches placed at exact intervals along both walls did their best to shed the darkness that filled the long channel that wound through the immense wall. The smoke from the torches rose in thin tendrils and quickly disappeared in the gloom. As they neared the exit the guards on duty came sharply to attention and saluted, light spilling in through the open portal was, for a moment too bright. A few blinks cleared up the sight just as always when they broke out of the tunnel and out under the clear sky of mid-morning.

Pon Tori'il, General of the Army, commander of all the human troops loyal to the Varshon, returned the salute with sincerity and the proper amount of decorum befitting his station. The group made its way along the road of inlaid stone blocks that would lead them to the first of the barbicans sitting astride the avenue that wound its way up the side of the mesa and to the home of the Varshon.

Passing through the heavily defended position, Pon looked out over the scene he had viewed at least a thousand times. Coming down off the high mesa the road was a series of switchbacks cut into the side of the rock. At each turn another barbican sat protecting the vital roadway.

There was no way to move up the roadway that wasn't under observation from above. Since it could be readily observed, missile fire from archers and a variety of catapults located in the fortifications along the edge of the mesa above each of them could rain down. They were presently manned, as they always were, by the Ogurth, fierce Mountain Trolls long in the service of the Varshon.

The general turned his gaze to the area beyond the mesa; it was a high plateau so the view was quite impressive extending for miles. The land around the mesa was clear for a mile in every direction. Every bush, tree and rock had been removed and the ground leveled to a fine degree.

Starting at the point where the mile area ended, various buildings and structures stood. Some were used for storage while others were stables and barracks; from there other buildings radiated outward forming the heart of the structure that supported the vast army loyal to the Varshon. Fields of various crops could be seen as well; it took a vast amount of food to keep the tribes fed. In the distance snowcapped mountains reared up to the north and to the west.

The group rode down the switch back road to the floor of the valley and selected the road leading away to the north. They rode at a brisk but unhurried pace. Pon enjoyed the feeling of the wind on his face as they rode. Once they were through the first mile they passed a variety of buildings and troops engaged in different activities, all of them moving with purpose, especially with the eyes of the senior general on them.

As they rode further north and slightly east they approached a punishment site. Pon knew that there were a number of locations just like this spread out all over the huge domain that the Varshon ruled. Looking past the four guards riding ahead of him he looked for and saw the colored pennon flying from the pole that held it aloft in the breeze, the cloth dyed red telling those who saw it the crime of those within -- desertion, a crime that the masters dealt with severely.

The site was a circular space thirty paces across bordered by rocks covered in the white wash common for many of the houses and other buildings. Only the Varshon or their tame Trolls were allowed to cross the boundary marked by the stones. It was death for any others.

As they rode closer Pon could clearly see the five men strapped to the logs holding them in a large **X** shape. Strong bindings made of leather restrained them; all of them held fast facing the high mesa and the home of the Varshon. It would be the last sight that any of the wretches would see, which Pon felt was fitting. He wasn't squeamish but slowly dying of thirst, your tongue swelling and cracking from lack of moisture was no way for a soldier to die. Even so, these five had made their choice and now they were paying for it. It would serve a good lesson for any others foolish enough to doubt that will of the masters was strong.

It was enough that each man was provided with shelter, food, and more importantly, a purpose. That the purpose was to fight in the service of the Varshon was meaningless, every man needed a purpose, why else would they live if not to do something?

As the condemned were left behind, Pon returned his attention to the upcoming inspection and promptly forgot about the prisoners. A myriad of details surfaced from the back of his mind, so he began to review them as he rode along. The distance to the camp fell away quickly.

The guards on duty at the gate had seen the group approaching and had sent word inside to the camp commander while the rest of the duty section hustled out of the guard room. They fell in on either side of the gate forming a hasty but impressive-looking honor guard.

The senior general had little time for foolishness and lack of attention to detail. He was well known for his ability to spot the one man in a unit who made a mistake. The guards came sharply to attention on either side of the entry way. They were Arakai and so held themselves to a higher standard than the other two tribes who served the Varshon did.

The first part of the formation passed through the gate and into the settlement that was a combination of living areas for some of the married troops and training arena. The remainder of the riders followed in very short order.

Kiris Suparn, the Arakai who commanded the camp, was informed of the visitor and grunted in response. He was intently watching a training session that was about to begin -- one that pitted one of his best Ri'al commanders against three opponents. The trio of attackers were teens who had recently returned from their first combat patrol, a raid against a goblin settlement. This could be very interesting.

About the same time, Pon and his entourage entered the stands of the arena. Kiris rose from his seat not only in deference to the senior rank of the man but also out of respect to the general. He had served under Pon during several battles some years earlier. The man was courageous and daring, he lead his troops from the front, and Kiris had personally witnessed Pon slay several goblin warriors. The man was no saddle general.

For his part Pon was happy to be out of the huge fortress and be among the soldiers that he would be leading into battle very soon. Staff meetings were important but a soldier needed more than conferences and planning sessions to sustain him. A real soldier wanted to be with others of his kind, training and fighting.

The last few months had taken a toll on the man that the Varshon had given operational command of their army to. The long days of planning seemed to be eternal. Pon hated that it took him away from the soldiers he commanded.

As the general approached, Kiris bowed deeply at the waist before the man he would gladly follow into battle without hesitation.

Pon saw the salute then said with a smile, "Rise friend, it has been too long!"

Suparn stood and braced wrists with Pon. The two had a quiet chat for several moments then Kiris turned to the Arakai around the arena who were still at attention as they should be, and ordered them to continue on with their duties.

He waved Pon toward a seat and told him, "This likely be of interest to ye'." Signaling the single man down on the floor of the sandy arena he gave him permission to begin.

Without returning the signal, the man looked at the three younger tribesmen grouped together about ten paces away. Looking at them directly he nodded once to let them know to begin. Without warning two of them launched themselves directly at him in an attempt to overwhelm him.

Anticipating that very tactic, the lean fighter quickly sidestepped the rush. As the two passed he shoved the nearest one, hard. This made the attacker lose his balance and tangle up with his partner. The two went down in the sand.

That's two for the moment. Not forgetting that one more attacker was present, the man could hear the sound of the sand being disturbed as the third youngster tried an assault from behind.

Just as the last trainee was in range the man spun and lowered his upper body lunging toward the sound. This movement caught the would-be assailant by surprise and open to attack. Striking full force into the torso of the teen he drove with his legs to give him maximum leverage.

The energy of the tackle drove the air from the lungs of the youth. An explosive blast of wind burst from his mouth. The man flipped the youth over his shoulder depositing him with a *thud* on the sand. Spinning quickly his mental clock had told him that the first two would be up off the ground by now and they were.

Wary now of the speed of the man the two youths tried a new tactic; they split up so that could catch their prey between them. One of them rushed forward with the intent of being able to occupy the single man while his partner came in from the other side and finished it. A good plan but it was already doomed to failure.

The man quickly sidestepped and spun giving him good position. He used it to deliver a strike to the side of the neck using a hard but not fatal chop with the edge of his hand. The youth stumbled and fell to the sound, out of the fight. The second youth fared no better as he tried to tackle the larger man. Superior size and strength were his downfall.

The man wrapped his arms around the teen and lifted him off the ground while purposely falling backwards to build up momentum. The youth could do little but be taken along. He was flung outwards landing heavily on his back several feet away, the air driven from his lungs.

The man was cat quick to come back to his feet, eyes sweeping the area around him to make sure none of his opponents were a threat. The trio of teens were still on the sandy floor of the arena.

Seeing that the youths were out of tricks for now, Kiris called an end to the session. At that word, several Arakai who had been watching from nearby moved toward the three teens still on the ground to check them for wounds.

The Arakai were fierce warriors, proud of their martial ancestry but sensible when it came to training. Hard training created injuries and those injuries could keep a man from taking his place in battle.

The man who had been the center of the action turned to look toward the seats where the others were watching. Suparn motioned him to join them in the stands. He moved briskly toward the short stairs leading up from the arena floor adjusting his uniform as best he could as he marched toward his commander.

As he neared, the others stood to welcome him. Stopping just short of them, the man waited for Kiris to speak. The camp commander smiled slightly as told his subordinate, "This is General Pon Tori'il, General of the Army."

Without hesitation, the man went to one knee, right fist held tightly across his chest and bowed his head. For his part Pon was a bit surprised at the display. This was the older way of saluting that had slowly gone out of style. It was by no means forgotten but rarely used in the current days. The senior general saw it as a genuine display of respect rather than a way of currying favor.

"Rise soldier." The man did as he was bid. He looked once to Kiris and nodded in deference. Suparn continued with the introduction, "General this is Bolgar Sparrs, Commanding 87th Ri'al, Hand of Red." Pon nodded in acknowledgement of the name and position. He looked the man over, he was a little over six feet tall, well-proportioned and his green eyes showed intelligence.

Waving the man to a relaxed position Pon sat as he took further stock of the Arakai before him. Down in the arena the three youths were being moved into the tunnel leading to the armory and staging rooms by several of the staff. All were unhurt but would still be checked by the resident apothecary to make sure. Training was important and at times dangerous but the Varshon would need every sword arm they had.

"So tell me, what is the condition of your unit Commander?" The Ri'al leader began to outline the depth of training, their overall equipment status and experience.

Pon listened and was impressed with what he was hearing but was careful not to allow the information to taken strictly at face value. All commanders were proud of their units and were capable of overlooking the unit's shortcomings. With that in mind Pon asked, "What are the weakest areas of your unit?"

Bolgar paused for the briefest of moments before answering, "That we don't kill enough of our enemies sir." Several officers of the general's staff found this comment arrogant but given the speaker was Arakai that was about the usual response.

Pon was intrigued. He had been inspecting units of all descriptions in the previous months as the gigantic southern army readied itself to move north but none of them had caught his interest as this Ri'al commander had.

"If I had a special job for you and your men could you take care of it?"

Bolgar never hesitated with his answers. "I command the best Ri'al in all the Arakai sir." A powerful statement given the high standards that the Arakai held themselves to.

Pon couldn't contain the look of uncertainty that this boast invoked in him.

"Would the general want to see with his own eyes?" the challenge hung in the air. Bolgar stood his ground, he was proud of his men. General or not, he wasn't about to back down.

Pon was intrigued by the man before him and getting more so all the time. So be it, a challenge had been raised and he took it up eagerly. "Very well, assemble your Ri'al and let us see."

Bolgar saluted his leader sharply and after the salute was returned he turned then marched off to carry out his orders. Pon watched him go and turned back to Kiris to find out more about the young cavalry commander. The two men were rapidly deep into conversation regarding Bolgar.

***

Making his way quickly to the trio of barracks where his Ri'al was quartered, Bolgar replayed the episode in his head. He knew that he had done nothing wrong and wouldn't have done anything differently. The Arakai was confident in the abilities of his men. He knew and trusted them.

All of them were combat veterans, unusual even among the highly martial Arakai. It had taken some doing to ensure that all of his men had seen battle but it had been worth it. They had battled goblins as well as scattered bandits. Everyone in his command had been with him at least two years which was also a little unusual.

Entering the first of the long barracks he sought out his number two. He asked one of the nearby soldiers where Rimm could be found. The

Arakai trooper came to attention and informed his leader that he was in the armory area. The Ri'al commander half smiled, figures, where else would Rimm be?

Moving through the communal dining area which doubled as a large classroom, the veteran Arakai passed some of his men who were engaged in a training session. He nodded in satisfaction. His men knew their duties inside and out but additional training was always a good thing.

Bolgar found his second in command exactly where the trooper told him he would be. Rimm, along with the senior armory hands, were inspecting a large shipment of arrows that had been delivered that morning. No detail was too small to overlook. Bolgar was pleased at the dedication that his men put into their duties. It meant something to be Arakai.

Stopping in the doorway, he watched as the powerful figure of his number two scowled as he looked through the arrows. Not surprising that Rimm would not be happy with the shipment; the man was a constant perfectionist. Anything that wasn't to his liking, which was nearly everything, got the same scowl.

Seeing his commander, Rimm nodded once then turned to the senior armory staffer. He told him to ensure all of the shipment was acceptable even if it meant taking them all to the archery butts and shooting them, and to toss any he didn't like. The man acknowledged the order and began issuing orders to his workers.

Bolgar was near the door waiting as Rimm approached with an arrow in hand. "These are worse than Ogurth spoor!" The two men went out in the common area, Bolgar holding out his hand for the offending item.

The quality was a little suspect on the arrow he was looking at but this was to be expected at times. Weapons of all types were being manufactured in quantities that often defied description. Bolgar had personally seen entire warehouse buildings full of nothing but arrows. The fletched projectile he was holding was of acceptable quality; Rimm was merely unhappy that the projectiles weren't perfect. That was his way.

Tossing the arrow on a nearby table, Bolgar began to fill Rimm in on the details of his encounter with the senior general. He stroked his chin as his commander spoke. Bolgar laid out a plan to have the Ri'al assemble on the nearby parade field. He emphasized that every man in their unit be present with full kit and horse.

For his part Rimm never said a word as Bolgar spoke. When he finished, Rimm nodded once then stepped back and saluted his superior. Bolgar returned the salute and nodded his dismissal.

Orders came in quick response. The three barracks housing their Ri'al burst into action as the men rushed to gather their equipment and their mounts. It took even less time than Bolgar had anticipated but he had once again underestimated the force known as Rimm. His second was everywhere at once, shouting orders, kicking backsides or whatever else was necessary to get the Ri'al moving and at a pace he was happy with.

Once the Ri'al was assembled and properly presented to Rimm's satisfaction, he turned and smartly marched to where his commander was standing at attention.

***

As they had waited for the Ri'al to form up for the inspection, Pon had a quiet discussion with his staff. *Be meticulous,* was what he ordered. He wanted them to see if this Ri'al was indeed as good as their commander had offered.

Pon gave several orders to different officers. Seeing that Bolgar was ready for him, he marched over to where the Arakai waited. Squaring himself up before the Ri'al commander Pon waited for the salute which was short in coming.

Bolgar reported to the senior general in a clear and distinct voice, "87th Ri'al, Hand of Red is ready for inspection sir!"

The breakdown of the formation was typical of the Arakai, each Hand was allocated one hundred Ri'al's and there were a total of five Hands, each one with a different color designation. Red was the elite of the five colored Hands of Arakai; was cavalry. The remainder of the hands were infantry.

"Very well. We shall see. Wait here commander. Stand easy." Pon turned and waved his staff forward to begin the inspection. He marched off toward the head of the first line of cavalry troops to see for himself the state of the men and their equipment.

Two of the officers begin randomly selecting thirty of the Arakai ordering them to fall out of the formation and to assemble off to the side.

Once they were there the small group was ordered to mount and head for the nearby archery range.

Bolgar saw this and standing in his position of isolation he grinned slightly, he had no concerns about that test. One of his personal pet projects was archery practice both standing and mounted. The officers doing the testing were about to be disappointed if they thought that any of *his* men would fail their examination. Bolgar firmly believed that proper archery was a force multiplier and worked his men hard at the archery butts over and over until they were up to his standard.

Other members of the staff were speaking with the various cavalry soldiers, asking about their training, randomly pulling out pieces of equipment to check the condition. It was slow going but Pon had ordered them to be very thorough and they always followed orders.

An hour or so into the inspection Pon had word sent to the Citadel via a rider of his whereabouts in case Anagir or any of the other senior Varshon wished to speak with him. The time allotted for the original tour of the camp had long since been used up and the general wanted to ensure that his masters knew where he was.

He grudgingly had to admit that so far this Ri'al was in fact everything its commander had promised and then some. The inspection wasn't over yet by any means but so far he had been pleased, even impressed a bit -- which wasn't the easiest thing to do.

It was late in the day before the inspection was over. Pon told Bolgar to stand his men at ease and to wait. The Arakai did so without question or hesitation.

The man who would be leading the southern armies gathered up his staff and moved them to the shade of one of the nearby trees outlining the large parade field to discuss their findings and to hear their opinions. The discussion lasted for nearly an hour as various points were brought up and analyzed. Details about equipment, training, morale and animal care were all covered.

Pon specifically asked about the thirty who had been taken to the archery range. One of the officers snorted in response, "Sir, those damned troops didn't miss a target, not one, no matter how we told them to shoot at, be it from foot or horse. If we had told them to stand on their head likely they would have hit the target." The comment brought a moment of light laughter from the officer group.

Pon was pleased to hear that. The task he had in mind was a delicate and dangerous one and would require the best cavalry unit he could find. He and Vinshee, the overall cavalry commander, had discussed this in detail several times with neither having the answer they were searching for, until now it seemed.

He put the question to the gathered officers and gauged their reaction. Three of them were quick to agree and the rest followed suit, not out of sheer acceptance. Pon brooked no cowards or yes-men on his staff and they replied from their belief that, in fact, they had found what Pon had been looking for. Nodding in agreement the senior general reached a decision.

Telling them to remain, Pon turned and marched back toward where Bolgar and his unit had been patiently waiting. Having watched the staff meeting with interest but not able to hear what was being said, the astute Arakai read their body language well. He felt certain that they were pleased with the inspection but still didn't know the purpose behind the general's inquiries. Noticing that the meeting appeared to be at an end he watched more closely then saw that Pon was marching toward him.

Bolgar came to rigid attention, did an about face turn and addressed his Ri'al, "Unit, come to Attention!"

The proud Arakai soldiers too had seen their general approach and were awaiting the command. The entire seven hundred and fifty man body snapped to the proper position within a half a heartbeat of each other. Seeing that, Bolgar was once again filled with the pride of being able to command such men. He reversed his direction and was standing at full attention when the general arrived. Saluting with all the decorum and pride he could muster Bolgar waited.

Pon returned the salute and then stepped around the Ri'al commander to address the Arakai. He ordered them to stand at ease and then he waved them to approach him. The troops were a little slow to follow the directive but once the first few began walking over to the general the rest quickly did the same. For his part Bolgar was curious. This was not the like the behavior of any general he had ever seen but in fairness he hadn't seen that many generals up close so...

The numerous Arakai circled the man who would be leading them into battle. Once Pon was certain all of them were present he signaled that they should kneel down. He wasn't seeking a way of demonstrating his authority or doing it to demand their obedience, those things he had already. Pon wanted them to kneel so that more of them would be able to see and hear him. When he saw that Bolgar too was beginning to kneel he motioned for him to remain standing. The Ri'al commander did as he was bid and remained standing.

The men didn't have to wait long for the general to begin, "87th Ri'al, Hand of Red, I greet you!"

A low but intense growl, so intense it was almost tangible was the response.

"My staff and I have been inspecting you and are pleased with what we have found. So much so that I have a job for you, a very special job."

The response from the seven hundred plus cavalrymen was a deep double thump as each man hit his own chest twice with a closed fist in acknowledgement. It was a purely Arakai trait. Pon knew this and had been expecting that exact response.

Bolgar looked around at his men and then fixed the senior general with a hard look, "Sir, we stand ready to do our duty!" As he spoke the proud Arakai soldiers stood and began to cheer.

Pon had his scout unit.

Chapter Ten
Travel Plans

Vankard

Vode Anners, High Priest of Vankard, walked steadily down the passage as he headed toward the royal hall in answer to the summons of the king. The recent events that had occurred when the majical guardian was released from the *Book of Hope* had unnerved many, earning the priests a further dose of enmity from some of those at court, not that they needed that.

Some things couldn't be helped thought Vode. The information gleaned from the ancient text has been frightening to the man who had made majic his entire life, the power written of, the new spells that even now his fellows were working on translating.

That thought brought back to mind one of the most intriguing discoveries that he made concerning some of the information in the *Book of Hope*. It took him some time but he had noticed something odd. There were areas of the blank pages in the rear of the book that seemed to shimmer as the light touched them.

At first he thought he was imagining it. Vode wrote it off to fatigue, blinked hard several times to clear his sight, then he looked again. *There, it did it again*! He was sure of it. This time the pattern was more distinct...angling his head to look at the pages from a canted perspective, Vode was surprised to see several words clearly visible. Surprised he sat upright and in doing so realized that he could not in fact see the words at all.

Leaning over again to previous angle he saw that the words were visible again. Rolling his head a little further over more of the words were visible, so he slowly increased the angle until all at once the entire page was visible. Vode smiled at the sight, he had never seen or even heard of such a manner of writing. The mage that had written the tome had to have been a powerful majic user!

A quick shiver as the High Priest realized both the burden and opportunity that having this level of majic available to a person would carry. Returning his full attention to the page Vode was further surprised by the fact that he could not only see the words on the page but could read them as well.

The wonder he had felt earlier returned and even expanded some. The spell was such that it allowed the reader to comprehend the words even if they didn't know the language! The High Priest was truly impressed that his majical forefathers were able to work spells of that magnitude. He left him feeling humbled and with not a small measure of awe.

The king had grudgingly allowed his priests some time to gather more information after the incident but he had now waited long enough. Odel Baragull, King of Vankard, wished to know what had happened in his castle and why. A trio of the castle staff stepped aside as the High Priest walked by. To them it was curious to see the High Priest without any retainers of any type.

Vode was determined to keep any repercussions that might come from what had happened fixed solely on himself. He was the Senior Priest and so it fell to him. Better to spare those of his order guilt by association if it came to that. Most of him felt that it wouldn't come to that but he was hedging his bet nonetheless. Levas had argued that he should be along to accompany his master but Vode overruled his request. The senior acolyte wasn't happy about the decision but accepted the orders of his master.

Two of the Thunderguards respectfully saluted the High Priest as he passed them, standing at their post guarding an intersection of hallways.

The royal protectors were an old and proud unit. Their name derived from the time of King Paresil who ruled nearly ten score years earlier. The realm was beset by attacks from seaborne raiders and during one of these attacks the king was cut off from the army by a block of the corsairs, a fierce group of pirates now long gone and all but forgotten.

During the battle a storm came up, a savage and terrible tempest that swept over the battlefield. The sky had been rent and torn with lightning; the air was alive with bolts of fire as heavy sheets of rain fell.

A group of warriors belonging to one of smaller, poorer families seeing the peril of their king fought their way through the corsairs and rushed to his side. As they formed a circle around Paresil three massive strikes of lightning hit the ground just beyond them and killed many of the invaders while sparing all the northmen.

In the confusion caused by the incredible blast of power those northmen in the circle attacked the survivors of the blasts despite being terribly outnumbered. Just as they struck down the first of them a peal of thunder so loud that it actually caused the battle to stop for a moment rolled down from the heavens. It was heavy and nearly a physical thing that reached down from the sky to touch them.

Some on both sides were unnerved by the sound and tossed their weapons aside trying to flee fearing the wrath of the Gods who they had made angry. The corsairs saw this as a sign and the survivors fled to their ships and never again troubled the shores of Vankard.

In reward for saving his life the king honored those who had come to his aid and decreed that from then until the last northmen went to the arms of Ralshon the Gatherer that the Thunderguards as they were now called were to be protectors of the King.

The High Priest walked through one of the open doors leading to the Royal Hall. Numerous advisors and court officials were in residence, most stopped what they were doing to look at the man that many of them felt was too powerful and a threat to their positions at court. Some had come to the audience hoping to see the High Priest put in his place. Others came for the show, while still others came to lend their support if needed.

Knowing all this, Vode merely smiled slightly and continued to make his way toward the raised dais where his sovereign awaited. He cared not for the politics of court but knew how to play the game as well. One did not rise to his rank without knowing how the winds often blew and how to change them if needed.

The room was nearly two hundred feet long so the journey to the other end took a few moments -- especially since Vode made sure he walked at a steady, dignified pace to help with the image of control and position he was projecting.

Numerous oil lamps and braziers were placed along the walls to provide illumination, the oil the northmen used was extracted from the boiled fat of whales. Vode had always thought that it smelled of berries; Levas thought otherwise but always deferred to Vode on that matter. The room was faced in white marble mined in the quarries north of the capital. The light from the lamps reflected on the highly polished wall surfaces which helped to brighten the room.

Starting at the half way point of the room every five paces along the wall a small alcove was insert into both sides of the Great Hall. These contained, finely sculpted in white stone, renderings of the previous kings of Vankard. Vode noted, as he did every time he was present in this room, the empty slot sixth down along the left side where the bust of Parem -- who some irreverently called Godslayer -- was absent. His reign was a brutal and violent one in which civil war came to Vankard for the only time in their long history.

The current line of rulers, including Odel came to power as a result of that uprising. Magla, the first of the new line of kings decreed that for as long as his line ruled no image of Parem was permitted to exist, so that would be a lesson to others to rule properly or be forgotten.

The royal hall was nearly half full, many of those present merely wished to hear the story first hand. Something new was welcome, little did they know that time had already started to run out for Vankard.

Stopping before the throne of the king, Vode bowed his head once deeply in respect to his ruler. The two had never been great friends but Odel had been careful to listen what his High Priest said on a wide variety of topics. Vode, until this point, had been careful to never annoy the king with his work.

Standing behind and slightly off to one side of the seated ruler was Thindar Norstaad, the military commander or Warlord of Vankard. He was a fanatical Baragull supporter but had always been respectful to Vode and his kind. The towering man was wearing burnished breast and back plate armor while a long sword hung ready at his side.

Conversation in the room died down as those present waited to hear the report of the cleric who some rumored was in trouble with the king because of the events earlier in the week. The king waved his return at the priest who raised his head. He looked his sovereign in the eyes and in a clear, respectful voice asked Odel "What is your command?"

The ruler of Vankard was careful not to allow emotion to taint his thinking. Simply put, the events of earlier had scared him but he was careful to avoid showing any signs of it, especially here. He told Vode it was his wish to be told the story of what had transpired. The priest nodded once and began.

Vode started with the seven nights of visions he had experienced, the images of places and people unknown to him. He took pains to use as much of his oratory experience as possible. There were some who doubted the divinity of the priest class and Vode was determined to use this opportunity to reduce that number as much as possible.

He described the sights in as much detail as he could. His voice rose and fell as he recounted the scenes of the visions. The better to get his ruler to understand what Vode was certain now was a coming time of danger for all of them.

The tale took some time while he spoke of his experience in the library, the release of the guardian, long bound within the *Book of Hope* and finally of what he found written in the sacred books but not about the new spells. That information was for now being very closely held to a select group of priests. Vode spoke of the discovery regarding the Varshon and their powers, the evil that they were capable of and how it could affect Vankard and the world if events were allowed to take place.

Odel listened intently without interrupting; he was leaning forward in his throne, chin held in one hand absently stroking his hand span-length beard as he heard the tale told. The man who ruled Vankard was becoming more disturbed the longer the account was brought out but still said nothing. He had no great love for the priest before him or his kind but he was careful not to allow this to enter his heart, especially now.

Vode continued on, "My Liege, the visions given me were of importance, of that there can be no question. The answers are likely beyond our borders and I feel that they must be sought out, no matter the policy of not going beyond the mountains gate."

This was the term that the northmen used for the single pass that led to the east and the outside world. A strong detachment of soldiers guarded the pass at all times to "discourage" any who might try and enter their land. If someone from Vankard left then they were gone from the hearts of the Northmen for good. Not many left and when someone did it was a somber time. The most well-known of those who had passed beyond the frontier was none other than Thindor's nephew, Gunnar, which the priest knew had caused the proud warrior a great deal of personal pain.

That statement brought a series of immediate reactions from those gathered. None by themselves loud enough to be clearly heard, but collectively the noise from the assembled throng rose sharply. So sharply, that Odel was impatiently forced to signal one of his attendants who thumped the end of a large pike on the floor. The metal shrouded end rang crisply against the metal plate set into the stones for just such an occasion. The sharp retort went out and commanded attention.

Silence returned immediately to the hall, it was well known that Odel did not suffer non-compliance with his wishes, especially in his own throne room. In the past offenders had been dragged bodily from the room to inhabit a cell in the lower levels of the castle. The man who ruled over the northmen gazed intently on the figure of the High Priest before him.

Baragull had listened without asking questions until his priest was finished speaking, but now it was his turn and he wanted some answers.

"Strong words, Priest. Does thou make jest of our history? Do not the writings of thy own Order speak of the evil of the Outside?"

That was the term politely used for lands beyond the mountains -- there were others less socially acceptable. Odel was clearly upset with Vode's statement but was trying to understand the reasoning behind it. Although quick to anger none could say truthfully that the ruler of Vankard wasn't fair. He waited for an answer and it came swiftly.

Vode replied, "My Lord, ever it is the members of my own order that are first to speak against travel beyond our fair realm, but this is something that cannot be answered within our borders. The events and places shown to me lay beyond our frontier and so it is there that the answers wait."

He knew that getting the next point across was crucial, "If what I have been shown is by the Gods, then these Varshon -- whatever they are -- truly exist, then all of us, not just here in the north but ALL the races and people of Dohrya are in peril." Hi voice rose to nearly a shout in the now eerily quiet hall. Vode was quivering with the emotion of what he was feeling and trying to express to the others. Evil was reaching out for them and ignoring it would not make it go away.

The king appeared thoughtful for a short time before the look was replaced by one of decision. He made sure that the priest was looking at him and with one hand made what to anyone else appeared to be a simple gesture of impatience; he raised two fingers of the right hand from where they had been resting on the armpiece of the throne.

Vode caught the meaning immediately: patience. It was one of the signals that his Order used. He knew that Odel had been taught part of the silent language that priests often used to communicate with each other. The signal also meant to wait, which was the meaning that Vode took from this arena.

The High Priest who had been standing with his arms folded together before him flicked one thumb in response. Odel caught the sign and then stood and looked quickly around the room before speaking, "Priest I must give thought to the words you have brought here before me. I will think on it. The audience is ended."

The closest attendant again struck the pike on the metal plate, twice this time to gather the attention of those too dim witted to be listening. That was not the case at this audience but it was not uncommon. Members of the staff began to clear the room of those in attendance. Guards swung the doors at the far end open and the throng began to head out through the waiting outlet.

It took several minutes for all those gathered to exit the room. Finally it was just the king, Thindor, the High Priest and several ranking aides remaining. Odel rose from his throne and headed toward one of the side doors leading off the large throne room. He was immediately followed by Vode and Thindor. The aides remained in place, waiting till the other men exited the room before following. Their job was to serve not to mingle. Within moments the large throne room was empty.

The king was agitated as he walked; his mood had been dark for several days. The majical event earlier in the ten-day had caused some damage to the palace, some of which had already been repaired. Work was ongoing non-stop to repair the remaining affected areas.

He, like many others in the palace, had been awakened by the passage of the majical being through the large structure. Roused from his bed to find his home in an uproar, part of the ceiling destroyed and then to be told that his own High Priest was at the center of the incident had not gone well. Then to have Vode openly speak of passing beyond the mountains to seek answers further aggravated the king.

Part of him was already questioning if what his High Priest had spoken of was possible and what the implications for his realm might be. Presently the men arrived at one of the reading rooms attached to the library. The room was at ease and quiet. The impending discussion warranted just such a place.

A pair of comfortable chairs were along one wall while finely spun tapestries covered two of the others. The last wall contained two large windows intended to allow as much light as possible into the room. The center of the room was dominated by a round table with four stuffed chairs circling it.

Once all the men were inside the room and the door secured, Odel wasted no time in asking the questions uppermost in his mind. He spun, fixing his gaze directly upon Vode. "Go beyond the mountain gate to the Outside? Are you certain of this?"

The High Priest had been anticipating a question along these lines so he was ready with his answer. "Yes Sire, we must go. If we do not, then all may be lost."

"If," the King's emphasis on the word was unmistakable, "you did go, what size of group would you take?"

Vode had already given some thought to that and was unsure of the total numbers. No one had taken an expedition beyond the Mountain Gate for several generations.

Thindor, speaking for the first time since they entered the room, said, "If you are allowed to go priest then go well armed and with no fanfare. Let none known of your journey." The others in the room weighed the advice and found it to be sound.

"Certain you are that this must be done?" Odel asked his High Priest.

Vode paused only long enough to answer in a manner befitting the seriousness of the situation. "Yes my Liege."

The king of Vankard was silent while grappling with the decision. He had witnessed the damage that the majical creature had caused to his castle, if that was even the smallest indicators of something worst that may be out there then something must be done.

For his part the king of Vankard still wasn't totally convinced of the need for this expedition but in his own way he did trust Vode. The two men were hardly friends but did respect one another. Vode had never overreached his authority and challenged Odel in any way so if he was saying this was something that needed done then…

The conversation lasted for some time. By the time it was concluded the basic outline of the logistics had been determined. Odel had viewed the damage to his castle personally as well as interviewing all the witnesses himself. He was convinced that it had been only one creature that had done all the damage -- and if there were more of these things out there, then it surely was a danger to his people. Odel wasn't the most popular ruler in Vankard's long history but he did pay more than lip service to caring for his subjects.

Another reason for permitting the trip was that Vode was a powerful figure in his own right. If the trip was as dangerous as he said, then it could be that the man might not return -- which would weaken the priesthood further and improve his own power base.

Odel had no way of knowing that the fate of his kingdom and its people was already sealed.

Vode had been careful not to push too hard but he knew that if he and the others were going to be allowed to go then planning and organizing needed to begin as soon as could be. There had been no timeframe associated with what he had been showed in the visions but his own feelings had made themselves very clear, there was no time to waste.

Odel nodded once and with a decisive turn looked to the others present. "Priest I give ye leave to make this trip, take who and what you need, let no expense be spared."

For his part Thindor was surprised, he had already decided that Odel wouldn't allow Vode to make the trip. *Today is an interesting day* thought the Warlord of Vankard.

Vode bowed deeply to his ruler, "Thank you sir. I will serve to my ability. Do I have your majesty's permission to begin my preparations?"

Odel signaled him to rise from the gesture of respect and told him that he had permission. "How soon might ye be leaving priest?"

"I hope to leave as soon as may be possible my lord, no more than three days hence." The king nodded. Before dismissal, he told his senior majic user to keep him informed. Vode promised to do so. Vode then left the room to carry out his planning.

Thindor waited until Vode had left and the door was closed before speaking, "I had not thought you would allow him leave to pursue this." The question of *why* was unspoken but very present.

Odel and Thindor thought very much alike but in this the king had caught his old friend off guard. Still not ready to give voice to all his thoughts on the matter, Odel only nodded as he looked at the now closed door.

Chapter Eleven
Assembly Hall

Karbel

The heavy rap of the Voice's gavel rang throughout the wide chamber, the tone solid and rich. The echoes died slowly in the far corners. The Assembly members present finally began to respond to the call for order and quiet as several of them began to break off conversations and seek their seats. Two more sharp blows were struck and the noise level in the great hall began to fall measurably as seats were found and taken. The visitor gallery in the wide balcony that extended out over the floor where the representatives were was slow to heed the call for quiet as decorum dictated.

Two noisy observers had to be warned sternly by one of the guards present to remain silent or be thrown out, literally. The reputation of the Assembly guards for just such actions was well known. Silence came to the pair immediately. The guard flashed the pair one more stern look before returning to his post at the top of the gallery. He would keep an eye on the two.

"Voice! Voice!" The call from the floor was clear and strong amid the silence of the hall.

Those present turned their attention to the man standing in the second row of the first quarter of seats, those reserved for the senior members of the Assembly. In practice it was for those members who had served the longest and with distinction, the reality was it was now reserved for the wealthiest and most powerful of the members "elected" to serve the needs of the people.

The wealthy, too, had needs and so it fell to these men, many of them among the richest in the kingdom to look after whatever it was that they wanted. The poor had few if any friends here.

The chamber was arranged in four tiered banks, each slightly higher than the one before it to allow those in the rear to see, each with the same number of seats so that no section could outweigh another, at least in theory. Wealth had long ago bought its way into what was originally created to give a voice to the masses. The raised tiers dominated the large room, centerpiece of the expansive Assembly building.

The rest of the building contained offices and meeting rooms to allow the members the space to work when they desired -- not as often as needed, although there were some members who did take their responsibilities of working for the people seriously.

"The Chair recognizes Member Rees." The man standing behind an ornate podium at the front of the large room solemnly acknowledged the call with a slight nod and then sat to listen to the speaker, sure that he didn't want to hear whatever the man had to say.

The man standing in the first tier was tall, almost painfully thin. He reminded some of the slender river grass stalks found along most waterways. Some had mistaken his slender build as a sign of weakness given their own more robust physiques. Those that erred in this way often found out quite harshly that there was no weakness present.

One hand lightly clasped the right lapel of the dark blue tunic he wore, the price of which would have fed a family of five for six months or more. The other hand rested lightly on the polished marble writing surface that formed the top of the desk before him, a practiced pose but a useful one. It was calculated to give those looking at him the full measure of his power, visible and more importantly, perceived.

Lynd Rees stood still for just long enough to give the effect without overdoing it, ensuring that all eyes were upon him before he spoke. He reflected that some minor theatrical background from his youth while attending the University served him well here.

'Voice,' the title of the Assembly member chosen to preside over all Assembly meetings, was considered the most powerful of them all. *Well, we will see about that* thought Rees. The current Voice of the Assembly was Loni Weslatt, a staunch friend and supporter of the king.

It had long been Rees' ambition to take over as Voice. Rees was a powerful, very wealthy merchant and landowner. His many business interests ran from one end of the kingdom to the other and beyond. His family was heavily involved in mining, agriculture, and metal works, at least legally. He was involved in a variety of other activities that were far from legal but each of these was carefully controlled and few records existed.

Speaking now to his fellows and to some of the visitors he had arranged to have there that day Rees began, "My fellow members, once again the weighty issue of finance lies before us. We are all familiar with why it necessary to impose taxes, require tariffs and levy fines."

Pausing for a brief moment as he gathered momentum, the politician continued. "Without these funds we are not able to construct buildings, erect defenses and do the work that allows this great state of ours to flourish." He refused to refer to Karbel as a kingdom; it was always the state or the realm with him.

Several of his cronies in the member section responded with a flurry of *hear, hear* just as he had instructed them earlier. Showmanship was ever important

Continuing on, "In view of this we must look upon our responsibility to oversee the affairs of the state with great deliberation. We hold a great trust. The peace that we enjoy provides us an opportunity and that opportunity is growth. To grow we must build and that takes funding."

Before those assembled could comment he smoothly continued, "That funding must come from somewhere and the likely place is the Army." He waited for those assembled to come to the obvious conclusion and while he waited he smiled thinly. One more strike against the power of the throne and he did it in full sight of everyone and only three others in the room knew about it.

Yes, it was going to be a good day.

Loni Weslatt knew what was coming but wasn't sure he had the support to turn away another cut in the army budget. This made the seventh attempt in the last year; unfortunately five of these had been successful. Peace could be a terrible thing at times. He settled deeper in his chair to gather his strength for what was coming sure that no matter the outcome it would be something he wouldn't care for.

***

Political maneuvering wasn't limited to Karbel. In the Elven capital of Ballanshire a high ranking delegation had just returned from a fruitless diplomatic expedition to the Free States, the modest sized human nation to their north. A report was being presented to the Elven king, Jendile Dalshorn.

The senior member of the delegation, First Minister Ehlo Sellenus was discouraged, and it was evident in his posture. His shoulders were slumped as he walked; his usual energetic stride was subdued as the elder statesman made his way to the council chamber to deliver the report to the king. He felt strongly that failure had been the only result of the trip, that failure weighing heavily on his mind as he moved along the richly paneled corridor.

Once everyone who had been summoned arrived and were seated, the First Minister began. Ehlo outlined the course of events that led to Jendile ordering the delegation being sent. He reminded those present that for at least the last two years there had been increasing tensions with their northern neighbors, trade shipments that had been refused or taxed excessively, reports of mistreatment of Elves traveling in the Free States -- and one report, never substantiated, of the murder of an Elven trader. There were rumors of increased military activity as well but these, too, were so far not confirmed.

Ehlo's report was very complete. He explained how they had traveled north and after crossing the Blazetail River entered the Free States. They were escorted to the capital, but were shown little respect despite being a formal delegation. Their housing was substandard and meals were much the same. When they did meet with the ruling council much of it was the Elves being lectured on their policy failures, their unfavorable trade balance, their aggressive behavior militarily and more. Two days of meetings were anything but productive.

Cutting the meetings short, Ehlo elected to return home. He and the others departed the morning of the third day. All the way from the capital to the river they were shadowed by a troop of cavalry.

One of the council members asked if the human troops threatened them. Ehlo told them that the mounted troops were careful not to directly threaten them but, yes, he felt their presence was an attempt at intimidation. The council member nodded his thanks at receiving an answer to his question. Ehlo asked if there were any other questions. There were none so he bowed once to the king then took his seat.

Jendile, the Elven king, sat quietly as Ehlo was speaking. That he was disturbed by the report was an understatement. There had never been excellent relations with the human realm to the north of the Homelands but this was something different entirely.

Discussions regarding the problem continued for several hours but no solution presented itself. Jendile called a halt to the session and thanked everyone for coming. The Elven king was in a foul mood and felt that there was trouble on the horizon for his people but had no idea how to prepare for it.

Jendile had no idea how right he was.

Chapter Twelve
Return to Quarters

Edora

The column of mounted Strikers moved with ease along the wide highway that led into the western gate of the large city. They had been gone from the city for nearly four ten-days and were eagerly looking forward to a night in their own beds after the long nights of sleeping on the ground. The last few days had been spent in assorted Legion outposts, since returning to the land ruled by the king of Karbel.

A number of the elite troops had been killed and more injured while they carried out their mission; many drinks would be later hoisted in their memory. The dead would be spoken of with humor, rancor, and finally with pride. They died as Strikers, sword in hand with enemies before them. That was all that any of them asked, a chance to kill the foes of their sworn liege all while getting paid to do it.

The former captives the Strikers had freed and the goods captured had been turned over to a Legion unit for disposition. The Strikers felt that since the regular army couldn't keep the problem from happening then the least they could do was clean up the mess.

Traffic of all varieties moved in both directions along the wide avenue of precisely set stone blocks resting on a bed of gravel; cargo wagons, small flocks of animals under the supervision of their owners, a detachment of Legion cavalry all going about their business. The day was warm and it was now past noon, the barracks but another hour's ride ahead and their mission would be over.

Everyone noticed the Strikers, the black and silver of their uniforms were distinctive and spoke volumes about both who and what they were. Strikers were a common sight in and around the city, which was the second largest of the six major cities of Karbel.

Shorin rode at the head of the three rider wide formation. The men were tired, travel stained and still had the look of battle about them, dirty uniforms and mending wounds the most visible signs that the defenders of the king had crossed swords with someone and lived to tell the tale if they wished to. That only a few of them would wasn't a large surprise. They were soldiers doing a soldiers job, it was their work, nothing special about killing people. Especially those that needed killing of which there never seemed to be a shortage.

Not a few smiles were present on the faces of the black and silver clad riders as many of them thought of the days off that they would soon be enjoying. It was a tradition among the king's men: after a mission involving combat, the unit commander had the discretion to allow his men leave.

Shorin smiled as he heard the familiar sound of one of the Strikers favorite songs being sung. It was one of the things that he had always found enjoyable. There was something about hearing hundreds of strong voices sing together. He idly listened as they rode toward the city catching part of one verse.

Riding the roads
Fighting the foes
We're ugly, mean, and loyal
We guard the kingdom

As the Strikers approached the gate, the Legion soldiers on duty hurried to move those in the press of the gates clear of the entryway. Two small wagons and their owners were unceremoniously rushed through to join the traffic on the west bound side. The wagon owners were left to mouth curses at the treatment they received. The sergeant in charge of the gate could care less what some cart driver had to say, soldiers were coming and so they had priority to enter.

He watched as the Strikers rode closer. They were a mean lot to be sure -- this thought from a man who had served eleven years in the Legions and was no stranger to the battlefield. A nod of the head in respect as the column rode by.

Clattering through the gateway, the troop rode up one of the avenues leading away from the portal and into the city proper. The men once again found themselves plunged in the depths of civilization as it existed in this part of the world.

The sights, sounds, and smells that were the product of thousands of people living and working in close quarters washed over them, shopkeepers hawking their wares, conversations in several different tongues on a dozen topics and much more.

The horses picked their way through the streets under the steady hand of their riders moving forward and around the press whenever possible. The taller structures on either side of the various streets blocked the direct afternoon sun at times, depending upon their placement. This created cooler sections of the avenues to ride through.

The Striker compound was in the southern part of the city near the main Legion barracks. It was behind its own wall and so once more Shorin and his men passed through a gate and beyond, returning the salutes of the duty guards. After the entire troop was through the gate and onto the parade area they filed off to form three lines facing their commander.

Once the men were in rigidly straight lines they came to attention. Shorin watched as his men assembled into the proper formation. Parun looked them over watching for something to correct but saw little they did wrong, but it wouldn't stop him from sharing some criticism with them later on lest they become complacent.

When the troop was properly formed the senior sergeant wheeled his mount about sharply then stopped. He saluted Shorin, "Sir, detachment all present and accounted for sir!"

The weary officer sat up in his saddle a bit straighter, precisely returning the salute of his senior sergeant. He looked his men over. They were dirty, wounded, and proud. Shorin loved his life and in no small part because of the quality of the soldiers like these that he was able to command.

He told them, "Men, we went and did a soldier's duty. We protected others and killed those that hunted the weak and the small. I'm proud of you, all of you. Check your equipment, tend to your horses and have a drink to celebrate being alive -- and to our fallen brothers. Leave for all of you!"

A short but heartfelt cheer went up from the ranks. Parun called for them to salute which Shorin returned with solemn dignity.

The arrival of the unit caused some excitement; the Strikers not on duty came out to see if their friends were among those to return. It was quickly obvious that a good number had not. Life in service to the king was rarely boring and often short, but that was a soldier's life. More so for the elite Strikers.

After making sure his horse was properly tended to, the Striker officer went to his quarters. He quickly bathed while wishing he could linger in the relaxing warmth of the water for much longer. He changed into a clean uniform. Once he was more presentable, Shorin made his way to the office of the commander to give his report on the patrol.

He had used some time the previous two nights while boarding at Legion posts to write up the details of the mission. The total length of the missive was nearly eight pages. Shorin tended to be a bit overly wordy at times when filing a report. He strongly believed that detail was important.

Arriving at the office of the commander he knocked once on the door frame of the open doorway. The customary aide was unusually absent. Inside, the senior Striker was standing while reviewing a large map of the area that hung from the far wall, a sheaf of papers held in one hand. He turned at the knock, then upon seeing Shorin he smiled a bit and waved him in.

Per standing orders the formal debriefing took place in the conference room just down the hall from the commander's office. Once word of the unit's return reached their ears, the ranking officers assembled. In short order the report Shorin had prepared was read and passed along to the other officers for their review as well.

Peer review of combat actions was not restricted to the Strikers, the regular army as well as the Black Guard did it, too. The one aspect of this that was unique to the Strikers was that there was a peer review group conducted at the sergeant level also. This was due to the fact most Striker detachments were commanded by senior sergeants, which were the true strength of the elite body. It was felt that using peer review allowed pertinent information, good and bad, to be passed along much quicker.

For his part Shorin sat and waited while the senior officers conferred, he had told his story to those present, answered their questions and now sat to see if there was going to be anything else for him.

He was tired. Sleep was a pleasant thought, but it wasn't just the physical aspect of the job that made him feel so exhausted. He had been a soldier for eight years serving Karbel -- only once in that time had he taken leave. Shorin had been giving that issue some thought of late; he had wondered if now was the right time to take some measure of where he was and what he was doing with his life. He thought so but wasn't sure.

His attention snapped back when Under-Colonel Tarvel, the commander of all Striker units stationed in Edora and senior Striker in the northern part of the Kingdom spoke, "Under-Captain Tallon,"

Out of respect, Shorin rose from his chair when his supervisor said his name. Whane Tarvel had spent many hours with him helping him to learn the mysteries of commanding fighting men. Shorin knew that he owed the man no small debt, so to stand was but a small measure of respect he could show right now and did so without hesitation. Tarvel noted this but said nothing, a small grin splitting his face.

"The members of this panel and I wish to commend you on a job well done and to recognize your intelligent handling of a delicate and potentially fatal situation regarding the captives. We salute you." With that Tarvel and other four officers present rose from their seats, came to attention and saluted the junior man standing before them.

For his part Shorin was appreciative of the respect the other officers were showing him but felt that he was just doing his duty the way a soldier was supposed to. Shorin solemnly returned the salutes of these were men he admired as well as respected.

The five ranking officers each came from around the table to shake the hand of the younger man. "Good job, son." and "Well done." were some of the compliments that he received as the others left the room to tend to other duties.

Colonel Tarvel waited till the members of the review panel were done before he came forward to shake Shorin's hand as well. He had been the younger man's commanding officer for almost two years and knew that something wasn't completely right with him. He seemed tired, out of sorts. Tarvel needed to figure out what it was. The Colonel suspected what the reason might be but wanted to talk to Shorin about it. The boy had a great deal of potential and so Tarvel had a responsibility to the Strikers to make sure that one of their best remained sharp.

"So what's next for you?" The question caught Shorin a little off guard; he was still doing a bit of mental wool gathering.

Tarvel saw the reaction and before the younger man could answer spoke again, "Likely haven't had a decent meal in some time, so let's fix that first. Come to my home tonight, be our guest for dinner."

Shorin immediately tried to think of a way out of the invitation. He didn't want to impose on the commander's hospitality and he was tired. Tarvel wouldn't take no for an answer and so Shorin found himself with a non-negotiable offer. "Yessir, be happy to come."

Tarvel told him the time to be there and dismissed him for the rest of the afternoon. Shorin thanked him then retreated to his quarters to take a much needed nap, leaving word with one of the orderlies that he be awakened at sundown.

***

Dinner was especially good. Denna, the Colonel's wife, had prepared a fine meal to welcome their visitor. Shorin had been to the Tarvel home before as a dinner guest and knew the Colonel's wife was an excellent cook, but tonight's meal seemed even better than usual. It did pick up his spirit some but both of his hosts could tell that something was troubling the younger man. Husband and wife shared a look that needed no words they had been married long enough that a glance spoke volumes.

Denna asked him, "When did you last take some leave Shorin? And I mean more than a day off, actual leave." The attractive brunette waited for the answer as did her husband.

The Striker Under-Captain actually had to stop and think about it...let's see it was before I went to Rhywe for the archery school so – "Uh, it was about four years ago I think."

Tarvel was a little upset at hearing that, for one reason he knew that Shorin certainly knew better than to have gone that long without taking some time off. He also made a note to have his staff review all the files of the Strikers under his command to determine when the last time they had taken some leave. He couldn't have his men becoming dull about their duties; leave was an important factor in keeping people refreshed and sharp.

Tarvel was a bit upset with himself also, as Shorin's commanding officer he should have realized that it had been that long. He vowed then and there that he would never repeat that oversight with someone under his command again. Well, making sure Shorin took leave, that was something that he could fix and he would start immediately.

For his part actually putting voice to the words 'four years' made Shorin realize that it had been far too long. This was something he had been thinking about recently and during this latest mission he'd had time to think on it at length.

One germ of an idea was to visit his family home place east of Edora. He hadn't been there in nearly six years, might be time to see it again. He recognized that no one he knew would be there -- his family had been killed by nomads when he was fifteen. Shorin himself was wounded during the attack that took the lives of his parents, both younger siblings and several hired hands. It had left the modest house and barn burned to ashes.

Realizing that the Colonel was speaking yanked Shorin back to the present, "...so we'll see what we can do about it. Now in regards to you, I feel that you have certainly accrued time enough, so I am hereby ordering you to take two months leave starting day after tomorrow. I will send a message to the appropriate people telling them you will be slightly delayed reporting to Eastmarch."

Shorin was caught completely off guard by the order. Two months off? Shades, what was he going to do with that much time off? He was thinking a ten-day, not *eight* ten-days for spirit sakes!

Denna saw the look of consternation on the face of their guest so she did something to help ease his mind, "Who's ready for dessert?" Her smile was warm and disarming as she signaled the maid to bring in the freshly baked pie.

The rest of the evening went easier for Shorin despite the fact that he was completely unable to get his commander to rescind his two month leave order.

Chapter Thirteen
Revival

Near the Citadel

The noise coming from the thousands of Alush who had been gathered in the large sporting venue was incredible; it pulsed and peaked as the soldiers moved forward into the stadia. They were jostling and pushing at each other as they headed by units for their assigned seats. The talk was loud and often vulgar as good natured curses and taunts were traded back and forth.

Discipline, a long standing Varshon principle was noticeably relaxed today, a deliberate ploy on the part of the masters, although a large number of Ogurth were present in the stadium just in case. A conscious bone thrown to their subjects, work them like hounds and then give them some leash, not enough to compromise their training but enough that the troops took notice.

The process of getting the massive structure full, used often for chariot races and gladiatorial matches, took a good portion of the morning. The coliseum seated nearly forty thousand and had seen its share of carnage over the years. The death matches were usually between slaves; often captured Northerners taught to fight and used as entertainment for the tribes and the masters.

At times the fighters were members of the three tribes, punishment for infractions or as a way of settling blood debts. The Varshon forbade the settling of blood feuds without their judgment. These feuds could spread easily among the honor bound tribesmen and damage the troop effectiveness.

The Ogurth, fierce mountain Trolls who served the Varshon, were quick to stifle any attempt to settle feuds usually with both parties being killed. This way, the guilty party was punished no matter what. It wasn't all that great for the innocent but it kept armed disputes to a minimum.

It was a cloudy day with a constant westerly breeze which helped to keep the smell from the thousands of poorly washed bodies from loitering, the odor already thick despite the open air construction of the venue. Food was being passed out to help with the festive atmosphere of the day. Trays of spicy sausages grilled and wrapped in warm yeasty bread were passed down the long rows of seats so that every man had several. No wine or other spirits were distributed but water was readily available -- serious drinking would come later in the day. The Varshon were old hands at keeping the tribes happy or at least productive and for them that was all that mattered.

Once the bulk of the bench style seats were full, word was sent to the Marshal of the Host who, along with select members of his staff, was waiting in the lavish apartment attached to the seating box. That special place was reserved for the senior members of the Varshon council when they partook of watching the spectacles that the venue hosted. The rich furniture and fine tapestries that graced the room were a broad world apart from the masses of drab, smelly soldiers that filled the stone seats outside.

Pon was speaking with Vareskel, the Varshon who led the Alush. Each of the three tribes that made up the Varshon army was overseen by a loyal and experienced Varshon. The pair had been discussing replacement levies and how they could be used.

Pon thanked the messenger and after looking for and receiving a nod of approval from Vareskel motioned to one of his staff, who bowed, then immediately went to start the proceedings. The aide exited a side door and headed down the short hallway and once at the balcony containing the musicians told the trumpeters waiting there to begin. He then waited to ensure that each signal was received and carried out per his standing orders.

The morning calm was shattered by the trumpet of two dozen long horns. The braying sound of the curtil horns cut the noise of the crowd and rose to the heights, the echo rolling back through due to the superb acoustics of the design.

First was one long steady call, followed by two short ones. The noise of the crowd dropped away like a bag of lead released from a great height, until only the sound of the wind-whipped banners flying from the upper points could be heard.

All eyes turned to the large seating box situated a quarter of the way around the oval wall from the wide gate that opened onto the sand covered event floor. A single figure slowly came into view from out of the shadows at the rear of the box. The walk was stately, the pace measured. The figure was Pon. Cheers began to erupt when those gathered realized who it was, as word quickly spread.

The Alush leapt to their feet to cheer for the general, the man who would lead them against the hated north and bring glory to the Alush nation. While not as numerous as the Arakai, the Alush were the most devout of the three tribes that served as troops for the Varshon. Their ancestors had been simple nomads who tended small flocks of goats and sheep, wandering throughout the deep south keeping to themselves.

It was the third year after the Elves had deposited their vanquished foes in the south that the Alush came into contact with them. By then the Varshon had established a sizable community and had tamed a good portion of territory around their settlements.

The first soldiers to see the tall, dark creatures, fierce in appearance, thought them evil spirits and fled. They brought more of their more skeptical brethren with them to show them what they had described and been laughed at for. The others did not laugh when they were surprised by a large number of Varshon that sprang from hidden positions to surround them as they moved through the forest.

The Alush who numbered in the thousands were quickly subjugated due in part to their own nature. They were herders and occasionally farmers; they had no means of resistance especially against those who were their superior in strength, cunning, and martial skills. The nomads had their wandering ways ended and were put to work by the Varshon raising food and flocks of animals.

Over time as their numbers were allowed to increase, the Varshon began taking some of the younger more malleable male children away and in time they became the first human soldiers to serve the masters, the Arakai and H'Roth coming later.

At a measured gesture from Pon, the coliseum occupants settled down and the noise again fell off to nothing. He contemplated for a moment the incredible feeling of power he held, tens of thousands of loyal trained soldiers hanging on his every word, his every gesture. The realization of it shook him and he reveled in the sensation.

This was the reward for the long years of training, fighting, and endless meetings. These were *his* soldiers; he never forgot his oath to the Varshon but this was what it was about for him. The masters had their reasons but him, here, now, this was all the reason he needed.

The feeling of leading tens of thousands and more besides into battle was so powerful he fought the urge to tremble from the feeling. Pure, raw power. It was enough power to shake the world, which they would do.

He looked over the assembled multitude, a rising wall of faces. Each of them was watching him and waiting for his next word or movement. Pon knew that this was one of many such events that he would attend in the coming weeks to ready the troops for the invasion of the north. His staff had notes on the various functions and events being staged to increase the morale and hone the loyalty of the tribes to its finest edge. The senior general didn't really mind, after all it did get him out of staff meeting and that fact alone made it worth something.

His gaze traveled from the lower reaches of the seats to the upper rows and from side to side taking in the sight of so many willing slaves – soldiers, yes, but in reality merely slaves for the Varshon to do with as they pleased. He had rehearsed this speech several times to check the inflection and spacing of the words; part of his training while growing up had been in speech and presentation.

The Varshon knew that whoever they chose to lead their army would have to possess skills in vocal manipulation and charisma when speaking. His impact in delivering it was important to help set the tone for the entire event.

"Friends and fellow soldiers, I welcome you today to this place…" He paused to let the anticipation begin to slowly build up. Pon continued "…for it is from this place that we will go north and bring down those that would be our betters. Those who would keep us from our destiny, our *right* to rule them! Who are they to tell us no?"

The Marshal of the Host then paused to allow some of the pent up emotion to vent as many of those gathered rose to their feet and shouted their answers. The volume was incredible as thirty thousand plus gave Pon and his masters the looked-for response. Loyalty was difficult thing to earn at times but this was showmanship, pure and simple.

He took a step forward coming to the edge of the richly carved stonework and raised one hand for silence. The difference in noise level from one moment to the next was almost beyond belief -- one minute it was so loud that the building actually shook from the energy, and the next it was so silent that it nearly made Pon question if had suddenly lost his hearing.

Nothing was said, the Alush were all standing and hanging on his every word, gesture, and suggestion. He waved them to their seats with his raised hand and on cue they sat. The movement of that many doing the same thing at the same time was impressive to say the least.

Pon allowed them to sit and adjust before speaking again. "Soldiers of the South, Warriors of the Alush, soon, very soon we will march north to claim our victory. The hand that wields the sword and notches the arrow are yours. North of here are those who sit and get fat eating food that should be yours! Collecting gold they did not earn. Gold that will be yours."

A growl was his answer to this. He continued. "Then my friends there is something else. Something that only real men, men like you understand -- the women of the north!" A savage yell followed this announcement. Looting and rape were the prizes of victory. Each man thought about a big-titted northern wench naked at his feet doing his bidding. That alone was worth fighting for.

Pon allowed them their moment of anticipation and quickly followed it with, "We will crush our enemies and when we do YOU will be the victors. YOU will be the strength that swings the blade that fells those of the north! Who goes with me?"

The crowd roared in response and once again came to their feet amid wild cheering. Pon signaled with the hand below the railing which was out of sight of the crowd. At the signal the trumpeters once again sounded a long call which added to the moment.

Some of the crowd were so swept up in the fervor they leapt over the railing trying to reach Pon himself to pledge themselves to the cause. Several forgot they were hundreds of feet in the air and fell to their deaths but the symbolism of the gesture was not lost on the others.

Pon signaled again and a different call went out from the curtils. This one was the call to attention which normally would bring an assembly to order instantly, but this time it was necessary to sound it twice more to rein in the highly enthused Alush.

In several places throughout the stands, officers found it necessary to physically restrain some of their troops to maintain order. This was all part of the plan. Train them to a sharp edge, indoctrinate them, restrain them, aim them at the target and then release them all at once.

Whip up the frenzy of hatred and give them a taste of superiority to help see them through the long march north and the battles that waited. Once a semblance of order was restored, Pon counted down from twenty five in his head to add to the drama that the troops were playing out without realizing it.

"My friends, only one thing remains for us. The most important thing in our lives, the one thing that for all of us is more important to us than our lives." He left the statement hanging deliberately and slowly turned as out of the shadows fully dressed in armor and festooned with his personal weapons came Vareskel.

Pon knelt and lowered his head to show his obedience. The Varshon strode forward slowly but with purpose evident in his stride. He was the embodiment of what the masters were. Regal and deadly all in one. This is what all those gathered worshipped.

The Alush all fell silent and bowed to their leader. Here was the one that would bring them to glory and honor.

As Vareskel came to the railing he reached down and touched Pon on the shoulder to release him from his salute. The general rose and took his place behind and to the side of the Varshon.

The large figure looked around the coliseum at his soldiers and their passion. Vareskel let them wait a moment longer, then in a loud, clear voice he shouted at them, "Who are you?"

The roar of tens of thousands of voices was nearly a physical force as they replied, "Alush, Alush, Alush…" Pon stepped forward and shook both fists in the air to encourage them and they responded even louder than before. The sturdy building shook as the assembled soldiers stomped and shouted as the fervor of the moment grabbed hold and held them in its power.

Pon listened and let them roar. He knew that many of them would not be returning from the war but it didn't matter. So long as they did what was needed, there were always more of them.

Chapter Fourteen
Departure

The Citadel

The morning was clear and bright as the sun climbed above the far horizon. Anagir was in a good mood as he went about finishing up a few small tasks. As he puttered, the reality of what today meant came over him again. The day had come at last, after nearly two thousand years. The time to move north to reclaim what was rightfully theirs had arrived.

Excitement had crept into Anagir the night before and kept him from any meaningful amount of sleep but he wasn't troubled by it. He found it somewhat interesting at how excited he was. The work and sacrifice of twenty centuries lay behind him while ahead was only victory and power!

The senior Varshon had long ago allowed himself to forget the truth about what had happened at G'mar, how Taranh had been forced to settle on using Anagir due to the loss of so many of majic users. How he had been trying to hide when the elder Varshon had found him and brought him along. The betrayal of Lykan Tee who had protected and sheltered him which led to Lykan's death. None of that was remembered. He was securely wrapped up in the persona that he had been careful to cultivate over the long centuries since the Varshon defeat at G'mar, that of warrior and leader.

He finished his morning routine, took a look around the room that had been his residence for so long then headed for the door. The belongings he was taking had been carefully packed and removed the night before so nothing would slow his departure.

Q-tra-All was waiting in the hallway outside of Anagir's quarters as he usually was every morning, an additional pair of guards with him. The Ogurth guards that were on duty outside his quarters were silent figures on either side of the doorway.

The wide portals swung open, the senior Troll immediately knelt, his massive frame going down on one knee to pay respect to the leader of those he and his kind served. The guards did not kneel; Anagir had long ago decreed that they were not to do that, can't protect someone if you are kneeling. After he was through the doors the portals began to close of their own accord. The spell controlling the doors had been in place for quite a long while.

Anagir was feeling quite expansive as he waved his loyal Ogurth servant to his feet. "Rise friend, rise, the day of our journey is finally here." The long time Varshon minion did as he was bid. Anagir motioned the guards flanking the portals to step aside which they did without hesitation.

Closing his eyes in concentration for a moment, the elder majic user raised his arm. With a series of intricate movements, he worked a spell. A swirl of bright green energy came into being a few inches from his hand, then it travelled the short distance to the doors. Once there the powerful spell seemed to latch itself to the doors; the swirl of green started to grow. It continued to expand outward until it covered both of the large portals; the mystic energy seemed to pause then expanded further moving across the walls that defined his living space. Lines of power straightened out to create a series of tightly interlocking bars that glowed brightly for an instant then faded until they were barely visible.

His entire residence was now sealed against intrusion.

Satisfied with his effort, Anagir lowered his arm. No one would be able to enter his rooms. The spell would provide greater security than even the faithful Ogurth. It would also mean that it would not be necessary to have guards there all hours of the day during the long absence.

Even if all went according to their plans Anagir knew it would be several long months at least before he was able to return. No reason to commit resources to guard what majic would safeguard. He had tied the spell to the force line that ran nearby so the spell would remain so long as it had majical energy to sustain it.

Turning from the door he started walking down the hallway with Q-tra-All following Anagir, as the way was led by the first pair of Ogurth.

Feeling expansive, the elder majic user began relating to his senior bodyguard about how it was when the Varshon had departed their capital of Imalla on the way to G'mar so many years earlier... "So when the trumpets sounded, the host stepped off as one and the power of the Varshon was displayed for all to see."

Q-tra-All said nothing as he listened, his keen eyes sweeping the passage ahead for any sign of trouble, but none was present. The remaining pair of guards followed a short distance behind.

After making their way through the expansive passageways of the structure and exiting the building, the Varshon leader and his escort made their way to the courtyard area without incident. There, transportation suitable to his station was waiting, as it should be.

Anagir stopped and took a deep breath; the morning air was clean and invigorating. He took in the sights around him. Numerous Ogurth were nearly finished loading several wagons that would accompany Anagir and his party. To the west a group of younger majic users were being given final instructions on their studies for the day before the instructor left to join his unit to travel north. To Anagir all seemed in place.

He turned to the handpicked teamsters that were driving his wagon, "Let us away!" then climbed aboard the custom built coach, his ever present Ogurth following.

The coach and its heavily armed escorts started moving toward the gate. Anagir was silent as he watched through the window as they made their way across the expansive inner courtyard.

I command all I see, thought the majic user. *All serve me and I will have my rewards. Those that oppose me are all done for. I shall rule all of Dohrya.* A measure of excitement crept into him as he contemplated that thought. *Yes, I shall rule.*

There was an additional joy taken in that he had accomplished more than Taranh had been able to at the height of his power. The student has surpassed the teacher. That it wasn't true was of no matter; Anagir believed it so it must be so.

He settled in to his seat a little deeper to improve his comfort and leaned back, enjoying the view out his window. The coach continued to make its way through the courtyard. As it approached, various servants and Ogurth all bowed in recognition of the passenger it carried.

The fortress was a massive construct so it took a little time for the coaches and escorts to reach the gates. As it did, a large honor guard of Ogurth were lined up on either side. As one, they saluted with their swords.

Anagir graciously acknowledged their presence with a full nod of the head. All was right in his world and so he was feeling particularly generous. In short order the coaches and escorts entered the wide tunnel leading to the outside.

Several days earlier Anagir had decreed that large numbers of the Varshon were to circulate themselves among the numerous army units to both encourage and remind them who it was that they served. The troops were eager to begin the journey; this is what they had been training for all their lives, to conquer in the name of their masters.

The massive host was on the move. The vanguard units, an Arakai Ri'al handpicked by Pon, and some mounted archers had already left heading north to serve as an advance screen for the bulk of the army, which had begun departing many hours earlier. Moving an army of this size, the largest one ever assembled, it would take nearly two full days for it all to be underway on the journey north.

After navigating the switchback road leading down from the top of the large mesa, Anagir's coach and retinue headed north. The steady pace of the well trained team of horses ate up the distance easily. There was no hurry, it would be a long journey but at last it was underway.

The elder majic user was visibly upbeat as he rode. The possibilities that lay before him seemed too numerous to count. There was no doubt present in his mind at all that the forces under his command would be victorious. All the possible variables had been foreseen and accounted for, the southern army was the largest ever assembled, and the power of the Varshon majic users was unrivaled. No there was nothing that could stop them.

Passing one of the staging areas, his guards shouted for those assembled to pay homage. Two thousand Alush instantly knelt in respect. Anagir told himself that was what true power was. Within minutes the Alush were behind him and other groups lay ahead but no one slowed his passage to slightest degree. Numerous mounted archers were riding well ahead of the procession to make sure that nothing interfered with its travel. Anagir watched the passing scenes through his window. Even at the height of his power Taranh failed to command an army such as this.

Waving over one of the escorts, the H'roth immediately swung his mount over and bowed as deeply as he could while maintaining control of the animal. Anagir told him to inform the driver to stop when they reached the command group; he wished to speak to Pon. The guard nodded curtly in recognition of the order and sharply urged his horse forward to pass along the instructions. Anagir settled back in his seat.

Yes, this is going to be a good day.

Chapter Fifteen
To Kill a King

Karbel

The assassins gathered in a dilapidated warehouse located in the eastern section of the large city. They had been trickling into the capital for the previous three days in preparation for their attack. The men had been careful to use all three of the gates, coming in singly or in very small groups at all different times of the day to allay any suspicion.

This was the first time that all of them had been together since just prior to crossing the Wystern river into D'Lohm, where they had split up into smaller groups to avoid detection. Each group had used a different route to ensure that at least several groups would reach the capital. Only one group had encountered a significant problem delaying them but they had still arrived in time to join in the attack. The group took a full day to do a final scouting of their target, double and triple check their equipment and to rest up.

Low lamps burned in a few places leaving much of the building's interior swimming in darkness. One shadowy figure slipped in and out of the scattered pools of weak light as he walked. His footfalls were light despite his size. As he walked more quiet shadows joined him. The tall figure was moving toward the largest open area in the old building. Once there he turned to face those that had been concentrating their numbers. A figure slid from the darkness to signal those gathering. They silently sorted themselves out and with little noise or fuss arranged themselves in rigidly straight lines facing the first man. The second man did a quick head count and minus the seven men he had on guard duty all of the group were now assembled.

He turned and with a bow informed his commander that all were accounted for. The leader returned the gesture of respect waving his second to his position. Pausing for a moment then motioning his men to close in around him, the man watched as they moved nearly silently despite their numbers. Pleased at their stealth, he allowed himself a small grin of satisfaction. This was most audacious act he and his kind had ever been ordered to undertake but he was confident of their success. It was as if they had been training for this event for their entire lives.

Once they were gathered around him he motioned them down. They sank down to the floor, legs folded under them.

"Brothers, we're once again together. It is good to see you. This task will bring us and our kind glory for all time. We will swing the blade that kills a king!"

A low but enthusiastic growl was the response. The assassins were well trained and experienced but had never undertaken a mission against a target so heavily defended as what they were about to.

"Make ready, let us leave this place, it is time."

The men rose silently, moving off to collect their equipment and supplies to take them to the wagons that were due to arrive momentarily. The drivers were part of their group so there were no worries about security.

The seven men on guard had already been notified to watch for the wagons. When the first one was seen word was quietly sent and final preparations got underway to leave. The transports had hardly stopped when the first of the assassins left the building. The rest slipped from the darkness to quickly but efficiently enter the wagons with as little noise as possible. Several bundles of equipment were handled by teams of the men to make the process quicker. The well wrapped packages were swallowed by the interior of the transports without fuss. With less than a sixty count all the wagons were loaded and the first of them was beginning to move. The four vehicle caravan departed the small warehouse district without incident.

The wagons, painted to resemble those that routinely hauled trash from its collection points around the large city, moved steadily but in no hurry just as their real life counterparts would. The drivers did nothing to attract even the slightest bit of attention to themselves. The mission was too important to have it spoiled by something as simple and stupid as rushing through the metropolis.

If they were stopped the story would be that this group of wagons was being sent across the city to have them in place for the morning rounds. Only one of the drivers spoke the local tongue and not well but it would have to suffice.

One of the drivers was relieved that they had practiced the route so many times over the previous ten-day having arrived long before the assault team. Karbel was a large city, the most populated city in the known world, so the practice was important. If they hadn't spent so much time driving the various routes near the castle it would have been easy to get lost, *but that is why the masters sent us* thought the man, *we never fail*. The reward promised for a completed kill was great, the largest they had ever heard of.

The trip through the streets took nearly an hour. Only once did they see a military patrol but were paid no mind continuing on their way. As their destination approached, the wagons slowed but never stopped. Again the long hours of practice paid off as the men leapt from the rear of the transports with their equipment to hurry toward the thick brush growing along the base of the towering butte. Once there they secreted themselves out of sight, weapons at the ready if case of discovery.

Tense moments passed as keen eyes watched for any signs of concern, ears pricked at the breeze for any hint of others nearby. The wagons continued on their way as if nothing at all was afoot. They headed toward the safe house, another warehouse in a different section of the city that those who survived the raid on the palace knew to head for.

Once the invaders were certain that no one had seen their exit from the wagons, the next phase of the plan got underway. One of the key defensive features of the palace was that it was situated on a high butte, not unlike the Varshon stronghold. The palace had been extensively scouted over the previous years by southern agents and it had been determined that trying to infiltrate the walls would be difficult at best.

However, the fourth wall which paralleled the western edge of the bluff was the weakest point in what was otherwise a strong fortification. In order to exploit that weakness it would be necessary to climb a near vertical stone face over a hundred feet in height and do so undetected. Rock climbing was a skill long taught to the assassins so this climb posed little challenge apart from being discovered.

Those assassins designated as lead climbers were already in place waiting the order to begin the ascent. Asumi, leader of the southern raiders reached out to either side of him to touch the man there, who in turn passed the silent directive on until it reached those it was intended for. Immediately several dark clad figures started their journey up the rock face. These men were the best climbers among the group; they would be the pathfinders that the others would follow. Each of them had a number of specially designed pins that would anchor the ropes that the others would use to climb up the rock wall.

Short handled hammers with rags wrapped tightly about the heavy head to reduce the sound were used to drive the pins into cracks between the rocks. Ropes were then fed through the openings near the upper end and then lowered toward the ground. This gave those below six different routes up the side of the butte which sped the process tremendously. With the necessity of moving nearly forty men up the cliff it was essential to have several paths that could be used simultaneously. The last man up each of the ropes was careful to pull it up behind him then secure it to the lowermost anchor pin so that anyone that happened to walk by the base of the butte would not stumble on it accidently. It was unlikely that the dark colored rope they used would be seen at night but these were proven tactics and so were strictly followed.

As the first climbers neared the top their pace become much slower and more deliberate to ensure that they were being as quiet as possible. The men of the south had no way of knowing for sure but it seemed very logical that this side of the fortress would have guards patrols as same as the other three did.

The scouts had not been able to gain access to the palace interior despite several attempts. Only some general knowledge of the interior layout was available to them which wasn't the best plan but it was what they had.

The half dozen pathfinders reached the edge of the butte and carefully peered toward the wall. A few torches and lamps lit portions of the area but there were still pools of darkness that could hide an attacker if he were careful. Timing the movements of the visible guards the six slipped over the edge and quietly crossed the narrow open space between it and the wall. Like most castles the upper reaches of the walls were not pure vertical. The ramparts and parapets extended over the edge of the wall which created an area invisible to those directly above unless the sentry leaned very far out from his position to look down.

One of the tools that the assassins had brought with them were sections of wooden poles about as thick as that of a man's calf cut to about the length of an arm if you measured fingertip to shoulder. On one end it was carefully cut down and smoothed, the other end had a metal band fastened to it forming a cup. Each end fit inside the end of another piece so that you could extend this pole for at least twenty feet before it became too unwieldy. Each piece had a metal rod inserted into it that extended out one side for about the width of two palms. By lining this up in an alternating fashion you created a ladder.

Once the first six reached the wall safely the next group readied themselves. To be able to scale the wall in numbers that made Asumi comfortable, it would be necessary to get at least two more groups up to wall so there would be enough ladder sections to create two of the climbing poles. The wall on this side of the fortress wasn't as high as its three counterparts; that oversight in design was about to have terrible consequences.

The second group made it to the wall without incident, the third was nearly discovered when one of their group stumbled on some rocks. The noise carried and one of the sentries looked over the wall but saw nothing so returned to his patrol, the dark colored clothing worn by the assassins serving them well. Those underneath the overhang were wasting no time; the two climbing fixtures were already assembled and ready. The remainder of the assassins were waiting below the edge of the bluff clinging to their ropes.

Asumi saw that his men at the wall were ready with the portable breaching tools. He watched as the patrolling sentry made his way past and when he was clear Asumi whistled lightly mimicking a small bird, indicating it was safe to move.

Instantly the eighteen men responded. Eight men took each pole and swung it out and up toward the parapet. Each team moved their ladder into position and leaned it against the wall. The remaining two men shimmied up the pole to open the way for their brethren. This was a drill practiced many times in all manner of conditions to make it second nature.

The first man made it to the top and let fly at the nearest sentry. The first Striker went down with an arrow through the throat. He fell heavily to the stone, the metal point of his spear clattered as it hit the stone. The assassins didn't hesitate. They were moving over the parapet before the body of the guard had hit the ground, not waiting to see if the sound was heard by anyone.

Asumi was moving in an instant as were those on the other five ropes. One of the nearby guards did hear the spear fall and when he looked over the edge of his post an arrow took him in the face killing him instantly Dark clad figures hurried up the ladders and began flooding into the castle.

Three archers stayed atop the stone barrier, eyes searching the surrounding area for targets, bows at the ready. Meanwhile more assassins poured into the castle, each group intent on their assigned tasks. The odds of their success improved with each man that slipped into the fortress. Asumi never hesitated once he was across the wall, a grin split his face beneath the black wrap intended to hide as much visible skin as possible.

Some of the assassins' first assignments were to set fires to create distractions. This tactic had been used a number of times during raids on assorted goblin hamlets in the south. Fire was a useful distraction when raiding deep into the heavily guarded goblins domains. Others headed directly toward their goal, the sleeping quarters of the king which was believed to be in the western portion of the fortress based on what little information that had been gathered.

The hour of the palace attack, two hours past mid-night, had been chosen to ensure that the king would be in bed and therefore in a fixed location. Trying to locate him in the large structure would prove fruitless; they had to attack when they were reasonably sure of his location since they didn't know the layout of the fortress.

One of the groups reached a storage room and quickly went to work placing their flammables around the room then struck a flame with a small kindling kit. Fire roared into life greedily feeding on the ample fuel. Smoke began to fill the room but the assassins were already on their way. They had made sure to leave the door partially open so that the smoke would escape the room and draw attention.

The king and queen were in their bedchamber for the night; both had been asleep for nearly three hours resting comfortably. The five Strikers standing guard outside their door were alert and focused as they were every night.

The assassins were getting closer to their target. Asumi and a large group of his men had been able to reach the area despite the roving patrols. It had been necessary for them to kill four guards and two of the palace staff to achieve this. Directions to the kings' chambers had been wrung from one of the staff who believed he would be spared if he spoke. He had been mistaken.

One of the roving Striker patrols smelled smoke and rushed to find the source. In doing so they ran into a group of assassins. A melee quickly ensued, the sound of which alerted other guards. One grabbed the short horn at his side and blew a blast. The tone echoed off the stone walls amplifying it.

That first notice of alarm was repeated by others. In the Duty Office some of those there rushed to the doorway to try and determine what the cause of the alarm was. The trumpeter stepped out on the short balcony and began to sound the notes for Full Alert and Palace Alarm. Others around the city repeated the calls, waking up large segments of the population as well as the military units in the area. The twenty five men of the Duty Section immediately gathered their equipment and headed toward the sound of the horn. The echo of boots hitting stone, as well as the rattle of their equipment, filled the hallway.

Asumi didn't know what had caused the alarm but put it out of his mind as he launched himself around the corner of the corridor. The four Strikers were now even more alert than they had been.

Assassins poured into the small corridor to try to overwhelm the royal protectors. The sharp ring of steel was heard as blade met blade. The fighting was immediate and close. In short order the corridor was filled by bodies and whirling blades as the Strikers tried to fight off the intruders.

The man at the end of the hall did exactly what he was supposed to do: without hesitation he slapped the wall mounted gate release mechanism with the side of his gloved fist. This unlocked the reel holding the last ditch security measure in place. A few feet in front of him a stout barricade of riveted iron straps fell into place from a slot in the ceiling of the short hallway.

In their room, Thadar and Shay were startled when the portcullis in the hallway outside slammed down. They had been awaked by the horn calls of moments earlier. The sound of the heavy iron barrier being activated shocked both into full consciousness, then action. If the barrier was needed, something drastic was going on.

Both of them abandoned the bed without thought slipping on whatever clothes were nearby. The fighting in the hallway could be heard now that the pair were fully awake.

Asumi was shocked to see the security device that they had known nothing of suddenly bar their way. The last of the four Strikers that had been on guard outside the private quarters went down, the fifth man at the end of the hallway had his weapon up and was waiting for them to do something. The assassin pointed at him, two of his men instantly raised their blowguns and fired. One of the darts hit while the second bounced harmlessly off the portcullis. The quick acting poison did its job on the guard. He slumped to the floor, shuddered a few times, then was still.

The sound of the horn alerted more than the Strikers. In his quarters Dwyn was surprised to hear shouts followed immediately by the ringing of what was most certainly sword on sword. Here? In the palace, at this time of night? That could only mean one thing and it wasn't good.

As he had been processing the thoughts he had leapt from his bed, quickly dressed in what was handy and armed himself. From the time he was awakened to dressed and pulling open the door was less than two minutes. Gripping his sword he yanked the handle swinging the stout door open and out of his way.

Almost instantly, the hallway before him was filled with a melee, several Strikers were battling seven unknown men. The Elf never hesitated falling upon one of the strangers from behind.

The man went down when Dwyn's blade found his lung. Shades, an attack force was *in* the palace! There was no time for further rumination as the battle in the hallway reached a peak. Shouts and curses could be heard along with the almost musical tones of sword on sword throughout the passageway. The Elf found himself pressed by one of the men. The pair traded cuts and parries which moved them around the narrow hallway.

In the barracks, more Strikers were assembling as quickly as possible, even as the sounds of sword fights, shouts and more horns could be heard. Asumi and his men were temporarily stymied by the iron barrier that blocked the hallway. Frustration at the delay didn't slow the thinking of the assassin; he turned and with a quick gesture waved his second forward to examine the workings of the accursed device.

Namii was a genius with mechanical constructs. With a flash he had climbed the portcullis like a ladder and was using a hastily grabbed oil lamp to scrutinize the pulleys and such.

In short order he had an idea. He slid a long thin dagger into the opening and cut one of the ropes. Now needing both hands, he hissed at one of the others to join him, which was quickly done. Passing the lamp over, Namii fished out some of the lightweight but strong cord that each of the assassins carried and with a deft touch tied it to the end of the cut rope. He nodded to the other and both hurried down.

Asumi saw what Namii had planned and waved several of his men into the corridor to help. He knew that they had to hurry, the palace guards were already on their way, and time wasn't on their side. A small group of assassins joined their brethren after making their way through the castle.

The Duty Section were nearly to the scene of the first alarm. The fire was being fought by several of the guards and staff but it was taking great effort to haul more water to the scene from down the hallway. Bucket after bucket of water was being tossed at the fire, as each load of water hit there was a rush of steam accompanied by a loud hissing sound.

Seeing that there was little they could do, the senior Striker told his men to split in two groups and make their way to the king's quarters. That took priority. A dozen or so men immediately headed toward a side passage while the remainder of the section headed off at a run using a different corridor.

They passed several of the staff who were frantically hauling more buckets of water toward the blaze.

In the narrow passageway Namii and several others took a firm grip on the rope and began to pull, slowly at first, but steadily the portcullis began to lift. Asumi saw the progress and readied his surprise. He was certain the door to the king's sleeping area would be a stout one and heavily barred as well. That factor had been taken into consideration already.

The assassin watched as the iron barrier was nearly half way up now. His mind flashed back to when he was summoned to stand in Anagir's presence before leaving the south.

The senior assassin had been ordered to report to Anagir's personal quarters which was virtually unheard of among the human troops that served the Varshon. Arriving, he was stopped by one of the Ogurth guards and searched carefully. The other sentry was vigilant during the check of Asumi's person. If he had shown the slightest hint of dangerous behavior he would have been killed instantly.

Once the search was completed the guard knocked once on the heavy door then waited. No sound was heard as the door swung open. The veteran assassin entered with one of the Ogurth behind him. He tried to quell his sense of fear and awe as much as possible. He was about to meet the supreme leader of the Varshon.

Anagir was waiting for him. Asumi took three steps into the room and then immediately went to one knee bowing his head deeply as a show of respect. The veteran assassin stayed there until Anagir bid him rise. As he did, the large Troll continued to eye him every moment. Asumi felt the stare of the guard on him but just barely -- to be in the presence of the Supreme Majic User was heady. The aura of the power that Anagir controlled was almost palpable.

Asumi said nothing; he had been carefully proctored on how to behave in the presence of the supreme one. The elder Varshon was savoring the moment as he often did when there was an opportunity to have his sizable ego stroked.

After a few moments Anagir asked his vassal a question, "What is the easiest means of confusing an enemy force?"

Asumi paused for half a heartbeat then answered, "Remove the head."

The senior Varshon looked pleased. Anagir was feeling expansive because the day to launch the attack on the north was rapidly approaching. The long centuries of patience were about to come to an end and Varshon dominance, specifically his own growth of power, was about to come to fruition. Walking from behind his large, richly carved desk Anagir waved the assassin forward.

As Asumi covered the distance between the two, he made sure to stop several feet short. He had been told in no uncertain terms if he violated what the guard considered Anagir's personal space that he would be killed immediately.

Using the tone he often used when he was teaching, Anagir began to lecture Asumi. "Much depends on the work that you and those of your kind will do in Karbel. Despite not knowing exactly what you will face, you will succeed. I have made sure of it."

With a half turn the Varshon leader reached over to lift a canister from the top of the desk. It was nondescript tube a bit shorter than the length of Asumi's forearm. He handed it to Asumi who slowly reached out to take it. The guard leaned forward a bit but stopped instantly with a look from Anagir.

Taking hold of the tube, Asumi looked it over. It was a few inches in diameter and inscribed with mystic symbols and words. A very ornate looking catch secured what appeared to be a cap on one end.

Being careful to handle it with caution, Asumi listened as Anagir began, "If you come to an obstacle that bars your path utilize this." He went to explain how to use what was contained within.

Asumi asked one or two questions regarding potential hazards during transport and was quickly assured that there would be no issues. As a means of dismissal Anagir passed his hand over the assassin in a gesture of blessing.

***

With that memory now behind him Asumi was ready. The portcullis was being held slightly above half way open, the bodies of the guards had been stacked up to form a wedge. Quickly making sure that the hallway was clear of his people Asumi leveled the container making sure to point the appropriate end toward the stout door that blocked their way.

Knowing they had little time, he worked the catch just as he had been instructed. In the same instant that the cap flopped open a ball of purple and orange fire erupted from the end. In less than a heartbeat the mystic battering ram flew down the short hallway striking the barrier.

The force of the blast was enough to shake much of the palace. The massive sound of the explosion rang loudly through the numerous corridors and was even heard in parts of the city proper. Many a face turned toward the fortress trying to see what was happening but that information was denied them.

The blast shredded the stout oak and iron door leading to the kings' anteroom. Thadar and Shay were fortunately not near the door when it was torn from its hinges and hurled with great force across the room. As the still significant sized pieces of the door traveled, it created a path of destruction. A small table and three chairs were crushed against the wall or flung out of the way. Thadar and his wife shared a look, what thunder was this?

Asumi and his men never hesitated, as soon as the way was clear several of them rushed down the short hallway only to be met by Thadar, who had correctly realized what was about to happen.

The first assassin to reach the end of the short passage was killed by a surprise blow from the king. Thadar knew that help would be coming but he had to hold them off; the opening was the logical place. If the invaders got into the room they could overwhelm him with their numbers. Asumi began trading blows with Thadar and the two went back and forth. The numerical superiority of the invaders was momentarily negated by the confines of the narrow passage, just as it was intended.

About that same time the first contingent from the Duty Section arrived. The scene was one of instant chaos as the two sides fought. Shouts, curses and sword finding flesh or steel created a storm of noise. Asumi was still trying to gain an advantage as he fought, the men behind him couldn't use their dart tubes without hitting their leader.

More Strikers were arriving nearly every moment and began to turn the tide against the assassins. Two of the three assassins behind Asumi turned then rushed back into the main corridor to try and stop the Strikers. Dart tubes whistled and a pair of the guards went down. Then it was sword on sword. The fight was spreading out to nearby passageways.

Shay was not content to stand idly by as her husband fought for their lives. She was not a stranger to the way of the blade; her father had started her and her siblings on weapons training early in their lives.

Grasping her blade, she favored a light but strong saber. She slid alongside her husband, and when the opening presented itself, she struck. Asumi was tiring and wounded but only slightly, he had scored several wounds on Thadar which evened the fight. He saw a woman come into view around the man he was fighting that he believed to be the king. Shifting his attack he tried to force Thadar to shift positions in order to protect his wife. Asumi reasoned she would be unfamiliar with the use of a sword.

That assumption quickly proved wrong when the senior assassin got his feet tangled up with the body of the man Thadar had killed. Being off balance for two heartbeats proved sufficient for Shay, her blade sank deep in his chest. Thadar used the moment to surge forward driving his shoulder under the guard of the invader. With solid contact he pushed the man backwards into the second man tying him up momentarily.

Asumi was shocked when the honed steel slid into his chest. Suddenly his body was filled with pain and he was being shoved backwards, his feet not working properly. Thadar stabbed the first few inches of his sword into Asumi's chest opposite from where his wife had struck to ensure that the man was good and dead. The second assassin had no choice but to move toward the open area behind him as the body of his leader was acting like a ram against him.

Ducking under the partially opening security gate, and then one final hard shove, and Thadar was clear of the narrow corridor. He tossed the limp body of the raider out of the way bringing his sword up in a quick short thrust into the second assassin who had been off balance and vulnerable. The man groaned as the steel bit then collapsed. Once Thadar was sure the man was no longer a threat withdrew his sword.

Thadar brought the blade up to a guard position as he hurriedly scanned the area immediately around him. The king felt the pressure against his hip and instinctively knew that it was his wife. Neither of them hesitated falling on a pair of the attackers from behind as they fought with some of the Strikers. Both men were quickly dispatched. The three Strikers turned their attention to the royals. Neither seemed too injured thank the gods.

With no thought to decorum, one of the guards essentially did to Thadar what the king had just done. The guard lowered a powerful shoulder and began shoving his ruler toward the opening of the narrow passage. The Striker knew that there were still assassins nearby, some as close as a double arm span.

Thadar was caught off guard and despite his desire to stay and join in the fight further found himself being moved backwards. The Striker increased the pressure he was using in order to keep the king moving. Shay saw this, she reached out as best as possible as she too was herded toward the corridor. The other two Strikers reacted as quickly, both of them turning outward toward the nearest fighting to take a position between the threat and the royals.

Once at the opening, the burly guard gave his ruler a hard shove to get him part of the way down the passage. When that was done, he spun about. Due to his size he filled the narrow space; the pair of Strikers with him took up positions immediately in front of him. The three guards had established a living wall right at the entrance of the short corridor.

Shay, who had managed to hang on to the tenuous hold she had established, now strengthened her grip. She was between the open area and Thadar. He was nearly frothing at the mouth to get back at those who had tried to kill them. These scum had come into *his* home, attacked *his* people and worse tried to kill *his* wife! Shay was saying over and over, "NO!" to her husband, she recognized the need to keep him alive.

Continuing to stay interposed between him and guards, she angled herself so that Thadar was forced to look her right in the eyes. When Shay knew that she had his attention she told him, *the people need you.* That simple statement was enough to give him pause, a brief one but it proved to be sufficient.

His breathing slowed, some of the tightness in his muscles dissipated, and his mental focus began to shift to the immediate. The sounds of fighting could still be heard from the hall beyond but it was diminishing. Taking a deep breath, Thadar shifted his head around that of his wife and at the top of his lungs shouted out, "Karbel and King!" Shay smiled at the outburst despite her ear ringing from the proximity to the source.

In the space beyond king's anteroom, the few surviving assassins were facing rapidly growing numbers of Strikers. There was no way they were going to be able to reach the king; knowing that they had failed and of the need for secrecy the three of them suddenly dropped their weapons right in the middle of the fight. All of them were killed before anyone could stop it. Dwyn arrived just as this occurred, he desperately wanted some of them alive so that they could be questioned but that was no longer an option.

Looking around the scene the Elf saw the carnage that had happened. Bodies, assassin and Strikers, were thickly littered across the stone floor. In some places it wasn't possible to see the floor the corpses were so numerous.

Dwyn saw the blockade that several of the Strikers had formed across the opening to the sleeping chambers. Around him Strikers were checking that all of the intruders were in fact dead. Dwyn told them that any found alive were to be kept alive at all costs. Others were checking the condition of the fallen guards searching for survivors. Some groans and moans could be heard so at least someone was alive.

The casualty count among the Strikers is going to be high, thought the Elf. One of the guards nearly fell after slipping on the blood-covered floor.

Stepping around some of the guards as well as the bodies he moved toward where the royals should be. Stopping at the human blockage Dwyn shouted, "Spear!" which was answered with "Shield" from beyond the guards.

At hearing the proper exchange of pass phrases the Strikers that formed the wall began to step aside to allow the tall Elf entrance. Without pause he hurried down the short hallway anxious to check on the condition of his friends.

Thadar was standing near dining table, Shay at his side. Both of them were still holding their swords. He did notice both swords were blood touched. Despite the usually stoic emotional stance of the Elder Race, Dwyn was visibly relieved to see the pair.

Before Thadar could begin to ask questions the Elf gathered the two to him in a hug. He gripped them tightly, his voice nearly caught in this throat.

Dwyn had been an advisor to Thadar since the king had been sixteen years of age. In those eight years he had become extremely fond of the human, so much that it even surprised him at times. Thadar was caught off guard by the display of emotion. The embrace lasted a few moments before Dwyn stepped back.

Thadar began to ask some of the many questions that he needed answers to. Soon the trio was deep in conversation.

***

Colonel Steele had been staying at the large Striker barracks in the city where he maintained an office. The evening meeting with some of his officers has run very late so he elected to spend the night there instead of returning to his room at the palace. When the initial alarm had been sounded from the stronghold he ordered a large number of the Strikers to come with him, all the while cursing himself for being away from the palace. He ordered the remainder of those at the barracks to Full Alert.

As they rode through the city they could occasionally see the fires from the fortress and once heard a sharp *Boom* sound as well. He urged his mount to go faster after hearing that. The senior Striker would find out later what had created that noise.

When he arrived at the palace he had nearly a full company of Strikers with him, over two hundred men. The guards at the east gate worked to get the massive portals open which took time. Knowing this, Steele had sent half of the men from the barracks with him to the other gate so that they could get as many Strikers into the large structure as quickly as possible.

The senior Striker didn't want to wait any longer so hurriedly dismounted while shouting for the first squad to come with him. The twenty one men rushed to follow their orders. He told the rest to get inside as quickly as they could and report to the Duty Officer.

Once down from his horse, Steele hurried over to the open man-size door and entered the palace with the others right on his heels. The gates were almost to a point of being open enough to ride through, the lead riders crowding the entrance to get inside as rapidly as they could. It wasn't hard to smell the smoke from the fires.

The portcullis was barely halfway up when the first of the mounted Strikers urged their horses within, lowering their own heads to pass through. The clatter and echo of the hooves on the stones filled the tunnel between the two sets of gates. Shouts and curses were in no small amount as four score riders hurried inside. A similar scene was taking place at the gate on the north side as well.

Once in the castle proper Steele set off for the royal quarters. He knew that at this time of night that would be the most likely place to find Thadar. The various corridors and passageways that he and the squad of Strikers traveled all showed some evidence of the night's chaos, bodies, fire damage, lingering smoke, injured staff members or other Strikers all being tended to.

The senior Striker felt his jaw set from the anger at what he was seeing. That this happened was his fault, he was the one in charge of royal protection and he had failed them. What to do about that had already crossed his mind but that would have to wait a bit. Checking on the welfare of the king came first.

Long minutes later Steele and the others arrived at the hall outside the royal quarters. The scene was still one of barely organized bedlam, wounded being treated, bodies of guard and assassins alike littered the floor while stern faced sentinels watched everything with weapons in hand.

Steele hadn't been prepared for this, so many of his men down. The sights of the black garbed corpses stopped him in his steps; eyes took in the whole view. His anger level went up another notch as did his level of guilt. Shaking that off for the briefest moment he started walking again, *have to check on the king.* Over his shoulder he told the squad with him to help out. The twenty plus Strikers immediately turned to doing what they were needed to do.

Steele moved past the half dozen guarding the short passage to the anteroom. *Barn's locked now*, he thought grimly. He had never felt such a sense of failure in his life, time to face the king and take what is coming.

The portcullis had been raised and temporarily secured so the senior Striker didn't need to duck his head as he passed through, leading into the room where he found the king, the queen, and Dwyn gathered near the dining table. Steele took two steps forward and knelt, lowering his head while lifting his sword with two hands up to the level of his head.

Steele was caught in an emotional storm, his honor demanded that he leave the king's service but his sense of loyalty made him want to stay, to be given the chance to make sure this type of incident never happened again. Thadar and the others saw the gesture.

The king had suspected that this is what Steele would do. Offer to resign in disgrace because of the attack; he would feel that it was a failure of his duty. Dwyn too could identify with how Steele was feeling; the Elf also felt that in some way he had failed the king.

As soon as he saw what his guard commander was doing Thadar stepped toward him. Grabbing hold of one wrist, Thadar pulled upwards to force the man to rise which he did. The king told him, "There shall be no further talk of this. We are alive and our trust in you is absolute."

The queen immediately echoed the sentiment of her husband, "It is. Now, rise."

The grip of the king wasn't painful but it was strong, Steele didn't want to stand but the combination of the words and the action of his king compelled him to ascend from his knee. Once he was up Thadar released his hold and offered his hand.

Steele was still hesitant but took the grip, wrist to wrist. He could feel the strength there and it brought him a measure of reassurance. There was no doubt that this attack would haunt him for a long time but the senior Striker had recovered enough to understand that he was needed, now more than he ever had been before.

One quick shake then Thadar turned to the others, "We have much work before us. Have Spree and Gunnar summoned at once please."

Steele had the pair sent for, then joined the conversation that was taking place. It would prove to be a long day for all of them.

Chapter Sixteen
Karbel

Coup

Riders rode hurriedly, almost recklessly, through the city spreading news of the attack on the palace. Word then spread like fever through an isolated settlement. Wild tales of death and horrible atrocities swept through the capital city from end to end. Stories told of those found in their beds, throats cut, bodies mutilated and women violated. The narrative grew in scope and ferocity with each telling so there was no way to separate truth from myth.

Those who were curious enough had only to step outside and look up toward the imposing mass of gray stone, the home of the king, situated high on the mesa above the city to see for themselves. Smoke could be seen rising from the fortress in several places even though it was still dark outside; the light rain of earlier had stopped and some of the fires shown red on the underside of the clouds. Many of the city residents wanted answers but most were more concerned about securing their doors and windows against any who might seek entrance. They huddled with their own, waiting for the dawn and more news, while imploring friendly gods to watch over them.

Blocks of heavily armed Legionnaires were just beginning to arrive from their nearby barracks to spread out through the large city in an attempt to maintain order, the heavy gates closing after allowing them entry. Their efforts were to be hampered by the many fires raging in various areas that pulled many of the soldiers away from other duties, just as the assassins intended. These fires had been set by several southern agents per their instructions, coordinating the arson to occur after the attack on the palace had begun. It was one of the many tenets used by the southerners; confusion is another wound that an enemy must recover from.

Fire was a very serious concern in a city built of mostly wood. The shabby construction and close quarters of some of the burning buildings made fighting the fires a difficult, if not impossible task. In many places throngs of residents were fighting the fires as best they could. Bucket brigades were started using whatever was at hand, pails, pans and even chamber pots.

In two locations the efforts were paying dividends as the fires were being controlled but this was more the exception. Smoke rolled upward to help darken a sky already filled with rain clouds. The underside of the clouds was lit by a dull red glow from the flames.

Several small riots had already broken out and looting was taking place as well and starting to spread. Desperate shopkeepers tried to protect their wares when they could. Many a merchant received a bucket full of bruises for their troubles, some got worse. The lack of any organized effort to inform the population of what news there was only fed the fervor of unrest growing steadily in the capital. The government wasn't withholding the information; no one had simply thought to send criers out to announce what news there was. This failure would lead to larger problems later.

***

Lynd Rees along with several members of his faction within the Assembly and three of his fellow conspirators who had been in the capital were gathered in his home. Several empty pitchers of fine wine and used crystal glasses sat unnoticed on a small table near the windows. The servants had been dismissed for now; business was at hand, dangerous business.

The group of conspirators were meeting in a private office of modest size that Rees favored for important work, located on the main floor of the fashionable structure. The Assembly members were in another room, Rees made sure that the two groups did not see each other. The men from the Assembly who were aligned with him were not a part of the conspiracy to remove the king. He instructed his staff to provide them with whatever they desired but they were not to leave the east end of the large house. The Council of Eight members were in the west end.

Rich paneling covered the walls, fine linen curtains now closed, graced the windows and their gilded frames. High banks of shelving contained numerous books and manuscripts. It was the room of a rich man, the trappings of power present in each item but for Rees it was simply part of his home.

Rees felt sure that his property was sufficiently protected, high stone walls topped with metal spikes surrounded the entire grounds and barricades reinforced the heavy iron gates at the front and a rear, a dozen men stood watch at each gate. Numerous high priced, well-armed mercenaries patrolled the grounds and inside the house watching for any trouble.

Mobs had already sacked several nearby estates then moved on to other areas. A mob had started to come up the main road toward his house but the sight of the well-armed, determined sentries gave the crowd pause. After shouting curses and tossing some stones at the guards the mob moved on to find easier pickings.

The Council members gathered were sitting around a table that occupied one end of the room. The discussion was sharp, "There will never be o' better time. This be a gift that we must use, now!" A thick hand, heavily calloused from years of handling tools, slapped down on the heavy table of richly polished chalba wood to accent the message.

This strong opinion was put forward by Orth Glan, a fabulously rich merchant and trader; he controlled vast tracts of land and employed thousands in his various enterprises throughout the kingdom and beyond. Glan was a longtime associate of Rees and no friend of the crown.

Finished with his statement he looked at each of the others seeking support in their expressions. He had invested heavily in preparing for the day when they would bring down the monarchy. Bribes, favors and debts had traded hands and not a small number of citizens had found themselves on the wrong end of a knife to advance their plans.

Glan had also recruited and supervised the training for nearly five hundred mercenaries who were currently quartered on one of his more remote estates in the northeast part of the kingdom. These men were all from outside of Karbel and owed allegiance to no one but Orth Glan. A fact he was careful to never hold over any of the other conspirators but one that they were all aware of. These men were to be the foundation of the security forces the members intended to use to protect their interests when they rose to power.

The men had been training hard for several months and were well equipped. Twenty of them were patrolling outside the Rees manor, even as the group was speaking, to help with security. Orth never traveled without at least that many with him. It helped to feed his immense ego to be seen with two tens of armed retainers around him. Most who saw this thought it pompous but said little for fear of drawing unwanted attention to themselves.

Serious nods and grim faces returned the searching look of Glan as the other men listened. Getting the group together hadn't been easy due to the unrest gripping the streets. Two of the men had already been visiting Rees on business matters when the trouble began. The others had found their way there using various routes and at times no small amount of force.

Rees did not nod but watched the faces of those who did. He knew that not all of their assets were in place but that an opportunity such as this, a deliberate strike into the heart of the palace by someone from outside their group, could be too good to pass up. Ever a cautious man by nature, even he had to admit that the chance dropped in their laps by this attack on Thadar was a rich albeit unforeseen prize indeed. Was it rich enough to risk what they had carefully planned for?

This meeting would determine that, despite the fact that several of the other conspirators were not present. Business had kept them from the capital for some time. The four men present represented the majority of the group so they felt it proper to discuss the plan.

Rees spoke for the first time in several minutes having been content to allow others to lead the discussion. "What resources have we in place here in the capital now?" A scroll containing that information was pulled from the small pile of them near the edge of the table and handed to Rees. The information was updated daily to ensure the data was close at hand, that foresight paid off now. He rolled it down and scanned the contents quickly but thoroughly. A small measured nod followed, "Not all that we would like but a sizable amount nonetheless."

The list detailed the men in their employ, assassins, traders and others who owed their allegiance to the Circle of Eight, the name a deliberate ploy on their part to mislead someone if they were to discover the conspiracy. If someone became aware of them they would only look for eight not the full number of them which would allow some to continue on with their work -- the downfall of the king.

He continued, "It can be done but not without risk, possibly considerable risk, and not as completely as we had wished due to the haste that must be employed, if we go forward at all. We don't know if he lives and that must be considered as well." The last words delivered in a light but serious tone.

He had spent a great deal of time, effort and no small amount of money to try and bring down the king. Rees was hesitant to expend all that had been done in useless half measures when patience could bring bigger dividends. Discussion was brisk and often sharp as various opinions fought for supremacy.

Finally a vote was called for after the group decided that even if the king lived his power base would be unbalanced and that should be enough to allow their plan to succeed if they struck quickly and with force.

Each man was given two stones, a small white one and a matched one of black. A velvet bag was passed around to each man in turn who placed a stone of the appropriate color in the bag under the table and handed the bag to the man to his right. Another bag was sent around the opposite way to collect the remaining stones to keep the balloting secret.

Once the first bag had gone around it was given to Rees who carefully emptied it onto the table. The others leaned forward to see the contents shaken free and determine their own fate. Four black stones gleamed dully in the oil driven flames of the overhead lamps. It was unanimous, proceed. If even one white stone had been present the plan would have been postponed. The method of voting kept the individuals secret if there was a dissenter.

Work began immediately; two trusted scribes were brought in and put to chore. Messages previously drafted were amended to reflect current information and signals arranged. Rees allowed the momentum of the moment to carry most of his co-conspirators forward. He would provide aid to them as agreed but he decided that he would allow the others to be more visible than he would be. He was unsure that their plans would work but the opportunity afforded them was nearly worth the risk.

After all, this may fail and he would be able to use the opportunity to his benefit even if it did. Were they to succeed then he would emerge from the shadows and claim the leadership role as he saw fit. He was a careful man and for a moment wondered if he was too caught up in the enthusiasm for his own good. *A good question*, he asked himself. Then giving it no more thought, returned his full attention to the matter at hand. Time was critical and to them no ally.

Runners loyal to House Rees were summoned and given the messages to deliver to various locations throughout the city. The men were given special instructions regarding the unrest taking place outside the walls of the estate. It was essential that all the messages get through.

The most important documents were to be carried by some of the conspirators themselves, the message text disguised amid lengthy, boring business terms so that anyone finding them would not realize the significance of what they had. Since much of the population of the kingdom could not read, it seemed a reasonable security precaution.

The most important messages would be carried to their contacts in the Legion; these would be carried by Orth himself.

***

Two Legions were assigned to the capital area while the other twelve were stationed throughout the realm, one near each of the other five cities and the remainder in forts and outposts near the frontiers. The kingdom was broad and maintained a large standing army unlike many other countries that used a small professional army and large numbers of reservists who were called up when needed.

Many members of the officer corps of the Second Legion, one of the two Legions assigned to the capital, were Rees sympathizers and supporters. Army life was hard with little reward; the pay while steady was never a large amount. A liberal spreading of gold and darnum -- a silvery metal mined heavily in the mountains near Plynth, much more valuable than gold -- along with promises of greater things to come was enough to sway some. It was hard to obtain a large, loyal following among the enlisted ranks but there were some, enough, it was felt, to give them additional strength of arms.

Those who were staunch supporters of the king were the ones who found themselves released from the army when the Assembly mandated lower troop levels, since it was the officers who decided who went. It was a perfectly useful and legal way to eliminate many royal supporters from among the lower ranks of the army while, faithfully carrying out the orders of the Assembly – of which Rees and two of the others present were members.

The other unit assigned to the capital was the Fifth Legion, known in the army as the Dragons; with them it was a different story entirely. Its commander, General Tal Lyn was a competent soldier, an avid royal supporter especially given that he was father of the current queen, Shay Lyn Skye. The officer corps of the Fifth had been handpicked by Tal and were without exception loyal to the realm. They could be a problem if things went the wrong way for them.

The Dragons had been moved into the Karbel area two months earlier as part of the scheduled rotation of units that the army undertook each year. Of the fourteen Legions that Karbel maintained, four were moved each year to different areas to help familiarize them with as many different parts of the realm as possible. Thadar had implemented this policy two years earlier and the Assembly had not seen fit to change it deeming it a sound policy. Rees smiled at that one. He had been one of those who felt at the time it was indeed a good policy. *Score one for the king* he had told himself.

This shuffling of units was another reason that the group decided to act. The Second was finally due for rotation in four months and would be going to garrison posts in the eastern part of the kingdom after sitting near the capital for several years. Their likely replacements were to be the Marauders of the Twelfth Legion, in which so far the Council had little in the way of paid supporters. So it was likely that the Twelfth would also remain loyal to the crown.

Timing, as in so many things, was crucial. Some of the pieces they needed were in place but were they enough? One critical piece of information that had not yet come out was whether or not Thadar lived. The palace staff was notoriously loyal and as such it was hard to obtain informers in their ranks. Rees was perturbed by the ability of the man to encourage that degree of reliability among those he met.

Another task that Rees decided that would be useful whether or not the king lived was for Loni Weslatt, current Voice of the Assembly, to die. It would be just another unfortunate murder on a night when they were happening all over the city. He did not say anything about it to any of the others. If nothing else was accomplished creating a vacancy atop the Assembly hierarchy could do much to aid their group, as well as further Lynd's own political ambitions --although he had a higher station in mind as his ultimate goal.

Rees had just the right group in mind for the job. He kept a foursome of experienced cutthroats that the others knew nothing about in the city for various tasks. He quietly summoned a runner while the others had moved over to the other table and were reviewing a map of the city discussing options. When the man came to the room he was given the message to carry to the others. Nothing was written down; the whole undertaking was to be done verbally. The wealthy conspirator had no concerns about the man's loyalty to him; Rees had saved him from a hanging after committing a murder by ensuring the witness would not be available to testify, ever.

The man took the message and left the room to deliver it. He had dealt with the four men in question previously and knew where to find them even if they weren't at the house they lived in provided for by Rees, or more precisely a fake company that Rees secretly owned. He planned his route mentally while heading for the stables. He normally walked but tonight speed was essential so being mounted was necessary.

Once he had secured a horse the man headed to the south wall where a small but stoutly secured gate was located. It was well hidden within the concealing foliage that had been carefully planted on both sides of the high wall to prevent unwanted eyes from casual glances. He had retrieved the key on his way out of the house and slid off the mount to unlock the solid gate. When this was done he led the horse through and secured the portal behind him, tucking the key deep into one of the high riding boots he wore.

Edging the horse forward carefully through the brush he checked to see if anyone was around before coming fully out onto the stone paved roadway. The messenger wanted no witnesses to how that he had left the estate. Certain he was alone for the moment he urged the steed forward and headed off in the direction of the house he was seeking. The night's work was just beginning.

***

Word began to reach those in the employ of the conspirators; messages long kept ready were sent to others in the group, weapons taken from their places of hiding, men hustled to carry out the tasks they had been paid for.

One such task was for several men in copies of the uniforms used by the messengers from the palace to ride to various locations in the sprawling city and once there to proclaim the death of the king in official sounding tones of somber note. This was to be done in as public a manner as possible.

Each of these men was accompanied by three others dressed in the uniforms of the Legion, complete down to the unit insignia. This wasn't hard since the uniforms were real, taken from Legion supply stocks by those in the service of Rees and the others. This would lend itself to the official appearance of the messenger and give those who heard the news more cause to believe what they were being told.

It was, in the opinion of the coup leaders, important that the masses be kept informed, at least of what they wanted them to hear. The power of the mob was not a tool to be thrown away before it could be properly used.

The false heralds began their chore of spreading lies in areas as far from the palace as they could, in rich areas, business districts but mostly in the shabby sections where the bulk of the poor denizens of the capital made their homes. These criers arranged themselves at intersections and with their "escort" stood to give out the word.

At first many residents stayed indoors fearing whatever was gripping the city but eventually curiosity got the better of many, and they went to hear for themselves or sent one to get the news. Silent forms ventured cautiously out of doors to make their way to where the news was.

The citizens had no reason to doubt what they were hearing. The messenger looked the same as those who had come bearing news often enough; the guards, steely eyed and watchful, in the uniform of the army. For those who wondered about the news the smoke rising from the palace was visible for some distance despite the hour and the weather. The rain of early evening had not returned but it was still overcast.

The news sounded official and it was delivered with a practiced tone of sorrow and hastiness. Many waited to hear the same proclamations made several times before returning inside, others stayed in case other news was coming. Talk among those gathered started at once: their ruler, murdered in his own bed by assassins, the palace ablaze and trouble in the great city.

The remaining Assembly members, most of them unaware of what was happening due to the late hour were sent word that the king had been killed. The same message, delivered by loyal Rees followers who quickly disappeared into the night once their message was delivered, asked them to come to the Assembly Building right away to convene in emergency session. Lynd used the Assembly members who had gathered earlier at his house to help garner support in the governing body for his actions. The men had been carefully coached by Rees in what to say and who to say it to.

Throughout the capital these representatives of government power and policy, many stirred from their beds, made their way through the city as best they could. Fires, looting, mobs and soldiers were seemingly everywhere. For some the trip to their chambers, usually a short quarter hour ride, turned into over an hour with danger not far off. Men at arms were close at hand and at times in use to move through some areas.

They gathered snippets of news, most false but with small grains of truth hidden within as they went which made it all the more maddening to try and figure out. What some of them saw on their journeys to the Assembly Hall told them more than any report could, however long.

Once at the Assembly building the growing number of members met with each other, all too often clamoring for the same news, what was going on, did the king live, who was in charge of the city. Two of the coup members had been escorted under heavy guard from the Rees manor to the Assembly to play out their role.

The conspirators were hopeful about their chances of success. At the proper time they would call for a new ruler to be elected in order to provide a steady head of state during this time of crisis. The king had no children and no male relatives so this was something that the group felt would be easy.

***

Orth Glan was making the journey across the city to contact their followers in the Second Legion to ensure that military support for their action would be present. His travel was hampered at times by throngs of anxious people clamoring for news. Trusted underlings had been given their assignments as well.

Not all of the desired assets were in place in the capital but the Council felt that what they did have in place would be sufficient. Much was riding on the outcome of tonight's work.

Rees had made his way to the Assembly Hall as well but stayed out of view of the others. His fellow coup conspirators and those loyal to him were still busy laying the ground work for him to be named as the new leader of Karbel. His office staff had strict orders to allow no one access to his chambers. A pair of well-armed guards in the outer office made it easy to enforce the edict.

In the palace the situation was very slowly being brought into a state of something that could be generously called control. Fires still burned in two locations but were being fought energetically by large numbers of staff and Strikers, the wounded who had been located were being treated while an extensive room by room search of the fortress was being conducted by grim faced troops.

In his anteroom Thadar was conferring with Dwyn, his wife, and Gunnar. The mood was dark, the conversation energetic. Earlier the king had watched as some of the bodies of the assassins had been carefully searched then removed. Angry that Steele had forbidden him to leave his own living area Thadar could do little but wait until more information was brought to him which wasn't happening nearly fast enough for his liking.

Any messenger sent to deliver news to the king had to wade through a sea of Strikers before being granted access. Steele had grabbed up nearly two dozen of his men stationing them both in the anteroom itself and the hallway outside. He had ordered a large contingent of the bodyguards to the palace from their barracks in the city as well as more units to the capital.

The senior Striker had already been informed that losses among his men were approaching nearly one hundred and that figure was still climbing. He was in the Duty Office overseeing the search of the palace while the king was meeting with the others; it was to be a long night for all of them.

***

At the Assembly Hall one of the conspirators was giving an impassioned speech to the others present, "…we must have leadership! We need to be acting not cowering in fear; it falls to us to lead!"

Shouts and questions filled the air as he paused. One of Lynd's staff was watching from the wing, he had been alerted what to watch and listen for. The coup member waved his arms for silence which took several moments to accomplish; those gathered in the hall were loath to give up their questioning. Several of the other Assembly members worked to help bring a modest level of decorum to the large chamber.

The speaker began again, "Friends, we are the government now, let us act like it, it is WE that speak for the people," pure fiction but it appealed to the enormous egos of most of those present.

The Rees staff member knew now was time, he turned and signaled to one waiting at the far end of the hallway. The man nodded once then headed for Rees office to summon his employer.

The speaker continued without missing a beat, "To that end we must elect a leader, a man who can bring us together and keep us safe and strong in this time. A man who has proven his devotion to this nation, I nominate Lynd Rees as the leader of Karbel!"

The response was immediate and loud, many shouts, some of approval while others were dismay. The naysayers were hurriedly shouted down by those in favor of the proposal. There was some pushing and shoving but the guards moved in quickly to try and break it up.

Emotions were running high in the chamber but to an experienced political observer it was easy to see that several definite groups had formed. These were not the usual groups of cronies and political hacks but at this moment those gathered believed that they did in fact constitute the government of Karbel.

In the meantime Orth Glan had finally been able to make his way to the headquarters of the Second Legion. He told the general to mobilize a few small units and get them on their way to the Assembly Hall immediately. It would take some time for the men to reach the Hall due to both distance and the chaos going on in parts of the large city.

Glan remained with some of the senior officers to further direct their actions. Control of the military was a key component of their plan; it took time to mobilize a full Legion. The conspirator was nervous, it was taking far too long, he was silently cursing the fool Legion Commander, and he should have had his officers and key sub-unit leaders better prepared for this. All the money that the Council had spent bribing their way to control of the Second was so far not paying much of a return.

Time was not their ally and it was slipping away. Orth fought to control his temper as he returned his attention to the orders being given and gave input as he saw fit based on his own experience, having served several years in the Legion when he was younger.

Rees waited in the wing with several of his staff and guards. Debate in the chamber was still brisk, even chaotic at times but he was certain it was almost time to enter. He carefully listened to the ebb and flow of the various conversations and shouting matches gauging the tide. Then it was time.

Nodding to one of the guards, the small procession entered the chamber. As soon as he was noticed the tumult increased by at least twice as much, the shouted questions all went unanswered. Some of those present tried to press close to Rees to speak to him but were held at bay by the guards and staff members. One or two had to be physically shoved back to allow Lynd room to pass without being slowed. The guards didn't care; they were well paid retainers so did their employer's bidding without hesitation.

Rees took a measured time to reach the open area in front of the first row of seats. There were cheers for him and a few boo's as well. He was careful not to react to those, trusting that his aides would take note of those members. They would be dealt with in good time. For now the matter at hand was to solidify his nomination with a vote.

It took several minutes for the clamor to abate sufficiently for a modicum of order to take hold. All the while Rees was standing silently working at projecting an image of calm leadership.

When he felt that the attention was sufficiently focused on him, Rees began to speak, "Friends, thank you all for coming and attending to your duties." No harm in stroking a few egos. "It has been reported that our leader, Loni Weslatt the Voice of the Assembly, as well as our beloved ruler Thadar Skye, have both been slain this night."

Before he could continue he was interrupted by a host of shouts, cries of outrage, and yells of all types. Members rose from their seats, two dozen conversations started up as a storm of chaos threatened to sweep through the large Assembly Chamber. Rees again stood quietly as he let the tempest run its course for a few moments gauging the timing of his next move carefully. The hue and cry was fierce, running the gamut from wails of despair to near exaltation. Rees had chosen his words with care to set up what he was going to do next.

The shouts and debates were nowhere near at an end when the senior member of the Council of Eight put the next step of his plan into action. With a decisive turn he moved from the front of the seating area up to the lectern area where the Voice of the Assembly usually sat to preside over the meetings.

A few of the gathered members saw him, ceasing their vocal output as they watched. With measured dignity mixed with a degree of dramatic acting, Rees ascended the fourteen steps to the lectern. As he did more and more of the gathered members fell silent. By the time he reached the top step to stand behind the podium the noise level in the room was significantly lower.

Nearly all the eyes in the room were on him as he intended. With a sense of hesitation that was all acting, he reached over to pick up the oversized ceremonial gavel that was the iconic instrument of the Assembly Voice. With a single determined swing he brought the hardwood gavel down on its sounding board. The *thrack* of the blow resounded clearly through the air, bringing the last bit of noise in the room to a still hush. Rees then laid the gavel aside, turning his sharp gaze on those in the room.

"Enough! We are the Assembly, the ruling body of Karbel and we now must lead!" Before any objections or outcry could gain traction he raised one hand to ask for silence. Pausing for an instant to increase his effect Lynd continued, "It falls to us; Karbel cannot be without leadership and WE are that leadership. We must step up at the critical time to do what needs done. Our people are deserving of our best and now, now is when we must be strong. We have been attacked and if the enemy's plan was to leave us adrift bereft of leadership then they failed!"

Cheers, some of them genuine, resounded.

The same Assembly member that had earlier called for Rees to lead again made his way to the speaking area in the open area in front of the seats. Waiting for a few moments and careful not to look at Rees at any point he began to wave his arms down in an attempt to quiet the room. It took several moments but those gathered mostly heeded the request for silence.

Once most of the chamber was quiet the man began, "We are agreed that action must be taken. To that end, I nominate Lynd Rees be named

Voice of the Assembly and that we all follow his lead in good faith. I call for a vote!"

Normal Assembly procedure was that once a vote was called for, then another member had to second the motion and then the Voice would grant permission or deny the request based on what the vote was. This time it went differently. Once the vote was called, several of those present all jumped up to second the motion, then they turned to those around them urging them to vote yes by chanting *Aye* over and over.

Slowly but steadily the chant gained strength, a small block of determined *No* voters were nearly physically assaulted by their colleagues caught up in the fervor of the moment. It took Rees sounding the gavel twice to bring some of the disorder to heel.

In the end, Rees was elected by a wide but not unanimous margin. Cheers and applause filled the room. As this was happening a contingent of Legionnaires from the Second made their way into the room. The appearance of the soldiers brought the room to a pause.

The senior officer who had been personally briefed by the Legion Commander went directly to Rees and saluted him. The new Voice of the Assembly and self-proclaimed ruler of Karbel returned the salute with all the gravity of the moment. "Captain, bring your men, there is much to do."

Rees and some of the others were then escorted from the chamber by the soldiers. They had much to do to gain control of the kingdom but the process had begun.

Chapter Seventeen
A Vision of Evil

The Deep South

Mryl Twinsteel shook his head to clear it before looking at the scene below him again. He was trying to convince himself it was in fact real, not some trick of hunger, fatigue or sickness of the head. He hadn't eaten much lately but he wasn't without food; yes, he was tired but he had been tired before. And as to the last, Mryl was almost wishing that what he was seeing wasn't real.

Like several of the others with him, they were laying on their stomachs peering through a screen of brush that covered the top of the hill, much like the thick shock of hair on a man looking at the plains that ran out away from the high, steep prominence. He turned his head to look at the men on either side of him for confirmation and they slowly returned his look of astonishment with looks of their own. The entire group present on the hilltop was made up of long time veterans but none of them had seen anything like this. No one in the north had in almost two thousand years.

The reason for their disbelief was the sight of what filled the valley below. An army was moving through the wide opening between the mountain ranges. Its size was nearly beyond description or even belief, vast blocks of cavalry rode the wings guarding the flanks while long winding columns of heavy infantry marched steadily along. The echoes of the drum beats used to set the pace for the infantry could be heard drifting up the hill on the wind. The rhythm of the marching soldiers could be felt in the ground the men were laying on.

The numbers of troops below the watchers on the hill continued to shock and amaze them. How could this be? Who could amass an army of this size and who was leading it? Where was it going and why? All these questions and more went through the minds of the hidden soldiers as they continued to take in the scene.

Mryl carefully looked over the area and estimated the valley was two miles wide and the army below him nearly filled it side to side! The leading edge of the army was no longer in sight while the tail end was yet to be seen. *Shades above, what have we gotten into?*

This particular patrol that he commanded had ridden deeper into the south than any other had ever dared. The reason for the risk, which now seemed overwhelming, was the information that they were obtaining on the enemy strength. An enemy that no one in the north even knew existed and now it was on the march, north.

An army this size meant nothing good for the Guard and especially Karbel. The Black Guard was a semi-independent unit that were responsible for protection of the southwest frontier of the kingdom of Karbel. As part of their duties they routinely patrolled the areas south of the Wystern River that marked part of the southern boundary of the realm. This territory was not officially claimed by any of the countries or nation states that dotted the broad expanse of the surface of Dohrya. The open country south of the river was a haven for slavers, smugglers and a host of others who existed on the other side of the law. The Black Guard were the law in that part of the world as well as serving as the eyes and ears of the king with whom they had a special arrangement. The Guard officer returned his full attention to the matter at hand as the count continued.

Licking his dry lips in an attempt to speak, the Black Guard officer returned to dictating notes on what they were seeing. He started out slowly but gained momentum as he went along. After several notations the man taking the notes who was behind them and couldn't see what they were looking at, stopped writing to look for himself, the numbers being given him seemed overly large, even crazy.

After sliding forward enough to part the bushes and see the host for himself he slid back and began to write faster taking pains to get the information correct the first time. Mryl smiled at the sight of his fellow soldier's shock, the smile disappearing all too quick in light of the situation.

All of the Black Guard troopers could read, write and do basic sums, it was part of their training. No illiterate soldiers were allowed in the Guard since it was necessary to often serve as scouts, a man who couldn't count couldn't give an accurate report. Those who enlisted who could not read or do sums found it added to their already heavy training program.

The Guard officer continued on with the count being verified by two of his men, one on either side of him. He blinked hard at the implication of what he was seeing. Tens, no, what could only be at least one hundred thousand troops were passing in view of them and only he and his small group of twenty three Black Guards knew about it. That was the equivalent of at least ten full strength Legions! Karbel only had fourteen Legions plus the Black Guard.

He shook his head slightly in disbelief as he continued to softly call out unit strengths, the scribe was writing quickly completely intent on his task. He had seen enough and each stroke of the pen only added to the dismay he felt.

The late afternoon sun provided plenty of light to scout by. It also meant that anyone looking at the hill would be looking nearly right at the setting sun, and so for the moment the Guards were invisible to anyone on the valley floor. Mryl knew that it wouldn't last for long and planned to take full advantage of it. They all knew it was vital to get the information back to their superiors and warn Karbel.

During the previous two years or so scattered stories and fragments of something going on in the mystery lands well below the Wystern had filtered to them from out of the south via travelers, merchants and mercenaries. Some of these tales had found their way to Kuln, home of the Guard, and a very faint picture began to emerge.

The tales were enough that the senior Black Guard leadership had authorized a series of long range patrols to investigate once and for all what, if anything, was happening in the south. The first four patrols found nothing of note and so it was decided to discontinue the effort until the fifth patrol didn't return on time. Time passed, one day, two days, a ten-day and then finally after fourteen days a patrol returned to the fortress home of the Guard with two survivors of the fifth patrol they had found while on scouting duty.

The wounded men were immediately taken to the healers for care, each had suffered serious injuries and were feeling the effects of shock and hunger despite the tending that the patrol members had been able to provide.

The story they had to tell was worth listening to once they had the energy to speak coherently. The fifth patrol, under the command of Mryl's brother in law, Hadrick, had pushed further south than the other patrols. At first there was nothing to worry about; they found no evidence of monsters, troops or anything of note. Hadrick had decided to push south for one more day and then if they still found nothing to return. They had already gone farther south than any other Guard unit ever had before, but orders were orders so they pressed still further south.

It was after mid-day when the trouble began. The Guard patrol which numbered an even dozen ran across a series of tracks. Hadrick and the others determined that a large infantry unit with accompanying supply wagons was the likely cause. It surprised them all since it was believed that the south was relatively unpopulated and what people there were down there were not organized, at least to the point of having formed military units.

Hadrick decided that this bore further investigation, the two soldiers who had been interviewed separately reported that everyone agreed; and so they began to follow the infantry unit. They tracked the mystery unit for two days as it went further south. Finally Hadrick said that they needed to return home. They had some information that needed to be shared and the dozen men broke contact and slipped away. Or so they thought.

The day after they left the infantry unit they were ambushed by some cavalry. During the fight nearly half the Guards were killed, a large number of the enemy paid the ultimate price as well but the patrol was in deep trouble.

The deep south was usually ignored by both the Guard and Legion due to the great distance from Karbel. There were enemies aplenty much closer to home so what went on south of the Wystern was often ignored out of sheer practicality; you fight the enemy that you see not the one that is at best a rumor.

The story that the survivors told couldn't be ignored, at least Mryl had felt strongly. There were times when he hated being right, this was definitely one of those times. Mryl knew what he was seeing was more than what the all the Guard could handle even with a Legion or three backing them up. Not that he doubted the ability of the Black Guard, nearly twelve thousand strong but against this, this … juggernaut, the Guard would find itself swarmed under like a handful of stones tossed in the Wystern, mightiest of all the rivers on Dohrya. They had to get the information gathered and survive to get it home where it could do some good. The north had to be told of what was coming.

The sight below the hill was nearly beyond the ability to describe. Blocks of heavily laden infantry and well mounted cavalry continued to pass below them, vast wagon trains of supplies and partially disassembled siege equipment was noted. Herds of cattle and sheep to help feed the men of the army were being moved as well, the smell from the animals so strong it even reached them at times on the hilltop. Several times the Guards saw fair size herds of horses, remounts for the cavalry, the numbers each time almost beyond belief as the scribe continued his work in earnest making sure the numbers were written properly. The soldier taking notes felt that no one would believe what he was writing but he faithfully wrote what his commander said, trying to quell his growing sense of apprehension as the numbers kept coming.

It was not healthy to be where they were for much longer and they all knew it. Wev Bandree, the senior enlisted Black Guard among the group, oversaw the effort to get the mounts ready. Saddles were checked and tightened, equipment situated and the horses watered. It would be a hard, fast and dangerous ride they were about to undertake. Better to make every preparation that they could, given the circumstances. It also helped to keep the men focused on their duties.

Copies of the notes were being prepared by two of the others so that as many as possible would be carried by the troopers so that if only a few got through then the information could be delivered. Word had already spread to the other Guards of what was being witnessed. Each had found a reason to slide up near where Mryl was and see for himself. One look was enough, for some too much but it was necessary. The veteran soldiers knew that the odds were heavily stacked against them and getting worse. Almost to a man they felt the numbers being hurriedly written down might have been too low.

The count continued as Mryl contemplated his options. He absently brushed his hand at a small swarm of tiny insects that were hovering near his ear; the high pitched buzzing sound they produced was something he hated. The noise subsided. Satisfied that he was free of them for the moment Mryl returned his attention to the situation he and others found themselves in.

He knew that the information would only be valuable if they could report it, everything depended on that. Several relays of heliograph teams were waiting for them, hiding from the prying eyes of any enemy. These teams were linked to form a long chain angled to the northwest. The last team had several riders waiting to carry any dispatches back to Blacktower.

Mryl had gone much farther south than the mission planners had intended which took the heliograph units out of range of the fortress home of the Guard. Mryl knew the information could move faster by the signal mirror system but to get the information he wanted he knew that going south, this far south, required breaking some of the rules. He knew he was in violation of his orders but he had fought hard to get this one patrol approved so if he was only going to get one chance he wanted to make sure it was a good one. A saying from his father came back to him all at once, *careful what you wish for boy-o!*

The location that they could contact the closest team was a very long day's ride away, and that was if nothing went wrong. Mryl thought as he looked at the army below that something going wrong was almost a certainty. He made a decision that the count was finished. There were more units coming but they had to go. Copies of the information were still being prepared to make sure that at least one set made it through.

There were two choices before them: wait until dark and try to ride through the picket lines out to the west, or leave now while there was still some light. The hill the Guards were on was steep, and trying it at night could be noisy and that was dangerous.

Better to leave while they could see at least a little and one more group of men on horseback would likely be confused as simply more of the southern troops, several small troops of whom had already ridden by on the western slope of the hill.

He hoped, more fervently than he ever had for anything in his life. He waved to the others and they slid back keeping low and once free of the ground cover headed for the horses.

Time to go.

Chapter Eighteen
Long Arm of the King

Karbel

Thadar and several of his top aides, Gunnar, Spree, Dwyn and
Colonel Steele were gathered again in one of the upper rooms of the
palace; the king's anteroom was still being cleaned up from the attack
and as such was unusable at the moment. There had been meetings
throughout the day; currently the men were discussing the recent coup
attempt although for someone to refer to it as a discussion would be in
most quarters a complete waste of time.

The debate was sharp in regards to what to do next. "Round up the
lot of them and toss them in cells!" Several sharp agreements could be
heard.

"No! If that happens then the law is being thrown out!" The
conversation swirled around the room; tempers were running a bit hot.
All of those gathered were well aware of how serious the situation was.

There had been an attempted coup, coming on the heels of an attack
on the palace by a large body of assassins, which cost the lives of many
throughout the city due to the fires and riots. It was unclear if the two
events were related but with the assassins dead they weren't able to be
sure. There had even been clashes between groups of Strikers and
Legionnaires from the Second who had been attempting to enforce orders
given by the Assembly, which resulted in deaths on both sides. It took
some time for that mess to be sorted out.

Steele had gone to the headquarters of the Second Legion with a large body of Strikers to personally see the Legion Commander. It took nearly an hour of discussion, some of which got quite heated, to finally convince the general that the king was in fact still alive and in charge.

Clean up and repair work to the castle was ongoing, trying to undo the damage done by the assassins. It would take some time. The casualties among the Strikers and palace staff alone numbered in excess of one hundred and thirty while the injury numbers from the city were still being compiled. The king was still sporting several dressings covering some of his own wounds.

Thadar had been listening to the various points of view; the king was tired and still angry. That someone would try to wrest control of the kingdom, *his* kingdom from him was enough to make him beyond furious. It had been his family that had forged Karbel into what it was today and that someone else believed that they could just take that from the line of Skye was too much.

Darnel, his father had often spoken to him of not making decisions in anger, how it would frequently lead to dangerous territory. Thadar was working very hard at remembering and applying that lesson right now. If he had his way every suspect member of the Assembly would be rounded up and jailed with the keys thrown away. The king knew that wasn't the right thing to do. It would be satisfying, no doubt of that but not the right thing to do, at least yet. Doing so could set a dangerous precedent.

There was some credible information to support the belief that at least some of the Assembly members had a direct hand in the coup attempt. One of the aides to a member of the conspiracy had been caught by mere chance. He had been trying to avoid one of the mobs that had filled the streets. So caught up in the moment his small entourage blundered into a Striker patrol. For some reason his retainers had attacked the soldiers. Forced to defend themselves the seven Strikers put down the four guards and detained the man who quickly confessed in an attempt to earn some leniency.

The man had handed over what documents he was carrying regarding the coup, implicating his employer. While damning, the papers did not name the conspirators and the man himself did not know the names of any of them either except for his employer. The information he did have was enough to get the investigation rolling, and as more information was obtained the scope of the inquiry grew.

Even as the men were meeting at the palace, units of Strikers were in the city hunting for those believed to be responsible. The city gates were shut and no one allowed in or out, by royal edict. Loyal troops from the Fifth Legion, Tal's unit, were in control of the gates as well as assisting the Strikers with security in the city. If those being sought were in the city they would be found.

It was believed that some of the assassins might still be loose in the city as well; they had to have had assistance from someone. Who that someone was still was an unknown but it seemed completely logical to assume that nearly forty men didn't spontaneously decide to all try to kill the king at the same time.

Additional Striker units had been rushed in to help secure the city and to aid in the search for the conspirators with more on the way. The soldiers of the Second Legion had been disarmed and confined to their barracks while an investigation of their actions during the previous two days was conducted. Tal was handling that, which was why he was not present at the meeting at the palace.

Listening to the men around him argue the various merits of their points back and forth was wearing on the head of House Skye, "Enough!" The king ended the debate; he had heard what he needed of the varied opinions to suit him.

Those in the room looked over to where their ruler was standing. Thadar stood silently for a moment gathering his thoughts then slowly began to speak, "I have listened; now it is time for action. There is much to do and little time. Colonel Steele," the Striker commander stepped forward immediately, "What is the progress on the hunt for the traitors?"

Steele explained that they had several people in custody who were already being questioned regarding their alleged role in the coup attempt. He then told those in the room that there was suspicion regarding several of the highest ranking members of the Assembly but none of them had been arrested yet. All were being watched carefully to prevent them from being able to leave their homes. Steele had issued orders that if any of them tried to leave their homes they were to be arrested immediately to thwart any chance of them being able to flee or hide.

Spree asked his friend, "So what about those we suspect? Going to bring them in for questions?"

The others looked to the king waiting for him to decide. Thadar sighed then told them that he would agree to sign arrest warrants for several members of the Assembly but stubbornly refused to issue blanket arrest orders. He knew that there were some in governing body that were loyal to him but not as many as there once were.

The king had already been given the news that his friend Loni Weslatt had been found murdered along with his wife. Someone had broken in and killed the couple the night of the attack on the palace. So far there were no clues to who the killers had been. So for now the Assembly was without its Voice. Thadar refused to acknowledge the election of Rees to the position that Weslatt had held for nearly three years -- a long time given the snake pit of intrigue and political wrangling of the Assembly.

There was only a small pause as the king signed several of the warrants already laid out on the table then affixed his seal, making the document official. Feeling emotionally drained and very tired, Thadar gave Steele permission to have the warrants carried out.

The loyal bodyguard saluted then gathered the numerous parchments sheets, nodding to the others he left to issue orders to his men. These arrests would be handled by the Strikers. Not knowing exactly who they could trust in the army it had been decided very early on that any arrests would be taken care of by the royal bodyguards.

Thadar thanked the others, "Friends, leave me now. I need to be alone for a time." They did as they were asked; Gunnar pulled the door closed behind him as he was leaving. Thadar waited for the door to close then sat heavily in one of the chairs and let his head roll forward until it was resting on the table surface. Gods above, he was tired…

***

Less than two hours after the warrants were signed Beaujay and the Strikers with him marched directly up the wide steps leading to the front of the Rees manor. The Senior Sergeant was eagerly looking forward to this, the arrest of one of those believed to be part of the coup attempt against the king. Traitors were the worst of scum and rich traitors made this so much better. He had been injured during the fight for the castle and lost several friends in the attack. That someone would try to take advantage of that burned at the Striker's principles. Time for a bit of payback and he didn't much care for whoever had to pay the bill.

The guards at the gate had tried to prevent the Strikers from entering the grounds but a short but spirited 'discussion' had taken care of them. Several of Thadar's elite troops now controlled the entry to the grounds of the large Rees manor.

As the Strikers reached the top of the steps Beaujay could see that some of the household guards were assembling outside the front doors. Nine mercenaries with bared swords were waiting. They formed two ranks of four with their leader, a tall man with an ugly scar on one cheek, standing two paces in front of his men. The sell sword had no intention of allowing his employer to be taken. A sword was held ready in his right hand, a heavy buckler shield in the left. Seeing the intent of the guards Beaujay almost smiled, so much the better. He tightened the grip on his sword as he advanced toward the waiting men.

The fight outside had been brutal and bloody so Beaujay was in no mood to dally with some loathsome household servant. "You can't come in here! This is the house of Rees! Stop, stop at once!" The man before him was of slight build and spoke to the Striker in a manner that Beaujay found a touch annoying. Like he was addressing someone of distasteful lineage or something you would scrape off your shoe. The elite soldier smiled a bit then stepped toward the man.

Lynd Rees noticed the sound of a disturbance in the foyer and moved to investigate. He had heard the clang of swords outside and was heading for the front of the expansive manor to determine what was happening. Nearing the large entryway a strange *thud* sound could be heard. It was occurring at regular intervals, the sound grew louder with each step. Whatever it was it was coming from the foyer area.

He rounded the corner to see Jafra Loong, one of his long time servants being held aloft by a Striker and slammed backwards into the wall over and over, that was what was producing the *thud* sound.

"Release him!" Beaujay looked over to Rees and with a sneer of contempt did exactly as he was told, tossing the little man he was interrogating into the wall with all the force he could. The majordomo struck the wall heavily and slid down to lie in a heap, a low moan slipped from his lips as he slid into unconsciousness.

"What is the reason for this intrusion?"

Taking his time Beaujay reached beneath his chest armor pulling the sealed arrest warrant out. "Lynd Rees you are under arrest, the charge is Treason against the Crown." He held out the rolled parchment document that was now somewhat flattened from being beneath the armor.

Rees knew that several of the others in the coup attempt had been arrested, including his friend Orth Glan who had been caught trying to bribe his way out of the city. He had no way of determining how much the authorities knew about his involvement in the coup attempt but he thought it best to try and play it off.

He turned to two of his household staff who were near the open front door telling them to see that Loong received proper care and to get the mess outside cleaned up. The two immediately nodded their understanding and starting toward where the major domo lay.

Finished with that, Rees told the king's man in a bored voice, "Very well, let us be off then."

Beaujay was surprised to say the least, this was not the reaction he had been expecting or he realized, hoping for. He motioned for two of his men to place Rees in irons.

***

In the palace, Spree was attempting to persuade Thadar of the need to rid himself of his largest political obstacle. The two were alone in the king's anteroom which had been cleaned up enough to utilize but was going to be without a door for at least another full day despite the near frantic work of the palace carpenters. It took time to fashion a door of that size and stature.

The discussion had been going on for the better part of half an hour and as Spree had anticipated Thadar was still resistant to the idea of removing the Assembly as a body. He felt that if he did that then he ran the risk of becoming a tyrant, that there must be checks and balances in government.

He and Spree had been over this ground before on several occasions but the king was forced to admit to himself that his friend and longtime advisor did have some valid points. One of those he was expounding on at that moment, "...so you see that if there is a single point of government then it becomes less confusing for those being ruled. They have no contradictory laws and edicts to worry about so their lives are simpler."

Before the king could answer, Spree continued by asking this question, "Do you recall why the Assembly was first formed and who did it?"

This gave Thadar pause for a moment; it had been nearly twelve years since the body was organized. A search through his memory produced the answers to both questions. "Yes, it was because my father had died, and I did." Spree smiled but didn't let his friend off the hook that easy.

"Tell me please *exactly* what the reason was it was recommended that you form the Assembly, think on it." The Dwarf reached for a nearby crystal pitcher to serve himself some wine, talking this much was thirsty work. He held the pitcher up to indicate if Thadar wanted some also; the king shook his head. Spree poured himself a healthy measure in a waiting goblet. Setting the tall container aside he took up the goblet taking in a deep drink. As he did he was watching the face of the other man.

For his part Spree had been waiting for just such an opportunity. He knew that Thadar would be resistant to the idea but in light of the events it might be possible to get him to understand that it was finally time to disband the Assembly. The Dwarf was no stranger to politics and human politics were even messier than those conducted by the Dwarves. *Who could have ever believed that possible?* he mused.

His father had been a member of the Council of Elders in the Dwarven capital of Thapx for several years so Spree had witnessed firsthand the twisted deal making that took place, including the circumstances leading to the betrayal of his father. After ensuring those responsible for the disgrace brought to his family's honor had been made to pay, Spree left the Dwarf capital.

Thadar had not thought about the issues regarding what happened following the death of his father in a battle with some of the Federation Clans for some time. This discussion was dredging up some painful memories. When Darnel, his father, had been killed leading a cavalry charge against a flank of the Federation army, Thadar had only been twelve years old. He recalled seeing the wagon that bore his father's body rolling through the gate of the palace. His mother and both sisters had been with him, standing alongside him in fact but in that instant he had never felt so alone in his entire life. The weight of ruling the vast kingdom had been dropped squarely on his shoulders. It was a burden he still felt.

After thinking on the question for a bit Thadar began to answer but before he could his mother entered the room. Without telling Thadar about it Spree had sent her a message earlier asking her to come to the palace.

When she entered, the Dwarf quickly placed the wine goblet on the nearest flat surface and bowed his head in respect. Thirea Skye smiled when she witnessed the act, she had often told Spree that it was not necessary or expected that he do that. The longtime Skye friend would hear nothing of the sort. He even did it when he was a guest in Thirea's home which was often. She would often pretend to be exasperated with him but inside she always appreciated the gesture knowing that it was done with sincerity and true respect to her. She and Spree were close friends who each enjoyed the company of the other.

Thadar had been so deep in thought it took a moment to sense another person entering the room. Then when he saw that it was his mother, he immediately bowed his head as well. Thirea thanked both men as she moved to stand near the table.

Dressed in a simple but elegant dress she interlocked her fingers then stood facing both of the men. She had overheard Spree's question, pausing in the short hallway for a moment to allow her son time to think. She then posed her own question. "So what is your main concern with disbanding the Assembly?"

For his part Thadar was prepared to bring up the objections that he had raised a few moments earlier with Spree but somehow each of them felt different now, diminished and not nearly as practical. He opened his mouth to speak but then slowly closed it as the reality of what he was thinking sank in.

She pressed on, "Could it be that you don't want to change something that you put in place yourself? That if you disbanded the Assembly that you have somehow failed?" Thadar was caught off guard by the question; it caused him to stop and consider that point. His mind went back and forth for a few moments as he wrestled with the issue. The question seemed to crystallize a number of thoughts and feelings he had been trying to ignore. Spree turned to Thirea while they waited and motioned toward the wine pitcher with one hand, she politely declined. The Dwarf nodded once in response.

Could she be right? Could that be the central issue I am not willing to admit to? It wasn't a pleasant thought to grapple with, but the more he did the more the truth of it clung to him like spilled honey, sticky and hard to remove.

Thirea allowed her son some time to give the matter thought; she knew how her son's mind worked. You couldn't talk him into anything quickly; you had to let him come to it in his own time. Certainly there were times that he made decisions quickly and decisively but weighty matters sometimes took him a bit.

The issue he was trying to come around the horns on was such a matter. It was no small thing he was contemplating but she knew that doing so would be the proper thing to do in the long run. Her husband had been a serious student of the school of the long run. Both of them had tried hard to instill that in all of their children. Since the death of Darnel it had fallen to her. She still missed him terribly and suspected that would never change.

Thadar realized that his mother was right; he had been avoiding that line of thought because he hadn't wanted to face the end of the road. The Assembly had become a mistake, a misguided body filled with corrupt, self-serving men and with their attempt to elect a leader to take over the kingdom it fell to him to correct the mistake.

"Mother, you are correct. I did not wish to face that choice but I *have* no choice. I never had a choice but refused to accept that, I was wrong."

Thirea was quick to reassure her son that being wrong wasn't evil, just human. The king of Karbel came to a decision and called for a guard who hurried in. Summoning a scribe the king paced a little waiting for the clerk to attend him. Spree and Thirea passed the time in quiet conversation.

When the man arrived the king had him sit at the dining table then taking a deep breath began to dictate. "Be it known, on this day, in this place I, Thadar Skye, Ruler of Karbel, do decree that from this day forward the body formally known as the Assembly is hereby disbanded. All power and authority of the realm is returned forever to the House of Skye."

The scribe took it down without pause, comment or visible facial expression, it was his job to record not opine.

Once the man was done writing, he nodded a single time to his sovereign, who had been waiting patiently. Thadar told the long time servant that he was finished. The scribe rose from his seat stepping to the side to allow Thadar to sign and affix his seal to the now official decree. There was no hesitation as the king finished, then told the man to have copies made and distributed immediately throughout the kingdom.

The clerk bowed to his king then to Thirea, gathered the document and his work tools. Thadar watched as the man left to carry out his orders. *I am changing the times we live in,* thought the son of Skye.

Chapter Eighteen
A Fresh Start

Eastmarch

Shorin had arrived a few days early to familiarize himself with what was about to be his new command. Everything he had seen so far told him that it was going to a good experience. The officer who he was to take over from in a few days when his leave expired had been doing an excellent job. The outpost was clean, well equipped and fully staffed with well-trained Strikers.

The new posting here in the southeast region of Karbel which was typically the quietest and slowest paced of the frontiers was just what he needed after his previous tour in the north. Taking the extended leave period had helped him a great deal; not that he had been given a choice by Colonel Tarvel.

Shorin was rested and much more mentally focused than he had been in some time. It had been a rough assignment on the northwest frontier but that time was now behind him.

Making his way across the compound the young Under-Captain was heading for the mess to get himself some lunch. He was taking a break from reading past patrol reports, a trick that Colonel Tarvel had taught him. By doing this he was able to get a better sense of what had occurred in the area in the months prior to his arrival. It also allowed him to get a feel for the personnel here at the outpost.

This station was similar in many regards to hundreds of others thickly scattered throughout the extensive kingdom. It served multiple functions, barracks, supply point, message station and defensive strongpoint. The outpost garrison was a full company of two hundred plus Strikers, a portion of whom were out on patrol as usual.

From this location Shorin was also in command of seven smaller garrison posts each housing a Striker platoon of seventy. This was in many ways a large step up in his responsibility levels. He had commanded troops before but not in these numbers or over such a wide area. But doing it in the area of the kingdom that was least active was a great training and learning opportunity for him. Shorin found that he was actually very excited about the upcoming change of command that would place him in charge of Striker operations in this area of the frontier.

To make the transition easier for Shorin, Tarvel had promoted Parun to Section Sergeant, a timely and well-earned rise in rank for the half-elven Striker, and transferred him to the same command that Shorin was going to after some well-deserved leave time. This would give Shorin a veteran non-commissioned officer he knew and was comfortable with to help run things.

Tarvel was smart enough to know that it was really the sergeants that made the Strikers function. Both of the men had earned a bit of respite from the heavy duties they had been shouldering; Eastmarch was the ideal place for them to continue their duties. Several other Strikers had also been transferred to Eastmarch from Edora as part of the regular rotation that the bodyguards underwent. This allowed the men to work at a variety of posts in different areas increasing their knowledge and skills.

While he was eating his lunch of fried potatoes and sausage Shorin reflected on some of what had transpired during his leave. He had elected to return to the area he was from originally, an agricultural area well north-east of Edora. When he arrived at the land that had once been farmed by his family, Shorin had been struck by a strong sense of loss. It occurred to him that he had allowed himself to lose touch with his own roots; this was where he was from, the farm once known as Weldon Fay. The Tallon's hadn't been rich by any means but they had been well thought of in the community and the home had been a loving one.

Turning his horse into what had been the lane leading to the house, he noticed that the grass had long since reclaimed the area where the house, barns and other buildings had once stood. Only the remains of a weathered stone pillar marking one side of what been the gate told him where to turn in. The trees lining the road were much taller than he remembered, they seemed well cared for, which Shorin found curious. He had not rented the property to anyone, so who was trimming and caring for the trees?

Dismounting, he found a place in the shade to secure his mount as well as the pack horse carrying his belongings. Then, he went looking around, stretching as he went. The ride had not been arduous but he had kept both horses moving at a steady pace.

A major portion of the reason he had come home was to pay his respects to his family, something he had only done in person one other time since leaving the farm. He knew that the Legionnaires that had responded to the nomad raid on the farm had buried his family before they left, taking Shorin with them to allow him to receive proper medical attention. *Where were they buried at…oh, maybe it's over by the…what is this?*

Shorin was totally unprepared for what he saw, the patch of ground that contained his family and the others was now cordoned off from the surrounding area by a low stone wall, each grave was trimmed, well-kept and had a rough stone marker.

The soldier was at a loss to explain the situation. Who had been keeping this up? It had been nearly ten years since the death of his family. He could tell that it hadn't been all that long since someone had trimmed the grass within the stone bordered enclosure. He had no other family he knew of so who was tending the small graveyard and why?

It surprised him as well as moved him immensely. The long years of hard service protecting Karbel from some of the worst that the world had to offer had hardened him well beyond his years. He had begun to lose his sense of feeling in regards to his own emotions. Life on the frontier often meant that kindness was shoved aside for the harsh reality of existence. Out there, kindness was a luxury that few had time to allow themselves.

For someone to take the time to collect the rocks, arrange them into a wall, construct the grave markers and then to keep the cemetery area well-tended meant more to him than he thought possible. *Who would have done this?* was a question that he kept coming back to as he stood looking at the scene. He never realized how long he stayed there.

***

Time passed as he sat quietly thinking about his life growing up.

The hard daily work of farming, which was all he had ever wanted to do, until that fateful day. A group of nomadic plainsmen had surprised the family shortly after the noon meal. The men put up as much of a struggle as they could, killing several of the raiders, but numbers and better weapons put them down one by one. The plainsmen then plundered what they could find and set fire to the buildings.

For his part, Shorin was ignored by the men thinking him already dead. A deep scalp wound poured blood out of proportion to the severity of the wound, making him look much worse off than he actually was. The same blow to the head that caused his wound also knocked him unconscious. That day was the first time he had taken a life.

Rising a little stiffly from sitting for so long he respectfully bid his family farewell, bowing to each of the graves in turn then returned to the horses, which were happily munching on the long green grass at their feet. Determined to find out who had been responsible for the great kindness he quickly untied then mounted the horse. Securing the long reins of the pack horse he rode back down the lane toward the road.

He was eager to get some answers for what he had found. Someone had been putting in their own time and effort to show his family respect and he wanted very much to tell them how much it meant to him. Once at the road he stopped his horses while he looked around. Nothing of note to the west but there, a little ways down the road to the east, a small cottage sat back from the road. That was as good a place as any to start his search. He headed in that direction at a steady pace, no reason to gallop. The day was warm and Shorin was relaxed, more so than he had been in some time.

***

His approach to the cottage had not gone unnoticed. A man, somewhat stooped by years of labor, came out of the small house. A woman whom Shorin assumed was his wife stood in the open doorway watching the rider as he came closer.

"Hail!" The traditional greeting was delivered a little slowly and with a touch of suspicion present in the old man's voice. Shorin raised his hand, open palm outward to signify his peaceful intent before swinging down from his saddle.

"Good day. I'd like to speak to you if I may."

The man turned sharing a look with his wife. This was somewhat unusual. Often when someone came by it was to deliver orders regarding work. To have someone stop by and ask to speak to them was almost unheard of.

The woman silently urged her man to speak. "Y-yes sir you can speak ta'us."

Shorin nodded his thanks, "I'm trying to gain some information about the people who used to live across the road." He turned as he pointed back toward where his family home once had stood.

The man looked confused for a moment then spoke, "Sir no one lived there in years. The family were killed. By nomads, good sir."

"Not all of them, I was there that day also. It was my family." At hearing that the man stood upright, the stoop of earlier suddenly gone. The woman nearly bounded out of the doorway, rushing up to stand with her husband.

"Could we be knowing your name good sir?" Her voice a bit shaky as the question came out.

The Striker realized he had failed to introduce himself. "I apologize friends, I'm Shorin Tallon." He deliberately left out the part about being a Striker, that wasn't important right now and since he was not wearing his uniform it was easier that way.

He had already picked up on the unease his presence had created with the couple. Shorin had seen it so often throughout Karbel it hardly registered anymore, the lack of respect that was shown to those considered peasants. Thadar didn't allow slavery in Karbel but in many locations peasants were virtually the same thing. Overworked, underpaid and forced to scrabble for a meager existence at best.

No sooner had the word 'Tallon' left his mouth than a toothy grin split the man's face. Shorin noted the lack of several teeth in the visage but the sincerity of it was hard to miss. The man rushed over to him, nearly knocking him down in his excitement. Even the woman was smiling and joyous.

"Young master Shorin! Good it be to see ya sir!" At hearing that appellation Shorin drew back in surprise. That was a term he had not heard in many years but it opened up a whole new area of memories and feelings for him, many of these had long lain dormant.

Young master Shorin was a term that one of his father's good friends had often called him. It was both a jest and an expression of respect as the Tallon's had been somewhat better off than the man and his family. *What was the name of the man who used to call me that...I know this, I know this – Hyl !*

"Hyl, Hyl Payson!" The smile on the man's face grew even wider at hearing that the son of his friend recalled him. Shorin wrapped the man up in a hug which he had not been expecting. The years of wielding a sword in combat had given Shorin a healthy measure of strength, one that Hyl was impressed with. The Striker lowered the man to the ground, both of them laughing happily at the reunion.

The wife invited him inside; Shorin took a moment to secure his horses before following the pair inside. A modest set of well-worn furniture was visible but Shorin paid it no mind. The Payson's were a little embarrassed at having company but their guest made himself right at home.

Now situated in the dining area, which was well lit by two windows, the three began to talk. Relaxing around the battered but clean dining table Shorin posed the question uppermost in his mind: did either of them know who had been keeping his family's graves cared for?

Hyl looked over at his wife across the table and sheepishly admitted that they had been the ones keeping up the graves. Shorin was deeply moved, so much so he had to close his eyes for fear of weeping. Hyl was worried that he had upset Shorin and began to apologize but a stop gesture interrupted him.

The Striker reached over the table to clasp each of them by the arm to better convey his feelings, "I have not the words to say thank you."

Hyl and his wife shared a look. They had simply been doing what friends did; Shorin's parents had been kind and generous people. Twice they had helped Hyl and Leigh survive through tough times and would never accept payment for it, telling their friends they did it because it was the right thing to do. The Payson's never forgot that kindness. Pulling himself together a bit, Shorin patted the man's arm.

Hyl was anxious to ask so many questions of his friend's son. The next few hours were spent telling stories and catching up on what had happened in the intervening years. One important fact that Tallon had been unaware of was that Hyl had believed him to have died from his wound. Word had come back to those in the area that the boy who had been taken by the Legionnaires had not survived. Shorin explained to them that he had been taken for medical care and that after he was well enough to travel he lied about his age and joined the Legion having no family to return to.

The time slipped past until it was late evening. Shorin joined them for dinner and after agreeing to stay with the couple at their insistence Shorin slept well that night. Better than he had in some time, in fact he slept a full hour past dawn which was rare for him.

During the day he helped Hyl with chores, something the older man told him several times was unnecessary but Shorin would hear none of it. The men fixed several fences as well as forked loose hay into the barn loft for storage. Hyl was grateful for the help; it would have taken him two full days to get done all that was accomplished that morning.

That afternoon Shorin turned his attention to the wood that needed to be chopped so it could be stacked and cured prior to use as firewood for the winter season. Hefting the axe he had just finishing sharpening Shorin thought for a moment about how different it was to be using the item as a tool and not a weapon.

There was a very satisfying feeling associated with splitting wood, he thought, as he steadied another wood round atop the stump Hyl used as a splitting block. One heavy swing with the axe sheared the forearm length of wood cleanly into two pieces, each of which went flying into their respective piles a few feet or so away. Shorin didn't realize he was grinning as he reached over for another unsplit length to continue the work.

Hyl was watching him from over near the house, Shorin had been steadily reducing the large pile of wood into split pieces for several hours almost without a break but somehow seemed relaxed and comfortable so he didn't bother him, besides he had other chores to do. A fact his wife would remind him of quickly if he didn't get back to his own work.

Leigh Payson insisted that he join them for dinner again. Shorin didn't want to impose himself any further than he had. The Striker almost felt guilty for taking up their time. For their part the Payson's were both very grateful to him for all the help. The repair work on the fence was a major improvement to anything that they could have done by themselves. And to get all the hay moved to the loft was a huge blessing to say nothing of the whole forest worth of now split firewood that Shorin had produced.

With some reluctance Shorin agreed to stay for dinner but only if they agreed to go with him into town the next day so that they could go to the market. Both of them agreed, the amount of work that had been accomplished since Shorin had been helping was enough that they could afford to take a rare day off from their labors.

The trip to town the next day was pleasant; the Payson's driving their small two wheel wagon with their friend riding alongside on his own horse. Once they arrived Shorin recalled much of the layout of the village. Hyl introduced him to several folks there that remembered him and his parents.

Arriving at the market place the trio spent two leisurely hours shopping for needed items. Shorin was very insistent that he be allowed to purchase some food to contribute to the Payson household to replace what he had eaten. He bought far more than what he was likely to eat if he stayed a full ten-day. Hyl couldn't talk him out of it no matter the tack he tried. Shorin had seen the state of their food stores and knew that this additional food would be needed. He also made several other purchases which he arranged to have delivered to his friends in a few days, a delivery schedule that would give him time to be well on his way south.

Shorin had no wish to embarrass his hosts but their life was one of struggle and sacrifice, he wanted to help them out in a way that would show some of the gratitude he felt toward them. The proprietors he made his purchases from assured him that the goods would be delivered as promised.

In the end Shorin stayed with his friends for almost five days helping out around their small farm. The sixth morning he joined them for an early meal telling them the previous evening that he had a long way to travel that day and wished to get an early start. He was speaking the truth but his journey southward would only be after he took care of some business in the nearby town. This was a decision he had come to a few days earlier and after mulling it over in his mind settled on it as a course of action.

The most interesting aspect of the morning however was when he first entered the dining area from his room. He was wearing his uniform since he planned to stop in town to conduct some business. Both Hyl and Leigh were almost shocked to see the military uniform on their guest. The black short sleeve tunic trimmed in silver resting over a chain mail shirt whose sleeves ended just above the elbow. The armor was black as well; once the mail was built it was dipped in oil and then baked to darken it. High dark boots into the tops of which dark trousers were fitted. Greaves protected both his shins. A broad sword belt of fine worked leather, along the top and bottom an evenly spaced row of silver rivets that circled the wearer. Armored wrist guards with filigreed silver designs were on both arms. He had foresworn wearing the customary breast and back plate armor since he was planning on traveling hard once he left Halaf, the nearby town.

During the previous days when the topic of what he had been doing in life had come up Shorin had been very non-specific, simply telling his friends that he was in 'government work'. The Strikers were often not seen in person by the vast majority of the population of Karbel on a day-to-day basis. This was due in part to the enormous size of the kingdom; another factor was that the elite soldiers were usually garrisoned in outposts near the frontiers. Certainly in the six large cities of the realm it was different; each of them had large Striker detachments stationed there. But in the interior rural areas some people had never seen a Striker up close.

This in turn led to the Strikers having a reputation that wasn't necessarily all positive. They were not regular army; they were not civil constabulary so there was sometimes a fear factor associated with those that served the king. Shorin had seen this reaction a number of times and worked to quell any fears or misgivings he had created.

While they ate the morning meal he explained to them that he had joined the Legion and from there had been accepted into the Strikers. Shorin failed to mention his rank; there was no need to tell them.

The Paysons were a little more relaxed after their guest talked to them. It was still a big surprise and a topic of much conversation between the spouses after Shorin departed. With a promise to visit again at some point, followed by sincere hugs and handshakes, Shorin left his friends and headed his mount and pack horse toward Halaf.

During their trip into town a few days earlier Shorin had determined that there was a land assay office, it would figure prominently into his plans. A brisk but enjoyable ride brought him to the assay office. He met with the head clerk and explained what he wanted done. After listening carefully the man located the appropriate file which held a copy of the land grant given to the Tallon's when they first took up residency at Weldon Fay.

The gift of the land was for years of service that his grandsire had provided to a member of the local nobility. In total the Tallon homestead was only twenty acres but it was prime farmland with its own spring and a running stream that provided year round water. The land had sat empty since the death of his parents. Shorin was informed that several people had inquired over the years about purchasing the land but since no one was certain if there was a living relative no sale was possible.

Shorin had the appropriate paperwork drawn up, paid the necessary fees, left a sealed letter along with a small heavy bag with the clerk and then inquired where the office of the magistrate was located. He was given directions and was then informed that the paperwork would be ready within an hour. Thanking the man for his work he bid him good day before heading off to find the magistrate.

The office was precisely where the helpful assay clerk said it would be. Shorin secured both his horses then stretched a bit before heading inside. He was immediately underwhelmed at what he saw; the room was ill kept, dingy and smelled musty. A figure was seated behind the desk so he moved in that direction.

"Hail, I have business that requires your attention."

The man who Shorin could now see was about forty or so, hadn't shaved in at least several days, but hadn't missed a meal in quite some time. The man hardly looked up at being spoken to.

"So what's all this about? I've no time for someone coming in my office ordering me 'round. Who do you think you are?"

Shorin was quite sure he knew the type of creature he was dealing with: a long time civil servant in an unimportant area of the kingdom who was quite full of himself and his minor position. So be it. He reached into a small pocket in his tunic and withdrew the small but weighty item within. Closing his hand around it he reached across the desk top to rest his hand on the center of the dirty ledger and dropped the contents of his hand there. Shorin withdrew his hand back across the desk and waited for the inevitable response.

The man leaned back at first as the man's hand neared him but quickly recovered when the hand stopped before reaching him. A glance upwards at the stranger who had entered his office then down at whatever it was that he had lain on the duty ledger. An idle scratch to the back of his head and the greasy hair present before reaching down to pick up the item. Hmmm, heavy thing it is, holding it up to better see what it was he gasped as the realization of what it represented hit him.

The small circle of metal, a little bit less than the width of his palm, was colorfully emblazoned with the full ornamental Striker seal. A shield shaped device divided into four quarters, the lower left was a solid field of black, the upper right filled in silver while the upper left sported a large death head skull underneath a crown and the final field contained a pair of crossed sabers. It was the official badge of His Majesty's Strikers and could only be carried by a member of the royal family or one of the Strikers. It was a prison term for any else to be caught with one.

Leaning half over the desk, which creaked theatrically under his weight, the Striker Under-Captain inquired, "Are you going to see to the King's business or does he need to find someone else who will?" The tone was light, almost bantering.

The magistrate belatedly realized he had far overstepped his limit with the tall, well-built soldier. The man nearly tripped as he tried to leap to his feet. "Sir, I, uh, didn't know. Dunkin Majus at the king's service sir." He held out the medallion to Shorin who slipped it back into his tunic.

Shorin explained to the pompous ass that he was to go to the assay office and wait there until the paperwork being prepared was ready no matter how long it took. Once it was completed he would *personally* take that paperwork, a sealed letter and the small bag already waiting there to the Payson farm east of town. Once delivered he would explain to them the meaning of the paperwork since it was highly likely that neither Hyl nor Leigh could read.

Majus nodded nervously as he listened to the instructions. He had grown sloppy and lazy about his duties over the years since there was little actual work to do.

Shorin then informed him, "I will personally be checking to see that this is done, magistrate, and if it isn't..." The implied message was quite clear; if it wasn't done then the magistrate would be looking for other work. Several quick bobs of the head confirmed that Dunkin understood the gravity of the situation.

Rising back up to an upright position Shorin thanked the man and told him that was all, he could go. The portly magistrate grabbed his coat and without so much as a word flew out the door. Shorin smiled as he saw the man forgo his comfortable wagon tied up outside to travel to the assay office. He dashed across the street as if hounds were nipping on his heels. Several of the town residents saw this as well causing a number of comments and smiles to be exchanged.

Dunkin was not the most popular man in Halaf by anybody's reckoning. Shorin then continued his journey south.

***

After arriving at his destination, the Striker found the meal hall for lunch. He found himself thinking about how his friends must have reacted to getting the papers and the small bag. The letter thanked them for their loyalty to his family, their hospitality during his visit and wished them well. The paperwork from the assay office transferred ownership of the Tallon land to Hyl and his family. Since it was owned free and clear they could maintain ownership of it no matter what. Shorin had also paid for the next two year's worth of taxes on the land as well as the back taxes which didn't amount to much at all but he wanted the Payson's to have no issues with it.

The last item was ten gold coines, often referred to as crowns. A reference to the design of a kingly crown that was present on each of the government issued coines. It was enough money to keep the couple going for some time. The deliveries of the purchased goods from vendors in town would further help them. These were new tools as well as a sow, calf and a draft horse.

Hyl and his wife were overwhelmed at the generosity of the gifts, especially the land. This meant that they were now property owners in their own right. No more having to work for someone else to try and eke out a meager living. The money, new tools and animals meant a whole new life for the couple who hardly slept that first night due to the excitement. Word quickly spread around town about the gifts and the good fortune of the Payson's who were by and large well thought of in Halaf.

Feeling better about the entire exchange with the Payson family the young Under-Captain returned his attention to his now nearly completed meal. He still felt badly about abusing his authority with the magistrate but justified to himself with the thought that if the man had been doing his job as his should it wouldn't have been necessary. A few bites remained which he quickly took in.

Finished with his lunch Shorin rose then deposited his plate and cutlery in the basket near the scullery and headed back to the office he was using until he took over. There were more reports to review, later that day he was scheduled to assist in a barracks inspection.

It was a very good day indeed.

Chapter Nineteen
Hazards of the Road

The Northern Plains

The Striker patrol was riding steadily through the long grass of the open plains, the lush green rising to knee high on their mounts. The nine riders were in no hurry, but being watchful at all times. It was near mid-day and the men had been riding since dawn. Since rising that morning they had encountered no one else save for a few rabbits which quickly scurried off, and with the exception of some hawks flying lazily high above them the men were alone.

This was the third day of their usual patrol with little to show for all the miles they had ridden since leaving their fortified outpost now some distance behind them. Their mission was simple, search for any signs of Federation troops, smugglers, slavers or any other trouble that could cause problems for the kingdom. It was unlikely that this far north there would be much to disturb the realm. This area was sparsely populated save for a few widely scattered farms whose residents stayed close to home.

Mehan Finn was riding alongside his friend T'shar. Three other pair of Strikers were riding two by two behind them while the remaining Strikers were some distance ahead scouting. The often jovial Finn was regaling his companions with yet another tale of his drinking exploits as they rode.

"So there we were trapped in the storeroom of the place, barrels and barrels full of fine wine and spirits – not to say that the selection was grand but they did offer some excellent choices especially a delightful red wine from…" Mehan continued on without a pause.

T'shar didn't say anything in response but he usually didn't. A large man, several inches over six feet in height and well built, he was the patrol leader. He had been a Striker for several years after a stint in the Legion. T'shar and Finn were often paired by choice, the two men worked well together.

They had met while serving in the Legion, Finn had used army service to escape a life of dry academic study. His father was a teacher at the university in Rhywe specializing in languages and felt that his son should be well versed in as many tongues as possible. As the child of a full staff member Mehan could attend the school for free and so his father made sure he did. The education paid off in some regards; Finn could speak several languages and could read nearly twice as many as he could speak. Three years of study was more than Finn could stomach so he left school, joined the Legion out of spite against his father who had planned for his son to become a teacher as he had. Mehan wanted no part of that life for himself.

The harsh reality of military life wasn't what the former student had imagined it to be but over time he improved and came to love the order and structure of the army. He fought in several actions against smugglers and goblins. It had been T'shar that helped him through the first year following basic training.

Mehan had been assigned to the same infantry Fist as T'shar. The big man took the bookish lad under his wing and his own gruff, silent way taught him how to be a soldier. Over time the two became good friends despite the enormous differences in their personalities.

Finn was as outgoing as they came, always with a joke, story or poem ready to recite; he was the center of attention no matter the setting. His dashing looks and quick smile guaranteed he never lacked for female companionship. By comparison the burly T'shar was quiet, almost broody. He would usually say only what he needed to and nothing more. He had been in the Legion for two years when Finn showed up in his life. Some speculated because the two were so opposite it was part of the reason why they were such good friends.

Finn was a lover of wine, all types and varieties; he loved to sample examples from as many different locations as possible. He could speak extensively on the art of wine making having made it a minor course of study at the university. Or rather at the many taverns he frequented which were located near the university.

T'shar had a different passion in life, he was a weapons master. He would practice for hours upon hours with a wide variety of weapons, swords, knives, axes, spears and more as often as he could. His skill was such that he was widely regarded as the finest swordsman in the Strikers, no small accomplishment given the talent throughout the ranks of those that guarded the king.

Finn was no slouch with the blade, thanks in part to the work that T'shar had done with him but his friend was in a class alone. Even the long bow, one of the most difficult weapons for anyone to master, was no problem for T'shar. The Legion didn't use the long bow but the Strikers did. Even when he was on patrol the veteran soldier found time for sword practice as he had the night before with several of the others.

The patrol continued on their way for almost another hour when one of the scouts appeared coming around the base of the low hill toward their front heading back toward them at a fast clip. T'shar ordered the others to increase their pace; horses were urged into a trot. No reason yet to bring them to a gallop that could expend energy that might be needed later.

Weapons were checked as the Strikers rode. The six men behind their leader also spread out so that when they met the scout rider the eight men were lined abreast.

In short order the two sides came together and the lone rider filling the others in on his discovery. "Smoke ahead, coming from the other side of those low hills. He's keeping an eye on it." The scout, Ian Hol, gestured over his shoulder in the general direction that he had just come from.

T'shar paused for just a moment, smoke meant fire and that could only come from something burning. There were no farms or settlements in this area; he knew that from experience having patrolled this area for some time. A quick nod of the head to show he had made a decision. "Take us there."

The scout spun his mount about and headed back in the original direction of travel. The others following close behind were all moving at a gallop. The well cared for mounts ate up the distance and in short order the men were at the base of one of the hills. Smoke was clearly visible from the other side.

The view offered from the low hill that the Strikers were now hidden atop told the experienced soldiers a great deal. A small collection of wagons were under attack, one of the wagons burning briskly which was what was generating the smoke. A thick circle of riders were globing the hastily drawn up wagon fort. Arrows flew in toward those gathered amid the wagons. A few arrows came back out from the inner circle; Mehan saw one of the circling riders catch an arrow which spilled him from his saddle. He landed heavily in the grass and didn't rise. Getting in a count he put the number of attackers in excess of thirty, hefty odds even for the Strikers. That they were going to help wasn't even an issue; there were people in need of aid and besides, ride away from a good fight? Not likely!

An added bonus was that Mehan recognized the coloring of some of the uniforms the riders wore -- marking them as members of one of Federation Clans, long sworn enemies of Karbel. Which Clan it was didn't matter, wolf, bear, hawk, dog, cat, chicken one of those stupid animal names they favored.

Mehan glanced over at T'shar who was studying the problem intently. A nod with the hint of a smile from his friend made Finn call quietly to the others to withdraw and return to the horses. Time to put their plan into action.

***

Inside the wagon fort Levas was working to control the bleeding from the wound in the thigh of the High Priest. The arrow was resting in the meaty part of the outer thigh, the bleeding had slowed considerably but Vode was still feeling light headed from the loss of blood. It was affecting his concentration enough that he wasn't able to form the complex spells necessary to help defend their makeshift camp.

Around him the efforts of those who could continued, as Vode watched one of his priests worked up a medium size Wind Sphere, this one about the size of a late season pumpkin. With no thought to his own safety the priest stood then with careful aim hurled the compact tightly wound orb of rushing air. It unerringly flew the distance between the wagons and circling riders so quickly the clansmen had no chance to avoid it. When it hit the super swirling air burst apart knocking three riders asunder so violently it killed two of the horses and all three of the riders.

The priest who had conjured the spell was so involved in watching his work he failed to duck down behind cover on releasing the incantation. An arrow found his throat felling him, then dying noisily a few moments later as the blood filled his airway. Vode lowered his head and tried not to weep. He had known the priest since he had been a second year student.

The surviving Thunderguards were doing their best to protect their charges. The attack by the unknown riders had come swiftly and with great cost to the proud guardsmen. Hurriedly drawing the wagons up into a small circle they had pulled in all their outriders setting up a hasty perimeter and were now dueling with their circling foes but their supply of arrows would run out at some point.

One of the royal guards loosed his arrow which took down another of the raiders. He hurriedly ducked his head correctly guessing that those on the outside would be eager to return his offering. Two arrows *plunked* into the wood of the wagon near his head. Grinning at Levas he nocked another arrow and popped back up to find another recipient. The senior acolyte was surprised at how humorous he found the exchange; the solider was almost enjoying himself.

The senior Thunderguard was watching the situation with a critical eye, she could tell that those encircling them were nearly ready to rush the wagons and deal with the defenders up close when one of her men shouted to her. She rushed over to where he was pointing. Several of the riders had suddenly and without apparent reason gone down. This caused those surrounding the northmen to become disorganized.

As she watched several more riders went down and failed to rise. Glancing around her the veteran soldier realized that it was nothing that either her men or the priests had done. Someone else was out there. Friend or foe didn't matter, they were killing the raiders -- so for now, friend. What else they might be would be figured out later, one crisis at a time.

The Federation riders also quickly understood that someone else had joined the fray and identified where the arrows were coming from that kept felling their brothers. A quick horn call changed their direction of travel and they all rode toward the low hill on which the Strikers waited. In doing so they exposed their backs to the Thunderguard archers who quickly took advantage of the situation, launching nearly a dozen shafts at the departing riders. Nearly half of the projectiles found purchase in flesh dropping the receivers from their mounts.

Another volley of arrows rained down on the Clansmen from the front emptying several more saddles, one of the riders catching the projectile in the chest which spilled him backwards off his saddle, he landed hard then tried to rise but couldn't. The balance of numbers was rapidly slipping away from attackers.

Two priests hurled spells at their tormentors, one of which caused further casualties. Levas took a moment to chide one of the two priests for his less than scholarly outburst after failing to fell a pair of attackers. The priest nodded in response to the chastisement but failed in his attempt to appear contrite.

T'shar had been carefully watching the Clan riders anticipating that they would do exactly what they did, break their formation then ride toward the Strikers atop the low hill in an attempt to overrun them with superior numbers. Having recognized the horsemen as belonging to one of smaller, less powerful Clans, T'shar knew them to be inferior warriors even compared to some of the other Federation members. He almost felt sorry for them at what was about to happen to them. Almost.

Grinning ever so slightly he barked out the order to mount. The other Strikers each let fly with an additional arrow in the direction of the oncoming gaggle of Clansmen then sprinted to their nearby waiting mounts. The ten troopers of Karbel were about to mix it up with the men of the Federation up close and personal.

Seeing an opportunity, the Thunderguard commander shouted orders at her men. The remaining soldiers hurried to comply, they were eager to ride out and meet their attackers to repay their hospitality. Several of the priests seeing what the soldiers were doing hurriedly began working at pushing one of the wagons forward to create an opening for the mounted men.

Within moments a cluster of the soldiers were ready to ride out. With a hearty cheer the Thunderguards galloped out of the enclosure chasing after the Clansmen who were now nearly to where the Strikers had been. Vode watched intently, trying to rise which caused Levas to forcefully urge him to remain where he was. The senior priest was in pain which kept him from standing and so with disgust and frustration plopped back to a sitting position.

After returning to the saddle, the two Sets, the smallest of the organization formations the elite Strikers used, lined up stirrup to stirrup to present the broadest front to the oncoming enemy horsemen. T'shar was carefully judging the distance until it was just about...now!

He swept his sword forward pointing at the approaching threat which was just arriving at the base of the hill, which alone would slow their mounts. As he did, the men of Karbel spurred their mounts and swept down the hill.

Having the additional momentum of riding down the slope added impetus to the weight of the Striker charge. The two groups of riders met head on, swords rang on sword as the two sides battled. The better trained, armored and heavier armed Strikers made quick work of several of the Federation troops.

Those of the Panther Clan still enjoyed numerical superiority but it was a thin margin and shrinking rapidly. The Striker charge carried them deep into the mob and a brutal melee ensued. Shouts, screams and curses filled the air along with the ringing of steel as sword found shield or the opposing sword.

With the Strikers now more or less in the middle of the Panther brothers, all attention was focused on them proving deadly for the Federation troops. The Thunderguards struck full weight from the rear of the melee catching a measure of the Panthers in a deadly vise. Both their opponents were heavily armored while the clan riders were clad only in boiled leather armor which failed to protect the wearer from determined attack.

The battle was not going well for the Clan members at all. Originally they held both the element of surprise and numerical superiority in their favor but both of those factors had now eluded them. One of the Thunderguards removed the head of his opponent with a hearty cut then urged his horse forward to help another of his kind.

Seeing the dilemma they faced, one of the Panthers wildly gestured to the others to escape. Several of them immediately spun their mounts toward a point that wasn't occupied by one of their attackers and spurred vigorously. One of them nearly made it but a sword swinging in from the side caught him in the side and laid him open like a melon exposing his ribs. Clutching the wound he fell from the saddle to collapse in the grass.

The small group of Federation riders who were still alive were riding for their lives as they tried to flee. T'shar let them go; he didn't want his men riding blindly in pursuit of the Clansmen. The men of Karbel had extracted a serious toll on the Federation riders and there was the still the matter of the caravan to deal with.

Seeing their attackers flee, the soldiers of Vankard edged back from where the Strikers were. There was still the matter of determining if they were friend or foe. Without speaking, the senior of them signaled to the others to return to the wagons. They did so without question, keeping a wary eye on the black and silver garbed men who had assisted them.

Mehan noted this, "Well there's a fine good morning and thank you." Those that heard the comment all laughed, several of the Strikers had dismounted to check that all the Clansmen that had fallen were indeed dead, those showing any signs of life were quickly dispatched. Another way to demonstrate Karbel's power and terror -- *mix it up with us and this is what will happen.*

T'shar too was watching the departure of the unknown soldiers. He had paid as much attention to them as he could during the fight. What he saw, he liked. The men fought bravely and seemed to be both confident and comfortable with their weapons. Their armor and equipment was of similar make and design, clearly they belonged to a larger body that was formally organized. The mounts were well cared for and strong. He didn't recognize them or any of the markings emblazoned on the shields, the most common of which of was a pair of inward facing stylized lightning bolts with a large war hammer upright between them.

He checked that all the cleanup of the wounded Clansmen was done then ordered his men to remount, which was done swiftly. Time to find out who these people were and what they were doing.

The small group of Strikers slowly rode forward until they were about thirty paces from the wagons. T'shar told them to make sure that the riders made no threatening gestures. He and Mehan urged their tired mounts onward. Levas and the leader of the Thunderguards walked out from the wagon circle to meet the strangers who had saved them.

Raising his open hand slowly as a gesture of peace and then pointing to himself, Mehan said, "Striker, Mehan Finn."

Levas was watching the other man as he spoke, Striker could be his rank or maybe his unit, Mehan Finn had to be his name. Laying his hand on his own chest, "Priest, Levas Hoosen."

Mehan nodded his understanding and gestured at his friend, "Striker, T'shar."

Levas then did the same with the woman who was the commander of the Thunderguards detachment, "Thunderguard, Allence Kellz."

Both of the Strikers were able to grasp that, now at least they had some idea of who they were talking to, or trying to talk to.

"We need help, many are injured. Is there a settlement near here?" The question coming from the senior acolyte.

Mehan thought he recognized some of the words. Finn spoke again trying to invoke a response so he could hear the stranger speak. "Where are you from?" A long buried fragment of knowledge was trying to burrow its way out and he needed to help it.

Levas didn't understand the soldiers but Vode had ordered him to speak to them so he continued to try, he repeated his statement. "We need help, many are injured. Is there a settlement near here?"

The words were completely foreign to T'shar but Mehan was listening intently. He realized he recognized some of the words or at least thought he did now if he could only remember from where. He gave the priest an impatient roll of the hand as if to say, 'more, give me more'.

For her part Allence was watching the strangers carefully. The northmen were far from home with many dead and wounded. The soldiers had helped them but it didn't mean she trusted them. Knowing that if they didn't get some help several more of the group would likely die, she commanded her nerves to remain calm and to help focus her thinking.

She had yet to say anything to the men opposite them but her keen eye picked out several details, all of the men were well armed and wore identical uniforms so they were likely members of an organized military unit. The big man to her left was the leader of the group, he had the look of one used to giving commands and being obeyed. The man speaking with Levas was making some progress with the language but it was taking too long.

Speaking for the first time the woman spoke directly at the man she had pegged as the patrol leader. "You," pointing at T'shar, "We need help, there are many wounded."

She mimicked the motion of someone being hit with an arrow

followed by the movement of a person being sliced with a sword. Knowing she had his attention she held up five fingers on one hand and then flashed four more fingers to indicate the number of wounded.

T'shar still didn't comprehend the spoken language but he clearly understood the gestures that the woman was making. Turning to Mehan, he told him to continue to speak to the other man. Spinning his mount toward the other Strikers he whistled and waved them to him before returning to face the woman.

T'shar ordered two of them to track the departed clan riders and to send word if any others were seen. Just as they were about to depart he told them that he intended to try and get the survivors back to the outpost. The rider pair, a set of twins, Sandor and Ian Hol, nodded once then rode away angling a few points west of north to carry out their orders.

The senior Striker then pointed at the wagons indicating that she should return there. He swung down from his saddle taking the reins in hand walking toward where the travelers were.

Allence nodded and told Levas to keep at it. T'shar knew that the clansmen would return in greater numbers at some point, he had to get these people away from here. The closest place to take them was the Striker outpost which was at least a full day's ride away but it was the best choice they had.

Levas and Mehan were continuing their exchange as each worked at better understanding the other. T'shar and the others were approaching the wagon circle, which was abuzz with activity. Several of what the Striker presumed were other priests of some sort and two of the soldiers, Thunderguards, were working at separating the burning wagon from the others to keep the flames from spreading. They were having some success.

Levas motioned for Mehan to dismount and follow him. He tossed his reins to one of the nearby Strikers who caught them. Finn told the rest of the men to stay put but keep their eyes open. Levas was listening intently to the man trying to gain as much insight into his speech as possible but it was proving more difficult that he hoped. He indicated that he wanted Mehan to come into the wagon circle by waving his hand in a 'come here, come here' motion.

The area inside the wagon circle was busy, wounded men were

being treated, several obviously dead bodies were being reverently moved and placed together, other people were hurrying about retrieving requested supplies. Mehan took it all in but was still wary.

Levas walked directly over to where a man was sitting, leaning up against a pile of assorted saddle bags. He was watching Levas and his companion intently but not to the point of staring. Mehan quickly determined that this was where his host was taking him.

The man was dressed in rich robes of a dark grey, a tightly wound compress was visible around the meaty part of the right thigh with a stain of blood that had bled through visible. One of what Finn assumed was another priest was tending to the man.

The wounded man appeared to be of middle age, with a close cropped head of dark hair sprinkled through with small splashes of grey. His eyes were keen.

Arriving at his destination Levas bowed once to his senior then turned to introduce the visitor. "Striker, Meehaan Finn, this is High Priest Vode Anners of Vankard."

The elite soldier noticed the slight mispronunciation of his name but paid it no mind. He did catch the name Vankard. That was a human realm well to the west, little was known about it. That was about all he knew of the place. Manners dictated his next action; he placed one hand over his heart and bowed a medium depth bow out of respect. Being polite cost him nothing but could gain them plenty.

Vode noted the sincerity of the gesture and thanked his visitor. Striker, was that a rank or organization name? The senior priest wasn't sure but that was for another time. He observed that Mehan was looking around and seemed to be poised to ask a question, he encouraged it with a look of understanding.

"How many in your group?" To further expound on the question the Striker pointed at Levas and held up one finger, pointed at Vode then raised another finger and then at the attendant treating Vode's wound raising a third finger. Mehan then pointed at the wagon area making a circle gesture ending a highly exaggerated shoulder shrug to emphasize the point of not knowing.

Despite his wound Vode hadn't lost his reasoning ability and surmised what the man was asking. He wasn't sure that providing the information was the correct thing to do but so far none of the black clad soldiers had done anything at all to warrant concern. "All total there are thirty or so of us remaining. Many were killed by the raiders; we thank thee for the help in driving them off."

Several of the words struck a chord in Finn. Then Mehan had it, the words he thought he had vaguely remembered were from the scrolls of Treelanh. The four scrolls were originally from Karkal in the northwest part of the kingdom. They spoke of a group of travelers that had come to the city nearly two hundred years earlier. The carefully written narrative outlined much of the journey that these travelers had gone through to reach Karkal. In the third scroll there were a number of examples of the language that the men spoke.

His father was considered something of an expert in foreign languages and the scrolls of Treelanh were a favorite of his, so Mehan had ample opportunities over the years to study them. Now he was wishing he had spent more time doing so, if he could dredge up more of that information it would be a huge help. He was certain that these men shared at least some of the same language as those that had ridden into Karkal long ago.

T'shar looked about, sizing up the condition of the people and transports he could see. He was convinced that time was not in their favor. The surviving Clan members may return with much greater numbers, no telling how many. They had to get moving and quickly.

"Kellz." She turned in response to hearing her name. The Striker waited until he was certain he had her attention. He pointed at her and made a circling motion with one finger to mean all of the rest of the encampment and then pointed decisively toward the southeast indicating his desire for all of them to head in that direction.

It took her only a moment to comprehend him but she did, giving him a firm nod of assent. Motioning him to follow, she led the way across the open space to where Vode was.

Mehan was quick to tell his friend that they were making progress. The senior Striker nodded but told him that it would have to wait; they had to get these people out of here, now. Finn knew why and agreed, this was definitely not a nice part of town to be stuck in. Several of the Clans routinely claimed this area as their own so it was possible that the ones they had dealt with earlier might not be the only ones around.

Vode knew that they couldn't remain in the area; he began to issue orders to Levas and Allence. The pair listened to the directives; Mehan too was listening with interest. The more of the language he heard the better his understanding, still spotty at best but improving. His academic studies were serving him well, at least at the moment. *Just be nice if they would do it quicker*, he mused.

Allence began to issue orders of her own in keeping with those given to her by Vode. Thindor himself had made it very clear to her that this mission was of vital importance to Vankard and possibly the world. Vode was not in her chain of command but the Warlord had expressed to her that it would be a good idea to pay close attention to what the High Priest had to say. It could be the difference between completing their task, and not coming home at all.

Wagons were hurriedly but efficiently reloaded, the wounded placed in several of the wagons. The weapons and usable supplies of the Clansmen had been gleaned as well. No reason to leave weapons behind and the supplies could be useful. The bodies of the dead priests and soldiers were reverently placed in one wagon that had been emptied of all goods and supplies. Proper burial for them was a must but there was no time to do it right now. The honored dead would be taken with them and given the proper rites when time allowed. T'shar made sure that the dead Striker was being brought along for the same reason. He had served with honor and would be given a formal military burial.

Within the span of an hour the small caravan was ready to get underway. T'shar had been conferring with Allence as much as possible given the language barrier. He had sent a Striker to each side of the formation to ride with the Thunderguard that Allence had assigned. This helped to better fortify their flanks. Mehan chose to ride with Levas who was now driving the wagon containing Vode. The Striker was continuing to try and push through the difference in speech so that the groups could better communicate.

T'shar was riding alongside the Thunderguard commander at the head of the double wide column of wagons. Allence had recommended to Vode that they shorten up the length of the procession since they had fewer to protect it. The High Priest agreed at once and instructed Levas to issue the appropriate orders since all the wagons were being driven by priests. The senior acolyte had immediately bowed before hurrying off to give the drivers their instructions.

Allence knew that even with the Strikers helping, not that she was totally convinced of their trustworthiness, the guards would be hard pressed to fight off another determined attack. Their best defense at the moment was to be somewhere else.

The site of the battle slowly but steadily fell away behind them until it was no longer visible. T'shar had figured that it would be at least eight or nine hour's hard push to get to the Striker outpost. He wondered if the Hol brothers had caught sight of any pursuit. A mental grin at the antics of the two, twins but so different in personality. Ian hardly spoke while Sandor was rarely quiet. Both were experienced, veteran Strikers that T'shar was certain that he could count on and had many times in the past.

His immediate concern was to get these people to safety.

Chapter Twenty
A Life Far Different

A Gaol, Karbel

It was dark, not so dark you couldn't see anything but very dim. Lynd Rees had been in his cell for some time, he was certain it had been at least five days but likely it had been longer, it certainly felt longer. It was hard to determine the passage of time even by trying to use his body's sleep rhythm; he had not seen the outside of this building or even sunlight since his arrival following his arrest on charges of treason.

When it was time for his captors to question him, which seemed to be whenever the mood struck them he was taken, shackled of course, to a room one level above this. It was a featureless cube of stone containing only a filthy table, two equally dirty chairs and several hard faced men who served the king.

Rees could hear the sound the slop cart slowly working its way down the passageway carrying its offering of what some, him not being one of them, called food. But since it was all that he had access to he endured the substandard fare without spoken complaint, better to strengthen his position when the time came and he was growing more secure in believing that time was indeed approaching. So far he had not given up one single piece of incriminating evidence against himself or any of the others.

His captors had not yet resorted to any overly aggressive physical means to try and retrieve any information. Rees believed that if they hadn't done it by now then they wouldn't likely go that route. They had slapped him around some and that he endured that indignity silently but with growing anger. The coup leader wasn't entirely sure why they hadn't resorted to more painful means but he wasn't going to question providence. Every day he held out the better his chances were so he continued to hang on.

A bowl and a cup were suddenly slid partly through section at the bottom of the heavy door created for just such a reason. Rees made himself wait until the rattling of the cart started up again signaling that the slopmate had moved on to the next cell. It took a fair measure of his self-control -- Rees was hungry, but by not pouncing on the meal as soon as it showed up he was demonstrating control and a sense of apathy.

Once he was satisfied that enough time had passed he collected the bowl, being careful not to inspect the contents too carefully. It was all he had to eat so whatever it was he had little choice, eat it or not but it was all that was at hand.

Taking the bowl and cup he moved back against the far wall and then carefully sat down as not to spill the contents of either. Rees took a sip of the water grimacing at the brackish taste but several days of having had only what they had fed him had removed much of his haughtiness at the meals provided. This was about survival, the meals were enough, just to keep him alive and that was all that mattered. He slowly ate the weak soup and then finished off the cup of water. Another bout of questioning was likely to take place that afternoon so he needed the energy. Once he was done eating the bowl and cup were returned to the opening at the base of the door.

Stretching expansively he felt some of the stiffness work itself out of the muscles of the back and shoulders. The mattress, stuffed with straw wasn't the most comfortable thing and tended to cause soreness. Holding the stretch for a few extra moments felt good, at least there was something positive about the day. Exhaling and releasing the muscles all at once gave him a mental boost. Rolling his head around a few times to prolong the tension removal he covered the short distance to the wall and slid down to a seated position thinking about his situation.

Only his anger at what was being done to him kept him going. The first two days of his captivity had been very hard to bear. When the guards first tossed him in the cell he was assaulted by the smell, stale sweat, old urine and fear. Then when meal time came around it was necessary for him to fight off several rats. He killed two of them by kicking and stomping on them. In the process some of his meager fare had been spilled and once he was done eating he flushed out the remaining pair of rats and killed them as well. The process took some time but at last he was alone in his cell or so he thought. The mattress wasn't filled with the cleanest straw and it was home to a variety of small bugs and fleas. Rees made himself deal with it, nothing was forever.

The ever present fear that had been with him since the Strikers had fought their way into his home was slowly subsiding. It was still present but less than it had been when he had first been brought to the gaol. His mind had been turning over plan after plan from the first moments of his arrest, each one examined then discarded until he had decided upon a strategy of indifference. He would answer the questions as he saw fit making sure to remember the details of previous answers so to maintain the continuity of his story.

Yes, of course he knew some of the others that he was asked about; they were fellow Assembly members as well as occasional business partners. A man of his social stature and political position came into contact with men from all over the kingdom; there was nothing illegal about that. He had nearly slipped twice but had caught himself without it costing him.

The questioning session that afternoon went on for hours but Rees was able to keep his outer demeanor calm, even appearing bored at times. This angered his captors but without the solid evidence that Thadar was demanding be produced so far there was little to use to convict the man. Some of the other conspirators had talked some in an attempt to lessen the charges against them but they had all refused to provide names of the others.

It was an unusual show of solidarity, each of the men felt that there were enough of the Council of Eight that remained free to carry out the groups plan and once that was done they would be set free. So despite giving up some information none of them had divulged who they had been plotting with.

Rees had been returned to his cell following the latest round of questioning to find his barrister waiting in the small room which was now lit with a lamp hung from the wall. He was also quick to note what appeared to be fresh food sitting on a clean napkin atop the small stool which was a new item of furniture in the room. His mouth began to water at the sight of the food but he worked at maintaining his composure as not to provide his captors with any sense of victory.

The barrister, Erl Fonn, a tall thin man with a slightly cruel visage watched silently as the guards brought his client in. They made him stand still as one of them removed his manacles and leg irons the other keeping a sharp eye on the prisoner and his visitor. The leg irons were completely unnecessary inside the gaol but the heavy shackles and chain served to remind the prisoner of his situation. Finished with unlocking the restraints the gaoler stood and moved off to the side of Rees.

Waiting for a few moments to see if the guards would go, Fonn spoke for the first time. "Leave us."

The command didn't seem to impress or encourage the guards to move. Fonn who had spent his share of time in various gaols and prisons assisting counseling clients around Karbel expected no less; in fact he'd have been mildly surprised if they had left the room.

In a voice filled a superior tone, "Per Royal Policy, Barristers are allowed unsupervised access to their clients for the purpose of assisting in their legal defense. Now leave us or I will be forced to mention this interference to the Senior Magistrate."

Both men shot him a hard look, one of them spitting on the floor in contempt as they grudgingly left the room. The heavy cell door was closed with a solid thump. Rees started to speak but Fonn raised one finger to keep him silent. The barrister was an old hand at gaol tricks, just because the door was closed didn't mean someone wasn't listening. Using the gap at the base of the door was a common tactic.

Fonn lifted the cup of water from the stool and tossed the contents at the bottom of the door. The water splashed through the opening but elicited no response or outburst so the barrister was reasonably certain that no one was listening, at least at the base of the door anyways. There was always the possibility that there was a way that someone was in the room on either side of the cell listening but there wasn't anything that either of the two men could do about it. Rees had watched the detection test with interest; it seemed that he had chosen his barrister wisely.

Erl turned to his client and motioned toward the food the smell of which had been driving Rees to distraction. Exhibiting a high level of self-control he picked up the plate and slowly began to eat the offered fare. After several bites Rees promised himself that he would never again take good food for granted. Fonn waited patiently for the other man to finish the meal, it was a common event when he visited clients.

Bringing fresh food was a way of displaying loyalty to the client, a total sham on his part. The only thing Fonn was loyal to was the fee that he was paid, which was always in advance in case of situations like this. The crown had ordered that all of Rees' property and money be seized until further notice. Proper planning had paid off for the long time legal representative. Without a doubt this case would be his highest profile defense and he had no intention of losing.

Fonn was no supporter of the king and this was his way of protesting, freeing those that the crown sought to punish. Fonn smiled slightly at the thought; if he won this case he could increase his fees by a sizable percentage.

Now that his client was finished eating the barrister was more than ready to get down to business. For his part Rees felt more energized and refocused, the fresh food helped but having gotten through yet another questioning session without slipping up then to be brought back to find his lawyer present gave the coup leader a large mental boost. Now he could pass along some instructions to those waiting on the outside as well as be caught up on what had transpired since his arrest.

Rees wasted no time with his first query, "How long have I been in here?"

Fonn didn't hesitate with the answer, with some clients you eased them into certain information but with others, such as this one it was best to give it to them straight. "It's been eight days since you were brought in."

The news was a little disheartening to Rees but not totally unexpected. He had felt sure it had been at least five days, still the situation wasn't unsalvageable. The next question didn't take long either since neither man knew exactly how long the barrister would be allowed to stay. "What news of the king and the others?"

The barrister began to explain the overall situation, the king lived despite having been wounded by the still as yet unidentified assailants and was expected to make a full recovery according to reports released by the palace. He had still not made a public appearance since the attack which had been a full ten-day ago. Rees said nothing as he listened; he was absorbing all the information. A royal edict had been issued dissolving the Assembly permanently.

The now former member of that body found that piece of news both interesting and angering. Interesting in that Thadar was showing a bit of political backbone which Rees found annoying and angering in that by eliminating the Assembly, the primary tool by which Rees and his associates used to undermine the monarchy, it set his goals back.

In regards to the others Fonn listed off the names of those arrested. Orth Glan was one that Rees had heard about prior to being hauled in but the others were new to him. Seems the king got some but not all, a thought formed in that instant. Rees focused on it, worked to bring it to maturity much like coaxing an ember into a full flame.

Yes, that may work and even if it doesn't it will still cause the king headaches that must be dealt with. Fonn had stopped his oration when he saw the thinking going on in the other man. He waited patiently, no reason not to, he had been well paid.

Rees took a step closer to the barrister and began to speak in a slightly lowered voice. He outlined a series of instructions regarding raising the public awareness and ire about the king's decision to dissolve the Assembly. Barely pausing, the prisoner also gave orders to have Fonn contact certain individuals and what to tell them.

One of the reasons that Fonn was so successful was that he had a nearly perfect memory which eliminated the need for written notes, a useful trait and one that aided in keeping him safer from government security forces. If there was nothing written down it was significantly more difficult to prove wrong doing.

Rees spoke for several minutes with little pause. Fonn was smiling now as he listened. Yes, that would be something that could work. He knew the appropriate people to speak to. When Rees was certain he had said all that was necessary he asked for a summary of the key points which was delivered flawlessly.

Fonn nodded once then turned to the nearby door pounding it hard twice and shouting for the guard. Rees told him thank you for the food. The barrister nodded elegantly as the heavy door was unlocked and opened. He stepped through without a glance at the guard; contact arrangements were already spinning around in his head.

Rees smiled widely in the reduced light as the door was closed and secured, his time was coming, all it would take was some patience on his part and that was something that he had in abundant quantities.

Chapter Twenty-One
Salvation

South of the Sea of Jolon

Pushing their mounts even harder, Mryl and his men finally crested the ridge and then, at last before them lay the long sought prize. Pulling in the reins to stop their exhausted horses, the Guards took in the sight. Sunlight danced and dappled on the surface of the water in a festival of colors that was so stunning it seemed to enchant the entire area. The edges of the vast lake that still carried the improper name given it long ago stretched away in the distance to either side.

All that lay between them and the water's edge were a few low hills and a scattering of trees. A breeze from the north came to them bringing the smell of water. The fresh aroma was like nourishment for the soul. Every one of them took in a deep breath, no smell of smoke, fire or death. Just clean, fresh air, something they had been riding toward and were nearly there, time to keep going.

The weary Guard troopers paused but a moment to savor this moment of beauty and delight. A measure of hope was rekindled in each of them, several smiles broke out. The pursuit had gained ground despite the horse-killing pace the men from Kuln had been riding. The effects were easy to see, sweat glistened from the back of every horse, deep breaths could be heard as the tired mounts rested as much as possible.

Every one of the Guards knew to be looking for a boat of any kind, something, anything that would take them out of the accursed south, each of them had more than their fill of it. The southern edge of the lake wasn't visible yet due to the low hills and so Mryl pushed them on.

Every one of them was alone with their thoughts as they tried to dredge up enough strength for one more ride, to coax their mounts for one more journey.

The renewed measure of hope gave them a little energy to keep going; completing the mission was all that was left. There were no thoughts of glory or fancy homecomings, not that that was what it was about anyway; it had come down to survival plain and simple. Ride north and try to find a way to cheat death one more time.

Wev was the last one off the top of the ridge as he looked back again to try and gauge the distance between them and what looked to be a sizable unit of southern cavalry, which could be seen pushing hard on the plains they had just left. His experience told him that they had no more than an hour behind and he was unsure about that given the landscape. He turned around and rubbed the neck of the tired horse he was astride and urged it forward once again. The sleek sides of the dark brown mare were heavily streaked with sweat but it headed down the hill at the prodding of the man on her back moving north once again.

The trip down the hill was much easier than the climb up and so the tired mounts were not pushed hard by the men of Karbel. It wouldn't do to have a spill now. The side of the hill was covered in an array of wildflowers, a wild mixture of colors that moved in the wind. The Guards moved through them as the hill ended and level ground presented itself. Once again they urged the horses into a trot and then a run to bring them closer to the water's edge. They had to reach the lake and then find a boat of some kind if one was there. If they didn't then the lake would stymie them to the north and force them to choose either east or west, and the pursuers could cut them off. Not an acceptable choice so the men pushed the mounts a little harder and prayed for a little, shades, a *lot* of help right now.

The distance to the lake fell away quickly since the ground was mostly level. Presently they found themselves riding a bowshot distance from the water. The light sparkled surface of the water danced in the wind in a wild twinkle of colors. Mryl and the others saw nothing that would serve as a craft so they moved on. The Guard officer had already decided that if they couldn't find anything right away that they would head east rather than west. It was only a slight diversion but since the pursuers likely knew who they were they might, might mind you, be more inclined to think that the hunted would head west toward home.

Moving closer to the water the tired group continued on. They rode along the shore, keen eyes peering ahead for something, anything, that would serve as transportation. Minutes passed, each one bringing the hunters closer and still nothing. Mryl knew that they were nearly out of time but there was nothing left to do but to keep riding and so they did.

Horn calls could be heard now, faintly but coming closer. Each man urged his mount to go faster. Death was coming and each wanted no part of meeting it just yet.

Wev was the first to see the boat. He turned and shouted at the others, pointing excitedly ahead. Hope suddenly sprung up in the group like water from a geyser. Despair and fatigue seemed to fall away. The boat was a decent size craft, easily large enough for all of them. A small group of men were present on the shore near where the craft was nosed in to help anchor it, gathered around a small fire cooking a hot meal, something that would be impossible aboard the wooden vessel.

The six men at the fire noticed the riders coming but thought little of it. They had recently returned from delivering a large group of spies and their load of cargo to the northern edge of the lake and were expecting a group of riders to take their report back south so the men felt they were in no danger. The masters controlled everything south of the lake so the sight of armed men bearing down on them meant nothing.

It was again Wev who saved them. He realized that the men were southerners and that they were not aware of who the Guards were. Turning once more in the saddle he got Mryl's attention and made sure that he understood that they would attack but only once they were right on top of the men. To help with this Mryl told them to slow down, every man complied at once. The tired horses had no issue with going slower. The Guards waved at the six as they approached to help lull the sailors into feeling safe.

The Guards approached carefully and with smiles displayed on their faces until they were nearly on top of the men huddled around the fire before striking. The fight was short, brutal and over in moments. The southerners were sailors not soldiers and the Guards made short work of them, the short melee a release of some of the pent up emotions that the northern soldiers had been dealing with. The bodies were quickly searched for anything of importance while others pulled the saddles from the horses and heaved them onboard the small ship. The horses were then turned loose to find their own way. A quick inventory of what they had found despoiling the bodies turned up a few short knives of poor quality, a well tooled leather pouch containing a map and several other pieces of parchment covered in a script unknown to any of them.

The final item raised their spirits somewhat, a large well filled pouch of thumbnail sized silver and gold coines. One of the troopers tossed it over to Mryl who was surprised at the weight of it. He tossed it up in the air then grabbed it again before tucking it carefully in his belt. The money could be useful if they survived to get out of the south.

Mryl saw that the meal, a poor stew, was bubbling away so he told the men to eat, quickly. The weary group disposed of the offered faire quickly and with no complaints, a few small ones maybe but only after they finished. The stew was not tasty but it was hot and that was something.

Wev inspected the boat after quickly eating his share. It was about fifty foot in length with a single mast. It was similar to a number of other craft that sailed the lake delivering cargo. It should be no problem for them to get it off the shore and underway since it appeared that it was barely beached. Several shapes could be seen beneath a large canvas cover forward of the mast that he would check out later.

The craft appeared to be capable of staying afloat but had not been well maintained by its now former operators. The deck was gouged and scarred in places by an unknown history of cargoes over the years. What was visible of the sail pooled around the base of the mast appeared dingy and crudely patched in places. Wev didn't even want to *think* about the smell coming from the lower level of the vessel.

All at once horns could now be heard much closer than the last time. Each man rushed to the boat before Mryl even had to say anything, the fire and the meager meal forgotten. It was time to try and go; the minutes they spent eating may prove to be their undoing. They cut the rope that was secured to a large rock further up the beach and all of them save Wev began to push the craft deeper into the water. It took several moments of pushing and rocking the craft in order to see the first signs of movement toward deeper water.

Another horn call was heard and that served to add to the moment. Effort which just seconds earlier seemed to be all they had now paled in comparison. The southies were close, too close by half.

Exhorting his men on, Mryl pushed harder as did the others. Muscles strained at the demands being placed on them. The boat now seemed to be one with the beach, it wouldn't move, it wouldn't budge. Another horn call rent the air. The first sound of hooves could now be heard.

Wev shouted at them to hurry. He could now see a large group, at least sixty in number, crest a hill to the west of them and begin down this side heading toward them. He screamed again at the others to hurry. Time was nearly gone and with no horses the remaining northerners couldn't run. Push for all gods' sake, push!

The boat came free of the beach all at once and two of the Guards were caught off guard falling in the water ending up soaked for their efforts. The rest rushed to wade through the water and climb on board grabbing their now dripping brethren. Several long oars were located and used to push the boat deeper into the water. Wev was at the tiller and he began to edge the boat around so that they could make their way north. He shouted instructions to several of the soldiers. Boots struck the deck as men ran to do as they were told.

Two of them raised the sail while several others collected their bows and quivers to answer any calls on them from the shore. The rest pulled hard at the oars to try and drive them away from the beach. Brawny arms bent at the long wooden paddles trying to bite deeper into the water. It was a choppy rhythm at first but as they stroked the pace evened out and they began to gain distance. The riders kept coming, horn calls filling the air alerting the other hunters to the location of the quarry.

A fair wind filled the sail and began to urge the small coastal freighter north but not fast enough to suit the passengers. The cavalry unit was still sending horn calls out to alert the other units to the prey.

The first group thundered up the beach unslinging their bows to try and stop the men of Karbel. A few arrows struck the boat but none found flesh. The lake swallowed a great many shafts without a thought as they fell short of their target. Mryl was in the rear with Wev gauging the distance between them and the receding shoreline.

Now free of the shelter of the hills the wind pushed the boat harder and a spray of white foam curled up from the bow as they picked up speed. The shoreline was now just a line on the far horizon as the men finally began to feel they had made it. Mryl had no idea exactly where along the southern edge of the lake they had been but he knew that north was safer than south. The day was warm, he'd had something to eat and he was alive, for now that was enough. He looked forward and saw that three of the men were already asleep having found themselves spaces that they felt adequate to rest on; another was slumped over one of the oars having passed into sleep where he sat. Exhaustion could only be fought off for so long.

He knew that he too needed some sleep and would get some soon but first to see to their situation.

Chapter Twenty-Two
News from the North

Northern Karbel

The Strikers at the small outpost were ready and waiting when the small caravan of wagons arrived. T'shar had sent one of his men on ahead to make sure that all was prepared, food, medical supplies and fresh horses in particular. A much larger escort of Strikers had ridden out several hours earlier to reinforce the small patrol.

Word had been sent via heliograph to both the local overall Striker commander as well as to Striker headquarters in Karbel earlier informing them that something important was happening and that further word would be forthcoming as soon as possible. In addition, riders had been sent out from the small garrison post to track down and recall the other two Striker patrols that were away from the outpost as well. T'shar still wasn't certain what was happening but, like the garrison commander, felt having as many of his kind around him was a good start.

Vode's wound was beginning to heal well; he was now much more in command of himself than when they had initially encountered the Strikers. To make the exchange of information easier, the High Priest had Levas bring Mehan Finn into the wagon he was riding in so that the three could talk as best as was possible. When the priest made the request Finn thought it a good idea but verified it with T'shar before accepting. The Striker weapons master immediately approved, he was certain these people had information of value and if having Mehan ride with them would get it faster then so be it. Whatever was going on with their guests could be important to Karbel and right now it fell to Mehan and the others to determine as much as they could.

Mehan had been working with the priest, Levas, on further breaking down the language barrier. One thing they had resorted to was a simple but so far reasonably effective process. One of them would hold up an item, cloak, sword, cup and so on then each of them would then tell the other what it was in their own tongue. This allowed both men to better understand one another and actually sped up the work quite a bit because it helped to provide each man more of the common words used. The Striker was now able to at least articulate some of his questions getting some answers and the same was true for Levas. Each had been keeping their superior updated as to their progress.

Allence Kellz had kept her remaining Thunderguards close to the wagons. She was grateful for the help these Strikers, interesting name, had provided but was still wary especially when the additional soldiers arrived to help escort them. These men were all Utlanders, a northman term for those who lived beyond the mountain gate, and as such were unknown to her. The woman wasn't paranoid but she had been tasked with keeping Vode alive, a mission that so far had not gone well at all.

The northmen had departed Vankard with no recent information on what was going in the rest of the world and so their maps, while topographically correct, were not of much real use. Travels through the Federation of Clans territory had been as close to a living nightmare as she had ever wanted to experience. The strange people, smells, and sights of the world, unnerved her more than she had thought it would.

The king had made a call for volunteers among the Thunderguards for those willing to undertake the mission.

She barely hesitated in stepping forward but had reconsidered her position several times since leaving Vankard; it was much too late now to change her mind. When the northmen had finally gotten through the more populated areas she had been able to relax a little thinking the worst was behind them.

The attack on the caravan had been unprovoked and unexpected, nearly sixty Clansmen had swept down on them as the group from Vankard moved northeast among some low hills. Several of her men had died in the initial wave as they did what they could to buy the others time by charging directly into the oncoming wave of riders, which surprised the raiders and considerably slowed their attack. Their sacrifice bought just enough time to circle the wagons and draw the other guards inside. The Strikers had arrived a little more than an hour or so after the initial ambush.

T'shar had shared his map with her, pointing out where they had been ambushed then drawing his finger along the route they were taking to a small point marked with a square with some kind of what she believed was a number beside it. He poked the map twice as his finger came to rest on the small square. This led her to believe that this was where they were headed.

The group of Strikers and northmen could see the outpost now. T'shar made sure that he pointed it out to the woman commanding the wagons guards. He had sensed her unease and recognized it for what it was, caution versus fear. If their roles had been reversed he was certain he would feel nothing different.

Allence saw where the Striker was pointing and in her tongue called her men to a higher level of attention. Having arrived at their destination she was even more wary now, good time for an ambush if one was coming. They would be on the Strikers' ground with walls around them.

To try and alleviate her concerns, T'shar suddenly rode in front of the first wagon well before it reached the open gates and signaled for it to stop. By placing his horse directly in front of the transport the driver had no choice. The priest was able to get the wagon halted before running T'shar down. The Striker weapons master dismounted and walked back to where Allence was. He motioned for her to follow him then to the wagon driver to stay put before he turned heading for the open gate. The Thunderguard was curious but elected to follow him, telling her men to watch themselves.

He walked next to her but made sure to not be too close and on the side opposite where her sword hung on her belt. T'shar was making every effort to keep suspicion out of her mind. They covered the distance in a few minutes, nothing was said between them. Allence took the time to take in the details of the outpost. One large watch tower she estimated to be at least thirty feet high, stout walls of what was likely mud- or stucco-covered logs, an impressive ditch that appeared to surround the fort. Not bad for what she assumed was a remote military station.

The pair entered the small fort; she wasn't bashful about looking around for any signs of an ambush. She didn't see anything out of the ordinary but that didn't mean she was satisfied.

The outpost commander, a veteran Section Sergeant was waiting for them. T'shar nodded to him then said, "Thunderguard Allence Kellz, Striker Section Sergeant Ortis."

The outpost commander slightly bowed his head toward his guest. "She's worried that we're bandits."

The Striker sergeant understood that; diplomacy wasn't his strongest suit but he knew a soldier when he saw one and the woman had the look. To try and alleviate her concerns the Section Sergeant did something unusual. Making sure that she was looking at him Ortis called one of the Strikers over. The man hurried over and when he arrived, Ortis told him to disarm. The soldier was a tad confused but did as he was told. He unbuckled his sword belt and then laid it on the ground. Thanking the man he told him to return to his post.

One after another the garrison commander brought his men to him and had them disarm. Allence quickly realized what he was doing and gestured to him to stop after the fourth man had laid down his arms. She smiled; this wasn't the action of someone with an evil intent. The Thunderguard nodded her head deeply to Ortis in recognition of his gesture.

He came to attention and saluted her in return. T'shar had watched the entire proceeding without saying a word. Turning in her saddle she caught his eye and pointed back toward the gate and by extension meant the others waiting. He bobbed his head once is response turning around and walking toward the gate with Allence following closely.

Walking through the opening he stepped out to where the others could see him and waved them forward. The priests looked to the Thunderguards who saw their commander, free and unharmed, so they nodded to the priests who shook the reins to get the horses going.

Vode was relieved at the prospect of getting additional medical attention for the wounded and a feeling of safety, however tenuous that security was. This world beyond the mountain gate from Vankard was as frightening and unknown as all the tales spoken of it but the High Priest knew that in order to reach their goal they must press on. Despite the large amount of information shown to him in the visions the single most important piece of knowledge, when these Varshon might move on G'mar, was absent so time was of great import and now they had less of it.

The small wagon train rolled through the gate, each one directed to a spot to minimize the amount of space being occupied. The courtyard area of the outpost wasn't all that large but Ortis didn't want any of the wagons to remain outside of the walls, this group had been through enough for one day.

The senior Striker watched as the last of the transports cleared the gates. "Close 'em," he shouted.

Several burly Strikers immediately began to pull on one of the large barriers to swing it shut. Allence was quick to dismount, moving to the wagon where Vode was resting to check on him. This entire undertaking was about the High Priest, a quick mental shudder when she recalled seeing him take an arrow. It had been the rapid action of his senior acolyte that had no doubt saved Vode's life.

Once the last wagon was through the gate it was closed and secured. Those from Vankard were dismounting, tending to the wounded as well as their tired horses. The Thunderguards were watching the Strikers closely but without overly obvious suspicion as they worked. The level of concern among the royal guards was high but Allence did what she could to reassure them.

Ortis had several of his men with him but so far had not moved toward the wagons as not to appear threatening. Kellz saw this and knowing that her people as well as the priests needed help impatiently gestured to him to come over. The senior Striker saw the hand motion then nodded to his men, the five of them headed for where she was working on helping unload some of the wounded.

The work of tending to those from Vankard took nearly two hours, the biggest headaches was the language barrier but judicious use of hand gestures worked through most of the issues.

Vode was resting comfortably in the commander's quarters. Sergeant Ortis had insisted that the senior priest use his own room to rest in and wouldn't take no for answer. The expedition leader was grateful for the courtesy and instructed Levas to relay that to the Striker which he did with a great sense of dignity. Ortis nodded deeply to them both out of respect.

Once the wounded were cared for and situated, there was finally some time for Ortis to speak to the patrol members more in depth. He found T'shar conferring with the Hol brothers and some of the others from the patrol about what had happened. Seeing the senior sergeant arrive, the conversation paused allowing Ortis to interject several questions. Sandor began to explain what had happened from the time they had first spotted the smoke. Ortis listened to the narrative holding further questions so that Sandor could speak uninterrupted.

Telling the tale took just a few minutes. Once he felt he had given all the information necessary Sandor paused to wait for any questions. The outpost commander still had some but was now confident he possessed enough of the story to formulate a much more accurate report. He told them all to get something to eat and stay together until he returned.

Without waiting for an acknowledgement he headed for the message center his mind already processing what information would be going into the follow up message to headquarters. Whatever these people were involved in seemed serious, there had already been two requests from higher command for further information but he had been stalling on a response to make sure it what he was reporting was as accurate as it could be.

Ortis had been a soldier for many years and something about this situation told him that it had bigger implications; he had learned to listen to his own voice of intuition and right now it was screaming at him.

After their sergeant had left, the patrol members took his advice and went to get something to eat. As they made their way to the outpost's kitchen area, which was open all the time to accommodate the varied guard schedule as well as the odd hours that patrols sometimes returned, the pace of the conversation slowed but never ended.

The small staff had been very busy preparing additional food to handle the sudden increase in population at the outpost. Each man in turn chose a few of the food items from the selections offered and moved on to find seating. Occupying one of the large tables in the eating area the discussion about what had happened continued. Various opinions were tossed out for examination by the others; some had merits while others were quickly rejected. With Mehan still with their guests it fell to Sandor to serve as impromptu moderator for the discussion.

While the others were eating another meeting of sorts was going on in the Duty Office. Mehan brought Levas and Allence over to the large map boards along the wall. There were several charts on oversized sliding boards that rolled into a slot in the wall. He pulled out one then pushed it back in not being the one he wanted at the moment. Finding the correct one, the Striker gave it a good tug to bring it out of its resting place. The map showed all of Karbel and the surrounding territories and realms. The map did not show the entirety of the continent but it was as accurate as the royal cartographers could make it.

He quickly located the approximate position of the outpost and stabbed that site with his finger telling Levas as best he could that it indicated where they were currently at. Allence and the priest were both surprised at the amount of information presented on the well-illustrated chart. It would seem that the Utland was significantly larger than either of them believed. It was a bit intimidating to both of the Vankard residents. It was possible that the map was a ruse to confuse them but that seemed more than a little ridiculous. There was no way that the Strikers could have known they were coming and so far they had done nothing but aid the northmen.

Mehan asked Levas to show him where they had come from. He started to raise his hand to point it out then lowered the hand while turning toward Allence. Levas relayed the request and she pursed her lips for a moment then nodded. For his part Mehan wasn't offended in the least, it was an unusual situation and as such some caution was well merited.

The senior acolyte placed the tip of one finger in the approximate location that Finn had indicated where the outpost was, from there he slowly pulled it across the map moving toward the west northwest. The Striker watched with interest as the pointer moved beyond Karbel's borders across Federation territory and continued on until it reached the neck of a narrow isthmus. There was just a moment's hesitation before the digit continued its journey; it tracked along further to the northwest.

Once the finger stopped moving Levas tapped it twice on the edge of the visible area above the isthmus and with a strong sense of determination said to Mehan, "Vankard." Finished with his map tour Levas lowered his arm and stepped back slightly.

Finn looked at the two to make sure he had their attention and once that he was certain that was the case he turned to the map. Using his finger as the pointer now the Striker began to outline the borders of his country. The pair from Vankard watched with great interest as their guide traced an extended line around a large area of territory.

Once he had come back around to the starting point he paused his finger, "Karbel".

For her part, Allence was more impressed than she hoped that she was showing. This realm, Karbel he called it – was a good sized place. She could see on the map what she believed to be the location of five, no, six cities. Vankard had one large city besides the capital of Ednon and two other reasonably sized population centers. Much of the populace lived in a thick scattering of villages and hamlets.

Levas too was impressed by the scope of not only Karbel but enormity of the Utland. He had never realized just how large it was, all those places and all those people…it was more than a little intimidating. And there were still areas not shown on this map as indicated the open areas at the edges of chart. So there were even more places and people than what was displayed. It was quite a bit to take in, the senior acolyte tried to digest it all. He was a little embarrassed to admit to himself that the education he had worked so hard to gain, improve on, and covet was lacking in some vital areas.

Finn continued his map tour by pointing at each of the various cities in turn and naming them, Karkal, Rhywe, Toras, Plynth, Edora and then finally Karbel. As soon as he mentioned the capital city Allence's face registered confusion. She turned to Levas whose face shared a look of confusion that mirrored hers. The city is Karbel? He said the realm was called that so which was it?

Levas asked that question as best he could in the halting manner of partially understood languages everywhere. Mehan actually did get the gist of what he was asking so tried to formulate a way to better clarify what he was trying to get across.

Pausing for a moment to allow his brain to chew on ideas, the three stood silent then all at once a notion presented itself. The pair from Vankard saw the change in body language which wasn't hard to notice. Mehan spoke the word for king in the northern tongue or at least what he believed was the proper word.

Levas wasn't sure what the Striker was saying so gestured for him to repeat it and he did. That time the priest did understand it and used the more commonly used term to Allence so that she understood what they were being told. Levas then spoke it with the proper inflection – *Angol*, which Mehan picked up on right away.

Speaking the word again while taking both of his hands and mimicking the gesture of placing a crown on his own head he said the word again. Nodding their understanding to the bodyguard he nodded once and with emphasis pointed to the capital city on the map – *Angol*!

He was attempting to get them to understand that this was where the king resided and ruled from. Double tapping the point on the map he said it again. Allence caught the significance of the inference and touched her finger to the map immediately next to his while saying the word aloud. Yes! Thank the gods she got it.

Tapping his finger again Mehan told them "Karbel!" and then drew a wide loose circle around the whole kingdom again stating, "Karbel."

The Thunderguard and the priest both smiled and nodded saying to each other at about the same time, "It's the capital city." For his part Mehan was relieved, progress was being made. Okay now on to the next part…

Ortis had received orders to provide an escort and transportation for his guests. They would be asked to come to the capital to meet with a senior delegation. A large detachment of Strikers who had already been dispatched from a post further south would meet them along the way to take over the escort. One of the Striker operated river craft was waiting at the Edora dock to take the party south to the capital. The outpost commander left the message center to find and notify the appropriate people.

Hell of a day…

Chapter Twenty-Three
Unlocking the Door

Near the Wystern

Anagir along with his immediate retainers were gathered on a low rise overlooking the river; necessary staff members were close in around him while fifty or so of the ever vigilant Ogurth formed a circle around their leader, standing a little farther out to give the Varshon leader some privacy. The Trolls were facing outward weapons at the ready, watching intently for any threat that might endanger Anagir. Another fifty of the massive figures stood at the ready nearby should they prove needed.

Q-tra-All, the Ogurth leader was taking no chances with the life of the one he was birth-sworn to protect. He stood several paces behind Anagir constantly taking in the view as well but from a different perspective. His trained and experienced eyes drank in all manner of details, topography, wind direction, movement of troops nearby, the conduct of those nearest to Anagir.

Now that the invasion of the north had finally begun his sole duty was to keep Anagir alive and get him to G'mar. He fully intended to ensure that happened.

From their vantage point the Varshon leader and the others could easily see the crossing point off to their right. A long line of troops, horses, and wagons stretched from the bridges that spanned the river away to the south to disappear in the distance.

Several large combat units, in particular heavy cavalry, under the direct command of Vinshee, the southern forces cavalry commander, had already crossed the river and were heading north to secure the flank of the invasion force. A wide screen of scouts had been sent out as well, heading in all directions above the river to report on any dangers.

Messengers from the various units already across reported in regularly to keep the leadership informed of their progress. So far only scattered and very disorganized resistance had been encountered and that had been crushed. Casualties to the southern forces had been very light but that was of no concern, they had troops aplenty to spare. It was that many less mouths to feed.

Anagir didn't care if every last one of the tribesmen died on the way north so long as he got to G'mar and secured the sacred books of power. The tribesmen were a means to an end, nothing more. He fought to curb the rising feeling of anticipation, it was still a very long way to the fortress but the deeply awaited day had come at last after nearly twenty centuries. Invasion of the north meant a return to the power that was rightfully the Varshon's and by extension, his.

More units were pouring over the wide pontoon bridges as the command group watched. Long lines of infantry marching six abreast with their spears tucked close to the body followed by more mounted units waiting their turn.

The pace of the movement was steady if unspectacular. One of Anagir's aides was checking units that passed them against a list written on fine parchment that listed the southern order of battle. It was a thick sheaf the younger Varshon held, a small inkwell secured to the side of the cleverly constructed table that rapidly folded up for carry to speed up the work. The keen eyes sought out another unit banner to add to the work he was charged with.

Two more of the bridges were being assembled with the end goal of having six of the massive constructs in place to facilitate the crossing and provide a secure means of moving additional men and supplies north. The barges that formed the foundation for these bridges had been built in secret at a site on the southern shore of the Sea of Jolon. Then when the time was right, they had been floated down the Wystern until they reached the site long since selected as the place the crossing was to occur. Once there the first barges were secured to the southern shore, a second barge tied to the first and so on.

Long, heavy braided cables of fiber secured the barges to the shore and each other. Dirt was then piled on top of gravel that had been brought in using wagons from the south to provide a road surface over the barges. The process was repeated over and over until the barges were topped with nearly three feet of gravel and soil. It was on this surface that the army passed into the north, the tramping of thousands of boot trod feet and iron shod hooves did the packing that formed the surface of the road material.

Slowly turning his head to look north again, Anagir could see that a number of tribesmen were engaged in installing defensive works on the northern bank to protect the bridgehead. The pace was energetic; dirt flew in copious amounts from hundreds of picks and shovels. A screen of mounted pickets guarded them while they labored.

A line of heavy transport wagons finished crossing and were immediately waved on to keep moving forward to clear the way for the next unit right behind them, some mounted archers of the H'Roth. Smaller in number compared to the other two tribes that served them, the H'Roth were superb horsemen and formed the majority of the Varshon led cavalry.

Anagir was generally pleased with the progress so far. Pon wasn't, but that was not a great surprise to the elder Varshon. The man who commanded the southern armies was a fanatic about details and always worked hard to please his masters, just as he should. The two had spoken just before Anagir had settled in on the rise to watch the crossing, he and his party would not cross until the morrow. Comfortable quarters, in as much as comfort could be provided, were even now being prepared for the elder majic user.

Many details had been worked out well in advance of the actual departure of the army, some of them many years in advance. Which paths to take north, how many men and horses, how much grain and meat to take and more. All of this had to be taken care of long before any army could move north to secure the Varshon destiny. An army of clerks and scribes, as well, had labored over the countless years to prepare the figures and to ensure that those figures became a reality. How to grow it, prepare it and then most important how to move all of it to keep it at the ready, so the army could make use of it.

The route they had taken to reach this point had been carefully scouted and any obstacles such as rocks or groups of trees had been removed or cut down. Nothing that would slow the army was permitted to exist. Pon was even now double checking the progress of the assembly of the other bridges and no doubt providing a measure of verbal "encouragement" to those laboring to finish the task.

Two dozen smaller supply wagons were crossing the river. They carried the equipment and basic supplies for a large field kitchen and the cooks to operate it. An army, especially one this large had to eat to keep functioning and to be able to fight. This unit, like the dozens of others, had only one job: get the troops something hot to eat and to do it quickly. It had nothing to do with compassion on the part of the Varshon, men fought better with something hot in their belly.

Aside from the report on the Black Guards who had escaped across the Sea of Jolon, all the news had been positive so far. Rumors that would have reached the capital of D'Lohm of the trouble approaching their southern border should never have arrived. A thick screen of scouts, mostly mounted archers, had deployed to the river well in advance of even the vanguard of the massive army. They had stopped the few who were on the southern bank of the river from crossing back to the north. Killing them was easier than dealing with prisoners.

The two ferry stops that served to aid those that did cross had been carefully watched for some time prior to the invasion. Anyone who crossed over to the southern edge were followed and then, when the time was right, killed. The stations themselves were left alone; when the time came these were seized with little difficulty and the ferries, low slung barges towed across by ropes connected to either end, were used to transport more of the invaders across the wide water barrier. It was important for the Varshon to make use of every crossing point they could. Many a southern spy heading north had used the ferries over the long years leading to this point.

The Varshon leader sat for some time watching the scene, the line of troops and equipment coming north seemed unbroken. Here and there a few wagons or other wheeled transports could be seen pulled off to the side undergoing repairs. The repeated sounds of whips could be heard as the draft animals were pushed harder. It wasn't uncommon for the whips to be used on the tribesmen either.

Every twenty five paces on either side of the long train from the south stood a fully armed Ogurth to ensure that no problems arose, and if they did to deal with them. The tribesmen knew the futility of trying to argue with one of the Trolls that the masters used as their enforcers. If a Troll gave an order, the best choice for the hapless man was to follow it. The alternative was death, period. A very large number of the mountain dwellers had come north with the army, none of the tribesmen knew how many but better to do what you were supposed to than risk the wrath of one of the Varshon's tame Trolls.

After several hours of watching, the chore broken only by a brief respite to eat a meal of flavored rice and highly spiced poucha sausages, the first of the heavy siege equipment, broken down for easier transport could be seen moving north slowly but with a dogged determination. Long team of oxen pulled lengthy carts that held sections of large catapults, siege towers and battering rams. Teamsters kept the wagons and carts moving at a steady pace.

A third bridge was now in operation which allowed for even more units to cross. For all their vast numbers, if a sizable force gained control of the northern end of the bridges the numbers would mean nothing with the majority of their strength still trapped below the river. The crossing must be successful, every time a soldier loyal to the Varshon stepped on northern soil the odds improved. It would be many hours until anyone would be happy with the balance of forces but for now it was going their way.

The latest message from Vinshee placed him some thirty leagues north of the bridges with no problems of significance reported. Tribesmen assigned to the engineers were erecting large upright oil braziers on either side of the wide column and at the bridges to ensure that that there would be ample light to work by once darkness fell. Mere darkness would not stop or even slow the invasion, timing was too important.

Anagir mentally urged the troops to hurry, speed was an ally. He sent a runner to determine how long it was before the fourth bridge was completed. He could see that the last two bridges were just getting underway and so would be some time yet before being finished, but certainly by morning. The man saluted and spun his mount about to carry out the wishes of his master. He rode recklessly down the grass covered slope to seek out the engineer in charge of the project. He feared no interruption; his tunic bore the personal signal of Anagir's staff which allowed him passage barred to virtually all others.

Meanwhile the invasion of the north continued.

Chapter Twenty-Four
A Walking Evil

Near D'Lohm

The storm tossed the rickety craft without mercy or respite. All of the Blacks Guards were tired, weak, and most were now at least mildly sick. All of them were on deck trying to do whatever they could to keep the storm tossed vessel in one piece.

The toll asked of them during the past ten-day had been high, so much so that each of them had not been able to rest much despite the need for it. Their narrow escape from the south had seemed something of a miracle at best. After sighting the massive army that the Varshon were using to invade the north, then slipping away to try and report it to warn those at home, the patrol had made it a fair distance before they were discovered. Then the chase was on.

Their numbers had been slowly diminished by attrition and twice more when Mryl had allowed volunteers to try and strike out on their own to reach one of the heliograph relay teams hidden along the trail north.

When the much reduced group of Black Guards had made it to the southern edge of the Sea of Jolon, managing to find a boat, they all felt that the worst was behind them and that they had made it. No more danger, a short boat ride and then homeward bound. The tired men had been making good time on crossing the wide lake that sat nearly astride the middle of the continent when the storm blew in and turned the once calm waters into an angry tempest that had them wondering if they would survive.

All of them had been desperately watching for some sign of land for some time. At last what appeared to be a shoreline could be seen during the lightning flashes, so Mryl ordered the helmsman to change course. It wasn't easy, the wind was not in their favor but they managed to change their course just enough that the craft began edging its way toward the now slowly growing shoreline.

Waves angrily slapped the vessel and during one long lightning release the Guard standing at the prow thought he saw what appeared to be several rocks sticking up from the swirling water. He immediately turned back toward the helmsman shouting a warning that was instantly lost in the wind, but others saw the frantic gestures and relayed the warning of some type of danger ahead.

Shouting for aid the man at the tiller pulled for all he was worth to try and alter the course. Two of the others leapt to his assistance and with the added muscle swung the rudder just enough to shorten the angle. None of them ever knew how close they came to hitting the rocks.

Suddenly the ship lurched to a halt as it came to rest against the slope of the shoreline. Several of the men were roughly tossed to the deck by the impact but no one was seriously injured. Mryl offered up a sincere prayer of thanks. He had been very worried that the storm might sink their vessel, now it appeared that they may live to see the morrow after all.

He waved his men to him, then shouting over the howling wind ordered them to all go below to the small berthing area to get some shelter from the weather, emphasizing the directive with hand gestures. No sense in them being exposed to the storm's fury. He followed them down; he had no intention of posting a guard on deck. If the enemy could find them in this mess, then so be it. Once below the men found what bed or deck space they could then collapsed, no thought or concern about the soaking wet clothing they wore. Sleep was more important.

After finding a spot, Mryl also laid down but sleep proved elusive. The wind rocked the vessel lightly as the storm continued. Twinsteel had been listening to his conscience a great deal of late, questioning the price paid in the lives of his men killed and sum still owed. When was the bill too high? What was the final price to be for duty fulfilled? That the information they had stumbled onto was of critical importance was beyond doubt but the price had been so high – so terribly high. He wrestled with the thoughts for a time then eventually sleep claimed him. Hours passed as the men slept.

The next morning when they awoke outside it was calm, the skies were still a solid overcast and grey but the high wind and rain were gone. The Guards began to climb out from below deck, moving slowly but moving none the less. They paused to take stock of their situation; they were finally out of the south but still needed to get word to Kuln and Karbel about the invasion. They didn't know where they were, had no horses, little food, and were physically exhausted so they had a few challenges but their sense of duty kept them going. It was all they had left but it would have to be enough.

Once they were all up and around Mryl had his men search the vessel from one end to the other to find anything that may be of use to them, food, weapons, water, blankets... anything at all. He pulled out the worn map that he had been carrying for ten-days on end. The heavy parchment sheet was tattered, faded in spots and generally well past the point of needing replacement but it was the only one he had so he carefully spread it out on a reasonably dry spot on the deck. Wev came over then knelt down next to his officer who was looking over the map. Mryl was looking at the northern edge of the Sea of Jolon in particular.

"Any idea where's we might be sir?"

That was the very question that Mryl had been trying to answer for himself. Truth be told he had no firm clue as to where he and his men were. The storm had tossed them about for hours so which part of the northern coast – he hoped at least it was the northern coast they were on -- was hard to say. The clouds were totally obscuring the sun so he couldn't even use that to get some sense of his bearings. His map wasn't greatly detailed but since it was all he had...blowing out a half breath the tired Black Guard pondered the question that his senior enlisted man had raised.

"I'm not sure, I believe that we're *somewhere* along here." His finger traced a line just above the surface of the map to avoid touching it to illustrate where he was talking about. The arc of the finger took in a large amount of territory but Mryl felt in his gut that they were likely somewhere east of where the Soling River emptied into the Sea of Jolon. He wasn't sure why he had that feeling but it was strong. If he was right they were beached on the coastline of D'Lohm, which meant that for the moment they were out of the south but it was a long way from home. It was a number of miles to the nearest friendly outpost of any kind but they were alive and that was something.

Returning his full attention to the immediate he told Wev that as soon as the men put together whatever was found he wanted to move inland to try and locate a population center of some type. The senior enlisted man nodded once in understanding, he stood, "I'll hurry the boys along."

Mryl watched him walk away to do just that. Now it was time for the next step in their journey, find a way to communicate with someone about what they had seen. He carefully picked up the map folding it tenderly before returning it to his bag, absently checking that the copies of the scouting report were present as well. They were, so that was good.

Wev had the men bring whatever they had found up on deck so it could be sorted. The pickings were somewhat slim, some food, mostly dried meat and some cheese -- enough for all of them for a few days at least. Along with that was several bottles of what they suspected was some type of wine or other spirits, some blankets, a pair of modest quality knives in matching sheaths and two small packs.

Mryl told them to bring it all. Within an hour they were on their way, single file through the brush and trees with one of their number ahead of them scouting the way. The day remained overcast as they walked; miles slowly fell by the wayside as the men continued on their way. The sleep they had been able to take in was helpful but all of them needed much more, so even with the urgency of their mission they couldn't move much faster for anything resembling an extended period.

Passing through a large stand of trees they moved out into a wide grassy plain, the weather remained overcast but not overly cool. The pace wasn't back breaking; the Guards were all too tired for that. Mryl wondered that they hadn't seen any settlements or even farms so far, he thought the area would have at least *somebody* living in it. But not so far…more walking.

Keeping them moving more east than north on the belief that it would be easier to find a populated area, Mryl saw the ground rising ahead of them with more woods in the distance. Wev and the others weren't talking much as they slogged through the knee high grass. This worried the Black Guard officer; their body language was telling him volumes, shoulders were slumped and heads weren't lifted as high as they should be for soldiers in unknown territory.

Calling for a break, Mryl motioned for them to gather around. He thought about giving them a rousing speech to try and lift their spirits but he found that he just didn't have it in him to do it. Besides it would likely come across as demeaning to the men; they were veteran soldiers who had much asked of them of late with more to come. They still had to get home.

Once the men were gathered around him Mryl said, "I know you're tired, I am too. At least we are out of the damned south."

A few hearty agreements followed that statement.

"We know what we need to do and right now keeping ourselves alert, awake, and moving are the priorities. And as a reward for all the hard work you've all put in, once we are home I believe I might be able to wrangle a day off or two for us all."

Some genuine laughter sounded which Mryl was pleased to hear. With that he told them to get a quick bite to eat then they would get going again. A meal of the dried meat and some cheese found on the boat was taken in.

When they resumed the march, the men seemed a bit more themselves. A measure of fatigue had been pushed back by the food and Mryl was grateful for that. The clouds were thinning, allowing more sunshine to poke through which lifted their spirits a bit more.

Within an hour of taking their repast the men found themselves beginning to move into another area of brush and trees as the ground rose a bit, sporting scattered hills, some of which seemed to be decent sized. The weather was cooperating somewhat, it was still solid overcast but it wasn't raining and the temperature had warmed up a bit so it was comfortable.

The man on point was trying to stay focused as he moved through the thickening brush. The fatigue factor had seriously eroded his ability to pick up on the fine details that he was there to see, the meal of earlier had helped. But he, like the others, was still operating at a physical deficit. Something ahead moved in the brush, he heard it which caused him to slow down to listen more intently.

Had he not been so tired he might have recognized the noise as a potential danger signal but his addled and fatigued mind missed the warning signs. The Guard moved toward the sound but before he could come around the rocks a loud, overpowering roar filled the air. A massive brown form suddenly towered above him with an earthshaking roar and a scream from him filled the air.

The others heard the commotion and they collectively began running toward the disturbance. The first two to reach the scene barely had time to determine what was happening before they were set on by a large attacker. Mryl was shouting at the others to hurry, he had his sword out.

The sounds of a serious fight could be heard coming from up ahead, none of the men had realized that as they had been moving through the increasingly thick brush and trees that they had allowed themselves to become much further strung out than they should have. That mistake was now compounded.

Wev turned sharply at hearing the sound; he spun round and took off at a full run heading in the direction of the sound. He crashed through the light brush and leapt the rocks that rose from the ground like a permanent crop in a forgotten field. As he ran a second wail came from somewhere ahead of him. Off to his right he caught a glimpse of one of the others running the same direction that he was as well.

The others came into the small clearing, eyes seeking the source of the danger; it took no time at all to identify the threat. One of the men was fighting what at first appeared to be two huge bears but the others quickly realized to their horror that it was in fact a pair of Dangals. The terrified Guard was frantically trying to keep two of the beasts at bay with limited success. His fellows wasted no time rushing to his aid.

The fight was now nine against the two Dangals, which while it seemed to favor the humans, was in fact barely a fair fight. Legends told of the fierceness of these creatures. A hybrid offspring mixture of majic and nature created long ago, what had once been a brown bear had become a terrifying beast. Each of the large animals had three sets of limbs and averaged nearly nine feet in height when standing erect, which is how they usually fought. The creatures were very territorial and apparently they felt that the humans were a threat to them so they attacked.

As Mryl and the others fought to survive the onslaught one of his men went down from a double claw swipe that nearly tore the luckless man in two. Four of the Guards were occupied with the second creature which was a smaller version of the other Dangal, a male. One of the Guards had wisely chosen to engage from a bit of a distance using his bow. Arrow after arrow was sent flying toward the enraged animals, most of them finding flesh but none penetrated a fatal area. The archer kept moving to try to get a better angle. He was running out of arrows but kept at it.

The other Guards arrived at last and joined the fight, up close and no quarter by either side. Roars and shouts filled the air as the fight continued. One of the men was working at distracting the beast so that two of the others could get an angle on the Dangals' blind spot. Another of the Guards was torn apart when he slipped trying to change positions. Wev yelled in fury when he saw the man killed.

The fight went on for several minutes with the archer getting in a lucky shot that penetrated through the eye of the larger Dangal which brought it down. As soon as it went down, the others turned their attention to the remaining animal. It took several more minutes before they were able to finally get in enough damage that the beast was slowed but the cost was high. Mryl ordered the men back to let the wounds take effect.

The Guards circled the beast warily trying to stay out of its reach. It took nearly a quarter hour for the blood loss to cause the female to stagger then slowly keel over. One of the men rushed in finish before Mryl could stop him. The beast had a bit of fight left, just enough to catch the man with a fierce bite and claw swipe, bringing him down. After that the others were content to let the beast die of its accord.

Mryl moved over to where the last wounded man lay. He reached down to gently brush the face with the back of his hand. A bloody hand stretched across the chest to grasp his arm by the wrist.

The man who lie there looked up and with his last breath spoke, "My Captain." Mryl felt the life leave him. The hand that had only heartbeats ago touched him slid open to lie on the chest almost in the manner of the salute that Karbel used to honor those of senior rank. The head gently rolled slightly to one side and then there was nothing.

The Black Guard tenderly reached up with a shaky hand and closed the sightless eyes that would see no more. Pain is gone from this one he thought. A tightness in his chest came over him as he stood, he felt weak and dizzy. There were no sounds, only the pounding of his heart in his ears as he tried to breathe in. Everything seemed to rush in on him. The bitter taste of bile rose in his throat that he was only able to choke back at the last instant. Mryl tried to blink away the tears that suddenly spilled unbidden from his eyes and blinded him.

The moisture that ran down his face cut runnels in the dirt and blood that marred his features. A dirty strand of his hair was stuck to his cheek by the blood that was there, warm and tacky. He lowered his head as the sobs born of anger, frustration and pain racked his body. His hand with no strength left in it opened, the sword dropping to the ground with a harsh ring of steel when the blade hit against a rock. Falling to his knees the Guard had not the strength to stand, this was the last. He couldn't take any more.

Around him the bodies of more of his men lie twisted and torn. Blood splatters were everywhere, on the trees, the rocks and the ground. In places the blood covered the surface of what it struck covering it completely. It was a garish sight and Mryl could not make himself turn away from. Six more of his own were gone, their lives ended in a desperate fight for survival that had claimed them, more of the loyal troopers that would never see home again.

More tears ran from his eyes, his chest heaving with exertion as the emotional gate he had been using to keep himself under control during the previous ten-days shattered and all the pent up emotions stormed over him. A wail of agony tore itself loose from his lips and he was like a beast sounding a cry for one of its own. The howl could scarcely be recognized as human, long and mournful.

Mryl beat the ground with his fists, dirt and dead leaves flying in the tumult. He was like a man possessed, anger and pain raged over him and there was little he could do but let it take him where it would. Another shriek tore itself from the man who had seen too much, lost too many. It was more than he could handle, reason and sanity were lost in a sea of pain.

He pounded the ground once more as he cried, his body rocked forward on his knees, no longer with the strength to raise his arms, he was emotionally spent. The burden of his choices had extracted too high a price.

Wev and the others watched the reaction of their leader, no one said anything. There wasn't anything that could be said. They felt the same way. Each man was alone with his own thoughts and feelings.

Mryl regained some measure of control, watching the surviving Black Guards place the bodies of the fellows side by side. They had served together in life and now in death they would remain comrades in arms. Covering the six bodies with stones took some time but there was no way that they would leave them. They had no tools to bury the men so a large cairn was the only option. Gathering up enough stones to cover all their friends took energy but they could do no less for the fallen.

There were only four of them left now: Mryl, his senior sergeant, and two troopers. The patrol had consisted of just over two dozen when they had departed from Kuln all those ten-days ago, Gods how long ago was that? He couldn't even clearly remember.

After sitting for a bit to recover their strength, the remaining quartet slowly began to stir. They all knew that they had to keep going. The run in with the Dangals had cost them more than a half a day and well more than that in flesh and spirit.

They moved onward through the woods as a group, no one on point. It wasn't a spoken decision but everyone wanted to stay together. After an hour or so of walking they found a sheltered spot near a small stream. Mryl merely nodded to the others, there had been no talking since they left the burial site.

A cold meal of rations and some water constituted dinner, then Wev had the others sleep, he told them in a low voice he would watch for now. The trio didn't argue, they simply lay down in the nearest location that looked even remotely promising and passed into sleep in short order. Wev sat in the growing darkness cursing the southern troops, cursing the Dangals, cursing the gods.

Night fell slowly as he guarded his friends.

In the morning, the spirit weary men awoke, Wev had been replaced by one of the troopers during the night. Mryl slept the entire night, the emotional release of the previous afternoon draining him to the point of utter collapse. A meager meal of more cold rations and water was taken in with little enthusiasm or talk. Once that was done each of them collected their equipment to continue their walk.

The four soldiers walked for about two hours when they came across the first signs of civilization in the form of scattered farms. A proper road soon presented itself which they began to follow, in what seemed short order a modest size settlement was visible. As the tired soldiers made their way into the village proper, numerous eyes were watching them with undisguised apprehension and some fear. Some scattered reports of trouble had already reached the village, wild tales of invasion, strange troops killing and burning.

Several burly men armed with a variety of implements stepped out from the front of the livery stable to confront the quartet of weary travelers. Mryl saw them and signaled his men to stand fast; he slowly raised his hands to show that he was not a threat. The other Guards did the same as several more villagers moved toward them.

Using the Common tongue Mryl began to try and explain their presence in the village. They were soldiers from Karbel and needed food, water, and horses. They had money and would pay. He spoke slowly at first but with a slowly growing confidence born of anger and dedication.

A man of middling age stepped forward, he was wearing a thick apron of leather and was holding a heavy hammer, likely the local blacksmith. In halting Common the man said he had some horses for sale, what was the color of their coine?

Using one hand only Mryl dug out the purse they had taken from the body of one of the southern sailors just before fleeing the south. He shook it twice so the man could hear the rattle. The blacksmith who also operated a small livery waved them forward but told several of his friends and townsmen to come also. Mryl got the message, no tricks or else. When the group reached the stable, the ironmonger called to his hand to bring out a horse. The animal was produced in short order. The temper of the blacksmith was well known which is why he had a hard time keeping help around the stable.

Mryl was disappointed when he saw the horse. It was definitely past its prime but right now he was in no position to be picky. He held up four fingers then made a circling motion to include himself and the other Guards to indicate that they needed four horses. In the end he paid more than what was a fair price but it didn't come close to depleting their funds, even with purchasing some fresh food which came quick when he showed he could pay.

Once the tired Guards were mounted, Mryl quickly explained to the gathered villagers about the coming southern army and that they would be well served making themselves ready to abandon their town if it proved necessary. He received more than a fair share of disbelief but he honestly didn't care. Asking directions to the Karbel frontier he nodded his thanks and then the four rode out.

Chapter Twenty-Five
Home and Hearth

Village of Arnoth

The long column of those from Karbel rode past several well-kept Elven farms and homes, all of them seemed to be perfectly placed in their surroundings. Stands of tall trees, some grown for use as oversized wind breaks, while others served as fences surrounded some of the houses, most of those painted in bright colors sat basking in the warm sun of mid-morning. Nothing was out of place, houses, barns, even the animals all idyllic in appearance something like a fancy painting on the wall of an affluent manor house, or so Shorin imagined.

Several of the residents had come outdoors to watch as the soldiers rode by. Shorin could see the curiosity carried on some of their faces as they talked among themselves, even as some pointed at the soldiers. Humans in this number and condition, heavily armed troops, the wounds on some of his men were heavily wrapped, dirty and blood stained, all had not been seen here for many more years than Shorin knew.

The steady clop of the horse hooves seemed to be coming from down a long hall, echoing and distant. He shook his head to try and wake himself up a little more with limited improvement. The effects of the last few days wore heavily on him, too little rest, poor food, and too much fighting.

They continued down the road and the tired captain could not help but notice the rich bounty of the area despite his fatigue. Several large well-tended orchards were situated on the northern side of the road and each tree seemed to carry an early weight of fruit, cherries, peaches and others weighed the branches down with their bounty.

The irony of the situation did not escape Shorin as he led the column at what some would very generously call a fast trot toward the village. It was the quiet beauty and calm of the peaceful farms and homes set against the ugliness of the war that was coming. He knew they were ahead of the southern cavalry but by how much he had no idea. Not nearly as far as he would like, of that he was sure. Several of his men were well behind to watch for their opposite numbers and give him some warning. Good lads all of them.

The troops rode side by side and moved steadily along. The village had appeared before them as they topped a rise in the road and began down the other side. Similar in layout to many human villages, with the inn and community buildings near the center, it was home to nearly nine hundred Elves, not counting those of the outlying farms which raised the overall numbers to well above a thousand.

The bright colors of the houses and gardens stood out in stark contrast to the long green grass surrounding the village. It was as if the town was an island of life in a vast sea of gently moving green. Even the brown dirt and gray gravel of the road seemed to fit in to the scheme somehow.

A wall of gray stone blocks circled the town, rising to the height of a tall man; Shorin immediately frowned at seeing that. It would need to be both heightened and strengthened to be able to hold off any type of determined attack if it might come. *If* - he asked himself; *when* may be the better question.

The village was sufficiently south that the nomads who rode the distant northern plains had not come this way in a considerable period of time. D'Lohm, the human kingdom to the southwest, was no aggressor so a heavier defense had not been needed for many years. At least until now, Shorin thought, peace can have a terrible price.

He shook his head to show his displeasure at the entire situation. He was a soldier, a Striker, but he was no lover of bloodshed. He fought because it was necessary; that he had killed many times was of no consequence, he never kept count of those whose life he had ended -- something that many of the troopers did. It was a badge of honor among them, the more the better. Shorin had certainly killed more than some, more than most if the truth was known, but killing just to kill was something he avoided.

The weary Striker, trying to refocus his thoughts, knew he would need somewhere to use as a base of operations from which he would be able to strike out at the all too rapidly approaching southern columns. He felt that it was likely to be multiple columns; the unit they had run into was obviously the vanguard for a large army. It was too big, too organized and well-armed for nomads.

Any army that size would use more than one column to move, it had to. It offered better mobility, increased offensive power and would be easier to forage for. He knew it was trouble, of that he was sure. The men of Karbel continued along the road, the village getting closer. Another reason for seeking out those in the area was to warn them.

According to his maps of the area, long since memorized, this village was the only habitation of size for some distance in any direction. It was the western-most of all the Elven towns and settlements while behind the Strikers in all directions lay only the vast miles of grasslands that made up the immense eastern plains of that part of the continent. The closest village belonging to Karbel was nearly a full day's hard ride away; none of the six large cities of the kingdom were situated in that part of the nation.

The Striker commander had sent three of his men off at different times bearing news of the invasion to that village and beyond but he didn't know if any of them had gotten through. It was likely that they could just now be arriving at the village if they did. He knew that they needed massive reinforcements but was certain they would be slow in coming when word got through to higher command.

First would be disbelief at the reports; that disbelief would then give way to inaction while someone decided what to do even if they believed the report. Then once they did decide to do something it would take time to assemble the forces to send.

Shorin shook his head in disgust at the situation. There was no doubt that they were in trouble and the overly tired man knew that he didn't have all the answers. Ruefully the admission came that even if he had all the answers he still didn't know what he would do.

So, for now this village, whatever it was called would have to do, his men and their mounts were sorely tired and badly needed some rest. Some of the riders were even now trying hard to stay awake, swaying in their saddles with exhaustion.

Even more urgent were the wounded he had which numbered at least fifty of the two hundred and nineteen riders. Some more so than others, a few he knew would not see morning no matter the help they might get. Most of those were from the Legionnaire unit that had been ambushed, whose survivors the Strikers had picked up and brought with them. They had been given all the care that had been possible during that time but hard fighting and riding had taken its toll.

Nearly a dozen of the Legionnaires and Strikers had been quickly buried without markers. The location carefully placed on his map so that later it would be possible to return and retrieve the bodies. The Strikers never leave their own, no matter the situation; it was part and parcel of who they were.

Leaving his men like that even though he had every intention of returning to claim them left Shorin feeling as if he had betrayed them and the Striker tradition somehow. He tried to push away the feeling of shame and succeeded if only a little, the decision ate at him, doubt clouded parts of his judgment.

***

A review of their situation replayed for what seemed the hundredth time. The regular army troop had been at the far end of their scheduled patrol along the southern edge of the kingdom near the border with D'Lohm, patrolling for smugglers and slavers when they began to encounter groups of refugees fleeing north into Karbel. The senior patrol member, a veteran sergeant, after speaking to various people in several such groups decided to head south to try and find out what was going on.

Shorin and his men, out on patrol of their own, had come across several large groups of people as well, most on foot heading north out of D'Lohm with little more than the clothes on their backs. They spoke of great trouble in the south and wild tales of invaders and were seeking safety elsewhere. This is what had sent the Strikers south crossing well into the neighboring country trying to find some answers.

The Strikers were doing that when they ran into the hornet's nest of southern cavalry. The Legionnaires had done the same hours earlier and had been ambushed by a unit of horsemen. Shorin, before entering D'Lohm, had sent word back to get more men and pass along what was being reported by the refugees. It wasn't until much later that he found out that those reports were never relayed. The young under-captain had repeatedly thanked the gods for the decision to consolidate his forces; the additional men had met him along the way. It was the only reason he had barely adequate numbers with him when he and his men had run into the southern cavalry unit.

After locating the main body of the cavalry several running fights and ambushes followed, stinging the invaders. It was a large unit, well over seven hundred men was his best guess despite their losses. He knew word would be sent out but the speed that events were happening seemed too fast for news to stay current.

To confuse the enemy the group rode to the northeast after breaking contact, Shorin felt it unlikely that whoever was commanding the cavalry would think him to flee that way. He earnestly hoped so anyway.

What the veteran Striker didn't know was that several of the nearest heliograph stations had already been attacked and destroyed by some of the advance units of the invasion force. The southern forces were well aware of the communications network that Karbel utilized, paying special attention to locating them prior to the invasion so attacking them would be possible. Word wasn't going to be passed along to the capital anytime soon.

The Striker column had picked up the pace when the village came into sight so they were now nearly at the gate. A small delegation of inhabitants had gathered at the western entrance to the settlement. The village had two, one each on the east and west sides. Word of the approaching soldiers had come in earlier from some of the outlying farms. The tall Striker could see that the number milling near the gate was increasing steadily. Entertainment comes in many forms and at the moment that would be us he told himself ruefully.

The tired man signaled for the troop to halt near the edge of the village. The riders halted as Shorin rode forward the last bit of distance and moved his horse off the road to speak with a tall Elf who had walked out from the front of the assembled villagers.

The Elf was dressed in plain but well-tended clothing and he carried himself well. A quiet air of authority seemed to hover about him, this was someone used to be being in charge. After the tall human had rode up to him and stopped, the Elf reached out and gently touched the tired horse on the nose and stroked him lightly. The mount lowered his head some to allow the gentle touch to reach between his ears.

The battered Striker sat slightly slumped in the saddle, both hands rested on the saddle horn as if to help hold him up. The tall Elf appeared to be of indeterminate age as many of his kind did. He could be a hundred and forty or four hundred it was hard to tell with some of the Elves. Having spent the last several years with Parun the human was better educated than most of his race concerning how to handle the exchange with what was obviously the village elder or chieftain. He knew this moment was important, he had to have the village for a base and so having this man on their side would be crucial.

The Striker officer locked gazes with the tall member of the Elder Race as he sat upright and then raised one hand open palm in salute and spoke, "Greetings and peace upon you Father-Elder, I am Captain Shorin Tallon of Karbel, His Majesty's Strikers." Shorin spoke in Merlik, the tongue of the High Elves, and delivered with a respectful bow of the head.

Pleasantly surprised at not only hearing his own language, but well spoken, the tall Elf stopped his ministering of the horse and bowed in return. Several of the closer Elves seemed surprised at such eloquent words coming from a soldier, a *human* soldier at that.

"I bid you welcome in the name of the town of Arnoth," he replied in Merlik welcoming the rider. A studied eye quickly looked the soldier over, his tunic was black with silver highlights over a short sleeve shirt of mail travel stained with dirt and blood that could be seen scattered all over the man. His face was long with fatigue and heavy burden. Keen eyes rode beneath the brows, eyes that missed little but were for now clouded from, Logas suspected, the lack of sleep and decent food. The long dark hair was stringy and filthy. His mount was tired and lathered from a long, hard ride. The gentle equine eyes watched him as well.

Shorin nodded politely in reply. The Elf introduced himself as Logas Kalantiere, the village elder and switched languages to that of Karbel. "How may we be of service?"

The question was polite, but direct. The Striker liked Logas immediately, no farting around with this one. In spite of the circumstances a small smile creased the weary face of the proud soldier. The smile lifted years of age from the grim visage of sweat and dried blood, only some of it his. Shorin paused for just a moment, knowing full well the weight of what he must tell Logas and how it would change forever the life of this village.

"I bring grave news, but first may we enter? I have wounded, some of them need help right away." As he spoke his head turned to the long column behind him and then back to the Elf.

Logas looked quickly at the soldiers then turned to several of those gathered outside the gate, speaking too rapidly for Shorin to follow despite his command of the language. Several of the Elves ran back into the village, others moved toward the column.

Logas bowed his head more deeply this time and asked forgiveness of the tall rider, he said he should have asked about their wounded right away and of course they could enter immediately. Elvish hospitality was well known throughout the lands, even if it was mocked in some less mannered quarters. The phrase "polite as an Elf" was high praise indeed in many circles.

Shorin turned in the saddle, waved the column forward with his left hand and turned back to their host. He bowed deeply as he thanked the Elf for his hospitality on behalf of his men. Logas returned the offered salute. The column slowed as it reached the gate. The unwounded riders filed off to the sides of the road, remaining outside the village to allow the wounded to come forward first and receive help. The wounded had been placed mainly in the middle part of the column to protect them if they were attacked again.

They quickly reached the high wooden gates and passed through being escorted by some of the Elves. More of the residents were appearing from inside the walls to assist the wounded as word spread through the village of the visitors and their needs. The Elves all wondered what was happening but it didn't keep them from aiding the soldiers in the meantime.

The senior Striker watched without a sound as the injured continue to move past him. An arrow wound, a sword slash, a long cut from an axe, the wounded seemed to just keep coming. He watched as one of his injured men, being held upright by the man to his left, he no less wounded than his companion, rode through the gate.

Shorin was as tired as they were, tired down to the depth of his soul. Sleep he knew would only help so much, but some of it would still be nice! Then again, so would having about of five hundred more Strikers with him. *Doing what I can with what I have…*

Tallon had seen death up close and enough bloodshed for several lifetimes the last few years in the service to his king and it was beginning to show. Fighting smugglers, slavers and potential assassins had slowly starting eating at his spirit some time back. Warfare had become his whole life; his skill at doing it was part of the reason that he was the youngest Under-Captain in the history of the elite Strikers. His name was often the first that came up when there were dirty jobs, the ones that needed a sword's sharp touch to remove. He spent far more time out on the frontier than he had in the city. Something that was fine with him but it was still a great deal for someone not yet twenty-five to carry.

The last several days had been especially bad, the close-in brutal no quarter fighting, ambushes, poor food and long hours of riding had taken their toll on men and mounts without prejudice. As part of the price Shorin paid for doing his duty he had started to become hard and unfeeling about most things. He could sense the change but not recognize it for what it was nor did he know how to alter it. Little did he know that what lie ahead would test him to his limits and beyond.

Logas was dividing his attention between the riders moving through the gate and the man astride the horse near him. He spent a few moments watching the soldier and studied him some without making it obvious. The man was tall, over six feet but a touch thin. His build suggested he was fit and what was present under the dirty tunic and armor was solid muscle. The face was dirty with mud and dried blood streaking the features somewhat. It was the eyes of the soldier that kept Logas looking, there was a haunted look present there, the young soldier had seen much in his, the elf guessed twenty or so seasons of life.

The Elves who had re-entered the village had gathered others, all of them were waiting for the wounded, more showing up as word continued to spread. A young Elf of only thirty or so summers, a pre-teen to these eldest of living creatures was ringing the large town bell with an unusual sense of urgency. The rapid strikes of the clanger adding to the clamor that had ridden into usually quiet, almost sleepy village of Arnoth turning the village on its collective ear.

More of the residents appeared, drawn out of their homes by the unusual disruption in their normally calm daily lives. The wounded riders were led to the center of the settlement and helped off their mounts. Some of the more seriously wounded simply fell off their horses, no longer with the strength to sit upright, landing heavily on the decorative paving stones that covered the avenue. Several Elves and some of their less wounded comrades rushed to help them.

The wounded were taken inside the inn that formed the southern edge of the square and carried to the various rooms to be tended to by the village healer and his assistant, neither of whom would see a bed for many hours after this.

Most Elves have some knowledge of the medical arts and some experience with healing especially with those injuries that the various inhabitants of the world sought to inflict upon each other, and they all pitched in to help with the numerous wounded. It is part and parcel of the world in this day. It hadn't always been so but it likely would continue, the awful effects of war had come to Arnoth.

The Elves started work at once on the wounded while others were pulling together the goods and equipment to begin preparing a meal for them and the rest of the soldiers, still others looked to the horses, many of them footsore and hungry.

Once the guest rooms were filled the common area of the inn was pressed into service for the wounded. The worst ones were placed in beds but some were stretched out on the long dining tables simply due to lack of space. The inn was not a large one compared to other towns but served an excellent local ale.

Several of the humans were led into homes along the street and made to lie down. Many fell asleep immediately despite their injuries and need for a meal and a bath. Some of the villagers led the numerous horses away to care for and feed them as well. The Elves were kind to animals and the love of a good horse was high on the list of important things.

After the wounded were inside the village, Shorin stiffly dismounted then stood next to Logas while trying to stretch his tired, aching muscles that had been subjected to no rest and a long, hard ride. The Strikers who had remained outside of the village were waiting on their horses lining both sides of the road leading into the village. The two leaders were standing near the gate when a sudden command startled the Striker captain. He whirled at the sudden sound; saw that his men, Strikers and Legionnaires alike were sitting at the position of attention, horses faced inward on both sides of the road.

Parun, who was halfway down the line, nudged his horse forward two steps and with deliberate movements slowly drew his sword using it to salute his commander. The rest of the Strikers and Legionnaires followed suit forming a canopy of glittering steel over the road. The effect on Shorin was instant, he felt much of the fatigue and mental fog that had been weighing on him vanish.

Dropping the reins of his horse, he took several steps forward to place himself in the middle of the road then pulled himself to attention while facing down the rows of his riders. He slowly drew the sword hanging at his side to return the salute of these men.

The pride the young Striker felt at that moment was nearly overwhelming. He saw the fatigue, the wounds and most of all the determination they all carried. Logas witnessed the tribute being paid to the tall soldier and he felt joy for the display but with it a sense of concern regarding the grave news that the soldier carried.

Obviously these men had seen battle recently and Logas wondered what it meant to his people. He feared the worst and as is often the case the worst was what was coming. There were many questions dancing through his mind. Chief among those was - why were these men here in their village?

The cities of Karbel were a fair distance to the west but the village had always welcomed friendly traders and travelers, no matter where they were from. The location of the town, in the opening between the arms of the massive Shyval mountain range, made it a natural stopping point for traffic in both directions. In fact there were several Dwarf and human traders in the village now.

But Logas sensed that these travelers would be very different indeed. No word had arrived in the village concerning raiders in the area, who Logas assumed were the ones that these men had fought. He would have to wait and hear it from this tall human. The thought of the village being attacked concerned him greatly; Arnoth had known peace for many years, now it appeared that was about to change drastically. His mind already turned over different plans and ideas regarding defenses.

After returning the salute from his men, Shorin waved his sword over his head and yelled out the battle cry of the Strikers, "King and Karbel!" The troops picked up the cheer and chanted it over and over, caught up in the moment.

They all knew that the southies were coming but they weren't here yet and for this moment what mattered is that they were there and alive. Swords waved wildly, cutting the air as the cheers continued for a few moments more. The release of pent up emotions was a welcome feeling, like taking the capstone off a natural water spring, as fear and anger were cast aside and the joy of being alive replaced it, at least for now. It had been a hard fought time and for the proud soldiers of Karbel revenge for their losses had to be taken.

A number of Elves had come to the gate to see what the shouting was about. Most did not speak the human tongue and those that did translated for the others. Some looked displeased at the open display of emotions but most seemed to understand. A few were dismayed at the brandishing of weapons, the Elves long a peaceful race. Logas noticed this and dismissed the thought; everyone was entitled to their own opinion. He knew from experience it was sometimes necessary to take up arms to defend your beliefs and homes and wondered if now was such a time? What disturbed him deeper was the notion that the choice may have already been made for them. A frown furled his brow as he considered that.

The cheering continued for several moments during which the Striker commander turned to speak to Logas. The Elf bid him welcome to the village with a wave of his hand toward the gate, a glint of a smile shown in his eyes. The Striker captain paused only long enough to sheath his blade.

A nod from Shorin and they were headed inside the walls. Behind them Parun was giving out necessary assignments. Posting outriders to watch for any sign of the southern cavalry was a high priority. The others began dismounting so they could rest.

One of the Elves near the gate took the reins of Shorin's horse and led it away with the promise of proper care. The Striker nodded his thanks and rubbed the flank as the horse was lead off for a meal and a much deserved rest and care. The chestnut colored flank shone with the sweat that marked the day's ride.

Logas walked down the street with his guest at his side heading toward the inn to check on the wounded, it was Shorin's first request as they walked through the open gates. Logas never hesitated as he escorted the soldier.

As they walked, Shorin took in the scene around him. The street was wide enough for four riders abreast and paved with different colored stones had been used to form varied patterns in the wide avenue. Several times as they walked it was necessary for them to stop or change directions to avoid bustling villagers or soldiers intent on their various errands. A number of horses were being led to the city park area since it was the largest open area in the walled village. The street was a bustle of activity of all types; Shorin felt bad upsetting the quiet village but deep down knew it couldn't be helped.

Once at the inn the two moved inside but made it no farther than the entry to the common room. Wounded were being tended all over the space, organized chaos reigned as calls for dressings, salves and sewing supplies abounded. Shorin watched the Elves as they worked to ease the suffering that these men were enduring. No words left his lips, the scene of bloody dressings, cries and shrieks of the injured and the distinct gentle tones of Merlik would stay with him till his last day. Logas said nothing as he stood with the man who had come to him for help. Two Elves apologized as they bumped into the pair as they entered the building carrying some of the requested items and then hurried inside with the badly needed supplies.

The Headman gently pulled Shorin out of the building by the arm and while his feet moved him outside the eyes of the Striker never left the interior of the room until the door closed and the sounds muted. Shorin turned to look at Logas, started to open his mouth to speak twice, but he couldn't speak the words -- as lost to him as if he was mute. Logas allowed him to collect himself and then with a wave of one hand suggested they continue. The Striker merely nodded once and with no little effort stepped off to follow his host who had started walking.

The activity level in the village continued to flow at a high pace. Logas spoke to several of the residents along the way while avoiding any mention of the serious news that the soldier had spoken of previously. It was early spring so the numerous trees and flowering plants that filled the village were alive with life. Flowers and other plants gave the air a sweet fragrance that came and went with the breeze.

Twice while walking, Logas was stopped by small groups of residents seeking clarification of his requests regarding their "visitors".

Both times he politely apologized for the interruption to his companion; Shorin understood completely and told his host so. Having several hundred troops suddenly show up could cause some confusion to anyone's day.

Shorin was very careful to return all the greetings he received from the villagers they passed who spoke to him; not all of them did but they were in the minority. It would be important to have the support of those who lived here and being polite cost nothing. Logas took notice of the effort being spent but said nothing, instead spending some to time to try and gain further insight on the young human soldier who had appeared at their door this day.

He gathered that the man was an officer, he was young, less than thirty to be sure and he was bothered by more than a few things. Logas felt he could only guess at what some of them were but patience would reveal truth, as the Elves said.

While they walked and talked Logas answered all the questions that his young companion asked regarding population, water supply, food availability, distance to the nearest unit of the army and on and on. As the answers poured forth Shorin became more convinced that the village would work as a temporary strongpoint from which to slow down the southern cavalry.

Finished with the extensive tour of the town Logas asked his guest "Would you accept the hospitality of my house and with me sup?"

Shorin was hesitant to accept with so much to do and was looking for a way to politely decline the offer when Logas continued, "My new young soldier friend, several things are obvious. You and your men have been engaged with a serious enemy, trouble is coming and you have not eaten well or rested for some time. You cannot lead if you cannot stand - your men are being fed and cared for. Should you not a moment take and do the same?" A small grin lit the face of the Elf as he spoke.

The Striker found no flaw with the question and so accepted the offer. He stopped in the street and with an exaggerated flourish born of exhaustion bowed to his host, his head bowed deeply and one arm sweeping grandly in the air.

"So be it, to sup it is." Shorin stood, a little embarrassed at the production he had made of the answer. He wrote it off to the exhaustion looking sheepishly at the older figure who was smiling at the display.

Logas liked the young human; in spite of the best efforts of his profession he had not completely lost his laughter. The Headman indicated the direction with a wave of his hand. Numerous residents were bustling about to see to the needs of the soldiers who were scattered throughout the town, some of those not needed by Parun had come into the town.

Some of these were in the park sleeping on the grass, most not even bothering to find the shady areas before laying down to sleep. Weapons and essential equipment were close at hand if needed. Horses were being tended nearly everywhere due to the number of them. Shorin sent word via one of his men for Parun to come to the house of the Headman when he was done with his duties. The elite trooper nodded and went at once looking for the senior sergeant.

Passing two side streets and finally turning onto a third, the pair walked by a few more houses before arriving before a small but comfortable looking two story cottage set back from the lane and fronted by a low stone wall. The house seemed warm and inviting from the outside.

Large rose bushes lined both sides of the walkway and along the front of the residence, blooms not yet open but many in number. Several other varieties of flowers, many already blooming, filled the various window boxes along the front of the home. A tall, almost regal looking fir tree lent a generous measure of shade to one side of the rich yard, deep green in color.

Logas preceded Shorin up the walk and once at the front porch opened the door and stood to the side while he bid Shorin enter.

After nodding his thanks, the Striker wiped the soles of his boots as best he could on the stone to clean them then stepped through and then inside. The interior was clean and orderly, the woodwork glistened of polish and care. A small fire was visible in the hearth of the main room tastefully set with rich furniture.

The Elf escorted Shorin to the dining area and waved him to a chair next to the table. Sunlight spilled in a large window and added a soft golden glow to the room. The tired man gratefully accepted the offer, he sat heavily, much more so than he had intended. Logas noticed this but said nothing, waiting till his guest sat before doing so himself.

A small bouquet of early season flowers were stylishly arranged in a vase on the table further brightening the room. Shorin thought back on the farm house he had been raised in and a spring of warm memories flooded over him including thoughts of his recent visit.

The door to the kitchen swung open and a figure stepped through. Shorin thought that he had heard a light footfall on the other side of the door and had started to turn his head toward it when it opened. The warm glow of the wooden doorframe seemed to shine around the figure that paused for just a moment to take in the scene and then stepped through the door which swung lightly closed behind the figure as she approached the table.

The tall Striker was suddenly aware of the fact that he had never seen a more beautiful woman in his entire life. Logas stood again as manners dictated, Shorin, still nearly mesmerized by the beauty of the woman lagged behind him badly in rising as well. The woman stopped just before the table, her footfall so light as to be nearly silent. This was the grace of an Elf personified.

She was dressed in a skirt of modest length, a soft medium green in color with a sleeveless blouse of the same hue. High brown boots gracefully covered her legs to about mid-calf. Her hair was incredibly golden in color and fell to her shoulder blades in the back, a simple silver circlet visible in her hair as the front curls framed her face.

It was her eyes that Shorin would remember forever. They were a sparkling blue; to him they seemed deep and clear as the mountain springs of the high country in the western region of Karbel with just a hint of laughter tossed in. Her hands were clasped together in front of her as she stood.

Logas introduced her as his daughter, Jehna. She reached out a delicate hand which Shorin started to take it as custom outlined but suddenly hesitated. The man who dealt in the business of war and death felt that his hands were too soiled with dirt and dried blood to take hers. Jehna noticed this and took his hand anyways; her touch was warm and alive.

The warmth of her touch flashed through Shorin and he held her hand longer than was necessary. He introduced himself and she smiled as he did.

She had heard the bell and had gone to investigate the cause of alarm seeing the first group of wounded being brought in. She knew that her father would be bringing whoever was in charge back to the house, so hurried back home arriving not long before the two. She could assist him in whatever manner she needed to, as she had done in the past serving as hostess when necessary, as now.

The smile she carried lit the room and shot through to his soul. The feeling was warm and powerful. The elder Elf asked his guest if he was ready to eat. Shorin, still taken with the beauty of the woman before him, missed the question entirely. Jehna smiled broader at this and then she asked their guest the question herself. Catching and mentally cursing himself for acting like a stupid schoolboy, the senior Striker accepted the offer of a meal and thanked his hosts for their hospitality.

Jehna gently disengaged her hand from that of the soldier to return to the kitchen to retrieve the requested fare. Shorin watched her go and numbly retook his seat while his gaze followed the fair Elf as she went back into the kitchen.

Logas gathered plates and utensils from a nearby cabinet then sat to eat with his guest to avoid being rude, having eaten a filling breakfast earlier in the day before the soldiers arrived. A large pot of hearty stew, fresh warm bread and rich butter were quickly hustled from the kitchen and set before them. The smell of the warm food flooded his mouth with spit as he realized he had not had a hot meal in nearly four or was it six days now? He couldn't remember, the last thing he had eaten was some jerked meat and even that was nearly two days ago. There simply hadn't been time to eat; staying alive had been the priority.

The young Striker did his best to remember some of his social graces and not shovel the food down, it was delicious and he was well past famished. His stomach nearly rebelled at first having had nothing warm in it for some time. He fought down the rush of nausea and briefly slowed down to allow the food to settle.

A large drink of water helped to calm his insides as well as help to begin to replenish his fluid levels. The cool well water tasted better than any wine or spirits he had ever had. The bread was fresh and sprinkled through with dill weed, an herb unknown to the soldier which he asked about, intrigued with the flavor.

Jehna joined the pair at the table after gathering the meal and she ate as well for the same reason as her father. The large pitcher of well water was refilled twice from the bucket kept in the kitchen to keep up with their guest. Shorin had trouble recalling the last time he had eaten so fine a meal, he had always favored rough peasant style faire and the stew was excellent, tender seasoned chunks of rabbit, heavy with vegetables mixed in a hearty broth. His body craved nourishment from the demands of the last few days and so he was far from full or finished when he stopped eating long enough to open a small pouch at his belt. He tossed two pinches of salt from it into his mouth, washing it down with a half glass of the sparkling water.

The soldier was aware of the body's need for the vital seasoning. Some of fatigue disappeared along with a measure of the weakness due to hunger. He was not completely better but it was helping. Strength began to fill him again as the nourishment began to take hold. It would take more than one meal to get the tired soldier back on his feet fully but this was a good start.

He gave Jehna a very sincere compliment on her food and she thanked him for his kind words but surely this was just simple village food? Shorin quickly assured her that if this was simple village food then a few kings may want to move in next door! Logas laughed at the words of the soldier who seemed to have relaxed some since he first saw the young human. She beamed at the praise and the genuine words that the soldier passed to her.

Shorin was well into a large unasked for but welcome second helping when a knock came at the front door. Logas started to get up to answer it when Jehna told him to stay, having finished her miniscule portion. She stood up waving both men down, crossed the room to open the door.

Standing before her was another soldier but unlike their current human guest this one was half-Elven. It was clear to Jehna that their new guest was of mixed blood, Elf and human, the height and bone structure of the soldier gave it away but she made no mention of it. After all, one cannot pick their parents.

Her father had taught her and her siblings tolerance and acceptance of those of mixed blood as part of that. Many Elves, often the most polite of all races, would openly shun an individual of mixed heritage with no thought to manners, some in the village already had when they noticed the parentage of the Striker sergeant.

Parun, long used to such behavior from his own people ignored those who lifted their collective nose at him. He had more important things to worry about than somebody's idea of social standing. The veteran soldier had dealt with prejudice like that his whole life so this was nothing new even if it was from his own people.

She bade him welcome and asked him in. He thanked her in Merlik and entered the house, stopping just inside the door and bowing once in the Elven style to pay respect to the residents of the house. Once an Elf had done this it was not necessary to repeat it again but the gesture caught Jehna's attention and she noted the respect being paid and smiled. Parun's response was a half grin that Jehna found warming. He asked if Shorin was here and Jehna told him he was and waved toward the dining area and the others.

Jehna lead the soldier to the dining area where he nodded deeply in respect to Logas as both village Headman and the household elder. Logas, having stood when he heard his daughter ask someone to enter, politely returned the gesture and bid his new guest to join them for the meal. Parun looked once at Shorin who nodded immediately his desire to have his senior sergeant join them.

The young officer knew that his friend had not eaten any better than he had and suspected that it was probably less. The lithe half-elf quickly settled into a chair at the end of the table thanking Jehna when she placed a heaping plate of stew in front of him, followed by a large slab of the fresh bread topped with butter. A tall glass of the cool water completed the setting.

Her presence seemed to fill the entire room as she looked at the two hungry troopers; it was not rare for the house to feel the weight of soldier's boots as her father was the village leader but human soldiers fresh from battle was new and not entirely comfortable.

In between bites the Strikers began to explain the situation regarding their soon to be unwelcome guests. Shorin knew that time was of the essence, but he was so mentally fatigued that he had needed the time to gather himself so that when the conversation regarding the situation did take place, he would be able to better articulate it. Having Parun there to tell the tale would help as well.

As more of the saga unfolded Logas stopped eating entirely and listened with a growing sense of concern. He looked at Jehna who mirrored his shock and worry; she found a seat near her father, never missing a word as the account poured forth.

War was coming to Arnoth and there was nothing they could do to avoid it. The elder Elf felt a flash of anger that these men had brought it with them but just as quickly tossed it aside as he realized that they would have had no warning at all. At least with the soldiers here the village had a better chance and it was not they who had started it.

Shorin left nothing out as he related the story; Logas heard the anguish in the younger man's voice as he spoke of the need to leave his men in unmarked resting places while the group rode away. Parun paused with the fork between his plate and mouth to remind his commander that it was the right thing to do at the time and it took courage to do it. He kept his eyes steady on those of the captain while he made the statement. Shorin was too tired to argue but still felt inside that he had betrayed the trust of those he commanded.

Jehna spoke for the first time since the story began to ask Shorin a question, hers was a simple one, "Did you do everything you could for them?"

The Striker replied at once that he had and as soon as he said it felt some of the guilt fade away as if by giving those words a voice it made more sense to him. Parun resumed eating with a short nod to Jehna to acknowledge the wisdom of the query. Logas watched as the thoughts of the man across the table from him worked themselves out.

For his part Shorin felt a little better after hearing what she had asked. He had done everything he could, he honored the men and what they fell fighting for and knew one day he would return to bring them home. Yes, he had done everything he could for them. Returning his attention to the last few bites on his plate he finished the meal with a gusto that had been lacking moments before, the burden on his heart now a touch lighter.

The Elven beauty caught the slight smile on her father's face as he approved of her actions. The pair of soldiers finished their meal and both thanked the pair again for the fine repast. Logas asked Shorin what his intentions were. The Striker pushed aside his now empty plate and began to explain what he had in mind. The four were soon deep in heavy conversation regarding the immediate future of them all.

After their discussion, Logas sent word for all the available residents to come to the town square right away. He rarely called for town meetings, preferring instead to deal with his neighbors in a more informal fashion; he customarily held about three formal town meetings a year. One just prior to the planting season, one usually just after harvest and the third was to oversee the celebration the village held at year's end.

The summons was hurriedly passed and most made their way to the center of the village. Some needed to stay with the wounded and asked to be informed of whatever news there was. Others promised to return with news as soon as they could.

At least four hundred of the residents and some of those from nearby farms had come in response to the earlier summons for help with the soldiers. Stepping up into the bed of a wagon so that he could be seen and heard by as many as possible Logas raised his arms to ask for silence. He slowly lowered them and paused before speaking to gather his thoughts and stave off for just one more moment the news he was about to bring and what it would do to their lives.

"My friends thank you for coming so quick. As you know, we have guests among us." The line delivered with a wry smile; there were several of the Strikers standing with Shorin near the wagon who was quietly translating for them.

"These men are soldiers of Karbel and bring grave news. They have fought several battles to the west of us and came here to seek our help and provide us warning." The burden of leading his people shown little on the face of the Headman but the burden was there nonetheless. The crowd was silent but expectant since some of them had heard from the other soldiers what had happened to them. Logas pressed on with the news.

"A large force of foreign soldiers is coming this way and could be here in no more than six hours or so. If they come they will likely attack us here, in our homes." He turned to look at Shorin who understood and climbed into the wagon with him.

The sight of the tall soldier silenced many in the crowd who had begun to speak among themselves at the news. The Striker took a deep breath and began to explain to them in Merlik which only helped his cause. He spoke directly but without haste what the situation was, how his men found and fought the coming troops, that the troops could only be the lead element for many more and he outlined the risks for them all. He spoke with a quiet elegance that surprised some, Logas among them in spite of their earlier conversation.

When he was done, Logas turned once more to the crowd, "The question before us is this: Do we stay and fight or do we leave the village and head east?" The question hung in the air for a brief moment before several voices cried out.

"Leave!"

"Stay and fight!" This seemed the more acceptable solutions as more of the villagers raised their voices in support of this choice. The calls for staying become louder and more pronounced. Logas allowed the responses to continue for a few more moments and then again raised his arms for silence; it took longer this time to quiet the crowd. For his part Shorin stood next to him in the wagon surprised at the passion level of the villagers but said nothing, it was not yet time for him.

"Friends, let me say this. I am for staying and fighting, this is our home and our place in the world." Several cheers went up and he quickly lifted one hand to ask for quiet again before he lost the momentum he was gaining.

"But if, and I mean if, we stay and fight we must look to the safety of the children and eld. We have a greater responsibility to them than ourselves, is that not so?" Several heads in the crowd bobbed up and down in acknowledgement of the statement. Logas had been elected Headman nearly fifty years earlier and several of the residents nodded at the wise words of their leader.

Discussion was brisk and for those of the Elder Race, spirited. In the end it was decided to stay and try and hold the village - no castle will stand if no one guards the doors. Word was to be sent via several of the younger Elves to the nearest farms, towns and villages of the danger and to alert whatever army units that may be in the area. It could be some time before they could get there but word had to be sent.

The message also asked for any who could come and help defend Arnoth, although Logas knew that this was likely a futile gesture. What help was available would be needed to ensure the safety of other locations as well as Arnoth. Still it doesn't hurt to ask. Groups were assigned and work details handed out. Those gathered began to leave the square rapidly to begin the tasks at hand.

Work proceeded at once in and around village to fortify it as best as possible. Arnoth was a farming community not a fortress. Despite the

Strikers request for them to leave, most of the women of the village stayed to help with the work.

The children had been gathered together; some belongings packed and under the supervision of the school master and several younger females had been sent to another village away to the east filling several wagons along with the wounded soldiers that could handle being moved. Several of the more elderly members of the community were persuaded to go with the children to "assist in their care". Several smiles had broken out when Logas used that ruse to move them from their homes and head them east and the perceived safety to be found there.

Shorin and Logas were everywhere at once it seemed. Logas had served in the Elven army many years before but had not forgotten the lessons he learned while fighting nomads and goblins, a scourge wherever they appeared.

The harried Striker knew that time was not his ally in this and pushed everyone hard trying to make up the difference. Dirt flew in copious amounts as a ditch took shape around the village, several hundred shovels and picks tearing at the rich loam. The soil was then moved via baskets and buckets inside the wall and dumped behind it to firm it up and raise the height. This would serve several purposes, a wide enough ditch meant that the southern cavalry would have to dismount to fight and that would rob them of their mobility. Time was not the defenders ally and so work proceeded without pause.

The Striker commander berated himself for the delay in speaking with Logas regarding the situation but it couldn't be helped now. The large numbers of the approaching cavalry already gave them a distinct advantage that Shorin wanted to remove or at least reduce as much as possible. All the spare lumber that could be found was being used to strengthen the two gates to stand up to whatever the invaders would attempt and to build mantlets to shield those inside the walls from arrows. Shutters were found to be nearly perfect for the task and many a house suddenly found itself without exterior window coverings.

Local craftsmen worked alongside the human soldiers who had been roused from their meager slumber, given a large plate of something hot to eat before beginning the labor that would give the hated Southerners a hard time. Wooden spikes were being driven into the wall to impale anyone trying to storm the barrier.

A party of about twenty Elves bearing long bows had ridden away heading to the west to serve as advance watch and give the enemy reason to delay his advance if possible. Shorin had argued against that but Logas told him simply that it was their land and up to them to defend, just as the humans would if the situation was reversed. The Striker captain merely shook his head at the logic but decided what was done was done.

A makeshift relay system had been set up with picket riders arrayed to the south and west looking for the southern cavalry. At the first sign of them the message would be relayed to the village. Shorin had been very forceful in explaining to the pickets that their job was to observe and report, nothing more, if they could do it and not be seen at all so much the better. Most of these were the younger Elves of the village and surrounding farms.

Food was being brought into the village as well since they did not know how long they might be under siege. This also served to deny these resources to the southerners who needed to eat and drink just as they did. Everyone had to eat; several piles of foodstuffs along with hay and oats were burning already outside of the walls. Smoke rose high in the sky which marked their location but it couldn't be helped. The Southerners would find them soon enough, better to be ready.

Weapons of all types had been removed from storage all over town. Many were family heirlooms but still functional. Several of the villagers were hard at work crafting additional arrows while still more were preparing spears and sharpening swords for the coming fight. The village metalsmith and his assistants were all toiling hard to repair what they could and fabricate more arrowheads. The ringing of hammers could be heard from one end of the village to the other. Smoke from the forge poured into the sky as the fires were stoked to the maximum. The orange glow of the fire was reflected in the grim, sweat stained faces of those rendering the hot metal into something useful and deadly.

The majority of residents were engaged in the preparation of the defenses but no one was idle. Even with the incredible longevity of the Elves, a few even living in excess of a thousand human years, none of the residents of Arnoth had personally participated in the Dark War. Even so, many had seen action against raiders at some point in the past having served in the Elven army or living in frontier towns such as this.

The lessons learned had been hard won and like some teachings, remembered in spite of all else.

Chapter Twenty-Six
A City in Peril

Luxia – D'Lohm

When word arrived in the capital of the small human kingdom that the southern provinces were being invaded the government was slow to react. D'Lohm had been at peace for quite some time with no enemy nations nearby. The closest thing to that were some rumors and wild stories of great evil taking place in the lands south of the river but those stories had been around for years so with nothing of substance proved there was little concern.

As more verified reports came in from the southern parishes to the capital, word began to spread throughout the populace of the danger. A hasty meeting of the king and his advisors did little to help the situation. They agreed to send some forces south to meet the threat but couldn't agree on whether or not to call up the reserves. The kingdom used a small standing army relying on a large reserve militia to fill out their army if and when the time was called for.

Precious time was lost as the troops were equipped and began to head south. During this time the Varshon-led army was pouring more and more manpower into the country from across the river with tens of thousands more to come. The balance of forces was very quickly in favor of those from the south due to the distance from the capital, where the bulk of what army D'Lohm possessed was located. The king wasn't always popular so he kept the bulk of his soldiers nearby in case of riots, which broke out at least every other year, it seemed.

When the lead elements of the units sent toward the river engaged the invaders they quickly found themselves in a serious battle. It culminated with the royal forces being forced to withdraw in the face of increasing enemy numbers. Word was hurriedly sent back to the capital that the situation was serious, very serious. Refugees fleeing from the ravaging southern army were quick to tell everyone they met to grab what they could and take to the roads as soon as possible to save themselves.

A few post riders had brought word to Luxia spreading the news, which only created fear and in not a few cases outright panic. The country had not fought a war in many decades so the populace was complacent about their own security -- now a huge problem.

Some with the means fled the city right away toward the north or the east. Anywhere that the enemy wasn't likely to be was preferable to being taken prisoner or killed. The vast majority of the city population didn't have the means to survive on the road but it didn't keep many from leaving the city as well. The roads leading away from the city were choked with frantic people, noisy animals and too much traffic hindering military movements in the area.

Days passed as more reserves were called up and fed into the grinder trying to stop or at least slow down the southern juggernaut but it was useless – the men of D'Lohm were poorly trained, poorly equipped and worse, poorly led. As a sizable segment of the invaders broke off from the main body heading toward the capital there was no stopping them.

All organized resistance to the invasion collapsed as units broke and ran, some deserted while others did their best to continue the fight. The enemy continued to move toward the city arriving nine days after the first reports of the invasion had come in. Once there, they laid siege to the city. The city itself had managed to pull together a meager, but for the moment, adequate defense consisting of a mix of regular army units and militia.

By this time the city residents were in complete panic. The city defenses were not constructed to withstand a significant assault, let alone a determined siege. It had never been necessary to fortify the city to a significant degree and now it was it was far too late.

The remaining residents of the city were running pell mell through the streets trying to find some measure of sanctuary, which was proving impossible. The defenders were severely hampered as they attempted to shift troops around due to the frantic throng in the streets. Screams and shouts filled the air as the city was tearing itself apart with civil unrest.

The southern infantry were massed just outside of bow shot from the rapidly shrinking city wall. Catapulted heavy stones were knocking large sections of the ancient curtain-style wall down. As the sections of wall fell the rubble formed a number of crude but very serviceable ramps that in short order the soldiers would use as entry points into the city.

Despite the ease with which the Varshon-commanded forces were winning the battle, it was here that a flaw in the overall southern strategy began to show itself. By pulling troops, siege equipment, and supplies out of the main effort the effectiveness of the march north was being diluted for little return.

Some of the catapult projectiles were landing beyond the wall smashing all they touched, homes, shops and residents. Fires had sprung up in a variety of locations, most were burning uncontested but a few were being tackled by *ad hoc* groups of desperate volunteers.

The senior D'Lohm general was at a loss to try to deal with the assault that he knew was coming. There weren't enough of his men to hold the city. He had sent the king out of the city the day before with a sizable escort in an attempt to save the man but it seemed likely there would be little for him to rule if he in fact survived.

The battering of the walls continued for nearly three solid hours. By the time the catapults stopped there was essentially no wall standing for several hundred yards which was far too wide an area for the beleaguered defenders to try and hold. As the last section of wall was collapsing the enemy infantry was up on their feet ready to attack. This was part of what they had been promised, loot and women and all of them were eager to get their share.

The Varshon commanding the assault had sent word that the lives of those in the city were of no consequence so the more of them that died the better. The proud infantry was more than ready to attack: this would the first significant city to be captured on the long march north but not the last as far as they were concerned.

The defenders were gathered in several locations on the inside of the wall waiting for the assault. Their plan was simple, stay in formations inflicting as many casualties as possible to slow down the enemy, keeping as close together as possible for mutual support. To a man it was plain that the city was lost but they were determined to exact as high a price on the invaders as they could.

What surviving catapults and other artillery they had was being saved for when the infantry came forward. Jugs of oils were hurriedly being prepared to give the enemy a warm reception. It was unlikely that they would be able to get off more than a few shots apiece before either the enemy was too close or the siege weapons knocked them out of action. Grim faces waited for the signal to unleash the flaming hell on the attackers.

The senior Varshon was watching as the last section of the wall they wanted down crumbled. A cruel smile split his face; it was time to erase this abomination of a city - let the northern realms burn! He turned slightly to the right looking toward the waiting trumpeter nodding once then returning to look upon the city. As soon as he saw the command the man raised his horn sounding a single long note.

The entire southern force fell silent which chilled the defenders to the core. The only sounds coming from the massed troops was the snap and pop of their banners in the wind. After sounding the note the trumpeter counting off to thirty in precise time then lifted the instrument to his lips again.

He blew a long single note followed by a three note call. As the last of the three notes was heard the infantry yelled as one. Then, they charged, shouting and screaming as they ran.

On the wall a concealed observer had been watching for just this moment, he was counting the seconds until the oncoming infantry would be in range. Gods there were so many of them…wait, wait – now! He jumped up frantically waving the large yellow flag to signal the catapults which all released within moments of each other, hurling their flaming jugs up and over the remains of the wall.

The leading elements of the charge were suddenly engulfed by oily bursts of fire and heat as the jugs hit. Hundreds of men were killed as the fire ended their lives, shouts and screams of the wounded and dying filled the air along with curses of anger as the unaffected witnessed the explosions.

A second volley was hurriedly readied then sent on its way. These too caused numerous deaths but there were just too many attackers and soon the first of them were at the rubble piles leading into the city. There was no hesitation as they began making their way up the stone ramps that would let them gain entrance to the enemy capital and the riches it held.

When the first of the invaders appeared at the top of the fallen walls they were met with volleys of arrows from the defenders but it was too little too late, a number of men fell from the aerial missiles but for every one that was hit there was a half dozen more who continued into the city. It was like a dark tide spilling into Luxia that was unstoppable.

The defenders moved forward to engage the southerners but due to their depleted assets, in the end it proved to be futile. There were simply too many attackers.

More and more of the southerners spilled into the city, searching for anyone resisting. All too often what they found were terrified civilians. The carnage was almost beyond description, men were quickly killed as were the boys, the women and girls suffered cruelly at the hands of the invaders.

From his vantage point south of the city, the Varshon commander had watched as his men stormed the enemy city taking some losses along the way. But they did as they were trained to do, which was to follow orders. This city was poorly defended which he was certain would not always be the case as they moved further north but this would provide excellent experience.

It was time to move into the city to supervise the collection of loot which would be sent south with the proper escort to the Citadel. This was a good day's work but there was a great deal more yet to do before they reached G'mar. With that thought he motioned to the Ogurth guards and his staff and began heading for the city.

Chapter Twenty-Seven
The Sound of Music

Arnoth

Bolgar had the senior surviving members of his Ri'al, along with those of the unit that had recently reached him, standing on the small rise that lifted a section of the dirt road running to the west gate of the village. From there they could see, when the smoke blew askew, into parts of the village. They were trying to gauge the number of defenders they faced, all of them sure it couldn't be enough to hold the town.

The Arakai of his command had been pulled back once again to regroup, allowing those of the recently arrived section of the second Ri'al to join them and coordinate the attack. The arrival of additional unit added to his overall strength but still did not give him a full strength unit since the new arrivals had suffered serious losses battling those of D'Lohm.

He intended to make the most of what he had. Bolgar had more than enough of this village, the delay, several hours now was costing him valuable time and worse, veteran soldiers. The scout leader needed all of those he had and more besides. Messengers had been sent south with updated information, while still others had been sent ahead to the northwest to scout then report back.

A nearby soldier stepped up and handed the unit commander a full canteen which he gratefully took with a quick nod of thanks. Pulling the cork stopper he poured some of the contents in his mouth and swished it around; the water was cut a third with wine to help sweeten it. The liquid cut the gummy taste brought on by the smoke and dust in his mouth.

Turning his head, Bolgar spat it out.

Lifting the container once more to his lips he drank deeply nearly emptying the vessel, the water felt like sweet ale. His body drank it in and a new measure of strength flowed in his muscles as the body soaked up the life giving fluid. Finished, he tossed the canteen back to the soldier, nodding his thanks while wiping his chin and lower face with the back of his hand.

After fortifying himself the veteran Arakai gave the matter at hand his full attention once again. He explained that he intended for an all-out assault this time, a heavy rush on the eastern end. The last three times they had pushed straight in from the west and it had not been successful so this time he intended to hit them hard from one side and while they were busy with that kick them hard in the ass with the other shoe.

Urban warfare was not well known among the tribes and fighting house to house was something they had practiced to some degree in the mock towns specially built for the purpose but this was different. Bolgar began to outline his plan; the others leaned in closer to hear more clearly, cruel grins showing their owners minds.

The attack was pushing the defenders hard; this time there were simply too many Arakai for the beleaguered force holding Arnoth to deal with. A hole was opened in the ranks of those fighting along the west wall and with a cheer some of the attackers poured in as Shorin fought with what he had to try to close the breach. More Arakai fought to expand their gain. The fighting was brutal, close quarter action without a respite.

Word of the breach came to Bolgar who was north of the town; he grinned savagely and immediately sent the twenty or so men with him to where the defenses had failed in order to help exploit the gap. He told them that as soon as they were over the wall to attack the west gate from the rear. This is what he had been waiting for -- inside the village the fight would be over quickly once either gate was opened. The score of southern cavalrymen hurried off to carry out the wishes of their leader.

Bowstrings sang so often that is sounded to some as if it was one long continuous bow shot. The sharp sound of steel finding steel could be heard over the shouts and curses as the assault reached the walls. Hastily constructed ladders were tossed across the crude ditch allowing the dismounted cavalry to run across the gap. All that was needed was luck and balance which for a horseman was natural -- luck or the lack of it was something only the gods could speak to.

Bolgar began to exhort his men in a louder voice than before telling them of the breach, *push forward* he shouted over and over. His blood was up; it was well past time to end this. This accursed village had cost him dearly and he intended to bring it to heel so they could continue on with their mission. He waved the nearest of his men to him then made his way across one of the ladders with the others close at hand.

***

Near the central part of the village Parun heard a scream then looked quickly around the corner of the house to see two of the attackers pawing one of the women of the village, their intent obvious.

The Striker felt his blood boil at the thought of what the men planned on doing to the woman, the knowledge of what had happened to his mother flashed in his mind. *No, not this time.* He was already moving toward them without thinking, no way would these bastards come here and have their way with the women, not while he held breath. The Striker slid around the corner heading toward the two men who failed to note the approach of the defender.

One of the men held the woman from behind cruelly pulling her arms backwards which forced her full bosom forward. His partner grinned in wicked anticipation, dirty hands pawed at the material of the blouse and the treasure it concealed. She tried but failed to free herself from the strong grasp of the Arakai holding her. Without warning the man groping her chest yanked hard and tore the blouse from her body.

Now with her ample chest exposed, Jehna was horrified at what was about to happen to her. She had no illusions about the intentions of these men and what it would mean to her. Twisting and pulling, she tried once again to free herself from the grip that held her arms but the hands that bound her proved too much for her strength. The two Arakai were laughing in anticipation of ravaging the Elven beauty. She could smell the bad breath of the man holding her, his rapid, almost panting breathing near her ear.

Parun was nearly upon them. He tightened the grip on his sword. The lean half-Elf was tired, his wounds sapping the strength from him. He knew that he must be quick or all was lost for the woman. Laughter from the two men filled his ears, his anger rushed up and without thought of plan or tactic he launched himself at the pair.

The one holding the woman was facing away from him so he had no idea of Parun's approach. His first warning of danger was the feeling of the Strikers blade as it severed his spinal cord. The Arakai rigidly jerked upright as the wound found him releasing his grip. Parun kept moving, with one hand pulled at the arm of the woman to try and get her to some perceived place of safety. Where that place was he didn't know but at the moment away from the two men was enough.

Seeing the startled look on the face of his partner the second Arakai was quick to recognize it for what it was. He yanked a hand axe from his belt and swung it wildly to create some space between him and this new threat. The body of his friend slumped to the ground in a heap as he began to die quite noisily.

The woman who had been an instant away from being gang raped was suddenly spun out of the way. Catching sight of the dirty black and silver uniform the southerner spat out a curse. This stinking soldier had cost the Arakai dearly. He could see the wounds on the half breed and spun the axe preparing to end this interruption and return to the woman. Parun was wearied but he was determined to finish this so that the woman would be spared.

The pair dueled back and forth, the weakened Striker able to keep the Arakai at bay initially due to having a sword while his opponent had only the hand axe. In addition Parun was working to keep himself between the woman and the southern cavalry soldier.

Realizing that he was at a disadvantage, Parun resorted to an old trick he had used several times over the years. Moving to his right he appeared to stumble which due to his wounds was closer to the truth than he had planned. The Arakai never hesitated; he rushed in seeing what he believed to be a fatal opening.

The Striker suddenly regained his balance slicing an upward stroke that caught the other man at the belt laying him open all the way to the shoulder. The Arakai fell backwards and died a few feet away as Parun went down to one knee. The exertion of the ruse took quite a bit out of him.

Jehna knelt down trying to help the Striker. She clung to him both in relief and trying to assist him. Not seeing a third Arakai approach Parun was trying to comfort the woman that in his fatigue he failed to recognize as Jehna Kalantiere, daughter of the village Headman. The first warning the pair had that something was amiss was Parun being stabbed deeply in the side. Jehna screamed when she realized what had happened. The force of the attack knocked him over, he lay on the grass shrieking in agony.

Knowing that his wound was mortal the veteran Striker felt his strength ebbing quickly away. The third Arakai was confident that the wound was fatal and that the cursed Elf was already a memory. He had turned his full attention to the comely beauty before him who, thanks to the now dead enemy soldier he wouldn't have to share with any of his own, at least for now.

A large dirty hand snatched hold of one delicate arm drawing her toward him. As she was pulled toward the imposing figure, anger took hold, with her free hand Jehna slapped him with all her might. Taking the blow full on the Arakai merely grinned at the woman, his stained teeth a horrible visage. Now wrapped in the arms of the brutish attacker Jehna was no longer afraid. Filled with a fury unlike any she had ever known the Elven beauty was determined to avoid the fate that seemed so certain.

Feeling his life drain away Parun knew that he had very limited time in order to try and save the woman since the stab wound had found a vital spot. Unable to properly move his body Parun was attempting to remove the last of his daggers from its customary place in his right boot. The Arakai was focused on Jehna and so was unaware of the desperate effort that the Striker was putting forth.

Wrapped up in the arms of the burly soldier there was little chance of breaking free so Jehna did something else. She lunged forward and with all the strength she could wield bit the right cheek of the man. Tasting blood she continued to bear down as hard as she could shaking her head back and forth to dig in trying to rend as much flesh as she could.

Howling in pain and anger, the Arakai immediately ceased his pawing and pulled at her to free her from his flesh. Yanking her by the hair he pulled which further added to the severity of the wound. Outraged that she would dare to defy him he swung one hand to smack her but she adroitly moved her head to the side trying to avoid the heavy blow which still sent her spinning back.

She landed heavily on the body of the Striker who had finally worked the long blade free of its confinement. Jehna looked into the face of the man who had twice saved her not realizing he was still alive until he mouthed the word 'knife' to her. The sensation of the cool metal on her bare skin shocked her. A weapon!

The Arakai was on her in a flash but due to the positioning of the woman was unable to see the exchange as the dagger was passed. Reaching down to roll her over so that he could have her, the flash of honed steel caught his eye far too late.

The blade sliced across his unprotected throat instantly producing a torrent of blood that sprayed outward. Both hands wrapped around the wound but there was no stopping the flood of crimson fluid. The Arakai staggered back then stumbled over the body of one of the two that Parun had killed. Watching the man fall away Jehna turned back to Parun, dropping the knife to try and treat his wounds.

Feeling for the source of his injury Jehna halted when Parun spoke, his voice a shadow of its self, "Stop, Lady."

Jehna looked into his face and with great feeling told him, "Thank you." She hugged herself to him.

Several moments passed, Jehna still holding him as the last of his life drained away. Tears filled her eyes as a thick billow of smoke wafted over them. She coughed a bit as she looked around at the three dead invaders and the body of the man who had saved her. Jehna leaned down and put her head on Parun's and lay still as the tears came.

To the east of the village a ragged formation of Elves were heading toward Arnoth as fast as their mounts could carry them. A small patrol of Lancers had been joined by villagers from two of the towns as well as those from some of the farms across the area. The collection numbered a little more than five dozen but others were riding to the aid of the residents of Arnoth as well. *Please let us be in time* was the prayer being repeated most often as they rode.

The senior Lancer wasn't sure what they were riding into but since word had arrived of a village under attack they had to respond. Looking to the south he saw another seven riders angling their galloping mounts to attach themselves to the slowly growing group.

One of the Elves from a nearby farm shouted at the Lancer that the village was just ahead. All of them had been able to see the smoke rising for some distance; it was thicker now, much thicker being close to the source. The Lancer suddenly had an idea; he signaled his trumpeter and shouted to the men to tell anyone with a horn to sound it. Word was hurriedly spread as best they could. It wasn't easy being at a full gallop and trying to shout over your shoulder but the others caught on.

The first horn call went up and was followed by another and then a third. The sweet notes carried far. He waved at them with one hand extorting them to continue.

Bolgar was certain that his men finally had the upper hand; nearly all of the Arakai survivors were inside the walls now and were battling with the beleaguered defenders who were continuing to fall back. Numbers were against them now and they knew it. Smoke drifted across his line of sight blocking his ability to see for any distance at all. Suddenly a flash of fire and light highlighted by screams of pain nearby. The first blast was followed by another; a rush of heated air blew into him. *What the...*

The riders heading west were ready for trouble; several of the Lancers were riding with bows held steady watching for any sign of the enemy. As the leading edge of the group topped the short rise just east of the town they saw the village and those attacking it. Five bowstrings sounded release as their arrows flew downrange toward some unsuspecting Arakai. Three men fell dead as the missiles found their targets.

The Lancers had been told to space themselves out among the other Elves and for the entire group to ride in a line abreast to try and fool the enemy into believing there to be many more of them than there actually were. Three of the riders held back and continued to sound their horns as part of this strategy.

The Arakai on the east end of the village were suddenly faced with the appearance of what to them seemed a large organized force. More arrows were launched in their direction from the riders.

In the village Bolgar now heard the horns and was turning to try and determine the source when another oil lamp came hurling toward him and the small group he was with. It hit on the wall of the house he was standing next to and burst, sending a cascade of burning oil out in a wide pattern. A splash of the fiery liquid landed on his neck. The pain was worse than anything he had ever felt.

A ragged scream tore loose from his lips as he tried to extinguish the fire at his throat. He frantically wiped at the burning fluid with gloved hands and was able to fling away much of the flaming oil leaving his gloves burning. He hurriedly shook them off as the fire bit at his flesh. One of his men hastily used a dirty scarf to put out the rest of the fire burning his skin. The pain he felt was incredible, the contents of a canteen were poured over the wound which removed some of the pain and much of the heat from the burned tissues on both hands as well as his throat. Two of his men were doing what they could to try and treat their commander's injuries.

The smoke was thick, hampering visibility for both sides. The senior Lancer with the group just east of the village knew that numbers were not in his favor but if they did nothing they would lose the element of surprise and any tactical advantage they may have. He waved the others forward shouting at the trumpeters to continue to call. If nothing else the continued horn calls would help summon whatever additional help that was coming to the proper location and possibly help mask their approach to the village.

The seventy or so Elves urged their mounts forward, the archers among them trying to do as much damage as they could but the wind and smoke was proving difficult to deal with.

***

Shorin had gathered several of his men and about ten villagers together; they were holed up in the inn along the main street. Using the tables and whatever else they could find they blocked the windows and doors trying to keep the attackers out. Shorin's biggest fear was that they would be burned out by the southern troops. He wasn't worried for himself; there were a number of seriously wounded in the building that they would not be able to move. He was long past the point of exhaustion but he kept himself going somehow.

Some of the invaders were hammering on the hastily barricaded door with a bench trying to breach the entrance. He yelled at one of the Elves to go upstairs and drop a lit oil lamp on them but for pity sakes don't get it too near the building! The villager grinned savagely as he rushed upstairs. Shorin shouted encouragement to the others.

On the eastern side of the village the Elves were now fully engaged with the Arakai there. The fighting was close and personal, no quarter for either side. The villagers and Lancers were giving a good account of themselves despite the majority of them not being trained soldiers. The Arakai were well trained but tired and disorganized so the odds for the outnumbered Elves were evened out some. A factor working in favor of the Elves, at least for the moment, was that due to their being on the eastern end of the village they had numerical superiority in that small locale. It was growing increasingly difficult to see as the smoke grew in intensity. Swords rang on sword as the fight intensified.

***

More Elves were slowly coming in to aid those of Arnoth; the messengers that Logas had sent out early were returning with what help they could. Two small groups, numbering about two dozen, arrived shortly after the Lancer led the larger group down to the village.

The new arrivals wasted no time in riding down toward the fight which further narrowly improved the balance of forces in that area. Slowly the momentum of the newly arrived reinforcements began to push the Arakai back. A stubborn stand at the remains of the eastern gate was broken by several of the Elves recklessly charging their horses through the line of defenders. Two of the riders were cut down immediately on the other side of the wall but the damage was done.

The Lancer shouted for them to push through; with a surge they did. Battling their way into the village, the Elves began to spread out engaging more of the Arakai.

As Bolgar was being helped to his feet his second, Rimm, came running over. "Sir, fresh reinforcements just hit the east end of the damned village!"

The Ri'al leader croaked out a question, "How – how many?"

The effort it took to speak was telling, the burns on his neck were incredibly painful. He was leaning against the nearest wall for support.

Rimm told him it looked to be at least one hundred with more coming. The confusion of the battle and the ever present smoke was the biggest factor for the huge inaccuracy in the count. He looked at his leader waiting for whatever the next order.

Shorin and the others had heard the horns and knew that at least some help had arrived. The oil lamp hurled down from above had for the moment taken the fight out of those trying to break down the door.

He looked at the others in the room with him, the Strikers were exhausted but each of them nodded in agreement. They had to go back out there, it might be too late but if they pressed the southies it might be enough to turn the tide.

Speaking in Merlik, Shorin asked the villagers to remain and guard the wounded. They all wanted to go with the Strikers but the sincerity of the request and the obvious threat of leaving wounded men unguarded sealed the deal, a grudging nod from one of the residents.

Two of the Strikers began to move some of the furniture that had been piled against the door earlier to try and fortify their position so that they could get out. The other men of Karbel were collecting themselves for what was coming - one last push.

One last stand.

***

Jehna was still holding Parun when the first of the recently arrived Elves ran by. The sound of running feet startled her to the point her head popped up, a whimper of fear escaped her lips. Two of the Elves were startled by the sudden movement of the woman thinking she was dead like those around her, the blood from the man she had killed still damp on her body.

Both men skidded to a halt, one of them looking around for any sign of danger. The second man slowly lowered himself while telling her that it was all right, she was safe. Jehna didn't fully understand what she was being told, the effect of the fight for the village was still more than she could process. More of the Elves were passing by as they sought out the Arakai.

Bolgar grabbed Rimm by the tunic sleeve pulling him close so he wouldn't have to talk so loud. In a halting voice he told him to order a recall and for all of them to regroup on the small hill west of the village. They had to try to preserve unit integrity. Rimm asked Bolgar if he needed any assistance -- but before he could answer, Rimm ordered the two nearby Arakai to stay with the commander no matter what. Then with a firm nod of the head, he left to carry out the orders he had been given.

The Strikers had the doorway cleared of the furniture; Shorin took a deep breath and told the man by the door to open it. Soon as it was wide enough to exit he was the first one outside leading his men. Side stepping around the still burning pool of oil, they were immediately beset by a handful of Arakai. The fighting was close quarter and brutal.

As the remainder of the elite troops came out of the scorched building the tide turned in favor of those of Karbel. Off to the west a new set of horn calls was heard, clear and sharp in the din of the fighting.

Around them, the Strikers noticed that the southies were turning away, running toward the west end of the village. The last of the Arakai that had been outside of the inn went down.

Shorin took a quick measure of what was happening. Those southern troops he could see were indeed all heading for the west end. A sense of hope rose from some deep place within him, maybe they had done it. "Follow me!"

He took off at as much of a sprint as he could manage, his Strikers right behind him. The two Arakai with Bolgar were supporting their leader as they too headed toward the west gate. Shorin and his men came around the corner at a trot, he saw the trio -- the rich cape of the man being helped by the other two caught his eye.

Hearing the running feet behind them one of the Arakai turned, seeing the Strikers he shouted to his partner who unceremoniously dumped his commander while spinning to face the new threat. Bolgar staggered to his knees, the pain of his wounds was all encompassing. His strength had all but left him as he found the ground, hardly able to rise.

Shorin never hesitated; he wanted the man in the cape.

One of the Arakai rushed him and the two traded blows with neither landing telling wounds. The rest of the Strikers joined the fray ending it in short order; three to one was pretty tough odds to face, but neither of the Ri'al members flinched as they took on all comers managing to hold their own for a few moments before being struck down.

The man in the cape was taken in and disarmed. Shorin visibly flinched at the sight of the ghastly burns on the throat of his prisoner. He told four of his men to take the man back to the inn and to treat his wounds right away and under no circumstances were they to leave him until he personally relieved them. Two of them lifted the man and took him under the arms to support him. The quartet of black liveried men headed off with their charge.

Taking the rest of the Strikers with him, Shorin again started for the west gate. The Arakai were trying to withdraw in good order but it was proving very problematic. The fires blocked several of the streets, dead and wounded littered the area making passage difficult at best and thick blowing smoke was still obscuring visibility.

Another group of Elves had arrived from the east; still mounted they circled around the north side of town where they were picking off Arakai with accurate bow shots as they could. Some of the others were pushing through the remains of the shattered town driving the enemy out.

Shorin and his men had joined up with some of the surviving villagers and part of the first group of reinforcements short of the west gate. Bolstered by the additional numbers the Strikers pushed the scattered Arakai free of the gate and out of the village at last. About that time the small party of mounted archers came into view from around the wall Shorin shouted at them to stop their pursuit. He wanted to consolidate as many friendlies as he could. If he allowed them to chase the Arakai they would likely be ambushed and lost.

A final volley dispatched two more of the southies before the Elves turned toward the gate and the waiting Strikers. Shorin leaned heavily against the now broken stone column supporting what was left of the gate. They had done it, held the village and survived.

So much to do but in that instant all he could do was close his eyes and take in a deep breath. He was alive...

Chapter Twenty-Eight
Character Flaw

Karbel

It had taken the Striker quite some time to arrive at one of the Legion outposts that dotted the frontier. He would have arrived much sooner but his horse had taken a serious fall when one of its hooves had gotten caught in the open burrow hole of a mole, and spilled him. The animal had suffered a broken leg, the man was sure he had at least bruised if not broken some of his own ribs in the fall as well. It had been necessary to slit the throat of the animal to end its suffering.

After that the man was afoot which slowed him considerably compared to being able to ride, and the importance of the message he was tasked with delivering made it all the more important. Walking with his injuries reduced his speed, further delaying word reaching the capital. But no one could fault the hardy soldier who kept pushing despite the circumstances.

Walking wasn't easy, the pain from the broken ribs made deep breathing torture but the man kept going. The Striker had been sent by Shorin to get word out of what was happening along with two others at various times. Neither of the other two had yet to reach help. One of them had been intercepted and killed by southern cavalry.

Seeing the outpost ahead reenergized the man. He had made it at last. Relief flooded through him and his pace increased, the pain faded some. At last word could finally be sent, it had been nearly a full day since Shorin had detailed him to deliver the message.

The tower guard was scanning the area when he saw what appeared to be a man approaching. He nudged his partner and with a grunt pointed toward the man with his chin. The Legionnaire nodded then leaned over

343

the edge of the tower and shouted down that there was someone coming. Both men turned their full attention to the man and the surrounding area; this could be some kind of trick.

Neither of the men saw anything out of the ordinary but that didn't mean there wasn't. The man was still walking toward them waving one hand over his head slowly but steadily to garner the attention of those in the outpost. His pace was steady as he continued toward the fort.

He was carrying something slung over one shoulder, he was wearing…was that a uniform? The second tower guard asked his companion, "Yeah, think it is. Looks ta' be a Striker."

There wasn't a Striker garrison anywhere near so if it was one of them he was a long way from home and on foot. The senior personnel at the station ordered the gate opened and so were waiting for the man who was now nearly where they were standing. When the man who was wearing what they could now clearly see to be a Striker uniform was about ten paces away he was ordered to stop which he did. He dropped the saddle bags that were slung over one shoulder glad to be free of the weight.

"State your business."

The Striker was tired but knew that this formality had to be observed in order to be granted access inside. Watchful eyes were alert for any sign of treachery.

"Hail," he said. "I bring ya message from my commander. Karbel's being invaded. A pissing ass big army from tha' south. Me captain sent me to get thee word passed along, lost me horse a few hours back."

The officer waved the man forward, this sounded serious. A lingering look over his shoulder as he escorted the Striker toward the station revealed nothing of concern but that didn't make him feel any better. He directed one of his men to take the man to the message center but waved him off, electing to take the man himself. This could be serious trouble. He began to ask questions to get a better understanding of the situation.

***

The message flashed its way along through the various stations and outposts north and west from the point of origin. It took several hours for it to reach its destination given the distance it traveled and that it had to been rerouted a few times since some of the stations had been destroyed by southern forces.

Once it arrived at military headquarters it was decoded and transcribed. The assistant Duty Officer who was covering for his superior who was taking an unusually long lunch read the message through. Chills filled him as the implications of what he was reading sank in. Invasion, the country was under attack.

He needed to inform someone, but Senior Captain Bordaz wasn't here. Who to tell…? Indecision took hold for a moment and then he realized that this message needed to be given to the commander, forget the chain of command. He left the Duty Office without a word; those present said nothing as they watched him leave.

The officer carrying the message ran through the hallways with the communication, clutched tightly in his right hand. The thrack of his boots striking the floor stones echoed dully in the passageway as he made his way through. Habit and instinct made him swing a step wider going around the corner to allow room for his sword, secure in its scabbard, to clear the edge of the wall. Several people in the hall were forced to move aside to create room for the runner who passed them without a courtesy word or glance. Angry looks followed the man down the hallway but he neither saw them nor cared.

The young officer saw the looks of interest on the faces of those he passed but ignored them. What he was carrying was too important -- if what he had read and been told was true, then it was more trouble than all of them could conjure. His eyes were constantly searching as he ran, trying to find… wait, there, yes, there he was.

"Lord Marshal!"

At the sound of the urgency in the voice, Balkon turned. He was standing with three other senior officers discussing a supply issue when the messenger found them. The Legion Marshal was perturbed by the interruption especially by a junior officer acting in such an inappropriate manner. Sakes, what are they teaching officers these days? Running through the halls and shouting like a buffoon.

The officer came to attention and held out the message form "Critical message you need to see sir."

Irritated, the Legion Marshal took the parchment and began to read…*Have received personal intelligence report of large unknown force approaching border from south…D'Lohm under attack…reports indicate my forces insufficient to stop… request additional Eleventh units sent my area immediately…Strikers report enemy already attacking Elven settlements…* The Marshal finished the message but failed to understand why the messenger was so upset, a small border raid and the local commander overreacting, explained why the man was sitting in some border hovel while real leaders were in more suitable posts.

As for sending more of the 11th Legion to the area, ridiculous, move an entire Legion on the word of a hysterical fool cowering in his border office? It was pathetic was what passing for officer material these days.

The messenger was waiting for his commander to give him orders; help had to be sent to the area. Balkon tossed the message back to the waiting officer with a look of dismissal. "Very well, now leave us."

The senior Legion general was mentally already on to the next issue, this one was of no consequence. He turned back to the other three officers to resume their conversation. One of them glanced over Balkon's shoulder to where the messenger was standing. The man was still there when Balkon realized that he hadn't left yet.

"Why are you still here? I said to leave us." The junior officer was no coward but to question the senior general in all the army did give him pause.

"Sir, what message do you wish sent regarding this attack?"

The Legion Marshal was quickly becoming perturbed at the man. What part of "leave us" did he fail to grasp?

"Do nothing, send no message, it is of no import. You. Are. Dismissed." The last three words were stretched out to emphasize them. With that he turned and walked off with the three officers in tow.

The younger man was fixed to the spot; he couldn't believe what had just occurred. Little did he know how much what had just happened would affect his career. Others were walking through the corridor, two of whom had to step around the still rooted messenger.

After a few moments he turned around to head back to the message center. A jumble of thoughts and feeling swirled in his mind as he retraced his steps. Uncertain as to what to do next, obviously there was something going on near the border but what else was there? The message was not an overreaction to something, at least that's how it read to him.

The fact that there were attacks on both D'Lohm and the Elves meant it had to be a serious threat; it was too much territory for it be nomads or some other small group. No this was something else; nearly to the message center he had a thought. The potential impact of it stopped him in his tracks. Could he really do that? *Should he?*

He stepped inside the message center and nervously looked around; no one seemed to be watching him. Straightening his back he walked to the scribe's desk and when the man saw him told to send the following message to, *what station was it again?* He couldn't remember so he had to glance at the message form in his hand.

The scribe waited impatiently despite the man at his desk being an officer. Oh there it is.

"Send this to Message Station 897. Send updated report on raid and all other information available this command. This is priority."

He nodded to the scribe who had finished writing it down and told him to send it off right away. The bored clerk rose from his desk and headed for the heliograph operator.

The Assistant Duty Officer knew that what he had just done could well end his career but he had to know what was going on down on the frontier. It sounded too serious to be 'nothing' as the Legion Marshal suggested.

The man was dedicated to his duty despite often being surrounded by those that did as little as possible and showed no measure of dedication to serving, certainly not to the level he did. He only hoped he had not brought an end to his career before it had really begun.

All he could do now was wait; it would be hours before they heard back from the distant frontier.

What would that message bring?

Chapter Twenty-Nine
Old Friends

Village of Arnoth

It was the smoke that led the terribly small group of remaining Black Guards to the shattered village. A high column of thick smoke rising from behind some hills off to the east of them; it served as a beacon of sorts that could be seen for miles in the clear mid-morning sky. The foursome rode in from the west narrowly avoiding a group of southern cavalry riding hard the other way, as a chorus of horn calls rang out somewhere east of them, the sound muted some by the distance.

The Guards hurriedly ducked their mounts into the remains of a once large fruit tree orchard, much of it now slashed and burned, and watched from within the sparse concealment of the remaining trees as the mounted men rode past without noticing them. Nervous hands gripped weapons tightly in case of discovery. It proved unnecessary as the cavalry continued oblivious to their presence.

The southern soldiers looked ragged and disorganized despite wearing the same uniforms, no outriders or even a point rider. Merely twenty or so men dressed the same, riding the same direction. Most of the riders appeared wounded in some fashion.

Mryl looked at Wev, a question posed on his face, but he withheld it. The veteran sergeant could only shrug his shoulders in response to the question unasked. He didn't have any answers worth voicing so said nothing.

Once the last of the riders were gone, the Guards cautiously emerged from the concealment of the remaining trees. They resumed their trek toward the source of the smoke following the pathway.

They rode forward slowly and with no small amount of uncertainty, all of them knowing that they could not outrun or outfight anyone right now. Both man and mount had been pushed hard, too hard, the last few days and all were near the breaking point, mentally and physically.

After purchasing the horses and some food in the D'Lohm village the four Guards had set out toward what they had been told was the direction of the Karbel border. At first they made good time despite the quality of the animal they had bought not being the best -- riding was better than walking -- and they hoped to find somewhere they could possibly trade the horses with some of the remaining coine for better ones at some point. They gradually starting moving through more small villages and settlements spreading the word about the coming southerners, which backed up the news that was arriving from the capital in bits and pieces.

They were able to trade the horses for better ones along with some additional food at a trading post they found in the late afternoon of the day after they passed the first village. They were tired but didn't want to stop which proved to be a fortuitous choice.

Less than three hours later the lead cavalry elements under the command of Vinshee started sweeping into the area. They were moving north with no resistance so they were actually arriving ahead of the news of the invasion in some places, inciting fear and panic as they rode in. The Guards were still working toward getting to the border and beyond but now they had a sizable number of enemy forces to their west and northwest cutting off that direction of travel.

More and more troops poured north forcing them further and further east, until at last they found themselves on the western edge of the Elven Homelands miles from where they wanted to be.

The four rode forward until they crested a small rise, spreading out so they were sitting side by side, they stopped their mounts to take in the scene. The Black Guards found themselves looking at the source of the smoke column; fires, some of them large, were burning unchecked in several locations in what appeared to once have been a modest size village.

The quartet tried to take in the panorama before them. Dozens, no, it had to be hundreds, of dead horses and their former riders littered the ground east of them clustered around the wall of the village, much of it crumbled down in places, bodies lay everywhere. It was hard to accurately gauge the number of corpses but it was a large amount.

The group exchanged glances, wondering what had happened here. It was like a vision from a horrible nightmare, the smell was incredible and strong, rotting blood, feces, spilled intestines and burnt matter all competed to sicken those unlucky enough to breathe in the mix. Two of the men reached for their scarves to tie over their lower face to help filter out the odors. None of the veteran Guards were squeamish but this was too much.

Smoke columns rose stronger as the wind died down. Several figures appeared at the remains of the gate on this side of what figured to be an Elven village. That assumption was based on the distance to the east that they had ridden, none of the Guards had ever been this far to the east so it was merely a guess on their part. Mryl motioned his group forward down the hill and toward what was left of the settlement.

Time to try and find out what had gone on here, and then see if they could get some fresh horses, maybe even some food before they continued on their way. They still needed to reach a message station somewhere across the border in Karbel. Time was clearly not on their side so it was best to use what time they had and press on. Riding into a village that had just fought a major battle against an unknown foe was not the smartest thing Mryl had ever done but the condition of his men and their mounts required it.

The horses had to pick their way carefully as they moved among the debris, discarded items of equipment, and the odd corpse as they went down the road toward the village. More figures appeared from inside the walls to accumulate near the breach in the wall that once held the gates. One of the gates was laying in pieces on the ground near the group of defenders.

It was clear to Mryl and the others from looking at some of the bodies that littered the area that these men had been connected in some way to the large army that the Guards had seen a few ten-days earlier on the other side of the Wystern and had been avoiding since landing in D'Lohm.

Mryl felt it likely that these men were part of the advance elements which meant that the main body of the southern army was still behind them Twinsteel was certain of that, as certain as he could be given the situation but the large numbers of enemy cavalry they had seen kept forcing the Guards east. Fatigue was sapping his ability to string together intelligent thoughts.

Overhead, numerous carrion eaters circled, eager for their feast, some of the more bold ones already at their grisly business. Squawks and squabbles among three of the large birds could be heard, each after the same large horse carcass a few dozen yards away. The smaller of the three extended and flapped his wings to try and intimidate the others but failed and returned to sharing bites with the others losing out on gaining sole possession of the prize. Mryl wondered about the symbolism of that, as he watched them feed.

Someone at the gate had seen them and sent word inside. A handful of soldiers, human and Elf -- *so it was an Elven village*, thought Mryl -- had begun to form a ragged half circle across the shattered gateway, weapons in hand. Most of them appeared wounded; some in more than one place, all appeared tired.

Mryl and the others were caught completely off guard by the sight of Striker uniforms; the tattered but distinctive black and silver tunics were a welcome but as of yet unexplained sight. Once again, he and the others shared a look. *My, how they do get around*, he thought to himself with no small measure of wonder.

Shorin received word that a group of riders were approaching from the west, the messenger too tired to mention it was only four. The exhausted Striker reached for his sword that lay nearby then managed only with a great effort to lift himself out of the battered chair he had found and headed for the gate with as much speed as he had, calling several nearby Strikers to go with him.

They moved through the gutted town as fast as they could which Shorin was sure at least faster than a newborn child could crawl. He smiled slightly at the thought in spite of the situation. The combination of fatigue and his wounds slowed him. He wanted to set a good example for his men by leading them but they were just as tired and injured as he so none of them moved too quickly. They'd had too much asked of them.

He knew if it was a sizable group they had no chance at all of holding them off. There was simply nothing left to fight with, many of his men were dead. Parun's face immediately came to mind but he put that thought away for now, most of the village destroyed and the majority of the villagers who remained behind to fight dead as well. The Strikers who remained were spent.

The group heading for the gate stepped around piles of bodies that stretched nearly the whole width of the street, side to side as well the length of the town. Shorin looked grimly at one such pair -- a villager with both hands tight around the neck of one of the southerners, who had plunged a dagger into the chest of the Elf -- the pair joined in death. Beyond them two of the villagers were helping one of the more seriously wounded as best they could.

As the riders neared the gate, one of the Strikers recognized what was left of the Black Guard uniforms they wore and sent word inside. The wounded Striker cautiously approached the small group of riders, a lopsided grin splitting his face, heavy with soot and dried blood. A strong limp from a deep leg wound left his movements awkward and stiff. The Guards stopped their horses a dozen paces or so from the group waiting outside the gate. The two groups eyed one another without comment.

Shorin arrived at the gate a few moments after the Guards did. Mryl looked over the damage done to the town and again at the piles of dead. Smoke still billowed upward from at least two dozen sources and blew across the scene at times.

The young Striker officer didn't recognize the leader of the Guards at first, fatigue and the disheveled appearance of the newcomers added to the problem. Besides, the Guards belonged in a completely different part of the world, no reason whatsoever to expect them here.

Mryl spoke first, "What goes, blackjack?"

A term for the Strikers, that some in the Legions often used as a quasi-insult against their counterparts. The Strikers however took it as a compliment. It was a common barb among those of the Guard and Strikers who shared a common heritage as royal protectors and similar uniforms, the Guard's red and black while the Strikers' were silver and black.

Shorin replied, "Not much you border hack. A little far from home, eh?" The senior Guard smiled slightly in response to the taunt then suddenly, he recognized the speaker.

"Shorin!" He jumped from his horse as best he could to rush to his friend. Shorin finally realized who it was that had been seated before him.

"Mryl!" Fatigue fell away for a moment as he too tried to hurry to his friend, the wounds slowing him. The pair met and clasped arms, wrist to wrist as was the style of the Guard. That done, they shared a hearty hug and much backslapping amid the laughter from some of those gathered. Smile broke out on all those present, a happy moment in the midst of so much pain and death.

***

The two men had been friends for several years; they had met when Shorin had gone to Blacktower, the Black Guard fortress, to attend his initial Striker training. They were both hard driven professional soldiers so a healthy sense of competition developed between them.

For Shorin the goal was to be a Striker, he wanted it worse than anything he had ever wanted in his life. For Mryl it was to be a better officer. He had already graduated from the School of the Order but was undergoing officer training. Shorin was a junior Legion officer who had already seen plenty of action so the two had plenty to offer the other. Mryl was no stranger to combat but doing it while commanding others was something unknown to him.

Mryl's father, Dougal, was a senior Black Guard officer who often led the Striker training sessions personally. The elder Twinsteel, a family name going back two generations to a Guard trooper who favored a pair of balanced swords, had overall responsibility for the Striker training.

Mryl's grandsire's skill was legendary among the Guard. So great was his fame that the king, Thadar's grandsire, gave him and his heirs the name Twinsteel for their house. It was a great honor to be so recognized in this fashion and all the members of the House took the responsibility seriously.

Mryl often carried a matched pair of swords as well strapped across his back. Some poked fun at the sight of the dual blades carried by the younger Twinsteel but it was always said with respect, carrying the two sabers was no mere gesture on his part to imitate an ancestor. He was capable of fighting with either hand and was deadly with both, though he favored his left slightly.

The original pair of swords were displayed in a place of respect above the mantle in the large family home, serving as the center piece of the family crest. A home that Mryl had not seen for many ten-days and often of late feared he never would return to again. Seeing Shorin returned a small measure of that hope.

Releasing each other they both stepped back one pace to look each other over. The story their eyes told them would be long and painful to be sure. The riders were asked to come inside the dubious safety of the walls while they tried to get everything sorted out.

Shorin still could not believe that out of all the people in the world that it would be Mryl to show up here...he shook his head at the thought. The Black Guard officer and his men were well beyond the scope of their assigned territory, normally the southwest border of the kingdom, more than a fair distance from where they now stood. Twinsteel hinted darkly at additional trouble coming which was something that none of them needed, but wouldn't say any more until he was told about what had happened here.

Shorin waved the others off their mounts and inside the walls. The tired Guards gratefully swung down from the saddles to shake hands with the now grinning Elves who had stepped forward to meet the friends of these humans who helped to save them.

The cluster of riders, Strikers, and villagers went through the now gaping opening where the west gates once stood and then stopped to look at the scene before them. Smoke and flames reached skyward in numerous places, no effort was being made to stop the fires, no one had the energy and most of them were beyond control in any case. Bodies, human and Elf, defender and attacker alike covered the ground that in some place was nearly a solid carpet.

Several groups were working at cleaning up the area, pulling bodies of the Strikers and villagers out of the patchwork of corpses to lay them aside together with their own. The bodies of the Arakai were left where they fell. Some of them had been hastily piled up outside the gate already but for now care of their own occupied the efforts of the tired defenders. Weapons were piled up in different places as the take from the dead grew and grew. The ringing of metal on metal could be heard as three more swords were added to the growing pile.

Shorin looked at the long row of bodies of his troops and could say nothing as another body was gently added to the chain. The price that had been paid for the village had been high and was continuing to climb.

A short distance from his Strikers lay the rows of villagers that stretched away into the smoke. The Striker and his friend watched as three more bodies were added to the already long row.

Mryl was curious but asked nothing yet of what had happened. He looked at Shorin and saw the look in his eyes. Several of those working there stopped when they saw that the Striker commander was watching.

Shorin looked embarrassed at being caught staring and then gestured to the group to continue on with the work of honoring the dead. He asked one of the residents to find Logas and tell him that guests had arrived and if he would to join them at the park. The Elf, a sword slash showing across the upper part of his left arm nodded at the human and headed off to find the village Headman.

Mryl for his part was impressed, he didn't know that Shorin could speak the Elf tongue; he knew he certainly couldn't in spite of the number of Elves that came through Kuln for Striker candidacy which on more than one occasion Mryl had thought both odd and interesting. Shorin caught the small grin his friend carried and merely shrugged in response saying he had fallen in with bad company and it stuck.

Mryl laughed, the first time he had done that in quite some time. It was agreeable and nearly foreign at the same moment, an odd sensation but not unpleasant. He could feel some of the tension and stress beginning to bleed away and it felt good.

Two Elves approached the group then spoke to Shorin asking him to have the others join them for some rest and food. The tired Striker turned to Mryl and relayed the request grinning a bit as he thought about how typical of the Elder Race – *the village is on fire but we have guests so let's make them welcome.*

Mryl in turn looked to Wev and passed along the invitation. The senior Black Guard enlisted man nodded gesturing to the Elves to lead the way. The two officers moved off to the side of the debris- and corpse-choked street to allow the others to pass. The small delegation moved deeper into the village to provide the Guards the promised items.

Shorin and Mryl watched them pass, each drawing some measure of strength from the presence of the other. The Striker then led them past a row of houses, most of them damaged, some burned down, located near the small park that had served as a temporary open air barracks for many of his troops right after they arrived at the settlement what seemed a lifetime ago. Smoke obscured the view at times as the wind swirled.

Once there Mryl had turned his tired horse loose to feed on the lush grass of the open park area while he and Shorin went looking around for something to sit on and talk. The two battered soldiers found a table and chairs that had belonged to one of the residents who had often taken in the evening breeze while sitting out of doors. The two sat heavily and both agreed as far as places went the one they were currently in was not bad.

About the time they sat, Logas and the senior surviving Lancer appeared around the corner of one of the nearby houses walking toward them. The Headman was laden with a large makeshift platter that formerly served as a kitchen cutting board, heaped with piles of cheese, fruit and several small loaves of what turned out to be reasonably fresh -- meaning it was only two days old or so -- bread piled on it.

Mryl and Shorin stood as manners dictated, Logas awkwardly tried to wave them down to remain sitting but the Guard felt it proper to stand to meet who ever this was, likely the village elder.

Logas placed the tray of food on the table before the two men. Rinard Golnar, the Lancer, carried two large pitchers of water with him and a couple of cups, none of them matching. These, too, were put on the table, then introductions were made.

Shorin handled the initial presentations. Mryl bowed to Logas and traded forearm grips with the Lancer, who were both impressed with the manners of Shorin's friend. Since the man had friends of this caliber it only added to his stature. Logas found himself thinking even more highly of the Striker which was surprising given the high standing he already held the human at. For his part, Rinard took in the stained and torn uniform worn by the man before him and recognized that he had traveled a hard road before arriving in their midst.

The four quickly found two more chairs, adding them to the table, and all sat. Logas attempted to apologize for the poor fare stating that he was sorry that the village was not able to offer more or better. Mryl nodded his thanks and without shame immediately took several large pieces of fruit and cheese, his body craving the nourishment. Shorin waited until his friend had taken his part then took several pieces of each as well having gone for many hours without something to fortify him; the last thing he had eaten was the excellent stew at the house of the

Headman, now heavily damaged during the attack.

Between bites, both men told Logas that what was before them was better than any king's feast. Rinard, who was now helping himself as well, agreed with a loud grunt. Shorin and Mryl both laughed at the sound from the hungry Elf who merely smiled as he shrugged while not slowing his eating one whit. The moment was a precious one for all of them, something funny amid the terrible death that surrounded them.

The fruit and cheese were several days old, a touch stale but not unhealthy, Shorin was sure he had never tasted anything better in his life. The long fight had left him wondering how much food and rest it would take to feel normal again and then he briefly considered what normal was anymore. Now was not the time to figure it out, simply eat, rest and worry about it later. The fruit and cheese tasted like something favored of the Gods as he savored the flavors. A small measure of strength was already building up within him as he ate more of the food.

After several minutes of nothing but silence as the four ate, the pile of fruit and cheese was significantly reduced. The bread too had vanished; all that remained was some crusty pieces, none of these large enough to be counted as much more than crumbs. The two pairs, human and Elf shared the company of the others merely by being near, having survived their various trials of late each was content for the moment to partake of the fare and feel glad to be alive albeit a little guilty given the losses each had suffered. That was much more than many of their contemporaries could say.

When at last the four stopped their steady eating and began to relax, Shorin, a cup of water in hand, asked his friend what he was doing this far from home. Before Mryl could begin Shorin turned to the other two present and told the Elves a little of the Black Guards and what they did so they would have some context for whatever story his friend was about to tell.

When he finished he turned to the Guard and explained quickly what he had told the two Elves since the entire summary had been in Merlik. Mryl nodded his understanding and at the wisdom of what Shorin had done. It had not occurred to him and he was too tired to think that deeply.

After Shorin finished, the Guardsman began to explain to his friend and the others the scope of his scouting mission, the reasons behind it, and finally what he and his men had seen while in the deep south. Mryl told them of the massive army he and the others had seen. The numbers seemed almost meaningless as he outlined the columns of cavalry, heavy infantry, light and medium artillery and supply trains without end it seemed. He outlined the desperate ride north to escape pursuit, finding the ship and the journey that had brought them here. It took several minutes for him to narrate the tale, the others waiting for him to finish before asking questions.

For his part Shorin sat mindlessly eating as he listened to his friend, the information being sorted out in his head. He knew that the information would be accurate having seen action with him during his training time at Kuln riding against some of the assorted goblins who lived south of the Jaggor Range. Mryl knew how to take a report as well as anyone. The information also tied in with what little he had managed to get from some of the refugees heading north out of D'Lohm. The two soldiers shared a look as Mryl continued the narrative.

Mryl then told them how he had started with over two dozen men and now it was just the four of them. His voice cracked slightly as he told of how some of them were lost and some of what they had been through, he looked down at the ground to avoid the eyes of the others while blinking away the bitter tears that had sprung from his eyes. He tried without success to make them stop, the body water cutting runnels through the dirt and sweat on his face. The others turned a blind eye to the display, there was nothing wrong with what he was doing; it was natural after what had occurred.

For his part, Shorin could say nothing to ease his friend's pain because he felt the same way. So many good men lost, it would be something else the pair would have in common for better or worse. Mryl lowered his head to cover the display of emotions as best he could, the well of emotions too strong for him to cap. The price he and his men had paid was too high for it not to tear at him.

Rinard nodded his understanding as well. Out of ninety one Lancers that had ridden into Arnoth, barely fifteen were alive and several of those were wounded seriously. He had been checking on them when the villager had arrived with news of the arrival of the humans friends from the west. He decided to go and see for himself when he found Logas gathering food and drink for them.

Shorin reached over and laid his hand on the shoulder of his friend; the Guardsman felt the weight and drew strength from it. Logas was deeply affected by the story that the young human told. He too felt guilty for the many lives lost here in the village; he had spoken out in favor of staying and fighting, his voice carrying with it great weight that many of the others had listened to. His once beautiful village was now a burned relic and hundreds of his friends and fellow residents dead in the ruins. For the rest of his days he would carry that guilt.

After a few moments to compose himself, Mryl looked up, wiped his eyes now red from the tears as Rinard and Shorin both poised questions. The Striker was translating since the Elf didn't speak Common as the Headman did. Logas was quiet as he listened to the information that had come at such a high price. Mryl answered the questions in between mouthfuls, the food while seriously depleted, not completely gone. Shorin then asked if there was anything unusual about what they had seen, anything outside the normal for an army on the move.

The message bearer thought for a moment and apologized to the others about his lack of ability to think clearly. The time for sleep had come and gone several times since he last lain down and that had been but a two hour nap. Logas and the soldiers with him nodded in grim understanding at the statement. All four of them were tired beyond the ability to explain it to anyone, even themselves if the need arose.

It was something only a soldier or someone who has been through battle could truly understand. A sudden flash of recognition shown in the eyes of the Guard member and his head jerked up as if to bring the thought to the top. He told the others that he had indeed seen something that he couldn't explain. The fatigue and hunger were slowing his wits as he fought to clear his head enough to answer the question coherently.

"I, I mean we, saw a whole bunch of large creatures, looked like really big men, sort of. They were large, I mean tall, really tall," excitement crept into his voice and the tone rose an octave as the tale continued. "…Each of them was at least seven or eight feet high but they weren't human or for that matter anything else I have ever seen."

He seemed far away when he spoke as his mind's eye went back to the scenes in the valley those long ten-days ago. He shuddered at the thought of the creatures. The others noticed the shiver but said nothing.

"The humans we saw were ordinary, just like us, nothing unusual there but these things… mostly dark in color but some were lighter. They seemed to be in charge wherever we saw them. The humans deferred to them and matter of fact, some of them had tattoos or paint on their upper arms. They were tall, round 'bout eight feet or so. Kinda looked like lizards or summin' like that."

He pointed to his own arm to show the location of the markings he had observed. The trio looked to one another and then back to Mryl. "I know it sounds like a madman's tale but I saw them and if I never saw them again that would be fine with me." He looked at the others and in a voice that was a whisper of itself said, "I've seen evil."

Logas who had listened more than spoken then asked Mryl in an off-handed fashion that immediately caught the attention of the others. "Were the other colors of these creatures a light gray and an off brown?"

The Elf refused to look at Mryl as he spoke. Rinard was quiet as well, a chunk of cheese held forgotten in his hand halfway to his mouth, the tension around the four suddenly heavy and pressing. Shorin looked at the Headman and then to his friend awaiting the answer but for some reason fearing what was coming.

"Yeah it was. How in shades did ya' know that?" The younger Twinsteel was wide awake now and a sudden queasy feeling leapt into the pit of his belly, the hunger of before gone as he stared at the elder Elf.

Logas seemed hesitant at first to reply to the question. He opened his mouth to speak but shut it without saying a word. He got up from his chair and walked off quickly leaving the two humans to wonder what in the name of the eternal darkness was going on, the rude manner of departure shocked Shorin knowing full well the high value the Elder Race placed on decorum.

They turned to look at the Lancer who suddenly remembered the cheese in his hand and shoved the whole piece in his mouth to keep from having to answer any questions. He chewed very slowly and with great deliberation to prolong the inevitable for as long as possible all the time avoiding their eyes.

Logas had moved away so quickly that neither man attempted to follow him. Shorin was trying to decide what to do next when Mryl asked him what had happened here at the village. The tired Striker paused for a few moments to gather his thoughts to answer the query with something resembling a sensible answer when as he was about to begin explaining, Logas reappeared from around the corner of the nearby building bearing a large book in his hands clutched close to his chest. He strode with a sense of purpose that belied his fatigue.

Shorin saw the open fear that the Elf carried in his posture and seeing it disturbed the Striker to the depth of his being. He knew from long talks with Parun that those of the Elder Race rarely displayed strong emotions openly and even during the height of the battle for the village Logas had not lost his composure.

Something in what Mryl had said frightened Logas to the point of showing his fear and that was something to take note of. If the Elf was afraid then pay attention he told himself. The trio waited as Logas approached, no one speaking at all.

The Headman reached the table but did not sit down. He looked intently at the two humans and then spoke carefully to Mryl, "I wish you to look at this and tell me if this was what you saw." The voice tinged with anticipation and a hint of something else, something darker. Rinard finally finished his mouthful of cheese and swallowed while silently watching the two men across from him.

The travelers from Karbel were fully on guard now as Mryl rose from his seat to stand before the Headman, telling him he would look at whatever he wished him to. Logas opened the large book and flipped through the heavy parchment pages a few at a time until he found what he was searching for.

Shorin was now convinced it was more than just what his friend had said that was giving Logas fits. The Elf located what he was seeking and with a slow hand turned the book around and held it out to the Guardsman, a slight tremor present that moved the book.

Mryl leaped toward him grabbing the book from his host as soon as he saw the drawings. He turned and slammed the book down on the table with such vigor several pieces of the remaining food jumped off the platter to come to rest on the table surface itself.

A strange look of wonder and fear shone from his face. "Yes! Yes that's it! That's what we saw." Excitement shot through him and he repeatedly poked the book with his finger restating his confirmation over and over. Shorin, who couldn't see what his friend was looking at from where he was, stood and moved over next to Mryl to look at what the book contained.

What he saw there amazed him - a large detailed drawing covering both pages of the open book illustrated several large creatures, one each in the previously mentioned colors. They were unlike anything Shorin had ever seen --large, powerful looking beings with long arms ending in three fingers and a thumb, bony ridges around the eyes and above the mouth gave them a hard look.

The eyes were what unsettled the proud Striker the most; they were a pale yellow in color and had a thin pupil like some lizards he had seen. Each of the figures was heavily muscled and wore a covering from the waist to what could be called boots of a type. One of the three had a series of rings painted or tattooed on the upper part of one arm in different colors that appeared to circle the arm. Several sentences of Merlik were written in the lower portion of each of the two pages. Shorin was able to read it quickly and a word he did not know leapt off the page: *Varshon*. That puzzled him, was that the creature's name or race?

The two humans looked at one another and then to the Elves who they realized with a start were both praying. Logas was standing with both arms lifted over his head which was tilted up to the sky.

The Headman was saying over and over "Great ancestors protect us."

The Lancer beside him was silent but obviously deep in his prayers, his hands clasp together and shaking with the fervor of his faith. Shorin and Mryl were truly afraid now, if this scared the Elves this bad then what did it bode for the rest of them?

Suddenly, so suddenly it startled the two men Logas dropped his arms and locked gazes with his guests, a wild light in his eyes. "We must go, leave here - leave now!"

The words carried a nearly frantic tone with them. Everything then seemed to happen at once, Logas turned then yelled for two of villagers who had been passing by. The unexpected command from their village Headman surprised both as weariness was momentarily forgotten at the intensity of the summons.

Rinard finished his ministrations and dropped his arms standing quietly to the side of the Headman, despair and fear creeping into his features. He seemed like a small child who had lost its way, waiting for someone to find him.

The elder Elf reached out and grabbed both of the villagers by the shoulders when they ran up and uttered a single word that would once again change the whole of the Elven nation, "*Varshonii!*" The Merlik word translated as "The Varshon Come."

It was a warning that came from the deep past of Elven history, a word not needed in the Homelands for over three centuries but known by all her inhabitants. A word that carried a long and bloody history with it, a phrase that was to those of the Elder blood evil itself.

The reaction was immediate and sharp. One of the pair broke from the strong grip on his shoulder and stepped back, a broad look of shock and terror full on his face as he tried to utter the word again as speech failed him. The second villager didn't move, didn't blink, his eyes fixed immobile on Logas as he tried to comprehend the scope of what he had just been told. The Headman looked at the two as if to confirm his words by the look on his face.

The gesture was not lost on the two men of Karbel. Shorin did not know the phrase he had heard despite his command of the language. Mryl for his part was trying to understand what was going on, he knew little of the Elves aside from stories and the ones who enlisted in the Strikers and came to Kuln. The fear he was seeing was real and deep, he didn't need to speak the language to understand that.

Food forgotten, Rinard unexpectedly turned and ran away from the table heading off to find his Lancers yelling at the top of his lungs for them to rally to him. Mryl and Shorin tried to keep up with what was going on around him. Mryl was at a particular disadvantage due to his inability to understand the language.

Both of the soldiers knew it was not good news, that much was painfully obvious but the shock of what they were seeing was nearly too much to handle. Events seemed to speed up and threatened to run away as the soldiers tried to comprehend what was happening. The thoughts of more food and some rest were rudely pushed aside by this new development that Logas was struggling with.

Logas released his grip on the villager and began to give his fellow residents orders in rapid bursts of Merlik. Shorin was able to keep up with most it, gather up food, horses, and wagons to get the wounded out, get them ready to move, now. Time is running out and we must go, now, hurry! The pair dashed off like an angered wraith was chasing them.

Mryl noticed the look of understanding come over his friend and waited impatiently for the translation. Shorin was silent, just trying to fully understand what he had heard. The Guardsman smacked his counterpart with the back of his hand to get his attention. Startled, the Striker looked at his friend who was staring at him quite intently.

When he got no response he shook Shorin to get his full attention, "Hey, me no speak Elvish, wha'd he say?"

Before he could answer Logas turned and told the two soldiers, "My apologies, let me explain, quickly though, we haven't much time."

He motioned to the pair to walk with him as he headed toward the town center. The men lost no time falling in on either side of Logas and the trio hurriedly trotted off as the story began. The Headman began with a short lesson in the history of the Homelands and its people and jumped around a little until he got to the heart of the issue.

"Nearly two thousand years ago the Elves fought a long and savage war with a race known as the Varshon. Those were the creatures you saw in the south. Varshon are users of dark majical arts and fierce fighters - they are cruel and without mercy."

Logas thought back on the stories his father had been told by his own grandsire from the time he had fought in the Dark War. Never in his worst dreams did Logas ever think he would have to worry about the return of the Dark Ones.

Logas could see that the humans did not fully comprehend the seriousness of the situation and tried to explain it to them, quickly. "Don't you understand? Don't you see? You saw Varshon with that army; that means they are coming again, here."

Both men got it this time and both nearly outdid Logas as they paled at the realization of what lie ahead. In a quiet voice, so quiet the other two almost didn't hear him Logas said "Darkness walks the land and we again live in fear of the night."

The trio hurried off to help with the evacuation.

***

The Strikers that could ride would head northwest to return to Karbel, the Guards riding with them, horses available in plenty due to losses among the Arakai. All the wounded except for the southern troop commander were being sent to the east. Logas promised Shorin that his men would be given the best treatment available. The young human formally thanked his former host with a deep bow and the Elven words of parting, "Fair Roads to thee". The village Headman returned the bow and then shook the hand of the Striker before heading for his horse.

Taking his leave of Logas, Shorin turned and was heading for his own horse when Jehna appeared from around the side of one of the wagons bearing the wounded and came running up to him. Shorin was somewhat startled when the beautiful Elf maiden called to him.

His mind was on a hundred other things and he had for the moment completely forgotten about her. Her hair was uncombed, her clothes didn't match and she was dirty but Shorin was certain she was even more beautiful to him than the first time he had seen her.

The first wagons were underway scrambling to the east, so time was running out. The two looked at one another and no words were spoken as they closed the distance between them and embraced. The mutual loss they shared in the death of Parun had brought them close, closer than either of them realized at the time. She was warm and alive and the tired, wounded, spirit-sapped Striker drew in all he could from her.

She snuggled deeper into his grasp and buried her head into his broad chest while he gently laid his cheek atop the golden tresses now discolored by soot. Despite the smoke he imagined he could just smell some of the flower-based soap she used on her hair. It was just enough to bring to mind better places and better times.

The wind picked up and tugged at her hair as the pair stood as one. Smoke from the fires still played havoc with trying to see at times, thick choking clouds of it blew across the scene blocking out the sun. Mryl had been getting the survivors ready to go and rode back to where he had expected to find Shorin.

The horse stood rider less and the Guard looked about for his friend among the wagons, smoke preventing him from seeing far. He continued to look around and then the smoke parted and there was Shorin, arms wrapped around an Elven woman. When they turned he could see her face -- gods above she was beautiful! The Guard stopped his horse, dropped his head and merely sat there shaking it back and forth. Only Shorin could find a girl amid the wreckage of a village right after a desperate battle.

Shorin looked down at Jehna and very slowly released his arms. She reached up and with a gentle hand touched his face and told him "Winds speed your journey."

Shorin felt her hand and the warmth of it seemed to touch something in him that he had not felt in longer than he had realized. For the moment, they were alone in that time and place, together, that they were from different worlds didn't matter, and that they were joined now was enough.

The wagon driver was yelling for her to hurry and that ended their moment. Shorin suddenly picked her up and carried her bodily to the front of the wagon and deposited her softly on the seat. The driver immediately shook the reins to get the horses going. She turned to watch him as the wagon pulled away.

With all the determination he had Shorin called after her "Look for me. I'll find you!" She waved in response.

The wagon picked up speed and several mounted Lancers rode up alongside as an escort. Rinard raised a hand in salute from his horse then headed east. Shorin stood watching till he could no longer see the group due to the smoke.

Mryl had been eyeing the exchange and rode over to where the Striker stood, leading a horse from his. The friends traded looks and then Shorin swung himself into the saddle. The two swung around and went to collect the men. It was time to go and the town of Arnoth now stood empty of living beings.

The Elves continue to head east while the Guard and Strikers that could ride headed west for the border, home, and likely another battle.

Chapter Thirty
The Road Ahead

D'Lohm

The elder Varshon had crossed the river several days previously, his coach and escort making excellent time. Anagir and his staff were moving north at a sedate pace compared to the combat elements of the Varshon controlled army. The tribesmen had been preparing hard for this moment for decades; they were capable for marching for hours without pause. The training had been brutally harsh, marching with double weight packs and weapons with little food, water or sleep.

This training was paying large dividends; the men were currently averaging nearly thirty leagues a day. At that rate they would be well inside Karbel in two more days if all went according to plan and so far it had been going well for the invaders.

There had been several good sized skirmishes as well as two full battles with the army of D'Lohm, in each case the southern army was victorious giving those defending their home country stinging losses and forcing them back. There had been casualties among the tribesmen but Pon and his superiors paid it no mind. Their own losses were expected and had been factored in.

All that was necessary was for Anagir to reach G'mar and secure the sacred books.

Pon had received word from the southern cavalry commander Vinshee that the heavy cavalry under his command had reached the Karbel border, crossed it without opposition and was continuing north. There had been no further word from the Arakai Ri'al leader…Bolgar, that's his name.

Pon had high hopes for the younger Arakai but so far only silence since his reports of being engaged by black clad human soldiers. The senior general felt confident that Bolgar had run into a unit of Strikers, supposedly elite troops belonging to Karbel. Hopefully Bolgar and his men triumphed; if not then Pon had been wrong about the young Arakai. He gave it no more thought -- there were plenty more where that one came from.

The elder Varshon had sent word for Pon to report to him. The senior general ordered his staff to keep him informed of any developments then headed off to answer the summons. He and his immediate retainers found horses waiting nearby which was as it should be. The senior general must have the ability to move about quickly should the need arise and being summoned by Anagir was certainly cause enough to move quickly. The senior Varshon could be quite particular about how those that served him responded.

Pon and his staff retainers stopped their horses well short of where the elder majic user was waiting. Long established protocol dictated that no one would ride up to the Varshon leader for security reasons even for those whose loyalty was assured such as the southern forces leader. The Marshal of the Host knew this of course; his training had been intense since a young age. Not the least of this had been learning the proper decorum for being in the presence of his masters.

The Varshon had long ago created the formalized rules regarding how their vassals would conduct themselves while in the presence of any Varshon, let alone the elder majic user. Pon well knew his own place and while he did command the combined human army it was only there to serve the masters.

Several grooms were waiting for the commander and his men. The soldiers barely acknowledged the servants; they were a full caste lower than themselves so not worthy of notice; so long as they did their job that was all that mattered. The command group dismounted and fell into a short double wide line behind Pon as he marched toward the waiting Varshon leader.

Anagir saw his commander approaching; he wanted to speak with him about a variety of topics. A small part of him wondered if what he was feeling was eagerness. The elder majic user had to stop and actually give that a moment of thought. *Could it be? I'm actually eager for this -* an interesting thought. He dismissed the emotion to return his attention to the form of his leading subordinate who was nearly upon him.

Those with Pon stopped well short of the senior leader; they hadn't been asked for so they waited. Q-tra-All watched the human approach, then properly and flawlessly bow to Anagir. Had he not done so the Troll would have shown no hesitation in reprimanding the commander on the spot.

The Ogurth were fanatics in their worship of the Varshon. The large mountain Trolls had been in service to them for more than five hands of generations. During a skirmish between the two groups, Anagir had used a spell to ensnare several of the attacking Trolls and hold them at bay with no effort.

To the Ogurth who valued strength above all else this was something completely new to them. No race had ever been able to stand up to them and now here was one creature stopping three Ogurth by waving his hand. The effect of the spell was immediate; all of the Trolls stopped fighting and laid down their weapons. The outnumbered Varshon were mystified but relieved, they had been hard pressed to hold their own against the fierce mountain dwellers.

Anagir saw this and used the opportunity to weave another spell, this one a fire spear. The Ogurth who witnessed this were shocked and awed. They had long ago mastered the ability to make fire but to create it without stone or fuel? What manner of creatures were these?

Anagir and the Varshon were taken with honor to the central town of the Ogurth nation and once there presented to the Elder Council whose members were the senior Troll of each of the five tribes of the Ogurth. They arrived in late afternoon; hundreds of Ogurth were in attendance watching from the stone benches of the large open air gallery.

Once there Anagir put on a display of various majical spells each more involved than the last culminating in the creation of the largest fire spear he could muster. It was taxing for him, the nearest force line was a ways off, but he managed to pull it together. The council members had been skeptical when the patrol members told their story but after watching Anagir work the majic they were cowed by what they had seen.

After conjuring another fire spear he launched it skyward. It traveled about a hundred yards then exploded lighting up the entire area for a few seconds. The thunder like clap was so loud and impressive several of the steady Trolls were nearly overcome with fear.

The council rose as a body then came down into the open floor area in front of the dais where they had been sitting. Once there they all knelt before Anagir, and as they did all of the assembled Trolls in the gallery did as well. This lead to some of the Varshon remaining with the Trolls to begin training their new subjects. In short order the entire Ogurth nation was subjected to the Varshon.

Pon waited to be told to rise which came in short order. He rose waiting to be spoken to as per the protocol. Anagir waved him forward and then asked him for a status report. The southern forces commander began to lay out the most current information for his master -- enemy troop strengths, distance that the lead elements of the army had travelled, how far they were from the Karbel frontier, and more. Anagir listened intently, his deep brown eyes fixed on Pon as he spoke.

The Varshon then asked him about the attack on Luxia, the capital city of D'Lohm. Pon hesitated for the briefest of moments before answering. Anagir noted the tiny delay, his curiosity was piqued.

The southern leader began to explain that the battle for the capital had gone well but their losses had been higher than anticipated, a good deal higher in fact.

"How much higher, commander?" The tone was direct and filled with authority.

Pon told him that they had suffered nearly eighteen percent higher losses than what had been projected. With a gimlet eye Anagir asked, *why had this occurred?*

Pon explained, "Sir many of the losses took place after the battle. A large section of Arakai and Alush were competing for some prize loot and it turned to armed combat. It took the Ogurth," a quick glance at the big Troll next to Anagir, "to restore order."

Anagir weighed his options; this was not supposed to happen. Squabbling like thieves over some baubles? This situation would require an example be set. Returning his full attention to his commander Anagir said, "I am not pleased. In fact, I am angered commander. What steps have you taken to correct this behavior? I am waiting…"

Pon hurriedly explained that as soon as he had been informed he had sent word that the commanders of both units were to be put to death and then a decimation was to be done to the units. This meant that one in every ten men were also put to death for the failure to maintain discipline. The units were then disbanded and their colors burned, the men disbursed to labor battalions and all the loot they had accumulated immediately transferred to the control of the Ogurth.

It was the fight and the resulting decimations that had been a major factor in the high casualty rate. Finished with his explanation Pon waited silently, his eyes fixed on the ground in front of Anagir's feet waiting for his master to speak.

Letting the man before him sweat a bit before answering, the Varshon leader considered what he had been told. Pon had actually been harsher on the men than he himself would have been and that wasn't a bad thing at all. It would serve as an excellent example to the others and he knew that the word would spread growing more garish with each telling. Yes, that would be an acceptable example for the others.

He told Pon, "My friend you did well, excellent job!"

Inwardly very relieved to hear that his work had been acceptable Pon lifted his head to look at his superior. "I give Thanks and Praise to the Varshon!"

A small smile cracked Anagir's face, it was important to give the menials a taste of kind words once in awhile lest they forget how it feels. "Now let us speak of other things…"

The two moved on a discussion of logistics. Pon was pleased at how much food was reaching the forward units, he mentioned two supply units by name for recognition. Anagir motioned to a nearby scribe who wrote the information down, a note would be sent to the unit commanders praising the men for their diligence.

The conversation lasted for several more minutes before Anagir thanked Pon for the information and dismissed him. Pon performed a proper salute and bow before leaving the Varshon's presence. He took his men to their horses and returned to the command area to receive an update on what had gone on in their absence.

Meanwhile, the army continued moving north.

Chapter Thirty-One
A Moment's Peace

Ballanshire

Jendile Dalshorn, the Elven king, his father Dural, and their guest, Dael Tjchanis, were just finishing an excellent meal of honey baked quail in one of the dining rooms of the palace, when a messenger from Arnoth arrived at the western gate of the capital city.

The massive barriers that shielded the city from the outside world had been closed as they were every night at the same time. The watchmen could hear the approaching sound of hooves coming up the long stone throughway. Three of the sharp eared Elves were peering ahead into the hidden dark that always came just after twilight, the night gloom mixed with a touch of fog which made seeing any distance difficult even for those of the Elder Race who all possessed excellent vision, even at night.

The rider suddenly appeared before the watch, coming hard out of the night, the rider so intent on staying mounted he missed what light there was coming from the torches and lamps atop the wall and those at the gate due to the conditions.

The slender figure atop the horse reined the mount in before they ran headlong into the gate. The three soldiers all frantically reached out to try and calm the agitated mount before it hurt itself or them. After a few tense moments of chaos one of the guards was able to grab the halter and started talking to the excited horse. His voice spilled out words of calm and care -- the Elves had a way with horses that was almost mythical in its apparent power to touch the heart and mind of the animal.

Despite the frantic pace of the ride the horse began to calm down as the soothing words continued. Strong hands rubbed the sweaty neck of the animal trying to get it to relax further.

Once the guard was able to make contact with the halter the other two backed off slightly to allow their fellow his work. The haggard rider was cloaked in a simple cape that reflected his travels; it was torn, dirty and smelled faintly of smoke and ash. The hooves of the tired beast were still active but growing less so as moments and more gentle words passed.

As the horse settled the rider seemed to lose strength and began to slide off his saddle. He nearly hit the cobblestone paved roadway but the other two guards caught him, barely. They gently pulled him up and supporting him on either side started walking toward the doorway leading to the guard post.

By now more of those on duty had been summoned or come on their own, fully a score of hardy Elves cleared a path for the two guards. The night captain met them just short of the door way, he moved aside telling them to take the rider inside and put him somewhere comfortable.

He then turned to the others, sharply telling them to stop standing about, see to your posts, double alert, and went back inside to question the rider himself. The nineteen soldiers broke up into sections and checked their weapons again as they rushed to carry out their orders. Something might be amiss so extra attention was warranted.

Once inside the guard house the rider was led to a chair, water was found and brought for him as well. The captain waited till the boy was able to drink which caused him to cough a bit. After he had composed himself he slumped in the chair, which the officer noted. Something was going on and for the moment the responsibility of finding out what was going on lay on him.

He looked the rider over, body language told him a great deal -- the youth was exhausted, hardly able to grasp the water cup; it shook slightly in his hand. He was speaking but in such a low tone it was hard to hear him. The captain knelt down and put his ear near the mouth of the messenger. The eyes of the officer got bigger and bigger the more he heard.

"Invasion, being invaded. The south, coming from the south. Need help –Varshon coming, get help." The same line repeated over and over.

Varshon? What in the name of – how could that be? Having heard the message several times now the captain stood, looking at his men. He knew that whatever was going on was serious. No Elf invoked the name of their most hated enemy without cause. Clearly something serious had happened and this boy had been a part of it.

Correctly surmising that this situation involved others well above his rank, the gate captain had the senior aide to the king sent for with a request to come to the gate immediately. Several additional messengers were summoned, he ordered that word was to be taken at once to each of the three remaining city gates and order the guards there be placed on full alert, no drill.

The trio of Elves saluted and left to carry out their mission, each headed for a different gate. The fourth messenger was told to report to the commander of the city garrison and request that the garrison also be put on full alert and that a complete report would be made to him as soon as was possible. The veteran soldier saluted and hurried off to deliver his news.

The two guards who had carried the youth inside were told to stay with him and if possible get some food in him. The captain knew that the quiet night of earlier was no more, and hoped that whatever was going on could be solved without more trouble. He looked over at the weary youth knowing that his wish wasn't likely to be granted. A growing feeling of unease filled the officer. He stepped out of the guard room to double check that the gates and immediate surrounding area was secure.

In due time Kellen Aidos, senior aide to the king, was notified that he was needed at the west gate on a matter of great urgency. Slightly surprised but calm at hearing the request, the Elf nodded once to the staffer then quietly excused himself from the room where the king and his guests were talking, making sure another of the household staff was nearby in case the men inside required anything.

The aide wondered what manner of situation could bring this request. Probing questions to the palace runner who had summoned him brought no further information. A pressing request from the guard captain for Aidos to personally come to the west gate as rapidly as possible was all that he knew. Double checking to ensure that the king and his guests had what they needed for the moment Kellen quietly excused himself, heading for the courtyard and the waiting transportation.

Exiting the palace, Kellen went to the carriage and told the driver to head to the west gate. The teamster and the guard who rode with him said nothing but the vehicle left with little pause. As the ride through the wide streets allowed him time to think, Aidos again wondered at the request for his person.

It was certainly not the first time he had gone to answer a summons during his years of service but it was the first one in some time. Why the west gate? Usually it was the south or eastern gate since the majority of the Elven Homelands lay to the east and south of the capital city. Patience and time will reveal all truth as the Elves liked to say.

He leaned back against the comfortable padding of the seat to endure the journey through the large city as best he could, knowing the trip would take nearly a third of an hour despite the lack of residents out and about at this time of day.

At the gate, Aidos was met by the waiting gate captain who introduced himself and thanked the aide for coming so quickly. A courtly nod of return, and with that he was taken to the room where the messenger was.

By now the youth had been able to eat a little which had lifted some of the fatigue and mental fog allowing him to compose himself. Aidos was introduced to the youth and in short order he was told in much greater detail what had transpired out on the frontier.

The tired rider relayed the message that Logas had sent. The senior aide was nearly shocked into silence. Such a thing could happen in this day and age? No matter, it wasn't for him to decide. This was something that the king must be made aware of as soon as possible.

The youth was taken directly to the palace by way of the same carriage that had brought Aidos, this time with a mounted escort to ensure nothing impeded the trip. Kellen resisted the urge to further question the youth as they rode. A number of questions were running through the mind of the longtime royal servant.

Once at the home of the royal family, the aide and two burly soldiers brought the exhausted messenger inside. The guards were practically carrying their charge in order to speed his passage through the expansive structure but not without care. Aidos was walking quickly, almost at a run. His training and sense of decorum forbade his running through the palace of the king but he was tempted, tempted as he had never been before. Varshon attacking the Homelands was almost more than he could fully grasp.

Upon reaching the door to the appropriate room he knocked twice then entered as Jendile preferred. Once in the room Kellen made the minimal bow to those inside. Tjchanis looked over from where he was seated to see Aidos enter. The longtime Dalshorn retainer, seemed – agitated? Dael turned his body to better see what was happening. Both Dural and Jendile saw the body language as well. Conversation died as the three waited for the man to speak.

Kellen stopped a few paces from the trio and without preamble told his king the tidings brought by the messenger, "My lords, forgive the intrusion but news of great import has arrived. The Homelands are under attack by the Varshon."

Reaction to the news was swift in coming.

Dael immediately stood at hearing the proclamation from the senior servant. The king and his father looked to one another then back at Aidos. About that time the guards arrived with the youth. Kellen waved the soldiers forward, motioning toward an empty chair. The duo hardly paused their stride to follow the directive.

Jendile was still trying to understand what his aide and friend was speaking of when two of his soldiers entered the room bearing a boy between them. They gently deposited him in the large chair opposite the couch. Dael was quickly able to gather much from the appearance of the messenger and his smell. A faint mix of smoke, sweat and dried blood. Tjchanis had smelt that same combination often enough over the years. Never once had that smell been accompanied by good news.

Jendile leaned forward in his seat asking what news the messenger carried. The long road from Arnoth had dulled the youth some but he answered quickly, he tried to stand as protocol dictated but Jendile waved back down.

Settling back into the chair the youth began, "My king, I am Neron – Neron Balt. I was sent to warn you. Our village was attacked; it was attacked by horsemen from the south. Human soldiers."

The youth was struggling to come to grips with many things at once, that he was alive was chief among those, the fact he was sitting in the palace and speaking to the King of the Elves was another. The long fight for the village had been a desperate struggle for survival. Neron had accounted himself well as had all those his age but many of his friends were now dead as was his father. The youth had a job to do, an important job Logas told him. The seriousness of the situation was a terrible burden to bear but there had been no one else that Logas could spare to carry the message.

Jendile rose from his seat, moved over to the youth then knelt next to Neron telling him that he was safe, he had made it. Aidos sent one of the soldiers for more food and drink for the youth. Dural edged closer, not wanting to miss a single word.

Neron nodded once and returned to his story. "Logas Kalantiere, Headman of our village, Arnoth sent me to warn you. He bid me speak these words to you '*The Varshon have arisen and are coming north with a massive army.*'"

Questions piled up but none were spoken. Jendile Dalshorn suddenly looked very tired, as if he had aged two hundred years in an instant, the pleasant memory of an excellent dinner so recently enjoyed completely forgotten.

Dael asked if there was anything else. Neron went on to explain that about the unit of Strikers that had arrived at the village bearing news of the invasion. He spoke at length about how they and the villagers fought for nearly a full day trying to hold off the enemy soldiers. He reached in his tunic and removed a parchment roll handing it to the king. Jendile wasted no time in unrolling the document; he stood up reading it aloud for the benefit of the others in the room.

"*My Lord, I, Logas Kalantiere, write this in haste and pray to all our ancestors it reaches your hand. A large force of southern soldiers is at this time moving north from beyond the Wystern River. I have knowledge of this thanks to the arrival at Arnoth of two human soldiers, one a Striker and the other a member of the Black Guard.*" Pausing his oration, Jendile asked, "A Black Guard? At Arnoth? That makes no sense; the Black Guard patrol the south-west of Karbel. Is that not so?"

The royal cousin was quick to assure his liege that was in fact the case. Dael was just as surprised, he had never heard of any of the Guards that far away from their home at Kuln.

Jendile returned to his reading. "*The Black Guard officer, Mryl Twinsteel is the leader of what remains of a Black Guard patrol that has tracked this army from the deep south. D'Lohm has been overrun and occupied by the Varshon and their human army. Twinsteel himself witnessed Varshon leading the human soldiers while in the south."*

Dural told Aidos to retrieve a map showing the western frontier area. The aide went over to an ornately carved cabinet on the far side of the room to get the requested item.

"Twinsteel reports the army numbers at least 80,000 possibly more than a 100,000..." Those gathered in the room were in disbelief. An army of that size was beyond the scope of reality. That was equal to a sizable percentage of the entire Elven population!

Jendile saw that Neron was holding out another document, this one was heavily stained, torn and wrinkled. Dael took this one and carefully unrolled it. It was one of the copies of the original sighting report that the Black Guards had written up several ten-days before while still on the hilltop watching the enemy army march past. Mryl had given it to Logas before leaving Arnoth.

Well educated, Tjchanis had no problem reading what was written despite it being another language. His eyes flashed over the numbers, heavy infantry, engineers, cavalry, siege towers, catapults, Trolls...*Trolls?*

Jendile watched as his cousin digested the information on the worn and dirty parchment. Dael glanced at his relation shaking his head in disbelief; this situation was beyond anything any of them had ever dealt with.

The king then returned to what he was holding. *"And I have sent a copy of his report. Mryl was careful to instruct me to tell you that what is on the report is not all of the southern army. His men watched for several hours before leaving to reach their own people so that they could report their findings. The courage of the humans in this is a tale for another time, had it not been for them everyone in our village would have been lost. The Striker officer, Shorin Tallon, is as brave as any I have ever known. He and the survivors of his command are headed to Karbel in an attempt to reach reinforcements that he had previously requested. We owe them no small debt of honor. I am heading east with what few of us remain. We request that troops be sent to the western frontier as soon as possible. All that may be spared. The fate of our people depends on it. I am, and remain Logas Kalantiere."*

Aidos was waiting with the map. Seeing that Jendile was finished speaking he brought the large, highly detailed map forward. Moving aside the cups and wine pitcher from the table near the couch, the group gathered around as the map was spread out

Arnoth was quickly located and pointed out. It was the westernmost of all the Elven towns and settlements. If the Varshon and their army were coming for the Elves they would have to pass through the wide valley between the massive arms of the Shyval mountain range north and south of Arnoth. An army of one hundred thousand - a force that large that could sweep aside the whole of the Elven Homelands.

There was no information in the message regarding the direction of travel of the enemy, what their location was, or how soon they would be in the Homelands proper. Those gathered that night left with more questions than there were answers.

Dural and his son began to discuss their options and response. At about the same time Dael grabbed an orderly telling him to have General Rale come to the palace with all haste. The household servant left the room immediately to carry out the directive. It mattered not a bit to him that the instruction had not come from the king. The orderly had been present as the messenger from Arnoth had explained about the Varshon. *Eternal Ancestors protect us,* he prayed while heading for the royal stables knowing full well some of the mounts were always kept ready. This was a message he would deliver himself.

The eyes of the royal cousin sought out the senior of the guards present. The Under-Captain was talking with several of his men. Tjchanis strode over to where they were.

The officer turned as Dael arrived. "Captain, order a full alert for the palace - now."

The officer never hesitated; he left the room immediately to carry out the order. The guards in the room stepped out to take up their positions. War had come to the Homelands and now it fell to those in charge to answer. After speaking with the man Dael returned to where the others were.

The three members of the royal family began earnestly discussing the situation. Additional questions came up as they reviewed the troop listing that Mryl had sent as well as compared the note from Logas with the highly detailed map that had been brought out earlier. The mood in the room was intense.

At that same time the alert that Dael had ordered was being carried out as additional guards rushed to their assigned posts. The Varshon were out there, they knew this now. Where they were wasn't known for sure but that fact that the ancient enemy had arisen was problem enough. The discussion continued without pause as the beginnings of a plan was sorted through.

***

Eathan Rale, the commanding general of the Elven army, arrived at the palace with several of his senior officers and a few guards. Once in the courtyard he and the others quickly dismounted then went inside.

Kellen Aidos was waiting for him, "General, the king and others are in the Manor Room."

Rale nodded his thanks and followed the Dalshorn retainer who led the way. The words of the messenger played through his mind as he traveled through the halls to meet with his king. *'Come to the palace at once on a matter of utmost urgency, the king requires you.'*

Not the most descriptive of summons but Eathan knew that the king was not one to request his senior general on a whim especially at this hour. Something was going on and he was about to find out what it was.

Kellen knocked once and without waiting for an acknowledgement opened the door to allow the general and those with him entry. The guards took up positions near the door once the officers were inside with the king.

As Rale entered he saw the current king, the former king, and Dael Tjchanis all gathered around a map. Their demeanor was determined, conversation stopped as the others arrived. Moving several steps into the room, the senior officer came to attention and saluted his ruler. Jendile returned the salute without speaking.

Looking over at his friend Dael was the first of the trio to speak. "War is upon us, the Varshon have returned."

Rale and his staff members were surprised, a reaction akin to shock in those of other races but he quickly recovered his bearing, "Where and in what strength?"

The officers that had traveled with the general moved forward to hear the news as well. Conversation in the room resumed as the king explained to all of them what they knew so far.

Within minutes, Rale had heard enough. "My Lord, several things need to be accomplished as soon as we may. The first of which is to order a general alert for the army, Next would be a call up of our reserves, as you know this takes time. The sooner we begin that process the better."

The general was looking across the table as Jendile listened intently to the man responsible for leading his military. Aidos waited to see if the general had any questions for Neron and when he didn't he escorted the exhausted youth out of the room, turning his care over to two of the night staff with orders that he be given anything he wanted then slipped quietly back into the room.

The younger of the two Dalshorn agreed with what Rale said. After the general finished his oration there was a quiet pause as the king weighed the choices.

The two men looked eye to eye across the table and then Jendile set his jaw as he answered. "Make it so, General. Order the army to maximum alert as well as publish the order calling up the reserves. However I must meet with the council before we settle on a course of action."

Eathan was confused, course of action? That was a simple one, take the army west and attack. He started to voice his concerns when the king spoke again. "General, you have your orders." The tone was direct with a hard edge.

Drawing himself to his full height Rale knew that the matter was for the moment at least, settled. He did have his orders so he saluted and once the king returned it he turned and marched from the room with the other officers in tow.

Dural waited until they left the room before speaking. He had in fact not said a word during the entire time the army officers had been present. Watching for the door to close he looked over at his son and without malice quietly told him, "That wasn't the best way to have handled that."

Jendile knew his father was right but having to speak with the council was something that he needed to do. The Elven army wasn't the biggest group of Dalshorn supporters in the Homelands. Many of the senior officers still felt that Dural had not given the army the respect they felt it deserved when he had been king. Some of them blamed the lack of action following the last great Varshon raid nearly three hundred years earlier on a lack of character.

Dural had not allowed the army to pursue the raiders back to wherever they had come from, as many of them had asked to. The king felt that it was unnecessary; the incursion had been halted and repulsed so there was no need for further bloodshed.

That raid had caught the Homelands by surprise and following the battle that turned the invaders back -- the Elven unit that took the brunt of the fighting was disbanded instead of being refitted. This left a very bitter feeling among many, some more so than others.

Dural recalled one junior officer in particular that had angrily spoken up about what the cost of failure would be. What was his name? The former king recalled the soldier clearly; he had lost a brother and his father during the fight that turned back the Varshon. When Dural refused to allow the army to follow their ancient enemies the officer vowed that he would never again wear the uniform stating that he would hunt them on his own.

Standing right there in the Council room he removed his rank badges and tossed them to the floor. *What was his name?* Dael and Jendile were discussing strategy while Dural sat there and tried to recall the name. It had been three hundred years but shouldn't be any reason to he should be able to – *Dwyn, his name was Dwyn*. The former king recalled with a small measure of satisfaction. He could clearly remember the reaction of the Council to the display that the officer had put on. Several other army members followed suit removing their rank and tossing them aside as well but it was Dwyn that had spoken the strongest about what to do regarding the Varshon. Wonder whatever became of him?

Dural shook his head to clear it of old thoughts; he needed to pay attention to what was going on at the moment. He stood and walked over to where the other two were deep in conversation. Soon the three were refining a strategy for dealing with the problem.

***

The messenger from Arnoth had been escorted out of the Council room after relating the story of the attack on the village by the southern cavalry and the information he had regarding the Varshon. An extensive period of questioning by the council members had followed the report. The young messenger had provided as much additional information as he could, casualties, property damage, crop loss, enemy weapons and more.

When the queries come to an end First Minister Ehlo politely thanked Neron for his dedication and sacrifice accompanied by a respectful bow of his head. The youth was taken away to get some much needed rest, it was now well past midnight.

Those gathered in the richly decorated room waited till the boy had been escorted away and the door closed before speaking among themselves regarding the news from the western frontier. Several points of view were presented, the debate continued for slightly more than an hour without a break.

Some of those in attendance advocated sending the army west as quickly as they could be mustered; others urged caution stating they didn't have enough information to commit the balance of the army. The king watched and listened as his advisors debated then a called a halt to the discussion.

One of the Council members, Kirth Wesylan had heard his fill. He had suffered for far too long through what he felt was the whining and spineless chatter of the other council members. He and his family had long been proponents of isolation, to end Elven interaction with the rest of the world permanently. It was time to bring this issue to an end once and for good, he came to his feet and spoke up without waiting for his turn, a serious breach of protocol.

"Enough of this!" His outburst brought all conversation in the room to an abrupt halt.

"Stories and fables, we sit and listen to this child speak of…of night monsters and myths! This is ridiculous and a waste of our time. One – just one village attacked by a few horsemen is hardly justification for sending our army to the western frontier. Those people shouldn't be there in the first place." His tone was venomous and dripped with sarcasm.

Enough was enough, time to end this waste of time and return to matters of real importance. He held his ground and in doing so dared any to oppose his stand. House Wesylan was an old and proud family; there had been a member of the family on the Council for hundreds of years without interruption.

Several of those present were shocked at the breach of decorum being displayed. Dural set his jaw and leaned forward to answer the statement made.

Jendile was about to tell the council member to retake his seat when

Dael spoke first, his voice low and full of malice, "Sit down, Hun'trel." There was no worse insult among the Elves, it called into question the honor of the person, their parentage all while equating them to being a Varshon follower.

The room was silent as the challenge was raised. Tjchanis looked across the table at the one standing. It was not only disrespectful of the king, but to the long-held council etiquette.

For years Dael had endured this self-righteous horse's ass drivel of segregation from the other races. He had long grown past the point of being tired of it. Isolationism was a stupid idea. The Elves were part of the world, and Dael felt strongly they should play a much larger role in it than they currently were. The Elves had cut themselves off from the rest of the world once before and Dael strongly believed the world was worse off for it.

The royal cousin had been patiently waiting for just such an outburst from Kirth. He knew that this long time outspoken opponent of the king would at some point slip and that day had finally arrived. Tjchanis was no stranger to politics and the intrigue that went with it, the circumstances to deal with the buffoon Wesylan had come at last.

Kirth was firmly convinced that his cause was right; move the frontier folk away from the border to the inlands and turn their collective backs on humans and others. This attack was merely further proof that he was right and had been all along.

So what if one pathetic little village had been razed? That was their problem. As for the ones who had been killed, they would serve as an excellent example of why the border should be abandoned. If they had been living in the east or south then it wouldn't have happened.

Wesylan wasn't afraid of Tjchanis, feeling that the so-called royal cousin was merely showing off for his betters. Kirth too had once served as a soldier and kept up his practice with a host of weapons on a regular basis. There were those who quietly agreed with his position on seclusion and their numbers and influence were slowly growing. The attack on this village would be the key to taking that issue to a much higher standing.

Kirth was already formulating his plan on how to best hold public meetings on the subject to help sway opinion. Not that he felt the majority of the masses were truly intelligent enough to comprehend the subject but once he could rally enough public support for his position he would force the issue with the Council. They must be made to listen; it was the right, and the only choice.

Jendile started to say something but suddenly stopped. He looked at his cousin and sensed that Dael had some plan in mind so he said nothing. Dural too was curious about what his nephew was up to but remained silent. The Elf that was next in line to the throne slowly stood and without taking his eyes from the figure across the table drew the dagger that rode his right hip and with a sharp flip of the wrist buried it in the wood of the chair that Kirth had vacated.

A glint of light reflected off the well-honed blade that now rested in a spot that would have placed it in the heart had Kirth been seated. The movement caused Kirth to jump back with a curse. He looked at the dagger, then to Dael. His eyes narrowed as anger rose up in him. How dare he!

Not afraid to accept a challenge, Kirth spat out the words, "Al Chargo Anya!" This was the ancient issue given to those seeking the challenge of arms, trial by combat. Kirth was sick of Dael and his kind, stupid soldiers whose only answers to a problem lay in the steel of a sword. If this is what he wished then so be it!

The other Council members looked to one another in surprise; this was not at all what they expected when roused from their homes at the summons of the king.

Arrangements were quickly made since as a matter of personal honor the duel took precedence over all other matters including those of state. There was a very specific and stringent protocol involving the custom. The two men were on opposite sides of the stone-ringed circle now laid out in the courtyard of the palace, measuring fifteen broad stepped paces in diameter. Torches flickered in the light breeze that carried through the courtyard, extra oil fired lamps had been brought outside as well to ensure adequate illumination.

Each combatant had one attendant present as per the long established rules of the challenge. Jendile was searching his memory for the last time that the challenge had been used in a council meeting and realized it was nearly eighty-five years earlier, and that one had involved words against the virtues of another man's wife. The husband had silenced his wife's accuser, successfully defending her honor.

This matter was entirely different and could prove very interesting as well as having the potential to be both beneficial -- in the loss of Kirth -- as well as damaging if Dael was the loser.

Not that he had any worries about his cousin; Kirth was healthy, fit, and a proven hand with a sword but Dael was a soldier, a warrior, and had been seemingly since birth. He had fought goblins, nomads, and monsters while serving the Homelands. Jendile knew of no finer swordsman than his cousin.

The Judge of the Challenge, in this case First Minister Ehlo, was to oversee the contest. It was usually the highest ranking person present at the time the challenge was issued who served as Judge. However in this case neither Dural nor Jendile could act as Judge since they were related by blood to one of the participants, so the position went to the next senior Elf.

The First Minister was no stranger to the proceedings, he had seen a number of these combat challenges in his many centuries of life but he couldn't recall one that he was anticipating as much as this one. His sharp mind was already calculating the win/loss factors based on who would win the challenge. The rules forbade him as adjudicator from placing a wager which was somewhat vexing; he hating missing an opportunity to win what he felt would be easy money.

Both men completed their preparations. By rule each contestant was allowed a shield and either sword or axe for the first exchange. The weapon not chosen was left in the ring to be used if the primary weapon was lost or damaged. If either of the two duelists lost their shield due to damage a temporary halt was called and a second shield was issued. If that one was rendered unusable then both parties were to continue with the fight with neither having a shield. If either of the combatants left the stone defined circle of their own accord they would be declared the loser then immediately put to death. However, if the person was knocked out of the ring as part of the combat a pause was called for him to reenter and the duel resumed.

The fight would continue until one of the two was dead. It was that simple, a surprisingly bloodthirsty ritual for those of the Elder Race known far and wide for their love of life. Armed guards stood nearby ready to carry out their duty if necessary.

Dael was calm as he studied his opponent. He knew that Kirth had served in the army so was no stranger to sword handling and had seen actual combat several times. Cautious not to underestimate him, Dael was confident without being foolhardy. That Kirth knew the sharp end of a sword was one thing, being able to defend himself with one was something else entirely.

Moving to the center of the stone marked ring Ehlo called the two forward from their respective sides. Each man moved to near the center to hear the Judge of the Challenge speak. "A challenge has been issued; may it be removed without trial by arms?"

Dael looked directly at his hated adversary answering in the proper form of the rite as protocol required, "No, the challenge shall end in blood." The First Minister nodded in acceptance, the choice whether to fight or withdraw was given to the one who had been challenged.

"So be it, challenge has been given and accepted." Turning toward Kirth, "Select your primary." As the originator of the ritual he would have choice of weapon, not surprisingly he chose the sword. "Return to your places and in all manners let honor be your guide."

Ehlo then turned and walked to the perimeter of the dueling area to be in a position to observe all the action. If as Judge he felt that either of the two combatants acted in a dishonorable manner he would signal the guards who would strike down the offender. A chair had been brought to allow him to sit and he did so that he could focus full attention on the match. The trial by combat was a serious matter and it required the proper awareness of all those involved.

Kirth looked at Dael and with a smirk told him, "Your precious Black Swords aren't here to save you again." Wesylan was making a reference to the large group of elite Elven fighters that House Tjchanis maintained that acted as Dael's personal guard. Dael merely smiled at the taunt but said nothing.

Jendile and the others watched intently as Ehlo looked to each of the men with a nod and a dropping of his raised hand signaled them to begin.

Gathering his shield and with sword in hand, Kirth advanced to near the middle of the arena. Dael did the same but kept himself several paces back from reach. Wesylan took measure of his foe, "I will be glad when this is over; you have been in my way for far too long. That ends now."

Dael didn't rise to the verbal bait. The two circled warily searching for an opening, any opening. The first attacks were mean to gain information, if I do this – then he'll do…

The duel continued unabated for several minutes with each man attacking and defending as needed. The sharp tones of steel impacting steel rang hollow as it echoed from the stone walls of the courtyard. Kirth surprised his foe with a strong backhand slash that tore the shield from his grip damaging the handhold on the underside rendering the shield useless.

Ehlo called an immediate halt to the fight while another shield was provided to Dael. Both men took advantage of the brief respite to drink something to refresh themselves. Their choice of drink reflected the difference in the two; Dael took a long, deep draught of water from the waiting pitcher while Kirth availed himself of a large flagon of wine.

Dael had to admit he was surprised at how well Kirth handled a blade. He had not expected this level of skill from the man. Dael wasn't worried, just more focused.

With a new shield in hand, the fight resumed and lasted for some time with neither man able to gain a significant advantage. The only breaks were for shield replacements, both of those were losses suffered by Kirth.

Per protocol, following the loss of the second shield by his foe Tjchanis was required to forfeit his remaining protective device as well. The royal cousin cast aside it with barely a thought, time to end this. The shield sailed a few paces to the side hitting the paving stone surface with a wooden *thump* then sliding to a stop within a length of itself.

Dael slid back to create a little distance between him and Kirth. While doing so he selected a High Guard position with his sword by lifting it with both hands to a point above his head. This put his hands at the forehead level meaning he could easily see what was coming. It was an archaic defensive position very rarely used in these times since in combat you were battling your opponent up close.

Wesylan saw the defense and without pause launched his attack, certain he had the bastard now. He chose a high cut expecting the angle to be difficult if not impossible for Tjchanis to be able to block. A powerful swing coming in from his right to sever the head and end the duel.

He was shocked at the sensation of ringing steel that stung his arms as his slash was deflected easily. The speed that Dael had maneuvered his sword had caught Wesylan completely by surprise. Before he could fully recover his guard the honed edge of the steel had raked him from left shoulder down to nearly the right hip opening a long gash. Blood immediately began to soak his shirt.

He staggered slightly back from the pain but was able to partially block the next attack as the advantage was pressed. The tip of Dael's sword found deep purchase in the thigh muscle of his opponent creating another opening.

Jendile and the others watched without comment as the fight continued. The duel had lasted longer than any of them had expected. The king had been more than a little surprised at the sight of his cousin sporting wounds, more so than he had believed possible. Kirth had been giving Dael a match but he could tell that the tide of the fight had swung; it was only a matter of time now and everyone there knew it.

Fear had crept into the eyes of Kirth. He was no longer confident of victory and could see his own death. Time and strength for one last attack -- gripping his sword with all his remaining might he swung awkwardly at Dael who nimbly stepped aside and with a horizontal slash severed the head of his opponent from his body. The corpse landed heavily on the stones while the head rolled several feet before coming to a stop, lifeless eyes staring into nothing.

His wounds aching, Dael stood over the body of his foe. *Now,* thought Dael, *we can get some real work done.* With that thought he turned and left the circle putting Kirth out of his mind.

Jendile motioned to several of the guards to assist the Wesylan household retainer in removing the remains. The body and head were to be collected and wrapped up for delivery to the family.

Once he had done that he turned to the remaining council members, "Gentlemen shall we return to our deliberations?"

Chapter Thirty-Two
The Voice of Home

Karbel

Gunnar still wasn't sure how to take the news; several days' earlier word had come into the capital that a group of travelers from Vankard, of all places, had been rescued by a Striker patrol well to the northwest of the capital. The group consisted of priests and soldiers on what was believed to be a quest of some importance. There was a language barrier but it was being worked through.

The northman had been away from the city when the first reports had come in regarding those that the Strikers had come across. Once it was determined where the caravan had originated it took no time at all for the king to have Gunnar summoned back to Karbel with all haste.

It had taken nearly two full days of hard travel to return to the capital in time to meet those from Vankard. Thadar had wished that his friend hadn't been gone, he would have sent Gunnar north to meet the travelers but that wasn't possible. He had only been back in the city for about two hours and the ship from Edora bringing their guests was due at any time.

The number of questions that Gunnar had regarding this news seemed to multiply the more he thought about it. What were they doing there? What was this quest they were talking about? Was it an approved expedition and if so who approved it and why? The questions far outnumbered the answers he had, which wasn't surprising since he had no answers at all.

For the northman, knowing that he would soon see some of his own countrymen for the first time since passing beyond the mountain gate leading out of Vankard didn't cause him anxiety. He had made peace with his decision to leave his homeland long ago. How those from his former home would react to him would be up to them.

In the past those few who had chosen to leave Vankard were not spoken of once they left, or treated kindly if they returned. The Utland was evil according to the tales that abounded in his own country and those electing to travel there must be affected as well.

T'shar, Mehan Finn and the Hol Brothers were part of the Striker group that were escorting Vode and the others to Karbel. Colonel Steele wanted to personally question those involved with the incident leading to the rescue of their guests.

Arriving at the docks after traveling down the Soling River from Edora aboard one of the two Striker operated vessels, the northmen were greatly impressed at the size of the capital city which they could easily see from the river as they came south. As the vessel had neared the capital, Vode and the others lined the rails taking in the sight.

The massive city wall was clearly visible from the dock area; it rose nearly fifty feet in height. Many of the travelers were feeling overwhelmed at what they were seeing. It wasn't hard for them to feel that way; Karbel dwarfed any city in Vankard as well as most of the other nations across the face of the known world.

After leaving the medium-sized sailing vessel, Vode and the others climbed aboard the waiting transport wagons and coaches then the group set out toward the palace. Mounted Strikers lead the way as well as riding alongside the visitors. The northmen were guests of the king so they had been told they had priority over other traffic into the city.

The masses of people in the streets were a bit unnerving to those from Vankard. That many people in one place was unlike anything they had ever experienced before. Edora was larger than the Vankard capital but Karbel was almost beyond their ability to comprehend -- it seemed to stretch to the horizon in every direction.

Vode and Levas were both taking in the sights and sounds from their coach seats. The senior acolyte was certain these were things he would never see again and found himself a touch sad at the realization, which made him pause. If the Utland was so dangerous and evil why was he feeling that way? He didn't have the answer which left him feeling uneasy.

T'shar had told Mehan to ride with the priests to answer any questions they had. The men used the opportunity to inquire about a wide variety of topics: how large the population was, what guilds if any operated in the city, how religious observation was handled, and more. Finn found himself hard pressed to answer some of their questions due to the continued language barrier but gamely battled on as they rode.

In due time the coaches and their escorts made their way through the city directly to the palace where Gunnar and Steele were waiting for them. They were escorted to the throne room which was not done to intimidate the visitors but out of necessity, the size of the group made it hard to fit them comfortably in a smaller place. Plus Gunnar had mentioned that since they were not in Vankard, the group would be feeling uncomfortable so being in an open area might help them feel more at ease.

Once those of Vankard were shown into the large room Steele looked at Gunnar to begin the meeting. Stepping forward the long-time advisor welcomed the guests, speaking in his own tongue again felt a touch odd for Gunnar. "Hail! Peace and long life to you." This was the traditional greeting among those of Vankard.

The High Priest, now entirely healed due to the ministrations of Levas, was the first to respond befitting his station as senior member of the group giving the traditional response. "Peace to you and your house."

Gunnar nodded his thanks and stepped forward to clasp wrists in the northman way. Vode complimented him on his command of the language. How was it that he spoke it so well? Gunnar knew this moment would come so why not get it over with – he took a half breath then told them, "I hail from Vankard, I am Gunnar Norstaad. Friend and advisor to Thadar Skye, King of Karbel."

That name was familiar. Vode pondered on it, where did he know that name from…wasn't there a – no it couldn't be! "You are Thindor's nephew!"

Vode was rarely surprised enough to let it show but this revelation was so unexpected he had no chance to harden his features. Two of the Thunderguard didn't even try to conceal their displeasure at hearing that Gunnar was one of them. To pass beyond the mountain gate was dishonoring his entire family.

Gunnar could see the disapproval that the guards were showing but couldn't care less what they thought, he had been asked by Thadar to speak with the visitors and so he would. Whatever it was had to be serious otherwise so many of them would not have left Vankard, especially if it was an approved expedition. So many questions that needed answers.

Vode only knew part of the story involving the departure of the man he was speaking to. Nearly ten years earlier a sickness took hold in several areas of Vankard including the village where Gunnar and his family, a wife and young son were living. Both of them caught the illness and after suffering greatly for nearly a ten-day passed away. Gunnar was grief stricken and angry that the northmen lacked the medical knowledge that might have saved his family.

He began to open speak out against the Vankard policy of isolation, a situation that did not endear him to his uncle Thindor. Gunnar was the elder son of Thindor's brother, who had passed away several years earlier. Thindor had no children of his own so Gunnar had been groomed to take over for his uncle when the time was right.

He continued to publically speak out until finally he irritated the king himself with his rants. Gunnar was called to palace and despite being in the presence of the ruler himself carried on with his tirade. Odell grew angry at the disrespect he was shown, so Thindor removed his nephew from the king's company.

The incident caused the Warlord a great deal of personal pain at seeing his own flesh and blood treat the king so poorly. Gunnar belatedly realized that he had greatly overstepped his bounds and formally apologized to his uncle. He tried to arrange an audience with Odell to offer his apologies but was rebuffed.

Returning to the village and his empty house Gunnar was forced to take stock of his life and found that he no longer had any desire to serve the royal court. He had alienated a number of now former friends and even some in his own family, including the parents of his wife which surprised and hurt him to no end. The grieving man became something of a hermit within his house, hardly venturing outside.

After a ten-day he came to the decision to leave. He kept the decision to himself; Gunnar was familiar with the dislike of those that chose to leave Vankard. He sent a long note to his uncle the day he left. Taking only those items he felt he would need, he left the rest to his younger brother and never looked back. He cleared the pass connecting Vankard with the rest of the world and headed toward the sun.

Gunnar traveled for several years before winding up in Karbel, a chance encounter with Thadar in a market place led to a long and deep friendship with the king despite the age difference, Gunnar being six years older than the monarch.

***

Food and drink had been set out for everyone, something Gunnar informed Vode of allowing him to make the announcement to his group which he did. Mehan Finn wasted no time helping himself, soon he had a heaping plate of assorted meats and cheeses in hand and a large mug of wine cut one quarter with water in the other. Others followed suit and soon the comfort level for the guests was improved as seats were found around some of the tables that had been brought in.

Levas took a seat at the same table as Mehan after checking that his superior had no needs. The ranking acolyte had some further questions about Karbel that he wished to discuss with his Striker counterpart.

After seeing if the High Priest wished any refreshments Gunnar asked Vode, "So what news do you bring sir?" He motioned to a waiting chair inviting the man to sit before he and Steele did the same.

The High Priest was a bit relieved to know that he was going to be able to better relay his concerns and thoughts due to the presence of Gunnar. How strange to find another northman here of all places but Vode didn't question providence, but offered a quick thanks to the gods. No slight against Mehan but the Striker hadn't been able to pick up enough of the tongue to adequately convey the information that Vode had, nor had Levas been able to grasp enough of the Karbel speech. Having Gunnar there would aid the process immensely.

Vode had been giving some thought on how to best present the information he had when the time was necessary. In the end he simply started at the beginning.

Speaking in his own tongue and allowing Gunnar to translate for Steele he began, "It would be best if I properly introduce myself. I am Vode Anners, High Priest of Vankard." Hearing that one sentence told Gunnar volumes, this must be an approved outing, there was no way that the High Priest would leave home unless it was. It also told him that whatever was going on was indeed serious.

He acknowledged the introduction and in turn informed the priest of Steele's name and station. The elder northman nodded once in due course to Steele who returned the gesture with the proper decorum.

With introductions finished Vode continued, "There are those of my Order that have in days past been shown visions of events and circumstances." This was a well-known fact among the northmen so Gunnar nodded his agreement.

Vode carried on, "Some while back I had a series of visions. Seven nights in a row they were shown to me." Keeping an ear cocked, Gunnar quietly brought Steele up to date on the conversation so far. The senior Striker nodded but said nothing.

Vode paused to allow the quick translation then resumed when Gunnar was finished. He didn't object to the short pauses, the information was too important and the encounter with these Strikers had led them here which may be the assistance they had belatedly come to realize they must have. That realization had come at a high cost in blood.

"During these visions I saw images of a massive fortress, on a scale well beyond what we have at home. There were scenes of a great battle between large armies and more scenes of the fortress during the fighting and long before." Without realizing it Vode was leaning toward Gunnar as he spoke, the implications of the experience still affected him deeply.

Steele was listening without being able to comprehend what was being said but he could read the body language very well and what he saw told him that the man speaking was worried and seemed sincere.

"Trying to understand what I was seeing took some time. I had to seek out additional information. You know of the Great Library, do you not?" Gunnar nodded, he had never been in it but his uncle had spoken of it several times. The massive repository was a treasure trove of knowledge.

Vode was a bit uncomfortable speaking of the next part but made peace with by electing not to disclose every fact regarding the two sacred books. "Within the library we found some information regarding the history of a great war that took place nearly two thousand years ago. The end of this conflict took place at a fortress well north of here, a place known as G'mar. The defenders had a dark and terrible plan to use a dark rite to change their use of majic."

While he was speaking Vode pulled up the small satchel that was on the floor next to his feet placing it on the table in front of him. Steele was curious as to what the man was going to pull out of the bag; he didn't have to wait long. Removing two rolled pieces of parchment from inside the leather bag he set them on the table then returned the bag to the floor.

Unrolling the first of them, Vode turned it around then spread it out on the table using assorted items from the table to weigh down each corner. Both Gunnar and Steele left their seats to gain a better view of what Vode was trying to show them. They moved to stand on either side of the seated man.

What they saw was a map, a hand copied chart that was a nearly exact duplicate of one of the maps from the Book of Iron but in a larger scale making it easier to use. This one showed the area of the continent where G'mar was located.

Both men studied the details outlined on the page. The fortress was well north of Karbel nestled in what appeared to be a small area surrounded by mountains and bordered by a body of water to the north of the bastion. A long, narrow pass came into the area from the south looking much like a funnel. To the west a much smaller pathway through the mountains led to the fortress. Vode gave the men a chance to look over the map while unrolling the second of the items he had removed from the bag. That was a highly detailed diagram of the fortress at G'mar itself.

After viewing the maps in the original book, Vode had been very impressed that Revas had taken the time and effort to go to that much trouble. He didn't do just a general map but had outlined and labeled the buildings as well as some of the many defensive features, both those the Varshon had installed as well as some of the original ones.

After the king had approved the expedition, Vode had both maps laboriously copied since he had no intentions whatsoever of removing the holy books from Vankard. The spells he found hidden in the Book of Hope were reason enough to make sure that the books remained secure. He had been working on learning some of them as time allowed; several of them were completely new to him.

Seeing that Vode had another map out both men turned their attention to it. They laid it atop the first one for ease of viewing. Steele's experienced eye picked out a variety of details about the defenses. A silent whistle from his lips as he acknowledged the work of those that had constructed the immense fortification. High walls, towers, a wide moat, overlapping fields of fire for catapults and other long range artillery, protected enclosures for troops to shelter in and more. The palace here in Karbel had many of those same features but nowhere near in the same number as he saw on the map before him or in that scale either. He marveled at the scope of the work that had created the location he was viewing.

Vode allowed the men to view the map, waiting until they spoke to ensure they had seen enough. Steele's view lingered on the map as he returned to his seat. Shades what an impressive place, a part of him was curious to see the place for himself.

He turned his attention back to their guests just as Gunnar was asking a question. "So what was the purpose of this rite that these, what did you call them again?" Vode told him. "These Varshon were attempting?"

This was something that the High Priest had been giving no small amount of thought to since first learning of the Cycle of Invocation in his research. It still gave him chills thinking of the immense power it would give the Varshon if they were able to accomplish their goal.

A quick swallow then he answered, "From what I was able to ascertain, if the dark ones were to complete the ceremony it would cause their majical abilities to grow, to expand by an order of tenfold or more. It would mean their spells would be unstoppable by anyone. They could use their majic to dominate all of the other races and rule all of Dohrya forever."

Gunnar swallowed hard at the implication of what he had been told. Steele was waiting for his friend to translate. The northman was having a hard time wrapping his head around the information. Vode reached out and took his arm which caused Gunnar to look up. The priest nodded toward the Striker.

He swallowed hard again then turned and relayed what he had been told to an increasingly worried audience. The Striker commander listened and then posed his own question which the transplanted northman relayed to the High Priest.

"What is your plan?"

The question was straightforward as was the quick answer. "To go to G'mar and stop this rite from taking place."

Gunnar was taken aback by the determination he heard in the voice of the High Priest. "Forgive me but with so few…" Vode interrupted him before he could finish the sentence.

"What we have will have to suffice, it is all we have."

Gunnar was silent for a few moments then made a decision. "I will speak to the king. He needs to know what you have made us aware of."

Gunnar asked the High Priest if he and others would be comfortable here for a turn while he spoke to Thadar. Vode told him that they would and thanked him. Before leaving the room Gunnar bowed to Vode who returned the gesture. The senior Striker stood at the same time and he too bowed to the priest before moving away from the table.

Steele began collecting his Strikers around him in order to further question them about the events leading up to this point taking them to a nearby table separate from where the northmen were gathered. He had a great many questions and his urgency was growing. The information that Vode had related was doing nothing but adding to that sense of haste.

Having T'shar and the others sit down Steele sat as well so he could be closer. Part of him felt like standing or pacing but now was not the time for that.

"I need to be knowing all that happened out there." He had of course read copies of the reports that had come in but he wanted more. T'shar began to fill his commander in on the events that had led to this point. Soon all the Strikers were deep in conversation as the information continued to flow.

Gunnar made his way to the small conference room where Thadar was working. Checking with the guard he found that the king was alone. He knocked once and then entered, a routine long established between the two men. Thadar didn't believe on standing on formality but Gunnar was conscious to show his friend the respect due a ruler.

Without preamble he told Thadar, "We have a serious problem." The longtime ruler of Karbel knew his friend well enough that for him to make such a declarative statement there was indeed something to be concerned about. The papers and work before him on the table now forgotten, Thadar turned his full attention to the matter that Gunnar had brought to him.

Gunnar began to explain, "As you know, those of my homeland are here now. I've just been speaking with them – they have uncovered a threat to us, all of us."

Thadar immediately pressed him, "Who, all of us? Karbel?"

The northman shook his head, "No, the entire world."

The two men shared a look of concern as the gravity of the situation weighed heavily in the room. "Tell me what you know."

Thadar listened with growing concern as his friend began to outline the threat. Gunnar spoke for several minutes without pause.

The ruler of Karbel was no fool, despite the fact that humans as a general rule had very limited ability to work majic he knew that wasn't the case for all of the other races. He knew that if another race was able to wield strong majic then all of his Legions could be rendered useless.

When Gunnar paused to allow Thadar to ask the questions that he knew were coming the king never hesitated, "What do you think we need to do to help them?"

The northman answered immediately "Send a sizable force up north to this G'mar place and see what can be done to stop these Varshon. If what the priest says is true we canna' take chances. We must help them."

The king listened to the words of his friend, agreement was quick in coming. With a decisive thrust of the chin and a firm timbre in his voice Thadar told Gunnar, "Give them whatever they require and do it quickly, keep me informed. I will meet with them shortly."

Gunnar nodded and withdrew from the room to return to the throne room. His mind was already formulating a list of supplies, men, horses, and more. The king had been quite specific, *whatever they require.*

The northman hoped that they weren't already too late.

Chapter Thirty-Three
A Problem Corrected

Karbel

Shorin, his men, and the surviving Black Guards were finally able to locate a working heliograph station. Both of the previous stations the group had managed to reach had been attacked then burned, likely by forward ranging southern cavalry, units very much like what they had battled while defending Arnoth.

It had been more than a little frustrating for the group – curse the damned southies! The weary Striker officer wasted no time sending in an updated report as well as requesting to know where to meet the reinforcements he had asked for earlier.

As they waited for a response Shorin and Mryl filled in the senior man who commanded the small outpost. Shock and disbelief were common emotions as the news spilled out, invasion, war and wide spread death. Those that had ridden in from the border were using the time to care for their tired mounts as well as providing better treatment to the injured among them.

The men of the outpost were rushing about to help as they could, be it serving food or helping with the wounded including the captured enemy commander. It was a chaotic time but there was much to do.

After several hours a reply came in. The duty officer at the palace sent back a reply acknowledging Shorin's report as well as asking what reinforcements he was talking about. As the message was being decoded the Striker was stunned to realize that apparently no one in the capital was even aware of the fact that a large invasion force was at that very moment making its way into Karbel. That there had already been casualties, that the Elves were under attack, any of it. What in the name of the eternal fates was going on?

It suddenly occurred to Shorin that the three Strikers he had sent to get the word out apparently hadn't made it to a working station and so must have been killed. That wasn't the case but that information was something the young commander wouldn't find out for many days.

Allowing his despair to get the better of him for the moment, the exhausted Striker officer slumped in the chair trying to gather himself. A heavy sense of anguish came over him. How could they not know? All the sacrifices and losses had been for nothing. He was faced with more questions than answers.

Mryl came over and knelt down on one knee next to his friend. Shorin held out the message form to him without looking up. Twinsteel read through it quickly. He too was shocked at the contents of page. If no one knew that meant that word had not reached Kuln either since they would have alerted the capital.

The Black Guard was just as tired and angry but he knew that they had little time. He told Shorin, "We have to tell them, we're the only ones that know." What was going on in the capital, Mryl wondered, but that was a discussion for another time.

Nodding in agreement, Shorin told the scribe to take down the following information. The clerk nodded his readiness and the Striker began to dictate the message. Mryl added bits and pieces to the message as well. It took several minutes to get enough information in the message to make sure those in the capital understood how serious the situation was.

In the communication, the Striker outlined the fight for the Elven village, the enemy troop estimates as well as their direction of travel, his current location, his plan for attacking the invaders and, at the urging of Logas, a very emphatic warning about the Varshon majical abilities -- then once again requested reinforcements, lots of reinforcements.

After Shorin was done he told the scribe to transmit it using the highest priority message coding that the station was entitled to use. He asked for a map of the local area which was hurriedly provided. The three senior men present began to outline plans and options while they awaited a response.

Mryl told the outpost commander to have someone put together packs of food, water, medical supplies and blankets; they might have to leave in a hurry. Shorin nodded in agreement, the man hurried off to get that taken care of. The two friends shared a look -- they weren't out of danger yet and they both knew it. In the meantime, they studied the map, discussed their options and waited for word from the capital.

***

In due time, the long message arrived in the Striker Duty Office from the heliograph station in the upper reaches of the palace. As the Duty Officer was reading over the shoulder of the clerk, he realized that something was terribly wrong out on the southern frontier and sent word for Colonel Steele. The officer told the runner that he didn't even care if the Colonel was naked, just get him here, now.

The first message that had come in left him very curious as to what was going on out in the border country. Now he knew. Suddenly the thought of how happy he had been while ignorant of the situation struck him. Returning his attention to the first parchment sheet he finished reading the message and then began rereading it, some small part of him hoping that it would get better the second time. It didn't. He debated sounding the alert but reasoned that the capital was a long way from heliograph station 241 so he waited. He and the clerk shared a look; the easy day of moments earlier was gone.

The Duty Officer glanced over at the map on wall but the map was no help. He ordered the clerk to send Shorin a message advising him that the notice had been received and the necessary people would be informed. The Striker took down the information and had it sent up to the heliograph for coding and transmittal.

The Duty Officer was silently cursing the time delay that was part of sending a message clear to the edge of the kingdom but it couldn't be helped. It had already been hours since the original message had arrived. Why hadn't more word come in if the situation was that serious? There was no way for him to know the answer but it didn't keep him from asking the question.

The Striker assigned as a runner hurried to find his commanding officer. Fortune smiled on him a bit as he found Steele in the second place he looked, the officer's mess. Presenting himself properly, the

Striker informed the Colonel that he was needed in the Duty Office at once.

Steele was a little annoyed at the interruption, he was trying to get something to eat prior to getting some scheduling done for a large rotation of Striker units but something in the way the elite trooper spoke made him decide to go right then. He put down his fork, stood up from the table and waved the trooper ahead. The two soldiers headed to the Duty Office, it would be many hours later before Steele finally remembered to get something to eat.

After his commanding officer entered the room the Duty Officer handed him the parchment sheets with both the first and second messages on them without a word. Steele thought this was odd but took the heavy documents with a touch of impatience and began to read. The officer had read them thrice, and had told the others in the room what it said. The contents of the message would be revealed soon enough so telling them now was not violating any state secrets. It would be pretty hard to hide the fact that the kingdom was being invaded.

Word had already started to spread among the palace Strikers; one of the duty section troopers went to inform those in the barracks. More of the black and silver clad soldiers came to the office area to try and find out more about the news.

The further Steele got in his reading the more concerned he got especially the section talking about the majical threat, he lifted his eyes from the page and, looking at the officer, got a curt nod in response then returned to his reading. Faster and faster his eyes flashed over the hastily written words until at last, mercifully the words ended.

Invasion. Karbel was being invaded.

Steele's hesitation lasted but a few heartbeats; here it was at last, finally, the reason for the assassination attempt. He had been puzzling that one out for some time, trying to determine a reason for the attack as well as who was behind it. Thought of an invasion had occurred to him but now it was much more than an idea. Shades…

The Colonel knew that there were several things that must be done immediately. He looked to the Duty Officer, "Full Alert, no drill, secure the palace and the city."

The man pointed at the Striker poised at the window with his horn in hand snapping his fingers once to emphasize the order. The trumpeter stepped out onto the short balcony, lifted his horn and began to blow out the call to signal the others within earshot. The clear notes went far and wide; the call was repeated throughout the area as other trumpeters echoed the alert.

Karbel was a large city and it took a little time for the message to reach those at the gates. As soon as it did, the duty guards began to immediately clear the area so they could close the immense barriers, which took time. Outraged citizens were simply told to move and shut up or were ignored. An unannounced closing of the gates at this time of day couldn't be a good thing. Maybe a drill -- but even if it was, they sure-as-a-goat's-ass-is-hairy would follow the orders. Steele liked to make an example of anyone not doing their duty, Striker or Legionnaire.

The palace duty section, twenty five Strikers that were to act as an alert force readied their equipment. The scene around the Duty Office was one of organized chaos for a moment as the armor clad soldiers rushed out to follow their long standing and well-practiced orders.

Steele, now turning to the Striker at the message desk, told him, "Full Alert to all our stations, all border posts, ours and the Legion. Tell them why."

Looking over at the large map of the kingdom hanging against the wall on which the locations of all message stations and Striker outposts were illustrated, Steele continued to speak. Grabbing the nearby Duty Officer with one hand Steele asked him which station Shorin was at and was told, then continued his dictation.

"All units at posts 87, 220 and 739 are to immediately report to Captain Tallon at Message Station 241. Posts 534 and 60 stand to at the Jubilee crossroads and secure it. And tell Shorin help is coming, good job, and get that information off to Kuln too – all of it." He told the scribe to get all of that out immediately using his personal authorization, go.

The Striker who had been writing as Steele spoke literally jumped up from the desk and ran out the door heading up to the heliograph station. Having Steele's authorization was essential. During full alerts, no messages were to be sent out of the palace except by Legion Marshal Balkon, Colonel Steele or either the king or queen.

Steele, who still held the parchment sheets in his hand, pointed at several members of the duty section telling them to come with him, then started walking toward the door. He told the Duty Officer to keep him updated on anything that came in, that he would be with the king. Then he was gone with six of his men in tow.

The hallways were alive with his troops as they worked to further secure the palace from any type of intruder. Steele had increased the size of the Striker garrison in the palace after the assassination attempt; having more loyal armed men near the king was not a bad thing.

Members of the palace staff had, of course, heard the alert horn sounded and kept out of the way as they too made their way to the places assigned to them during alerts. A full alert had not been necessary since the infiltration of the palace by the assassins. Hearing the alert, several of the staff nearly broke down in fear. They had lived through one assault on the castle and dreaded another.

After leaving the Duty Office, the senior Striker had gone directly to the royal living quarters where he knew the king and queen were waiting. As soon as the notes sounded for the Full Alert the king's bodyguard entered the room where he had been in a meeting and moved him to the royal quarters over his verbal protests. The queen had been brought there from one of the sitting rooms she often used for meetings and entertaining.

Thadar had gone with his bodyguards but not without resenting it. He was well aware of the orders that Steele had given all the Strikers, a Full Alert means that no one in or out of the palace. He and Shay were to be taken, by force if necessary, to their quarters and once there to wait until further notice. As he moved through the hallways toward his own living quarters he noted the numbers of Strikers and how they kept the staff at a distance.

Thadar didn't like being held above his subjects but recognized that at times it was needed, even required. It served as a reminder to those around him of the power of his position. The king was not one to laud his title over others, it was a quality that many felt added to his power, not detracted from it as some believed. This situation was different. A Full Alert was not done lightly so even if it was a drill the level of intensity increased.

Gunnar and Spree had been present in the palace as well, hearing the alert horn they went immediately to the Duty Office to try and find out what was going on. Both of them were well known to the staff and security forces so they were able to reach their destination within moments of each other despite coming from different areas of the palace. The tall man and the stout Dwarf were staunch supporters of the king and a Full Alert could only mean something ill for him and his realm.

Entering the busy room after making their way through the throng of Strikers from the duty section in the hallway outside both of them could immediately feel the tension and noted the increased activity.

Two Strikers were busy plotting something on the large fabric map of the kingdom hung on one wall. Pieces of colored ribbons in various sizes were being pinned to the map, each color meant something different. Red ribbon meant an enemy force; Gunnar could see a great deal of red ribbon. Blue, representing friendly forces, were present but in small, scattered numbers as indicated by the widely separated, very short ribbons. The local ratio of force was clearly in favor of whatever enemy this was.

The attack was coming up from D'Lohm on the south-east border, why would they be attacking us? It was a modest size human kingdom, not exactly friendly with Karbel but certainly not enemies, at least on this scale. Reports didn't indicate that their army was all that large either, most certainly not of the size that the red ribbons would indicate. What in the name of sacred ancestors was going on? If this was a drill that Steele had laid on it was a damned good one but there was something about what was going on told the man that wasn't the case, it had a different feel to it.

The Duty Officer noted the entry of the pair and quickly moved over to where they were looking at the map. Without formality Spree demanded to know what was happening. The Striker officer, Lain Tanic, gave them a rundown on Shorin's messages. With a toss of the head, he indicated the information being posted on the map by the two troopers. Around them other Strikers were conducting their duties; several of the elite troopers came and went out of the office for various purposes during the impromptu briefing.

About that time a runner from the heliograph station brought a follow up message from Shorin, this one sent in plain language. Gunnar waited impatiently while Tanic read through it. He finished reading then handed it to the northman to read for himself. Gunnar thoughtfully knelt down to allow Spree to read it at the same time.

It contained a much more detailed listing of southern unit strengths and overall numbers courtesy of the report carried by Mryl. The Striker Under-Captain had deliberately inserted a passage explaining the source of the numbers and requested that a message be sent to Kuln informing them of the status on the surviving Black Guards along with the names of the men.

As the two men read the lengthy report the implications were immediate. Karbel was in serious trouble, an army that large could conquer the entire kingdom and a great deal more. Spree looked at Gunnar who shared a look with the Striker officer. No words were spoken. All three turned to look at the map…

Steele, unaware of the advent of the new message, had arrived at the section of the palace that the king and queen used as living quarters. The residential area consisted of a sleeping chamber, an anteroom, meeting rooms and a modest size dining area. The ruling pair often preferred to eat in the smaller, less ceremonial chamber in place of the large formal dining room located two floors above them that could seat as many as seventy. As usual the five Strikers responsible for the security of the entrance to this part of the palace were in place and alert.

The Striker Colonel stopped, telling the six men with him to spread out. The men paired up, then moved to take up positions at the three nearby corridors that led to this part of the palace. Temporarily satisfied that the area was reasonably secure Steele went down the short hallway nodding to his man stationed at the far end, then passing into the anteroom. He was not surprised to find Thadar waiting rather impatiently for him.

The senior Striker handed his king the messages without delay or comment. The ruler of Karbel began to read the news that would change the course of his kingdom for a very long time. Shay slid over next to her husband to be able to see the message as well. The pair read the communication, shared a look and then looked at Steele. The queen gasped as the realization of how serious the situation was struck her.

As it happened the junior Legion officer who had delivered the news of the invasion the day earlier to Balkon came by the Duty Office to see Lain. He was already in the palace and had of course heard the alert but wanted to say goodbye to his friend before leaving the capital. He was being sent to the northwest frontier by order of Balkon.

Following the exchange in the hallway after the Legion Marshal refused to accept the validity of the invasion warning, the junior officer had spoken forcefully about the need to do something. Balkon wanted him sent away as a lesson to others about respecting their place. Besides that way the man would be far away and could tell no one of consequence of what happened in the hallway. The other officers present at the time were all cronies of the Marshal so that was no issue.

Entering the office shortly after the third message had been read he knew something was terribly wrong. He walked over to Tanic and noted the expression that all three of the gathered men had. Could it be more of the same news?

He had tried to get more information but per Balkon's orders no further news of the invasion was to be asked for. In fact due to the destruction of several stations in the frontier area no means short of dispatch riders to move information in that area of the frontier was available. He saw the situation map and the ribbons denoting the correlation of forces.

A deep sinking sensation filled him; it had to be the same news. His country was being attacked and that pompous, stupid, air-brained excuse for general...

Tanic noticed his friend and quickly excused himself from the presence of Spree and Gunnar. Without preamble he said, "You shouldn't be here right now, serious problems on the frontier, invasion."

The Legion officer spoke with little conscious thought to his decision to go forward about saying something, "Yes I know, we've known since late yesterday."

Tanic couldn't believe his ears, "Yesterday! Yesterday? Why in the name of spirits didn't someone say something?" The last words were loud and angry.

Gunnar caught the outburst; he walked away from the map where he and Spree had been working with the Strikers to plot the new information. He went to where the two men were talking. Once there he asked what the issue was then was hesitantly filled in on what had happened the previous afternoon regarding the message and Balkon's response.

A lengthy discussion followed which ended when Gunnar left to inform the king, taking the younger Legion officer with him as well as the message detailing the enemy numbers. Gunnar was certain that the king was going to be at least moderately vexed at the news.

***

"He did *what?*" The tone of the question left no doubt about the state of mind of the person asking it. Trying to speak again Thadar couldn't, he was so upset that it was impossible to form a coherent sentence.

He stopped trying, closed his eyes, taking in a deep breath he lowered his head and rolled it slightly so that his chin was pointing toward his left shoulder. The king stood this way for a moment and then slowly began to release the held breath, now with a little more control he opened his eyes and in a measured voice asked the question again, each word spoken slowly.

"Balkon - did - what?" Shay standing near her husband could feel his body almost vibrating with the anger he was feeling. She too was upset but stayed silent resting one hand on his arm for a moment to give him strength and support as a selection of choice foul language crossed her mind concerning the action or rather the shocking lack of it by the Legion Marshal.

Gunnar looked at his friend and began to explain it further detail. The northman told him how word of the invasion had been sent to the capitol via heliograph yesterday and had been ignored believing it to be only a minor cross border raid.

The Legion Marshal had not requested confirmation of the message, he not alerted any of the regional commanders, he had not chosen to inform anyone at the palace and then tried to exile the officer who wanted to say something. The only reason the palace had known of the invasion was when word arrived via the Striker communication staff after a message sent by an Under-Captain Shorin Tallon who had finally reached a working heliograph station.

Steele, Shay, and the junior Legion officer were all silent as the king was told of the grievous failing of his senior general and then of the follow up message outlining the enemy numbers. Gunnar held out the message outlining the strength of the enemy army.

Thadar took it and could scarcely believe what he was reading. His eyes lifted from the page more than once as he tried to comprehend the enormity of the forces arrayed against his kingdom. At least part of this vast force was already *in* Karbel with more or all of it to follow.

Holding the parchment sheets he asked those in the room, "What are the chances that this..." shaking the papers, "...is the Varshon army coming north?"

Gunnar and Steele shared a quick look, each nodding. Gunnar spoke, "It would seem that Vode knew what he was speaking of. Good thing we had the warning they carried."

The king nodded his agreement; enough of this for now, action was needed. He tossed the parchment toward the table dismissing it from his mind for the moment. Steele adroitly gathered in the document, the information would be vital later on as they tried to figure out how to defeat the invaders.

Thadar's mind was churning; he analyzed a variety of different choices, rejecting some, modifying others as he went. In very short order he had the beginnings of a plan, time to put some of into action.

"First thing, order a full alert for every Legion and Striker unit, every one of them! Give them the reason why, then muster ALL of our reserve forces, everything we have down to the last militia levy. It will take us some time to get together enough troops to fight an army of that size! Next get this, Shorin, some reinforcements as soon as possible. And someone bring me Balkon, now!" The last word was almost a hiss as it came past the lips of the king.

Gunnar went to carry out the orders taking the Legion officer with him wanting to make sure the man was available should a tribunal hearing be ordered against Balkon. Steele remained with Thadar to help organize their strategy for repelling the invasion; detailed maps of the frontier area had already been sent for. Thadar was then informed of what steps that the senior Striker had already ordered.

For his part Gunnar figured to take care of the king's order to have Balkon sent for personally. He headed for the duty section area to collect a few Strikers to "assist" him with that particular task. That Gunnar disliked the Legion Marshal only added to the feeling of pleasure at what he was certain would be the end of Balkon's posting as senior army commander -- and who knows, maybe even his life. Gunnar tried not to grin too much at that thought given the circumstances of the day.

***

Legion Marshal Balkon was at his headquarters in the city when word arrived of the Full Alert. He was vexed at the interruption, he had some work to do and having to deal with a no-notice drill was to his way of thinking, beneath his station.

During a Full Alert his responsibility as Legion Marshal was to ensure that all Legion units within the city and those of the two Legions housed just outside the city were ready to respond to whatever the situation was. If it was not for the fact that a personal report had to be given to the king himself by Balkon on the results of an alert, the Legion Marshal wouldn't bother even paying attention.

So here he was once again forced to deal with matters of little concern best dealt with by those far beneath his rank. *Why do I put up with such things?* was a question he often asked himself. He had sent runners to determine the status of the Legion units in and around the capital. Best to get this foolishness over with as soon as possible and return to matters of consequence so that he could move on to more pleasant things.

He was speaking with his staff when the doors to the room were swept open without notice, causing all conversation in the room to cease. Balkon was already annoyed due to the drill but to be interrupted like this in his own headquarters was intolerable!

He was ready to tongue lash the clumsy aide that had allowed this happen when the figure of Gunnar Norstaad appeared in the open doorway. What in spirit's sake was this boot licker doing here?

His unasked question was answered without preamble. "General Balkon, the king requires your presence at the palace, immediately."

Balkon and the others noted the presence of the Strikers waiting just outside the room. The Legion Marshal told the others that he would be at the palace and to send word on the status of the Legion units as soon as it came in. He was assured that it would be done. Taking his time, the Marshal gathered his uniform cloak and then went with the northman to see the waiting king.

Departing the headquarters building the senior officer was directed to the waiting coach that had brought Gunnar. Both men climbed inside, Balkon going first since he felt that was proper, he was an officer and the other man was just a friend of Thadar's with no official standing. Once both men were inside the driver shook the reins to get the horse team moving. There was no talking during the trip, Gunnar didn't want to give away any hints or suggestions as to what was coming. And Balkon, firm in the belief that the foreigner was of no consequence, refused to engage in conversation with him.

When the group arrived in the courtyard of the fortress that served as both home and work place of the king, they exited the carriage. The adviser quickly asked the guard if he knew where the king was.

The Striker was ready with that answer, "His anteroom sir."

Nodding his thanks Gunnar led the way as he, Balkon, and several of the Strikers headed toward the private quarters area of the palace where Thadar awaited. The walk through the expansive building was silent. Once the men arrived at the living quarters the pair were ushered straight in.

Thadar, who had been busy with organizing a response to the invasion, looked up to see Balkon. Thadar drew the reins on his anger tighter before speaking. Steele and the other senior Strikers in the room were silent as they watched the show.

The heir to the house of Skye wasted no time with pleasantries or protocol. "Was there a message received yesterday that said Karbel was being invaded?" The eyes of the king never wavered as they bore on the senior general.

For his part Balkon to think for a moment before answering, *what was that...? Oh yes, that...* "No sir, an incomplete message that may or may not have talked about a small border raid was all."

Still not understanding how serious the situation on the southern border was, Balkon was comfortable with his answer and so was puzzled when the king asked again. "Did you or did you not get a message that spoke of invasion?"

Thadar was angry; he didn't care if the whole world knew it. Balkon was struggling a bit to come to grips with the circumstances despite his experience at commanding a situation to his advantage. What was all the fuss about? I was dragged away from my headquarters for this?

"My Lord, a message was received that spoke of a raid, nothing more. We suffer border raids all the time I cannot be held responsible if some lowly area commander failed to provide the proper information because he was too busy cowering behind his desk."

Thadar was not surprised at all that Balkon was so quick to put the blame on someone else. It was typical for him. Gunnar said nothing but his expression of disdain was plain to see. Balkon was standing near the dining table but closer to the king than the northman was and so missed seeing the look.

"When the message came in did you ask for clarification?" Thadar knew from questioning the junior Legion officer that the general had not but wanted to hear Balkon's answer.

"Sir, the message seemed complete. Some troops had crossed the frontier, beyond that what else needed asked?"

The king's anger was checked for the moment, replaced by surprise then incredulity - what else needed asked? Did that pompous mule really just say that? A full day of warning gone, pissed away because of this self-serving ass licker...

Taking a different tack Thadar posed another question to the general. "So answer me this, general. Which was it, the message was incomplete or complete? You are told that troops, armed foreign troops have crossed the frontier and yet did not ask for more information or order an alert or even send out a patrol?"

Balkon's finely honed sense of self-preservation was suddenly running in high gear. He was starting to understand that message he had so blithely dismissed the previous day must have been more serious than he thought.

Balkon was caught in his own story now and didn't know how to best extricate himself. He tried speaking but the harsh glare of the situation had him fixed. Reverting to form the general pulled himself fully erect and set his shoulders. "Sir, I did what I felt was best with the information I had. I won't apologize for that. That I didn't have all the information wasn't my fault."

Not seeing how he had just left himself completely exposed Balkon stood his ground. Thadar had been searching without success for a reason to have the Legion Marshal removed from his post but his powerful political connections had been enough to keep him safe. That was now no longer the case with the dissolution of the Assembly. He had meant to take care of this problem prior to this but had been overwhelmed with other issues, which had been a mistake he realized.

Gunnar was enjoying the moment despite the cause of the situation. Seeing one of the biggest thorns in Thadar's side about to be removed made the king's man very happy.

Thadar was quiet for a moment; he closed his eyes and lowered his head, time to deliver the sentence. Opening his eyes then fixing his gaze steady upon the Legion Marshal he told him, "General, I understand you not having all the information, that is the job of your men to get you that." Balkon didn't say anything but nodded slowly.

"The number of failures on your part in this situation is both disappointing and unforgivable. It was your job to train them to know what to do. It was your job to make sure that proper information was collected and then passed along. It was your job and your lack of action has put this nation at great risk. The kingdom has been invaded, by those same forces you so casually dismissed yesterday! It is a massive enemy army and because of your incompetence we are just now finding out about it! You are a disgrace to that uniform so I will ensure that is not a problem again!" He paused for emphasis. "Serus Balkon, by royal judgment you are hereby charged with Insubordination, Malfeasance of Office and Cowardice before an Enemy."

Thadar only paused long enough to take in a breath before continuing. "You are stripped of your rank and title; you will be taken to a holding cell to await your trial."

The now former Legion Marshal couldn't believe what he was hearing, that this worthless – he opened his mouth to speak but before he could utter a word, a hand grabbed him by the shoulder and he was spun around. As he was turning a fist crashed into his mouth nearly felling the man who staggered from the force of the impact.

Thadar looked over at Gunnar who had delivered the blow. The northman had gotten in the last word in a convincing manner. It wasn't something he could do while Serus was still a general but now... Balkon was clutching at his painful jaw and mouth area with both hands. No one had laid hands on him in a very long time. Thadar glanced at Steele who then motioned to the guards.

Several Strikers stepped forward to take custody of the royal prisoner. He was hustled quickly but efficiently out of the room on his way to the dungeon.

"Feel better?" The king asked his friend who was slowly flexing his hand to work out the stiffness caused by the stout blow. Gunnar only smiled and then turned his attention to the map on the table.

Thadar looked to one of the Strikers, "Send immediately for General

Lyn have him report to me here right away please."

The man saluted and without waiting for a return salute left the room to carry out the order. Steele gave that some quick thought. Tal Lynn was the most experienced and capable general in the army by far. He lacked the political connections that Balkon had enjoyed which meant that he had been hated by many in the Assembly and he was Thadar's father-in-law to boot. This was shaping up to be quite the day.

"So let us look at this." Thadar gestured at the map and those gathered around the table turned their attention to more planning.

***

At the message station Shorin and Mryl had read the communication telling them that help was on the way. They were glad that the word had gotten through and that help was finally coming. That it would be many hours before any significant help arrived didn't matter. Reinforcements were finally on the way.

The two tired friends were sitting at a table in one corner of the main room of the small outpost. Two plates, holding the remains of a hurried meal, sat forgotten pushed to the side. The small garrison of the station had gotten hot food to the others that had ridden in with the two officers. The wounded were still being treated as best they could be with the rudimentary skills and supplies available. The battered Strikers were seeing to their travel worn mounts and to what meager defenses there were. All of the men had been pushed far beyond what any of them had experienced before.

Mryl laid his head down on the table. He was just going to close his eyes for a moment, one quick moment. Shorin saw his friend slump as fatigue took hold. As exhausted as he was, the Striker knew he had to stay awake to oversee things.

Several minutes later one of the clerks found Shorin to hand him a message that had come in. The Striker was still sitting, his head slumped backwards against the wall. He was sound asleep. The clerk left the two men alone and went to find his own commander to give him the message.

Chapter Thirty-Four
Help is Enroute

Eastern Karbel

The men were tired; their journey had been long and by no means an easy ride. The mounts clearly showed the effects of the travel, their flanks were shiny with sweat, breathing was hard and rapid.

Without waiting for his horse to come to a complete stop the patrol leader dismounted. He was so tired his boot hung up for a moment in the stirrup causing the Striker to stumble as he climbed down from the saddle nearly sending him flat onto the cobble stone covered courtyard of the regional governmental office. Recovering his balance at the last moment, the lean Elf silently cursed then letting it pass.

There was no time for his attention to be split. The news he carried was far too important. The other patrol members were bringing their mounts to a halt; the walls of the surrounding buildings as well as those of courtyard, amplified the noise in the center area of the small plaza.

The sudden arrival of the patrol had caused a tempest of activity. Grooms were hurrying forward to assist in caring for the horses. Shouts for healers and curses seemed to be in equal number.

The Elf knew that his place was with his men but he had to get the information they had fought and died for to those in a position to be able to use it. Entering the building he grabbed one of the nearest passersby, spinning the man to him so that he could look him directly in eyes. In a harsh voice he demanded to know where the commander's office was.

This wasn't the Elf's usual duty area so he was unfamiliar with the layout. Startled at first by the movement, the man was a little slow on the uptake; this was further compounded by the unforgiving tone; the Elves, were long known for their manners and reserved demeanors.

Failing to get the needed information from the inexplicitly mute servant, the Striker released with the man with a guttural growl and headed further into the building shouting for the commander. Now free to resume his previous duties the servant followed the progress of the uncharacteristic Elf with his eyes and when the Striker was out of sight, the servant shrugged and went on about his business.

The hurried calls for the commander brought her out of her office. She had been reviewing the details for the deployment of the Strikers under her command when a commotion was heard outside in the hallway. Seeing the officer, the Elven Sergeant changed directions and moved those in his way.

"Ma'am!" Turning toward the sound she waited till he approached. A correct but hurried salute was given and returned. The other officers that had been present in her office were bunched just inside the open doorway listening to the exchange.

He didn't hesitate, "Invasion! There's a massive enemy force moving just a bit west o' Sutter's Creep heading to the north. Heavy infantry, cavalry, siege equipment and more – be the biggest force I've ever seen."

Senior Captain Pantos, the area commander, had several patrols out already trying to determine the location of the reported invasion army. Urgent heliograph messages had been pouring in the last day or so. The first one had been a shock; a forwarded report from another Striker unit outlining the basic details of a very large army that had already overrun D'Lohm to the south and was moving north. The report had also stated that the western Elvish settlements and the Black Guards were under attack as well. It was their job along with all other military units in the region to attack the invaders and try and repel them.

Pantos listened then turned decisively to the other officers, "Full Alert! Mount everyone we have, get a message with the particulars off to Karbel, now!"

There was no panic just action as they spread out to carry out their orders. She motioned for the junior officer to remain. The Captain collected the sergeant telling him to show her on the map precisely where he last saw the invaders.

Those in the capital desperately wanted and needed any and all the information that could be provided regarding the enemy- location, size and composition, speed of travel as well as in what direction they seemed to be heading. Several large cities were potentially in the path of the invaders and it would take some time to muster sufficient troops to engage and then beat back the foreigners.

The pair went into the office followed by the Under-Captain where she led them to a large wall map and stepped aside to allow the patrol leader better access. The experienced non-commissioned officer studied it for a brief moment then with certainty placed a long finger directly on the spot he and his men had their most recent run in with some of the enemy troops and began to narrate his report.

The junior officer wrote out notes as more specifics were provided. "...The leading elements were heavy cavalry, we saw at least four thousand of them, followed up by heavy infantry formations. There were at least seventeen to twenty thousand just in the column we could see. There was another column further to the east we couldn't get a clear look at that seemed to be least equal numbers and possibly another but that I'm not sure about. Too much cavalry to be able to work our way around." He paused to let that information sink in. Through the window the sound of bugles could be heard as the post was being alerted.

***

After the message arrived from the capital explaining that their warning had been received and that reinforcements were on the way, Shorin and the others did what they could to ready themselves for what was coming. They knew it would likely be hours before any sizable amount of support would reach them.

All of the men were worn out; sleep had been taken in what increments it could be as had food. The outpost wasn't large or particularly well-fortified so the small staff and the Strikers worked at making what upgrades they could -- which wasn't much but it was something.

Several of the men worked at caring for the horses as best they could, the mounts had been pushed hard in the previous ten-day so they too needed a rest and some proper care.

The same was true of the wounded, the more seriously injured had been carefully loaded in the single wagon that the message station maintained and sent on their way with a small escort toward the nearest sizable garrison where it was hoped that they would be able to receive better care. Shorin was certain that some of them wouldn't survive the trip but it was the best option available to them, there were simply no facilities for treating wounded at the station.

The captured enemy commander was among those that had been sent off. Shorin felt it was important that he be taken for better care with the hope that he may provide some useful information. He had given the escort leader very specific orders regarding the care and safety of the prisoner. It was vital that he be sent on to the capital as soon as possible.

The tired Striker leader had already sent a message to Colonel Steele in Karbel asking that a coach be arranged to transport the man and his guards. He hadn't received a reply yet but was confident that the senior Striker would quickly grasp the importance of the prisoner. Shorin was certain enough of that fact that it had been necessary for him to face down several Legionnaires who had been intent on harming the prisoner.

As the Strikers had fled north they had run into a Legion patrol that had tangled with some of the southern army as well. They had taken heavy losses and the survivors were angry, so when they found out that there was a wounded enemy soldier with the Strikers they attempted to take him.

The Striker leader placed himself in their path until several more of his men joined him. The angry Legionnaires were denied their prize.

Mryl worked with Shorin on preparing their own plans. As part of that, several men had been sent south to scout for any enemy troops but none had reported back yet. Not long after arriving, Mryl sent a message to Colonel Tagg explaining their situation. Unknown to either Twinsteel or Tallon, another long message had already been sent directly to Kuln from the capital to better explain the overall situation.

Colonel Tagg had sent a short reply expressing his gratitude for the dedication they had all displayed and his sympathy for the losses. The message stated that he would personally speak to the each family regarding the lost patrol members. The message ended with a short sentence that Blacktower was under siege by an unknown force from the south.

That short passage caught both Mryl and Shorin by surprise. The men knew how strong the defenses were at Blacktower. What really worried both of them was who the attackers were.

The two friends discussed the thought. It quickly made sense to both of them that the force attacking Kuln had to be connected to the large army making its way north. While riding north from Arnoth following the battle, Mryl had been very specific in laying out the details and scope to Shorin of what he and his men had witnessed down south. The veteran Striker had absorbed the information and in return had shared what he and his men had undergone in their running skirmishes with the southerners as well as during the conflict for the village.

Walking around outside the small communication station Shorin encouraged his men to get as much rest as possible. He spoke with them in small groups and individually, letting them know that the capital had been notified and that help was on the way. He thanked them for all their efforts but didn't shy away from telling them that a much larger fight was coming in the very near future.

Making a point of taking and answering any questions that his men had, the Striker worked to reassure his men all the while not willing to admit it to himself about how serious their situation was.

Shorin was still trying to properly cope with the emotional drain that the recent events had placed on him. The fighting, the lack of sleep or proper meals, and worst of all, the amount of death he had seen. He had lost a goodly number of his men, which ate at his soul. For the moment he worked at keeping his focus on those that were still alive and the unknown of what lie ahead. More than once the memory of the beautiful Elven woman, Jehna, came to mind as well -- the single positive that he had to hold on to. The tired soldier clung to it.

As he was speaking with another small group of Strikers, Mryl came and found him. He was carrying a message form that he handed to his friend. It was from Colonel Steele at the capital, it outlined in detail what units were on the way to him, what some of the other regional troop deployments were and the approximate arrival time of the reinforcements. It also stated in very specific terms that he and his men that had done a very good job so far and to keep at it.

Shorin smiled mirthlessly at the thought, keep at it…sure what's getting a few dozen more of his men killed, that's all of them I have left. Calculating the amount of time that had elapsed since they had sent their message to the capital, toss in the decision making time there, time for word to go out to the various outposts and garrisons, and the time it would take them to muster their forces and begin the journey to his present location, Shorin determined that it would be at least another two – three hours before the first of any sizable contingents of reinforcements would arrive.

Mryl stood by quietly as he watched his friend read the message then process the information before speaking, "So round 'bout three hours or so?"

Shorin smiled weakly before nodding his agreement. Time enough to try and get in a little more sleep.

Chapter Thirty-Five
A New Challenge

Karbel

The size and scope of the planning meeting had required the group to move from the king's anteroom up to the Throne Room, which could easily accommodate them. The tables and chairs that had been moved in when Vode and the other northmen had been there a few days earlier were still in place, so it made it the logical choice for a meeting location.

Thadar had resisted the suggestion to move the focus of their planning work to army Headquarters. The king was still angry at much of the senior Legion leadership for their failure to react to the current crisis. So much so, that he didn't want to step foot in that building because he wasn't sure that he would be able to contain his temper -- which would distract him.

There was going to be a serious cleaning of the senior ranks when he had the time to do it properly but that time wasn't right now. His kingdom had been invaded and that was where his focus was and needed to remain. But after that...

After relieving Balkon of his position as Legion Marshal, Thadar knew that in order for the army to operate effectively he would need to appoint a new Marshal. It was essential that the army have a single, central commander.

Fortunately he didn't have far to look to find the right man to fill that slot. Earlier he had sent for Tal Lynn, the commander of the Fifth Legion. Tal was a veteran of numerous battles and skirmishes; he cared passionately about the men under his command and was respected in numerous circles. Yes, he would do nicely and that he was Thadar's father-in-law didn't hurt either, no trust issues at all with Tal.

After the general arrived at the palace, he was shown to the throne room. Once there he found a number of Strikers and others around the room working on various reports and maps. The king was gathered up with Steele, Dwyn, Spree and a handful of others including his own daughter, the queen.

It was with no small amount of pride that Lynn looked at his eldest child. She had grown into her role as queen nicely and he was very proud of her as he had always been. Looking over quickly she saw her father, flashing him a quick smile before returning her attention to the discussion.

Arriving at the table, Tal came to attention to report to his ruler. Thadar saw the senior general approach and straightened up himself to properly return the salute he knew was coming.

Once that was take care of he said, "General, stand at ease, glad you are here we can use your help."

Lynn nodded once in recognition of the statement then asked, "What's the overall situation?" He was quickly filled in on what they knew, what had been done so far and what they suspected.

Listening intently, he waited until he was certain that everyone was finished then spoke, "Sire, those are good steps but there is a pressing issue that must be addressed. There is no time to waste on this -- you need to appoint a new Legion Marshal. I can recommend several qualified generals that would be good choices if you would like me to sir."

Tal was a bit caught off guard by the silent grins and knowing smiles that broke on the faces of all those gathered around the table. *What in the world is...*

Thadar spoke up and further confused the veteran soldier, "Thank you, General. That will not be necessary, I have already selected a new Marshal, and notifications have already been sent out." Before Tal could ask the king continued, "My new Legion Marshal is you, congratulations."

Tal was rarely caught off guard but that announcement certainly did. Handshakes and congratulations began immediately but were halted when Shay Skye slid over to her father and embraced him. The assembled group of soldiers and advisors all watched as a daughter hugged her father with fierce pride. Tal was the right choice and that was for sure. It was high time that a real soldier occupied the senior commander slot.

Tal was surprised; pleased to be sure but at the moment was enjoying the hug of his daughter. He returned the embrace briefly then released her, there was too much to do to indulge in the moment.

Coming to attention he stated with a heavy sense of gravity "Sir, I accept this post with my promise to you that you shall always be given my best."

The king told him, "You have ever given me your best in many ways." Shay beamed as she looked upon her husband. "Now let us return our attention to the matter at hand."

The group sorted itself around the table in short order, the discussion of the invasion force and how to deal with it resumed in earnest.

There was a review of what information they had so far which wasn't as much as any of them wanted. In addition word had come in from Kuln that the Black Guards were under attack as well by a large unknown force that was attempting to seize the crossing point over the Wystern. It wasn't difficult to put together the notion that the attack on Kuln, the invasion and the attempted assassination attempt were all related.

In various Legion and Striker posts all across Karbel troops were hurriedly collecting weapons and supplies for transport to move toward where the invaders were. Information was sketchy but the news that Karbel had been invaded was more than enough motivation. It would take some time for the various reservists to be notified and have them gather at the appropriate facilities in order to be issued their armor and weapons. It would take more time to form the units up then move them to where they would need to be.

Some of the units would be coming from quite a distance away taking as much as a full ten-day to move to a position that would make them available. Since no one knew exactly what the invaders plans were, now that they were inside Karbel the residents and defenders of Plynth and Toras were frantically working at readying their cities for a possible attack and siege in case the invaders moved in that direction.

As the others were talking Tal was studying the map with a determined look on his face. Something in how the enemy was moving north was bothering him. There was an intangible that didn't make sense to him.

What information had come in told them that so far the movement of the large force had been steadily north, little to no deviation in their travel. Possibly it was an attempt to draw the Legions in and deal with them piecemeal, which wasn't a terrible plan but that didn't feel right to the newly promoted Legion Marshal, either. Tal had learned a very long time ago to listen to his instincts and at the moment his gut was telling him that what he was seeing wasn't right. He didn't know for sure what about it wasn't correct, but something wasn't as it should be.

Looking up from the map he asked what the current Legion deployments were; he was quickly handed a sheet containing the information.

Rapidly reading through it, he realized they had a problem: the Second Legion was moving to intercept the invaders but additional units including his own Legion were too far away to provide adequate support. His instincts were now screaming at him, he saw it now clearly: defeat in detail.

When a unit is broken into smaller and smaller units with each one then being attacked by a significantly larger unit – crap, the Second was moving in too soon. The Second was in over its head and he had to act now Tal prayed he had enough time.

"Sire I must leave immediately!" Thadar and the others fell silent as each looked at the Marshal. "I need to take the Fifth and whatever else we have available to assist the Second! I, uh, fear that they may be in far over their head."

The king considered the thought for a terribly brief moment then nodded in understanding. A decision was quick in coming.

"General, do as you see fit and may the Gods watch over you. I will send word to have the Second hold their position until you arrive."

With that, Tal came to attention and saluted his son-in-law who returned the salute with all the enormity demanded of the situation. He shook hands with the man entrusted to secure his kingdom. Shay stepped over embracing her father who returned the hug then left the room to carry out his plan.

The king and the others still in the room watched him leave then returned their attention to the maps and the planning. The Legion Marshal's statement about the Second Legion was quickly agreed with, that unit was unsupported, and against the juggernaut that the invaders represented it could mean serious trouble. A runner was sent to the heliograph station to have the orders sent to the Second.

Tal hurried through the passageways of the castle. His aides had been waiting outside the room having been summoned by the king without the general's knowledge. They were men that Tal knew and trusted, their presence gave the older man strength.

As they walked he filled them in on what information he had, what he suspected and what he had planned. Taking the most direct route to the courtyard, the men arrived a few minutes later. Grooms had their horses ready; none of them wasted any time mounting.

Tal turned to the senior man, a full Colonel, "Martus, go immediately to Headquarters, send orders to the Second to hold position -- the king's doing it as well but do it again -- fill the staff in on what I am planning then coordinate getting the units massed. Check on the reserves as well. Go, my friend!" A quick salute then he headed his horse for the gate; the others were close behind him.

Tal and the others passed through the gate, the new Legion Marshal returned the salutes of the Strikers then they rode the wide avenue leading down from the butte. At the bottom of the road they passed through the open gates at the lower barbican, then moved on into the press of the nearby road.

The three soldiers headed for the east gate to the city so they could catch up with the Fifth that had moved out nearly an hour earlier heading toward the distant invading army. Tal was worried; he was growing more and more concerned about the welfare of the Second Legion but at the moment there was little he could do.

He focused on getting his horse through the crowd. That much he could do. *By all the Ancestors, let us be in time* he prayed.

Chapter Thirty-Six
A Hard Day's Work

Eastmarch

It was early evening; the sun was slowly sinking, making its way toward the distant horizon masked by a line of low clouds that were already starting to obscure the glowing orb. Shorin and the others who had ridden into the Message Station with him the previous day had managed to eat and steal a little much needed rest. It hadn't been enough of either by any means but it was something.

The most positive aspect of the day so far, beyond finally establishing contact with the capital, was that the first of the promised units had been trickling in for the last two hours or so -- a platoon here, a pair of squads there, but they kept coming. As each additional group of armed soldiers arrived the small spark of hope that Shorin had been carefully guarding and nurturing grew ever so slightly.

There had been little time for him to process all the events of the last few days. The only thing the Striker was certain of was that there was a great deal of work to do in the coming days. More riding and fighting was ahead for him and the others but at least he had survived to this point, if that were to change then so be it – but he was damned certain it wouldn't come cheaply.

Now that at least some of the reinforcements had arrived, Shorin and Mryl were able to start formulating how to go after the enemy invasion force in a meaningful way. Both men knew they had nowhere near enough manpower to stop the entire southern army but at least they would be able to start hitting back in some type of measurable way.

Having a few hundred more of their fellows around was improving their moods a great deal. Karbel was slowly but steadily responding to the invasion but it was only a beginning. The actions of units just like theirs would be very important in the coming days.

Shorin and Mryl were meeting with the other unit commanders to brief them on the enemy strength, tactics and what their own plans were regarding how to go about attacking them. Some of the other unit leaders were equal in rank to both of them but orders from the capital had made it clear that Shorin was in charge.

Mryl had already decided to stay with Shorin till the end of whatever was ahead. He felt it owed that to the men he lost and if truth be told to himself as well. Earlier in the day he had ordered Wev and the remaining Black Guards to leave and head home. The three men looked at one another and remained where they were. Mryl was angry for a very brief moment that they would disobey his order but the moment rapidly passed. Words failed him as he struggled with the strong emotions just nodding in thanks for their loyalty. Nothing more was said about them leaving, they were in it together.

As soon as the first unit had arrived, Shorin sent a number of them out as scouts to try to determine the location of the enemy force. The men had been given very specific instructions that their mission was information gathering not combat. If it looked like they were going to be discovered then they were to ride away. It didn't sit well with the men but Shorin explained that if the enemy didn't know that they had been discovered it would be easier to attack them later. *Surprise and revenge is a real bitch* he told them which elicited several smiles before he sent them on their way, confident they would follow his orders.

Additional messages had come in at various times during the day as other heliograph stations were either attacked or more scouting reports were distributed from other locations. Each of these events were carefully plotted on the large area map in the main room of the message station. It helped to fill in details of what was taking place but the precise location of the main enemy force was still unknown.

Shorin and Mryl were telling the other officers that what they planned to do was keep their force as intact as possible to shadow the main body of the invaders. Then picking a time and place of their choosing, attack. Then repeat the process as often as they could.

They both felt strongly that if they could do that then it would be possible to inflict casualties well in excess of their own numbers. Hit hard then melt away, do it again and again as a way of sapping the enemy strength. All of them knew that more help was on the way but what they needed to do was try and buy the army time to consolidate.

Shorin was quick to acknowledge that there were a number of unknowns that would come into play once they got underway - topography, enemy troop levels, weather, and so much more. There were nods of agreement from several of the other unit leaders but he reminded them those bastards were in *our* country, and now it was going be *our* turn.

He went on to further explain that once the scouts brought back word on the enemy, they would be moving out regardless of the time. So would they make sure that all of their men had eaten, horses were fed and watered. Thanking the others he dismissed them to return to their units.

Mryl was nearby. The tired Striker turned to his friend who asked him, "What now?"

Shorin wasn't sure himself but until the scouts returned with definitive information the best course of action was to wait. It galled him to do it, but that was what he told Mryl they would do, wait.

The Black Guard understood the situation and the emotional need to do something, anything. But right then all they could do was wait. Another advantage of waiting was that more units joined them improving their numbers. After the last few days of fighting and riding to have to be this inactive was difficult to adjust to.

The two veterans shared a quiet moment as the evening deepened the low sound of night insects could be heard as both of them were alone with their own thoughts. A trio of Strikers passed nearby saluting the two officers who returned the salutation without speaking.

Twinsteel motioned toward a pair of chairs that had been dragged outside to make more room inside. The two tired men sat down savoring the sensation of not having to be on their feet. Shorin leaned forward resting his head on his clasped hands with his elbows on his knees, the toll of the previous ten-day would take some time to work off. Neither spoke for a few moments just taking in the company of the other.

Now that he had the ability to think on matters not immediately related to staying alive Mryl posed a question. "So who was the woman in the village?"

Thinking about Jehna made Shorin smile despite the fatigue, it was so automatic to do so that he didn't realize he was doing when he looked up at his friend.

"Ahhh just the daughter of the Headman is all."

Mryl wasn't fooled for a moment, he had seen the two embrace, the power and meaning of it, and that smile on Shorin's face, wasn't usual especially lately. Lifting one eyebrow to show his disbelief the Black Guard pushed the issue challenging his friend's assertion. "Oh just the daughter of the senior villager huh? I guess that hug and promise to find her was what? Being a gentleman?"

The two shared a short but sincere laugh at the question.

For his part now that Mryl had brought up the subject openly Shorin realized he wasn't reluctant to discuss Jehna. She had been on his mind throughout the day -- where was she? Was she safe? Where would he look to find her? These were just questions on his mind.

The one thing he was absolutely certain of was that once this business with the invaders was taken care of he would be heading back to the Homelands to seek her out.

Knowing that his companion wasn't about to let the topic drop Shorin gave in some, "Her name is Jehna Kalantiere. Her father is Logas, him you met."

Mryl nodded in acknowledgement but said nothing to allow his friend to continue.

"I met her at their home when I first arrived. Gods above, she is the most beautiful woman I've ever seen. No slouch in the kitchen either."

The smile on his face was growing the more he spoke about her. His mind was replaying all the words they had shared, the feeling of warmth in her hand, her body pressed into his when they embraced, the sudden emptiness in his heart as he realized it might be some time before he was able to be with her again.

Turning to look at Mryl he told his friend "I will find her."

Hearing the level of determination in the statement, Twinsteel was a bit surprised. She had obviously made a very deep impression which was all the more meaningful given the mess that they had all found themselves in.

He reached over to squeeze Shorin's shoulder in support telling him "We'll get through this so you can find her, I promise."

Shorin didn't say anything but nodded once in agreement. *Yes, by all the Gods, we will.*

***

One of the men who worked at the station stepped outside then stopped to allow his eyes to adjust to the darkness. Seeing Shoring the man hurried over to where the two men were sitting.

"Sir, there's a message you should see."

Taking a deep breath then blowing it out before standing, the tired Striker stood as did Mryl. Pointing the man toward the door the pair followed him.

Once inside the building the station commander handed Shorin a message form then waited. Angling it to catch more light from the lanterns and so that Mryl could read it as well the pair scanned what was written there. It was from Striker Headquarters in the capital:

Scattered scouting reports indicate that enemy force is heading slight west of north. Possible army is larger than reported and believed to be fully inside Karbel at this time. Estimates – not confirmed - put enemy force size at nearly ninety thousand total strength. Strongly suggest that you remain on eastern flank of invader striking as often as possible. All repeat all kingdom reserves are being called up to provide reinforcements. Four Legions are moving to intercept invaders; additional Striker units are also enroute to assist. Best wishes and keep this command as informed of your location and plans as much as is practical.

Steele

For his part Mryl whistled silently, ninety thousand was a staggering number. He was the only one present who had seen the enemy force and he had long realized that what they had seen in the south was only a portion of the invaders, but to try and comprehend that figure was almost too much. That made it the largest force he had ever heard of bar none.

Stopping that juggernaut would be a living nightmare but they had no choice. They had brought the war to Karbel not the other way round.

Shorin was having several of the same thoughts, he asked the room knowing they all knew the contents of the communication what they thought. None of the clerks said anything but the station commander licked his lips then spoke, "It's too much, too big to stop."

Shorin had to give the man credit for having the guts to put a voice to the concern that many, if not all them, were feeling. Pausing for a bit before responding the Striker officer knew that a wordy speech would be too much, too inappropriate for the situation.

When he did speak it was short and to the point, "That may be case. But we'll have to find out."

With that he took the message form as he headed for the door with Mryl close behind. He went to inform the other unit commanders of the information.

Chapter Thirty-Seven
Sleight of Hand

Eastern Karbel

Landa Turgo, the general commanding Karbel's Eleventh Legion, was a very angry man. Since initial word had arrived a few days earlier regarding an invasion of the kingdom, things had not gone well at all for those tasked with protecting it.

Scattered reports of large numbers of enemy forces had begun reaching the area headquarters at increasing intervals shortly after that. Many of the reports were incomplete or worse, contradictory, which added to the frustration the general was feeling. The southeast frontier was usually considered the least active militarily which is why his unit was so widely dispersed. There had never been an armed conflict with D'Lohm so the Eleventh had been more focused on stopping smuggling which was easier to do by using large amounts of smaller patrolling units.

It had taken time to assemble his forces, most were well disbursed to cover as much of the border as possible. Normally that policy worked well to provide manpower over a large area of the frontier. However at this particular time it was proving to be a very large hindrance.

Some of the units of the Eleventh had already engaged the enemy but were unable to significantly hinder their progress, while taking losses out of proportion to their own numbers. It galled Turgo greatly but he had been forced to order his men to withdraw to prevent them from taking the full brunt of an enemy attack. He needed time for the other units to reach him so that his Legion was as close to full strength as possible.

There had already been several skirmishes with enemy scout units and once with a flank guard section. In each of those fights the men of Karbel had been victorious but that wasn't stopping or even slowing the invaders. It seems as though every time they fought a unit another two came up to replace it. The main body of the enemy force was well inside the Karbel border still moving north and so far the Eleventh had not been able to do anything of significance to alter that.

Turgo was in communication with the capital keeping them updated on what information he had as well as his own plans. To further complicate the overall situation, a large number of refugees -- some reports put the number well into the thousands -- were crossing over into the perceived safety of Karbel from D'Lohm trying to escape the invasion.

Their movement was at times hindering his troops plus many of them were scared and desperate which only added to the turmoil. Some of the refugees were wounded and in need of care but he had to make the difficult decision to order his men to ignore their needs. It was harsh but the efforts of the soldiers had to be on fighting the enemy. Humanitarian concerns would have to wait, no matter how pressing they were.

Among the command group of the vast southern army, Anagir was deep in thought as he listened to Pon talk about the growing amount of resistance that the southerners were facing. More and more of the troops of Karbel were mobilized and deployed which was slightly slowing down the advance, which to this point had actually been going well.

The southern army had been traveling faster than their own estimates despite dealing with scattered defending units at different times and taking some losses. The hard training that the Varshon had the tribesmen doing for so long was paying dividends.

Even knowing that they were somewhat ahead of schedule caused some doubt to creep into the mind of the senior majic user, curse these humans – do they not realize that they are defeated?

There was still more than sufficient time to reach G'mar -- which had been well factored into the planning -- retrieve the ancient scrolls then make the preparations for the celestial alignment which was necessary for the invocation. The elder Varshon closed his eyes as he gave the situation thought.

The delay, while a nuisance, wasn't actually anything resembling a serious problem. However it was causing Anagir a sense of unease, certainly not panic, but maybe better described as anxiousness. Pon and the others fell silent as they waited for their leader to continue.

At this rate the travel time to where he needed to be meant waiting while the army slogged their way through all the obstacles of terrain and defenders which the elder Varshon felt was beneath him. There was a secondary plan in place to travel to G'mar. It had been put in place really at the last minute but in theory it was sound.

According to the secondary plan, Anagir and a select group would split off from the army and head to a prepared location on the Ghora River well north of Plynth where two sailing vessels were waiting, fully supplied and crewed by a group of select agents familiar with the north. They would sail north on the river until reaching the Wind Sea then head west until they reached the fortress. It would shorten the trip by at least two full ten-days if not more.

The more he contemplated the idea the more it appealed to him. By the time the army arrived, the preparations for the majical rite would be completed then he would be able to conduct the ceremony unhindered. After that, with his power increased so significantly, nothing would be able to stop the Varshon from conquering the world. The image of him standing on the wall at G'mar with the army bowed before him, yes, that suited the situation and it was fitting that all should bow to him. So be it…

Turning to one of his aides, Anagir told him to summon all the senior majic users to him as soon as possible. The vassal saluted the master then headed off to carry out the task. Waving Q-tra-All over to him, the massive Ogurth responded immediately to the summons. When the Troll arrived he bowed his head as he listened to the words of the Elder Varshon.

Anagir told him to personally select a detachment of Ogurth and tribesmen, they would be his escort to G'mar using the ships. The large figure listened without speaking, he knew of the plan, had it memorized in fact so was already aware of what was needed, how many troops the ships would hold, what additional supplies would be necessary and so speaking was unnecessary. All that was required was for him to carry out the wishes of his sworn leader.

When Anagir was finished, he nodded to acknowledge it was acceptable for his minion to take his leave which the Ogurth did without ever speaking. The senior majic user returned his attention to the matter he had been working on prior to Pon's arrival with the situation report.

A small but growing sense of anticipation was present in the Varshon leader, to be back at G'mar and this time to be in total charge, to have everyone there obeying *him*. He allowed the pleasant thought to linger before grudgingly allowing it slip away. Anagir knew that it would be at least five more days of travel -- possibly one or two more -- before they reached a point that it would be possible to depart for the location where the vessels would be waiting for them.

The time was of no concern; they were through D'Lohm and now moving deeper into Karbel. He turned his attention to what he would speak to his senior majic users about. Certain that their opponents were ignorant of the overall plan of his army Anagir wanted to take steps to further protect the secret of the overall goal.

It took nearly an hour for all of the senior majic users to be located and for them to make their way to where Anagir was waiting. Feeling expansive he didn't begrudge the time at all, it was somewhat out of character for him but no one said anything, they didn't dare.

Gathering the nearly two dozen or so Varshon to him Anagir began to explain his plan, he and some of them would be taking the ships to G'mar while the remainder of the group would be in charge of the other majic users but the key point is that in order to preserve the secret of their majical potential they were not to employ majic against their foes. Doing so could alert the humans to what was really about to take place.

Several of those gathered looked to one another in confusion, one question uppermost in their minds. *What would it matter if the humans knew they possessed majic?* Anagir saw the looks, telling them they were free to speak.

One of them hesitated slightly then spoke, "Wouldn't the use of majic make it easier and faster for the army to overcome the defending troops?"

The Elder Varshon nodded once in recognition of the wisdom of the question then told them, "It is possible, even likely, but by using only the force of arms it would keep our greatest weapon a secret. Besides, it wouldn't hurt for the tribesmen to bleed a bit -- that is their purpose."

Several heads nodded in understanding, the agreement wasn't unanimous but that didn't matter in the least. Anagir's decision would be what was followed and obeyed.

Centuries of training and indoctrination had brought about a level of obedience to the will of the senior majic user that was unchallenged. The last of those Varshon who had opposed his rule had long since been removed or otherwise silenced. Some of them had suffered particularly gruesome fates which served as a lesson to many of the others, obey or suffer.

Anagir smiled as he explained further, "Friends, by not using our most powerful resource now whatever forces we will face after reaching G'mar and completing the rite, will likely be more apt to combine their forces to face us. When that happens we will crush them. If we use the majic now it will demonstrate to them what we are capable of. So doing this is not only tactical but strategic as well." Now more of the majic users understood the logic of their leader.

Telling them of his plan to use the alternate transport method to reach the fortress, Anagir outlined what he expected of them while he was gone. Before dismissing them they were told that in the next day or so those who would accompany him would be notified so they were to be ready to go.

Each of them were now eager, almost anxious for what lie ahead just as Anagir had planned. It was sometimes necessary to provide a level of enticement for one's minions.

Chapter Thirty-Eight
Black Guards at War

Kuln

The morning dawned bright and clear. The storms that had drenched the area during the night had blown through and were gone. It was cloudy but not a solid overcast.

Tagg looked down from his spot on the battlements to survey the scene on the south side of the river again. Eager eyes from the men on either side of him looked on as well. What they were seeing pleased none of them, least of all their commander.

As the sun rose higher in the eastern sky it revealed more of what had occurred during the darkness hours.

"Make sure all of this is being sent to the capital." Tagg's voice was calm as he spoke but the scribe at his side understood the seriousness of what they were watching.

Blacktower was under siege for the first time in its history and the enemy, whoever in the name of the spirit they were, seemed quite determined to press their attack. The assault he was observing was the third such attempt at seizing the vital drawbridges that spanned the Wystern. If they were able to do that it would drastically alter the situation.

The Southerners had brought up several heavy bridging trusses during the night; each was at least fifty feet in length. Tagg whistled silently, that had to have taken some doing. He found himself impressed despite the circumstances.

If properly employed they could span the distance between the southern shore and the island astride the middle of the river allowing the southerners access to the land spit. Once there, they could repeat the crossing and gain access to the northern shore of the Wystern without having to occupy the sturdy fortifications that dominated the small island.

Certainly the men there would do all they could to disrupt the crossing, but Tagg had to admit it was a good plan and not one that they had foreseen to defend against. *The wonders of modern warfare*, Tagg mused to himself and no one in particular, a scowl riding his face as the thought rose up.

The Black Guard commander knew that doing something effective against enemy would be difficult, but not impossible. Blacktower commanded the heights and the road leading up from the river but he was still worried. The attackers were up to something but he didn't know exactly what.

He had quietly sent more men and supplies to the smaller fortress on the island during the night and now was glad he had, it would remain to be seen if they could get more men and supplies in there tonight. The entire battle could hinge on the ability to control the island that formed the natural anchor for the two bridges across the way.

Workmen were preparing the drawbridge on the northern side of the river for destruction if it proved necessary; Tagg would have no problem with making sure the southerners could not use it. He was confident that the men in the fortress on the islet would be able to hold out even if the northern drawbridge was destroyed.

Over the years the fortress on island had been upgraded and strengthened with every possible defensive measure the Guards could provide. Tagg had already realized that one of the shortcomings was the lack of substantive defensive measures on the southern bank but that was a problem for another time. His gaze turned to the area beyond the river, the look of displeasure on his face growing.

One thing that the southern forces had been investing serious time and effort into since their arrival was creating a series of defenses so that now there was nearly a complete line of trenches and strongpoints guarding the northern flank of the attacking army. The entire area forward of the trenches was a mass of wooden stakes driven into the ground at an angle to stop any mounted attack. In several places it was obvious that the stakes had been placed to create lanes that would force the attacker into following a path of the defenders choice.

Tagg frowned at that. It meant that any foray across the river would meet stiff resistance and would likely be driven off with heavy losses. It was also apparent to see that numbers favored the attacker despite the fact that Guard numbered slightly over twelve thousand men. Many of those were at their posts seeing the same things that Tagg did. It was a stalemate, at least for now.

The catapults and other artillery in the large fortress that were in range of the crossing were all dropping missiles, flaming oil and large rocks on the southern forces as the attack continued. One interesting facet of the enemy plan was only having those forces immediately involved in the action forward, the remaining units were only sent forward at the double as needed to reduce the time they were in range of the powerful defensive artillery.

As if on cue, a section of heavy infantry began running for the center of the melee. The battle went back and forth for some time with neither side gaining a serious advantage. Then a series of horn calls brought the southern forces back from the river.

So far the defenders on the small island that held the heavily fortified waypoint and bridge mechanisms were holding their own quite admirably, given the size of the enemy force. One factor that was working in the favor of the Black Guards was that due to the depth of the river and the very strong current that was present year round, the attackers were limited to a small area that they could attack from, which negated their superior numbers. The same factor worked for the southern forces in return, there was a single point of attack that the Black Guards could use so it evened out the tactical issue.

He continued to watch for quite a while, just as the Varshon hoped he would. Meanwhile the southerners kept digging. After another hour or so of watching Tagg asked his senior officer to take over and to keep an eye on things. The Under-Colonel nodded his understanding. Tagg then headed in to have something to eat.

He wasn't especially hungry earlier that morning but he knew from experience that it was smart to eat hearty when you could during times of combat. You had no way of knowing when you may be able to do so again.

As he passed through into the center section of the large fortress he motioned to one of his senior officers who stepped up beside him as they walked.

"What do you think?"

Dougal Twinsteel, who was the fourth highest ranking Black Guard and a well experienced soldier, spoke up immediately. "Sumthing be wrong. Their attacks wer' no well-coordinated or supported as they should be. If they had be then they may have carried the island."

Colonel Tagg nodded in agreement but said nothing. The same thought had occurred to him as well. The enemy force had not asked for a parley which wasn't unusual but was a bit unexpected.

The veteran commander had also been mentally composing a long message to go to the king, updating him on what had occurred over night and during the morning. The Guards had been made aware of the invasion that had overrun D'Lohm was now taking place in eastern Karbel. The scope of the invading army was unlike anything he had ever seen or even heard about. Then suddenly he found yet *another* enemy force on his own doorstep.

It had to be part of the same group.

What would be the odds that two large organized and independent forces would appear at the same time and attack Karbel? Tagg wasn't much of a gambling man but he was reasonably sure that it was unlikely.

The Guards commander knew that his friend and mentor had been worried; his son, Mryl, had been missing for some days then word came in from Karbel that he and a few survivors had turned up in Eastmarch of all places. The same message brought with it some dire news about what the patrol had discovered while still in the south.

Dougal hadn't let the concern show, and Tagg knew that it was unlikely that he would have. Mryl was a good soldier, in fact he was one of the best in the entire Black Guards and that was no minor accomplishment. The fact that he hadn't been heard from for some time prior to his showing up where he did wasn't a fluke or laxness.

The loss of several patrols including one led by Dougal's son-in-law, Mryl missing, and now a large enemy force laid siege to them. The events were connected -- Tagg was certain of that.

The pair continued on to the message center where the Black Guard commander told the clerk he had a dispatch to send. Nodding his readiness to begin writing, the clerk lifted his quill. Once Tagg had the bulk of the message dictated he asked the clerk to read it back to him which he did. Dougal waited until the man was finished then suggested the addition of two small items that the Guard commander readily agreed to. The clerk wrote the information down and then with a nod Tagg let him know it was time to send it.

The clerk pulled out the current code book to begin the laborious process of encrypting the lengthy text. Tagg thanked the men present; there were always at least two men present in the message center for security. If one had to relieve himself, then a guard was called in. No one was to be alone with the code books by himself at any time.

As a security feature there was always a fire going in the corner fireplace no matter the weather, if there was the slightest chance of the books being captured then they were to be tossed into the fire to be destroyed.

Dougal waited until his commander was through the door before following. The men headed for the officer mess continuing their discussion about the tactics used during the assault. By the time they had finished eating the message had been encoded and transmitted.

As soon as the enemy forces had been sighted Blacktower and its companion town, Kuln, had been placed on alert. Additional security troops had been sent to the town and the message stations just in case. The first four message stations on the line to the capital were staffed by Black Guards.

Life in the southern area of Karbel had suddenly gotten very dangerous. Heavily armed mounted patrols watched the northern banks of the river just in case the enemy was somehow able to get troops across. No reports of attempts to cross the river had come from any of the patrols but Tagg was keeping a sizable contingent of troops standing by just in case such a report was received.

The rest of the day passed without another attack. The man who led the Black Guard was strangely puzzled by what had happened so far. He called for an officer council to discuss the situation. It took about an hour to get all of the men gathered; once they were there was little doubt about what they were going to talk about.

Tagg wasted no time with formalities asking his men what they thought of the situation. Discussion went back and forth around the room as opinions varied on what the enemy forces' objective was, as well as what the Guards needed to do to bring the fight to them. The meeting ended without a firm plan which didn't please the Black Guard commander but he knew what his officers were thinking which had its own value.

There was no attack the following morning which broke the pattern of the previous three days. Then word came in of additional enemy forces arriving from the west which was not something that they expected at all. While rushing to the battlement to see for himself, Tagg admitted that had been a brilliant move, bringing forces around the Jaggor Range to the south and then to come down on them from the west instead of the east or south.

He grudgingly gave them credit for the planning. They knew that the majority of the scouting efforts had been in those two directions. The Guard patrols hadn't detected them and that was no small task. It must have taken several ten-days for the infantry to move around the mountains, north to the river and then down toward Kuln from the direction of Arandon. It was also likely the cause of the disappearance of two of his patrols. They were on long range scouting missions to the west so they could have run into these southerners and been destroyed.

Once the additional forces had arrived, no effort to attack had been made. A series of large, well-fortified camps had been built in a wide half circle well beyond the trench line. These camps were teeming with soldiers erecting tents of various sizes, arranging supplies and drilling with their weapons. A number of men could be seen in the trenches as well.

Tagg felt that this was not the action of an army about to commit to an attack any time soon. They would have sufficient warning before an attack came so what was the southern commander up to? Tagg didn't know and it bothered him right down to his soul. His counter-attack options were shrinking. The veteran officer felt he was being forced into a box.

That was a feeling Tagg cared for not at all.

Chapter Thirty-Nine
A Desperate Journey

Karbel

Once Thadar had made the decision to support the travelers in their attempt to stop the Varshon, a great deal was rapidly undertaken. Gunnar had already been talking at length with Vode regarding the travel arrangements as well as the plan on what to do once they reached the fortress. Despite the Vankard tradition of shunning those who had gone beyond the mountains, the High Priest reasoned that since they were all beyond the borders of home that it was both counter-productive and foolish to worry about that now.

Gunnar and Vode, along with input from Levas, had compiled a list of supplies that they felt it would be wise to take with them on the trip to G'mar. Obtaining what they needed wasn't hard since they had the full backing of the throne.

Men and materiel were collected and then loaded on the two Striker-operated vessels that plied the Soling River. Once that was accomplished they set sail up the river. The trip took nearly a full day; they enjoyed a strong wind blowing from the south for much of the time which shortened the trip.

Orders had been sent ahead of time to have fresh horses, as well as appropriate carriages and wagons, waiting for the group when they arrived at Edora. At the direction of the king Steele had also detailed a full company of Strikers from the Edora garrison to accompany the group, along with T'shar and the others from the patrol who had all volunteered.

The Strikers and dock workers were waiting when the ships docked. Kelyvn Nahn, the Under-Captain commanding the company of Strikers, came aboard right away to report to Gunnar. He had been sent very specific orders by Steele explaining that whatever Gunnar or the High Priest wanted or needed *he* was to personally make sure it happened. Those were the direct orders of the king.

Finding the man he was seeking on the raised stern section of the medium sized ship, the officer came to attention introducing himself. Gunnar nodded in response giving his own name then shook hands with the man who then handed over the message form. The form detailed Colonel Steele's instructions, which the king's advisor quickly scanned over so that he understood what had been said. Finishing that up, the two began to discuss the situation as work began around them in earnest.

Space had been cleared at the busy river docks ahead of time so that both vessels could be unloaded as rapidly as possible. It seemed as if the ships were barely tied to the wharf when the first bundles of goods were going down the gangplanks to the waiting wagons.

Soon a line of men, Strikers and stevedores, had formed to expedite the unloading. Shouts and a few curses filled the air as the work progressed. Some of the Strikers were deployed as security, forming a half circle out from the expansive dock area to keep out anyone not authorized to be there. Additional Strikers were in place along the first part of the roadway north to help speed the passage of the expedition.

There were several other cargo ships tied up nearby so activity in the area was quite high as nets of assorted merchandise were going back and forth between the dock and ships. The air smelled strongly of drying fish, sweat and damp of the wide river.

After several minutes of talking with Nahn, the king's advisor saw the High Priest. He paused in mid-sentence with the Striker to motion his fellow northman over. Curious, Kelyvn turned to see a man of medium height dressed in rich robes approaching at a steady dignified pace. Gunnar waited until Vode joined them then made introductions.

When Nahn realized that this was the man Steele had been talking about in his orders, he immediately came to full attention then bowed respectfully telling the High Priest that he and his men were at his disposal. For his part Vode bowed in return as Gunnar translated what the officer had said.

After hearing what was said he responded, "Thank you Captain, it means a great deal to us that your king would provide us the capable service of you and your men." The Striker bowed again at hearing the honor being paid to him and his men.

As the three were speaking about the trip, Levas came up to have a word with his superior. When he joined them, Vode introduced him to the Striker officer who politely bowed in response.

As he returned the courteous gesture the senior acolyte was again impressed with the quality and character of the people of this, Karbel. It was so completely different than their time riding through the Federation territory. The people here were open, friendly and helpful. All those stories that were so often repeated in Vankard about the evils of the Utlanders now seemed so foolish and, to his own embarrassment, made his own people seem somewhat backwards.

Nahn used the opportunity of Levas joining them to go and check on the progress of the unloading. Politely excusing himself, the tall officer headed for the dock.

Vode, Gunnar, and Levas watched as the various bales, barrels, bags and such, were moved. Having a full company of Strikers, some two hundred plus men in addition to those from Vankard meant a hefty amount of supplies needed to be taken. At one point Levas excused himself from the others to go oversee some of the priests so that they may lend a hand with the unloading as well.

For his part Gunnar was apprehensive about the trip, he had begun to trust the High Priest, not doubting the sincerity of what Vode believed to be necessary, but would they be in time? What would be waiting for them when they reached this G'mar place? How many troops would the enemy have there? Too many questions with not nearly enough answers to suit him.

He turned his attention back to the activity on the vessels. It appeared much of the cargo had been offloaded already; knots of men were working at placing the goods and weapons into the various transports. Gunnar grabbed up his bag then headed for the gangplank to join Vode and the others who had left the ship a few minutes earlier.

Once the wagons were full and the cargo secured, Gunnar informed Vode that they were ready and asked if they could depart. The High Priest was careful to notice the level of respect that his fellow northman was showing him and the others.

Gunnar had been consciously deferring to the priest whenever practical and had not disputed any of his orders in front of any of the others including Levas. Vode was both impressed and a bit surprised; this was Karbel and not Vankard. Here he was the guest, and it was Gunnar who enjoyed the favor of the king. The senior member of the group quickly but with the dignity befitting his station climbed in his waiting coach. Once in he had Levas join him.

The door to the carriage was closed and he then nodded to Gunnar that he was ready to depart. Vode had spoken with the advisor to the ruler of Karbel earlier asking him to join them in the carriage. Gunnar politely turned down the request citing his reason as it would be easier to stay in communication with the Strikers if he too was mounted but as time permitted he would join them.

The High Priest nodded in agreement at the thought and before he could comment Gunnar had leaned in slightly then in a lower voice told the priest that it would also lessen the issue of the priest being in such close quarters with one of the shunned among some of the other northmen.

Vode saw the wisdom of the statement, a sense of shame filled him at the realization that it was true. The long standing prejudice against those that had left Vankard -- was it outdated? He wondered. No answer presented itself but the priest suspected he knew what he would say the next time the topic came up. Vode had nodded his understanding of the statement.

Gunnar was already on his horse, he quickly glanced around to make sure that the others were ready. Satisfied that they were, he signaled to the senior Striker who then waved the others forward and with that the long journey to G'mar was underway.

The group quickly made their out of the busy dockyards area and headed north, it was to be a journey of nearly a full ten-day as they intended to travel through the night as well as much as possible. Word had come that the Varshon army was already in Karbel so none of group knew what they might be facing when they arrived at the fortress.

Another issue was that none of them had been there before so where they were going wasn't an exact science. Gunnar planned to follow a path that would take them in proximity to a number of government locations, most of which coincidentally were equipped with heliograph stations so they could stay as updated on the overall situation as possible and be able to relay messages as needed.

He knew that several teams with portable heliographs had been detailed to go north as well and would be waiting near the frontier at a pre-arranged location with more troops to provide security for the communicators. If they ran into trouble or, gods willing, were successful then word would need to be sent to Thadar as rapidly as possible.

As the group traveled north a screen of Strikers rode ahead of them to clear the road of all traffic of any type. This was no time for niceties, no one was injured but not a small amount of hard feelings were left in the wake of the groups' passage.

Everyone on the road was hurriedly ordered to make way for the caravan. Their orders had come directly from the king; they were to avoid delays at all costs. The mission had to succeed -- the fate of the kingdom was at stake.

Vode had already shared what information he could from his visions with Gunnar, none of which had occurred again since leaving Vankard. The High Priest found that more than a trifle annoying. Now that he was on the path that the visions had set before him a little more insight would have been nice.

Vode was feeling a little blind, his lifelong belief in the higher power of the gods had been tested since he and the others crossed through the mountain gate into the Utland. He kept those thoughts to himself but the further down the path they found themselves, the more the spark of worry that had arisen, grew.

Miles slowly but steadily fell away as they travelled north. The first dozen miles or so after leaving the dock area saw a thick band of population. Once they were through that the land began to open up around them as the long column passed into more of the agricultural area that Edora was widely known for. Twice during the day the group stopped long enough to have the wagon teams replaced with fresh horses so that they could continue as rapidly as possible.

At the second stop which was late in the evening as they were taking in a hurried but hot meal, all of the mounted troops had their horses exchanged as well, which took quite a few hands to accomplish. The whole process took over an hour but it was necessary. There were still several hours of daylight left so Vode and the others planned to use as much of it as possible.

Leaving the livery station behind, the group continued on their way. The process was repeated for the next several days as they headed north toward G'mar.

Chapter Forty
Battle Call

Eastern Frontier

Legion Marshal Tal Lyn, who was for now also still wearing the hat as commander of the Fifth Legion, had gathered what survivors of the Second Legion that could be found and added them to his own ranks. They had continued to head northeast to try and intercept the southern columns, which were marching steadily northward through eastern Karbel.

Adding the survivors to his own ranks had improved his overall strength level while adding a few options he didn't have before, especially in regards to his cavalry. But thanks to his scouts Tal knew that he was still badly outnumbered. By exactly how much the veteran soldier didn't know but was sure that it would be a significant amount. It couldn't be helped though; Karbel had been invaded and it was his duty to try and correct that.

The senior general had sent out orders to ensure that no one battalion received too many of the men from the shattered Legion; he also made sure that the Third battalion had received none. He had something special in mind for them and the survivors could further complicate what was going to be hard enough to accomplish.

The men from the Second had already been broken once. It was not the fault of the men but once defeat was tasted it was a difficult thing to remove. They had been forced to run; it may not take much to make it happen again. Better to spread them out to reinforce his line companies and allow for a greater reserve. A strong man standing on either side of you could do wonders for confidence. The general was counting on that fact, very heavily, hopefully not too heavily.

He had some of his staff searching for any senior officers from their sister unit so he could personally question them as to what happened. Several of the junior officers were already waiting for him but he was unsure how much help they would be.

Lyn wanted and needed all the information he could get about their opponents as well as why the Second didn't follow their orders to hold their position to wait for help. Word had already been circulating around that much of what remained of the command staff from the Second had fled when it became apparent that the situation was out of hand. Ran away! Leaving their command at the mercy of an unforgiving enemy -- only the action of a handful of junior officers had allowed those that survived to escape.

It shamed Tal badly to hear that Legion officers had run, leaving the men to their fate. He had never heard of such a thing before. The Legions had a proud history but this was almost too much to believe.

Tales had been floating around the army for some time regarding certain members of the Second Legion command staff -- that they had been given their posts as a political reward and some were deep in the pockets of wealthy patrons. It had even suggested that certain officers of the Second had been part of the coup attempt against the king. He had found the tales hard to believe but the proof before him was damned hard to ignore.

Seven of every ten men of the Second were dead or wounded, most dead. Several wagons normally used for transporting food and equipment had been hastily emptied to make room for some of the more seriously wounded who were even now being treated as well as the situation allowed. A few of these were already heading west under escort.

There were not very many wounded. The attack by the southern forces had been very thorough; the grass and other plants in the area would grow high for several years after this due to the amount of blood spilled into the soil. Tal shuddered slightly as he recalled the scene where they found the remnants of the Second.

Bodies littered the area, some piled three deep in places. Many of them had been struck by multiple arrows, a macabre crop of fletchings that rose from the long grass. Tal was determined to try to not let that happen to his men, but that was yet to be seen.

The cavalry had placed themselves between the remaining infantry and the enemy to protect them from any further strikes after the southern columns had continued on their way north. Some of the supply wagons were damaged and many of them burned. The overworked medical staff was losing patients simply due to lack of attention. Tal had immediately sent the entire medical staff of his Legion to help with the wounded, hopefully saving many but the losses that day were great and very likely to be added to.

Enough! He had a job to do; he drove the thoughts from his mind and focused on his task at hand.

After his scouts had reported the enemy position to a fine degree, Tal chose the location to make a stand. The southerners had a number of scout units deployed so it was necessary to deal with several of them before arriving at the place he wanted to use. His own location was no secret to the approaching army group but that didn't matter.

He eliminated the enemy units out of simple necessity, he didn't want anyone behind him when he made his attack, and it had the added feature of killing that many more of the southern tribesmen. Numbers were already out of balance in favor of the enemy so every one killed only helped the men of Karbel. Kill another ten thousand more and it would be only eight to one against him. He would take all the help he could beg, borrow or steal.

The Legion commander knew that the coming fight would be crucial to the survival of the realm. If he failed and lost his Legion, then Karbel would be facing an invasion with nothing in the way. He couldn't allow that to happen. This would be the most serious crisis he had ever confronted.

Nearly all of the mounted units of the Second were intact since they had been separated from the infantry when the attacks that pounded them down came. They could be of great use if the right opportunity presented itself.

Now that his Legion was in place the horses were quickly being fed and watered to keep them as fresh as possible. The cavalry could be crucial to the success of the battle that was to come. Tal knew two more Legions were coming to reinforce him but for now he and the Fifth were alone with the enemy. The odds were not in their favor but this was the best Legion in the army.

He sent a runner to remind the Third battalion commander to ensure that the equipment matter they had discussed had been taken care of. The proud Legionnaire saluted and rode off to carry out his assigned duty. The general was sure that the matter would be handled and handled properly but a good commander always checked on the details and Tal was a good commander.

After arriving at the location he had selected earlier based on the scouts reports and careful use of his maps, Tal used a bit of showmanship to have the entire Legion move over the crest of the low hills en mass accompanied by a loud chorus of horn calls. This gave those watching the appearance of first nothing and then suddenly a wide well-ordered force on the enemy's left flank.

The effect was immediate, the lower half of the Alush column marching to the left of center stopped to deal with these interlopers before returning to their march north.

The Legion General arranged his men on the east side of a series of long, low hills that ran fairly north-south to the west of the large southern columns. Long rows of infantry were standing shoulder to shoulder, their large metal clad shields arranged in front of them giving the formation the look of a giant turtle shell, dark and scaly.

He watched his enemy deploy from marching formation into solid blocks of heavy infantry that took shape slower than what he anticipated. His own men would have done it nearly twice as fast, but as he studied the enemy with a practiced eye several things became apparent.

The first of these was that only half of the left column had deployed to face him, the center and right side columns continued to march north with the remainder of the third column joining them as well. Damn, he had hoped to slow down two of the columns or at least one full one; he knew that three would not be possible.

Still, that one half of the column facing him had more than triple his numbers. *Well quantity did have a quality all its own,* he thought wryly.

Another issue was that a large number of enemy cavalry were now milling about on his extreme right, lurking out there beyond triple bow range but they could still be a problem. He thought briefly about shifting one of the reserve companies to the right but held off. He knew from experience that the army that shifted its reserves last was often the victor.

The wily veteran knew that he did not have a great deal of reserves to begin with, even with the men from the Second, so for now he would wait. It was possible that the cavalry was bait to get him to shift some reserves. He did order that his company of Rhywe archers be placed on that side.

The bowmen that hailed from the southernmost of Karbel's cities were master archers and he had specifically recruited a full company worth for his Legion while stationed near the city two years earlier, each was worth two regular archers. One uses what tools are available.

The southerners had not shown any brilliant tactical thinking so far but with numbers like they had to work with it really wasn't necessary. His men had completed their deployment along the forward slopes of the low hills. Archers were ranged along the crests to provide covering fire and with the elevation, Tal judged it to be around a hundred feet or so above the plain, it would increase their range somewhat. It wasn't much but he would take any advantage he could gain.

Three rows of swordsmen were ranked just to the rear of the blocks of pikemen that made up most of nine thousand men of his Legion. The infantry would protect their fellows from any who got past the long phalanx of sharp steel.

Tal intended to use the long infantry pikes to keep the southern troops away as long as possible, break their formations and tie them down. The sword bearers could then move forward to strike at the stalled mass while staying within the pikes themselves. That way his archers would inflict what damage they could on the enemy as well especially along the flanks.

The heavy infantry across the way were still shaking themselves out but it would not be long now before they began their advance. He had a number of light catapults along and these were being assembled as rapidly as possible, against a host the size of the one arrayed against him these proven engines of death could help to improve the odds.

It hadn't been easy getting them up the slopes of the hills but liberal use of the whip on the draft animals and not a small amount of manpower got the job done. The risk wasn't in getting them up the hill but rather getting them down. If it had to be done in a hurry then they would likely have to be abandoned.

The catapults had been sent out to the wings of his formation along with their wagonloads of solid shot and fire pots. Their location would add to the defense of his flanks. If the enemy tried to rush him the catapults could help disrupt their formations.

The general had no illusions about stopping the enemy completely; his job was to delay them for as long as possible and inflict as many casualties as they could to buy the other Legions time to join up with him. Then they could start thinking seriously about stopping the invaders.

Keeping his unit together as a viable force was foremost on his mind.

His eyes scanned the scene below him again. It appeared the southern troops planned to sweep the field with nothing but numbers and force of arms alone. Tal believed that even though his men were better trained and equipped it would still be possible for the blocks of infantry now approaching to swarm him under as they did the men of the Second.

Orders quickly went out the wings of the formation to where the catapults were now assembled and ready for use. Immediately they began to lob unlit fire pots out at angle from their location. Tal could hear the heavy *thraack* sound as each arm snapped forward to release their cargo. The clay jugs shattered on impact spraying a mixture of oil and naphtha all over the ground.

The catapults, arranged four to each side, were tossing the jugs as fast as they could. The crews were moving the light siege engines slightly each time so that an area as wide and long as possible was being saturated with the flammable material. The crews were careful with the tensioning as not to break the jugs too early as the arm swung forward to deliver the fragile containers downrange.

***

Across the way the southern infantry commander was with his officers, all of them laughing at the terrible accuracy of the Legionnaire artillery. So much for the vaunted Legions of Karbel -- the first one couldn't fight and now this one couldn't see! He was sure that they would crush the units before them just as had been done to the other Legion.

He and his units had seen limited action since entering Karbel but now it was their turn. The Alush general knew that he outnumbered the men on the hills more than three to one and so he was confident of victory. March forward, strike them hard with archers and then move forward to crush them underfoot with a general assault.

The rain of clay jugs continued to fall on both sides of his formation but had slowed as his men got closer. The infantry blocks were now aligned and rapidly advancing toward the west. Steady drum beats set the pace as the distance between the two sides shortened.

A few rocks now began to rain down on the lead squares of approaching infantry from the catapults. Most weighed in the area of forty pounds and when they hit the force tore into several men at a time. Limbs and even heads were torn away by the projectiles that rained down on the infantry. Several holes opened up in the marching blocks that were quickly filled as men from behind rushed forward to erase the gaps, leaving the formations uneven just as Tal planned. It also moved men into positions different from what they were used to which degraded a unit's effectiveness a little more. Not much in the grand scheme, but Tal would happily take every bit of an advantage he could create.

The casualties while fairly insignificant in number were designed to also shake the confidence of the approaching troops. They were taking losses without the ability to respond while they closed the distance between them and those from Karbel. The infantry blocks themselves often finished what the solid shot started. The men were so tightly massed together that most of those wounded who fell were trampled by their fellow soldiers to lie unmoving on the carpet of grass.

The heavy drum beats that accompanied the southern troops sounded over and over as they advanced toward the men of Karbel one steady step at a time. A determined looking block of pikes filled the middle of the Legion line. It was heavily supported by shield- and sword-bearing infantry and was forward of the main line by nearly two hundred feet.

The Alush commander saw this and wondered what his opposite number could be thinking, it would be easy to crush this group and further improve the odds against him. It would also serve to demoralize the rest of the soldiers arrayed along the hills. The ploy was so obvious that he didn't see it for what it was.

He ordered the two middle sections of his infantry to close on and destroy the block of pikes, just as Tal hoped he would. Colored flags snapped as they were twisted and waved to pass along the orders. The mass of infantry changed directions slightly to comply with the orders leaving a gap in the Alush line which would be important later on.

As the enemy marched closer and closer the commander of the Third battalion signaled his men. When he judged the time right, a double horn call sounded. The sword bearing infantry which had been waiting behind the pikemen rushed forward along both sides of the pike blocks which were twin formations sixty men wide and eight deep that now stepped together forming a solid front. Five ranks of pikes were lowered as one, presenting a bristling wall to the southerners who were still coming straight on toward them. The sword and shield men now in position formed a deep U shape around the pikemen. Once in place they locked shields and drew their swords. Their backs were to the phalanx so that they faced outward, a grim brisling hedge of sharpened steel, sunlight glinting from many a sharp edge.

The remaining three rows of pikemen, separated from the rear of their kind by nearly ten paces hefted their weapons and awaited the word. Tension was thick and heavy but the men stood steady awaiting the now nearby enemy.

The commander of the Third battalion, positioned astride his horse just behind the pike block watched as the enemy infantry approached and knew it was time to spring the little surprise he and Tal had planned earlier. He signaled a trumpeter who quickly lifted his horn and sounded a different two-note call.

Before the echo of the second note could fade the rear three ranks of pikers, three hundred sixty men in all, stepped forward and hurled their weapons, long javelins, toward the approaching infantry blocks. This was a different tactic than what was usually done. The sword men usually handled the javelins but Tal felt that timing was too critical so the pikemen did it this time. If the sword carriers had done it then they would not have been time for them to resume their formation around the pike block and the entire unit could have been lost.

The invading troops were caught by surprise as the iron tipped wood shafts fell like a heavy obscene rain. The approaching infantry tried to raise their shields to ward off the missiles. But unlike the men of Karbel who carried curved, heavy, nearly man size shields, the Alush carried much smaller round bucklers which failed them badly, being better suited for fending off sword blows.

The long iron rods backed by a heavy wooden shaft punched right through the shields or missed them completely to find purchase in flesh. Whole sections of one approaching infantry formation were sundered by the first flight of the missiles. Many of the southern troops were merely wounded but they were unable to continue forward and that was as good as killing them.

A second flight of the deadly weapons was launched right after the first and they too found many targets. Many of those who had been wounded by the first flight now went to join their ancestors as new wounds presented themselves, one man staggered about screaming wildly, a javelin lodged in his head. The long iron shaft was tainted red. He screamed and screamed until someone cut his throat to shut him up.

Parts of the enemy infantry formations were ragged and uneven as they tried to continue forward. What officers that survived were struggling to get the men in line and fill up the spaces left by the deadly missiles.

More of the wounded were trampled by their fellows as they continued forward to strike at the Legionnaires. Shafts of metal tipped death continued to rain down. Dressing their ranks as best as possible, the proud Alush continued forward, cursing the Legionnaires for cowards grimly determined to repay the blood debt.

The weight of the wooden shaft served to bend the iron shaft once the missile struck something solid which prevented their use by an enemy, so the invaders suffered terrible numbers of casualties with no way to repay the blood. Grim faced southern tribesmen tightened their grip on sword and axe as they marched toward the men of Karbel now close enough to see each man's face clearly.

The shafts had torn up the blocks that formed the middle of the approaching line but had not done damage to the wings of the formation that now made contact with the locked shields of the sword bearing infantry positioned around the pikes, as they tried to crush the block. The push forward by the Alush was brutal and was met with grim determination by the men of Karbel who knew full well the odds against them.

The Legionnaires too had a debt to collect on and southern blood was the coine they demanded. The press of the southern forces was fierce as each of them tried to pay back the gift of the javelins. Blood ran freely on both sides of the line as the contest for control of the battle raged. If you were wounded your choice was simple, fight on or die. There was no time or energy to deal with anyone who was hurt.

The third battalion commander signaled the trumpeter again who blew a four note call then repeated it twice to ensure that it would be heard of the din of the battle. This ordered his unit to commence the second part of their planned action. Javelins now began to rain down steadily on the enemy infantry fighting along the flanks but several ranks behind those engaged with his sword bearers.

This served to try and isolate sections of the forward ranks of the Alush and deny them the advantage of numbers they enjoyed. A steady drum beat kept the air filled with a heavy sound to mix with the shouts, screams and horn calls. The wings of the formation were now passing the pike block in the center of the line and moving steadily toward the main Legion position.

Tal, who had been watching the advancing infantry very carefully, now unleashed another of his surprises. He signaled one of the trumpeters that were always near his side. The rider lifted his horn and blew a series of long calls that were repeated three times to guarantee that the intended party got the message.

The right flank catapults responded first followed immediately by those on the left. The catapult crews quickly changed their ammunition from rocks to more clay jugs of the flammable liquids. Once this was done and the jugs were in the basket the artillery men lit the top of the jug from a nearby torch readied for just such a time. The arms were then released and the flaming jugs were hurled into the area that had been presoaked with flammables earlier.

When the clay pots landed and broke they ignited the grass with a vomitus roar and a great flash of heat that burned many of the nearby troops to death. Huge billows of smoke immediately rose into the air from both fire beds as a wide swath of flame roared into life along both flanks. This cut off the southern cavalry and forced some of the approaching infantry back.

In several places men who had marched through the flammables were now themselves burning as the fire rapidly spread. From his vantage point on the hill Tal would see some of these running about in agony as the flames ate at their flesh. Smoke poured into the sky, black and oily, blocking the view of the Alush archers who had been moving up to support the infantry attack.

The veteran Legion commander knew that the sight of burning men running wildly about would demoralize some of the others and that would work for him too. If a man was concerned about anything other than what was directly in front of him, at that exact moment he was vulnerable.

The flames and smoke broke apart several large formations of the enemy infantry which allowed his front line units to concentrate their full attention on the men they were engaging. Several sub-unit leaders used their own initiative to move their men forward and strike at the southern line exacting a terrible price then melting back into line.

The Legion archers were now having a serious effect on selected areas of the approaching troops forward of the fire. The powerful composite bows that the men of Rhywe used were falling men with every shot it seemed, the metal tipped shafts punching through armor to find warm flesh beneath.

Tal swept the field again with his eyes to check the progress of his soldiers; time for the next move in his plan. He knew that gaining and keeping the momentum in this fight was vital, if he allowed his opposite number to dictate the battle then he and his men would likely lose. Time seemed to ebb and flow as the battle raged. Sounds of shouts, curses and the constant ring of steel on steel could be heard across the battlefield.

After earlier receiving word that the watering of the horses was finished, Tal had ordered his cavalry, all of it, to move around to the north side of his formation which placed it on to the left of the Legion line. Much of it had remained behind the hill to keep it hidden from view until it was needed. He ordered it forward now.

The third battalion was still holding its own in the center of the line against the blocks of infantry trying to swarm it under. The veteran troops would lunge forward one step, their pikes pressing the enemy back and then after each lunge back up two steps. This had the effect of forcing the advancing Alush to bunch up and intermix their units while trying to get at the pikemen, as well as to draw them closer to the ranks of Legion infantry that lined the hills now just seventy paces away.

The flanks of the pike blocks supported by the heavy line of swordsmen on either side kept the southern infantry at bay. Steel flashed repeatedly along the lines as the two sides clashed. Many of the Alush were down with more joining them. No quarter was asked or given on either side. The movement was acting like a vacuum drawing more of the enemy into the center away from the flames and into the strength of the Legion line. More of the incendiary bombs landed among the advancing infantry wreaking havoc and death with each blast of chemically-fueled fire.

The Alush commander didn't like what he saw. His infantry was stalling, parts of the formation were farther forward than others and so they presented no firm front to the Legion while flames had cut off other sections of his command. He couldn't order his archers to fire for fear of striking his own troops. Smoke from the fires denied him the ability to see what was happening in some areas.

One of his aides rushed over and pointed excitedly. The general shifted his gaze and to his horror saw a large number of enemy cavalry pouring over the hills on his right in a wide formation. They were a rolling mass of hooves and armor and aimed straight at his unsupported right flank which was stalled due to the fire. His own cavalry was deployed far to his left and so for the moment useless against this new threat. He cursed soundly and signaled for a trumpeter to order some of his units to shift directions to handle the cavalry.

The wide arc of Legion cavalry was still coming over the hill and gaining speed as part of the Legion left flank came in contact with the Alush -- who were now disorganized due to the work of the Third Battalion which had back stepped its way to rejoin the rest of the unit. A solid mass of pikes and swords tore into the enemy infantry while arrows and more javelins rained down killing dozens in every volley. The work was bloody as men on both sides of the steel fell.

More heavy infantry pushed forward to strike at the Legion line as the weight of Alush began to be felt along Tal's entire front. This was in spite of the flames which were dying out in places and left gaps that some of southerners leapt through to get at the men of Karbel.

The bulk of those from the south was wider than the Legion line and in places ambitious unit commanders ordered their men to curl in and strike the sides of the waiting formation to try and envelope the men of Karbel just as had been done to the Second earlier by one of the other columns.

Archers, lofting their shafts from high up on the hills, were continuing to take a terrible toll on the tightly packed mass below, the heavy shafts sometimes passing through one man into other. Shouts and screams mixed in the air with the sharp clash of metal on metal.

The Alush commander was still having a hard time seeing what was happening to his men, the smoke from the fires lay thick in places. He shouted for his horse and it was brought forward instantly. Lithely swinging into the saddle the commander gathered up his aides and other staff by eye and they rode forward to try and obtain a better view and regain control of the battle.

The Legion cavalry raked the extreme right side of the invaders line like a scythe felling wheat. Many a long lance came away bloody as Karbel rode along. Once clear of their charge the first sections peeled off to dress their line and swing back in the opposite direction and catch the flank again. This also served to shield the Legion left from the other columns which proved unnecessary as they continued marching north.

Pon was unconcerned with the action of a single Legion; he had manpower enough to absorb the losses and then some. The dead ate very little and made their supply situation easier. He ordered Vinshee to deploy some cavalry to their rear and was informed that this was already done. The Marshal of the Host merely nodded and kept riding, their goal was ahead not behind.

As the Alush commander and his staff rode through the smoke, a section of cavalry suddenly appeared before them. Recognition took little time; the riders wore the red and tan of Karbel. Swords were swept out of the southern scabbards as the two groups came together amid shouts and curses. The southerners were far outnumbered but fought bravely.

A few moments was all it took and with the loss of their commander the advantage truly turned to the men of Karbel. Two of the riders stopped and dismounted, once down they ran over to where the body of the fallen general lay and lifted the torn and bloody Alush battle flag from the grass along with one of the captured standards from the Second Legion.

The men of the south had been bearing it alongside their own as a way of shaming those they had crushed earlier. It was necessary to pry it from the hand of his aide but the man didn't mind, he was minus his head. The pair ran back with their prizes intent on getting them to their own general as soon as possible, along with word regarding the fallen commander. The veteran sergeant in charge of the platoon immediately ordered them all to withdraw and report to the command post. They spun their mounts and headed off to the west to loop around the fighting still taking place and report their news.

Tal had been watching carefully, judging when the time was right to order the withdrawal. His men had exceeded his expectations; they had dealt the invaders a serious blow. There had never been any intent to take on all of the columns. The Fifth would have suffered the same fate as the Second and for nothing.

This way he had returned the favor with interest. It was now more important to ensure that his unit survived as a fighting force. Help was coming but not yet. Now he had to disengage from this fight to get ready for the next one. He waved for a trumpeter.

Chapter Forty-One
Bed Rest

Karbel

The wounds on his neck were bringing about less pain but the burned area was still causing a good deal of discomfort. Bolgar suspected that would be the case for some time. Someone from the hospital staff had been in to check on his injuries not long before.

The Arakai found that his curiosity about his situation was growing. The fear he felt, fear that he would never admit to even under pain of death at being tortured for information, was slowly fading. For some reason those in authority wanted him alive and well.

The former Ri'al commander was certain this was simply a different method of getting at what he knew. He reminded himself to be wary of their trickery. Those who served the Varshon had been given extensive briefings about the cunning and viciousness of those in the north as well as the cruelty of the ruling class.

Bolgar was very well acquainted with how the Arakai and the Varshon dealt with prisoners; torture was often used to extract information. He expected no less of his captors now that the invasion of the north was well underway.

Bolgar could move around the small but airy room he occupied which he did as often as possible to help stave off the boredom. He did physical exercises several times a day to keep his fitness up which also helped to kill some time. The forced inactivity was hard on him; Bolgar was used to being very active. This confinement was wearing on him.

Soon after being brought in, one of the staff had told him he was not to leave the room, or at least that is what he imagined she was saying. The language barrier was still a problem but he was slowly learning the basics of the Karbel speech. He was certain that he wasn't going to be allowed to just walk around wherever he wanted to, so being told to stay put was a mere formality.

A pair of guards was posted outside in the corridor; hard looking men who seemed quite acquainted with violence. Bolgar expected nothing less. They handled themselves and their weapons and other equipment with a level of experience and skill, this had brought a nod of respect from the Arakai the second day after he was moved to the private room. He knew professionals when he saw them.

This caused him to think again on the Striker, that term he had already picked up on during the ride north to the enemy capital, who had commanded the defense of the village. A worthy opponent for sure, the craftiest he had ever encountered.

The man had ensured that his wounds had been treated and throughout their travel away from the frontier went out of his way to see that he had been treated respectfully, even at one point physically placing himself between several soldiers and his wounded prisoner. The proud soldiers were angry and seeing one of the enemy close at hand brought that anger to the front. Several other Strikers backed their officer up before the Legionnaires could reach him.

Bolgar had been forced to admit that he had received far better treatment than he would have given the Striker if their roles had been reversed. That realization had been slow in coming as well as a bit painful when it did. A strong sense of honor was one of the main character traits that he had always prided himself but the Arakai found it somewhat unsettling to realize that he might not have done what this Striker had.

Rising from the bed, he once again traced his steps over to the window to look out on the view. He didn't bother checking again to see if there was a way to break out of his captivity. He had already explored the room and situation carefully. There was only the single door which was locked from the other side and no possibility of escape via the window. He was on the third floor of the building so jumping was out of the question and there was nothing at all within reach on the outside wall that he could potentially utilize to scale down, even if he could remove the bars on the window. His captors had thought of that ahead of time.

The sun was passing from overhead toward afternoon. A few clouds were scattered here and there but it was comfortably warm with a slight but steady breeze coming in the open window. The hospital section he was in overlooked a small park and what appeared to be a barracks of some type. He had observed numerous men dressed similar to what the Strikers had been wearing, so he surmised that it was one of theirs. He was in fact correct but had no way of knowing that for certain.

A hard knock on the door, just prior to the lock bar being slid, turned his attention from the window. The door was opened by one of the guards who immediately sized up where the single occupant was located prior to entering the room. Seeing that he was near the window and so several paces away, he entered. It wasn't fear but respect for what the man was capable of. He was an enemy combatant, a commander at that so being mindful of that was only good sense.

Close on the heels of the guard was one of the physicians who had been treating his wounds. The second guard was not far behind the healer. He moved off to the side so that the two protectors were flanking the doctor who was oblivious to what they were doing.

Bolgar was watching the entrance of the men with a casual expression carried on his face but his mind was taking in the details. So far he had not been able to spot a weakness in how it was done but he was certain that at some point he would and that hope kept his spirits up. He had every intention of escaping and returning to the south and home. During the trip to the capital city he had managed to pull together a wide variety of scraps of information both military and economic that he would be able to pass along to his superiors. Besides that, escaping was his duty. It was part of the Arakai code of conduct, duty was always and ever the first call.

The healer was a man of middle height with an ample waistline and a ready smile. He had also been working with Bolgar on language skills as he had time since it was a hobby of his. The physician could speak conversational Merlik, Common, and even a few phrases in the thick Dwarf tongue. The former Ri'al commander was sure this was merely to make it easier to interrogate him. He went along with the ploy, being able to speak some of the northern tongue would make it easier on him once he was able to escape. There were some in the south that could speak the language but never enough so it would be something else he would be able to bring with him on his return. He absently wondered if he would be given command of another Ri'al before turning his full attention to his visitors.

The physician with the rather grandiose first name of Rathelmos due to having two parents with a rather self-inflated perception of their own social standing, smiled pleasantly at the patient. When he had first been brought in he was suffering from not only the burns but some fever related to the wounds. They had gotten him cleaned up then tackled the fever bringing it under control in two days while doing what they could for the burns. Unfortunately there was nothing they could do about the extensive scarring on the man's neck but he was still alive so that was something.

He had been intrigued when he was told who and what the patient was. It was also made clear to the healer that it was very important that the man survive. Rathelmos had been a little put out at hearing that from the senior Striker officer. He was a healer, making sure that people survived was what he had dedicated his life to and to have that, as well as his professional competence questioned, irked him. If they didn't want the man to live, why bring him to the hospital in the first place? *Typical military thinking*, he had mused.

Rathelmos repeated the words of greetings he used every day. The Arakai had taken to trying to mimic those words as a way of learning the uncouth language of the north. Listening to the accent that his patient had was endlessly fascinated to the healer. It wasn't like any other inflection that he had ever come across before in his life.

Both of the guards remained silent vigils during the exchange, it was the same each time the man came to see the prisoner. Better to keep quiet, being able to observe any errant movements that the man might make. Gods above knew that the healer wouldn't see it coming until it was over by a good while.

Waving the man toward the bed Rathelmos politely waited until he was seated to step forward to examine his burns once again. Less red areas than before, good sign. He gently probed the edges of the scar tissue noting the reaction which was always less than before. Bolgar knew the routine by now. He worked at decreasing his reaction to the wounds a little bit each time as a way of increasing the level of complacency that his healer felt. It was a small step but it was one of the few things that the proud Ri'al leader had some measure of control over, so he was working to exploit it to whatever gain it might bring him.

Determining that the wounds were healing nicely the healer stepped back nodding while he pointed at the neck area so that Bolgar could see what he was doing. He explained that he was pleased with what he was seeing. Comprehension was a bit slow in coming but it did come to which the patient nodded once in understanding causing the good doctor to beam, his efforts at teaching the man to learn the language were paying off.

Telling him that he would check on him later, Rathelmos turned from the man abruptly then went to the door impatiently waiting for one of the guards to open it for him. One of them did, doing his best to keep the prisoner fully in sight as he did so. Once he had the door opened the doctor exited without a word of thanks. The guard furthest from the door moved over to where his partner was then stopped next to him to allow the one who had opened the door to leave the room first. In that manner at no time was one of them stepping in front of the other which would cause a momentary blind spot. They knew to be cautious.

Once they were both outside, the lock bar was slid back in place with a solid sound. Bolgar rose from the bed crossing back over to window to continue looking outside slowly repeating the words that the doctor had used trying to get them just right and burned into his memory. He was determined to escape from this place.

Just because he hadn't found a way yet didn't mean there wasn't one.

Chapter Forty-Two
Saddle Sore

North of Karbel

The ride north to the fortress was grueling, endless mile upon mile of grassland broken by only scattered groups of trees and hills. They didn't even see any farms or hamlets; this part of the large continent was essentially unsettled.

The group from Karbel had decided to take a course that would keep them on the extreme eastern edge of Federation Clan territory despite the need for speed. The reasoning was that if any of the clansmen caught sight of several hundred heavily armed troops from Karbel they would likely attack which could delay the group or worse keep them from reaching G'mar at all – unacceptable, so the extra miles were a compromise.

It was a concession that Gunnar was regretting. He was sore and saddle weary but they had no choice but to press on despite personal discomfort made worse by the pace they were riding. Several times before crossing out of Karbel the group exchanged horses so that the fresh mounts could be ridden hard to make the journey in as little time as possible. At the northern edge of the kingdom there was a large selection of horses waiting for them, these were marshaled north with them to provide a remount for everyone as well as the wagon teams.

Sleep was another issue; the men were only averaging about five hours of sleep a day which was beginning to show. Gunnar had spoken with Captain Nahn regarding that. The Striker made the case that despite the necessity for speed due to the unknown deadline, that arriving worn out and mentally fatigued wouldn't do them any good much less anyone else. It was too important.

The longtime advisor to the king realized that the man was correct. He told Nahn that when they got close he would stop them to allow for one, he emphasized the *one*, full night's sleep. That was as much of a concession on the subject as Gunnar was willing to make to which the officer agreed.

The tired northman knew that the weariness was temporary and in the grand scheme of all that was taking place it was a very minor concern. He and the others were all that were available to try and stop these Varshon from completing their ceremony so making the time to allow everyone to rest was a necessary risk.

As they continued riding north he reviewed what he knew of the route they were using to help pass the time. They had left the capital heading north to Edora using the river, mounted up there then began the long ride. They had changed horses several times to allow them to travel rapidly. Sticking to the roads of the kingdom helped to ease their passage but once they reached the edge of the frontier it was open grasslands for miles and miles.

They were riding east of what they knew to be Federation territory. Before departing the capital Levas, Gunnar, Allence and a few of the Strikers from the patrol that had found the northmen had spent several hours in deep study of every map they could find in the palace that showed the slightest bit of detail regarding their anticipated route and destination. As they looked over the charts additional questions were raised so some of the histories and notes were sent for from the university. The request for the written materials was accompanied by a summons for the senior researchers to bring the materials themselves so that they could be consulted. While the group waited for the information from the university to arrive the discussion went back and forth regarding the route that they should take to the north.

Vode was feeling much the same as Gunnar despite his traveling conditions being much more comfortable than those making the trip on horseback. In truth he was forced to admit to himself that it was much more than the mild inconvenience of riding in the plush carriage, it was the fear of what they would find when they reached the ancient fortress. Would the enemy already be there? Would the ceremony have taken place and if so would it then be too late?

The High Priest was worried about these Varshon, no one knew any details about them, how strong their majic was, what manner of spells and incantations they could conjure and so many more unknowns but they had no choice but to continue on. Vode settled deeper into his seat as he turned his gaze to the view out the window allowing his mind to wander just a bit.

Allence was still unsure about their entire mission but said nothing of her doubts to anyone. The trip from Vankard had been a mix of emotions; the loss of so many of her men had been a sharp blow to her. Her family had long been soldiers, the line going back for many generations. Her ascent into the officer ranks of the Thunderguards had not been an easy one but she had worked hard, proven herself and so when the opportunity to serve on this expedition came she stepped forward.

Thindor Norstaad himself had spoken to her privately for nearly an hour about the journey. For the Warlord of Vankard to take the time to speak to her as he did meant a great deal to her and always would. The two had discussed the requirements, logistics, manpower and most importantly her duty to Vode.

When the High Priest had been wounded during the ambush she felt her heart drop. Vode was her responsibility and if the Strikers had not come along then she wasn't sure if they would have been able to survive the attack -- ending their already meager change of stopping the enemy ceremony.

When she thought about the Strikers her first thoughts often seemed to be about the patrol leader, the one named T'shar. When she realized how often she thought about him she chided herself for the girlish thoughts but over time she came to see him in a different light. Quiet, confident, handsome even rugged looking, was it possible she was beginning to have genuine feelings for him?

When they were in the capital city she had gone looking for some of her men, when she came across them doing some weapons drills with T'shar and a few of the other Strikers. She was able to watch him without his awareness of it as he handled the blade, explaining a few techniques to the group. He was very proficient with the sword; Allence watched for some time before slipping away.

She had later asked Mehan about it when she and Levas were having dinner with Finn. He explained as best he could with the language issue that T'shar was the finest swordsman in all of the Strikers, describing the long hours he spent training with all manner of weapons. After making the declaration he paused for moment then told them that if he had to describe his friend he would call him a weapons master.

It took Levas a few moments to work through the term but he kept at relating to his countrymen the concept behind the words. She picked up on it not disagreeing with the assessment based on what she had seen of his fighting and then teaching.

Shaking her thoughts free of the good looking soldier for a bit, Allence took a long look at the area they were riding through. Nothing to see of note but more grass, two low hills about two leagues to the northwest and some scattered trees. The weather was on their side it would seem. It had rained on them the second day after leaving Karbel but since then it had been clear and dry which only helped their progress.

She and the remaining Thunderguards were riding on either side of the coaches that were carrying Vode and Levas as well as the other priests. She and her men were, in turn, flanked by a number of the Strikers. Gunnar was up near the front of the formation with the senior officer.

Each morning the command group had a short meeting to discuss anything that need to be taken care of, outline the travel route for the day, and so on. This morning's meeting had been a little longer than any of the others, save the very first one. Knowing that they were now getting close to that G'mar place the discussion had gone back and forth about what the actual plan regarding how they would handle the attack if the enemy was already in place or what defense they would try to use if they arrived first.

All of them acknowledged that, because they didn't know which situation they would find when they arrived, that caution should be their best approach. Once they arrived at the southern end of the pass they would send scouts forward then once the way was clear move to the northern end, repeating the process with the scouts to clear the area between the pass and the fortress.

Once at the northern end of the pass they should be able to determine what their next course of action was. For not the first time,

Allence was happy about having several hundred Strikers with them.

It had been something of a bitter surprise to her when about six days earlier she had realized how poorly prepared the group from Vankard had been in setting out on the mission. What they should have done is brought a much larger contingent of soldiers and supplies. *We had been both very naïve and arrogant to think we could just venture out into the world we literally knew nothing about, travel to the fortress defeat these Varshon and then happily traipse back home, stupid of us.* Part of her was wondering if they had enough men with them now but it was too late to worry about it, much too late.

Hours passed as more miles fell away behind them bringing them all that much closer to the entrance to the pass. Gunnar had announced at the morning gathering that they would likely be there the day after tomorrow so it would be important to have additional flank guards and outriders sent out to make sure that they would not be surprised.

The Striker Captain – uh, Nahn, *why could she not remember his name?* Anyway, he told the northman that had already been ordered and that the men were in place. Gunnar had nodded his thanks to the professionalism of the man. Allence was impressed in spite of her own socially induced reluctance to embrace the Utland and those who lived in it.

Having been told from birth that all that lay beyond the mountain gate was evil, she was still hesitant to admit that wasn't the case at all. Certainly the trouble they had while still in Federation of Clans territory -- she had learned the name after arriving in Karbel -- had done nothing to change her opinion. Once they had begun dealing with the Strikers and by extension Karbel the complete opposite had been the case.

Her mind kept turning over all the mix of emotions, sights and sounds they had encountered while she absently reached for one of her water bags, she was thirsty. Taking in some of the lukewarm liquid helped to rewet her mouth and made her feel a bit better. She retied the bag to her kit as they continued moving.

In the lead coach Vode was talking with Levas about some of the ramifications of the journey so far. Of all the northmen it was Levas who had been the most impacted by the travel beyond his home. The senior acolyte had always been a forward thinker, more accepting of new concepts and ideas than many of his peers. When the need to travel to

G'mar became apparent he was secretly excited. Growing up, he had often wondered what life in the Utland was like. He had been careful to not scoff openly at the notion that everything outside of Vankard was bad. If that was the case then would not the evil have overwhelmed their kingdom as well?

When they had been taken from Edora down the river to the capital city he had been taking in the scenes as often as he was free from his duties to Vode. This was truly a once in a lifetime opportunity that he wanted to gather as much from as he could. Riding into Karbel from the docks he and Vode could scarcely believe what their eyes were showing them.

The soaring building, some of them five stories high, the incredible throngs of people, even people of different colors and twice he had seen Elves!! He had thought at one time in his life that he would never see an Elf and there right in front of him had been a pair of them having a conversation with one of the shopkeepers along the street. It appeared to him to be an ordinary, everyday conversation -- it wasn't until later after the surprise and wonder of seeing the members of the Elder Race faded that it occurred to Levas that it was an ordinary event here in Karbel. It turned out that what was normal in one place wasn't all that common in every area.

Discovering that the use of majic was unknown to much of the people of the world was also a bit of a shock. He had been asked by Vode to inquire if it would be possible to consult with Karbel's majic users and after doing so was told there weren't any, none. It was a complete fact of life in Vankard that majic was there to be used as necessary. Drought was unknown in their country; if an area was overly dry then a group of priests would summon rain to help the farmers with their crops, if a fire broke out then the majic users would be called on to help extinguish it if they were available, and so much more. Upon being told there were no majic users it made Levas feel a bit out of place, different from those around him in a way that was hard to define even for himself.

Vode was attempting to deal with some of the administrative issues that went along with being the head of a large order of priests. There were transfers, promotions, requests for new buildings, and on and on. The men had of course not dragged the files along when they traveled but Levas possessed a keen memory which allowed him to serve the High Priest well.

Both men knew that what they were doing may be pointless, neither may survive what was coming but it at least gave them a way to pass the time as they rode.

"Yes I agree that the chapel at Blaganth needs to be enlarged, but he is asking for an entire new chapel capable of seating what seems to be the entire population of the region!" Levas smiled as his superior vented a bit, the senior priest in that area of the country had a reputation as being rather full of himself -- the request for the new chapel had less to do with needing a new building, which they did, versus having a bigger, newer chapel than many of his contemporaries. The conversation went back and forth on the topic.

Near the front of the formation Nahn was debating whether or not to send out even more scouts. He had been pleased when he had told Gunnar that morning that he already had anticipated the need for more security. The orders he had gotten from Colonel Steele had been perfectly clear. It was his responsibility to make sure that the mission succeeded. *Win or don't come home* wasn't said but it sure read that way to him. He wasn't terribly worried about it on one hand because if the mission failed he figured he and his men would all be dead so it wouldn't matter. He settled on not sending out more scouts for now but in a self-compromise agreed that it didn't mean he couldn't send more later on.

Meanwhile they continued north…

Chapter Forty-Three
A Little Side Trip

South West of Toras

The main body of Karbel's army was moving a bit south of east heading to intercept the invasion force when the command group who were riding with the king were surprised when he suddenly reigned in his mount. He brought his horse to a slow walk before stopping.

Steele shared a look with Tal and Dwyn neither of whom had any more answers than the Striker. Thadar looked deep in thought as if he was wrestling with an idea that was trying to get out but playing at hard to get.

The king looked to those who he depended upon, a decision firmly in place in his mind. "Send another scouting group out, a fast group; we have to know what is going on, this is wrong. They are not making sense with these attacks, why move to attack Toras? Why not Karbel itself?" The king shook his head. "No, this is wrong. It does them no good to attack one of the cities when we know that their goal is G'mar."

The others shared a glance between them and then looked upon their leader. Thadar saw the look and with a small note of exasperation present in his voice tried to further explain, "Do you not see? This invasion is not designed to conquer territory, it is intended to tie *us* down, the army...."

He left the sentence unfinished as recognition of the ploy sank in and the others realized the extent of the situation. They had all allowed themselves to think of the enemy force in a single dimension, an invading army. Thanks to Vode they were aware of the true objective, now they were out here in eastern Karbel slugging it out with the mass of southern troops when the real threat all along has been far to the north at G'mar.

Steele jerked his reins over to the side and urged his mount to a run as soon as he could. He was shouting for several of his senior officers which hurried to meet him. Thadar was suddenly hoping that the extra forces he had told Steele to send with Gunnar would be enough. How could he have been so stupid?

The longtime ruler of Karbel was extremely angry with himself; he had been given the information but had chosen to only see what he wanted to. Yes, the invasion force was a real concern but it wasn't the primary concern. Taking a few deep breaths, he tried to regain his focus. He grudgingly gave the enemy credit; they had managed to fool him.

Steele ordered that four groups of Strikers to head out immediately; Tal was doing nearly the identical thing with his own men, the more scouts out there the better. Thadar had three full strength Legions and a healthy amount of reserves totaling almost another full Legion with him so overall he felt that they were in good shape to deal with the invaders – and that was not counting the Strikers that were along which numbered over three thousand.

Despite being surrounded by thousands of his soldiers the king of Karbel was feeling very alone and isolated at the moment. The responsibility for the safety of his subjects and the realm rested with him, and Thadar was very upset with himself for not handling the crisis properly. All that they, and more to the point *he*, had done since learning of the invasion was react.

The enemy was controlling the pace of the entire invasion. Thadar realized that he had done exactly nothing to change that dynamic. He had let his anger and pride get in the way, these people had invaded his kingdom and it offended him so his reaction was like that of a youth. You hit me, I hit you in return.

His fury at the situation was almost more than he could bear. Thadar possessed a strong temper but he had never been angrier in his entire life than he was at that moment. Consciously slowing down his breathing the sole male Skye worked hard at gaining some measure of control. Focus, what Thadar needed was to focus on what they must do next, he had to think. The king nudged the horse a little to move the two of them away from the group.

Tal started to follow but Thadar held up one hand to signal his desire to remain alone. The Legion Marshal stopped his mount to allow his son-in-law the private time he desired.

For his part Tal, too, was a very unhappy man. The longtime soldier had fallen into the same trap as his king, only seeing the invasion as a one dimension threat. His Legions had been slow to effectively respond to the invasion, the low point of which was the serious casualties inflicted on the Second which had suffered enough losses to render the Legion combat ineffective. The Eleventh which had responsibility for the border had been brushed aside; they were now following the massive invasion force but had been unable to effect the enemy in any meaningful way. And now he and other senior officers had all been made to realize that the thrice cursed pox ridden southerners had suckered them. Tal was a more than a bit unhappy, with good reason.

Moving away from the others gave Thadar at least the illusion of some privacy and space which was hard to achieve given that he was amidst a sea consisting of thousands and thousands of his men. He had managed to throttle his emotions somewhat which was slowly giving way to clearer thinking, Thadar tried to analyze the entire situation but it was still too personally near for him to do it objectively, he would need some help.

With a jerk of the reins he spun his horse about to bring him back to the command group. Tal and the others didn't have to wait long for their ruler to speak, as he pulled up he looked at the group which consisted of Tal, the generals commanding the three Legions, Dwyn and several senior officers from both the army and the Strikers. Steele had not yet rejoined them.

"We know this is an elaborate attempt at misdirection. What do we know about the situation, the whole situation?" Tal speaking for the others began to outline what information they had. The Black Guard had been investigating reports of strange activity in the area well south of the river; they had lost contact with one of the patrols then found some survivors who reported on those that had attacked them. Another patrol was sent south to try to determine what was taking place. Thadar was nodding as each point of fact was repeated, for some of those present this was the first time they were hearing details about what had happened leading up to this point.

Tal continued reviewing the information – contact was lost with the follow up patrol as well. Word had come in from one of the outposts on the D'Lohm border from a Striker unit who had engaged what was believed to be the lead elements of a large invasion force. Balkon had disregarded the information – Thadar scowled at the mention of the former Legion Marshal's name but said nothing as his senior general spoke further. This information was confirmed when the survivors of the follow up Black Guard patrol, who had slipped through the invasion force, met the Striker unit. That unit had helped defend an Elven village then they had made their way to an operational message station sending word to the capital of the invasion the following day.

At about the same time, the group from Vankard had brought word to the capital of what they had learned regarding the Varshon plans to conduct some type of majical ceremony that would allow them to increase their majical ability by a significant degree, the long term goal being to overrun the world.

The king was listening intently not speaking since he had asked the initial question. The High Priest and a sizable escort were dispatched to the location where the ceremony was to take place to try and stop it. As the invasion force continued to move north they encountered the lead Legion units brushing them aside. A call up of all reserves and military units was ordered then several Legions were sent east to stop the invasion force which was where they were at now.

Once he was certain that Tal was finished speaking Thadar addressed those present, "First I want to apologize to all of you – I made some decisions that were based on personal feelings and not what was best for the realm. That was my mistake and my responsibility. All of you deserve better from your king and he is truly sorry." No one said anything for a few moments until Dwyn, who had been silent the entire time, spoke up.

"It is a man of strength who admits he was wrong. It is a king who must bear the weight of ruling so many. You have done it well for many years and will continue to do so." He bowed his head while placing his fist over his heart in the manner of the Elves, the others present all saluted in the appropriate manner as well.

Thadar was humbled to be in the presence of such men and to be able to command them. He promised himself that he would never make another such mistake as this one, as he proudly returned their salutes telling himself to do better, be worthy of these men and so many others.

Listening to the chronological list of events raised several questions for the king who posed the first one to the group "What is the purpose of the enemy invasion force?"

Dwyn was the first to speak telling the group the purpose was to escort the majic users north to G'mar. Thadar nodded his agreement, his anger of earlier now moving behind him as he worked out the enemy plan.

"True but that is not the only reason. If need be they could have simply slipped over the borders in secret to make the journey."

Tal picked up the line of thought –"I agree, sire, but if they did that, then they would be a world away from their own forces. I'll be the first one to admit my complete lack of knowledge when it comes to the use of majic but I don't care how much majic you can fling about if there are enough people against you then you'll fail."

There were several nods of agreement then Thadar presented another question, "So if the enemy goal is to reach G'mar, then why are they moving toward the northeast away from where we know they need to go?"

One of the Legion commanders then spoke up telling his king that if the enemy's goal was to misdirect our forces then by appearing to threaten one of the kingdom's cities they know we would have to react to that movement.

Hearing the key point in what the man said the king snapped his fingers then pointed at him to emphasize the moment. "General you are absolutely correct, *by appearing to threaten* is the entire point. We know what their goal is but if we did not then it would make total sense to us for them to move toward one of our major cities would it not?"

Several quick nods of agreement solidified the thought for him.

"So knowing that their movement to the northeast is a feint what is our next move?"

Tal spoke for the group, "Sire I recommend that we stop and wait right here." He pointed one finger straight down to emphasize the suggestion. That was an intriguing idea which appealed to Thadar. It would allow them to consolidate their own forces on ground of their choosing, and it could also force the southerners to react to what *they* were doing for a change, in place of it being the other way around as it had been since the invasion had begun. Yes that was their best option.

"General Lyn, order our troops to stop and hold position immediately." Tal and the other generals all saluted then rode off to carry out the king's orders.

Shortly after that Steele returned to the king's side. Thadar looked over at his chief protector; the two having been together long enough that there was a level of unspoken communication between them. Steele knew that Thadar wanted to hear about what he had just checked on.

"Sir, there be several large scouting parties now on the way -- south, east, and northeast to check on what the southies are up to. Tal sent scouting parties as well plus what we already had out so we'll know for sure within a fair time."

He absently rubbed the neck of his horse while explaining to the king what had taken place. What he didn't tell Thadar was that he had also ordered several formations of Strikers to close in around where the king was so that he was further protected. Steele knew that the Legion troops they were in the midst of were a very strong barrier but he was taking no chances at all with the life of the king or his family for that matter.

After the assassination attempt several ten-days prior he had increased not only the garrison at the palace and in the capital but the size of the protective details for the king, the queen, his mother and both of his sisters. Neither Avila or Thirea made a fuss at all but Darnella was fit to be tied, she already felt that a half dozen heavily armed men around her all the time was far too intrusive, so when Steele added an additional four bodyguards to the detail she was mad enough to spit teeth. She confronted him about it using very unladylike language to express her displeasure with the matter.

For his part Steele had fully been expecting the visit and the tirade. He allowed her to rant and rave to her heart's content taking no offense at her words. The Strikers were responsible for the safety of the royal family and that was all that mattered to him. Once she was done Darnella stormed out of his office questioning his parentage in a voice loud enough that anyone within shouting distance was able to hear it. Moving additional Strikers around the king now was the proper thing to do despite the presence of so many Legionnaires.

The two men sat quietly for several minutes listening to the sounds of distant horns signaling the Legions. It took time for that many men to be notified and a bit more for the orders to be carried out. The wind was blowing from the north steady enough that it was moving the heavy cloth of the king's banner as well as the nearby Striker banner. Thadar turned to one of the senior officers informing him that he wanted all of the troops fed a stout hot meal as soon as possible, they may have to be on the move for an extended period meaning cold rations in the future, so get them a proper meal now.

The Colonel saluted then wheeled his horse about to carry out the order. Steele nodded in agreement signaling to one of his own officers who had heard the king's order. Pointing in the direction of the main body of Strikers, Steele indicated that he wanted the same directive carried out. Two of his officers saluted then departed to accomplish the task.

Thadar and Steele sat quietly as they waited, there was little to do at the moment. Leaning back slightly in his saddle he lifted his head looking skyward, as he did he caught sight of a large eagle. He watched as the proud bird soared effortlessly, slowly making its way north. With a half turn of his head he glanced at his own banner, the eagle was symbol of his House.

How fitting indeed that I should see that now, he thought, *how fitting indeed.*

Chapter Forty-Four
Help Unseen

Karbel

The small but well supplied group of men had been planning and preparing for nearly a full ten-day. Now it was nearly time to put their plan into action. One of their own had been captured; it was their duty to help set him free. That the prisoner wasn't Alush as the agents were mattered not at all. The man – a Ri'al commander no less, was a loyal servant of the Varshon and so must be set free.

There was little conversation as each of them continued to double check the supplies and equipment that they planned on using. It was very important that in rescuing their comrade that their overall mission here in the capital city not be compromised. It would be just a few short hours until they put the plan into action.

It was late afternoon, nearly time for the evening meal. For Bolgar the day had been similar to the previous ones, two visits a day by one of the medical staff to check on his burns which he had to admit were healing and three meals delivered quite punctually. Even his interrogators had not been to see him today.

He could faintly hear the cart that brought the food. Bolgar was a little hungry and the food here wasn't terrible. More meat than what he was used to eating but he wasn't complaining about it. Something other than water to drink would be nice; a tall glass of Percha, a strong distilled spirit the Arakai favored, would be very welcome. Being a prisoner was bad enough for Bolgar but the inactivity was wearing on his patience, the longtime soldier exercised several times a day more as a means of passing the time than staying in shape.

Out of habit he was standing as the door was unlocked. The guard opened the door slowly as he usually did, watching for any sign that the man in the room was going to try and escape. As much as he wanted to, so far the proud Arakai had yet to devise a way to do it.

Once the guard could see where the room's occupant was, he swung the heavy door the rest of the way open then stepped inside. The second guard was diligently watching his partner's back so he was not able to see what the kitchen orderly behind him was doing. Neither had a concern about the orderly -- he had been working at the facility for some time and had never been any kind of a problem which was all by intent. Bolgar could hear but wasn't able to view it due to the bulk of the second guards body being in the way.

As the guards entered the room the orderly pulled a small tube from his apron pouch. Holding it near his mouth he got both of the guards to turn his way, "Hey!"

As the men turned he placed one end of the tube in his mouth and blew hard moving the tube in a line from one man toward the other. A fine bluish powder formed a small cloud that enveloped the upper bodies of both men. As they turned to challenge the orderly, Bolgar was surprised when both of the guards suddenly became limp and slumped to the floor as the small cloud rapidly dissipated into nothing.

The man who had brought the meal cart caught one of the men while trying to catch the other but was unsuccessful. When the second man hit the floor there was the usual thump associated with a body hitting the ground. The first guard was lowered to the guard to reduce the noise.

The orderly quickly stepped over and closed the door to the room then signaled for Bolgar to remain quiet. The Arakai did as he was told – the surprise of the action caught him off guard for a moment but that didn't last long. Escape was suddenly possible! It was his duty to return to the south. He had been searching for a way but these accursed people had been too well prepared to allow that to happen until now.

Bolgar found himself grinning at the prospect of freedom. The surprises weren't over for the Arakai as the orderly came to a rigid attention and saluted in the southern manner. Long ingrained habit took over as Bolgar returned the salute. The man then offered his hand which was heartily shaken; still holding the grip, the orderly stepped closer and in the tongue of the Alush quietly told the soon to be former patient that they needed to leave – now.

Bolgar was ready. His rescuer released his grip and then opened the door. He checked the hallway then nodded once to indicate that the passageway was clear.

Pulling a change of clothes out from its hiding place in the cart he tossed it to Bolgar who caught it then began changing clothes as quickly as he could. As soon as he had tossed the clothes the other man pulled the meal cart into the room to remove it from the hallway and out of view.

When he had exchanged his hospital garb for what the Alush had passed him, Bolgar was handed a stout dagger. He quickly hid it in his waist band under the shirt then was given a stack of assorted dirty dishes; the orderly likewise took a double handful. The two went out the door pulling it closed as best they could with a tug from one foot.

Moving at an unhurried pace the pair walked single file with the orderly leading the way. It took Bolgar several moments to realize that his companion had altered his body language, his head and shoulders were drooped to better project the image of a menial at work. He quickly copied the act as best he could which also helped to hide the burns on his neck lest that raise suspicions.

His mind was racing, an Alush here? How could this be? Questions swirled about in his mind before a suitable answer presented itself. He must be one of the spies that the masters had in place here in the enemy capital. The information that southern forces operated with was updated from time to time, this must be one of the men who helped to gather it.

The Varshon had established cells of spies in a variety of locations in the north long ago. It had taken time for the effort to start paying dividends and the long travel time between Karbel and the Citadel sometimes rendered the information collected moot but that couldn't be helped. Bolgar found himself once again praising the planning of the masters.

Wordlessly they moved past several of the staff who hardly gave them notice. Bolgar was sure they would recognize him as a patient and mentally prepared to attack them if they gave warning but no one acknowledged the men from the kitchen. The Alush, who had been working at the hospital for over a year as part of his cover while assigned to a southern intelligence gathering group stationed in the capital city, headed for the stairs that would lead them down ostensibly to the kitchen but in reality to the outside and freedom for the man following him. It would obviously be his last day working there since the guards had seen his face but that had been factored into the planning.

All of the group worked at different jobs across the large city, it gave them additional income as well as the opportunity to gather information for their masters. Political intrigue, economic and military intelligence, all flowed south to waiting ears. Much of the information used to plan the invasion had come from units just like this one from a number of cities in the north not just Karbel.

The two men continued to move, unhurried but walking at a steady pace. They were simply two functionaries going about their work, unworthy of notice, which is exactly what they needed to appear to be.

For all his combat experience Bolgar was nervous -- this wasn't what he was used to. He had done his share of scouting enemy territory while fighting the goblins but this felt different. Being confined for several ten-days now since his capture, the proud Arakai was determined not to be caught again. His companion hissed at him to relax, Bolgar was chagrined as he realized he had been walking so fast that he had nearly run into the back of the other man.

Forcing a silent but deep breath out he worked to regain his composure. The pair reached the stairway then started down making sure to stay to one side so others on the staff could travel unimpeded. Each step took Bolgar closer to freedom; time seemed to drag as they continued down. At the second landing a group of nurses were heading up, the southerners stopped then moved to the corner of the landing to allow the women to pass. One of the nurses smiled at the kitchen workers as the five women walked passed. Giving the nurse's time to be several steps up, the duo continued on their way down the stairs.

Once they reached the bottom floor, the Alush took them via the less used hallways toward the kitchen. If someone had been paying direct attention it may have seemed strange to them that the men took that path to the kitchen but no one questioned the pair. It was nearly time for shift change; those that worked during the day had their minds on getting home which is precisely why the escaped was planned for this time of day.

Moving without haste the two men continued on their way. Just before they entered one of the doors, the southern agent stopped then quickly told his companion to do exactly what he did and speak to no one. Bolgar nodded then before he knew it in they went. The kitchen staff was also winding down their day, their attention was on getting the area prepared for the next day's meals, so when the two orderlies entered scant notice was given. Moving to the sink area the dirty items were quickly but quietly placed down then with a single jerk to the head the Alush indicated for Bolgar to follow.

The pair exited through the same door through which they had just entered. Neither spoke as they walked. Bolgar was curious as to what was happening but kept his tongue still. As they moved down the hallway he could hear voices from several people conversing, he understood scattered pieces of it but certainly more than he could when he had arrived.

With a hand the Alush slowed his Arakai partner down as they approached a door on their right that he quickly opened then stepped inside, out of view of Bolgar who stepped forward to come inside. As he reached the open door the Alush appeared with a light coat in either hand one of which he handed to the other man who slipped it on as they resumed walking. Furtive glances about confirmed that they were for the moment alone in the hallway.

Reaching the back door they passed outside without being challenged. The guards were on the third floor with the prisoner so there was no need to have additional guards present at the doors. With a quick glance at the building that he had been held in Bolgar, smiled as the men melted into the nearby crowd, the first genuine smile he had worn in some time as the pair moved deeper into the late afternoon throng.

Spending the night in one of the locations the group used as a safe house, Bolgar felt better than he had in some time. He was still in the enemy capital city but at least he was free of his captors for the first time in several ten-days. After leaving the hospital his Alush counter-part took Bolgar via a circuitous route to the northeast section of the city to a small warehouse.

Over the course of night Bolgar spoke at length with those present as well as receiving some additional treatment for his burns which he had to grudgingly admit were healing well. The Alush who put on some of the salves known to the southern tribes told him as much as well, also letting him know that there would be extensive scarring to which Bolgar nodded his understanding. The doctor in the hospital had told him that too, or at least that is what he believed that the man had been saying.

Something else that made the evening better was the men had several bottles of Percha -- one of which Bolgar happily helped himself to, along with the modest but filling meal that was provided as well. He was shown extensive maps of the capital and eastern Karbel.

Bolgar asked about the progress of the invasion. The Alush relayed what information they had, which wasn't much. There was much talk in the capital about what was happening, some of it was correct but the vast majority of the news was wrong but it was being spread as if it was truth from the lips of the king himself. Bolgar spent some time dictating much of the information he had gleaned during his journey to the capital. The Alush promised to pass it along as soon as they could. Bolgar slept better that night than he had in some time.

Getting the man out of the sprawling city had been planned in advance. The group had decided to use the north gate as it was furthest from the hospital they had freed Bolgar from. It was felt that that would be the least likely exit that the escaped man would be using as it was the opposite direction from which he had come from.

Taking him through the well-guarded gates would take a bit of subterfuge but it could be done. Now that the invasion of the north was underway by the masters, security had been heightened all around the large city.

To get their high-value cargo safely out of the city the southern agents were relying on a proven ploy. He would be placed in a secret compartment hidden below the bed of the wagon which was loaded with a mixture of ordinary trade goods. The wagon had been used successfully several times to get select contraband and the occasional person in or out of the city without attention.

Before climbing into the hidden spot Bolgar bowed to the others in respect for their courage and duty. The boards were replaced then the goods hurriedly but carefully placed on top. There was no way for him to get out without assistance, it didn't set well with the independent minded man but he knew there was no choice.

Once the cargo, living and otherwise, was secure the wagon left the warehouse. The ride through the cobblestone paved streets proved to be quite jostling to the two men handling the wagon and even more so for their hidden passenger who had little room to move around and even less padding but each endured the travel as best they could.

The wait for those lined up wanting to leave the city was long, nearly an hour as each man was carefully checked to make sure he wasn't the escaped prisoner. The guards at all the gates had been provided sketches of the man that had been done soon as after his arrival at the hospital.

Hard-eyed Legionnaires compared the face of every man wanting to leave with the skillfully done drawing, being told to pay particular attention to his neck since the escaped man had been burned there. When it was finally their turn to be checked the southern agents did exactly what they needed to do to fit in, they complained about the extra security bemoaning how honest traders were being harassed and it wasn't right that those that paid taxes be poked and prodded.

The Legion sergeant paid them little attention once he was certain that neither looked like the man in question. The goods in the wagon were searched to ensure that the prisoner wasn't hiding there, then they were allowed to pass through. Each of the agents noting the heavily increased manpower near the all-important entrances to the city, both of them counting the guards to be certain of the count. That was an item to be included in their next report.

Moving out of the shadow of the large city wall the wagon continued on its way, supposedly heading to the farming villages south of Edora to sell their goods as they had told the guards when asked. There was a line of people and wagons waiting to gain entry into the city as well but it was much smaller than those wanting out.

After the wagon had traveled for nearly an hour and a half north of the large city it turned onto a side road then continued on for a bit. In the compartment Bolgar was feeling very closed in, there was little air flow and it was growing quite warm in the small space but he endured the travails. The night before the complete escape plan had been explained so despite being trapped in the hidden space Bolgar knew that it would come to an end at some point, he merely had to trust in the Alush agents.

Eventually the wagon turned into a small farm with a ramshackle house and equally bedraggled looking barn which was where the wagon headed. Once inside, the waiting man closed the doors one at time to conceal the activity inside. As soon as the wagon was brought to a stop one of the Alush climbed into the back to begin removing the trade goods. Time was important. They needed to get Bolgar on the road as soon as was possible. It was a long ride to the frontier.

Securing the wagon team, the second teamster moved to the back to assist in the removal of the goods which now went faster. The third man had the doors closed but there was plenty of light to work by as some of the roof was gone spilling generous amounts of sunlight into the building.

The three men worked steadily to remove the tools, metal works, linens, and other sundry items from the area over which Bolgar was hidden. In short order they cleared the space allowing the panel to be removed. As it was, the now released man blinked several times from the light. He worked to stand up, which took a bit of doing. The bouncing and jolting had stiffened him up some but with a helping hand he came out of the grave-like space.

Moving slowly as he regained his circulation, Bolgar looked around taking in the scene. The barn had seen better days but that wasn't important in the slightest. What did matter was that he was now free and out of the enemy capital.

The third man who had been waiting for them at the barn had brought a pair of horses. One of them was well prepared with provisions which was to be Bolgar's means of transport to the frontier, and if need be, beyond.

The three men all climbed out of the back of the wagon. One of them handed Bolgar a purse which he tucked in his belt. A selection of clothing in different sizes and styles had been waiting for him at the warehouse so he was well clothed for the journey. It was obvious that the Alush agents were highly prepared.

He was then given a sword to accompany the long knife from the hospital that he had retained. Holding the blade made him feel good; it was as if a part of him had been missing but now that had been rectified.

A map was unrolled showing the Ri'al commander exactly where they were presently and what roads he should take to get him headed in the proper direction for the frontier and the army. The horse was brought forward; he looked the animal over carefully pleased with what he saw. It was well taken care of, healthy, and appeared to be strong. While he was doing that one of the men went near the doors peering out as best he could through the assorted holes to check for any signs of people nearby. Seeing no one he opened one door then stepped back inside.

Taking the reins in hand Bolgar turned to the trio "I shall report of your faithfulness to the masters, thank you for your help and duty."

After being handed the map he shook hands with all three in turn. He mounted the horse then urged it out the open door. Outside with the directions fixed in his mind, a horse under him, a free sun on his face, Bolgar turned his horse for the road and then the border.

Time to go home.

Chapter Forty-Five
A Season of Change

G'mar

Days earlier, as they had traveled north from Edora, Captain Nahn had circulated among the Strikers explaining to his men all the details of why they were going north as well as what they might expect to run into once there. The reaction had been little different from his own, surprise, anger and then determination. Having some idea of what they might be riding into didn't necessarily change their chances but the senior Striker believed in keeping his men well informed, his reasoning was the more they knew the more intelligently they could react and respond.

Finally arriving at the entrance of the gradually narrowing pass that led to the fortress, Nahn sent the thirty plus handpicked Strikers forward into the pass working in small teams of three. Theirs was a two-fold mission, locate and kill any enemy sentries as well as sending word back of any enemy movement in the pass.

The senior Striker was confident in the abilities of his men, they were all veterans and just as important, all Elves. The ability of the Elder Race to move quietly and unseen was a key part of his selection process. He and the remainder of the expedition waited anxiously.

They waited for nearly five very long hours before word came back that the way was clear. After the scouts had eliminated the few guards who had been hiding in various locations throughout the pass leading up from the south, the group made their way toward their goal. The supply wagons and coaches had been left behind near the entrance to the pass with a guard detachment with orders to send word if any other enemy troops were seen -- and if they did see any high tail into the pass.

No need to try and hold the southern end of the pass, there wasn't enough manpower remaining to do so, making the priority if trouble was seen to get word of the sighting north. It may be possible to hold the northern, narrow end if needed.

Time was not on the side of those who had traveled from Karbel. The fact that there were pickets to send warning of anyone approaching was evidence enough that the enemy must be present at the fortress. In what strength no one knew but there was no choice, they had to press forward.

As the Striker scouts reached the northern edge of the pass they were very cautious, eyes anxiously scanning for any sign of trouble. Tense moments passed as they watched for the slightest indication of discovery but none came. The Strikers had been able to kill the remaining sentries without being detected.

The Monitor in charge of the section silently motioned his men forward. There was a sizable group of trees off to the right front of the men which blocked the view of the pass from the fortress, which is where they headed. If there were any more of the enemy sentries about that was the likely location for them to be. Word was quietly passed back to the main body of the group of what was happening. The Elves spread out as they moved to the body of trees, alert for any enemies hidden within the concealing shadows.

Gunnar, Captain Nahn, and those from Vankard received the report from the scouts at about that same time. The Striker officer had just come up to them regarding the removal of the southern sentries as word from the advance element arrived. Nahn immediately excused himself to head to the mouth of the pass. He was keeping Gunnar and the priests in the middle of his men to better protect them.

Everyone was edgy; trouble could come at any moment. He was glad that several additional platoons of Strikers had been attached to his command as they had moved north. The more soldiers the better as far as he was concerned.

As soon the main body of the group arrived at the northern entrance to the pass they were directed to the concealment of the tree growth. Nahn didn't hesitate as he waved the others forward. Moving such a large group into the trees hadn't been easy but it had been accomplished.

At the trees, the riders dismounted then pulled the horses into the cover of the large forested area, working hard at keeping them as quiet as possible. Surprise was their only meager advantage. When the group was gathered in the southern end of the forest, Gunnar told him to send a small scout group forward immediately. He was informed that several of the men had gone forward on their own as soon as they had reached the trees.

The northman smiled slightly, so typical of the elite troops. He asked Nahn to double check that all of the men and their mounts were well hidden in the trees, then stepped away from the others to make some of the checks himself. The three northmen waited in silence for any news each alone with their own thoughts.

The Hol brothers returned from the scouting mission. They had been gone far longer than Gunnar, T'shar, or any of the others were happy about. The news they returned with was grim; there were a number of sentries randomly patrolling the walls and at least a half dozen or so were posted at the gate. If they could get close enough then numbers favored those of Karbel but how to traverse the open distance from the northern edge of the trees to the fortress unseen was the challenge.

Ian reported that it might be possible to move a modest number into a position three bow shot lengths from the walls amid some trees but it would be chancy at best -- but it was likely their best option.

A quick conference among the group leadership lead to the conclusion that an open assault on the gate wouldn't work. They had to be able to take the gate and hold it for the bulk of the group to be able to gain entrance. It wasn't the greatest plan ever formulated but it was what they had. They knew they had no way of knowing when the sentries in the pass would be relieved so the risk of discovery increased every moment they delayed. Therefore, waiting for nightfall was out of the question.

The problem of how to get a small group near enough to the gate without being seen was the next order of business. Several suggestions were made but were quickly discarded as being impractical.

Vode and Levas shared a look, one that Gunnar picked up on. "What? Do you know of a way?"

The High Priest barely hesitated before telling them there was a spell that could, he emphasized that *could*, allow them to move a small group, no more than say, seven or eight close enough to the gate guards to allow them to attack them.

Gunnar looked to the others, then made the decision; he nodded to the majic user, it was all they had.

The group that would seize the gate consisted of T'shar, Allence Kellz, the Hol brothers, Mehan Finn and two other Strikers. The Strikers had politely but quite firmly told Gunnar to stay with the northmen. Gunnar wasn't happy about it but stayed put, as did Vode.

Vode had intended to be the one with the group but to his surprise Levas told him *no*. The senior acolyte was quite firm regarding this. He told his superior that the whole reason for them to be there was to ensure that he, and he alone could be on hand to personally deal with the Varshon, going to the gate would be the job for another.

The High Priest who had worked with Levas for many years was both moved and angered by the younger man. Moved that he was concerned for Vode's safety and angered that he wanted a chance to personally take on some of the southerners. But he quickly saw the point, bowing his head once in thanks.

After asking those nearby to please step back a little and gathering the chosen to him, Levas began to concentrate. Working the spell wasn't difficult but it did require a high degree of focus. The priest had specifically asked to see the body of one of the enemy sentries earlier; this is what he would use as the basis for what he was attempting.

Vode watched from nearby, this wasn't a spell that was used often, primarily because it had certain negative connotations for some people. That the priests could make themselves look like someone else didn't set well with others. There were also security concerns, someone using the spell could be an assassin but the priests still practiced the spell albeit only when no one else outside the order was present --which was the case with several of the spells they used. Not everyone in Vankard was comfortable with the power that the priests held which was often due to fear of the unknown.

Levas could feel the incredible amount of power that the confluence of the five -- Eternal Ancestors above *five* force lines -- offered up. He had of course known of this from the writings in the books of the Great Library, but to be here in person and to experience it for himself was something that was beyond his scope, far beyond it.

There were three places in Vankard where two force lines crossed; one of them was where the priest's main stronghold and training academy was quite deliberately located. Being careful to open himself up just a fraction to the available power he continued with the spell. His mind focused on the image of the dead sentry, how he was dressed, the smell of the man, the appearance of his weapons and equipment.

As each piece of the imagery fell into place in the mind of the senior acolyte -- who was a strong majic user in his own right -- the others in the small group felt a multitude of tingling sensations on their skin; it wasn't unpleasant just different. Levas continued the enchantment, this was the first time he had worked the spell over so many at one time. The stakes for getting this wrong were immense. A light sheen of sweat could be seen on his face as the moments passed.

Nahn had sent word to those nearby to keep noise and movement to an absolute minimum to avoid any distractions. It wasn't hard for those closest to follow the order; they were entranced by what they were seeing. The use of majic was virtually unknown in Karbel, it was widely accepted that those of the race of Men had lost the ability to work mystic forces -- it was an untrue but widely held belief.

To his surprise Mehan realized that he could no longer recognize those with him. Each of the others except for Levas were now similar in appearance to the dead sentry. A few slight differences such as the height of each person varied the appearance but from a distance there would be no way someone would know they were not who they appeared to be, or so he fervently hoped.

Several minutes passed then it was done. The group was as majicaly cloaked as was possible. As he finished the spell the majic user exhaled loudly, the effort had been much but he had done it. Vode looked on pleased at the work of his trusted aide.

The High Priest knew that he could hardly have done a crisper spell himself. His sense of hope rose slightly. Their chances of success had just increased, marginally, but it was an increase nonetheless. T'shar wasted no time motioning the others toward the fortress. Making their way north through the old growth forest they passed the last line of concealed Striker pickets who wished them luck as they passed. T'shar and the others heard but didn't acknowledge the salutation.

The now-enchanted group slowly but steadily approached the gate.

The guards could see some of their own coming closer with what appeared to be a prisoner dressed in robes of some type. His hands appeared to bound in front of him, one of the soldiers shoved the prisoner to keep him moving. *Wonder what this was?*

The gate sentries were now more alert than before. If their fellows had a prisoner then there might be others around. The men had been personally instructed by one of the masters to keep the gate guarded at all costs and all of them intended to fulfill their duty. Weapons were checked as eyes swept the area for anything amiss. Despite having several powerful majic users with the group, there were only a few dozen guards accompanying Anagir so vigilance was essential.

The group from Karbel didn't hurry as they continued to shorten the distance to the all-important gate. Mehan was watching the walls for any sign of alarm, nothing yet but that could change in an instant. The weight of the moment was causing him to sweat heavily. Weapons had been readied before they left the trees.

Levas was keeping his head down as T'shar had earlier suggested, better to appear to be cowed to further allay the suspicions of the guards. The acolyte stumbled then fell at one point which wasn't an act, a small root had snagged on his boot causing the misstep. The group paused to pick up their charge; Levas was breathless as he worked to maintain the spell, the fall nearly allowing his concentration to waver but his training sustained him. Once the priest was upright again a rough shove got him moving forward.

T'shar was in the front of the group along with Allence, the Hol brothers were on either side of the "prisoner" with Mehan and the remaining two Strikers following close behind.

When they were at the gate, before any of the men there could speak, T'shar struck first. A knife buried itself in the throat of the man nearest him as he swept his sword out to deal with the others. Mehan, Allence and the Hol Brothers all pounced on their opposing numbers. The other two Strikers each let a long knife fly toward their chosen targets before they too struck.

Levas had been told that the instant the fighting started he was to rid himself of the ropes that were wrapped loosely in place on his wrists, then get to the nearest wall and stay there. He was to drop the image spell at the same moment so that if a different spell was needed he would be able to conjure it and there would be no chance of one of the attackers being mistaken for one of the guards.

The fight for the fortress access was over in what seemed mere seconds, the eight guards lay dead scattered across the entrance of the tunnel. The assault group listened intently for any sign that their attack had been heard. Seconds passed as hearts pounded, *did they do it?*

Two of the bodies were hurriedly but quietly pulled back into the tunnel opening so they wouldn't be visible from above. Eyes looked upward at the stone ceiling trying to peer through it to the battlement with ears cocked. *Did the others hear? Are we discovered?*

Moments passed as they listened then, Sandor and Ian began to make their way down the tunnel along with Mehan and the other two Strikers. The twins were looking for what they hoped would be a passageway leading up to the ramparts so they could try to secure the section of the battlement nearest the gate. That would further add to the security of the others who would be following in short order.

Giving the twins a few moments to scout T'shar turned to Allence and with a firm nod gave her the go ahead to signal the others. He then headed up the passageway to follow Mehan, leaving the two from Vankard to keep this end of the tunnel secure.

As soon as T'shar and the others left, Gunnar told Nahn to bring all of the men forward to as close to the edge of the trees as they dared, but for spirit's sake do it quietly. Once the signal came they had to move rapidly, no horns, just speed. It was the same tactic they intended to use if the small group failed.

They had to gain entrance and the gate was their only acceptable option, the walls were too high to scale with any speed so a horse bound dash was what their options had been reduced to. It was risky either way but they had come to the conclusion they had little if any choice.

The area between the fortress and the trees was mostly open ground save for a few scattered trees so that worked for those of Karbel but it was still a fair distance to travel and there was only the one opening on this side of the wall so it all depended upon a single chance. Terrible odds but one works with what one has.

At the gate the Thunderguard officer never hesitated as she pulled the crimson cloth from where it had been tucked under her sword belt. She began waving it briskly over her head as she looked anxiously at the distant tree line -- making sure she was still in the tunnel as not to be visible from any of those on the battlements above.

Mehan had the other two Strikers move further down the tunnel to scout and if necessary engage anyone they found. Each of the men with Finn had bows at the ready just in case. The relief for the sentries in the pass had to be coming soon; it had now been several hours since they had been killed.

Who knows how long it had been since they began their shifts so as each minute went by the chance of discovery increased. Finn had to work up some spit to wet his very dry mouth; he had seen his share of action in the past but this mission was unlike any he, shades *anyone,* had ever done. Eyes scanned ahead looking for the slightest evidence of trouble as he stepped around a pile of debris from the wall.

Seeing the signal from the assault team, Gunnar waved the others forward then focused his entire being on getting to the gate, spurring his mount into action. He may not have been allowed to be part of the group that seized the gate but he was damned sure going to be the first man through it.

One, then four, then a dozen, then tens of dozens of horses erupted from the concealment of the trees, all of them heading directly for the gate. The sentries on the walls couldn't miss that sight and they didn't -- one of them began shouting and pointing frantically at the cavalry charge which was all it took. Another hurriedly tugged a horn from his belt letting forth a long call as the other guards ran toward the point on the battlements nearest to the gate readying their weapons as they ran.

As the first of them approached the spot above the tunnel entrance, he was suddenly set on by Sandor Hol. The brothers had finally located a means to work their way upward to the wide walkway from the entrance tunnel then lay in wait. Sandor burst from the stairway entrance catching the startled Arakai off guard. The Striker sliced him deeply across the upper arm spinning him around. Ian was right behind his sibling finishing the first man off, then the others were on them.

After signaling the others Allence waited until she saw them emerge from the trees then told Levas to follow her. It took the priest a few moments to understand what she wanted, the violence of moments earlier when the guards were killed were certainly not his first exposure to the uglier side of life but seeing it that close up had been startling.

She was already moving down the tunnel shouting again for him to follow; that bark shook him out of his reverie and got him moving. Allence planned to go up to assist the Hol brothers; she had counted the guards on the battlement carefully while they had been walking up so she knew that the twins would be outnumbered. Plus she wanted to be out of the tunnel when the Strikers came thundering through, far less chance of being run down.

T'shar had joined the other three at the northern end of the tunnel when they heard the alarm horn blaring forth above them. *Dinner's in the fire now.* The nearby soldiers began to move toward the tunnel opening in response to the alarm. The pair of Striker archers let fly at the nearest ones, who fell not even seeing who killed them.

Allence and the senior acolyte had a difficult time locating the opening that led upward in the darkness of the wide passageway but he solved that problem with a quick spell that illuminated the tunnel. "There!" she shouted. The pair ran for the doorway. Gunnar saw the flash in the darkness of the tunnel wondering what it meant but he knew it didn't matter, they had to keep going.

The charge across the open space was nerve wracking. The Strikers had no way to scout inside the fortress so what was waiting for them was unknown. For all they knew the courtyard was lined up side to side with enemy troops -- far too late to worry about it now. The ground was shaking from the impact of the thousands of individual hooves as the charge narrowed the gap to the opening.

A few arrows reached out from the wall, felling a pair of riders, but did nothing to slow the charge. Gunnar along with the leading elements of the mounted force reached the opening in the wall slowing only enough to prevent someone from being crushed into the wall.

The tunnel was wide enough for nearly a dozen riders setting stirrup to stirrup. The echo of the horse's passage grew in timbre as more and more of them filled the tunnel. At its peak, it was a long peal of terribly loud rolling thunder.

Bursting into the courtyard, the Strikers immediately began to fan out. Gunnar pulled out of the charge to the left as he exited into the sunlight, he needed to be able to see what was going on. His eyes anxiously scanned the courtyard for the enemy. It didn't take long.

Some of the men of Karbel were engaged by the nearest southerners while others rode deeper into the courtyard. The scene was chaotic and loud. Seeing the group of mounted humans Q-tra-All angrily bellowed, the force of his outburst seemed to fill the wide courtyard and beyond the Ogurth, with them all echoing the outrage of their chieftain.

The sound was primal and terrifying.

***

Anagir was surprised to see the human soldiers entering the fortress. He had taken possession of the sacred books shortly after they had arrived the previous day; all of the materials were under tight guard in one of the buildings. Standing over the remains of Lykan Tee, his longtime protector, the senior majic user only smiled as he looked over the results of another of his betrayals. He had tricked the loyal soldier into being killed by the protective spell that guarded the sacred books. The spell had been diverted into the luckless protector. The books, last touched by Taranh, now were his, and his alone.

The guards had been given implicit orders that only he was to be allowed near the scrolls. When the alarm horn was sounded he and one of the senior majic users were inspecting the area so that they could determine what needed done to conduct the rite. The Ogurth leader ordered Anagir's escort to get him to safety. One of the big Trolls stepped in between the two Varshon and the threat, urging them to move toward safety. The four guards surrounded the senior majic user to shield him from the menace as they began to move away from the tunnel which was now disgorging mounted riders. The remaining Ogurth began to move toward the invaders.

The Strikers all saw, in fact there was no way any of them could miss seeing the massive forms wrapped in armor. None of the humans had ever seen one of the Ogurth before despite one of them serving in the Strikers. The sight was enough to freeze their blood.

T'shar was judging the beast as an opponent, analyzing what saw. Big, likely very strong, heavy armor, and thick skin, this wasn't going to be easy. Who would face off against their leader was never a question -- it would be him. He changed direction to move toward the fearsome threat shouting for Mehan and the others nearby to follow him.

Nearly two dozen Strikers began running toward the Trolls. Hidden southern archers were making their presence known as men fell here and there across the southern end of the courtyard as the battle deepened.

T'shar recognized the authority of the central figure moving straight at him. The Strikers met the five angry Ogurth head on, the encounter quickly proving deadly for several of the men from Karbel. The Trolls were consummate warriors long in the service of the Varshon. That these puny ones would attempt to interfere with the masters was the greatest of offenses.

Shouts, screams and curses filled the air as the two sides engaged. Q-tra-All and his opponent traded blows, neither finding flesh as both took quick measure of their situation. For his part Mehan was terrified as he fought his own Troll, the looming figure above him was a living nightmare, big, smelly, and heavily armed.

T'shar was careful to avoid the loose gravel near his boots, no time to slip and fall. If he did the big Troll would have him for sure. In all his years, the weapons master had never fought an opponent like this. The massive Ogurth was powerful and surprisingly quick for his size. The swing of a large hammer made T'shar dodge to the side just avoiding being crushed to a pulp.

Up on the battlements the Hol brothers were barely holding their own, each of them were wounded, several bodies lay scattered nearby as mute testament to the ferocity of the fight for control of the location. Ian stumbled over one of the bodies falling backwards, his opponent was moving in for the killing blow when suddenly the point of a sword burst from his chest. Allence gave the blade a slight twist to allow it slip out easier then turned her attention to the nearby area after freeing the blade. For the moment the four of them were alone on that section of the wall.

On the run up the stairs she told Levas that the best thing he could do was engage any of the other guards further away to allow her and the Strikers to deal with those in close proximity. Without answering her the priest began to work up a spell to have ready when they reached the top.

Exiting the stairway so close behind her that he was nearly her shadow, Levas quickly sized up the situation then let the windball loose down the battlement where it flew unerringly striking two of the approaching Arakai. One was knocked backwards off his feet so hard his head bounced off the stone surface knocking him unconscious instantly. The man who had been to his right was far less lucky.

The power of the windball was greater than any that Levas had ever created. The access to the multiple force lines took getting used to and the priest hadn't had that kind of time. He had worked the spell as his experience allowed but with access to so much power what he unleashed was many times stronger.

The second man was lifted off his feet then hurled over the wall without effort; he frantically clawed at the empty air to no avail falling the long distance to the rocky ground below and dying on impact. Only chance spared the third man who had been closer to the courtyard side of the battlement and several steps behind the other two. He was forced to lower his head and fight to regain his balance as the rush of wind howled over him.

Allence joining the fight bought Ian enough time to come to his feet. The three of them were for the moment engaged with a single enemy apiece. Levas was readying another spell as the ringing of steel on steel filled the air.

As he was being hustled toward the safety of the building interior Anagir felt his anger grow -- *who were these insolent worms to intrude!* Stopping in his tracks he told the others to step aside as he worked up a powerful spell. The Trolls were reluctant to obey but the other Varshon told them to follow the order. Concentrating on the spell Anagir worked it up then with a decisive thrust of his arms forward released it toward the charging soldiers.

The powerful mystic blast struck part of the Striker charge, men and horses were hurled in all directions killing nearly a score of each, the force of the blast shaking the ground slightly. The other Varshon majic users were now joining the fight as well, as more of the black clad soldiers fell.

Feeling the majic tinge to the first blast which was almost a physical sensation, the senior acolyte shifted focus. He rushed to the edge of the battlement trying to locate the majic user who had unleashed the incantation while readying a far different spell from what he was conjuring moments earlier. The other priests from Vankard who had accompanied the group were searching out their opposite numbers as the battle in the courtyard intensified. Anagir was working up another spell as was the majic user with him; the Ogurth took on a different formation to better shield the pair. This was where they would make their stand.

Once he was inside the fortress having been made to wait for the Strikers to clear the way, Vode began searching for the senior Varshon majic user. Little known to those outside of the priesthood was their ability to transmit short messages in the form of images to one another over short distances, usually less than a mile but it was a significant advantage. This was a very closely guarded secret among those who could wield majic.

The High Priest was attempting to use that ability to hone in on his opposite number. The process wasn't easy nor was it straight forward. One had to concentrate on the process. It was similar to a compass point seeking north. The images could be strong, almost painful at times. Several times as he was looking around, slowly turning his body in the process, he came across images of dark figures, each was fleeting -- so fast at first he wasn't even sure that he had even seen it.

Then suddenly there was no doubt.

He had felt the intensity of the first blast; it was powerful, more so than anything he could conjure. A figure with a dark aura, far darker than anything the High Priest had ever seen, made its presence known. Vode fought down a strong sense of revulsion, this was going to be more difficult than he had allowed himself to believe.

Fixing the location of the dark figure in his mind, Vode told the priests and Thunderguards with him to follow. The group moved out away from the relative safety of the wall into the courtyard proper. The last of the Strikers had entered into the open area; numerous melees were taking place across the wide area. Shouts, screams and curses could be heard along with the ringing of steel on steel as the fights deepened.

Dust from the passage of the numerous horses choked the air in places, another mystic blast shook the ground but Vode remained focused on the task at hand. It was up to him to end the threat to them all. The weight of that burden was heavy. The small group from Vankard stayed together as best they could as they moved with Vode.

Mehan and the ones with him were trying to attack the big Troll from all sides at once to gain some advantage over the massive creature. It was working to an extent but for every serious blow one of the Strikers landed it seemed that the Troll would repay the wound in kind by killing or seriously wounding one of the soldiers. It seemed much the same with the others nearby as well. The one exception was the fight between T'shar and Q-tra-All -- those two were alone with each other going back and forth with neither side gaining an advantage.

Vode and his group worked through the dust and fights, the Thunderguards getting drawn into one such entanglement helping the Strikers to dispatch a lone Ogurth before continuing on their way. As they neared where the first mystic blast had struck they were forced to work around the piles of shattered bodies that had been men and their mounts.

The smell of the carnage was sharp and immediate; the result of the spell was grisly in the extreme. There was not a single body left whole. Vode tore his eyes from the sight and when he did – there! He saw his opponent for the first time with his own eyes. About a bow shot distance with several more of the big guardians, the evil one was readying another spell which caused the priest to react instinctively raising a wall of power between his group and the dark conjurers.

***

T'shar was focused as he had never been in any fight he had ever been in. The fight with the other four Trolls had moved a short distance away leaving him and his towering opponent with the immediate area all to themselves. Both of them were now wounded but neither in a significant way. Instinct and experience told the veteran Striker he needed to add to his offense so he snatched the short handled axe from its spot on his belt giving him an edged weapon in either hand. The two were slowly circling seeking a means to get inside the guard of the other but so far that had proved ineffective.

Gunnar was with a group of Strikers dealing with about ten of the tribesmen. One disadvantage that the southerners faced was that of sheer numbers, there were now over two hundred Strikers in the courtyard while those that had accompanied Anagir numbered less than eighty total with a number of those already removed from the fight.

The nephew of the Vankard Warlord was truly in his element as the fight progressed; his adversary was a skilled fighter and judging by the visible scars no stranger to battle. The Alush was determined to kill the northerner pressing his attack which forced Gunnar backwards where he tangled feet with one of the Strikers causing him to trip. Before his foe could finish him off a pair of the royal bodyguards both stabbed the man from behind killing him instantly. Gunnar nodded his thanks then regained his feet to join the fight.

***

When Vode raised the protective barrier he was instantly singled out to Anagir, who recognized the skill level of the man. Changing his point of aim, he released the spell, another powerful blast toward the small group barking at the nearby majic user to do the same. The hex covered the distance in the blink of an eye. When it struck the barrier the combined majical forces sounded like a peal of thunder erupting right over one's head, it was that loud and close. An array of bright sparks in a multitude of colors erupted at the point of impact.

Up on the battlement Levas didn't hesitate, he bolted toward the opening to the stairway leading down to the tunnel so that he could join the fight. Allence had been working to treat the wounds of the twins with the priest helping when he suddenly jumped up from where he had been treating Sandor who was propped against the wall. She didn't realize the senior acolyte could move that fast. Frustrated at not being able to join him she turned her attention to stopping the flow of blood out of Ian who had been injured even worse than his brother. She wasn't sure that either of the men would live but that didn't stop her from trying to save them.

The force of Anagir's blast striking the barrier nearly knocked all of the group down but they managed, just barely, to keep their feet. Vode yelled at his priests to send a mix of windballs and firespheres and don't stop! The five priests began to hurl the ordered items at their targets with mixed results.

The other majic user with Anagir dropped his own blast spell to quickly raise a modest size but strong wall of mystic energy of his own to shield he and Anagir. The first strikes of the elemental majic bounced off but each one took with it a piece of the shield reducing its effectiveness. Each time one of the majical objects made contact with the shield, a dazzling pyrotechnic display was produced, each short lived but intense.

Mehan was watching carefully as the big Troll feinted then move to strike one of the men. All those god-awful sword lessons from T'shar paid a dividend when Finn drove his sword home through the momentarily lowered guard, catching the Ogurth in a vital spot that made it falter. The instant it did several of the other Strikers pounced, each inflicting a serious wound, the combination of which was finally enough to bring the Troll down for good, collapsing with no small effort.

Finn was breathing heavily as his withdrew the sword from the body of the Troll; sweat stung his eye which he angrily wiped away. The fight wasn't over yet – "Let's go!" Two of the other Trolls were still alive.

Anagir was growing angrier; the plan that had been so carefully drawn up, trained for, sacrificed for, was being threatened. He hurled another blast toward the barrier protecting the small group of majic users, this one even more powerful than the last, which itself had been stronger than the one prior to it. The Varshon majic user was becoming consumed by the challenge, he wasn't thinking clearly, all that mattered was the death of those who had interfered with plan and his rise to absolute power.

The entire battle in the courtyard had been reduced to him and the man opposite – nothing else existed in that moment.

Levas was running down the stairs as fast as possible while his mind was racing. The battle was continuing in the courtyard and now his mentor was likely involved. As the senior acolyte, his place was at Vode's side but he couldn't get there fast enough despite the all-out effort he was running with. When he reached the bottom of the stairs he stumbled over some of the fallen stone that littered the area, using his arm to steady himself by reaching out to the wall, he kept going.

The two blasts that Anagir had hurled at the barrier had done their intended job. The High Priest had been forced to pull it some to maintain the same amount of protection but the second of the new spells that hit was more powerful than he had anticipated.

The force of it had knocked them down which dropped the barrier. Confident that he had killed them all, Anagir turned his attention to some of the other fighting, unleashing another of the spells toward a group of Strikers and catching them full force killing them all. Two of the Ogurth roared in triumph seeing the effects of the blast.

As he fought to regain both his feet and focus, the senior majic user from Vankard realized that he couldn't go directly at the enemy. He was simply too powerful to take on in that way so a new plan was needed, quickly.

Rolling on his side to get up Vode was tossing suggestions aside almost as quick as he was making them – *no won't work – no too slow – no not that one – no wait! That one might work* – without conscious thought he adopted a new strategy.

He shouted at the Thunderguards to all use their bows and

concentrate their arrows on the second Varshon. He was the one shielding the evil one, and if he didn't have the protection then their combined efforts would likely be enough.

Vode told the other priests to be ready to attack on his signal. The seven soldiers didn't hesitate as they all readied their arrows.

The senior of the soldiers yelled for them to release. Vode waited a moment for the arrows to travel before he told the priests to release as well. Seven shafts sped their way toward their target who had his back toward them as he was readying another spell. Three of the seven arrows found their mark one of the trio hitting the majic user in the throat which tore open the flesh. Blood cascaded down his chest. He gurgled weakly as his life left him.

One of the Trolls saw this and was turning to see where the threat was when the windballs and firespheres hit the group.

Anagir was surprised, even shocked, when two of the elemental orbs struck near him tossing him and the guards to the ground. One of the unlucky Ogurth had been the recipient of multiple strikes which took him out of the fight with serious wounds. The other three were battered by the majic but remained able to fight. One of them reached down picking Anagir up, breaking long standing protocol against touching the senior majic user, but it never registered with Anagir.

A second flight of arrows was close behind the first but now that they were aware of the danger the Trolls covered up with large shields so the arrows bounced off harmlessly. As soon as he was on his feet Anagir let loose another spell toward the northmen.

The speed of the conjure caught them off guard. The blast was poorly aimed but still caused injuries, several of the priests were hurled away taking them from Vode's side. He was himself injured in the blast as well. Had the blast been even slightly better targeted, they would have all been killed. The Thunderguards had been knocked over like leaves in a stiff wind. Some of Vode's wounds began to bleed but he pressed on.

Still slightly dizzy the northman's next spell wasn't aimed well but it did help the situation some. He had tried to hit the Varshon with a different type of spell, this one soil based. Those of Vankard used almost exclusively elemental majic whereas with the Elves it was more of a White majic. The particular spell Vode had hurled was intended to open up the ground to swallow the target but he missed, mostly. When the spell hit it was off target in that it failed to affect Anagir but it did burst near the three Ogurth.

The ground immediately around them began to give way, so rapidly they didn't have time to react. With a tearing sound a fissure opened up beneath the three guards who shouted as they fell. Anagir saw them disappear into the mouth of the ground and disappear as the dirt flowed back together like water leaving no trace of the fissure or his guards.

Anagir flung another blast spell out of reflex which struck near the northman injuring him further; the heat of the blast singed his face and clothing. The impact of the blast knocked the wind from his lungs filling with chest with a thousand needle like pricks from the inside. The pain was intense, almost exquisite but he remained conscious.

Vode knew time was short; his wounds were gnawing at his strength. The loss of blood in particular was becoming a real problem; he was beginning to feel light in the head just as he did when he was wounded by the arrow during the travel to Karbel. Not able to completely focus could be their undoing and Vode was completely aware of that fact.

He was the only one present who could stand up against the Dark One, swords and arrows would not do it, this was about him and now it was time, his time.

He steeled himself for the pain that would come with what he was about to do, there was no choice only duty and that was to win, be triumphant or the whole of the world would lose. He took in as deep a breath as he could and with great effort began to push himself up from the ground.

The High Priest struggled to his feet again and this time he vowed he would not fall or fail. An idea suddenly came to mind and he tried to concentrate on it, form his mind around the thought, work the idea into fruition. Sweat ran down his face from the effort he was exerting. Vode tried to slow his breathing to better focus as he rose to his full height gathering himself with the power and full majestic import of his office – he was the High Priest of Vankard and this was his time.

His eyes never wavered from their watch of the Varshon who had turned away after the last strike thinking that the man who had opposed him was finished.

Anagir sensed something and turned back toward where the man lay and saw the human slowly rising from the ground - he couldn't believe it. Disbelief and no small measure of wonder rushed about in him as he watched; too surprised to summon another spell.

The priest regained his feet locking eyes with him, only anger returned the look he sent across the way. In his mind Vode could see the shimmering dark aura that the Varshon was surrounded by – for that moment he was no longer afraid. He turned that fear into anger, and that became resolve.

The Varshon thought that his last strike should have finished the man, *of all the impudence!* Anagir hadn't felt anger like this in all his life, the utter arrogance of the *human* across the square from him nearly beyond him, couldn't the pathetic fool see he was defeated? That ALL of the humans were defeated, that he was their master? Enough, who was this insect to challenge *ME*? Smoke still rose from the spot where the energy bolt had burned through the mystic shield and tasted Vode's flesh.

The High Priest raised a shield between himself and the Varshon again; this time instead of the wide wall that he had used before it was only a barrier barely wider than he was. This way he still had a measure of protection but it used much less concentration than the full shield.

Vode had been trying to gauge the extent of the power his opponent was capable of. This had caused him to lose focus on the immediate which was that it was allowing the dark one to dictate the terms of the fight, the one he was losing.

To win he must turn the tables and be the one dictating the terms. If he did not, then all was lost.

Then he had a thought, one of the spells that he had recently learned, one of those from the Book of Hope. Yes, that was it, he didn't have time to mull the idea, it was what he had. Beginning with a simple spell, one of almost childish use by moving his hand in a growing circular motion in front of him, the human majic user sent a long tongue of bright red and orange flame in the direction of his foe.

The spell did no damage but it wasn't intended to, it was a distraction, a cheap, flashy diversion. It did what it was intended; it blocked the line of sight for the Varshon momentarily. Anagir hardly stepped aside as the weak flame cloud roiled toward him but failed to cover the distance between the two combatants breaking apart in a showy but ineffectual mass of flames and smoke. *Pathetic*, he thought while summoning the next spell, one that would crush the life out of his antagonist and end this farce of a duel.

The battle had moved the two around the courtyard during their fight which had, unknown to either of the two majic users, arranged them in a highly curious location. Between the two adversaries was one of the areas of majic created during the battle two thousand years earlier. It was invisible to the naked eye as were the most of the others but this was one of the less familiar of the anomalies.

Some areas generated by the unstable blend of the two different types of majic were nulls, where no majic of any kind would work. Others had caused some of the stones to melt as if they were water, in places the air itself had been affected, causing it to solidify and fall to the ground in pieces. The last of these anomalies were far fewer in number than the null areas but were in many ways far more dangerous.

One of the unforeseen effects of the blending of the different majical incantations was to form areas of intensely focused power. Spells invoked within these areas, or power passing through, was magnified to many times their original level as if they were light sent through a lens. A lesser trained majic user could find that the spell they released could rival the greatest majic users easily. It was just such an area that Vode and Anagir had unknowingly placed between them.

Vode's injuries were sapping his strength, he fought to maintain his balance and work the new spell in his head. The flame lance, a long dense spear-like creation formed of pure majical fire, leapt from Vode's fingers across the distance between the two and suddenly as it hit the focus area the spear disappeared from sight as if it never existed. Anagir, who had been surprised by the appearance of the mage's weapon, suddenly stopped when the lance which had been heading directly at him vanished.

A cruel grin of anticipation curled his lip at the thought of the failure of the human when at thirty or so paces in front of him the air began to swirl with color. It grew brighter as the color intensified. Anagir had to squint to see what was happening because the colors were so bright.

The light became so intense that he was unable to see, hand held before him as he tried to block out the powerful illumination. The spell he had been ready to cast was forgotten as he fought to keep out the light. Others around the courtyard were so distracted by the light they momentarily stopped fighting, many of them trying to shield their eyes from the brightness.

Before the Varshon could move or react a shaft of mystic flame almost three feet in diameter erupted from the focus area and enveloped the upper half of the Varshon leader's body. Anagir screamed in pure agony as he was burned with a power rivaling that of the sun. The force of the magnified fire spear hurled him nearly a hundred feet from where he had been standing while burning him severely.

The shaft of fire winked out of existence as instantly as it had come into being, everywhere that the fire had touched was marked. All the foliage along the path of the mystical flame was either ablaze or withered to ash; even the stone of the distant wall was scorched and blackened from where the blast had struck it smoke rising from the now heated stone.

The Varshon leader landed heavily on his back and then slid nearly twenty paces, in places smoke and flame rose from his body. Anagir was barely conscious as the pain, indescribable in its detail and depth had time for but one thought as the darkness rushed up to claim him, '*I'm afraid*', then the crushing weight of death clutched him.

Vode was as shocked as the others who were watching the fight from their various locations in the courtyard. The flash of light was so powerful it had lit up the entire courtyard despite it being during the day, causing all the remaining fights to cease as each party tried to determine what had just occurred.

T'shar seized on that brief opening attacking with all his remaining strength in a last gasp effort. The Ogurth had been distracted just enough to allow a gap in his defense but it was the singular moment the Striker weapons master needed. The honed edge of T'shar's blade found the neck, slicing deeply as it penetrated the thick skin. Black blood gushed from the wound as the Troll felt the bite of the sword. One massive hand clamped over the wound but it did little to staunch the heavy flow of blood. The battered Striker moved in to finish his opponent but it proved unnecessary. The combination of wounds was sufficient to finally bring the Ogurth down.

The fights resumed as the distraction from the spell ended. Nahn, Mehan, and the rest of the Strikers had their hands full with the other Varshon and Ogurth despite having them well outnumbered. A few melees were being fought around the courtyard, the battered Striker officer could see what could only be the bodies of a large number of his men motionless on the ground all across the southern end of the courtyard.

The utter ferocity of their foes was unlike anything these Strikers had seen before but there was still work to do. Yelling for those nearby to rally he sprinted toward the largest group brawl still underway with a growing number of Strikers joining the charge.

Gunnar and Levas saw the death of the Varshon majic user just as the other had. The release of that much majic was impossible to miss. When the body of the creature came to a rest they could see the smoke and even a few small flames rising from it. *Let this be the end of it,* Gunnar thought as he moved as quickly as his own wounds allowed.

Please let this be the end...

Chapter Forty-Six
Epiphany

Eastmarch

Bolgar wasn't sure where he was. It was possible that he had already passed the border between Karbel and D'Lohm but he had no way of knowing for certain. He was hungry, very little had passed his lips for three days other than some water and it hadn't been exactly clean and fresh but it was what he could find.

Fortunately it turned out to not be unhealthy but it had worried him. Becoming sick while alone in the wilderness was not a good idea at all. He had seen many men die over the years, a number of them from illness. Part of the training he had undergone while growing up was endurance -- young Arakai are taken deep into the wilds and left to fend for themselves. Those that survived then moved on to the next phase of training. Not a few of those undergoing the test failed. That experience was helping to keep him alive.

Spending the last ten-days or so traveling through Karbel after leaving the capital had made Bolgar begin to question some of the so called facts that he had been told his entire life. One of the things that he and generations of Arakai had been told was of the wretched slavery that those of the north endured at the hands of cruel overseers, none of which he witnessed as he rode.

Certainly there were rough conditions that many of the peasant class lived in but seeing the people come and go as they wished belied the stories he and the others had been fed. Seeing the well-stocked markets, flourishing farms and generally robust agricultural development of region after region also allowed doubt to creep into the tales of famine and malnourishment they were informed was prevalent.

The more he rode through Karbel the more he was forced to admit that much of what he had been raised on simply wasn't true. His emotions were slowly moving from disbelief to wonder onto anger. Who was he to question the words of the masters? Even so, the truth of what his own eyes were seeing was forcing him to question many things which he wasn't comfortable with but it was what he had.

The Arakai kept moving, senses on increased awareness; it was the smell of the smoke from a camp fire that caught his nose. Maybe they had food, he moved forward toward the smell, recklessly not paying attention to what was around him as he hurried along.

The smell was elusive, twice he had to stop and backtrack his own path trying to locate it again. Each time he sniffed the air as if he was a trained hound seeking a blood scent. The hunger and thirst had been tormenting him for days; meals had been few and far between since leaving the more populated areas. His training in field craft had kept him alive so far by allowing him to find edible roots, berries and such but the thought of a hot meal was almost torture.

Topping a small rise he identified the source of the smoke below him was a small ragged circle of wagons. The wheeled transports were about two long bow shots from where he was standing. The wind brought him the smell again, this time much stronger than before. Something was definitely being cooked and that thought moved Bolgar off the elevated ground moving directly toward the encampment.

As he got closer he could see that the wagons were not in good repair, one of the horses was tied to the outside of the circle which made it easy to steal, poor security. The animal was thin and looked very tired as it weakly plucked at the grass at its feet.

Bolgar thought briefly about how he had lost his own horse a few days back and was once again displeased to admit that he wouldn't have had to walk this far if he had remembered to tie the horse up before falling asleep. That he, an Arakai cavalry soldier would forget to do something so basic as properly secure his mount was a sign of how fatigued he was. The horse carried his supplies so when it wandered off during the night Bolgar was left with little to sustain himself.

Despite being hungry the Arakai stopped before walking into the wagon circle. He called out using the Karbel speech, "Hallo." Being careful not to shout he used his training to modulate his tone so that it carried the necessary distance. It didn't take long to get a reaction.

A shriek from the woman nearest to him created even more activity as she ducked out of his sight. Two men with long handled hay forks slowly approached with their implements held at waist level pointed at him.

Bolgar was armed but slowly raised his arms away from his side to try and signal his non hostile intentions. The men were wary, glancing at each other frequently as if to reassure themselves by the presence of the other. The points of the tines on each implement wavered slightly as the men came closer. One of the men motioned downward with his tool which Bolgar took to mean they wanted him to go to his knees. He exhaled loudly but did as he was directed.

Several others approached while the first two with the hay forks kept a guarded eye on him. He tried several words in succession with little response. Then one of the newcomers said something, Bolgar believed it was a greeting. He belatedly realized that these were likely refugees from D'Lohm which used a different tongue from that used in Karbel.

The language barrier was proving to be a problem but slowly he was making headway. Fortunately he still had his belt purse so keeping one hand upright he used his non sword hand to slowly draw out a pair of small gold coins from the purse and mimicked the motion of someone eating which got a nod from two of the refuges.

The duo with the hay forks motioned with them for him to rise which he did slowly making sure to not appear threatening. With a jerk of the head one of the men indicated for him to step inside the wagon circle. Several of the men were close by, none of them appeared armed but that didn't keep the tired Arakai from being wary. They could just as easily kill him for his weapons and coine so he remained as vigilant as he could.

They lead him to a spot near one of the wagons; he sat down without being told. Some of those who had come out to inspect him drifted away but none of them very far. In short order he was brought a bowl of stew and a small piece of bread. He handed the coines to the woman who had given him the food. She immediately stepped back after taking the money which rapidly disappeared into the pocket of her tattered apron.

Bolgar wasted no time spooning up some of the food. It certainly wasn't the best stew he had ever had but as he was filling his mouth again he thought about the fact that it was certainly better than what he'd eaten the last two days – all a matter of perspective. A chipped clay mug of water was brought over which he politely nodded his thanks for. Having some hot food going in him was providing an almost immediate lift to the spirit, his body was soaking up the nourishment it needed.

He was well into the second bowl of the mediocre stew when Bolgar heard the horses before any of the others did, his head automatically turning to better identify the direction. From the southeast, at least a half dozen horses, maybe a few more, riding at a quick but not full on stride. Standing, his action drew the focus of several of the men around him and they too stood and listened intently.

Others in the small camp fell silent as the noise of the horse hooves drew nearer. With a decisive motion Bolgar pointed at two of the children and waved them toward one of the wagons as he tossed aside the bowl. The man nearest to him immediately nodded and began to give the others orders. The quiet meal of moments earlier was gone as women sought out their offspring. None of the men in the encampment were soldiers but several weapons appeared from their storage places.

Bolgar hurried to the communal fire pit and tossed in several more pieces of wood. He wanted more light to better handle whatever was coming. Children were crying as the sudden activity startled them. All of the travelers had seen what had happened in their own country and believed that they were safe having crossed the border in Karbel. The smell of fear was clearly evident to Bolgar; he took it in but dismissed it as a distraction. He was in his element and that gave him its own sense of purpose.

The unseen horsemen had picked up their pace, the thunder-like sound of multiple hooves striking the ground was close, almost on top of them. Then suddenly there they were nine riders at the edge of the flickering firelight. One of them was motioning to the others who were spreading out in both directions trying to circle the small encampment. With a start he recognized the riders as Arakai. The clothes as well as the markings on their mounts Bolgar knew was from one of the cavalry units in the Hand of Red, a different formation than his own Ri'al but distinctly Arakai.

Coarse laughter was coming from several of the mounted men who were tossing a clay jug of some liquid that Bolgar presumed was likely percha, a strong distilled spirit favored by the Arakai, back and forth.

To see what some of his kind had become was hard for the former cavalry commander to deal with. These once proud soldiers of the Varshon were now acting like bandits and petty thieves. His shame at seeing his onetime brothers was quickly overwhelmed by the anger rising up in him. The refugees had done nothing to deserve this, this group wasn't a military unit - the Arakai were doing this for sport!

Without coming to a conscious decision, Bolgar pulled his sword and began running toward one group of riders. He was fixated on the four men clustered together. He saw nothing else as he covered the distance. Without realizing it he was shouting at the men using the Arakai tongue, Hazhel, cursing them for cowards and questioning their honor.

This caught the attention of two of the riders who turned to see a sword wielding figure racing toward them. One of the two grinned thinking that finally here was some sport, up till now they had only found farmers and weak city dwellers to prey on. Selecting one of the riders with his back toward him Bolgar launched himself off his feet. His sword found purchase in flesh nearly severing the riders' spinal column spilling him from the saddle screaming in agony as he fell.

The other three saw the result of the attack belatedly understanding that this man was indeed a threat, the percha they had been swilling down in prodigious amounts earlier dulled both their wits and reflexes.

After taking down the first man, Bolgar continued moving. His path took him around the rear of the first horse and into the midst of the remaining three Arakai. A wild swing with his sword left one of the trio with a long slash wound to the thigh but still mounted. A ragged curse came from the man as he clutched at his wound with both hands trying to staunch the flow of blood.

The former Ri'al commander rolled to his right along the ground which carried him between the legs of yet another horse. Bolgar stabbed upward and slashed opening the belly of the now mortally wounded equine. As the sharpened edge of the steel found its flesh the horse reared up in a vain attempt to evade what was killing it. The shriek of the animal was heard for some distance. As it fell over to one side the Arakai rider wisely flung himself loose of the saddle and pitched backwards to try avoid being taken down with his mount, something that would almost always result in serious injury to a rider. He landed heavily, knocking the wind from his lungs with a painful rush.

Bolgar kept rolling trying to avoid being landed on by the horse as well. Certain that he was now clear of the risk that the horse posed he sprang upright to his feet but staggered a little as a bit of dizziness from his repeated rolls took him.

A shake of the head to clear his mind and help his focus as the remaining two riders angrily sought him out. His anger clouded everything, it was like a red mask over his ability to reason. He charged toward the pair heedless of his own safety. He could hear the shouts and screams from some in the camp.

As the two men rode toward him at a quick clip Bolgar held his course until the last moment then darted to his left just in front of the oncoming horse, swinging his sword along a horizontal plane. The move surprised the man who was expecting him to be trapped between the two horses. A frantic move with his sword barely turned the slash Bolgar was trying to make but it bought the intoxicated man a few seconds but those seconds were his last as the return slash caught him across the back biting deeply.

The other riders were making a sport of taunting the unfortunate refugees by yelling and shouting at them while wheeling their horses around the small encampment. The frightened civilians did their feeble best to keep the armed riders away from them. When the last of the four riders went down Bolgar chased down one of the nearby horses knowing it would be easier to fight the others if he was mounted as well - that was his element.

The horse he was trying to catch shied away at first but within three steps the former Ri'al commander had it caught and was in the saddle. He wasted no time urging the horse into a gallop, aiming it directly at the next group of riders who unfortunately for them had all their focus on the people in the wagon circle.

Crossing the distance, Bolgar had no plan just an intense desire to kill as many of the riders as possible. There was no thought to his own survival as he bore down the men, his sights fixed directly on the nearest man who began to turn at hearing the approaching horse but he turned slightly late.

His eyes grew instantly wide as he saw the man who was literally flying at him; Bolgar had launched himself out of the saddle to tackle the man. There was no time to react as he was taken from the saddle with the man landing on him driving the air from his lungs. He was laying there stunned trying to gasp for air when the blade of a long knife found his heart ending his life.

The other riders were startled at the sudden attack; the group of nine had been reduced by several already. Hurriedly pulling the blade from the chest of the man, Bolgar spun about, a sense of near calm now filling him as if killing the latest man drained the blood lust from him. Both of the nearby men saw the look, each of them was no stranger to battle but the look they saw on the face of the man who was slowing standing reflecting the light from the campfire was as close to living death as either of them had ever seen.

The yellow red of the fire caught the blood on the blade he gripped tightly as his gaze found the eyes of the pair. Speaking to the men in Hazhel he told them that they had lost their honor, they were to take the others and leave or this would be the where they would all die.

The two shared a look; this was as far from what they expected when they decided on a whim to attack the small encampment. What was to be a few hours of fun killing, raping, and pillaging, had quickly turned into something else entirely. Nearly half of them were dead due to the grim faced stranger who was speaking to them in their own tongue telling them to leave and shaming their honor.

The confrontation had captured the attention of the other riders who slowly rode over to be with their fellows. Slowly those from the wagon train came up behind Bolgar, all of them. He felt their presence but didn't take his gaze from the men on horseback.

Bolgar spoke slowly but with a heavy tone of authority once again told the men that they needed to leave. The refugees were sporting what weapons they had, their courage increased by the action and attitude that the stranger was displaying. The five remaining Arakai were now less haughty as they faced those they had intended to kill.

Some of the refugees began to edge forward, whatever they had grabbed up to arm themselves gripped in their hands. Feeling the movement Bolgar knew that he needed to get the men moving away before the civilians rushed them which would likely result in deaths and injuries to some of them, which he wanted to avoid. The people had already had their country invaded, their lives disrupted to the point they had to flee from their homes and now they were being hunted for sport. No more.

He took one step forward, stopping the others behind him with a raised hand. Looking each of the men in the eye he got the tone of what he wanted to express without speaking a word. One of the men turned his horse away then was followed by the others. Bolgar watched the body language trying to judge if they were shamming the action or not, he wasn't positive but he was leaning toward them actually leaving.

Once they were beyond the light from the bonfire the refugees moved forward to surround the tired Arakai thanking him profusely. He was overwhelmed by the sea of emotions but was slowly allowing the pent up tension to bleed off.

After a few minutes of jubilant celebration, Bolgar raised his arm to try and signal for silence which took a few moments to take hold. Making sure those of the wagon were looking at him he pointed at the body of one of the Arakai holding up his own blade to try to convey his meaning.

When none of the others caught his meaning Bolgar quickly moved to the body picking up the sword that lay near the open hand. He lifted it to show the others what he was talking about then stepped over to where the leader of the group was who was watching his movements closely.

Stopping a few feet away from the man he reversed the weapon, handing to the man hilt-first who slowly but with a steady hand reached out to take it from him. Once he had released the blade Bolgar pointed to the other bodies then lifted his own sword again. The group leader nodded in understanding then quickly told the others to check the bodies for more weapons. Men and women began to spread out to do as they were told.

Once the swords and knives were gathered up, the group was now slightly better armed. With a tired wave of his hand in the general westerly direction Bolgar indicated that they should all leave. His message wasn't lost on the others.

They realized that they needed to leave, Karbel was hopefully taking in those that had managed to flee the invaders, it was still too close to the frontier for safety. It was going to be a long night but Bolgar felt a keen sense of duty.

Getting what was left of the small group to safety was now his only purpose in life.

Chapter Forty-Seven
Endgame

Northern Karbel

It was mid-morning as Thadar was conferring with his advisors and senior commanders about what to do regarding the formation of southern troops nearby; they had already attacked and defeated two other smaller groups of southerners the previous day.

Now that reinforcements were arriving in a more orderly fashion, Thadar had an increasing number of troops at his disposal and he was better able to replace his casualties. The king was listening to suggestions on how to best attack when a Striker marched up.

He stopped then came to attention and saluted waiting to be acknowledged. Thadar saw the man, returned the salute and motioned him over. He handed the king a message then stepped back to see if his ruler wished to send a reply, Thadar excused himself to the others present then unfolded the note and began to read.

'Varshon leadership killed, ceremony stopped. G'mar in friendly hands. No chance of ceremony happening. Will explain all when reunited. Suggest you contact Varshon nearest you and relay information. Might cause confusion among southern armies. Sending troop south with items able to provide confirmation with all possible speed. Am heading south myself once this location secure. Request additional forces be sent here to keep location secure.'

Gunnar

Thadar was surprised by the message, and felt a glimmer of hope. A relay of portable heliograph teams had been sent north with Gunnar and those of Vankard which is how Thadar was able to get the message he held in his hand.

He glanced at the day and time of the message, it had been sent yesterday. G'mar was quite a distance away, explaining the long delay.

Realizing that the others were waiting on him Thadar blinked twice to help refocus himself then spoke, holding up the paper as he did so, "It would seem that those that went north were successful. Gunnar says that the Varshon leadership has been killed and the ceremony stopped for good. He also suggested that we inform the Varshon nearby. How does that affect our choices now?"

The command group which included Dwyn, Tal, Steele and several Legion generals were excited at the news, smiles and a few joyful laughs were heard as they realized that the greatest threat they had ever faced had been eliminated. Shortly they began to discuss the new information and how it influenced their plans.

It was several minutes before Thadar realized that he should send Gunnar a reply. Motioning the Striker over he told him to inform Gunnar that the message was received and that forces would be sent north. The man saluted and then headed for the nearby message team.

Within short order it was decided to take Gunnar's advice and let the Varshon know what had happened at G'mar. The southern army group that they had been planning on attacking was the largest group in the area. It was easily half again their number despite the reinforcements that had arrived.

Thadar told Steele to send two Strikers carrying a flag of truce to a point where the southerners could see them and wait there but not to endanger themselves. The man who ruled Karbel didn't trust those of the south to honor a request for a meeting but it was all they had to go on. The Striker commander nodded once and left the officer's group to carry out his orders. The discussion returned their attention to the map that showed the local terrain and what information they had regarding enemy troop dispositions.

In the southern camp Pon was notified that a herald had been spotted. He had been trying to pull together scattered reports on enemy strength in the area as well as organizational information on his own forces. The last few days had been taxing to say the least. Repeated attacks from the forces of Karbel had inflicted moderate losses which was to be expected, but the attacks were also affecting unit integrity to a degree that was problematic.

Adjustment had been ordered to try and compensate the balance of forces but it also meant that some units were now a mixture of men from different units who were not used to working together. That in turn lowered the efficiency of the units making them less combat ready but this deep into enemy territory they had no choice but to continue as best they could.

Several of the Varshon were with him when the news came in that those from Karbel wished to parlay. He was told that two black clad soldiers displaying a flag of truce were waiting just beyond bowshot. Looking over to the senior of the Varshon present he received a nod granting him permission to go and speak to the herald.

He was feeling very confident so he took his time, no reason to hurry. Pon reasoned that by now Anagir had been able to complete his work and that those of Karbel having suffered at the hands of the now unstoppable Varshon were anxious to sue for peace so that they might lick their wounds and save their pathetic lives.

He sent word for three of the men from his personal guard to accompany him, no reason to be foolish, the men of Karbel had fought bravely he was willing to grant but the outcome of this war was inevitable. The Varshon were too powerful to stop -- but that didn't mean the enemy would remain honorable and not try to harm him.

***

A runner brought word to Thadar that a small party of southerners was approaching where the Strikers were waiting. Nodding, he decided to take only a small group with him to go and meet whoever they were sending. Thadar chose Steele, Tal Lyn, and Dwyn, the choice of the Elf was a deliberate one. He knew it would rattle the southerners but more importantly it would give his friend the opportunity to face those that served the Varshon. That was something he had been denied the chance to do three hundred years earlier, three centuries is a long time to wait. No more. There was also the issue that Dwyn knew some of the speech that the Varshon used.

The king and his chosen companions mounted, then headed out to where the Strikers were waiting. The wide line of Legion troops watched as Thadar and the others rode toward their parlay. Those of the north arrived about the same time that those that had rode over from the Varshon forces did.

Thadar took measure of the man at the head of the small entourage; this one was clearly in charge. How he sat the horse, the way he carried himself spoke volumes, Pon was doing the same thing, sizing up his foe. Younger than he thought but no matter, he was here to find out what they wanted.

Shifting his gaze to the others in the party he recognized the Legion uniform on one of them and that the next one was a Striker while the third was....anger rose up in him at seeing Dwyn. The member of the Elder Race sat quietly on his mount looking directly at Pon enjoying the reaction his presence created.

The senior general couldn't contain his anger and in the tongue of Karbel asked, "Why is that here?" referring to Dwyn.

Thadar turned his head to look at the Elf who slid his eyes over to catch the movement. He and the king had come up with a plan to further shake up the Varshon and their lackeys. Dwyn would do the talking for Karbel forcing whoever the southerners sent to deal with him.

The Elf edged his horse forward some then spoke to the man who commanded the southern army, the potential language barrier no longer an issue, "Your plan had failed, your leaders were killed at G'mar and the ceremony prevented. You have lost."

Pon was surprised at the bold statement; this is what they were going to try? A lie so weak that he couldn't believe that they would offer it, they were so pathetic. This was all they had? He snorted in response to the Elf's declaration. It didn't dawn on him at first that they were speaking of things they should have no knowledge of. Dwyn never hesitated, trying to build and keep the momentum of the conversation in his favor.

"Here are the terms offered, take them or not. You and your Varshon leash holders either take what's left of your rabble and head home or face us in battle and be crushed, your choice."

Pon was stunned; this upstart so called king was being openly defiant as well as disrespecting him by allowing this thrice cursed Elf to speak to him. Turning toward Thadar the senior general asked him in

Common, "Does this one speak for you? Are you not man enough to use your own tongue?"

Thadar spoke to the southerner for the first time, "I am more than man enough. You are unwelcome intruders in my kingdom. I would rather you fight so that we may kill more of you." His gaze never wavered from the man sitting on his horse across from him. The king had said all he intended to say.

The southern general was angry when he jerked the reins around to turn his mount. He would waste no more words on this one. A hardy kick got the horse going. The three soldiers with him turned and followed without a word each keeping an eye on those from Karbel.

Riding away Pon was carefully judging the distance until it was just about right, "Kill him!" The order loud enough for all three of the H'Roth archers with him to hear but no one else. The trio immediately turned their mounts to allow themselves a better angle on the target.

Pon kept riding knowing he was well out of range of the Legion line so was in no personal danger. Those of Karbel had waited with the Strikers, watching as Pon rode off. They were talking among themselves when one of the Strikers shouted, "Watch out!"

He spurred his horse hard to get it to move quickly enough. The bodyguard had seen the three archers stop and pull their bows. The arrows were released about the same time he shouted leaving him little time to act.

The Striker closed part of the distance to the king and leapt off his horse arriving at Thadar the same moment as the first of the three arrows. One of them struck the king's horse which immediately shied to the side heading for the ground. Another of the missiles found flesh, the Striker who had shielded Thadar yelped in pain, the arrow lodged deep in his thigh, the last of the deadly projectiles missed and stuck in the ground.

The others around the king were caught off guard by the sudden attack. Thadar and the Striker were taken to the ground with the horse as it fell. The king was barely able to kick himself clear, avoiding serious injury.

The already wounded soldier wasn't so lucky, a ragged scream of agony came out as the mortally wounded horse carried him to the ground pinning his now formally uninjured leg beneath it. The H'Roth archers sent another volley on the heels of the first and then galloped their horses at the small group from Karbel while drawing their sabers.

Steele and the other Striker were moving to place themselves between Thadar and the approaching riders. One of the second flight of arrows found Tal's horse. The Legion Marshal managed to escape injury when jumping from the beast, it wasn't the first time he'd had a horse killed beneath him.

Dwyn was down from his mount trying to help Thadar get the wounded Striker free hoping not to be struck.

Pon kept moving while his men worked at carrying out his order. Whether or not the king lived he planned to move the entire force forward in a general attack. No time to plan out a formal strategy, this was the time for aggressive action.

As soon as he was in shouting distance Pon began yelling orders, at first he wasn't seeing any reaction to his commands but then movement like the waves in a pond after a stone was tossed in the amount of movement spread. As he got closer several officers ran out toward him. He pulled his horse up and turned slightly pointing back at where the parlay group was, "Attack, general attack all units, NOW!"

The officers hesitated for a moment but the look of intensity along with the command voice was enough. The men turned shouting orders as they went. The southern forces began to shake themselves out in response to the directives.

Pon was searching for a trumpeter – there! He rode over, "Attack, all units attack!" The signaler hurriedly licked his lips then raised the horn. Crisp notes broke the air which was repeated by other trumpeters. More of the southern formation which numbered well in excess of fifty thousand was forming up and sluggishly moving forward but it would take time for that many to be mobilized.

The three archers were nearly to Steele and the Striker at his side. Tal had rushed over and shouted at Dwyn to help the Strikers, he would help Thadar. The Elf never hesitated, leaping the dead horse while drawing his blade. Steele was judging the best way to handle the men riding hard directly at them. The man with him solved the problem for him; the Striker swung his own horse sideways right in the path of two of the oncoming attackers. One of them slammed directly into the living barrier. The force of the impact killed both horses spilling all three riders.

The knot of horses and men was a whirlwind of activity with riders tossed about and horses going down, dust and grass billowing up and outwards. The third H'Roth faced off with Steele trying to cut him down.

The air was filled with shouts and the ringing of steel as the fight intensified. The Striker who had moved his mount into the path of the oncoming archers was at a serious disadvantage; the collision had not only killed his horse but had knocked the wind from his lungs. He was trying to gather himself but one of the H'Roth was on him. The southerner drove a thrust past his feeble guard and ended the life of the Striker.

For his part Dwyn found that his opponent was a seasoned fighter, the two traded blows with neither one able to score a decisive wound on the other. Steele was able to gain a quick advantage on the third man and sliced him deeply on the torso forcing the H'Roth into a defensive fight.

Thadar and Tal managed to free the injured Striker from beneath the downed horse. The fight was getting closer to them as they worked; the harsh tone of steel was unmistakable. Once he was free, Thadar told Tal to remain with him while pulling his own sword to aid his men.

The H'Roth who had killed the Striker saw the king and rushed him covering the short distance in no time. Thadar barely had time to see what was coming before the man was on him. A slash caught the king across the upper arm which raised his ire, his chain mail shirt wearing the blow; he parried the next slash and then attacked using the anger as extra fuel.

The leading edges of the massive southern army had shaken themselves loose and were now advancing at a steady pace toward their enemy with more of their own close behind. The distance between them and the small melee was growing progressively smaller. Tal saw this and knew that they all had to leave very soon or they would be in range of enemy archers. He struggled to help the badly wounded Striker toward one of the remaining horses, crap on a shingle, we don't have enough horses for us all!

The injured Striker saw this and tried to resist the help that Tal was providing to get him to move. He wanted the others but especially the king to be able to escape. He told Tal to leave him, save the king!

As soon as the waiting Legion officers saw the archers turn to fire on the king, anger took them. They began to shout orders to the various units to come to alert. As this was happening a group of Strikers immediately took off at a hard gallop toward the king. Nearly two dozen men were urging their mounts forward with reckless abandon.

Meanwhile the wounded archer had been finished off by Steele who turned his full attention to the struggle between Thadar and his adversary. The king was now wounded in two places and had been forced into a defensive posture. Steele caught the man from behind, ramming his sword through the body of the southerner. The archer stumbled, dropped his sword and a vomit of blood and spit erupted from his mouth as he fell.

About that same time Dwyn was able to finally gain a good position using it to finish his own opponent who fell to the grass dying noisily.

The small group were battered and breathing heavy. Tal shouted to get their attention while pointing at the approaching threat from the east "We have to go, now!"

The others saw the frantic pointing then saw for themselves what he was exercised about. *Damnation! We have to get out of here! Go, Go!*

A scramble toward the few horses was barely underway when the first of the galloping riders from their own lines arrived. Seeing the wounded , several of them hurriedly dismounted, barely waiting for their horses to come to a halt before doing so.

Thadar rushed over to the wounded Striker ignoring the man's pleas to leave him. Several men lifted him to a seat behind one of still mounted riders. Thadar yelled at the front man to *go, go!* He complied using one hand to steady his passenger as best he could. Two others went with them riding as closed as they dared to help stabilize the load.

"Mount up!" Shouts and curses as those afoot rapidly worked to sort out seating on the remaining horses. Several of the arriving riders circled around to put themselves between the group and the threat. A few arrows were starting to land nearby, the accuracy improving as the range diminished. One of the men caught an arrow in the side but managed to stay astride his horse.

Thadar and his men were scrambling aboard the excited mounts. He shouted, "Rally! To me!" then pointed toward the safety of their own lines.

Arrows were landing much closer and in much greater numbers. It was possible to see the faces of some of those marching toward them. The men of Karbel urged their horses forward, hooves tossed dirt and grass behind them as the group moved westward. As Thadar was turning to judge the distance another of his men was hit, spilling him from the saddle. Anger burned at the sight of the proud soldier killed before his eyes knowing there was nothing he could do.

The Legion generals had ordered their men to stand to when the archers had fired on the parlay group so the Legionnaires were ready for what was about to take place. Shields were raised, swords gripped, arrows readied and nerves steadied. Horn calls, the thunder of the cavalry and more filled the air as the king and his group approached finally having ridden out from under the enemy's bowshot. An opening was made as men sidestepped to allow them entry. Thadar lead the way, he was anxious to get to a spot he could see what the enemy was doing as well as get the wounded cared for.

Time seemed compressed as he rode through the thick lines of his soldiers toward the rear. It galled him to have to have fled but they stood no chance out there in the open. It served no purpose to die in that manner, he was angry beyond words at the invaders. He wanted them to die, all of them, every stinkin' pox ridden motherless son of them.

Thadar was angry but focused. This invasion was the largest challenge to his rule since taking his father's place. He would not be the one to lose the kingdom, not this day, no that would not be his legacy. His mind was already churning over various strategies and tactics.

Reaching the rear of the first section of the Legion line Thadar and the others reined in their mounts, shouts for healers were quick in coming. A flurry of activity surrounded the group as men dismounted to help the wounded and take control of the excited horses. It was chaos for a few moments but with the help of others the situation began to sort itself out.

Thadar checked to make sure the wounded were being taken care of then moved to find the senior staff with Tal and the others in tow. The enemy had closed the gap considerably, close enough for archers on both sides to begin their work. Scattered groups of arrows were being exchanged with casualties being taken by both armies.

Once contact was made between the front lines the fight began in earnest. The sharp sound of sword on sword could be heard amidst the shouts, curses and screams from the wounded and dying of both sides. The Legion formation continued to hold its ground as another wave of attacks broke on the forward edge of the line.

Numbers favored the southerners but lacking a formal attack plan their numbers were not serving them as well as they could have. The better organized and formed Legion units were responding to the attacks in a coherent fashion which helped to negate their numerical inferiority. The Legion Marshal watched with a practiced eye waiting for the right moment to order the next part of his strategy. Almost there – not yet...

Now! Now was the time, Tal smiled grimly as he ordered his center unit to slowly withdraw. It took time for the effect of the order to be visible but slowly they could see it. The middle of the Legion line was moving to the rear and as it did it was drawing more and more of the southern forces in. This caused their flanks to be longer and longer leaving them more exposed. Thadar saw the strategy and grinned, it was almost time to really punish them. A little more, that is right, just a bit more, there! Now General!

Tal gave the order; multiple horns rose as one and sounded a long three note call that carried far across the tumult of the battle. Those the order was meant for heard it and sounded their own horn call, *Charge!!* Several thousand Legionnaires on rested mounts leapt forward, sharpened lances glinting in the sun as they thundered forward.

Pon was growing concerned as the battle progressed, his men were making gains but they hadn't been able to break any section of the Legion line as yet. Casualties were high on both sides but all he was concerned about was crushing his master's enemies. He dispatched a pair of runners with orders for separate units then was turning to confer with one of the Varshon when they all heard the multiple horns distantly sound. They didn't have to wonder long what that signal was meant to convey.

An aide pointed toward the southern forces right flank. Pon and the others saw the sharp lines of the advancing cavalry aimed directly at their weakened line. One sharp curse escaped his lips before he shouted for Vinshee but the handpicked cavalry commander was already moving toward his men to counter the Legion thrust shouting for his staff.

Pon was pleased, he was certain that his able subordinate would be able to turn the charge. Returning his attention to the senior Varshon he asked his master what his orders were. The two were deep in conversation in moments.

Thadar was just about ready for the final act in this drama, calling for a messenger he told the man to take the hastily written note to the commander of the reserve formation which had been held in place and as yet not seen action.

That was about to change, the note ordered him to move forward attacking the southern left flank and work at rolling it back toward the center of the battle. The courier saluted and headed off to carry out his assigned task. The king and those nearby watched as the battle unfolded further. There was little that they could do at this point but watch, it was the actions of the individual soldiers that would win or lose the battle.

The lines went back and forth as the fight continued, the discipline and training of the Legion troops were able, barely, to offset the numerical edge that the southerners had. The front lines ebbed and flowed back and forth. It took some time for the reserve formation to move into position but it made its presence known immediately by striking at the overextended left flank of the invaders. No quarter or pardon was asked for or given by either side as the battle intensified.

Tal was speaking with a runner as he watched a segment of the conflict then he paused as he focused on the action. He nearly changed part of his order but decided against it, nodding to the runner as he gave him a quick squeeze on the arm then pushing toward his mount. The courier dashed for his horse to deliver the order.

Slowly the tide was turning against the invaders. The Legion cavalry charge shredded a large measure of the southern right flank; the counter attack led by Vinshee was repulsed with heavy losses including the southern cavalry commander who was brought down by a pair of lances that pierced his armor. A number of the Varshon and Ogurth even joined the battle turning the battle for a time but superior training and the anger of fighting on their home soil brought it back around to those of Karbel. A large number of Varshon and their loyal Trolls were killed along with their human vassals.

Thadar kept the pressure up as the hours passed. He moved his left flank forward as well as ordered his middle section to advance which pushed the invaders hard, too hard for them to resist. Slowly at first but steadily the men of Karbel, Legionnaire and Striker alike, began to gain ground as the afternoon passed on toward evening.

During this time the king received word that the units he had ordered down from the north were approaching, only about an hour or so march away. He knew that once they arrived he would have enough men to end the threat for good but he had to continue to keep the pressure up. His men had been fighting for far too long but he couldn't risk disengaging them without allowing the southern forces time to regroup and possible counter-attack.

This was the fight that would break the invaders once and for all if it was handled properly, Thadar knew they had to keep fighting.

Pon and the others struggled to rally their battered forces ordering them to withdraw to the south per the direction of the senior surviving Varshon. Moving north was no longer an option. Scouts had reported that they had sighted at least one but likely two full strength Legions moving in from the north which had to be the ones from Toras and Plynth. *Sacred ancestors what else could go wrong?*

The once proud Varshon army had been beaten, they had to pull back to regroup against increasingly strong formations of Legion and Striker units. Pon wasn't certain how it had happened but it had and now all that mattered was getting as many of his men out of Karbel alive as possible.

Chapter Forty-Eight
A Bloody Sword

Eastern Karbel

The long days of riding and fighting had taken a heavy toll on all of them but there was more work ahead the enemy was still in Karbel in strength. Shorin felt that parts of it were a blur, all mixed together and he wasn't sure if he would ever be able to sort out the memories and feeling of the experience – if he survived.

That issue had been put to the test several times in very recent memory. The fighting had been up close and very personal. He and his men were tired, dirty and hungry but still in the saddle.

He and a large unit of Strikers had been shadowing the retreating southern forces hitting them as hard as they could to whittle them down. Several things had become glaringly obvious to the veteran Striker officer and others. The southern army was noticeably less organized than when they had been moving north, they were leaving a wide trail of broken equipment as well as dead and wounded men in their wake.

The lack of movement discipline that the southerners were displaying was shocking but Shorin wasn't being overly picky. *What was bad for them was good for us,* he thought as he watched from the bushes atop the small hill and grimly smiled as the thought that it was about to get very bad for them came to mind.

Unbelievable that they wouldn't have flank guards to keep what was about to happen to them from occurring. He and the other Strikers had ridden to a point ahead of the Varshon army picking a spot to wait in ambush.

Hidden from view by the scrub brush atop the small rise, Shorin was watching the lead element of the enemy force. Kneeling to lower the odds that someone would be able to spot him the tired soldier was talking to himself, *keep coming, that's right just a little further, a little further...wait, wait....now!*

He swept his upright arm down to signal the massed archers at his back. A swarm of long shaft arrows rose into the air from behind him then went well over his head toward the unsuspecting enemy unit. It didn't take the southerners long to realize they were under attack again.

Hurried shouts and panicked voices could be heard as they saw the incoming missiles, there was little they could do to avoid being hit. Shields were raised in attempt to ward off the deadly shafts which proved less than effective since the buckler style shield was intended to protect the user from sword blows not arrows. Many of the nearly four hundred arrows found flesh in one form or another.

Dozens and dozens of the Arakai infantry went down for good all over the massed formation. Anger and confusion reigned amid the rain of deadly shafts.

The second volley was on its way before the first one landed. Hours and hours spent at the archery butts had honed the Striker skills to a fine edge, and now those long days of training were paying off. The retreating Varshon led forces had been under repeated attacks during the withdrawal from the north and it was happening again. Some of the units had seen more than their share of attention from the soldiers of Karbel while others, like this particular unit of heavy infantry hadn't seen as much action to this point as many others but it made no difference to those from Karbel, these were still enemy troops on their soil.

As the follow up volleys of arrows continued to kill and injure some of the invaders, the Strikers were prepared to head back to the waiting horses to withdrawal if a serious counter-attack took place. Despite the casualties they were inflicting the Strikers were still vastly outnumbered which is why they were using slash and move tactics.

It allowed them to sting the larger force nearly at will but it wasn't all one sided. Earlier in the day a sizable force of southern cavalry had caught a mixed unit of Legion and Striker troops forcing a protracted fight resulting in major losses for the men of Karbel. Despite withdrawing there was still plenty of fight in southerners.

The enemy commander began issuing orders as soon as he saw the arrows fly; a large formation of cavalry broke from the main body heading directly toward where Shorin and the others were. Fortunately that is exactly what the veteran Striker expected them to do, it's what he would have done if the situation was reversed. Nodding to the waiting trumpeter the man blew a pre-arranged three note call. Immediately, all of the men changed aim and let fly at the approaching horsemen, then half of the Strikers headed for their horses. The remaining men quickly fired off two more volleys to cover the retreat then they too dashed for their waiting mounts.

The long shafts fell among the leading edge of the charging H'Roth causing some losses but more important created chaos as the wounded and dying horses tripped creating a ripple effect of disorder in the ranks behind them.

Shorin and the others were moving to their horses the instant the second volley had left the bows. There was no panic but a healthy sense of self-preservation hurried the Strikers along.

As the last of them reached their horses Shorin waved his men forward, it was time to get out of there. The chorus of the massed hooves tearing at the ground was like thunder, dust and grass filled the air behind them as they headed at a full gallop to the southeast. The H'Roth forces had been able to regroup and were continuing their pursuit. The southern cavalry force was significantly larger than the group that Shorin commanded.

As the minutes passed, the gap between the pursuing horsemen and their prey was growing smaller as the H'Roth gained on the Strikers. Shorin was looking over his shoulder to judge the distance, the cursed southies were entirely too close for his liking they had been able to regroup far quicker than he had anticipated. Just a few more minutes at this speed -- he faced front urging his tired horse to go faster. The wind whipped his hair as he lowered his head concentrating on being one with his mount.

The leading element of the Strikers rode into a modest size gap between a pair of wide, low hills. The enemy commander saw this, signaling his trumpeter to send orders to the others to change formation. He intended to follow them right into the gap then crush them. The b'lara horn sounded and the well trained cavalrymen responded immediately, their formation altered into more of a column from the wide side by side manner they had been in.

Shorin glanced back once more to see the southern forces almost within bow shot. *Almost there, keep going, keep going.* He was nearly through the gap when he saw what he had been praying for. A savage smiled split his face as he began to slow his mount, it was about to get interesting.

As the leading edge of the southern cavalry cleared the gap surprise and horror filled them, the men in front tried to slow down but it was far too late, the trap had been sprung. Because they didn't have scouts riding forward the H'Roth rode blindly into the ambush. Hundreds of waiting Legionnaires armed with pikes were angled to form a wide V shape on the other side of the hills. There was no time for the enemy to effectively react as the metal tipped shafts found flesh, the scream of men and horses filled the air as more of the riders pressed through the opening to find themselves being attacked. Shorin and his men had dismounted to rush back to help solidify the Legion line.

Archers filled the air with arrows which could hardly miss, so tightly packed was their targets. More and more of the H'Roth were trying to come through the gap but were stymied by the seething mass of flesh, equine and human, fighting for their lives. The Legion line was being pushed back on all sides but they were holding. The senior Legion officer sent his remaining infantry forward to help steady the line. In the pocket the struggle was epic; men were dying at a horrific rate as steel bit flesh.

Shorin along with the Strikers were joining the fight, a wedge of southern cavalry broke through a section of the left side of the pike line. Shouts of exaltation quickly turned to anger and fear as the gap was sealed by a heavy rush of Legion infantry. The H'Roth commander was attempting to withdraw his men when a pair of arrows found him spilling him from his horse.

A measured series of horn notes had the men of Karbel begin to slowly but steadily push forward. The cavalry trapped in the pocket were now being squeezed. Several sections of Legion cavalry joined the fight striking at the rear of the enemy force after looping around one of the hills.

Shorin shouted at those nearest him urging them on, the fight wasn't close to being over but they had to finish the fight soon so that they could all withdraw to the next location. His sword found the ribs of one of the cavalrymen biting deeply ending the man's life.

Yanking the bloody blade free he pushed forward deeper into the fight with a fierce shout, "Karbel and King!"

Epilogue
Choices

Kuln

Tagg looked again at the message in his hand and wondered if someone had lost his mind -- but couldn't say that the information he had read was bad news, well at least it wasn't bad news for Karbel.

The veteran soldier looked up from the parchment and then over the parapet down at the scene below him. Smoke blew across his field of vision again as the wind shifted blocking the scene for a moment before clearing again as the twisting veil of smoke moved. The fires that were eating the first set of bridge trusses had really taken hold burning fiercely, but it would be some time before the fire completely claimed the massive wooden beams.

The man who led the Black Guard could see the steady work that the Alush -- early the previous morning they had finally learned who it was that had laid siege to them -- had accomplished on the island midway between the north and south banks of the river. Large, stout mantels had been erected to protect the workers who had been trying to improve the work on the hasty trusses that had survived to cross the gap between the island and northern shore. Many of these lay askew from hits registered by the catapults, the shattered wood mixed with the bodies of many of the engineers who had been laboring to improve their earlier works. Some of their surviving comrades could be seen moving furtively about to avoid being on the receiving end of an arrow or something larger.

Tagg signaled for the artillery commander who hurried over. He ordered his subordinate to cease firing on the attackers below so they could go and parley. Arrows and some catapult shot rained down from the castle walls but for now it was harassing fire only. The man immediately saluted and turned, shouting at his men to stop their work. It took just a few moments for word to spread and the scattered barrage to end. Tagg sent word for his horse and those that would accompany him. This will be interesting he thought as he headed down from the parapet.

Picking his way down the serpentine roadway to the meeting with the enemy commander, as a sign of strength he only took a handful of retainers with him including Dougal. The old soldier's wits had saved them at least twice and deserved to be there at the end of the fighting if this was to be the end. They rode smartly but without undue haste as the road surface was pockmarked with craters from shots of the southern catapults.

Colonel Tagg waited until the enemy commander arrived. The southern commander had kept him waiting for nearly an hour thinking that his opposite number had come to surrender himself and his fortress. Feeling expansive, General Digil had taken the time to eat prior to making his way across the makeshift bridges to meet Tagg, unaware of the news that awaited him. The heliograph system of Karbel was vastly superior to the horse borne messengers that the southerners employed providing the Black Guard leader with an enormous advantage.

The Alush general had studied everything the Varshon had on Tagg numerous times to try and learn as much about him as possible. He had been forced to admit to himself that he was a little surprised the Guard was giving up already. It was true that his men had finally seized the island and done some damage to the main fortress but it was unlikely that it was enough to cause Tagg to wither.

Something else was going on but he felt confident, his Varshon master had told him that he would remain out of sight for now. Digil agreed, he was a great deal sharper than many of his counterparts, keeping the Black Guard commander ignorant of the presence of the Varshon for as long as possible was a shrewd move, little did he know that it had been a small patrol of these same Black Guards that had sighted the massive southern army before it had even left the south later informing those in the north.

Digil had no way of knowing that Tagg had been informed of the existence of the Varshon and their plans in great detail. No this meeting was not going to go his way at all.

The two men faced off with about five paces between them. Tagg opened the dialogue, "I have a message that should be of interest to ye'."

Digil snorted contemptuously as his aide translated Tagg's words. For his part the senior Black Guard wasn't surprised at the reaction. A number of messages had been pouring in from Karbel in the last few hours explaining much of what had happened in the north as well as more of the reasons behind it all. His intelligence staff had been working through the night to compile the information in a usable manner. What Tagg had read so far was almost beyond belief. Majical ceremonies and an enemy thousands of years old...shades above.

When word had come in several ten-days earlier what Mryl Twinsteel and the remains of his patrol had found, in Elven territory of all places, first there was joy but shortly after that additional word arrived that a massive army of southern troops had invaded Karbel. It was about that time that word reached Tagg of a large force approaching the river crossing. Things got a bit interesting shortly after that. He returned his full attention to the man standing with his guards.

"If it's of no interest to you then it may be of interest to your Varshon master." Tagg waited for that to hit. As the translator spoke Digil's expression moved from contempt to surprise which was quickly covered but not before Tagg saw it.

What Digil was unaware of was that the Varshon majic users had been unsuccessful in retrieving the sacred books and completing the rite they were going to attempt, and that G'mar was in the hands of the northerners. In fact nearly all the senior Varshon that had accompanied the army north were dead. The huge southern army was fractured and had been defeated by Karbel, the remnants of it were slowly being driven south under harassing attacks of various Legion and Striker units.

Digil was quickly trying to come up with a retort to the Varshon allegation. The man was a proven tactician but intrigue on this level was not his strong suit. Tagg didn't let him have the chance to recover his mental balance; he needed to push his opponent even further. "I offer you the chance to withdraw your forces back to the south. If you don't then we'll do it. I know about what the plan was, I know about the Varshon, I know about the majik ceremony, I know everything so if you wish to speak then have your master --" the colonel had deliberately chosen that word to further provoke his foe, "-- come forward so we can talk, I am through dealing with underlings."

The Alush translator hurriedly swallowed before rendering Tagg's comments into his own tongue. The general had a strong temper and what the man had said was sure to ignite it. Tagg just smiled as he waited for the response.

***

Shorin, Mryl and their men were in southeast Karbel assisting a group of villagers who had suffered an attack from one of the southern units as it had returned south. The damage to the small town was extensive, much of the farming community had been burnt to the ground and many of the residents killed.

The soldiers were helping to treat the wounded as well as search for those that were missing. A number of horrific stories had been told of atrocities, rape, murder, arson and theft. All of it further fueled the fires of anger that the Strikers felt as they worked. Many of them had fought some of the Varshon led forces at some point over the previous ten-days.

Patrols were scouring the area for any sign at all of the return of the enemy. Shorin had received reinforcements in the form of several large units of Strikers that had been rushed in from outposts throughout the region and beyond with even more on the way. The size of the kingdom was proving to be a significant hindrance to moving large formations of troops in a timely manner. There were still sizable numbers of invading foreign troops to deal with but at the moment the work of helping the survivors was the most important thing they could accomplish. There would be time to deal with the southerners later.

For his part Thadar, watched as another wave of his cavalry struck at the flank of a large body of southerners inflicting further casualties. This group of enemy soldiers was noticeably less organized than some of the other units they had been in contact with.

It was still two days ride to the frontier but the remains of the Varshon army were in full retreat while more troops arrived to strengthen Thadar. He fully intended to keep striking them as they made their way out of his kingdom. Every enemy soldier that was killed was one less that might threaten them again someday. He signaled another unit forward to hit the enemy in the opposite flank. He was determined to kill as many of them as possible.

A freshening wind from the west stirred his hair as he watched the slow movement south continue. But with each step, it took them closer to the frontier and out of his kingdom.

ABOUT THE AUTHOR

Mark A. Smith

This book is his second fiction work; he has previously released an alternative history novella, *Roma Victrix* which has sold internationally. In addition he is the author of *Preparedness: The Basics and Beyond* an internationally selling work addressing the area of personal preparedness and safety. He resides in Oklahoma and has a son.